AUG 09 2017

D0913685

THE YEAR'S BEST DARK FANTASY & HORROR

2016 Edition

SPRINGDALE PUBLIC LIBRARY
405 South Pleasant
Springdale, Arkansas 72764

OTHER ANTHOLOGIES EDITED
BY PAULA GURAN

Embraces
Best New Paranormal Romance
Best New Romantic Fantasy
Zombies: The Recent Dead
The Year's Best Dark Fantasy & Horror: 2010
Vampires: The Recent Undead
The Year's Best Dark Fantasy & Horror: 2011
Halloween
New Cthulhu: The Recent Weird
Brave New Love
Witches: Wicked, Wild & Wonderful
Obsession: Tales of Irresistible Desire
The Year's Best Dark Fantasy & Horror: 2012
Extreme Zombies
Ghosts: Recent Hauntings
Rock On: The Greatest Hits of Science Fiction & Fantasy
Season of Wonder
Future Games
Weird Detectives: Recent Investigations
The Mammoth Book of Angels and Demons
After the End: Recent Apocalypses
The Year's Best Dark Fantasy & Horror: 2013
Halloween: Mystery, Magic & the Macabre
Once Upon a Time: New Fairy Tales
Magic City: Recent Spells
The Year's Best Dark Fantasy & Horror: 2014
Time Travel: Recent Trips
New Cthulhu 2: More Recent Weird
Blood Sisters: Vampire Stories by Women
Mermaids and Other Mysteries of the Deep
The Year's Best Dark Fantasy & Horror: 2015
Warrior Women
Street Magicks
The Mammoth Book of Cthulhu: New Lovecraftian Fiction
Beyond the Woods: Fairy Tales Retold

THE YEAR'S BEST DARK FANTASY & HORROR

2016 Edition

EDITED BY PAULA GURAN

PRIME BOOKS

SPRINGDALE PUBLIC LIBRARY
405 South Pleasant
Springdale, Arkansas 72764

THE YEAR'S BEST DARK FANTASY AND HORROR: 2016

Copyright © 2016 by Paula Guran.

Cover design by Stephen H. Segal & Sherin Nicole.
Cover art by Fergregory.

All stories are copyrighted to their respective authors,
and used here with their permission.
An extension of this copyright page can be found on pages 523-524.

Prime Books
Germantown, MD, USA
www.prime-books.com

Publisher's Note:
No portion of this book may be reproduced by any means, mechanical,
electronic, or otherwise, without first obtaining the permission of the
copyright holder.

For more information, contact Prime Books:
prime@prime-books.com

Print ISBN: 978-1-60701-471-3
Ebook ISBN: 978-1-60701-477-5

Contents

Introduction: The Dark Dangerous Forest • Paula Guran • 7

Sing Me Your Scars • Damien Angelica Walters • 11

There is No Place for Sorrow in the Kingdom of the Cold
         • Seanan McGuire • 24

The Scavenger's Nursery • Maria Dahvana Headley • 46

Black Dog • Neil Gaiman • 57

1Up • Holly Black • 90

The Three Resurrections of Jessica Churchill • Kelly Robson • 106

Windows Underwater • John Shirley • 121

Ripper • Angela Slatter • 134

Seven Minutes in Heaven • Nadia Bulkin • 208

Those • Sofia Samatar• 218

The Body Finder • Kaaron Warren • 230

The Deepwater Bride • Tamsyn Muir • 237

Fabulous Beasts • Priya Sharma • 259

Below the Falls • Daniel Mills • 284

The Cripple and Starfish • Caitlín R. Kiernan • 294

The Door • Kelley Armstrong • 307

Daniel's Theory About Dolls • Stephen Graham Jones • 313

Kaiju *maximus*® : "So Various, So Beautiful, So New"
         • Kai Ashante Wilson • 333

Hairwork • Gemma Files • 349

The Glad Hosts • Rebecca Campbell • 359

The Absence of Words • Swapna Kishore • 370

Mary, Mary • Kirstyn McDermott • 382

Cassandra • Ken Liu • 403

A Shot of Salt Water • Lisa L. Hannett • 417

Street of the Dead House • Robert Lopresti • 430

The Greyness • Kathryn Ptacek • 447

The Devil Under the Maison Blue • Michael Wehunt • 457

The Lily and the Horn • Catherynne M. Valente • 466

Snow • Dale Bailey • 478

Corpsemouth • John Langan • 491

Acknowledgements • 523

Other Notable Stories: 2015 • 525

INTRODUCTION:
THE DARK DANGEROUS FOREST

Paula Guran

The dark dangerous forest is still there, my friends. Beyond the space of the astronauts and the astronomers, beyond the dark, tangled regions of Freudian and Jungian psychiatry, beyond the dubious psi-realms of Dr. Rhine, beyond the areas policed by the commissars and priests and motivations-research men, far, far beyond the mad, beat, half-hysterical laughter . . . the utterly unknown still is and the eerie and ghostly lurk, as much wrapped in mystery as ever.

—Fritz Leiber, "A Bit of the Dark World" (first published in
Fantastic Stories of Imagination, February 1962)

If you are new to this series (and these introductions), take my word: we've already established that neither *dark fantasy* nor *horror* is really definable. Any definition you might apply is apt to be debated anyway. Perhaps more importantly, both terms are—by the very nature of what they describe—always evolving, changing, mutating, transforming . . .

The spectrum of whatever we might consider dark fantasy or horror is extraordinarily expansive. "The dark dangerous forest" is vast and teeming with strange and fabulous flora and fauna; some of it familiar, some unnameable, most of it weird. This allows enormous latitude to execute the unique purpose of *The Year's Best Dark Fantasy and Horror*.

This year we have thirty works of fiction (ranging in length from less than three thousand words to more than thirty-two thousand words) published in 2015 from twenty-six different sources. We run the gamut from whispers of fear to profound dread, historical horror to grim scenarios of the future, explorations of small relationships to considerations of the inexplicable. There are delvings into both death and immortality, examinations of past mythologies and the invention of utterly new ones, sobering speculation as well as some smiles and dark drollery . . . and a great deal more.

The prose styles range from straightforward to deceptively effortless to elegantly decadent to exquisitely poisonous to intentionally Gothic and others in between and outside those modes.

Random notes made as I was re-reading, copy editing, arranging, and doing the other mysterious things editors do:

• Many of the stories might be said to deal with monsters or the monstrous, but none of them deal with typical monstrosity, except for, perhaps, some of the human monsters. (Perhaps it is appropriate to recall that *monster* comes from the Latin *monstrum*, from the root *monere:* "warn; instruct." Monsters were first identified not only as abnormal abominations, but also as divine portents of impending evil or aberrance in the natural order.)

• Several ghosts appear, a couple of aliens, some witches, a seer, and there is even a vampire story (albeit the vamps are neither classic nor sparkly).

• At least three are identifiable as "Lovecraftian," however none of these mimic H. P. Lovecraft, nor are they similar stories. (In fact, many readers will probably not even realize they are "lovecrafty" at all.) Since there were around fifteen anthologies of Lovecraftian tales published in 2015—not to mention other venues that published such stories—there were a number of stories of this type to choose from this year.

• Six or more are set in, or partly set in, the future. Some of these could be termed "science fiction," but at least one is more fantastic than scientific.

• Four deal with environmental issues; two with surviving the end of the world as we know it.

• Nine or so are set in the past (history is, after all, primarily horrific), and several of those evoke earlier literature or literary figures.

• This overlaps with the point just above, but other than the Lovecraftian stories, there are also a few "tributes" to earlier writers.

• Two stories involve dolls; that is due to Ellen Datlow's excellent *The Doll Collection* anthology.

• Only one story has computers in it.

• The sea plays a role in four of the stories.

• Racism is a theme in two selections; gaming in another two. Two stories deal with heroes.

Make what you will of all that. But don't worry, just because stories fall into groupings from my little list—they have little else in common.

This year, for the first time, I'm including a list of stories from the year that are also notable. (See page 525.) I'm not calling them "honorable mentions"

—no offense to those who use the term!—because, to me, the phrase connotes a commendation for something of exceptional merit, but still not deserving a top honor or "prize." This isn't a competition or a ranking. The notables stories are also among the "best" of those published in 2015. It is far from a complete list! (Also check the introduction and content of my *The Year's Best Science Fiction & Fantasy Novellas: 2016* for some long dark fiction I may have forgotten to include here.) One reason I have hesitated compiling such in the past is that I inevitably will forget to note or miss some great stories. Consider this an experiment.

Why aren't these stories here? Four of them appear in Rich Horton's *The Year's Best Science Fiction and Fantasy: 2016*—the big sister of this series and also published by Prime Books. (We already duplicated one story this year.) Obviously, I don't have enough room for them all; more specifically, I can only include a limited number of longer stories, so some on the list were sacrificed due to length. Others are by authors already included; some anthologies had several great stories and I couldn't include them all, a few, well, I didn't catch up with them until too late . . . etc.

Of course, you already have quite a bit of fiction right here in your hands and/or in front of your eyes to consider before looking for more. Enjoy!

Paula Guran
11 April 2016

I'm certain they call him the good doctor, but they're not here at night.
They don't know everything.

SING ME YOUR SCARS

Damien Angelica Walters

This is not my body.

Yes, there are the expected parts—arms, legs, hips, breasts—each in its proper place and of the proper shape.

Is he a monster, a madman, a misguided fool? I don't know. I don't want to know. But this is not my body.

The rot begins, as always, around the stitches. This time, the spots of greyish-green appear on the left wrist, and there is an accompanying ache, but not in the expected way. It feels as though there is a great disconnect between mind and flesh, a gap that yearns to close but cannot. I say nothing, but there is no need; Lillian's weeping says it with more truth than words.

The hands are hers.

"Please don't show him yet. Please," she whispers. "I'm not ready."

"I must," I say. "You will be fine."

"Please, please, wait until after the party."

I ignore her. I have learned the hard way that hiding the rot is not acceptable, and while the flesh may be hers, the pain is mine and mine alone. I remember hearing him offer an explanation, but the words, the theories, were too complex for me to understand. I suspect that was his intention.

Lillian will still be with us; she is simply grasping for an excuse, any excuse at all. I understand her fear, but the rot could destroy us all.

My stride is long. Graceful. Therese was a dancer, and she taught me the carriage of a lady. I pass old Ilsa in the hallway, and she offers a distracted nod over the mound of bed linens she carries. All the servants are busy with preparations for the upcoming annual party, which I'm not allowed to attend, of course.

I wonder what sort of fiction he has spun to the servants. Am I an ill cousin, perhaps, or someone's cast-off bastard that he has taken in? Either way, I'm certain they call him the good doctor, but they're not here at night. They don't know everything.

They never speak to me, nor do they offer anything more than nods or waves of the hand, and none of them can see my face through the veil I must wear when I venture beyond my rooms. All my gowns have high necklines and long, flowing sleeves; not a trace of flesh is exposed.

For my safety, he says. They will not understand. They will be afraid and people in fear often act in a violent manner. His mouth never says what sort of violence he expects, but his eyes do.

When I knock on the half-open door to his study, he glances up from his notebooks. I shut the door behind me, approach his desk slowly, and hold out Lillian's hand.

"Oh, Victoria," he says, shaking his head. "I had hoped we were past this. This configuration is as close to perfect as I could hope."

I bite my tongue. Victoria is not my name, simply a construct.

I asked him once why he had done such a thing; he called me an ungrateful wretch and left his handprint on my cheek. I wonder if he even knows why. Perhaps the answer is so ugly he has buried it deep inside.

Without another word, he leads me to the small operating theater, unlocks the door, and steps aside to let me enter first. The room smells of antiseptic and gauze, but it's far better than the wet flesh reek of the large theater. My visual memories are vague, but the smell will not leave, no matter how hard I try to forget.

I sit on the edge of the examination table without prompting. His face is grim, studied, as he inspects the wrist, and even though his touch is gentle, I watch his eyes for signs of anger. I know the rot is not my fault, but innocence is no guard against rage.

He makes a sound deep in his throat. Of sorrow? Condemnation?

Lillian weeps, then begs, then prays. None of which will make any difference.

The rot binds us to him as the stitches bind them to me. A prison, not of bars, but circumstance. I have entertained thoughts of the scissors and the thread, the undoing to set us free, but I have no wish to die again, and neither do the others. While not perfect, this existence is preferable. And what if we did not die? What if our pieces remained alive and sentient? A crueler fate I cannot imagine.

He scrapes a bit of the rot away, revealing a darker patch beneath. When he lets out a heavy sigh, I note the absence of liquor on his breath.

He busies himself with the necessary preparations, and Lillian begins to cry again. The others remain silent. He paints the wrist with an anesthetic, which surprises me. My tears have never stopped him from his work. I close my eyes and feel pressure. Hear the blades snipping through the stitches. Smell the foul scent of decay as it reaches out from beneath.

He places the hand in a small metal tray, then coats the remaining flesh in an ointment that smells strongly of pine and wraps it in gauze.

"We shall know in a few days.

Diana's worry is as strong as mine. Lillian tries to speak but cannot force the words through her sorrow and fear.

When the anesthetic wears off, the skin gives a steady thump of pain from beneath the gauze and I do my best to ignore it.

"At least it was only the one," Grace says.

"You wouldn't understand," Lillian snaps.

"What if it spreads?" Diana asks.

Molly mutters something I cannot decipher, but it makes Lillian weep again.

"Hush," says Therese. "Remember Emily? She had reason to weep. You do not."

Sophie laughs. The sound is cruel. Hard.

"Stop, please, all of you," I finally say. "I need to sleep. To heal."

Heal is not the right term, perhaps *remain* would be better.

"I'm sorry, Kimberly," Lillian says softly.

The sound of my real name hurts, but not as much as the false one. At least Kimberly is, was, real.

The rest apologize as well, even Sophie, and fall silent. I toss and turn beneath the blankets and eventually slip from my bed. The others say nothing when I open the small door hidden behind a tapestry on the wall. The passageway is narrow and dusty, and spiders scurry out of my way; it travels around the east wing of the house—the only part of the house where I'm allowed—then leads to the central part, the main house. There are small covered holes here and there that open to various rooms, to carpets my feet will never touch and sofas I will never recline upon. The passageway also goes to the west wing of the house, but the rooms are unused and the furniture nothing more than cloth-covered shapes in the darkness.

The only doors I have found lead to bedrooms—mine, his, and one other designed for guests, although we never have guests stay—and one near the music room.

There is, as always, a race in the heartbeat, a dryness to the mouth, when I creep from the passage and make my way to the servants' entrance. The air outside is cold enough to take my breath away as I follow the narrow path that leads to the gate in the outer wall. There is another path that leads down the hill and into the town, but the gate is locked.

I pretend that one day I will walk through the gate and down that path. Leave this house behind; leave him behind for good. But if I ran away and the rot returned, who would fix me? The rot would not stop until it consumed me whole.

I know this for truth because he left it alone the first time to see what would happen, and the rot crept its way up until he had no choice but to remove the entire arm. Her name was Rachael, and he removed both arms so he could then attach a matching set.

Most of the windows in the town are dark. The church's steeple rises high, a glint of moonlight on the spire. I have heard the servants talk about the market, the church. Beyond the town, a road winds around a bend and disappears from sight.

My parents' farm is half a day's travel from the town by horse and carriage. It would be a long, difficult walk but not impossible. I wonder if Peter, my eldest brother, has asked for Ginny's hand in marriage yet. I wonder if Tom, younger than I by ten months, has stopped growing (when I fell ill, he already towered over all of us). I wonder if my mother still sings as she churns butter. And my father . . . the last thing I remember are the tears in his eyes. I hope he has found a way to smile again; I wish I could see them all once more, even if only from a distance.

I wait for someone to speak, to mention escape and freedom, but they remain silent. After a time, I return to my bed and press my hand to Molly's chest. The heart belongs to someone else, someone not us. Sometimes I think I feel her presence, like a ghostly spirit in an old house, but she never speaks. Perhaps there is not enough of her here to have a voice. Perhaps she simply refuses to speak.

I wish I knew her name.

Although the stump shows no more signs of rot, he doesn't replace Lillian's hand. It makes dressing difficult at best, but I manage.

After supper, when all the servants have gone, I join him in the music room. I sing the songs he has taught me. Melodies which were strange and awkward at first now flow with ease; foreign words that fumbled on my tongue now taste of familiarity.

He accompanies me on the piano he says belonged to his mother. Only two songs tonight, and after the second, he waves his hand in dismissal, and I notice the red in his eyes and the tremble in his fingers. Perhaps he is worried about the party.

When he comes to my room in the middle of the night, I hide my surprise. He usually doesn't touch me unless I'm whole, but by now I know what is expected, so I raise my chemise and part Therese's legs. When he kisses my neck, I pretend it belongs to someone else. Anyone else. The others whisper to me of nonsense as a distraction. Thankfully, he doesn't take long.

After he leaves, I use Lillian's finger to trace the stitches. They divide us into sections like countries on a map. The head, neck, and shoulders are mine; the upper torso, Molly's; the lower torso, Grace's; Diana, the arms; Lillian, the hand; Therese, the legs and feet; Sophie, the scalp and hair.

I make all the pieces of this puzzle move, I feel touches or insult upon them, but they never feel as if they belong completely to me. He may know how everything works on the outside, but he doesn't know that they are here with me on the inside, too. We plan to keep it this way.

Once a week, in the small operating theater, he has me strip and he inspects all the stitches, all the parts. He checks my heart and listens to me breathe. I hate the feel of his eyes upon me; it's far worse than enduring his weight in my bed.

Not long after he brought me back, I tried to stab myself with a knife. At the last moment, I held back and only opened a small wound above the left breast. Stitches hold it closed now.

He says the mind of all things, from the smallest insect to the largest animal, desires life, no matter the flesh. He says I am proof of this.

But it was Emily's doing. She was with me from the beginning, and she was always kind, always patient. She helped me stay sane. Like a mother, she whispered soft reassurances to me when I cried; told me I was not a monster when I insisted otherwise; promised me everything would be all right. She taught me how to strip the farm from my speech.

He tried hard to save her, carving away at the rot a bit at a time, but in the end he could not halt its progress. She screamed when he split apart the stitches. I did, too. Sometimes I feel as if her echo is still inside me and it offers a small comfort. Therese is kind, but I preferred my walk when it carried Emily's strength.

"I will unlock your door when the party is over," he says.

I nod.

"You will stay silent?"

"Yes."

"I would not even hold this party if not for my father's insufferable tradition. I curse him for beginning it in the first place, and I should have ended it when he died."

I know nothing of his father other than a portrait in the music room. He, too, was a doctor. I wonder if he taught his son how to make me.

The key turns in the door. I sit, a secret locked in with the shadows.

Even from my room, I can hear the music. The laughter. I creep in the passageway with small, quiet steps, extinguish my lamp, and swing open the spyhole. The year before, I was recovering and did not know about the passageway; the year before that, I was not here.

I twine a lock of Sophie's hair around my finger and watch the men and women spinning around on the dance floor, laughing with goblets of wine in hand, talking in animated voices. He is there, resplendent in a dark suit, but I don't allow my eyes to linger on him for too long. This smiling man is as much a construct as I am.

"I had a gown like that blue one," Grace says. "Oh, how I miss satin and lace."

"Please," Lillian says. "Let us go back. I can't bear to see this. The reminder hurts too much."

"Hush," Molly says.

"I wish we could join them," Diana says.

Sophie says, "Perhaps he will bring us some wine later. And look, look at the food."

Therese makes a small sound. "Look at the way they dance. Clumsy, so clumsy."

I sway back and forth, my feet tracing a pattern not from Therese, but a dance from my childhood. I remember the harvest festival, the bonfire, the musicians. My father placed my feet atop his to teach me the steps, and then he spun me around and around until we were both too dizzy to stand.

Therese laughs, but there is no mockery in the sound. I close my eyes, lost in the memory of my father's arms around me, how safe and secure I always felt. I would give anything to feel that way again.

The music stops, and my eyes snap open. A young woman in a dark blue gown approaches the piano, sits, and begins to play. The music is filled with tiny notes that reach high in the air then swoop back down, touching on melancholia. It's the most beautiful thing I have ever heard. Everyone falls silent, even Lillian.

Then I see him watching the girl at the piano. His brow is creased; his mouth soft. I hear a strange sound from Sophie. She recognizes the intensity of his gaze. As a kindness, I let go of her hair. Does he covet this girl's arms? Her hair? Her face?

Lillian begins to weep again, and it doesn't take long for the rest to join her. All except Sophie. She never cries.

"He will not," I say.

"He will do whatever he wants. You know that," Sophie says.

"She is not sick," Grace says.

"Neither was I," Sophie hisses. "He saw me in the Hargrove market. He gave me *that* look, then I woke up here."

"But you do not know for certain," Therese says. "The influenza took so many."

"I was not sick." Sophie's voice is flat. Then, she says nothing more.

Hargrove is even farther away than my parents' farm. I bend my head forward, and Sophie's hair spills down, all chestnut brown and thick curls. My hair was straight and thin, best suited for tucking beneath rough-spun scarves, not hanging free, but still I cried when he replaced it.

He is drunk again. His voice is loud. Angry. I pull the sheets up to my shoulders and hope he doesn't come to visit. When he is drunk, it takes longer.

Sometimes I want to sneak into his study and take one of the bottles and hide it in my room. On nights when I can still hear my mother saying my name; when I can remember the illness that confined me to my bed and eventually took my life; when I recall the confusion when I woke here and knew something was wrong.

But those nights happen less and less, and I'm afraid I will forget my mother's voice completely. Would she even recognize me with Sophie's hair in place of my own? Would she run screaming?

• • •

On Sunday morning, I creep through the passageway. Step outside. The servants have the day off, and he has gone to mass. Even here, I can hear voices in song. I remember these songs from my own church where I sang with the choir. I have never known if he heard me somehow and chose me because of my voice, but I remember seeing him on the farm in my fifteenth year when Peter broke his arm, two years before the influenza epidemic.

"We should leave," Sophie says.

"Yes, we should run far away," Lillian says.

"And where would we go?" Molly asks.

"Anywhere."

Therese laughs. "And who will fix us if we rot?"

"Better that we rot away to nothing than remain here," Sophie says.

The others start speaking over each other, denying her words. In truth, I do not know what I want. When I head back inside, the voices outside are still singing and those inside still arguing.

Days pass, then weeks. The stump remains rot free, but he says nothing of it, only nods when he does his inspection.

He spends his days in the town, ministering to the sick. I spend mine in the library, reading of wars and dead men and politics. Rachael taught me how to read; now Sophie helps when I find myself stuck on a word.

"Wake up."

His voice is rough, scented with whiskey.

"Now?"

"Yes, hurry."

"No, oh, no," someone says as we approach the small operating theater, but I cannot tell who it is.

He tears away my chemise. Pushes me down on the table.

"But there is nothing wrong," I say.

"Don't let him do this," Lillian screams. "Please, don't let him do this to me."

He lifts a blade. I grab his forearm, dig Lillian's nails in hard enough to make him wince.

"Please, no."

He slaps me across the face with his free hand. The others are shrieking, shouting. Lillian is begging, pleading, screaming for me to make him stop. I grab his arm again and try to swing Therese's legs off the table. He slaps me twice more and presses a sharp-smelling cloth over my mouth and nose. I hold my breath until my chest tightens; he pushes the cloth harder.

I breathe in, and everything goes grey—*I'm sorry, Lillian, so sorry*—then black.

I wake in my bed, the sheets tucked neatly around me. The others are weeping, and Lillian is gone. I choke back my tears because I don't wish to frighten the newcomer.

"What has happened to me?" she asks. Her voice is small and trembling.

"What is your name?" I ask.

"Anna," she says.

"Welcome to madness," Sophie says, her voice strangely flat.

"Hush," Molly says.

"Who is that? What is this? Please, I want to go home."

"I told you," Sophie says, still in that strange, lifeless tone. "We should have run away."

"Where am I?" Anna says. "How did I get here?"

I try to explain, but nothing I say helps. Nothing can make it right, and in the end, we are all weeping, even Sophie, and that frightens me more than I could have imagined.

I don't see him for several days. The music room remains dark, the door to the operating theater locked. I retreat to the library, lose myself in books, and pretend not to hear Anna cry. We have all tried to offer support, but she rebuffs every attempt so there is nothing to do but wait. Eventually, she will accept the way things are now, the way we've all been forced into acceptance.

There are no signs of rot along the new stitches. They're uneven both in length and spacing—not nearly as neat as the others—but they hold firm. Anna's hands are delicate with long slender fingers, the skin far paler than Diana's. The weight is wrong; they're far too light, as if I'm wearing gloves instead of hands.

I miss Lillian so very much. I didn't even have a chance to say goodbye.

When he enters the library, I notice first his disheveled clothes, then the red of his eyes. He tosses my book aside, drags me to the music room, and shoves me toward the piano.

"Tell her to play."

Everyone falls silent. Surely we have heard him wrong.

"I don't understand."

He steps close enough for me to smell the liquor. "Tell Anna to play," he says, squeezing each word out between clenched teeth.

I sit down and thump on the keys, the notes painful enough to make me grit my teeth. I poke and prod, but Anna is hiding the knowledge deep inside, and I cannot pull it free. I offer a tentative smile even though I want to scream.

"Shall I sing instead?"

He groans and pulls me from the bench. The skirts tangle and twist, and I stumble. He digs his fingers into my shoulders, brings my face close to his. "Did you truly believe I didn't know? I have heard you speak to them. I know they are in there with you. You tell her to play. Or else."

"Never," Anna says.

Therese's legs are no longer strong enough to hold us up, and I sink to the floor. He smiles, the gesture like a whip. Eventually, he stalks from the room, and I sit with Diana's arms around me.

Sophie hisses, "Bastard."

"You must teach me how to play," I tell Anna.

"I will not."

"Please, you must. If you don't, he will kill you."

"It doesn't matter. I am already dead."

"But he may kill us all, and we don't want to die."

The others chime in in agreement.

"I do not care," Anna says. "I will give him nothing. He killed me. Don't you understand? He killed me!"

"Yes, I do," says Sophie. "We do. But this is what we have now."

"I do not want this. It is monstrous, and you, all of you, you're as dead as I am."

"Please," I say. "Teach me something, anything that will make him happy. I'm begging you, please."

She doesn't respond.

Three more trips to the music room. Three more refusals that leave me with a circlet of bruises around the arms; red marks on my cheeks in the shape of his hand; more bruises on the soft skin between breasts and belly. The others scream at Anna when he strikes me, but she doesn't give in.

She is strong. Stronger than any of us.

• • •

The fourth trip. The fourth refusal. He pulls me from the bench with his hands around my neck. His fingers squeeze tighter and tighter until spots dance in my eyes and when he lets go, I fall to the floor gasping for air as he walks away without even a backward glance.

I wake to find his face leering over mine. I bite back the tears, begin to lift my chemise, and he slaps my hand.

"If you cannot make her play, I will find someone else who will." He traces the stitches just above the collarbone, spins on his heel, and lurches from the room.

I sit in the darkness and let the tears flow. I don't want to die again. I will not.

I creep into the passageway and make my way into the kitchen. Cheese, bread, a few apples. An old cloak hangs from a hook near the servants' entrance. I slip it on and pull up the hood before I step outside. The air is cold enough to sting my cheeks, too cold for the thin cloak, but I head toward the gate, searching the ground for a rock large enough to break the lock.

Perhaps my mother will scream, perhaps my father and brothers will threaten me with violence, but they cannot hurt me more than he has.

I'm five steps away from the gate when he grabs me from behind. All the air rushes from my lungs. I draw another breath to scream, and his hand covers my mouth. He leans close to my ear.

"I had such high hopes for you. Perhaps I will have better luck with the next one."

I fight to break free. The gate is so close. So close.

He laughs. "Do you have any idea what they would do to you? Even your own parents would tear you limb from limb and toss you into the fire. If I didn't need the rest of them, I'd let you go so you could find out."

He presses a cloth to my mouth, and I try not to breathe in.

I fail.

I wake in the large operating theater. The smell is blood and decay, pain and suffering. I scream and pound on the door, but it's barred from the outside. I sink down and cover my eyes; I don't want to see the equipment, the tools, the knives, and the reddish-brown stains. There are no windows, no hidden doors, no secret passageways. There is no hope.

I have no idea how much time passes before he comes. "This is your last chance," he says. "Will you play?"

"No," Anna says.

"Please, please," the others beg.

"I will not."

"She will not play," I say, my voice little more than a whisper.

He smiles. "I thought not." He closes the door again.

Does he mean to leave us locked here until we die? I bang on the door until tiny smears of blood mark the wood, then I curl up into a small ball in the corner.

I wake when he opens the door again and drags something in wrapped in a sheet. No, not a something. A body. I lurch to my feet.

"No, no, you cannot do this. Please."

"I can do whatever I want. I made you, and I can unmake you."

He approaches me with another cloth in his hand. I know if I breathe this time, I will never wake again. Sophie is shrieking. They all are.

I stumble against a table and instruments clatter to the floor with a metallic tangle. I reach blindly with Anna's hand, find a handle, and swing. He steps into the blade's path, and it sinks deep into his chest. He drops the cloth; his mouth opens and closes, opens and closes again, then he collapses to the floor as if boneless. Anna lets out a sound of triumph, but I cannot speak, cannot breathe, cannot move.

"No, no," Sophie shouts. "What have you done?"

Therese and Grace scream, Diana lets out a keening wail, Molly babbles incoherencies that sound of madness, and all the while, Anna laughs.

His eyes flutter shut, and his chest rises, falls, rises. I drop to his side and pull the blade free, grimacing at the blood that fountains forth. His eyes seek mine. His mouth moves, and it sounds as if he is trying to say, "I'm sorry," but perhaps that is only what I wish he would say.

Nonetheless, I say, "I'm sorry, too."

Then, I begin to cut.

"Thank you," Anna whispers, right before the blade touches the last stitch and she is set free. I close my eyes for a brief moment to wish her well on her journey, but there is not enough time to mourn her properly.

My stitches are clumsy, ugly, but they seem sturdy enough for now. His hands are too large, the movements awkward, but gloves will hide them, and soon I will know how to make everything work the way it's supposed to.

He whispers he will never tell us how. We laugh because we know he will eventually; he will not want his creation, his knowledge, to fall apart or to rot away and die. He mutters obscenities, names, and threats, but we ignore him.

We are not afraid of him anymore.

In the ballroom, I set fire to the drapes and wait long enough to see the flames spread to the ceiling and across the floor in a roiling carpet of destruction.

"Where shall we go?" Therese asks.

"I don't know," I say.

Sophie gives a small laugh. "We can go anywhere we wish."

The heat of the blaze follows us out. The air is thick with the stench of burning wood and the death of secrets. The promise of freedom. We pause at the gate and glance back. A section of the roof caves in with a rush of orange sparks, flames curl from the windows, and the fire's rage growls and shrieks.

When we hear shouts emerge from the town below, we slip into the shadows. This is our, *my*, body, and I will be careful. I will keep us safe.

Damien Angelica Walters' work has appeared or is forthcoming in various anthologies and magazines, including *The Year's Best Dark Fantasy & Horror: 2015, Year's Best Weird Fiction: Volume One, Cassilda's Song, The Mammoth Book of Cthulhu: New Lovecraftian Fiction, Nightmare Magazine, Black Static,* and *Apex Magazine. Sing Me Your Scars,* a collection of short fiction, was released in 2015 from Apex Publications, and *Paper Tigers,* a novel, in 2016 from Dark House Press.

Sorrow is surprisingly malleable, capable of adjusting its shape to fit the box that holds it, but it fights moving from one place to another, and it has thorns. Sorrow is a bramble of the heart and a weed of the mind . . .

THERE IS NO PLACE FOR SORROW IN THE KINGDOM OF THE COLD

Seanan McGuire

The air in the shop smelled of talcum, resin, and tissue, with a faint, almost indefinable undertone of pine and acid-free paper. I walked down the rows of collectible Barbies and pre-assembled ball-jointed dolls to the back wall, where the supplies for the serious hobbyists were kept. Pale, naked bodies hung on hooks, while unpainted face plates stared with empty sockets from behind their plastic prisons.

Clothing, wigs, and eyes were kept in another part of the shop, presumably so it would be harder to keep track of how much you were spending. As if anyone took up ball-jointed dolls thinking it would be a cheap way to pass the time. We all knew that we were making a commitment that would eat our bank accounts from the inside out.

I looked from empty face to empty face, searching for the one that called to me, that whispered, *I could be the vessel of your sorrows*. It would have been easier if I'd been in a position to cast my own; resin isn't easy to work with compared to vinyl or wax, but it's possible, if you have the tools, and the talent, and the time. I had the tools and the talent. Only time was in short supply.

Father would have hated that. He'd always said time was the one resource we could never acquire more of—unlike inspiration, or hope, or even misery, it couldn't be bottled or preserved, and so we had to spend it carefully, measuring it out where it would do the most good. I could have been making beautiful dolls, both for my own needs and to enrich the world. Instead, I spent my days in a sterile office, doing only as much as I needed to survive and stay connected to the Kingdom of the Cold.

My head ached as I looked at the empty, waiting faces. I had waited too long again. Father did an excellent job when he made me, but my heart was never intended to hold as much emotion as a human's could.

"Perfection is for God," he used to say. "We will settle for the subtly flawed, and the knowledge that when we break, we return home." Because we were flawed—all of us—we had to bleed off the things we couldn't contain: sorrow and anger and joy and loneliness, packing them carefully in shells of porcelain, resin, and bone. I needed the bleed. It would keep me from cracking, and each vessel I filled would be another piece of my eventual passage home.

Times have changed. People live longer, but that hasn't translated into longer childhoods. Once I could have paid my passage to the Kingdom just by walking through town and seeing people embracing my creations, offering up their own small, unknowing tithes of delight and desolation. Those days are over. Father was the last of us to walk in Pandora's grace, and I do what I must to survive.

A round-cheeked face with eyes that dipped down at the corners and lips that formed a classic cupid's-bow pout peeked from behind the other boxes. I plucked it from the shelf, hoisting it in my hand, feeling the weight and the heart of it. Yes: This was my girl, or would be, once I had gathered the rest of her. The hard part was ahead of me, but the essential foundation was in my hand.

It didn't take long to find the other pieces I needed: the body, female, pale and thin but distinctly adult, from the curve of the hips to the slight swell of the breasts. The wig, white as strawberry flowers, and the eyes, red as strawberries. I had clothing that would fit her. There was already a picture forming in my mind of a white and red girl, lips painted just so, cheeks blushed in the faintest shades of cream.

Willow appeared as I approached the counter, her eyes assessing the contents of my basket before she asked, "New project, dear?"

"There's always a new project" I put the basket down next to the register. "It's been a long couple of weeks at work. I figured I deserved a treat."

Willow nodded in understanding. The women who co-owned my favorite doll shop were in it as much for the wholesale prices on their own doll supplies as to make a profit: I, and customers like me, were the only reason the place could keep its doors open. I prayed that would last as long as Father did. I couldn't shop via mail order—there was no way of knowing whether I was getting the right things, and I couldn't work with materials that wouldn't work with me. I'd tried a few times while I was at college, repainting Barbie dolls with shaking hands and a head that felt like it was full of bees. I could force inferior materials to serve as keys to the Kingdom, but the results were never pretty, and the vessels I made via brute force were never good enough. They couldn't hold as much as I needed them to.

My total came to under two hundred dollars, which wasn't bad for everything I was buying. I grabbed a few small jars of paint from the impulse rack to the left of the register. Willow, who had argued Joanna into putting the rack there, grinned. "Will there be anything else today?"

"No, that's about it." I signed my credit card slip and dropped the receipt into the bag. "I'll see you next week."

"About that . . . "

I froze. "What about it?"

"Well, you know this weekend is our big get-together, right?" Willow smiled ingratiatingly. "A bunch of our regulars are bringing in their kids to share with each other, and I know you must have some absolutely gorgeous children at home, with all the things you buy."

I managed not to shudder as I pasted a smile across my face. The tendency of some doll people to refer to their creations as "children" has always horrified me, especially given my situation. Children live. Children breathe. Their dolls . . . didn't. "I can't," I said, fighting to sound sincere. "I'm supposed to visit my father at the nursing home. Maybe next time, okay?"

"That would be nice." Willow barely hid her disappointment. I grabbed my bag and fled, and this time the bell above the door sounded like victory. I had made my escape. Now all I had to do was keep on running.

The cat met me at the apartment door, meowing and twining aggressively around my ankles, like tripping me would magically cause her food dish to refill. Maybe she thought it would; it's hard to say, with cats.

"Wait your turn, Trinket" I shut and locked the door before walking across the room—dodging the cat all the way—and putting my bag down on the cluttered mahogany table that served as my workspace.

Trinket stopped when I approached the table, sitting down and eyeing it mistrustfully. The tabletop had been the one forbidden place in the apartment since she was a kitten. She badly wanted to be up there—all cats desire forbidden things—but she was too smart to risk it.

The half-painted faces of my current projects stared at me from their stands. Some—Christina, Talia, Jonathan had bodies, and Christina was partially blushed, giving her a beautifully human skin tone. Others, like Charity the bat-girl, were nothing more than disembodied heads.

"I'm sorry, guys," I said to the table in general. "You're going to need to wait a little longer. I have a rush job." The dolls stared at me with blank eyes and didn't say anything. That was a relief.

Trinket followed me to the kitchen, where I fed her a can of wet cat food, stroked her twice, and discarded my shoes. I left my jacket on the bookshelf by the door, hanging abandoned off a convenient wooden outcropping. I was halfway into my trance when I sat down at the table, reaching for the bag, ready at last. The tools I needed were in place, waiting for me. All I needed to do was begin.

So I began.

The doll maker's art is as ancient and revered as any other craft, for all that it's been relegated to the status of "toymaker" in this modern age.

A maker of dolls is so much more than a simple toymaker. We craft dreams. We craft vessels. We open doorways into the Kingdom of the Cold, where frozen faces look eternally on the world, and do not yearn, and do not cry.

I learned my craft at my father's knee, just as he'd learned from his father, and his father from his mother. When the time comes, when my father dies, I'll be expected to teach my own child. Someone has to be the gatekeeper; someone has to be the maker of the keys. That was the agreement Carlo Collodi made with Pandora, who began our family line when she needed help recapturing the excess of emotion she had loosed into the world. We will do what must be done, and we will each train our replacement, and the doll maker's art will endure, keeping the doors to the Kingdom open.

I fixed the face I'd purchased from Willow to the stand and began mixing my colors. I wanted to preserve its wintry whiteness, but I needed it to be a living pallor, the sort of thing that looked eerie but not impossible. So I brushed the thinnest of pinks onto her cheeks and around the edges of her hairline, using an equally thin wash of blue and grey around the holes that would become her eyes, until they seemed to be sunken sockets, more skeletal in color than they'd ever been in their pristine state. I painted her lips pale at the edges and darkening as I moved inward, leaving the center of her mouth gleaming red as a fresh-picked strawberry. I added a spray of freckles to the bridge of her nose, using the same shade of pink as the edges of her lips.

She was lovely. She'd be lovelier when she was done, and so I reached for her body and kept going.

Somewhere around midnight, between the third coat of paint and the first careful restyling of the wig that would be her hair, I blacked out, falling into the dreaming doze that sometimes took me when I worked too long on the borders between this world and the Kingdom of the Cold. My hands kept moving, and time kept passing, and when I woke to the sound of my cell phone's alarm ringing from my jacket pocket, the sun had risen, and a completed doll sat in front of me, her hands folded demurely in her lap, as if she was awaiting my approval.

Her face was just as I'd envisioned it in the store: pale and wan, but believably so, with eyes that almost matched her lips gazing out from beneath her downcast lashes. I must have glued them in just before I woke up; the smell of fixative still hung in the air. Her hair was a cascade of snow, and her dress was the palest of possible pinks. She was barefoot, and her only ornamentation was a silver strawberry charm on a chain around her neck. She was finished, and she was perfect, and she was just in time.

"Your name is Strawberry," I said, reaching out to take her hands between my thumbs and forefingers. "I have called you into being to be a vessel for my sadness, for there is no place for sorrow in the Kingdom of the Cold. Do you accept this burden, little girl, so newly made? Will you serve this role for me?"

Everything froze. Even the clocks stopped ticking. This was where I would learn whether I'd chosen my materials correctly; this was where I would learn if they would serve me true. Then, with a feeling of rightness that was akin to finding a key that fits a lock that has been closed for a hundred years, something clicked inside my soul, and the sorrows of the past few weeks flowed out of me, finding their new home in the resin body of my latest creation.

It's no small thing, pouring human-size sorrow into a toy-size vessel.

Sorrow is surprisingly malleable, capable of adjusting its shape to fit the box that holds it, but it fights moving from one place to another, and it has thorns. Sorrow is a bramble of the heart and a weed of the mind, and this sorrow was deeply rooted. It held a hundred small slights, workdays where things refused to go according to plan, cups of coffee that were too cold, and buses that came late. It also held bigger, wider things, like my meeting with Father's case supervisor, who had shown me terrible charts and uttered terrible words like "state budget cuts" and "better served by another placement." Father couldn't handle being moved again, not when he was just starting to remember his surroundings from day to day, and I couldn't handle the stress or expense of moving him. Not now, not when I was already out of vacation time and patience. Lose my job, lose the nursing homes. Lose the nursing homes, and face the choice so many of my ancestors had faced: whether to share my space with a broken vessel who no longer knew how to reach the Kingdom, or whether to break the last dolls binding him to this world, freeing their share of his sorrow and opening his doorway to the Kingdom one final, fatal time.

I could send him home. No one would call it murder, but I would always know what I had done.

It was a hard, brutal concept, one that had no place in the modern world, but I had to consider it, because Father had always told me that one day it would be my choice to make. Life or death, parent or duty—me or him. And I wasn't ready to decide. So I poured it all into the doll I had crafted with my own two hands, and Strawberry, darling Strawberry, drank it to the very last drop. I couldn't have asked for anything more than what she offered, and when I felt the click again, the key turning and the doorway closing, I had become an empty vessel. My sorrows were gone, bled out into the doll with the strawberry eyes.

"Thank you," I murmured, and stood. I carried her across the room to a shelf of girl dolls who looked nothing like her, yet all seemed somehow to be family to one another: There was some intangible similarity in their expressions and posture. They all contained a measure of sadness, decanted from me through the Kingdom and into them over the course of these past three years. I set Strawberry among her sisters, adjusting her skirt and the position of her hands until she was just so and exactly right, as if she had always been there.

Then, light of heart and step, I turned and walked toward my bedroom. It was time to get ready for work.

The day passed in a stream of tiny annoyances and demands, as days at the company where I worked as an office manager so often did.

"Marian, do you have that report ready?"

"Marian, is the copy machine fixed yet?"

"Marian, we're out of coffee."

I weathered them all with a smile on my face. I felt like I could handle any challenge. I always felt that way right after I opened a channel to the

Kingdom. People like my father and I used to be revered as surgeons, the doll makers who came to town and helped people remove the parts of themselves that they couldn't handle anymore. The bad memories, the pain, the sorrow. Now he was a senile old man fading away by inches and I was a woman with a strange, expensive hobby, but that didn't change what we'd been designed to do. It didn't close the doorway.

"Hi, Marian."

The sound of Clark's voice wrenched me out of the payroll system and sent me into a state of chilly panic, my entire body going tense and cold with the sudden stress of living. *No, no, no,* I thought, and raised my eyes. *Yes, yes, yes,* said reality, because there was Clark, useless ex-boyfriend and even more useless coworker, standing with his arms draped across the edge of my half-cubicle like I'd invited him to be them, like he was some sort of strange workplace beautification project gone horribly wrong.

"Hello, Clark," I said, as coolly as I could. "Is there something I can help you with?"

"You can tell me why you're not answering my calls," he said. "Did I do something wrong? I know you said you didn't want to be serious. I didn't think that meant cutting me out entirely."

"Please don't make me call HR," I said, glancing around to be sure no one was listening. "I said I didn't want to see you socially anymore. I meant it."

"Is this because I said your doll collection was childish and weird? Because it is, but I can adjust, you know? Lots of people have weirder hobbies. My little sister used to collect Beanie Babies. She was, like, twelve at the time, but it's the same concept, right?"

I ground my teeth involuntarily, feeling a stab of pain from the crown on my left rear molar. I had sliced half of that tooth off with a hot knife when I opened my first doorway to the Kingdom. Early sacrifices had to hurt more than later ones to be effective. "No, it's not," I said stiffly. "I told you I didn't want to talk about this. I definitely don't want to talk about it at work."

"You won't take my calls, you won't meet me for coffee, so where else are we supposed to talk about it? You haven't left me anywhere else."

He looked so confident in his answer, like he had found the perfect way to get me to go out with him again. I wanted to slap him across his smug, handsome face. I knew better. I flexed my hands, forcing them to stay on my desk, and asked, "What do you want me to say, Clark? That I'll meet you for coffee so we can have a talk about why we're never going to date again, and why I'll report you to HR for harassment if you don't stop bothering me?"

"Sounds great." He flashed the toothy smile that had initially convinced me it would be a good idea to go out with him. I should have known better, but he was so handsome, and I'd been so lonely. I'd just wanted someone to spend a little time with. Was that so wrong?

No. Everything human wants to be loved, and wants the chance to love someone else. The only thing I did wrong was choosing Clark.

I swallowed a sigh and asked, "Does tonight work for you?" Better to do it while I was still an empty vessel. If I waited for the end of the week, I'd have to pull another all-nighter and add another girl to my shelf before I could endure his company. That would be bad. Not only would the cost of materials eat a hole in my bank account that I couldn't afford right now, but the strain of opening a second doorway so soon after the first would be . . . inadvisable. I could do it, and had done it in the past. That didn't make it a good idea.

"So what, first you play hard to get and now you're trying to rush me? I thought you said you didn't like games." His smile didn't waver. "Tonight's just fine. Pick you up at seven?"

"I'd rather meet you there," I said.

"Ah, but you don't know where we're going." Clark winked, pushing himself away from the wall of my cubicle. "Wear something nice." He turned and walked down the hall before I could frame a reply, the set of his shoulders and the cant of his chin implying that he really thought he'd won.

I groaned, dropping my head into my hands. He thought he'd won because he *had*. I was going out with him again. "What the hell is wrong with me?" I muttered.

My computer didn't answer.

The bell rang at 7:20 p.m.—Clark, making me wait the way he always had, like twenty minutes would leave me panting for his arms. I put down the wig cap I'd been rerooting and walked to the door, wiping stray rayon fibers off my hands before opening it and glaring at the man outside.

Clark took in my paint-stained jeans and plain grey top, his jovial expression fading into a look that almost matched mine. He was wearing a suit, nicer than anything he ever put on for work, and enough pomade in his hair to make him smell like a Yankee Candle franchise.

"I thought I told you to put on something nice," he said.

"I thought I told you I was willing to meet you for coffee," I shot back. "Last time I checked, the dress code at Starbucks was 'no shirt, no shoes, no service.' I have a shirt and shoes. I think I'll be fine."

Clark continued to glower for a moment before shouldering his way past me into the apartment.

"Hey!" I yelped, making a futile grab for his arm. It was already too late: He was in my living room, turning slowly as he took in all the dolls that had joined my collection since the last time he'd been here, some three months previous. I tried not to open a doorway to the Kingdom more than once a week, but sometimes it was hard to resist the temptation, especially when I had more than one trouble to decant. Dolls like Strawberry held sorrow, while others held different emotions—anger, loneliness, even hope, and love, and joy. Positive emotions took longer to grow back and had to be decanted less frequently, but they were represented all the same.

Clark's examination took about two minutes before he focused back on me, disdain replaced by pity. "This is why you broke up with me?" he asked. "I mean, you said it was because of the dolls, but I thought that was just a crappy excuse, you know? The weird-chick equivalent of 'I have to wash my hair on Saturday night.' But you meant it. You like plastic people better than you like real ones. There's something wrong with you."

"My dolls aren't plastic," I said automatically, before I realized I was falling back into the same destructively defensive patterns that had defined our brief relationship. I glared at him, shutting the door before Trinket could get any funny ideas about making a run for the outside world. "You want to have this talk? Fine. Yes, I chose my dolls over you. Unlike you, they never tell me I'd be pretty if I learned how to do something with my hair. Unlike you, they don't criticize me in public and then say they were just kidding. And unlike you, they shut up when I tell them to."

"You really are a crazy bitch." He strode across the living room, grabbing the first thing that caught his eye—pretty little Strawberry in her mourning gown. His hand all but engulfed her body. "You need to learn how to focus on real things, Marian, or you're going to be alone forever."

"You put her down!" I launched myself at him as if he weren't a foot taller and fifty pounds heavier than I was. I was reaching for Strawberry, trying to snatch her out of his hand, when his fist caught me in the jaw and sent me sprawling.

I'd never been punched in the face before. Everything went black and fuzzy. I didn't actually pass out, but the next few minutes seemed like a slideshow or a Power Point presentation, and not like something that was really happening. Static picture followed static picture as I watched Clark stalk around my apartment, grabbing dolls off the shelves. When he couldn't hold any more he walked over to me, looking down, and said, "This is what you get."

He kicked me in the stomach, and then he was gone, taking my dolls with him, and I was alone. At some point, I came back to myself enough to start crying.

It didn't help.

Trinket stuck her nose through the curtain of my hair and mewled, eyes wide and worried. I sniffled, wiping my eyes with the back of my hand, and sat up to pat her gently on the head. "He didn't hurt me that bad, Trinket. I'm okay. I'm okay."

I was lying to myself as much as I was lying to the cat: I might be many things, but I was distinctly not okay. I picked myself up from the floor inch by excruciating inch, finally turning to take stock of the damage.

It was greater than I'd feared. Fifteen dolls were missing—at least one from every shelf, as well as one of the unfinished dolls from my table.

Relief washed over me when I saw that. At least not everything he'd taken was a weapon. Shame followed on relief's heels. He'd stolen fourteen full vessels, fourteen doorways into the Kingdom of the Cold, and I was relieved that it wasn't one more? What was the difference between fourteen and fifteen when you were talking about knives to the heart? Fourteen would be more than enough to kill. The only question was who.

If I was lucky, he'd accidentally kill himself, and all my troubles would end . . . but that might leave full vessels floating around the world outside, ready to be found by someone who didn't know what they were holding. Open a vessel improperly, and everything it contained would come flooding out. And there were many, many improper ways to open something that had been closed.

I wanted to go after him. I wanted to demand the return of my property, and I wanted to make him pay. I glanced to the remaining unfinished dolls, assessing the materials I had, automatically counting off the materials I'd need. Forcibly, I pulled myself away from that line of thinking. Revenge was satisfying, but it would be hard to explain if he had some sort of bizarre accident, and I'd already been reminded that I couldn't take him in a fair fight.

Hands shaking, I pulled out my cell phone and dialed the number for the police. When the dispatcher came on the line, voice calm and professional, I began to tell her what had happened.

I made it almost all the way through the explanation before I started to cry.

That night was one of the worst I'd had since Father started getting bad. We'd both known what his lapses in memory meant, but we'd denied it for as long as possible, he because he wasn't ready to go, me because I wasn't ready to be alone. Every keeper of the Kingdom eventually develops cracks. It's a natural consequence of being a vessel that's been emptied too many times. There's a reason we don't use the same doll more than once for anything other than the most basic and malleable emotions. That was the reason I couldn't make myself a new doll, one big enough to hold my shame and grief and feelings of violation. I'd emptied out my sorrow too recently. I was too fresh, scraped too raw, to do it again.

The officers who came in answer to my call were perfectly polite. They took pictures of the empty spaces on my shelves and of the bruises on my face and stomach, and if they thought the number of dolls still in my apartment was funny, they had the grace not to laugh in front of me. Eventually, they left me with a card and a number to call if Clark came back, and the empty promise that they'd see what they could do about getting my stolen property back. One of them asked me, twice, about filing a restraining order. I refused both times.

I didn't sleep. All I could do was lie awake, staring at the ceiling and thinking about the dolls who had been entrusted to my care, now lost in the world with their deadly burdens of emotion. They were so fragile. They had to be if they were going to properly mirror the fragility of the human heart, and do the jobs that they were made for.

When morning came I rolled out of bed and dressed without paying attention to whether my clothes matched. My face hurt too much for me to bother with makeup, so I left it as it was, bruises like smeared paint on the side of my jaw and around the socket of my left eye, and exited the apartment with my head up and my thoughts full of nothing but vengeance.

A shocked hush fell over the office when I arrived. I ignored the people staring at me as I walked to my desk. Something white was trapped under the keyboard. I pulled it loose, only to gasp and drop it like it had scalded my fingers.

Strawberry's whisper of a dress fluttered to the floor, where it lay like an accusation. *You failed us,* it seemed to say. *You didn't protect. You didn't keep. You are no guardian.*

I clapped my hand over my mouth, ignoring the pain it awoke in my jaw, and fought the urge to vomit. Bit by bit, my stomach unclenched. I bent, picked up the dress, and walked calmly down the hall to the door with Clark's name on it. He had an office; I had a cubicle. He had a door with a nameplate; I had a piece of paper held up with thumbtacks. I should have known better than to let him buy me that first cup of coffee. Even if I didn't have that much sense, I should have known better than to let him take me out for dinner even once. I was a fool.

Foolishly, I raised my hand and knocked. Clark's voice, smooth as butter, called, "Come in."

I went in.

Clark was behind his desk, a broad piece of modern office furniture that was almost as large as my worktable at home, if not half as old or attractive. He looked . . . perfect. Every hair was in place, and his tailored suit hung exactly right on his broad, all-American shoulders. His eyes darted to the scrap of fabric in my hand, and he smiled. "I see you found my present."

"Where are my dolls, Clark?" I'd meant to be more subtle than that, to approach the question with a little more decorum. Father always tried to tell me you got more flies with honey than you did with vinegar, but he'd never been able to make the lesson stick, and the words burst out, hot with venom and betrayal. "You had no right to take them."

"And you had no right to call the police over a little lover's spat, but you did, didn't you?" The jovial façade dropped away, leaving the snake he'd always been staring out of his eyes. "I was going to give them back. As an apology, for losing my temper. I shouldn't have hit you, and I know that. But then the cops showed up at my apartment saying you'd filed a domestic violence complaint against me. I'm sure you can see why I didn't like that very much."

I stared at him. "I didn't file a domestic violence complaint against you, *Clark*, because you're not any part of my domestic life. I filed an assault charge. You didn't just hit me. You beat me down. Where are my dolls?"

His smile was a terrible thing. "I'm not part of your domestic life. How would I know where your silly little toys ended up? As for your trumped up charges, my lawyer will enjoy seeing yours in court. Now you might want to get out of my office before I tell HR that you're harassing me."

Wordlessly, I held up Strawberry's gown, daring him to say something that would deny he was the one who'd left it on my desk.

"What, that? I found it in my car and thought you might want it back.

You know how it is with grown women who play with dolls. They're just like children. Leaving their toys everywhere."

He sounded so smug, so sure of himself, that it was all I could do to not to walk around the desk and snatch his eyes from his head. I kept my nails long and sharp, to make it easier to position delicate doll eyelashes and reach miniscule screws. I could have had his eye sockets bare and bleeding in a matter of seconds.

I balled my hands into fists. I was my father's daughter. I was the keeper of the Kingdom and the maker of the keys, and I would not debase myself with this man's blood.

"This isn't over," I said.

Clark smiled at me. "Actually, I'm pretty sure it is," he said. "Bye, now." There was nothing else that I could do, and so I turned, Strawberry's dress still clutched in my hand like a talisman against the darkness that was rushing in on me, and I walked away.

The rest of the day crept by like it wanted me to suffer. My eyes drifted to Strawberry's dress every few seconds until I finally picked it up and shoved it into my purse, hoping that out of sight would equal out of mind. It didn't work as well as I'd hoped, but it made enough of a difference that I was able to complete my assigned work and sneak out the door fifteen minutes early. Thanks to Clark, I had lost track of fourteen filled vessels. I needed to find them, and that meant I needed help. There was only one place to go for that.

My father.

The Shady Pines Nursing Home was as nice a place to die as money could buy, with all the amenities a man who barely remembered himself from hour to hour could want. I had made sure of that. Even though I was keeping him alive past the point when he was ready to go, I wasn't going to make him suffer.

Part of what that money paid for was an understanding staff. When I presented myself at the front desk an hour after visiting hours, a long white box in my hands and a light layer of foundation over the bruises on my face, they didn't ask any questions; they looked at me and saw a dutiful daughter who had experienced something bad, and needed her father.

"He's having one of his good days, Miss Collodi," said the aide who walked me through the well-lit, pleasantly decorated halls toward my father's room. "You picked an excellent time to visit."

I could tell he meant well from the look on his face—curious about my bruises but eager not to offend. So I just smiled, and nodded, and said, "I'm glad to hear that."

We stopped when we reached the door of Father's room. The aide rapped his knuckles gently against the door frame, calling, "Mr. Collodi? May we come in?"

"I told you, the doll house won't be ready for another three days," shouted my father, sounding exactly like he had throughout my childhood: aggravated by the stupidity of the world around him, but trying to improve it however he could. "Go away, and come back when it's done."

I put a hand on the aide's shoulder. "I can handle it from here," I said. The aide looked uncertain, but he nodded and walked away, leaving me alone with the open doorway. I hefted the box in my hands, checking the weight of its precious burden—so few left, and no way to make more—before taking a deep breath and stepping into my father's room.

Antonio Collodi had been a large man in his youth, and that size was still with him: broad shoulders and a back that hadn't started to stoop, despite the deep lines that seamed his face and the undeniable white of his hair. The muscle that used to make him look like a cross between a man and a bear was gone, withered to skeleton thinness; his clothes hung on him like a shroud. He was standing near the window, hands curled like he was working on an invisible doll house. I stopped to admire the workmanship that had gone into him. I must have made some small sound, because he turned and froze, eyes fixing on my face.

"I'm your daughter," I said, before he could start flinging accusations.

He usually mistook me for Pandora—a natural misunderstanding, since I looked exactly like she did in the painting that we had been passing down, generation to generation, since the beginning. He didn't like being visited by dead people. He said it was an abomination, and a violation of our compact with the Kingdom of the Cold, which some called "Hades," where the dead were meant to stay forever. "Daddy, I need your help. Can you help me?"

"My daughter?" He kept staring at me, dawning anger melting into amazement. "You're beautiful. What did I make you from?"

"Bone and skin and pine and ice," I said, walking to his bed and putting down the long white box. I rested a hand on its lid. "Pain and sorrow and promises and joy. You pried me open and called me a princess among doors, and then you poured everything you had into me, and kept pouring until my eyes were open." I remembered that day: waking on my father's workbench, naked and surrounded by bone shavings, my teeth tender and too large in my little girl's mouth, my face stiff from the smile it had been painted wearing.

My family has guarded the trick to calling life out of the Kingdom for centuries, since Pandora brought it to us and said she was too tired to keep the compact any longer. No one you didn't make with your own two hands can be trusted. That's the true lesson of the Kingdom, and what I should have remembered when Clark smiled his perfect smile and offered me his perfect hands. But my father made me too well, and when he bid me to become a woman, a woman I became. If I'd stayed a doll of bone and pine, Clark would have had no power over me.

"Yes, that's how you make a daughter," said my father, following me across the room. "Is that why I'm so empty?"

"Yes," I said. "I'm sorry."

"I should be in pieces by the road by now."

"I still need you." I took my hand off the box and opened the lid, revealing a blue-eyed boy doll. He was dressed in trousers and a vest a hundred years out of date, and his face was painted in a way that subtly implied he had a secret. I undid the ribbons holding him in place and gingerly picked him up. He weighed more than he should have for his size, and my hands shook as I held him out toward my father. "There are five of these in the world. That's why you can't go. If you break this one, there will only be four, and you'll be one step closer to entering the Kingdom."

We doll makers were supposed to be at peace there, finally home among our own kind. We were supposed to be rewarded for the things that we had done while we pretended to be human. I didn't know if that was true . . . but I knew that the humans lived for the promise of Heaven with much less proof of its existence than we had of the Kingdom.

Pandora and Carlo Collodi had been real people, flesh-and-blood people. Pandora had carried a vase like a broken heart, meant to contain all the dangers of the world, both sweet and bitter. She had been tired from her wandering, from years on years of struggling to recapture the evils she had accidentally released. Carlo Collodi . . .

He had wanted a daughter. Of such necessity are many strange bargains born.

Father took the doll. I didn't look away. This was on me; this was my fault, because I was doing this to him. I could have crafted my child as soon as it became clear that the vessel of Father's thoughts had cracked. I could have set him free. I was the one who wasn't willing to let him go.

"Oh, my brave boy," he murmured, cradling the doll in his hands. "Your name was Marcus, wasn't it? Yes, Marcus, and you were a vessel for my anger. The world was so infuriating back then. . . . " He raised the doll, pressing his lips against the cold porcelain forehead.

It felt like the temperature in the room dropped ten degrees, the doorway to the Kingdom of the Cold swinging open and locking in place as all that Father had poured into that blue-eyed boy came surging out again, filling him. He stayed that way for almost a minute, lips pressed to porcelain, drinking himself back in one sip at a time. The chill remained in the air as Father lowered the doll, and the eyes he turned in my direction were sharp and clever, filled with the wisdom of two hundred years of making dolls to hold every imaginable emotion.

"Marian, why am I still here?" he asked. All traces of confusion were gone. The sad, broken vessel was no longer with me, and I rejoiced, even as I fought not to weep.

The dolls he had filled before he had broken grew fewer with every visit, and his lucidity faded faster. I was running out of chances to call my father back to me. "Four dolls remain, Father," I said, rising and sketching a quick curtsey, even though I was wearing trousers. "Until they're used up, you can't finish breaking."

"Then use them. Stop wasting them on me. I command you."

"I can't." I straightened. "I would if I could. I love you, and I know my duty. But the world has changed since you were its doll maker, and I can't do this without you. I need to be able to ask my questions, and have someone to answer them."

He frowned. "Have you made a child yet?"

"Not yet. I can't." Once I made myself a child—made it from bone and skin and pine and ice, like my father had made me, like his father had made him—my own cracks would begin to show, and my essence would begin leaking free. A vessel can only be emptied so many times. The creation of a child was the greatest emptying of all. "I'm not ready. But Father, that isn't why I came. I need your help."

"Help? Help with what?"

I took a deep breath. This was going to be the difficult part. "There was a man at my office. . . . "

I spilled out the whole sordid story, drop by terrible drop. The smiles, the flirtation, the dates for coffee that turned into dates for dinner that turned, finally, into Clark deciding he had the right to start dictating my life. From there, it was a short progression to him knocking me to the floor and stealing my dolls.

Father listened without a word, letting his precious moments of lucidity trickle away like sand. When I was done, he inclined his head and said, "You have been foolish, my Marian. But you're young as long as I'm in this world—children are always young when set against their parents—and I can't fault you for being a young fool. I was foolish, too, when I had a father to look after me." He held out his empty doll. I took it. What else could I have done? He was my father, and he wanted me to have it. "You know what you need to do."

"I don't want to," I said weakly—and wasn't that why I'd come to him? To find another way, a better way, a *human* way, one that didn't end with someone broken and bleeding in the street?

But sometimes there isn't any other way. Sometimes all there can be is vengeance. "You have to," he said gently.

I sighed. "I know." The empty doll was light as a feather, nothing but a harmless husk. I could sell it to a dealer I knew for a few hundred dollars, and watch him turn around and sell it to someone else for a few thousand. It didn't matter who profited, or how much. All that mattered was that this shattered little piece of my father's soul would no longer be in my keeping. One more doorway, permanently closed.

"Now come, sit with me." My father sat down on the edge of his bed, gesturing for me to return to my previous place. "I don't have long before the cracks begin to show again, and I would know what you've been doing with your life."

"All right," I said, and sat, settling the empty doll back into his box.

Father reached for my hands. I let him take them. We sat together, both smiling, and I spoke until the understanding faded from his eyes, and he was gone again.

There are always consequences when you spend your life standing on the border of the Kingdom of the Cold.

I spent the night at my worktable, a rainbow of paints in front of me and Charity the bat-girl's delicate face looking blindly up at the ceiling as I applied the intricate details of her makeup, one stroke at a time. She'd been waiting for the chance to be complete for months, but I'd passed her by time and again to focus on newer projects. I'd always wondered why. It's not like me to leave a doll languishing for so long. Now I knew: Charity had a purpose, and until the time for that purpose arrived, I would never have been able to finish her.

Charity was meant to be my revenge.

Morning found me still sitting there, now drawing careful swirls on the resin body that would soon play host to her head. Her wings would get the same treatment before they were strung into place. She was less a bat-girl than a demon-girl, but "Charity the bat-girl" had been her name for so long that I couldn't stop thinking of her that way. I reached for my silver paint, and cursed as my hand found an empty jar.

"Shit."

I'd been working without pause and hadn't stopped to assess my supplies. Charity needed the silver to be properly finished. I glanced at the clock. The doll shop would be open in ten minutes. This was their big gather-day, but I could be in and out before anyone had a chance to notice that I was even there. I wiped down my brushes, capped my paints, and stood. Just a few more supplies and I could finish my work.

The drive to the doll store took about fifteen minutes, minutes I spent reviewing what I was going to buy and how I'd explain why I couldn't stay if Willow or Joanna asked me. I was deep in thought when I got out of the car, walked to the door, and stepped inside, only to be hit by a wave of laughter and the smell of peppermint tea. I stopped dead, blinking at the swarm of people—mostly women, with a few men peppered through the crowd who moved, chattering constantly, around a series of tables that had been set up where the racks of pre-made doll clothes were usually kept. A second wave hit me a moment later, this one redolent with sadness, and with the smell of cold.

My stolen dolls were here.

I shoved my way through the crowd, ignoring the startled protests, until I reached the table. There they were, all my missing vessels, even Strawberry, although someone had re-dressed her in a garish red and white checked dress. All fifteen were set up as a centerpiece, surrounded by a red velvet rope, as if that would ensure that people looked but didn't touch.

"Marian?" Willow's voice came from right behind me. She sounded surprised.

I couldn't blame her for that. I had other things to blame her for. I whirled, pointing back at the table as I declared, "Those are my dolls! How did you get my dolls?"

Willow's expression changed from open and genial to closed and hard.

"I'm afraid I don't know what you're talking about, dear. Those dolls were sold to us by a private collector, and you've always been so adamant about not showing or selling your work that I can't believe you'd have sold this many to him. They're a fine collection, but they're not yours."

I ground my teeth together, pain lancing from my damaged molar, before I said, "Yes, they are. They were stolen from my apartment two nights ago by my ex-boyfriend. I filed a police report. We can call the station and get them down here; I'm sure we'll find your 'private collector' matches Clark's description."

Her eyes widened slightly at his name. I resisted the urge to smack her.

"He didn't even lie about his name, did he? Clark Hauser. You probably wrote him a check. You'll have a record." I shook my head. "You had to know those weren't his. I bought most of these materials *here*, and they are not common combinations. You knew. But you took them anyway." The crowd around me was silent, watching. I turned to them. "Think they'd buy your dolls, too, if you got robbed?"

"We didn't know they were stolen," said Willow. "We bought them legally. We—"

"Give the lady back her dolls," said a weary voice. Willow turned, and we both looked at the dark-haired woman in the workroom door, leaning on her cane. Joanna focused only on me. She walked slowly forward. It felt like she was studying me, taking my measure. She stopped about a foot away and said, "Doll maker. That's what you are, isn't it? You're the doll maker."

I nodded mutely.

"I always wanted to meet one of you." She waved a hand at the table. "They're yours. Take them. I knew we couldn't keep the collection as soon as I put my hands on it. They're dangerous, aren't they?"

I nodded again.

"Then get out of my store. Was that all you came for?"

I found my voice and managed, "I needed some silver paint."

"Take that, too. Call it our apology." She smiled thinly. "When you take your revenge, doll maker, don't take it on us. Willow, get the lady her paint." Willow hurried to obey.

I looked at the crowd, and then back at Joanna, and said, "Thank you."

Joanna smiled. "You're welcome."

Restoring the vessels to their proper places made me feel infinitely better, like a hole in the world had been closed. I apologized to each of them, and twice to Strawberry: once as I was stripping off that horrible checkered dress, and again as I placed her back on her proper shelf. I felt their approval, and the approval of the Kingdom beyond.

Silver paint in hand, I sat down and got back to work.

Crafting a vessel for the self is easy, once you know how. It requires understanding your own heart—a painful process, to be sure, but your own heart is always close to hand. Crafting a vessel for someone else is an uphill struggle, and I felt it with every stroke of the brush. I mixed the last of the silver paint with blood taken from the small vein inside my wrist, and it made glittering brown lines on Charity's skin. There was a moment right before the designs drew together when I could have stopped; I could have put down the brush and walked away. But Clark had struck me, had stolen from the Kingdom, and he had to pay for what he'd done.

I dressed Charity in a black mourning gown and placed her in a long white box, covering her with drifts of tissue paper. Then I fed Trinket, left the apartment, and drove to Clark's house. I left the box on his doorstep. I didn't look back as I drove away.

Clark didn't come to work on Monday. That wasn't unusual. Clark didn't come to work on Tuesday either. People were talking about it in the break room when I came to get my coffee.

Wednesday morning, I called in sick.

The key Clark had given me still fit his lock. I let myself in. There was Charity on the floor, full to the point of bursting, and there was Clark next to her, eyes open and staring into nothingness. He was still alive, but when I waved my hand in front of his face, he didn't blink.

There was nothing left in him.

"You shouldn't open doors you don't know how to close," I said, bending to slide my arms under Clark and hoist him to his feet. He would have been surprised to realize how strong I was. "It's dangerous. You never know what might happen."

Clark didn't respond.

"I never told you where my family was from, did I? We're doll makers, you know. We go all the way back to a man named Carlo Collodi. He wanted a daughter, and he used a trick he learned from a woman named Pandora to open a door to a place called the Kingdom of the Cold. It's a good name, don't you think? There's no room for sorrow there. The people who live there don't even understand its name. He called forth a little girl, and as that girl grew, she learned so many things the people of the Kingdom didn't know." I carried Clark to his room as I spoke.

"Sometimes that little girl sent things home to them. Presents. But more often, she used the things her lather had learned from Pandora. There's too much feeling in the world, you see. That's what Pandora really released. Not evil: emotion. So the little girl collected feeling like a cistern collects the rain, and when she held too much, she pulled it out and sealed it in beautiful vessels. Sorrow and anger and joy and loneliness, all held until her death. We can't contain as much as you can. We're not made that way. But we need something to pay our passage home." Home, to a place I'd never seen, with halls of porcelain and nobility of carved mahogany. We were revered as craftsmen there, and all we had to do to earn our place was keep repaying Pandora's debt, catching the excess of emotion that she had released into the world, one doll at a time.

I unpacked my father's last four remaining dolls before I unrolled the bundle that held my tools, pulling out the first small, clever knife.

"Every vessel holds a piece of the maker's soul. We pack it away, piece by piece, to keep us alive after we cut out our hearts and use them to make a child. Our parents' dolls give us the scraps of soul we'll need to create a new one for the baby. They're not the only thing we need, of course." The scalpel gleamed as I held it up to show him. "Puppets come from blocks of wood. Rag dolls come from bolts of cloth. What do you think it takes to construct a child?"

Clark never even whimpered.

There was a message from Father's nursing home in my voicemail when I got back to the apartment. I didn't play it. I already knew what it would say: the apologies, the regrets, the silence where my father used to be. That didn't matter anymore. My chest ached where I had sliced it open, and I rubbed unconsciously at the wound, looking around the room at the rows upon rows of dolls filled with my living. They would sustain me now that I had no heart, until the day my daughter was ready to be the doll maker, and I was ready to stop patching the cracks left by her creation.

She snuffled and yawned in my arms, wrapped in a baby blanket the color of tissue paper. She'd have Clark's perfect smile and perfect hair, but she wouldn't have his temper. I'd given her my heart, after all, just like my father had given his to me.

The police would eventually notice Clark's disappearance. I'd left no traces for them to follow. A good artist cleans up when the work is done, and I had left neither shards of shattered porcelain nor pieces of dried, bloodless bone for them to track me by.

I walked to the couch and sat, jiggling my daughter in my arms. She yawned again. "Once upon a time," I said, "there was a man who wanted a son. He lived on the border of a place called the Kingdom of the Cold, and he knew that if he could just find a way to open a door, everything he dreamed of could be his. One day a beautiful woman came to his workshop. Her name was Pandora, and she was very tired . . . "

The dolls listened in silent approval. Trinket curled up at my feet, and the world went on.

Seanan McGuire is a prolific short story author and collector of deeply creepy dolls, which fill her room and watch her sleep at night. Mysteriously, she does not have many nightmares. She has released more than twenty books since 2009, so it's possible the lack of nightmares is due to a lack of sleep. You can keep up with her at seananmcguire.com, or follow her on Twitter for pictures of her doll collection and her massive Maine Coon cats.

The last of the river dolphins. The last of the poisonous frogs. The last of the polar bears. The last of the Siberian tigers. The last of the dodos, gone two centuries now. The first of these.

THE SCAVENGER'S NURSERY

Maria Dahvana Headley

A boy finds a baby in the garbage. It's hotter this summer than it was the summer before. Everyone in the city is trying to get to the country, because in the city, the rat population is exploding. Rats themselves are exploding, though not of their own volition. Sometimes rats swallow explosives. Sometimes explosives are wrapped in little bobbles of food.

The boy, Danilo, has been doing some work in this regard. Rats are a renewable resource. Today, he's tracking a big rat up the mountain. Beneath his sandals is a hill of plastic and peelings, rubber, blank screens, glass formerly glowing, now reflecting nothing but sun. He looks through red knock-off sunglasses labeled GUCCY. His feet skid on something. Something across the hillock ignites, and he looks suspiciously at the area, judging distance. Fine. No wind today.

This mountain can be seen from space. It has a name, and on maps, it's part of the topography. It's only when you get closer that you can see it for an assemblage, invented earth. Secretly, the boy calls the mountain after himself: *Danilo's Bundók*, as though he's the first explorer to reach its summit. Beneath Danilo's feet, the mountain shudders. A quiver, a coursing, and garbage slides.

In the town below, roofs clang with tin cans, and automobile parts thunder down. It's a storm of junk.

As the avalanche subsides, Danilo becomes aware of something at his feet, pushing out from the layers of refuse. The rat, he thinks, ready for it. It's long as his forearm. He nearly spears it, a wet black thing, its skin shining, blurry, dazzled eyes opening. But it isn't a rat. It is an animal, its flesh hard and soft at once, like a banana bound in iron.

He'll take it home, he thinks, and make it a pet. He's owned other pets, some friendly, some feral. There's a chicken in his history, smut-feathered, beak shiny and perfect, and when he owned that chicken, he stroked it until he lost custody and it became a soup. This pet won't be eaten. There's nothing about it that looks edible.

The thing blinks, showing pale yellow rubbery eyelids, somewhat transparent, and Danilo reaches out and picks it up. It shifts, comforting itself against his fingers, and he thinks *Baby?*

Danilo once held his sister over his shoulder, her silken cheek resting against his neck, her fuzz of hair brushing his face, and so he tries to hold the thing using the same method. He jogs it a bit, and coos, shifting his sack to the other shoulder. Below him, metal roofing vibrates in the sun, hot and glittering, but where he is, far above the town, he's king of the bundók.

He considers his new pet. It's not a monkey, though it has a tail, and grasping fingers. It has a feathery black fringe around its neck, and small rough horns made of something very solid. No teeth, but a clamping mouth, the sort of mouth that would cause a bruise were it allowed to bite. It is very ugly.

Danilo knows he hasn't seen everything. He hasn't seen the stars, though he knows they exist, or once did. On the mountain, he found a tourist magazine with a yellow jacket, and photos of places all around the world, including the bottom of the sea, where a glowing jellyfish orbited in the dark, like a balloon caught in a current, floating higher and higher until the clouds took their color.

Antennae tendril against Danilo's face, radio, television, insect, whisker, he can't tell, but they belong to the baby. The little thing stares up at him, and he feels powerful. He might put the baby down and leave it here in the sun, or he might take it and save it. It's his choice.

It makes a sound, a gurgling crow. Then it begins to cry. Danilo gives it a bit of his T-shirt to suckle at, and it clamps its mouth down on that, nursing at the dirty cotton, smacking. He considers for a moment, and then wraps the baby in the rest of his shirt, constructing a small sling. He makes his way, bare-chested, down the mountain toward home.

As Danilo descends, the mountain pulsates. He looks around, wondering if there's a relief organization bulldozer bringing dirt to cover over some particular toxicity, but shortly, the quivering stops, and he continues, the baby sleeping against his chest.

• • •

The last of the river dolphins. The last of the poisonous frogs. The last of the polar bears. The last of the Siberian tigers. The last of the dodos, gone two centuries now. The first of these.

A small boat moves like a hungover partygoer in Times Square on New Year's Day. Nets stretch out to take samples from the patch—bones and tangles. It's a glittering gyre, colorful bits of wrapping, and metal-lined sacks.

It's the end of the world as we know it, and I feel fine, somebody's music shouts from the cabin, and somebody else yells "Fuck off, Jack. That song's banned from this boat and you know it."

"I miss the nineties," says the somebody, unrepentant.

On deck, Reya Barr sifts fingernails through her fingers. A container of decorated plastic press-ons fell from a Chinese ship six months ago, and here they are, as predicted. She's mapped their theoretical progress on a current chart, but no one ever knows what the ocean will do, not really. She reads the pale pink ovals, one letter at a time. B-R-I-D-E. As though a woman might need to look down midway through her wedding and read her fingertips to tell herself who she is. She puts one on each finger, and crimps her fingers into claws. It's for the money, this cruise. Her student loans are due. BRIDE. Her other hand's all glitter lightning and storm clouds.

This is a particular kind of expedition, a sponsored sail though a plastic sea. The goal is to confirm that the garbage patch is growing, and also to confirm that it's drifting toward Hawaii. Everyone already knows this, but this is science; one hypothesis requires confirmation before another can be made. The scientists are mapping the boundaries of the mass. Garbage flows over the water like something fluid, but it's also distinct, each piece something that can be captured in a net, examined.

She imagines garbage crossing thousands of miles, drawn to this place. A kind of magnetic desire, drawing like to like. The world is collapsing under plastic ducks. Hula hoops. Water bottles. Were she plastic and thrown into a gutter, Reya might be drawn here herself. She'd sail across the sea, until she arrived in this civilization of crumple.

She leans far out over the rail, squinting at something shiny moving in the garbage. Maybe a gull or a trapped fish. There's an ancient smell out here—rot, salt, and darkness.

There's a kind of weird beauty in the reinvention of an ocean. It's not as though things have never changed before. It isn't as though what she floats on wasn't once ice. And the land she walks on, when she's at home? That land was covered with ocean, the sand full of bones of the sea.

She thinks about that when she feels like pretending that none of this is really going to have repercussions. There was oil geysering up in the Gulf of Mexico; the oil was in the news for a while, and then mysteriously gone, as though some giant mouth beneath the ocean sucked it away. It isn't lost. That much oil doesn't get lost. But the world is content to believe that water is big enough to win.

Reya has vials full of water thickened with photodegraded plastic, a slurry of children's toys and dildoes, of baggies, shiny leggings, medical tubing and plankton, and all of it looks like the same thing. It looks like water.

Sometimes she dreams of dropping to the bottom, where none of the world has yet gotten, but even the deepest vents are full of mermaid tears and microplastic. The arteries of the earth are clogged with hotel room keys.

The world's ending, yeah. It's begun to bore her, the sort of horror that's dull when considered too deeply from the deck of a research boat out in the middle of the Pacific.

The thing in the garbage patch is still moving. She watches it idly. There was a storm last night, and today the mass has rolled over. New things are visible, bodies of gulls and fish skeletons, dead jellyfish wrapping about indecipherable gleam. She aims her camera at the thing, zooming in on its motion and filming it. She'll post it to the vessel blog. Look at this, expedition donors, this bit of plastic that looks like an animal. *Look at this un-thing that looks like life.*

The un-thing looks back at her.

"What," she says, quietly, and then her voice rises. "What the hell is that?"

It's not a seal. It's not a shark. It's not anything like anything.

A cloud drapes itself over Mexico City, yellow with gasoline and cigarettes and souls. It hangs there like something solid, low enough to graze the skyscrapers, putting them to their original task, that of touching the fingers of god. But the cloud is not birthing a god; it's birthing another cloud—small, dark, heavy, wet.

In an office building in London, a janitor pushes a wastepaper bin down a hallway. Inside the bin, a plastic sack of shredded accounts rustles against coffee grounds, newspapers. Its heart is full of decapitated payables, receivables, half words and splintered sentences, crumpled muffin wrappers, its blood copy machine toner and printer ink.

The newborn lies at the bottom of the bin, too wobbly to support its own limbs. The janitor swipes a mop along the floor and dumps wastepaper baskets, and each time wastepaper joins the mass, the baby at the bottom of the bin grows bigger.

Danilo puts his garbage baby into a box and feeds it fruit. It rattles and bares its tiny tin teeth. His sister looks into the box, once, and gives him a look of confirmation. Yes, Danilo is a devil on earth. Yes, he would adopt a thing like this thing. She runs from the room spitting tattle like she's a can full of crickets.

Danilo's mother looks into the box, but doesn't really see. It's dark. All she can make out is tail and a fringy black ruff. "That'll get too big," she says. "Better put it out now and save yourself the pain."

"I'll keep it just a little longer," Danilo says.

"Don't get attached," says his mother, knowing he will. These are the sorrows of having a son. Daughters are more bloodthirsty.

So the baby grows. The mountain outside shudders and shakes, shedding layers of garbage, earthquaking, and the baby cries. Danilo worries about it. He isn't feeding it the right food. He gives it a Coke. It whirrs like a motor, and grows fat and sleek on sugar. It sleeps in his bed. It eats a bicycle tire, then a bicycle, broken and twisted after a run-in with a car. Danilo looks at it, assessing its appetite. The mountain is there, and periodically a particularly succulent piece of garbage surges up through layers, a gift for the baby's belly.

Reya reaches over the rail, the fake-fingernails three inches longer than her fingertips. The un-thing swims to her. She hauls it aboard. The garbage gyre roils, and then is still. The creature is small and light, its body covered in aluminum wrappings and fingernails, bones of fish, a bit of kelp, a tentacle of some dead cephalopod caught in a net. It has a black beak, and large, lidless hazel eyes.

The other scientists examine it, brows furrowed, tweezers taking samples. They argue. It's a gull covered in oil; maybe it drifted in from the Gulf. No, it's some other seabird, messed about in garbage and plastic. At last, they decide that it is—it must be—a creature that's been mutated by the plastic water. They photograph it, post the photo to the vessel's blog, and then send the photo to NOAA, asking for backup. People take notice. A contingent rises up and screams about the end of the world, beast numbering, signs.

The un-thing curls in Reya's stateroom, wrapped in a heat blanket, opening its beak periodically for food. Its tentacle twists around the bottle. The only woman on the ship, and here she is, feeding a baby. She's appalled, repulsed, guilty. She can't bring herself to think about what sort of baby it is. It'll become a paper in *Nature*. She'll be the head author. Career-making. New species. She looks at its glassy doll eyes. There was a container of five thousand drink-and-wet baby dolls lost from a ship late last year. She'd originally thought of tracking the baby dolls instead of the fingernails, but decided it was too much metaphor, mapping a sea full of fake babies.

Though she should've known they were coming, Reya isn't expecting it when the helicopter lands on their pad and the uniformed men get out. They'll take the un-thing away from her, probably to a laboratory to be dissected. She looks into the baby's eyes. If anyone's going to kill it, dissect it, display it, it will be her.

Reya carries it onto the helicopter. She cradles it all the way to Washington. She feeds it Styrofoam cups and foil-wrapped candies. She doesn't croon to it or lullaby it. She learns it. That's her job. Does it have reflexes? Yes. Can it speak? Also yes, a mynah, a mimic. She knows things about it that the other scientists don't. It's intelligent. She'll be damned if she lets it pass through her fingers without . . . without, what? She wants to know where its mother is. It didn't come into being out of light and photosynthesis; it was born from the patch. The creature's mother is drifting toward Hawaii.

In the laboratory, Reya looks at the creature, and the creature looks back. It opens its mouth, stretches its jaws, and crumples itself back into a ball. It lives in a tank beside the tanks of the seagulls and the ocean fish to which the lab is comparing its DNA. Reya doesn't feel sympathy for it. It's more complicated than that, and also simpler. She feeds it a classified document, which gives it codes for entry into any locked door in the building. Later, the baby will use the codes to open its cage and rustle out. Later in the night, it will become a Top Secret, but for now, she passes it a latex glove, and watches as it sinks its teeth into it.

A heap of cell phone parts glimmers green as beetle shells. Children sort them. A goat minces its way through a thousand ghost voices, recorded messages crushed into oblivion, texts, naked photos, emails, and pleadings. The goat's white-yellow fur is splashed with turquoise powder from a festival

SPRINGDALE PUBLIC LIBRARY
405 South Pleasant
Springdale, Arkansas 72764

that's now over. It nibbles at a bit of metal, faintly annoyed at the new thing rising from the heap of broken. Children crouch on their heels and watch as a newborn creature stands, twelve feet tall, flashing in the sun. It opens its mouth and screams, and all across the sky, satellites tremble.

This one, at last, hits the international news, but is dismissed as a hoax. Hysteria. Mass hallucination. Some sort of Techno-Environmentalist Bigfoot. Eyes roll in the countries that still have all the money. The creature in the photo is convincing, and that is to the credit of whoever made it, but that's all.

The monster crawls into the forest, its feet tender still, bruised by rocks. After a time, some of the children creep into the trees to feed it. Children are better at feeding monsters than adults are. They don't have the burden of suspicion.

Danilo finds the baby standing in his bedroom one day with a rat in each of its claws. They struggle, upside down.

"Rats aren't food," he tells it, suddenly anxious. He can't tell whether or not the rats are explosive. The baby is six feet tall now, but still doesn't sleep through the night. Its long tail is whippy, and it knocks things down.

It's becoming difficult to keep the baby quiet in his room, though it folds itself small when it sleeps, and he's reminded again of the tiny creature it was when it was born. It requires bottles of oil and dirty water. It needs gasoline. When Danilo fails to feed it on time, it bites at itself. When he fails to feed it what it wants, it bites at him. He feels exhausted by responsibility.

It eats the rats. They explode inside its belly. Danilo cringes, hands over his face, simultaneously hoping for freedom and fearing disaster, but the baby doesn't die. It grows bigger.

In a forest in Montana, a newborn made of sawdust, splinters, engine oil and bird's nests encounters a thing with a chainsaw. It picks the thing up, looks at it curiously, considering its purpose. Satisfied, it crumples the thing in its giant hand, and throws it away, off the logging road and into the river, where it floats for a moment—a bright, chaotic piece of red and white garbage. The body sinks, slowly, and the fish eat it.

The rest of the logging crew is speechless for only as long as it takes to dial the police, who bring news crews along with their sirens.

The monster stands in the place where it was born. Is it confused? Does it care? It is unclear. The newborn's still standing there when the loggers surge around it and cut it down.

Hysteria begins with that footage, worldwide.

Danilo's baby eats more than its weight, making its way onto the mountain at night, scavenging cars. It speaks to the mountain, until, one day, the mountain itself stands up, raining down on all the people surrounding it, and walks away from the place it has always been. The mountain carries its baby in its hands, and Danilo, standing in the doorway of his school building, covers his eyes.

Danilo goes about his business, what business there is. Rats explode. His family flees the city. At night, he looks out and as the world gets darker, the stars are, for the first time in his life, occasionally visible.

Reya Barr lets the monster take her with it when it leaves the lab. It carries her in its arms, and she looks up into its glassy eyes. When it opens its beak to speak it says *Bride*. It says *love*. It says *sleep*. It swims out into the sea, and she rides on its back, free of her student loans, her publication graphs, the way she prayed for an article a year, the scientists who've told her, despite her accomplishments, that she's not their equal. She still thinks of dissecting the monster, but now she feels like a dissected object herself, a doll made of soft materials and stuffed with batting. A thing fallen off a ship and floating. She no longer minds. She sings the song from the rock-and-roll band, the end of the world song, and the garbage monster, the mimic, sings with her.

"And I feel fine."

There are guns, of course, and bombs. There are thoughts of nuclear strikes, but the summer is hotter and hotter, and at first, the monsters aren't killing many people. Those they do kill, they crush efficiently, placing them in sloping piles in the dirt.

Scientists and politicians deliberate. They try bombs, but bombs do nothing. They try poisons and guns. One monster curls up into tiny pieces of garbage, and then resurrects from each piece, a thousand-headed hydra, an impossible excess. More emerge newborn from buried trash, destroying houses and buildings. The earth wears a mantle of paper and plastic, tin cans, DVDs, and all of it is hatching. Perhaps the cold will kill these creatures made of useless things. The research supports it. Blooms have always ended and waters have always run clear again. Eventually, even plagues of locusts starve and fall out of the sky, and the humans, what humans remain, will do as they've always done. They will shovel.

Live and let live, say some.

Already dead, say others.

Use everything, say still others. The people on Earth who've been living in places where everything has already been used look out across the dry plains at the dry crops. They move into caves. They set fires around the perimeters of their camps and villages, because the only thing that keeps the creatures away is fire. Those people survive. The ones who are used to excess do not. They hide amongst their own stockpiles, and there, the conditions are right for births. Even a scrap of paper forgotten might yield a newborn. Even a toothpick, or a rind. Even the dead might yield a newborn, and in a city with an underground full of pauper's unmarked graves, things shake and stir and skeletons assemble into horses, large enough for the monsters to ride.

These are new conditions to become accustomed to, but this is the planet shifting. Earthquakes have flattened cities. Cities have been murdered. The ice has melted. The world adjusts, after screaming and panic, to a new normal. The monsters keep to themselves, and most of the remaining population of the planet does not eventually care. The garbage sleeps at night, and sometimes someone tries to kill it with a gun, or with a knife, but it doesn't die. The rivers run and drift into the sea. Lazy twisted currents, water traveling into lakes and into sky. The garbage moves through the water and rain from the clouds, floats and drifts, and slowly makes a changed world out of mess.

The documents from this period are public now. The deaths—called *mysterious*—of the team of scientists sent to examine that first sea-born baby, the way they were, months after they harvested it from the Pacific Patch, crushed in its tentacles and torn by its beak, the way the hazel eyes blinked when its head moved to swallow them.

The way Reya Barr, the scientist who fetched the baby from the water, was the only one spared as the laboratory was torn apart from the inside out, returned to metal and glass, and how that broken metal and glass rearranged itself into something new. The way more babies were born from this new garbage, and how they emerged from the building, flooding the parking garages, swarming down the street, overturning cars as they moved, turning the cars into wrecks, turning the wrecks into more of themselves.

A bloom of babies. A swarm. A plague.

And can joy be read between the lines of the official prose? Vindication, certainly. The world was indeed ending. Certain of the official documents reflect that conviction. Everything was beginning again. Slates were wiped clean.

The President gave an address, of course, an Emergency State of the Union, but as he spoke, he realized that all he could say was that people should stay away from the garbage.

Fresh Kills landfill walked into New York City, miles tall and miles deep. In Rome, Monte Testaccio shook off the trees on its back, and stood up to trample, its body made of the shards of ancient amphorae, once full of olive oil, now coated in lime.

The rules of the world changed. There was an evolution, a shift in everything.

The last of the senators. The last of the secretaries. The last of the chieftains. The last of the burlesque dancers. The last of the astrophysicists.

The first of these.

The cities empty. The streets stop moving. The nights get quieter and darker. Danilo is one of the last left in his city, and as he grows older, sometimes he sees the garbage mountain walking, moving past his shack, and beside it, the smaller body of its baby, walking with long strides, a slipping thing with a hard shell, horns, a black plastic fringe fluttering in the hot breeze. Beyond the city limits, there's a new mountain, this one made of human bones, and in its layers the rats move as they always have, turning the secrets of centuries to sediment.

Somewhere in the Pacific, Reya Barr floats on a raft made of detritus, her back supported by plastic bottles, held above the surface by the fingers of soda rings. Her hair is long and white now, and it trails into the deep, and her eyes are blind from too much sun.

Some things are still as they've always been on earth. There are fewer people, but they still fight and still fuck. Some people are frightened of the dark, and some are not. In one of the cities, a human throws something away. A dog finds it in the garbage, snuffles it and barks, and a gleaming, clattering creature kneels and picks the garbage up, carries it away, cradling it, rocking it.

As it's carried, the human baby cries, a thin cry, and then it's soothed by the thing that has found it. This green-skinned creature sings out a lullaby in all the former languages of the world, for *more signal*, for

Can you even hear me? And

Fuck you, just go and fuck yourself if you're going to be like that I'm telling you I'm done and

I love you so much, oh my god I love you so much and

I'm going to tell you something I've never told anyone before and

The creature opens its mouth wider and vibrates to all the satellites, to everyone who has ever occupied the place it occupies now. It holds the human baby in its metal hands, and talks to the sky.

I'm losing you, it trills in every language ever spoken through telephony. *I'm losing you.*

Maria Dahvana Headley is a *New York Times* bestselling author and editor whose books include *Magonia, Queen of Kings, The Year of Yes*, and with Kat Howard, *The End of the Sentence*. With Neil Gaiman, she is the editor of the anthology *Unnatural Creatures*. Upcoming is *Aerie: A Magonia Novel*, and *Beowulf* adaptation *The Mere Wife*, as well as a short story collection, with Farrar, Straus & Giroux. Her Nebula and Shirley Jackson Award-nominated short fiction has been anthologized in many year's bests. Her work has been supported by The MacDowell Colony, and Arte Studio Ginestrelle, among others.

He imagined the black dog squatting on the roof, cutting out all sunlight, all emotion, all feeling and truth. Something had turned down the volume in that house, pushed all the colors into black and white.

BLACK DOG

Neil Gaiman

There were ten tongues within one head
And one went out to fetch some bread,
To feed the living and the dead.
                                    —Old Riddle

I
The Bar Guest

Outside the pub it was raining cats and dogs.

Shadow was still not entirely convinced that he was in a pub. True, there was a tiny bar at the back of the room, with bottles behind it and a couple of the huge taps you pulled, and there were several high tables and people were drinking at the tables, but it all felt like a room in somebody's house. The dogs helped reinforce that impression. It seemed to Shadow that everybody in the pub had a dog except for him.

"What kind of dogs are they?" Shadow asked, curious. The dogs reminded him of greyhounds, but they were smaller and seemed saner, more placid and less high-strung than the greyhounds he had encountered over the years.

"Lurchers," said the pub's landlord, coming out from behind the bar. He was carrying a pint of beer that he had poured for himself. "Best dogs. Poacher's dogs. Fast, smart, lethal." He bent down, scratched a chestnut-and-white brindled dog behind the ears. The dog stretched and luxuriated in the ear-scratching. It did not look particularly lethal, and Shadow said so.

The landlord, his hair a mop of grey and orange, scratched at his beard reflectively. "That's where you'd be wrong," he said. "I walked with his brother last week, down Cumpsy Lane. There's a fox, a big red reynard, pokes his head out of a hedge, no more than twenty meters down the road, then, plain as day, saunters out onto the track. Well, Needles sees it, and he's off after it like the clappers. Next thing you know, Needles has his teeth in reynard's neck, and one bite, one hard shake, and it's all over."

Shadow inspected Needles, a grey dog sleeping by the little fireplace. He looked harmless too. "So what sort of a breed is a lurcher? It's an English breed, yes?"

"It's not actually a breed," said a white-haired woman without a dog who had been leaning on a nearby table. "They're crossbred for speed, stamina. Sighthound, greyhound, collie."

The man next to her held up a finger. "You must understand," he said, cheerfully, "that there used to be laws about who could own purebred dogs. The local folk couldn't, but they could own mongrels. And lurchers are better and faster than pedigree dogs." He pushed his spectacles up his nose with the tip of his forefinger. He had a mutton-chop beard, brown flecked with white.

"Ask me, all mongrels are better than pedigree anything," said the woman. "It's why America is such an interesting country. Filled with mongrels." Shadow was not certain how old she was. Her hair was white, but she seemed younger than her hair.

"Actually, darling," said the man with the mutton-chops, in his gentle voice, "I think you'll find that the Americans are keener on pedigree dogs than the British. I met a woman from the American Kennel Club, and honestly, she scared me. I was scared."

"I wasn't talking about dogs, Ollie," said the woman. "I was talking about . . . Oh, never mind."

"What are you drinking?" asked the landlord.

There was a handwritten piece of paper taped to the wall by the bar telling customers not to order a lager "as a punch in the face often offends."

"What's good and local?" asked Shadow, who had learned that this was mostly the wisest thing to say.

The landlord and the woman had various suggestions as to which of the various local beers and ciders were good. The little mutton-chopped man interrupted them to point out that in his opinion *good* was not the avoidance of evil, but something more positive than that: it was making the world a better place. Then he chuckled, to show that he was only joking and that he knew that the conversation was really only about what to drink.

The beer the landlord poured for Shadow was dark and very bitter. He was not certain that he liked it. "What is it?"

"It's called Black Dog," said the woman. "I've heard people say it was named after the way you feel after you've had one too many."

"Like Churchill's moods," said the little man.

"Actually, the beer is named after a local dog," said a younger woman. She was wearing an olive-green sweater, and standing against the wall. "But not a real one. Semi-imaginary."

Shadow looked down at Needles, then hesitated. "Is it safe to scratch his head?" he asked, remembering the fate of the fox.

"Course it is," said the white-haired woman. "He loves it. Don't you?"

"Well. He practically had that tosser from Glossop's finger off," said the landlord. There was admiration mixed with warning in his voice.

"I think he was something in local government," said the woman. "And I've always thought that there's nothing wrong with dogs biting *them*. Or VAT inspectors."

The woman in the green sweater moved over to Shadow. She was not holding a drink. She had dark, short hair, and a crop of freckles that spattered her nose and cheeks. She looked at Shadow. "You aren't in local government, are you?"

Shadow shook his head. He said, "I'm kind of a tourist." It was not actually untrue. He was traveling, anyway.

"You're Canadian?" said the mutton-chop man.

"American," said Shadow. "But I've been on the road for a while now."

"Then," said the white-haired woman, "you aren't actually a tourist. Tourists turn up, see the sights and leave."

Shadow shrugged, smiled, and leaned down. He scratched the landlord's lurcher on the back of its head.

"You're not a dog person, are you?" asked the dark-haired woman.

"I'm not a dog person," said Shadow.

Had he been someone else, someone who talked about what was happening inside his head, Shadow might have told her that his wife had owned dogs when she was younger, and sometimes called Shadow *puppy* because she wanted a dog she could not have. But Shadow kept things on the inside. It was one of the things he liked about the British: even when they wanted to know what was happening on the inside, they did not ask.

The world on the inside remained the world on the inside. His wife had been dead for three years now.

"If you ask me," said the man with the mutton-chops, "people are either dog people or cat people. So would you then consider yourself a cat person?"

Shadow reflected. "I don't know. We never had pets when I was a kid, we were always on the move. But—"

"I mention this," the man continued, "because our host also has a cat, which you might wish to see."

"Used to be out here, but we moved it to the back room," said the landlord, from behind the bar.

Shadow wondered how the man could follow the conversation so easily while also taking people's meal orders and serving their drinks. "Did the cat upset the dogs?" he asked.

Outside, the rain redoubled. The wind moaned, and whistled, and then howled. The log fire burning in the little fireplace coughed and spat.

"Not in the way you're thinking," said the landlord. "We found it when we knocked through into the room next door, when we needed to extend the bar." The man grinned. "Come and look."

Shadow followed the man into the room next door. The mutton-chop man and the white-haired woman came with them, walking a little behind Shadow.

Shadow glanced back into the bar. The dark-haired woman was watching him, and she smiled warmly when he caught her eye.

The room next door was better lit, larger, and it felt a little less like somebody's front room. People were sitting at tables, eating. The food looked good and smelled better. The landlord led Shadow to the back of the room, to a dusty glass case.

"There she is," said the landlord, proudly.

The cat was brown, and it looked, at first glance, as if it had been constructed out of tendons and agony. The holes that were its eyes were filled with anger and with pain; the mouth was wide open, as if the creature had been yowling when she was turned to leather.

"The practice of placing animals in the walls of buildings is similar to the practice of walling up children alive in the foundations of a house you want to stay up," explained the mutton-chop man, from behind him. "Although mummified cats always make me think of the mummified cats they found around the temple of Bast in Bubastis in Egypt. So many tons of mummified cats that they sent them to England to be ground up as cheap fertilizer and dumped on the fields. The Victorians also made paint out of mummies. A sort of brown, I believe."

"It looks miserable," said Shadow. "How old is it?"

The landlord scratched his cheek. "We reckon that the wall she was in went up somewhere between 1300 and 1600. That's from parish records. There's nothing here in 1300, and there's a house in 1600. The stuff in the middle was lost."

The dead cat in the glass case, furless and leathery, seemed to be watching them, from its empty black-hole eyes.

I got eyes wherever my folk walk, breathed a voice in the back of Shadow's mind. He thought, momentarily, about the fields fertilized with the ground mummies of cats, and what strange crops they must have grown.

"They put him into an old house side," said the man called Ollie. *"And there he lived and there he died. And nobody either laughed or cried.* All sorts of things were walled up, to make sure that things were guarded and safe. Children, sometimes. Animals. They did it in churches as a matter of course."

The rain beat an arrhythmic rattle on the windowpane. Shadow thanked the landlord for showing him the cat. They went back into the taproom. The dark-haired woman had gone, which gave Shadow a moment of regret. She had looked so friendly. Shadow bought a round of drinks for the mutton-chop man, the white-haired woman, and one for the landlord.

The landlord ducked behind the bar. "They call me Shadow," Shadow told them. "Shadow Moon."

The mutton-chop man pressed his hands together in delight. "Oh! How wonderful. I had an Alsatian named Shadow, when I was a boy. Is it your real name?"

"It's what they call me," said Shadow.

"I'm Moira Callanish," said the white-haired woman. "This is my partner, Oliver Bierce. He knows a lot, and he will, during the course of our acquaintance, undoubtedly tell you everything he knows."

They shook hands. When the landlord returned with their drinks, Shadow asked if the pub had a room to rent. He had intended to walk further that night, but the rain sounded like it had no intention of giving up. He had stout walking shoes, and weather-resistant outer clothes, but he did not want to walk in the rain.

"I used to, but then my son moved back in. I'll encourage people to sleep it off in the barn, on occasion, but that's as far as I'll go these days."

"Anywhere in the village I could get a room?"

The landlord shook his head. "It's a foul night. But Porsett is only a few miles down the road, and they've got a proper hotel there. I can call Sandra, tell her that you're coming. What's your name?"

"Shadow," said Shadow again. "Shadow Moon."

Moira looked at Oliver, and said something that sounded like "waifs and strays?" and Oliver chewed his lip for a moment, and then he nodded enthusiastically. "Would you fancy spending the night with us? The spare room's a bit of a box room, but it does have a bed in it. And it's warm there. And dry."

"I'd like that very much," said Shadow. "I can pay."

"Don't be silly," said Moira. "It will be nice to have a guest."

II
The Gibbet

Oliver and Moira both had umbrellas. Oliver insisted that Shadow carry his umbrella, pointing out that Shadow towered over him, and thus was ideally suited to keep the rain off both of them.

The couple also carried little flashlights, which they called torches. The word put Shadow in mind of villagers in a horror movie storming the castle on the hill, and the lightning and thunder added to the vision. *Tonight, my creature*, he thought, *I will give you life!* It should have been hokey but instead it was disturbing. The dead cat had put him into a strange set of mind.

The narrow roads between fields were running with rainwater.

"On a nice night," said Moira, raising her voice to be heard over the rain, "we would just walk over the fields. But they'll be all soggy and boggy, so we're going down by Shuck's Lane. Now, that tree was a gibbet tree, once upon a time." She pointed to a massive-trunked sycamore at the crossroads. It had only a few branches left, sticking up into the night like afterthoughts.

"Moira's lived here since she was in her twenties," said Oliver. "I came up from London, about eight years ago. From Turnham Green. I'd come up here on holiday originally when I was fourteen and I never forgot it. You don't."

"The land gets into your blood," said Moira. "Sort of."

"And the blood gets into the land," said Oliver. "One way or another. You take that gibbet tree, for example. They would leave people in the gibbet until there was nothing left. Hair gone to make bird's nests, flesh all eaten by ravens, bones picked clean. Or until they had another corpse to display anyway."

Shadow was fairly sure he knew what a gibbet was, but he asked anyway. There was never any harm in asking, and Oliver was definitely the kind of person who took pleasure in knowing peculiar things and in passing his knowledge on.

"Like a huge iron birdcage. They used them to display the bodies of executed criminals, after justice had been served. The gibbets were locked, so the family and friends couldn't steal the body back and give it a good Christian burial. Keeping passersby on the straight and narrow, although I doubt it actually deterred anyone from anything."

"Who were they executing?"

"Anyone who got unlucky. Three hundred years ago, there were over two hundred crimes punishable by death. Including traveling with Gypsies for more than a month, stealing sheep—and, for that matter, anything over twelve pence in value—and writing a threatening letter."

He might have been about to begin a lengthy list, but Moira broke in. "Oliver's right about the death sentence, but they only gibbeted murderers, up these parts. And they'd leave corpses in the gibbet for twenty years, sometimes. We didn't get a lot of murders." And then, as if trying to change the subject to something lighter, she said, "We are now walking down Shuck's Lane. The locals say that on a clear night, which tonight certainly is not, you can find yourself being followed by Black Shuck. He's a sort of a fairy dog."

"We've never seen him, not even on clear nights," said Oliver.

"Which is a very good thing," said Moira. "Because if you see him—you die."

"Except Sandra Wilberforce said she saw him, and she's healthy as a horse."

Shadow smiled. "What does Black Shuck do?"

"He doesn't do anything," said Oliver.

"He does. He follows you home," corrected Moira. "And then, a bit later, you die."

"Doesn't sound very scary," said Shadow. "Except for the dying bit."

They reached the bottom of the road. Rainwater was running like a stream over Shadow's thick hiking boots.

Shadow said, "So how did you two meet?" It was normally a safe question, when you were with couples.

Oliver said, "In the pub. I was up here on holiday, really."

Moira said, "I was with someone when I met Oliver. We had a very brief, torrid affair, then we ran off together. Most unlike both of us."

They did not seem like the kind of people who ran off together, thought Shadow. But then, all people were strange. He knew he should say something.

"I was married. My wife was killed in a car crash."

"I'm so sorry," said Moira.

"It happened," said Shadow.

"When we get home," said Moira, "I'm making us all whisky macs. That's whisky and ginger wine and hot water. And I'm having a hot bath. Otherwise I'll catch my death."

Shadow imagined reaching out his hand and catching death in it, like a baseball, and he shivered.

The rain redoubled, and a sudden flash of lightning burned the world into existence all around them: every grey rock in the drystone wall, every blade of grass, every puddle and every tree was perfectly illuminated, and then swallowed by a deeper darkness, leaving afterimages on Shadow's night-blinded eyes.

"Did you see that?" asked Oliver. "Damnedest thing." The thunder rolled and rumbled, and Shadow waited until it was done before he tried to speak.

"I didn't see anything," said Shadow. Another flash, less bright, and Shadow thought he saw something moving away from them in a distant field. "That?" he asked.

"It's a donkey," said Moira. "Only a donkey."

Oliver stopped. He said, "This was the wrong way to come home. We should have got a taxi. This was a mistake."

"Ollie," said Moira. "It's not far now. And it's just a spot of rain. You aren't made of sugar, darling."

Another flash of lightning, so bright as to be almost blinding. There was nothing to be seen in the fields.

Darkness. Shadow turned back to Oliver, but the little man was no longer standing beside him. Oliver's flashlight was on the ground. Shadow blinked his eyes, hoping to force his night vision to return. The man had collapsed, crumpled onto the wet grass on the side of the lane.

"Ollie?" Moira crouched beside him, her umbrella by her side. She shone her flashlight onto his face. Then she looked at Shadow. "He can't just sit here," she said, sounding confused and concerned. "It's pouring."

Shadow pocketed Oliver's flashlight, handed his umbrella to Moira, then picked Oliver up. The man did not seem to weigh much, and Shadow was a big man.

"Is it far?"

"Not far," she said. "Not really. We're almost home."

They walked in silence, across a churchyard on the edge of a village green, and into a village. Shadow could see lights on in the grey stone houses that edged the one street. Moira turned off, into a house set back from the road, and Shadow followed her. She held the back door open for him.

The kitchen was large and warm, and there was a sofa, half-covered with magazines, against one wall. There were low beams in the kitchen, and Shadow needed to duck his head. Shadow removed Oliver's raincoat and dropped it. It puddled on the wooden floor. Then he put the man down on the sofa.

Moira filled the kettle.

"Do we call an ambulance?"

She shook her head.

"This is just something that happens? He falls down and passes out?"

Moira busied herself getting mugs from a shelf. "It's happened before. Just not for a long time. He's narcoleptic, and if something surprises or scares him he can just go down like that. He'll come round soon. He'll want tea. No whisky mac tonight, not for him. Sometimes he's a bit dazed and doesn't know where he is, sometimes he's been following everything that happened while he was out. And he hates it if you make a fuss. Put your backpack down by the Aga."

The kettle boiled. Moira poured the steaming water into a teapot. "He'll have a cup of real tea. I'll have chamomile, I think, or I won't sleep tonight. Calm my nerves. You?"

"I'll drink tea, sure," said Shadow. He had walked more than twenty miles that day, and sleep would be easy in the finding. He wondered at Moira. She appeared perfectly self-possessed in the face of her partner's incapacity, and he wondered how much of it was not wanting to show weakness in front of a stranger. He admired her, although he found it peculiar. The English were strange. But he understood hating "making a fuss." Yes.

Oliver stirred on the couch. Moira was at his side with a cup of tea, helped him into a sitting position. He sipped the tea, in a slightly dazed fashion.

"It followed me home," he said, conversationally.

"What followed you, Ollie, darling?" Her voice was steady, but there was concern in it.

"The dog," said the man on the sofa, and he took another sip of his tea. "The black dog."

• • •

III

The Cuts

These were the things Shadow learned that night, sitting around the kitchen table with Moira and Oliver:

He learned that Oliver had not been happy or fulfilled in his London advertising agency job. He had moved up to the village and taken an extremely early medical retirement. Now, initially for recreation and increasingly for money, he repaired and rebuilt drystone walls. There was, he explained, an art and a skill to wall building, it was excellent exercise, and, when done correctly, a meditative practice.

"There used to be hundreds of drystone wall people around here. Now there's barely a dozen who know what they're doing. You see walls repaired with concrete, or with breeze blocks. It's a dying art. I'd love to show you how I do it. Useful skill to have. Picking the rock, sometimes, you have to let the rock tell you where it goes. And then it's immovable. You couldn't knock it down with a tank. Remarkable."

He learned that Oliver had been very depressed several years earlier, shortly after Moira and he got together, but that for the last few years he had been doing very well. Or, he amended, relatively well.

He learned that Moira was independently wealthy, that her family trust fund had meant she and her sisters had not needed to work, but that, in her late twenties, she had gone for teacher training. That she no longer taught, but that she was extremely active in local affairs, and had campaigned successfully to keep the local bus routes in service.

Shadow learned, from what Oliver didn't say, that Oliver was scared of something, very scared, and that when Oliver was asked what had frightened him so badly, and what he had meant by saying that the black dog had followed him home, his response was to stammer and to sway. He learned not to ask Oliver any more questions.

This is what Oliver and Moira had learned about Shadow sitting around that kitchen table:

Nothing much.

Shadow liked them. He was not a stupid man; he had trusted people in the past who had betrayed him, but he liked this couple, and he liked the way their home smelled—like bread-making and jam and walnut wood-polish—and he went to sleep that night in his box-room bedroom worrying about the little man with the mutton-chop beard. What if the thing Shadow had glimpsed in the field had *not* been a donkey? What if it *had* been an enormous dog? What then?

The rain had stopped when Shadow woke. He made himself toast in the empty kitchen. Moira came in from the garden, letting a gust of chilly air in through the kitchen door. "Sleep well?" she asked.

"Yes. Very well." He had dreamed of being at the zoo. He had been surrounded by animals he could not see, which snuffled and snorted in their pens. He was a child, walking with his mother, and he was safe and he was loved. He had stopped in front of a lion's cage, but what had been in the cage was a sphinx, half lion and half woman, her tail swishing. She had smiled at him, and her smile had been his mother's smile. He heard her voice, accented and warm and feline.

It said, *Know thyself.*

I know who I am, said Shadow in his dream, holding the bars of the cage. Behind the bars was the desert. He could see pyramids. He could see shadows on the sand.

Then who are you, Shadow? What are you running from? Where are you running to?

Who are you?

And he had woken, wondering why he was asking himself that question, and missing his mother, who had died twenty years before, when he was a teenager. He still felt oddly comforted, remembering the feel of his hand in his mother's hand.

"I'm afraid Ollie's a bit under the weather this morning."

"Sorry to hear that."

"Yes. Well, can't be helped."

"I'm really grateful for the room. I guess I'll be on my way."

Moira said, "Will you look at something for me?"

Shadow nodded, then followed her outside, and round the side of the house. She pointed to the rose bed. "What does that look like to you?"

Shadow bent down. "*The footprint of an enormous hound,*" he said. "To quote Dr. Watson."

"Yes," she said. "It really does."

"If there's a spectral ghost-hound out there," said Shadow, "it shouldn't leave footprints. Should it?"

"I'm not actually an authority on these matters," said Moira. "I had a friend once who could have told us all about it. But she . . . " She trailed off.

Then, more brightly, "You know, Mrs. Camberley two doors down has a Doberman Pinscher. Ridiculous thing." Shadow was not certain whether the ridiculous thing was Mrs. Camberley or her dog.

He found the events of the previous night less troubling and odd, more explicable. What did it matter if a strange dog had followed them home? Oliver had been frightened or startled, and had collapsed, from narcolepsy, from shock.

"Well, I'll pack you some lunch before you go," said Moira. "Boiled eggs. That sort of thing. You'll be glad of them on the way."

They went into the house. Moira went to put something away, and returned looking shaken.

"Oliver's locked himself in the bathroom," she said.

Shadow was not certain what to say.

"You know what I wish?" she continued.

"I don't."

"I wish you would talk to him. I wish he would open the door. I wish he'd talk to me. I can hear him in there. I can hear him."

And then, "I hope he isn't cutting himself again."

Shadow walked back into the hall, stood by the bathroom door, called Oliver's name. "Can you hear me? Are you okay?"

Nothing. No sound from inside.

Shadow looked at the door. It was solid wood. The house was old, and they built them strong and well back then. When Shadow had used the bathroom that morning he'd learned the lock was a hook and eye. He leaned on the handle of the door, pushing it down, then rammed his shoulder against the door. It opened with a noise of splintering wood.

He had watched a man die in prison, stabbed in a pointless argument. He remembered the way that the blood had puddled about the man's body, lying in the back corner of the exercise yard. The sight had troubled Shadow, but he had forced himself to look, and to keep looking. To look away would somehow have felt disrespectful.

Oliver was naked on the floor of the bathroom. His body was pale, and his chest and groin were covered with thick, dark hair. He held the blade from an ancient safety razor in his hands. He had sliced his arms with it, his chest above the nipples, his inner thighs and his penis. Blood was smeared on his body, on the black and white linoleum floor, on the white enamel of the bathtub. Oliver's eyes were round and wide, like the eyes of a bird. He was looking directly at Shadow, but Shadow was not certain that he was being seen.

"Ollie?" said Moira's voice, from the hall. Shadow realized that he was blocking the doorway and he hesitated, unsure whether to let her see what was on the floor or not.

Shadow took a pink towel from the towel rail and wrapped it around Oliver. That got the little man's attention. He blinked, as if seeing Shadow for the first time, and said, "The dog. It's for the dog. It must be fed, you see. We're making friends."

Moira said, "Oh my dear sweet god."

"I'll call the emergency services."

"Please don't," she said. "He'll be fine at home with me. I don't know what I'll . . . please?"

Shadow picked up Oliver, swaddled in the towel, carried him into the bedroom as if he were a child, and then placed him on the bed. Moira followed. She picked up an iPad by the bed, touched the screen, and music began to play. "Breathe, Ollie," she said. "Remember. Breathe. It's going to be fine. You're going to be fine."

"I can't really breathe," said Oliver, in a small voice. "Not really. I can feel my heart, though. I can feel my heart beating."

Moira squeezed his hand and sat down on the bed, and Shadow left them alone.

When Moira entered the kitchen, her sleeves rolled up, and her hands smelling of antiseptic cream, Shadow was sitting on the sofa, reading a guide to local walks.

"How's he doing?"

She shrugged.

"You have to get him help."

"Yes." She stood in the middle of the kitchen and looked about her, as if unable to decide which way to turn. "Do you . . . I mean, do you have to leave today? Are you on a schedule?"

"Nobody's waiting for me. Anywhere."

She looked at him with a face that had grown haggard in an hour. "When this happened before, it took a few days, but then he was right as rain. The depression doesn't stay long. So, just wondering, would you just, well, stick around? I phoned my sister but she's in the middle of moving. And I can't cope on my own. I really can't. Not again. But I can't ask you to stay, not if anyone is waiting for you."

"Nobody's waiting," repeated Shadow. "And I'll stick around. But I think Oliver needs specialist help."

"Yes," agreed Moira. "He does."

Dr. Scathelocke came over late that afternoon. He was a friend of Oliver and Moira's. Shadow was not entirely certain whether rural British doctors still made house calls, or whether this was a socially justified visit. The doctor went into the bedroom, and came out twenty minutes later.

He sat at the kitchen table with Moira, and he said, "It's all very shallow. Cry-for-help stuff. Honestly, there's not a lot we can do for him in hospital that you can't do for him here, what with the cuts. We used to have a dozen nurses in that wing. Now they are trying to close it down completely. Get it all back to the community."

Dr. Scathelocke had sandy hair, was as tall as Shadow but lankier. He reminded Shadow of the landlord in the pub, and he wondered idly if the two men were related. The doctor scribbled several prescriptions, and Moira handed them to Shadow, along with the keys to an old white Range Rover.

Shadow drove to the next village, found the little chemists' and waited for the prescriptions to be filled. He stood awkwardly in the overlit aisle, staring at a display of suntan lotions and creams, sadly redundant in this cold wet summer.

"You're Mr. American," said a woman's voice from behind him. He turned. She had short dark hair and was wearing the same olive-green sweater she had been wearing in the pub.

"I guess I am," he said.

"Local gossip says that you are helping out while Ollie's under the weather."

"That was fast."

"Local gossip travels faster than light. I'm Cassie Burglass."

"Shadow Moon."

"Good name," she said. "Gives me chills." She smiled. "If you're still rambling while you're here, I suggest you check out the hill just past the village. Follow the track up until it forks, and then go left. It takes you up Wod's Hill. Spectacular views. Public right of way. Just keep going left and up, you can't miss it."

She smiled at him. Perhaps she was just being friendly to a stranger.

"I'm not surprised you're still here though," Cassie continued. "It's hard to leave this place once it gets its claws into you." She smiled again, a warm smile, and she looked directly into his eyes, as if trying to make up her mind. "I think Mrs. Patel has your prescriptions ready. Nice talking to you, Mr. American."

IV
The Kiss

Shadow helped Moira. He walked down to the village shop and bought the items on her shopping list while she stayed in the house, writing at the kitchen table or hovering in the hallway outside the bedroom door. Moira barely talked. He ran errands in the white Range Rover, and saw Oliver mostly in the hall, shuffling to the bathroom and back. The man did not speak to him.

Everything was quiet in the house: Shadow imagined the black dog squatting on the roof, cutting out all sunlight, all emotion, all feeling and truth. Something had turned down the volume in that house, pushed all the colors into black and white. He wished he was somewhere else, but could not run out on them. He sat on his bed, and stared out of the window at the rain puddling its way down the windowpane, and felt the seconds of his life counting off, never to come back.

It had been wet and cold, but on the third day the sun came out. The world did not warm up, but Shadow tried to pull himself out of the grey haze, and decided to see some of the local sights. He walked to the next village, through fields, up paths and along the side of a long drystone wall. There was a bridge over a narrow stream that was little more than a plank, and Shadow jumped the water in one easy bound. Up the hill: there were trees, oak and hawthorn, sycamore and beech at the bottom of the hill, and then the trees became sparser. He followed the winding trail, sometimes obvious, sometimes not, until he reached a natural resting place, like a tiny meadow, high on the hill, and there he turned away from the hill and saw the valleys and the peaks arranged all about him in greens and greys like illustrations from a children's book.

He was not alone up there. A woman with short dark hair was sitting and sketching on the hill's side, perched comfortably on a grey boulder. There was a tree behind her, which acted as a windbreak. She wore a green sweater and blue jeans, and he recognized Cassie Burglass before he saw her face.

As he got close, she turned. "What do you think?" she asked, holding her sketchbook up for his inspection. It was an assured pencil drawing of the hillside.

"You're very good. Are you a professional artist?"

"I dabble," she said.

Shadow had spent enough time talking to the English to know that this meant either that she dabbled, or that her work was regularly hung in the National Gallery or the Tate Modern.

"You must be cold," he said. "You're only wearing a sweater."

"I'm cold," she said. "But, up here, I'm used to it. It doesn't really bother me. How's Ollie doing?"

"He's still under the weather," Shadow told her.

"Poor old sod," she said, looking from her paper to the hillside and back. "It's hard for me to feel properly sorry for him, though."

"Why's that? Did he bore you to death with interesting facts?"

She laughed, a small huff of air at the back of her throat. "You really ought to listen to more village gossip. When Ollie and Moira met, they were both with other people."

"I know that. They told me that." Shadow thought a moment. "So he was with you first?"

"No. *She* was. We'd been together since college." There was a pause. She shaded something, her pencil scraping the paper. "Are you going to try and kiss me?" she asked.

"I, uh. I, um," he said. Then, honestly, "It hadn't occurred to me."

"Well," she said, turning to smile at him, "it bloody well should. I mean, I asked you up here, and you came, up to Wod's Hill, just to see me." She went back to the paper and the drawing of the hill. "They say there's dark doings been done on this hill. Dirty dark doings. And I was thinking of doing something dirty myself. To Moira's lodger."

"Is this some kind of revenge plot?"

"It's not an anything plot. I just like you. And there's no one around here who wants me any longer. Not as a woman."

The last woman that Shadow had kissed had been in Scotland. He thought of her, and what she had become, in the end. "You *are* real, aren't you?" he asked. "I mean . . . you're a real person. I mean. . . "

She put the pad of paper down on the boulder and she stood up. "Kiss me and find out," she said.

He hesitated. She sighed, and she kissed him.

It was cold on that hillside, and Cassie's lips were cold. Her mouth was very soft. As her tongue touched his, Shadow pulled back.

"I don't actually know you," Shadow said.

She leaned away from him, looked up into his face. "You know," she said, "all I dream of these days is somebody who will look my way and see the real me. I had given up until you came along, Mr. American, with your funny name. But you looked at me, and I knew you saw me. And that's all that matters."

Shadow's hands held her, feeling the softness of her sweater.

"How much longer are you going to be here? In the district?" she asked.

"A few more days. Until Oliver's feeling better."

"Pity. Can't you stay forever?"

"I'm sorry?"

"You have nothing to be sorry for, sweet man. You see that opening over there?"

He glanced over to the hillside, but could not see what she was pointing at. The hillside was a tangle of weeds and low trees and half-tumbled drystone walls. She pointed to her drawing, where she had drawn a dark shape, like an archway, in the middle of clump of gorse bushes on the side of the hill. "There. Look." He stared, and this time he saw it immediately.

"What is it?" Shadow asked.

"The Gateway to Hell," she told him, impressively.

"Uh-huh."

She grinned. "That's what they call it round here. It was originally a Roman temple, I think, or something even older. But that's all that remains. You should check it out, if you like that sort of thing. Although it's a bit disappointing: just a little passageway going back into the hill. I keep expecting some archaeologists will come out this way, dig it up, catalog what they find, but they never do."

Shadow examined her drawing. "So what do you know about big black dogs?" he asked.

"The one in Shuck's Lane?" she said. He nodded. "They say the barghest used to wander all around here. But now it's just in Shuck's Lane. Dr. Scathelocke once told me it was folk memory. The Wish Hounds are all that are left of the wild hunt, which was based around the idea of Odin's hunting wolves, Freki and Geri. I think it's even older than that. Cave memory. Druids. The thing that prowls in the darkness beyond the fire circle, waiting to tear you apart if you edge too far out alone."

"Have you ever seen it, then?"

She shook her head. "No. I researched it, but never saw it. My semi-imaginary local beast. Have you?"

"I don't think so. Maybe."

"Perhaps you woke it up when you came here. You woke me up, after all."

She reached up, pulled his head down towards her and kissed him again. She took his left hand, so much bigger than hers, and placed it beneath her sweater.

"Cassie, my hands are cold," he warned her.

"Well, my everything is cold. There's nothing *but* cold up here. Just smile and look like you know what you're doing," she told him. She pushed Shadow's left hand higher, until it was cupping the lace of her bra, and he could feel, beneath the lace, the hardness of her nipple and the soft swell of her breast.

He began to surrender to the moment, his hesitation a mixture of awkwardness and uncertainty. He was not sure how he felt about this woman: she had history with his benefactors, after all. Shadow never liked feeling that he was being used; it had happened too many times before. But his left hand was touching her breast and his right hand was cradling the nape of her neck, and he was leaning down and now her mouth was on his, and she was clinging to him as tightly as if, he thought, she wanted to occupy the very same space that he was in. Her mouth tasted like mint and stone and grass and the chilly afternoon breeze. He closed his eyes, and let himself enjoy the kiss and the way their bodies moved together.

Cassie froze. Somewhere close to them, a cat mewed. Shadow opened his eyes.

"Jesus," he said.

They were surrounded by cats. White cats and tabbies, brown and ginger and black cats, long-haired and short. Well-fed cats with collars and disreputable ragged-eared cats that looked as if they had been living in barns and on the edges of the wild. They stared at Shadow and Cassie with green eyes and blue eyes and golden eyes, and they did not move. Only the occasional swish of a tail or the blinking of a pair of feline eyes told Shadow that they were alive.

"This is weird," said Shadow.

Cassie took a step back. He was no longer touching her now. "Are they with you?" she asked.

"I don't think they're with anyone. They're cats."

"I think they're jealous," said Cassie. "Look at them. They don't like me."

"That's . . . " Shadow was going to say "nonsense," but no, it was sense, of a kind. There had been a woman who was a goddess, a continent away and years in his past, who had cared about him, in her own way. He remembered the needle-sharpness of her nails and the catlike roughness of her tongue.

Cassie looked at Shadow dispassionately. "I don't know who you are, Mr. American," she told him. "Not really. I don't know why you can look at me and see the real me, or why I can talk to you when I find it so hard to talk to other people. But I can. And you know, you seem all normal and quiet on the surface, but you are so much weirder than I am. And I'm extremely fucking weird."

Shadow said, "Don't go."

"Tell Ollie and Moira you saw me," she said. "Tell them I'll be waiting where we last spoke, if they have anything they want to say to me." She picked up her sketchpad and pencils, and she walked off briskly, stepping carefully through the cats, who did not even glance at her, just kept their gazes fixed on Shadow, as she moved away through the swaying grasses and the blowing twigs.

Shadow wanted to call after her, but instead he crouched down and looked back at the cats. "What's going on?" he asked. "Bast? Are you doing this? You're a long way from home. And why would you still care who I kiss?"

The spell was broken when he spoke. The cats began to move, to look away, to stand, to wash themselves intently.

A tortoiseshell cat pushed her head against his hand, insistently, needing attention. Shadow stroked her absently, rubbing his knuckles against her forehead.

She swiped blinding-fast with claws like tiny scimitars, and drew blood from his forearm. Then she purred, and turned, and within moments the whole kit and caboodle of them had vanished into the hillside, slipping behind rocks and into the undergrowth, and were gone.

V
The Living and the Dead

Oliver was out of his room when Shadow got back to the house, sitting in the warm kitchen, a mug of tea by his side, reading a book on Roman architecture. He was dressed, and he had shaved his chin and trimmed his beard. He was wearing pajamas, with a plaid bathrobe over them.

"I'm feeling a bit better," he said, when he saw Shadow. Then, "Have you ever had this? Been depressed?"

"Looking back on it, I guess I did. When my wife died," said Shadow. "Everything went flat. Nothing meant anything for a long time."

Oliver nodded. "It's hard. Sometimes I think the black dog is a real thing. I lie in bed thinking about the painting of Fuseli's nightmare on a sleeper's chest. Like Anubis. Or do I mean Set? Big black thing. What was Set anyway? Some kind of donkey?"

"I never ran into Set," said Shadow. "He was before my time."

Oliver laughed. "Very dry. And they say you Americans don't do irony." He paused. "Anyway. All done now. Back on my feet. Ready to face the world." He sipped his tea. "Feeling a bit embarrassed. All that Hound of the Baskervilles nonsense behind me now."

"You really have nothing to be embarrassed about," said Shadow, reflecting that the English found embarrassment wherever they looked for it.

"Well. All a bit silly, one way or another. And I really am feeling much perkier."

Shadow nodded. "If you're feeling better, I guess I should start heading south."

"No hurry," said Oliver. "It's always nice to have company. Moira and I don't really get out as much as we'd like. It's mostly just a walk up to the pub. Not much excitement here, I'm afraid."

Moira came in from the garden. "Anyone seen the secateurs? I know I had them. Forget my own head next."

Shadow shook his head, uncertain what secateurs were. He thought of telling the couple about the cats on the hill, and how they had behaved, but could not think of a way to describe it that would explain how odd it was. So, instead, without thinking, he said, "I ran into Cassie Burglass on Wod's Hill. She pointed out the Gateway to Hell."

They were staring at him. The kitchen had become awkwardly quiet. He said, "She was drawing it."

Oliver looked at him and said, "I don't understand."

"I've run into her a couple of times since I got here," said Shadow.

"What?" Moira's face was flushed. "What are you saying?" And then, "Who the, who the *fuck* are you to come in here and say things like that?"

"I'm, I'm nobody," said Shadow. "She just started talking to me. She said that you and she used to be together."

Moira looked as if she were going to hit him. Then she just said, "She moved away after we broke up. It wasn't a good breakup. She was very hurt. She behaved appallingly. Then she just up and left the village in the night. Never came back."

"I don't want to talk about that woman," said Oliver, quietly. "Not now. Not ever."

"Look. She was in the pub with us," pointed out Shadow. "That first night. You guys didn't seem to have a problem with her then."

Moira just stared at him and did not respond, as if he had said something in a tongue she did not speak. Oliver rubbed his forehead with his hand. "I didn't see her," was all he said.

"Well, she said to say 'hi' when I saw her today," said Shadow. "She said she'd be waiting, if either of you had anything you wanted to say to her."

"We have nothing to say to her. Nothing at all." Moira's eyes were wet, but she was not crying. "I can't believe that, that *fucking* woman has come back into our lives, after all she put us through." Moira swore like someone who was not very good at it.

Oliver put down his book. "I'm sorry," he said. "I don't feel very well." He walked out, back to the bedroom, and closed the door behind him.

Moira picked up Oliver's mug, almost automatically, and took it over to the sink, emptied it out and began to wash it.

"I hope you're pleased with yourself," she said, rubbing the mug with a white plastic scrubbing brush as if she were trying to scrub the picture of Beatrix Potter's cottage from the china. "He was coming back to himself again."

"I didn't know it would upset him like that," said Shadow. He felt guilty as he said it. He had known there was history between Cassie and his hosts. He could have said nothing, after all. Silence was always safer.

Moira dried the mug with a green and white tea towel. The white patches of the towel were comical sheep, the green were grass. She bit her lower lip, and the tears that had been brimming in her eyes now ran down her cheeks. Then, "Did she say anything about me?"

"Just that you two used to be an item."

Moira nodded, and wiped the tears from her young-old face with the comical tea towel. "She couldn't bear it when Ollie and I got together. After I moved out, she just hung up her paintbrushes and locked the flat and went to London." She blew her nose vigorously. "Still. Mustn't grumble. We make our own beds. And Ollie's a *good* man. There's just a black dog in his mind. My mother had depression. It's hard."

Shadow said, "I've made everything worse. I should go."

"Don't leave until tomorrow. I'm not throwing you out, dear. It's not your fault you ran into that woman, is it?" Her shoulders were slumped. "There they are. On top of the fridge." She picked up something that looked like a very small pair of garden shears. "Secateurs," she explained. "For the rosebushes, mostly."

"Are you going to talk to him?"

"No," she said. "Conversations with Ollie about Cassie never end well. And in this state, it could plunge him even further back into a bad place. I'll just let him get over it."

Shadow ate alone in the pub that night, while the cat in the glass case glowered at him. He saw no one he knew. He had a brief conversation with the landlord about how he was enjoying his time in the village. He walked back to Moira's house after the pub, past the old sycamore, the gibbet tree, down Shuck's Lane. He saw nothing moving in the fields in the moonlight: no dog, no donkey.

All the lights in the house were out. He went to his bedroom as quietly as he could, packed the last of his possessions into his backpack before he went to sleep. He would leave early, he knew.

He lay in bed, watching the moonlight in the box room. He remembered standing in the pub and Cassie Burglass standing beside him. He thought about his conversation with the landlord, and the conversation that first night, and the cat in the glass box, and, as he pondered, any desire to sleep evaporated. He was perfectly wide awake in the small bed.

Shadow could move quietly when he needed to. He slipped out of bed, pulled on his clothes and then, carrying his boots, he opened the window, reached over the sill and let himself tumble silently into the soil of the flowerbed beneath. He got to his feet and put on the boots, lacing them up in the half dark. The moon was several days from full, bright enough to cast shadows.

Shadow stepped into a patch of darkness beside a wall, and he waited there.

He wondered how sane his actions were. It seemed very probable that he was wrong, that his memory had played tricks on him, or other people's had. It was all so very unlikely, but then, he had experienced the unlikely before, and if he was wrong he would be out, what? A few hours' sleep?

He watched a fox hurry across the lawn, watched a proud white cat stalk and kill a small rodent, and saw several other cats pad their way along the top of the garden wall. He watched a weasel slink from shadow to shadow in the flowerbed. The constellations moved in slow procession across the sky.

The front door opened, and a figure came out. Shadow had half-expected to see Moira, but it was Oliver, wearing his pajamas and, over them, a thick tartan dressing gown. He had Wellington boots on his feet, and he looked faintly ridiculous, like an invalid from a black and white movie, or someone in a play. There was no color in the moonlit world.

Oliver pulled the front door closed until it clicked, then he walked towards the street, but walking on the grass, instead of crunching down the gravel path. He did not glance back, or even look around. He set off up the lane, and Shadow waited until Oliver was almost out of sight before he began to follow. He knew where Oliver was going, had to be going.

Shadow did not question himself, not any longer. He knew where they were both headed, with the certainty of a person in a dream. He was not even surprised when, halfway up Wod's Hill, he found Oliver sitting on a tree stump, waiting for him. The sky was lightening, just a little, in the east.

"The Gateway to Hell," said the little man. "As far as I can tell, they've always called it that. Goes back years and years."

The two men walked up the winding path together. There was something gloriously comical about Oliver in his robe, in his striped pajamas and his oversized black rubber boots. Shadow's heart pumped in his chest.

"How did you bring her up here?" asked Shadow.

"Cassie? I didn't. It was her idea to meet up here on the hill. She loved coming up here to paint. You can see so far. And it's holy, this hill, and she always loved that. Not holy to Christians, of course. Quite the obverse. The old religion."

"Druids?" asked Shadow. He was uncertain what other old religions there were, in England.

"Could be. Definitely could be. But I think it predates the druids. Doesn't have much of a name. It's just what people in these parts practice, beneath whatever else they believe. Druids, Norse, Catholics, Protestants, doesn't matter. That's what people pay lip service to. The old religion is what gets the crops up and keeps your cock hard and makes sure that nobody builds a bloody great motorway through an area of outstanding natural beauty. The Gateway stands, and the hill stands, and the place stands. It's well, well over two thousand years old. You don't go mucking about with anything that powerful."

Shadow said, "Moira doesn't know, does she? She thinks Cassie moved away." The sky was continuing to lighten in the east, but it was still night, spangled with a glitter of stars, in the purple-black sky to the west.

"That was what she *needed* to think. I mean, what else was she going to think? It might have been different if the police had been interested . . . but it wasn't like. . . Well. It protects itself. The hill. The gate."

They were coming up to the little meadow on the side of the hill. They passed the boulder where Shadow had seen Cassie drawing. They walked toward the hill.

"The black dog in Shuck's Lane," said Oliver. "I don't actually think it is a dog. But it's been there so long." He pulled out a small LED flashlight from the pocket of his bathrobe. "You really talked to Cassie?"

"We talked, I even kissed her."

"Strange."

"I first saw her in the pub, the night I met you and Moira. That was what made me start to figure it out. Earlier tonight, Moira was talking as if she hadn't seen Cassie in years. She was baffled when I asked. But Cassie was standing just behind me that first night, and she spoke to us. Tonight, I asked at the pub if Cassie had been in, and nobody knew who I was talking about. You people all know each other. It was the only thing that made sense of it all. It made sense of what she said. Everything."

Oliver was almost at the place Cassie had called the Gateway to Hell. "I thought that it would be so simple. I would give her to the hill, and she would leave us both alone. Leave Moira alone. How could she have kissed you?"

Shadow said nothing.

"This is it," said Oliver. It was a hollow in the side of the hill, like a short hallway that went back. Perhaps, once, long ago, there had been a structure, but the hill had weathered, and the stones had returned to the hill from which they had been taken.

"There are those who think it's devil worship," said Oliver. "And I think they are wrong. But then, one man's god is another's devil. Eh?"

He walked into the passageway, and Shadow followed him.

"Such bullshit," said a woman's voice. "But you always were a bullshitter, Ollie, you pusillanimous little cock-stain."

Oliver did not move or react. He said, "She's here. In the wall. That's where I left her." He shone the flashlight at the wall, in the short passageway into the side of the hill. He inspected the drystone wall carefully, as if he were looking for a place he recognized, then he made a little grunting noise of recognition. Oliver took out a compact metal tool from his pocket, reached as high as he could and levered out one little rock with it. Then he began to pull rocks out from the wall, in a set sequence, each rock opening a space to allow another to be removed, alternating large rocks and small.

"Give me a hand. Come on."

Shadow knew what he was going to see behind the wall, but he pulled out the rocks, placed them down on the ground, one by one.

There was a smell, which intensified as the hole grew bigger, a stink of old rot and mold. It smelled like meat sandwiches gone bad. Shadow saw her face first, and he barely knew it as a face: the cheeks were sunken, the eyes gone, the skin now dark and leathery, and if there were freckles they were impossible to make out; but the hair was Cassie Burglass's hair, short and black, and in the LED light, he could see that the dead thing wore an olive-green sweater, and the blue jeans were her blue jeans.

"It's funny. I knew she was still here," said Oliver. "But I still had to see her. With all your talk. I had to see it. To prove she was still here."

"Kill him," said the woman's voice. "Hit him with a rock, Shadow. He killed me. Now he's going to kill you."

"Are you going to kill me?" Shadow asked.

"Well, yes, obviously," said the little man, in his sensible voice. "I mean, you know about Cassie. And once you're gone, I can just finally forget about the whole thing, once and for all."

"Forget?"

"Forgive *and* forget. But it's hard. It's not easy to forgive myself, but I'm sure I can forget. There. I think there's enough room for you to get in there now, if you squeeze."

Shadow looked down at the little man. "Out of interest," he said, curious, "how are you going to make me get in there? You don't have a gun on you. And, Ollie, I'm twice your size. You know, I could just break your neck."

"I'm not a stupid man," said Oliver. "I'm not a bad man, either. I'm not a terribly well man, but that's neither here nor there, really. I mean, I did what I did because I was jealous, not because I was ill. But I wouldn't have come up here alone. You see, this is the temple of the Black Dog. These places were the first temples. Before the stone henges and the standing stones, they were waiting and they were worshipped, and sacrificed to, and feared, and placated. The black shucks and the barghests, the padfoots and the wish hounds. They were here and they remain on guard."

"Hit him with a rock," said Cassie's voice. "Hit him now, Shadow, *please.*"

The passage they stood in went a little way into the hillside, a man-made cave with drystone walls. It did not look like an ancient temple. It did not look like a gateway to hell. The predawn sky framed Oliver. In his gentle, unfailingly polite voice, he said, "He is in me. And I am in him."

The black dog filled the doorway, blocking the way to the world outside, and, Shadow knew, whatever it was, it was no true dog. Its eyes actually glowed, with a luminescence that reminded Shadow of rotting sea-creatures. It was to a wolf, in scale and in menace, what a tiger is to a lynx: pure carnivore, a creature made of danger and threat. It stood taller than Oliver and it stared at Shadow, and it growled, a rumbling deep in its chest. Then it sprang.

Shadow raised his arm to protect his throat, and the creature sank its teeth into his flesh, just below the elbow. The pain was excruciating. He knew he should fight back, but he was falling to his knees, and he was screaming, unable to think clearly, unable to focus on anything except his fear that the creature was going to use him for food, fear it was crushing the bone of his forearm.

On some deep level he suspected that the fear was being created by the dog: that he, Shadow, was not cripplingly afraid like that. Not really. But it did not matter. When the creature released Shadow's arm, he was weeping and his whole body was shaking.

Oliver said, "Get in there, Shadow. Through the gap in the wall. Quickly, now. Or I'll have him chew off your face."

Shadow's arm was bleeding, but he got up and squeezed through the gap into the darkness without arguing. If he stayed out there, with the beast, he would die soon, and die in pain. He knew that with as much certainty as he knew that the sun would rise tomorrow.

"Well, yes," said Cassie's voice in his head. "It's going to rise. But unless you get your shit together you are never going to see it."

There was barely space for him and Cassie's body in the cavity behind the wall. He had seen the expression of pain and fury on her face, like the face of the cat in the glass box, and then he knew she, too, had been entombed here while alive.

Oliver picked up a rock from the ground, and placed it onto the wall, in the gap. "My own theory," he said, hefting a second rock and putting it into position, "is that it is the prehistoric dire wolf. But it is bigger than ever the dire wolf was. Perhaps it is the monster of our dreams, when we huddled in caves. Perhaps it was simply a wolf, but we were smaller, little hominids who could never run fast enough to get away."

Shadow leaned against the rock face behind him. He squeezed his left arm with his right hand to try to stop the bleeding. "This is Wod's Hill," said Shadow. "And that's Wod's dog. I wouldn't put it past him."

"It doesn't matter." More stones were placed on stones.

"Ollie," said Shadow. "The beast is going to kill you. It's already inside you. It's not a good thing."

"Old Shuck's not going to hurt me. Old Shuck loves me. Cassie's in the wall," said Oliver, and he dropped a rock on top of the others with a crash.

"Now you are in the wall with her. Nobody's waiting for you. Nobody's going to come looking for you. Nobody is going to cry for you. Nobody's going to miss you."

There were, Shadow knew, although he could never have told a soul how he knew, three of them, not two, in that tiny space. There was Cassie Burglass, there in body (rotted and dried and still stinking of decay) and there in soul, and there was also something else, something that twined about his legs, and then butted gently at his injured hand. A voice spoke to him, from somewhere close. He knew that voice, although the accent was unfamiliar.

It was the voice that a cat would speak in, if a cat were a woman: expressive, dark, musical. The voice said, *You should not be here, Shadow. You have to stop, and you must take action. You are letting the rest of the world make your decisions for you.*

Shadow said aloud, "That's not entirely fair, Bast."

"You have to be quiet," said Oliver, gently. "I mean it." The stones of the wall were being replaced rapidly and efficiently. Already they were up to Shadow's chest.

Mrr. No? Sweet thing, you really have no idea. No idea who you are or what you are or what that means. If he walls you up in here to die in this hill, this temple will stand forever—and whatever hodgepodge of belief these locals have will work for them and will make magic. But the sun will still go down on them, and all the skies will be grey. All things will mourn, and they will not know what they are mourning for. The world will be worse—for people, for cats, for the remembered, for the forgotten. You have died and you have returned. You matter, Shadow, and you must not meet your death here, a sad sacrifice hidden in a hillside.

"So what are you suggesting I do?" he whispered.

Fight. The Beast is a thing of mind. It's taking its power from you, Shadow. You are near, and so it's become more real. Real enough to own Oliver. Real enough to hurt you.

"Me?"

"You think ghosts can talk to everyone?" asked Cassie Burglass's voice in the darkness, urgently. "We are moths. And you are the flame."

"What should I do?" asked Shadow. "It hurt my arm. It damn near ripped out my throat."

Oh, sweet man. It's just a shadow-thing. It's a night-dog. It's just an overgrown jackal.

"It's real," Shadow said. The last of the stones was being banged into place.

"Are you truly scared of your father's dog?" said a woman's voice. Goddess or ghost, Shadow did not know.

But he knew the answer. Yes. Yes, he was scared.

His left arm was only pain, and unusable, and his right hand was slick and sticky with his blood. He was entombed in a cavity between a wall and rock. But he was, for now, alive.

"Get your shit together," said Cassie. "I've done everything I can. Do it."

He braced himself against the rocks behind the wall, and he raised his feet. Then he kicked both his booted feet out together, as hard as he could. He had walked so many miles in the last few months. He was a big man, and he was stronger than most. He put everything he had behind that kick.

The wall exploded.

The Beast was on him, the black dog of despair, but this time Shadow was prepared for it. This time he was the aggressor. He grabbed at it.

I will not be my father's dog.

With his right hand he held the beast's jaw closed. He stared into its green eyes. He did not believe the beast was a dog at all, not really.

It's daylight, said Shadow to the dog, with his mind, not with his voice. *Run away. Whatever you are, run away. Run back to your gibbet, run back to your grave, little wish hound. All you can do is depress us, fill the world with shadows and illusions. The age when you ran with the wild hunt, or hunted terrified humans, it's over. I don't know if you're my father's dog or not. But you know what? I don't care.*

With that, Shadow took a deep breath and let go of the dog's muzzle.

It did not attack. It made a noise, a baffled whine deep in its throat that was almost a whimper.

"Go home," said Shadow, aloud.

The dog hesitated. Shadow thought for a moment then that he had won, that he was safe, that the dog would simply go away. But then the creature lowered its head, raised the ruff around its neck, and bared its teeth. It would not leave, Shadow knew, until he was dead.

The corridor in the hillside was filling with light: the rising sun shone directly into it. Shadow wondered if the people who had built it, so long ago, had aligned their temple to the sunrise. He took a step to the side, stumbled on something, and fell awkwardly to the ground.

Beside Shadow on the grass was Oliver, sprawled and unconscious. Shadow had tripped over his leg. The man's eyes were closed; he made a growling sound in the back of his throat, and Shadow heard the same sound, magnified and triumphant, from the dark beast that filled the mouth of the temple.

Shadow was down, and hurt, and was, he knew, a dead man.

Something soft touched his face, gently.

Something else brushed his hand. Shadow glanced to his side, and he understood. He understood why Bast had been with him in this place, and he understood who had brought her.

They had been ground up and sprinkled on these fields more than a hundred years before, stolen from the earth around the temple of Bast and Beni Hasan. Tons upon tons of them, mummified cats in their thousands, each cat a tiny representation of the deity, each cat an act of worship preserved for an eternity.

They were there, in that space, beside him: brown and sand-colored and shadowy grey, cats with leopard spots and cats with tiger stripes, wild, lithe and ancient. These were not the local cats Bast had sent to watch him the previous day. These were the ancestors of those cats, of all our modern cats, from Egypt, from the Nile Delta, from thousands of years ago, brought here to make things grow.

They trilled and chirruped, they did not meow.

The black dog growled louder but now it made no move to attack. Shadow forced himself into a sitting position. "I thought I told you to go home, Shuck," he said.

The dog did not move. Shadow opened his right hand, and gestured. It was a gesture of dismissal, of impatience. *Finish this.*

The cats sprang, with ease, as if choreographed. They landed on the beast, each of them a coiled spring of fangs and claws, both as sharp as they had ever been in life. Pin-sharp claws sank into the black flanks of the huge beast, tore at its eyes. It snapped at them, angrily, and pushed itself against the wall, toppling more rocks, in an attempt to shake them off, but without success. Angry teeth sank into its ears, its muzzle, its tail, its paws.

The beast yelped and growled, and then it made a noise, which Shadow thought would, had it come from any human throat, have been a scream.

Shadow was never certain what happened then. He watched the black dog put its muzzle down to Oliver's mouth, and push, hard. He could have sworn that the creature stepped *into* Oliver, like a bear stepping into a river.

Oliver shook, violently, on the sand.

The scream faded, and the beast was gone, and sunlight filled the space on the hill.

Shadow felt himself shivering. He felt like he had just woken up from a waking sleep; emotions flooded through him, like sunlight: fear and revulsion and grief and hurt, deep hurt.

There was anger in there, too. Oliver had tried to kill him, he knew, and he was thinking clearly for the first time in days.

A man's voice shouted, "Hold up! Everyone all right over there?"

A high bark, and a lurcher ran in, sniffed at Shadow, his back against the wall, sniffed at Oliver Bierce, unconscious on the ground, and at the remains of Cassie Burglass.

A man's silhouette filled the opening to the outside world, a grey paper cutout against the rising sun.

"Needles! Leave it!" he said. The dog returned to the man's side. The man said, "I heard someone screaming. Leastways, I wouldn't swear to it being a someone. But I heard it. Was that you?"

And then he saw the body, and he stopped. "Holy fucking mother of all fucking bastards," he said.

"Her name was Cassie Burglass," said Shadow.

"Moira's old girlfriend?" said the man. Shadow knew him as the landlord of the pub, could not remember whether he had ever known the man's name. "Bloody Nora. I thought she went to London."

Shadow felt sick.

The landlord was kneeling beside Oliver. "His heart's still beating," he said. "What happened to him?"

"I'm not sure," said Shadow. "He screamed when he saw the body—you must have heard him. Then he just went down. And your dog came in."

The man looked at Shadow, worried. "And you? Look at you! What happened to you, man?"

"Oliver asked me to come up here with him. Said he had something awful he had to get off his chest." Shadow looked at the wall on each side of the corridor. There were other bricked-in nooks there. Shadow had a good idea of what would be found behind them if any of them were opened. "He asked me to help him open the wall. I did. He knocked me over as he went down. Took me by surprise."

"Did he tell you why he had done it?"

"Jealousy," said Shadow. "Just jealous of Moira and Cassie, even after Moira had left Cassie for him."

The man exhaled, shook his head. "Bloody hell," he said. "Last bugger I'd expect to do anything like this. Needles! Leave it!" He pulled a cell phone from his pocket, and called the police. Then he excused himself. "I've got a bag of game to put aside until the police have cleared out," he explained.

Shadow got to his feet, and inspected his arms. His sweater and coat were both ripped in the left arm, as if by huge teeth, but his skin was unbroken beneath it. There was no blood on his clothes, no blood on his hands.

He wondered what his corpse would have looked like, if the black dog had killed him.

Cassie's ghost stood beside him, and looked down at her body, half-fallen from the hole in the wall. The corpse's fingertips and the fingernails were wrecked, Shadow observed, as if she had tried, in the hours or the days before she died, to dislodge the rocks of the wall.

"Look at that," she said, staring at herself. "Poor thing. Like a cat in a glass box." Then she turned to Shadow. "I didn't actually fancy you," she said. "Not even a little bit. I'm not sorry. I just needed to get your attention."

"I know," said Shadow. "I just wish I'd met you when you were alive. We could have been friends."

"I bet we would have been. It was hard in there. It's good to be done with all of this. And I'm sorry, Mr. American. Try not to hate me."

Shadow's eyes were watering. He wiped his eyes on his shirt. When he looked again, he was alone in the passageway.

"I don't hate you," he told her.

He felt a hand squeeze his hand. He walked outside, into the morning sunlight, and he breathed and shivered, and listened to the distant sirens.

Two men arrived and carried Oliver off on a stretcher, down the hill to the road where an ambulance took him away, siren screaming to alert any sheep on the lanes that they should shuffle back to the grass verge.

A female police officer turned up as the ambulance disappeared, accompanied by a younger male officer. They knew the landlord, whom Shadow was not surprised to learn was also a Scathelocke, and were both impressed by Cassie's remains, to the point that the young male officer left the passageway and vomited into the ferns.

If it occurred to either of them to inspect the other bricked-in cavities in the corridor, for evidence of centuries-old crimes, they managed to suppress the idea, and Shadow was not going to suggest it.

He gave them a brief statement, then rode with them to the local police station, where he gave a fuller statement to a large police officer with a serious beard. The officer appeared mostly concerned that Shadow was provided with a mug of instant coffee, and that Shadow, as an American tourist, would not form a mistaken impression of rural England. "It's not like this up here normally. It's really quiet. Lovely place. I wouldn't want you to think we were all like this."

Shadow assured him that he didn't think that at all.

VI
The Riddle

Moira was waiting for him when he came out of the police station. She was standing with a woman in her early sixties, who looked comfortable and reassuring, the sort of person you would want at your side in a crisis.

"Shadow, this is Doreen. My sister."

Doreen shook hands, explaining she was sorry she hadn't been able to be there during the last week, but she had been moving house.

"Doreen's a county court judge," explained Moira.

Shadow could not easily imagine this woman as a judge.

"They are waiting for Ollie to come around," said Moira. "Then they are going to charge him with murder." She said it thoughtfully, but in the same way she would have asked Shadow where he thought she ought to plant some snapdragons.

"And what are you going to do?"

She scratched her nose. "I'm in shock. I have no idea what I'm doing anymore. I keep thinking about the last few years. Poor, poor Cassie. She never thought there was any malice in him."

"I never liked him," said Doreen, and she sniffed. "Too full of facts for my liking, and he never knew when to stop talking. Just kept wittering on. Like he was trying to cover something up."

"Your backpack and your laundry are in Doreen's car," said Moira. "I thought we could give you a lift somewhere, if you needed one. Or if you want to get back to rambling, you can walk."

"Thank you," said Shadow. He knew he would never be welcome in Moira's little house, not anymore.

Moira said, urgently, angrily, as if it was all she wanted to know, "You said you saw Cassie. You *told* us, yesterday. That was what sent Ollie off the deep end. It hurt me so much. Why did you say you'd seen her, if she was dead? You *couldn't* have seen her."

Shadow had been wondering about that, while he had been giving his police statement. "Beats me," he said. "I don't believe in ghosts. Probably a local, playing some kind of game with the Yankee tourist."

Moira looked at him with fierce hazel eyes, as if she was trying to believe him but was unable to make the final leap of faith. Her sister reached down and held her hand. "More things in heaven and earth, Horatio. I think we should just leave it at that."

Moira looked at Shadow, unbelieving, angered, for a long time, before she took a deep breath and said, "Yes. Yes, I suppose we should."

There was silence in the car. Shadow wanted to apologize to Moira, to say something that would make things better.

They drove past the gibbet tree.

"*There were ten tongues within one head,*" recited Doreen, in a voice slightly higher and more formal than the one in which she had previously spoken. "*And one went out to fetch some bread, to feed the living and the dead.* That was a riddle written about this corner, and that tree."

"What does it mean?"

"A wren made a nest inside the skull of a gibbeted corpse, flying in and out of the jaw to feed its young. In the midst of death, as it were, life just keeps on happening." Shadow thought about the matter for a little while, and told her that he guessed that it probably did.

Neil Gaiman is the *New York Times* bestselling author of the novels *Neverwhere, Stardust, American Gods, Coraline, Anansi Boys, The Graveyard Book, Good Omens* (with Terry Pratchett), *The Ocean at the End of the Lane*, and *The Truth Is a Cave in the Black Mountains*; the Sandman series of graphic novels; and the story collections *Smoke and Mirrors, Fragile Things*, and *Trigger Warning*. He is the winner of numerous literary honors, including the Hugo, Bram Stoker, and World Fantasy awards, and the Newbery and Carnegie Medals. Originally from England, he now lives in the United States.

*In games, we know we're not supposed to give up, not until we've won . . . We
know that if we don't give up, we'll win. There's always a solution. There's
always a way. That's why games are great and this sucks.*

1UP

Holly Black

When people die, you just press a couple of buttons and bring them back to
life. You reset the game. That's how games work. Restore from your last save
point. Restore from the beginning. Start over.

Your people are never just gone.

That's what I think of as I look at the photograph of Soren resting on top of
a coffin. His family is Jewish—well, other than his stepmother—so they don't
have open casket funerals. I've never been to a closed casket one before. I'm
used to seeing the waxy faces of my dead relatives, made up with red lips and
red cheeks, like they're waiting for true love's kiss to wake them. According to
my phone, Jewish law prohibits embalming or removing any organs or doing
anything but wrapping him in a shroud and putting him in the ground. That's
why we aren't allowed to see him, I guess. He'd look too dead.

I can't help being sad, though. We've never met in person. And now, I
guess we never will.

In games, we know we're not supposed to give up, not until we've won
out against the big boss and the credits start rolling across the screen. We
know that if we don't give up, we'll win. There's always a solution. There's
always a way. That's why games are great and this sucks.

Even as I listen to the rabbi talk, even as I watch Soren's grandmother dab
her rheumy eyes with Kleenex, even as I hear everyone say his nickname—
Sorry Sorry Sorry—over and over, I can't help trying to figure out how to
fix this.

Just last week, he sent me a message: YOU HAVE TO COME FOR THE
FUNERAL. PROMISE ME. It was the first message I'd gotten from him in more
than two weeks. Still, I messaged back that there wouldn't be any funeral,

that he was going to get better and we were going to meet up at PAX East in the winter like we'd all planned. But then there was the death notice. That's why me and Decker and Toad met up in Jersey and made the drive down to Florida together.

We'd never even met Soren in person, be we were still his three best friends in the whole world. Even if no one from his real life knows us.

Black ribbons get torn and pinned onto mourners. After they lower the casket into the ground, dirt gets tossed, and we go over to his house to visit his family while they sit shiva.

It's mostly old people. A greying great-uncle with bristling nose hairs. A hysterically weeping second cousin. Aunts who run the coffee maker and take the plastic off trays of cold-cuts. Uncles who smoke outside with a girl who tells us she's Sorry's cousin, back from art school for the funeral. No one else talks to us.

Sorry's stepmother sits in the center of a sofa, her shoulders rigid as relatives comfort her, tell her what a wonderful nurse she was to Sorry those last months when things went from bad to worse, talk about her inner core of strength. Someone has given her a Styrofoam cup of coffee. I wonder if it's hot. I wonder if the coffee is burning her hand and she hasn't even noticed yet.

Sorry's father sits alone in a corner, looking at his phone. He's wearing a black pin-striped suit with a paisley tie that looks more appropriate for a business meeting than burying a kid.

We obviously didn't know what to wear either. Decker dressed in a too-small black blazer over black jeans and a black T-shirt. He looks like he's going to a concert.

Toad is about what I expected from his avatars and message board signature. Big and shy with a small, untrimmed goatee that extends to his neck. He wears the same thing every day—jeans, funny/ironic nerd shirt and a flannel open over it. It doesn't even occur to me he's going to change for the funeral and he doesn't.

I'm in a black shirt dress that my mother lent me. It's boring, which is apparently the point. I have on pantyhose too—medium brown, to match my legs—and my big clunky black boots. Mom told me I couldn't wear boots to a funeral, but I left the pumps she loaned me in the trunk of Decker's car. Maybe I shouldn't have.

None of us fit in at Sorry's place. I can't imagine Sorry fitting in here either—not the Sorry that we knew. Of course, he was sick for so long that maybe it didn't matter.

Three years, stuck in his bedroom, too ill to go to high school or do anything teenagers are supposed to do but play games and hang out online.

Me and Decker and Toad drift toward that bedroom, not sure what else to do. We've never been there before, but we know it instantly by his posters of *Resident Evil, Arkham City, Left 4 Dead,* and *Warcraft.* We talk in hushed voices about how weird it is to be in his room for the first time.

"Maybe we shouldn't have come," Toad says.

I sit down on his bed. "I know what you mean."

Decker flops on the plush carpet of the floor, resting his head against a plush alien chestburster.

I can't quite put my finger on what I think of Decker now that we've met in person. He's some bizarre combination of cute and pretentious. He has a put-on British accent and insisted we navigated our way here with real maps, instead of just using the navigation on our cell phones. We got lost twice, until finally, Toad turned off the sound on his phone and pretended not to be looking at it.

I wonder if Decker notices that I'm a girl. I wonder if he likes girls. Before Sorry died, we would sometimes send each other flirty messages, so maybe it's not okay that I wonder that.

Maybe it's not okay that we're going to have a long drive back and we're going to argue about which Marvel movie they should make next and stop for junk food and fast food and we're going to be sad about Soren, but happy that we went on a road trip together.

My mom insists that my friendships online aren't real. She says that until you meet someone in person, you don't *really* know them. I don't agree, but I think that belief is part of the reason she let me come on a three-day road trip with two boys. I'm supposed to call her every night at seven and text her three times a day, plus she spoke with Decker and Toad's mothers before she agreed to let me come; I think she believes this is my one shot at having IRL friends before college.

Sitting there, I wonder how I am supposed to feel. I cried when I first heard Sorry was dead, but I haven't cried since. My eyes were dry when they lowered the coffin into the ground, even though I told Sorry things I never told anyone, things that I don't know if I will tell anyone ever again.

It just doesn't seem real that he's gone.

It's hard to cry when I my brain still can't accept the truth.

After a while, Toad turns on Sorry's computer. "Lot of parental controls on this thing. And it's not connecting to the internet."

"That sucks," I say. I wonder if there's something wrong with it. I wonder if that's why he didn't message us more or come online to game these last few weeks. I thought it was because he was tired from being sick, but the idea that we couldn't be there for him—that *I* couldn't be there for him near the end of his life—because of a stupid broken cable modem makes me want to punch something.

Across from me a corner of one poster has peeled back, rolling up. I wonder if Sorry's dad is going to box all this stuff up and put it in the attic. I wonder if his dad is going to box all this stuff up and just throw it out.

Toad opens a few more things and types a little. "Weird," he says, frowning at the screen.

"What?" demands Decker from the floor.

"I don't know," says Toad, rubbing his head. "Look."

He's opened up a game on Sorry's computer. It's an interactive fiction game—what people used to call text games, like *Zork*—but not one I've ever seen before. But no matter what it is, Toad shouldn't be messing around on his computer, opening his files and stuff.

"What are you doing?" I ask.

"I was trying to find his password for *Diamond Knights*," Toad says without missing a beat.

"You were going to make him donate his whole inventory to one of your characters, weren't you?" Decker says. "Asshole. We're at his fucking funeral."

"I'm an asshole," says Toad. "This is known. But I didn't find his passwords, did I? I found this, right on the desktop. Look."

We crowd around the computer, peering at the screen.

THE LAZARUS GAME by Soren Carp
You are sad.
>|

"He wrote a game?" Decker says. "Did any of you guys know he wrote a game?"

Toad shakes his head. "I didn't even know he liked this kind of thing."

Neither did I. Interactive fiction games aren't all that impressive to look at. They're just blocks of text with a blinking cursor after, waiting for you to make the right choice—the clever command—that will unlock the rest of the story. They used to be made and sold by big companies, but they don't make enough money for that anymore. Now they're pretty much just made by the people who love them.

"Look around," I say. "Type in 'L' for 'look.'"

He does.

You are wearing black, standing in a kid's bedroom. There are nerdy posters on the walls and nerdy stuff all around you. One of the posters is curled up at one corner and you think you might be able to see writing on the other side.

>|

The poster I was looking at just a moment before.

I slide off the bed while the other two are still staring at the screen. I gently pull the poster free of the blue sticky stuff adhering it at three out of four points. Then I turn it over.

The back has been written on in Sharpie.

YOU HAVE FIVE HOURS TO WIN.

THE CLOCK STARTED WHEN I WENT IN THE GROUND.

GRAB THE FLASH DRIVE AND GO.

GO NOW BEFORE SHE FINDS YOU.

My heart starts hammering in my chest. Decker starts to roll up the poster.

"What are you doing?" Toad says. "They'll notice it's gone."

"So what?" Decker keeps rolling, crinkling the poster in his haste. "So they think we're poster thieves."

"Where's the flash drive?" I demand. "We need to find the flash drive."

"No, wait, this doesn't make sense." Toad looks around the room, like he's wondering if there's going to be some kind of hidden camera.

I go over to the desk, ignoring Toad. Loose change, breath mints, paperbacks, nerdy toys (including a figurine I sent him of a brown-skinned manga girl I wanted him to think looked like me), and a Hot Wheels car that had clearly been modified so that a USB connection stuck out of its rear bumper.

"Got it," I say, picking up the car.

"Wait," Toad says and I pause. "Shouldn't we check what's on it first?"

"Don't worry about that," Decker says. He tries to push open the window—I guess so we can slip out in the most criminal way possible—but it doesn't budge. Toad turns off the computer.

I shove the flash drive in the pocket of my dress. As I am shutting the desk drawer, the door to the room opens.

Sorry's stepmother is standing in the hall, a startled smile pulling at her face. "What are you three doing in here?" she asks.

"We just—" I start, but I don't know what to say. This is the exact kind of situation that I'm bad at. This is why I started staying inside and talking to people over the internet in the first place. My tongue feels heavy in my mouth. I want to crawl deep in my clothes, curl up, and hide.

Her gaze goes to the wall where there isn't a poster anymore, and then to the drawer she saw me close. Her expression sharpens and she stops smiling. "Who are you?"

"We're Soren's friends," Decker says.

"None of you ever visited here before." After a moment of silence, she steps back from the doorway and continues in her brusque voice. "I am going to ask you to leave. Now. We're all very upset and whatever you're doing—we don't have time for it. Be glad I don't have the energy to pursue this further."

"Sorry," Toad says, sliding past her into the hall, head down. I follow him, unable to do anything else. I feel shamed, even though I know we weren't doing anything wrong. Sorry made us promise to come. Sorry left us the flash drive. He wrote a message just for us: *go now before she finds you.*

Out in the hall, I feel like a coward.

Decker is standing in the middle of the room, staring at Sorry's stepmother, eyes blazing. He looks like he's trying to swallow words before they crawl out of his mouth.

"Come on," I say.

Finally Decker makes a motion like he's zipping his lips closed and swings toward us. I keep glancing back to make sure he stays with us and as I do, my gaze falls on something I didn't notice before. There's a lock on Sorry's door—a brass dead latch—on the wrong side. The side that would have locked Sorry in.

My head starts to pound and I can feel the sweat under my armpits. As I walk out the door, my gaze sweeps over the black-clad people in the living room.

It occurs to me that maybe Sorry was sure he was going to die because he thought that someone was about to murder him.

We get back in Decker's car—a beat-up Impala with inside upholstery held together mostly with duct tape. We don't speak. Decker starts the engine and drives in what appears to be a random direction.

Finally, after long minutes of silence, Toad says, "I'm sorry. I freaked out."

Decker says, "I wanted to punch that bitch in the face."

And I say, "We need to see whatever is on that flash drive."

A few minutes later, Toad and I are on our smart phones, trying to find a place with internet that also serves food. There's not a lot of choices, but there's always Starbucks. We head to the nearest one. This time Decker doesn't say anything about us navigating with our phones.

We all have laptops, but there's only one free outlet, so I pull out my MacBook Pro and Decker and Toad crowd around. My laptop is covered in stickers; just the familiar sight of them makes me feel better. I flip open the case, type in my password and shove the flash drive into the USB.

The game starts up again.

Words appear on the screen of my computer.

You are sad.
>|

I type in "L" again.

You are wearing black, standing in a kid's bedroom. There are nerdy posters on the walls and nerdy stuff all around you. One of the posters is curled up at one corner and you think you might be able to see text on the other side.
>|

I try something else this time. *Why am I sad?* I type.

Some guy you know from the internet is dead.
>|

I raise my eyebrows and look at Toad and Decker. Sorry had clearly intended us to find this, just the way we did, but why? *X poster*, I type, "x" being standard shorthand for examine.

The back of the poster looks like a crazy person has written it on. It seems to indicate that you have a deadline to complete this game. I guess you'd better hurry.

>|

Decker raises his eyebrows. "I don't like this. I don't like anything about this."

"What do I do next?" I ask them.

"Take the flash drive from his desk," says Toad. "I mean, that's what we really did, right?"Right," I say, my fingers on the keys.

You've already taken it or you wouldn't be playing this.

>|

"I don't think there's anything else here. Exit the room," Decker says, blowing out a frustrated breath.

Toad stands up, heading toward the counter. "I need cake for this," he says. "And caffeine."

"Good idea," says Decker, reaching into his pocket for wadded up cash. "Get me a latte. And get Cat . . . what do you want, Cat?"

"Cappuccino with a lot of extra shots," I say and start typing to exit the room in the game.

You are in the living room. More sad people wearing black. One of them isn't as sad as she seems, however.

>|

Talk to Sorry's Stepmother, I type without anyone needing to suggest it.

What would you like to ask her? Type the number to ask the question or type "X" to say nothing.
1. Do you still have your MasterCard?
2. How come you tried to murder your stepson?
3. How come Sorry's father is never home anymore?
4. Did something happen three weeks ago?
5. Are you a diabetic?
>|

I turn the computer so Decker can see the screen. Toad comes back with our order. His pink and white piece of cake is enormous.

"Uh, two, obviously," Toad says, taking a big bite of it.

Sorry's stepmother looks at you like you're a worm stranded in a puddle after rain.

"That's ridiculous," she says. "Surely if I did that there would be proof. Surely someone would have noticed. Just because he got sick a few months after I married Aaron and then got progressively sicker until he died, just because I was in sole control of his care, just because I love the attention I get when he's unwell, just because I locked him in his room and disconnected his cable modem three months before he died, none of that means anything."

>|

"Do you think that's what his game is? The proof?" Decker says, between swigs of latte. "Are we supposed to take his game to the police?"

"Then why would we need to play quickly?" I shake my head.

"Maybe his stepmother's going to destroy evidence," Toad replies. "Maybe the game is going to tell us how to stop her."

"Then why doesn't it?" I ask, frustrated and sick to my stomach. All those times we chatted and he never said a thing—not *one single thing* about what was going on. "Why not just spell it out? Why all of this?"

"I think he made the game for us," Decker says. "His stepmother wouldn't understand it, but we would. I don't think there is any proof. I think he just wanted somebody to know."

The idea of that being true is awful. "Why not tell us in chat?"

Decker shrugs.

"Remember what I said about the parental controls?" Toad said. "I bet she was tracking what he said."

I type *talk to Sorry's stepmother* again. I pick number three.

Sorry's stepmother gives you a kindly smile.

"You have to understand how hard it is to have a sick son and not be able to do anything to help him. I think he thought it was easier to concentrate on his work."

>|

No real information there.

I go through the options again and ask about the diabetes.

Sorry's stepmother looks surprised.
"Is this about all the insulin I ordered from Canada? That was for my cat! What cat? Oh, she's around here somewhere."
>|

Disturbing.

My next question is about what happened three weeks ago although I am not sure I can bear knowing.

Sorry's stepmother actually looks troubled.
"You should have seen the expression on his face when I came into the hospital room. He'd been feeling better that day and I guess he'd seen me inject something into the bag attached to his drip. It was just vitamins, but I think he—well, never mind. I was bringing him green Jello. He looked at me and it was like he was seeing me for the first time."
>|

I go through the options one more time and choose the only one left, the question about her credit card.

Sorry's stepmother looks surprised.
"Do you know something about those fraudulent charges? I swear I never ordered tetrodotoxin. I don't even know what that is."
>|

"What's with the tetro-whatever?" Decker eats a piece of the strawberry cake Toad procured and takes another sip of his latte. "Is that what she killed him with?"

I open up my browser, log into the internet, and search for *tetrodotoxin*. I frown at the screen. "It's some kind of toad neurotoxin. Poisonous."

"But what about the insulin?" Toad asks. "I don't get this. Which one did she use? Does he not know? Are we supposed to figure it out, like in a murder mystery? Doesn't Sorry remember how dumb we are? He's got to just spell shit out."

"Yeah," I say, barely paying attention. Typing words in the game is enough like chatting to Sorry online that it allows me to—almost—pretend he's not dead. And yet, the whole game is a reminder that he is.

The Lazarus Game. I guess this is Sorry's way of rising from the grave to name his murderer.

Find proof, I type in, but the game doesn't seem to know what I am looking for.

Go to dining room, I type in. It still doesn't know what I am looking for.

Go to kitchen, I type. Still, nothing.

Go to funeral home, I type, which seems grim. I'm almost relieved when it doesn't work.

Exit house, I type. Finally, this time I get something else, a menu of options.

You are standing outside on the patchy lawn in front of Sorry's house. Cars are parked out front, like there's a party going on inside, although you know it's a pretty grim party. It's afternoon and the Florida sun is beating down mercilessly. You're starting to sweat.

Where would you like to go? Type the number to travel or type "x" to stay where you are.

1. The Police Station
2. The Hospital
3. The Graveyard
4. The Hardware Store
>|

"What the hell?" I say. "The hardware store?"

Toad and Decker had started discussing something in low voices, but stopped abruptly when I spoke. They both leaned in to look at the screen.

Toad whistles. "I can't believe you think having the option of going to the hardware store is worse than going to the graveyard."

"Uh," Decker said, blinking at the screen a few times. "Can you google that toad poison again?"

"How come?" I ask.

Instead of answering, he opens his bag and pulls out his own laptop. "Spell it?"

I do and he starts clicking. After a few minutes, his face goes blank, then an expression of horror flashes across it. I can't even fathom what he could have found. What's worse than being poisoned by your own stepmother?

In fairy tales, stepmothers are wicked, jealous, untrustworthy bitches with poisoned apples, but my mom remarried six years ago, so I am pretty sure not all stepparents are like that. My stepdad drops me off at school most mornings. Some days we get coffees and donuts and sit in the parking lot eating them until the bell rings, just talking. I couldn't imagine him wanting to hurt me. But I guess Sorry's stepmother seemed nice too, until she didn't.

"I think you better look at this," Decker says, turning his computer and pointing to the screen. "Read that part."

I look where he's pointing. There were cases of people being given tetrodotoxin and seeming to die, but actually being in a state of near-death, conscious the whole time. For a while, it was even alleged that tetrodotoxin was an essential ingredient to brainwash people into thinking they were zombies.

"Now read this part," he says and pulls up another window. It has the amount of time a person can last with the air in a coffin. Five and a half hours.

"Fuck you," I say. "He's dead. We saw him buried."

But I am thinking of the message he left for us on the back of the poster. The one with the time limit we didn't understand.

YOU HAVE FIVE HOURS TO WIN.
THE CLOCK STARTED WHEN I WENT IN THE GROUND.

And I think about the options of places to go—the police station where we could report his stepmother (if we had proof) for making him sick, the hospital where we could go to try to find that proof and might stumble on something else, something that would send us to the hardware store and then the graveyard.

The graveyard.

Decker snorts. "But if he faked his own death then he'd have to seem—"

"Whoa," says Toad, interrupting him. "What? Faked his own death? Both of you need to stop communicating brain-to-brain and spell things out for me."

"No," I say, standing up and jerking my power cord out of the wall. "We need to go. We need to go now!"

We get to the graveyard just as the sun is starting to set. The sky is shimmering with gold, gleaming on our Home Depot shovels in the backseat. I feel like we're on a real adventure, the kind that people in real life don't go on. This is the kind of thing that only happens in video games and right now, I get why. No one in real life would ever want to feel like this.

I am scared we're going to be arrested and I am terrified of what we're going to find inside his casket. We get out. We get our brand-new shovels.

The dirt is fresh, easy to scoop. My heart is hammering.

We're awkward at first, none of us used to this kind of physical work. We're the kids who spend our free time in front of our computers. We're the kids whose moms are always going on about "needing fresh air and vitamin D." My arms hurt and I don't know how to swing the dirt away in the right rhythm. We smack our shovels into one another's more often than not, sometimes hard enough to sting my hand. Still, we keep going.

"What if he comes back as a zombie?" Toad asks.

I give him a look.

"It could happen! He's using some kind of zombie drug and we don't know what else is in his system. This is how outbreaks happen."

I just keep digging. Decker shakes his head.

Sweat rolls down my neck. I keep hearing the noises of cars going by in the distance and nearly jumping out of my skin.

"Okay, well, what if he's not awake yet?" Toad asks. I realize that he's talking to talk, that it's his way of managing his nerves. It's funny, on the drive down he was quiet and I figured that was how he normally was. But robbing a graveyard turned him into a chatterbox. "Like, we know this stuff wears off, but how long does it take? And won't he look dead until then? How are we going to get him out of here if he looks dead? I don't want to touch him if he's like that."

"Let's just try not to get arrested," Decker says quietly. "I heard Florida jails are no joke."

"My mom will kill me if I get picked up by the cops for messing with a grave," I say and Decker laughs.

For a moment, it occurs to me that this is crazy. That maybe my mother is right about friendship, because I do feel differently about Decker and Toad now that we've been together in real life. Now that we've heard the timbre of one another's laughter. Now that we've learned one another's Starbucks order and how we like our burritos at Chipotle and who can burp the loudest. Now that I learned how far they were willing to go for someone they never met. After all of this, it makes me realize that we didn't know Sorry at all.

We're putting ourselves in the way of a whole lot of trouble for someone we've never met.

Then my shovel hits wood.

"Sorry?" Toad calls softly. His voice shakes.

But either Sorry can't hear us or he can't reply, because there's no sound but traffic from the nearby road and wind ruffling the thick leaves of the nearby palms.

Squatting down, we start to clear dirt so that we can open the casket itself. By now, I am one big ball of sweat and my mother's dress is caked in dirt. My stockings ripped at the knee without my even noticing.

As I move earth, I have these moments of total immersion in what I'm doing and these other moments where I am totally aware that this is a crazy thing to be doing and I must be crazy for doing it.

Then the casket is cleared and there's no way to avoid our real purpose. We're going to open up a coffin and it's possible we're going to see a corpse. In fact, as we get ready to wedge open the wood with our Home Depot crowbar, even though I know exactly why we decided to do this, it seems inconceivable to me that we're going to see anything but a corpse.

"Get back," Toad says, wedging the crowbar under the lid. We give him some space.

And then, with a splintering sound, the lid is off and I am seeing Soren Carp in the flesh for the first time. His eyes are closed, long black lashes sweeping his cheeks. His hair is kind of a mess and he's wrapped in linen. He looks pale, his lips tinted blue.

"He sure doesn't smell dead," Toad says.

And even though it sounds rude coming out of his mouth, it's a relief that it's true. There is no scent of rot blooming in the air.

"We've got to call 911," Decker says, looking down at Soren's face. "He poisoned himself. He could still die."

I shake my head. "We can't. If he's in a hospital, his parents would get notified."

His stepmother was his guardian, the one who'd been making all his medical decisions. We had no legal right to make any decisions and, in fact, the police would probably take us away for questioning. They might not even really listen to what we were saying until it was too late.

"We should have played the rest of the game," Toad says. "I thought it was stupid that we could go to all those places, but we probably should have figured out what he wanted us to do."

Decker goes down on one knee next to Sorry's body. "What do you want us to do, buddy?" he whispers.

I almost expect Sorry to get up and tell us, but he doesn't. He doesn't move at all.

Toad turns in my direction. "Say something to him."

"Me?" I edge over to the casket. "What should I say?"

Toad clears his throat. "He liked you."

I am too surprised to know how to respond.

Toad waits for me to respond and when I don't, goes on. "I don't know if he ever even went out with a girl. I mean, he's fifteen and he's been sick for three years. So unless he was making it with girls at twelve, probably not."

"What's that supposed to mean?" I ask.

Toad shrugs. "I don't know. I just mean, he had good reasons for not telling you—one of those reasons being that he's got no game. But I know he liked you . . . *likes* you, so he'd be more likely to listen if you were the one talking to him."

I glance toward Decker. He looks like he wants to ask me something, but he doesn't.

I lean over and put my hand on Sorry's arm. His skin is cold from being deep in the ground. "Hey," I say. "It's Cat. We played your game, but now it's your turn. Time to wake up."

He doesn't move.

"We're risking our asses for you," I say.

"Nice," Decker says. "How about saying we love him?"

"How about saying *you* love him, Cat? How about 'if you wake up, I will give you a big, fat, sloppy kiss,'" Toad says.

"Shut up," I tell him.

"Soren," Decker says. "Listen, if you wake up, *one* of us will give you a big, fat, sloppy kiss. I can't guarantee it will be Cat, but one of us will definitely do it. I am ready."

"Soren," Toad says. "Listen, how about this—if you *don't* wake up, one of us will give you a big, fat, sloppy kiss and I can guarantee it *won't* be Cat."

We can't help it, we start laughing. We laugh helplessly, the relief like the release of a leg cramp.

Then, abruptly, Soren starts to cough.

I suck in my breath so sharply that I nearly choke. Toad yelps. Decker falls backward onto his ass.

A moment later, Sorry is turned on his side, puking his guts up. I have never been so happy to see someone vomiting. I crawl over to smooth his hair out of his face. His skin feels cold and clammy and when he turns to look at me, his eyes are bright with something like fever.

"You guys are insane," he says, the words slurred, then flops down face-first in the dirt.

It turns out that I do know him, even though we've never met before in person. It turns out that he knows us too.

And it turns out that sometimes, you do get to start from your save point. You do get another life.

You are standing in the graveyard with your friend, who until very recently, you thought was dead. Soon the police are going to come. Soon, he's going to have to go to a hospital, even though he hates hospitals. Soon, he's going to have to explain how he did it, how he knew he was going to die and decided to try to trick his way out of a locked bedroom in the most gruesome way possible. Soon he is going to have to thank you, even though there is no way to ever really thank you enough. But for right now, he just stands next to you and you all look up a little, into the middle distance. The wind blows your hair back from your faces and you strike a super badass pose.

<<You win the game.>>

To play again from the beginning, press "X."

Holly Black is the author of bestselling contemporary fantasy books for kids and teens. Some of her titles include The Spiderwick Chronicles (with Tony DiTerlizzi), The Modern Faerie Tale series, the Curse Workers series, *Doll Bones*, *The Coldest Girl in Coldtown*, the Magisterium series (with Cassandra Clare), and *The Darkest Part of the Forest*. She has been a finalist for an Eisner Award and the recipient of the Andre Norton Award, the Mythopoeic Award and a Newbery Honor. She currently lives in New England with her husband and son in a house with a secret door

The posters of the dead and missing girls on the cigarette cabinet had stared at her all summer. At first they creeped her out. But then those girls disappeared into the landscape. Forgotten.

THE THREE RESURRECTIONS OF JESSICA CHURCHILL

Kelly Robson

"I rise today on this September 11, the one-year anniversary of the greatest tragedy on American soil in our history, with a heavy heart . . . "
—The Honorable Jim Turner

September 9, 2001

Jessica slumped against the inside of the truck door. The girl behind the wheel and the other one squished between them on the bench seat kept stealing glances at her. Jessica ignored them, just like she tried to ignore the itchy pull and tug deep inside her, under her belly button, where the aliens were trying to knit her guts back together.

"You party pretty hard last night?" the driver asked.

Jessica rested her burning forehead on the window. The hum of the highway under the wheels buzzed through her skull. The truck cab stank of incense.

"You shouldn't hitchhike, it's not safe," the other girl said. "I sound like my mom saying it and I hate that but it's really true. So many dead girls. They haven't even found all the bodies."

"Highway of Tears," the driver said.

"Yeah, Highway of Tears," the other one repeated. "Bloody Sixteen."

"Nobody calls it that," the driver snapped.

Jessica pulled her hair up off her neck, trying to cool the sticky heat pulsing through her. The two girls looked like tree planters. She'd spent the summer working full time at the gas station and now she could smell a tree planter a mile away. They'd come in for smokes and mix, dirty, hairy, dressed in fleece and hemp just like these two. The driver had blond dreadlocks and the other had tattoos circling her wrists. Not that much older than her, lecturing her about staying safe just like somebody's mom.

Well, she's right, Jessica thought. A gush of blood flooded the crotch of her jeans.

Water. Jessica, we can do this but you've got to get some water. We need to replenish your fluids.

"You got any water?" Jessica asked. Her voice rasped, throat stripped raw from all the screaming.

The tattooed girl dug through the backpack at Jessica's feet and came up with a two-liter mason jar half-full of water. Hippies, Jessica thought as she fumbled with the lid. Like one stupid jar will save the world.

"Let me help." The tattooed girl unscrewed the lid and steadied the heavy jar as Jessica lifted it to her lips.

She gagged. Her throat was tight as a fist but she forced herself to swallow, wash down the dirt and puke coating her mouth.

Good. Drink more.

"I can't," Jessica said. The tattooed girl stared at her.

You need to. We can't do this alone. You have to help us.

"Are you okay?" the driver asked. "You look wrecked."

Jessica wiped her mouth with the back of her hand. "I'm fine. Just hot."

"Yeah, you're really flushed," said the tattooed girl. "You should take off your coat."

Jessica ignored her and gulped at the jar until it was empty.

Not so fast. Careful!

"Do you want to swing past the hospital when we get into town?" the driver asked.

A bolt of pain knifed through Jessica's guts. The empty jar slipped from her grip and rolled across the floor of the truck. The pain faded.

"I'm fine," she repeated. "I just got a bad period."

That did it. The lines of worry eased off both girls' faces.

"Do you have a pad? I'm gonna bleed all over your seat." Jessica's vision dimmed, like someone had put a shade over the morning sun.

"No problem." The tattooed girl fished through the backpack. "I bleed heavy too. It depletes my iron."

"That's just an excuse for you to eat meat," said the driver.

Jessica leaned her forehead on the window and waited for the light to come back into the world. The two girls were bickering now, caught up in their own private drama.

Another flood of blood. More this time. She curled her fists into her lap. Her insides twisted and jumped like a fish on a line.

Your lungs are fine. Breathe deeply, in and out, that's it. We need all the oxygen you can get.

The tattooed girl pulled a pink wrapped maxi pad out of her backpack and offered it to Jessica. The driver slowed down and turned the truck into a roadside campground.

"Hot," Jessica said. The girls didn't hear. Now they were bitching at each other about disposable pads and something called a keeper cup.

We know. You'll be okay. We can heal you.

"Don't wait for me," Jessica said as they pulled up to the campground outhouse. She flipped the door handle and nearly fell out of the truck. "I can catch another ride."

Cold air washed over her as she stumbled toward the outhouse. She unzipped her long coat and let the breeze play though—chill air on boiling skin. Still early September but they always got a cold snap at the start of fall. First snow only a few days ago. Didn't last. Never did.

The outhouse stench hit her like a slap. Jessica fumbled with the lock. Her fingers felt stiff and clumsy.

"Why am I so hot?" she said, leaning on the cold plywood wall. Her voice sounded strange, ripped apart and multiplied into echoes.

Your immune system is trying to fight us but we've got it under control. The fever isn't dangerous, just uncomfortable.

She shed her coat and let it fall to the floor. Unzipped her jeans, slipped them down her hips. No panties. She hadn't been able to find them.

No, Jessica. Don't look.

Pubic hair hacked away along with most of her skin. Two deep slices puckered angry down the inside of her right thigh. And blood. On her legs, on her jeans, inside her coat. Blood everywhere, dark and sticky.

Keep breathing!

An iron tang filled the outhouse as a gout of blood dribbled down her legs. Jessica fell back on the toilet seat. Deep within her chest something fluttered, like a bird beating its wings on her ribs, trying to get out. The light drained from the air.

If you die, we die too. Please give us a chance.

The flutters turned into fists pounding on her breastbone. She struggled to inhale, tried to drag the outhouse stink deep into her lungs but the air felt thick. Solid. Like a wall against her face.

Don't go. Please.

Breath escaped her like smoke from a fire burned down to coal and ash. She collapsed against the wall of the outhouse. Vision turned to pinpricks; she crumpled like paper and died.

"Everything okay in there?"

The thumping on the door made the whole outhouse shake. Jessica lurched to her feet. Her chest burned like she'd been breathing acid.

You're okay.

"I'm fine. Gimme a second."

Jessica plucked the pad off the outhouse floor, ripped it open and stuck it on the crotch of her bloody jeans, zipped them up. She zipped her coat to her chin. She felt strong. Invincible. She unlocked the door.

The two girls were right there, eyes big and concerned and in her business.

"You didn't have to wait," Jessica said.

"How old are you, fifteen? We waited," the driver said as they climbed back into the truck.

"We're not going to let you hitchhike," said the tattooed girl. "Especially not you."

"Why not me?" Jessica slammed the truck door behind her.

"Most of the dead and missing girls are First Nations."

"You think I'm an Indian? Fuck you. Am I on a reserve?"

The driver glared at her friend as she turned the truck back onto the highway.

"Sorry," the tattooed girl said.

"Do I look like an Indian?"

"Well, kinda."

"Fuck you." Jessica leaned on the window, watching the highway signs peel by as they rolled toward Prince George. When they got to the city the invincible feeling was long gone. The driver insisted on taking her right to Gran's.

"Thanks," Jessica said as she slid out of the truck.

The driver waved. "Remember, no hitchhiking."

September 8, 2001

Jessica never hitchhiked.

She wasn't stupid. But Prince George was spread out. The bus ran maybe once an hour weekdays and barely at all on weekends, and when the weather turned cold you could freeze to death trying to walk everywhere. So yeah, she took rides when she could, if she knew the driver.

After her Saturday shift she'd started walking down the highway. Mom didn't know she was coming. Jessica had tried to get through three times from the gas station phone, left voice mails. Mom didn't always pick up—usually didn't—and when she did it was some excuse about her phone battery or connection.

Mom was working as a cook at a retreat center out by Tabor Lake. A two-hour walk, but Mom would get someone to drive her back to Gran's.

Only seven o'clock but getting cold and the wind had come up. Semis bombed down the highway, stirring up the trash and making it dance at her feet and fly in her face as she walked along the ditch.

It wasn't even dark when the car pulled over to the side of the highway.

"Are you Jessica?"

The man looked ordinary. Baseball cap, hoodie. Somebody's dad trying to look young.

"Yeah," Jessica said.

"Your mom sent me to pick you up."

A semi honked as it blasted past his car. A McDonald's wrapper flipped through the air and smacked her in the back of the head. She got in.

The car was skunky with pot smoke. She almost didn't notice when he passed the Tabor Lake turnoff.

"That was the turn," she said.

"Yeah, she's not there. She's out at the ski hill."

"At this time of year?"

"Some kind of event." He took a drag on his smoke and smiled.

Jessica hadn't even twigged. Mom had always wanted to work at the ski hill, where she could party all night and ski all day.

It was twenty minutes before Jessica started to clue in.

When he slowed to take a turn onto a gravel road she braced herself to roll out of the car. The door handle was broken. She went at him with her fingernails but he had the jump on her, hit her in the throat with his elbow. She gulped air and tried to roll down the window.

It was broken too. She battered the glass with her fists, then spun and lunged for the wheel. He hit her again, slammed her head against the dashboard three times. The world stuttered and swam.

Pain brought everything back into focus. Face down, her arms flailed, fingers clawed at the dirt. Spruce needles flew up her nose and coated her tongue. Her butt was jacked up over a log and every thrust pounded her face into the dirt. One part of her was screaming, screaming. The other part watched the pile of deer shit inches from her nose. It looked like a heap of candy. Chocolate-covered almonds.

She didn't listen to what he was telling her. She'd heard worse from boys at school. He couldn't make her listen. He didn't exist except as a medium for pain.

When he got off, Jessica felt ripped in half, split like firewood. She tried to roll off the log. She'd crawl into the bush, he'd drive away, and it would be over.

Then he showed her the knife.

When he rammed the knife up her she found a new kind of pain. It drove the breath from her lungs and sliced the struggle from her limbs. She listened to herself whimper, thinking it sounded like a newborn kitten, crying for its mother.

The pain didn't stop until the world had retreated to little flecks of light deep in her skull. The ground spun around her as he dragged her through the bush and rolled her into a ravine. She landed face down in a stream. Her head flopped, neck canted at a weird angle.

Jessica curled her fingers around something cold and round. A rock. It fit in her hand perfectly and if he came back she'd let him have it right in the teeth. And then her breath bubbled away and she died.

When she came back to life a bear corpse was lying beside her, furry and rank. She dug her fingers into its pelt and pulled herself up. It was still warm. And skinny—nothing but sinew and bone under the skin.

She stumbled through the stream, toes in wet socks stubbing against the rocks but it didn't hurt. Nothing hurt. She was good. She could do anything.

She found her coat in the mud, her jeans too. One sneaker by the bear and then she looked and looked for the other one.

It's up the bank.

She climbed up. The shoe was by the log where it had happened. The toe was coated in blood. She wiped it in the dirt.

You need to drink some water.

A short dirt track led down to the road. The gravel glowed white in the dim light of early morning. No idea which way led to the highway. She picked a direction.

"How do you know what I need?"

We know. We're trying to heal you. The damage is extensive. You've lost a lot of blood and the internal injuries are catastrophic.

"No shit."

We can fix you. We just need time.

Her guts writhed. Snakes fought in her belly, biting and coiling.

Feel that? That's us working. Inside you.

"Why doesn't it hurt?"

We've established a colony in your thalamus. That's where we're blocking the pain. If we didn't, you'd die of shock.

"Again."

Yes, again.

"A colony. What the fuck are you? Aliens?"

Yes. We're also distributing a hormonal cocktail of adrenaline and testosterone to keep you moving, but we'll have to taper it off soon because it puts too much stress on your heart. Right now it's very important for you to drink some water.

"Shut up about the water." She wasn't thirsty. She felt great.

A few minutes later the fight drained out of her. Thirsty, exhausted, she ached as though the hinge of every moving part was crusted in rust, from her jaw to her toes. Her eyelids rasped like sandpaper. Her breath sucked and blew without reaching her lungs. Every rock in the road was a mountain and every pothole a canyon.

But she walked. Dragged her sneakers through the gravel, taking smaller and smaller steps until she just couldn't lift her feet anymore. She stood in the middle of the road and waited. Waited to fall over. Waited for the world to slip from her grasp and darkness to drown her in cold nothing.

When she heard the truck speeding toward her she didn't even look up. Didn't matter who it was, what it was. She stuck out her thumb.

September 10, 2001

Jessica woke soaked. Covered in blood, she thought, struggling with the blankets. But it wasn't blood.

"What—"

Your urethra was damaged so we eliminated excess fluid through your pores. It's repaired now. You'll be able to urinate.

She pried herself out of the wet blankets.

No solid food, though. Your colon is shredded and your small intestine has multiple ruptures.

When the tree planters dropped her off, Gran had been sacked out on the couch. Jessica had stayed in the shower for a good half hour, watching the blood swirl down the drain with the spruce needles and the dirt, the blood clots and shreds of raw flesh.

And all the while she drank. Opened her mouth and let the cool spray fill her. Then she had stuffed her bloody clothes in a garbage bag and slept.

Jessica ran her fingertips over the gashes inside her thigh. The wounds puckered like wide toothless mouths, sliced edges pasted together and sunk deep within her flesh. The rest of the damage was hardened over with amber-colored scabs. She'd have to use a mirror to see it all. She didn't want to look.

"I should go to the hospital," she whispered.

That's not a good idea. It would take multiple interventions to repair the damage to your digestive tract. They'd never be able to save your uterus or reconstruct your vulva and clitoris. The damage to your cervix alone—

"My what?"

Do you want to have children someday?

"I don't know."

Trust us. We can fix this.

She hated the hospital anyway. Went to Emergency after she'd twisted her knee but the nurse had turned her away, said she wouldn't bother the on-call for something minor. Told her to go home and put a bag of peas on it.

And the cops were even worse than anyone at the hospital. Didn't give a shit. Not one of them.

Gran was on the couch, snoring. A deck of cards was scattered across the coffee table in between the empties—looked like she'd been playing solitaire all weekend.

Gran hadn't fed the cats, either. They had to be starving but they wouldn't come to her, not even when she was filling their dishes. Not even Gringo, who had hogged her bed every night since she was ten. He just hissed and ran.

Usually Jessica would wake up Gran before leaving for school, try to get her on her feet so she didn't sleep all day. Today she didn't have the strength. She shook Gran's shoulder.

"Night night, baby," Gran said, and turned over.

Jessica waited for the school bus. She felt cloudy, dispersed, her thoughts blowing away with the wind. And cold now, without her coat. The fever was gone.

"Could you fix Gran?"

Perhaps. What's wrong with her?

Jessica shrugged. "I don't know. Everything."

We can try. Eventually.

She sleepwalked through her classes. It wasn't a problem. The teachers were more bothered when she did well than when she slacked off. She stayed in the shadows, off everyone's radar.

After school she walked to the gas station. Usually when she got to work she'd buy some chips or a chocolate bar, get whoever was going off shift to ring it up so nobody could say she hadn't paid for it.

"How come I'm not hungry?" she asked when she had the place to herself.

You are; you just can't perceive it.

It was a quiet night. The gas station across the highway had posted a half-cent lower so everyone was going there. Usually she'd go stir crazy from boredom but today she just zoned out. Badly photocopied faces stared at her from the posters taped to the cigarette cabinet overhead.

An SUV pulled up to pump number three. A bull elk was strapped to the hood, tongue lolling.

"What was the deal with the bear?" she said.

The bear's den was adjacent to our crash site. It was killed by the concussive wave.

"Crash site. A spaceship?"

Yes. Unfortunate for the bear, but very fortunate for us.

"You brought the bear back to life. Healed it."

Yes.

"And before finding me you were just riding around in the bear."

Yes. It was attracted by the scent of your blood.

"So you saw what happened to me. You watched." She should be upset, shouldn't she? But her mind felt dull, thoughts thudding inside an empty skull.

We have no access to the visual cortex.

"You're blind?"

Yes.

"What are you?"

A form of bacteria.

"Like an infection."

Yes.

The door chimed and the hunter handed over his credit card. She rang it through. When he was gone she opened her mouth to ask another question, but then her gut convulsed like she'd been hit. She doubled over the counter. Bile stung her throat.

He'd been here on Saturday.

Jessica had been on the phone, telling mom's voice mail that she'd walk out to Talbot Lake after work. While she was talking she'd rung up a purchase, $32.25 in gas and a pack of smokes. She'd punched it through automatically, cradling the phone on her shoulder. She'd given him change from fifty.

An ordinary man. Hoodie. Cap.

Jessica, breathe.

Her head whipped around, eyes wild, hands scrambling reflexively for a weapon. Nobody was at the pumps, nobody parked at the air pump. He could come back any moment. Bring his knife and finish the job.

Please breathe. There's no apparent danger.

She fell to her knees and crawled out from behind the counter. Nobody would stop him, nobody would save her. Just like they hadn't saved all those dead and missing girls whose posters had been staring at her all summer from up on the cigarette cabinet.

When she'd started the job they'd creeped her out, those posters. For a few weeks she'd thought twice about walking after dark. But then those dead and missing girls disappeared into the landscape. Forgotten.

You must calm down.

Now she was one of them.

We may not be able to bring you back again.

She scrambled to the bathroom on all fours, threw herself against the door, twisted the lock. Her hands were shuddering, teeth chattering like it was forty below. Her chest squeezed and bucked, throwing acid behind her teeth.

There was a frosted window high on the wall. He could get in, if he wanted. She could almost see the knife tick-tick-ticking on the glass.

No escape. Jessica plowed herself into the narrow gap between the wall and toilet, wedging herself there, fists clutching at her burning chest as she retched bile onto the floor. The light winked and flickered. A scream flushed out of her and she died.

A fist banged on the door.

"Jessica, what the hell!" Her boss's voice.

A key scraped in the lock. Jessica gripped the toilet and wrenched herself off the floor to face him. His face was flushed with anger and though he was a big guy, he couldn't scare her now. She felt bigger, taller, stronger, too. And she'd always been smarter than him.

"Jesus, what's wrong with you?"

"Nothing, I'm fine." Better than fine. She was butterfly-light, like if she opened her wings she could fly away.

"The station's wide open. Anybody could have waltzed in here and walked off with the till."

"Did they?"

His mouth hung open for a second. "Did they what?"

"Walk off with the fucking till?"

"Are you on drugs?"

She smiled. She didn't need him. She could do anything.

"That's it," he said. "You're gone. Don't come back."

A taxi was gassing up at pump number one. She got in the back and waited, watching her boss pace and yell into his phone. The invincible feeling faded before the tank was full. By the time she got home Jessica's joints had locked stiff and her thoughts had turned fuzzy.

All the lights were on. Gran was halfway into her second bottle of u-brew red so she was pretty out of it, too. Jessica sat with her at the kitchen table for a few minutes and was just thinking about crawling to bed when the phone rang.

It was Mom.

"Did you send someone to pick me up on the highway?" Jessica stole a glance at Gran. She was staring at her reflection in the kitchen window, maybe listening, maybe not.

"No, why would I do that?"

"I left you messages. On Saturday."

"I'm sorry, baby. This phone is so bad, you know that."

"Listen, I need to talk to you." Jessica kept her voice low.

"Is it your grandma?" Mom asked.

"Yeah. It's bad. She's not talking."

"She does this every time the residential school thing hits the news. Gets super excited, wants to go up north and see if any of her family are still alive. But she gives up after a couple of days. Shuts down. It's too much for her. She was only six when they took her away, you know."

"Yeah. When are you coming home?"

"I got a line on a great job, cooking for an oil rig crew. One month on, one month off."

Jessica didn't have the strength to argue. All she wanted to do was sleep.

"Don't worry about your Gran," Mom said. "She'll be okay in a week or two. Listen, I got to go."

"I know."

"Night night, baby," Mom said, and hung up.

September 11, 2001

Jessica waited alone for the school bus. The street was deserted. When the bus pulled up the driver was chattering before she'd even climbed in.

"Can you believe it? Isn't it horrible?" The driver's eyes were puffy, mascara swiped to a grey stain under her eyes.

"Yeah," Jessica agreed automatically.

"When I saw the news I thought it was so early, nobody would be at work. But it was nine in the morning in New York. Those towers were full of people." The driver wiped her nose.

The bus was nearly empty. Two little kids sat behind the driver, hugging their backpacks. The radio blared. Horror in New York. Attack on Washington. Jessica dropped into the shotgun seat and let the noise wash over her for a few minutes as they twisted slowly through the empty streets. Then she moved to the back of the bus.

When she'd gotten dressed that morning her jeans had nearly slipped off her hips. Something about that was important. She tried to concentrate, but the thoughts flitted from her grasp, darting away before she could pin them down.

She focused on the sensation within her, the buck and heave under her ribs and in front of her spine.

"What are you fixing right now?" she asked.

An ongoing challenge is the sequestration of the fecal and digestive matter that leaked into your abdominal cavity.

"What about the stuff you mentioned yesterday? The intestine and the . . . whatever it was."

Once we have repaired your digestive tract and restored gut motility we will begin reconstructive efforts on your reproductive organs.

"You like big words, don't you?"

We assure you the terminology is accurate.

There it was. That was the thing that had been bothering her, niggling at the back of her mind, trying to break through the fog.

"How do you know those words? How can you even speak English?"

We aren't communicating in language. The meaning is conveyed by socio-linguistic impulses interpreted by the brain's speech processing loci. Because of the specifics of our biology, verbal communication is an irrelevant medium.

"You're not talking, you're just making me hallucinate," Jessica said.

That is essentially correct.

How could the terminology be accurate, then? She didn't know those words—cervix and whatever—so how could she hallucinate them?

"Were you watching the news when the towers collapsed?" the driver asked as she pulled into the high school parking lot. Jessica ignored her and slowly stepped off the bus.

The aliens were trying to baffle her with big words and science talk. For three days she'd had them inside her, their voice behind her eyes, their fingers deep in her guts, and she'd trusted them. Hadn't even thought twice. She had no choice.

If they could make her hallucinate, what else were they doing to her?

The hallways were quiet, the classrooms deserted except for one room at the end of the hall with forty kids packed in. The teacher had wheeled in an AV cart. Some of the kids hadn't even taken off their coats.

Jessica stood in the doorway. The news flashed clips of smoking towers collapsing into ash clouds. The bottom third of the screen was overlaid with scrolling, flashing text, the sound layered with frantic voiceovers. People were jumping from the towers, hanging in the air like dancers. The clips replayed over and over again. The teacher passed around a box of Kleenex.

Jessica turned her back on the class and climbed upstairs, joints creaking, jeans threatening to slide off with every step. She hitched them up. The biology lab was empty. She leaned on the corkboard and scanned the parasite diagrams. Ring worm. Tape worm. Liver fluke. Black wasp.

Some parasites can change their host's biology, the poster said, or even change their host's behavior.

Jessica took a pushpin from the board and shoved it into her thumb. It didn't hurt. When she ripped it out a thin stream of blood trickled from the skin, followed by an ooze of clear amber from deep within the gash.

What are you doing?

None of your business, she thought.

Everything is going to be okay.

No it won't, she thought. She squeezed the amber ooze from her thumb, let it drip on the floor. The aliens were wrenching her around like a puppet, but without them she would be dead. Three times dead. Maybe she should feel grateful, but she didn't.

"Why didn't you want me to go to the hospital?" she asked as she slowly hinged down the stairs.

They couldn't have helped you, Jessica. You would have died.

Again, Jessica thought. Died again. And again.

"You said that if I die, you die too."

When your respiration stops, we can only survive for a limited time.

The mirror in the girls' bathroom wasn't real glass, just a sheet of polished aluminum, its shine pitted and worn. She leaned on the counter, rested her forehead on the cool metal. Her reflection warped and stretched.

"If I'd gone to the hospital, it would have been bad for you. Wouldn't it?"

That is likely.

"So you kept me from going. You kept me from doing a lot of things."

We assure you that is untrue. You may exercise your choices as you see fit. We will not interfere.

"You haven't left me any choices."

Jessica left the bathroom and walked down the hall. The news blared from the teacher's lounge. She looked in. At least a dozen teachers crowded in front of an AV cart, backs turned. Jessica slipped behind them and ducked into the teachers' washroom. She locked the door.

It was like a real bathroom. Air freshener, moisturizing lotion, floral soap. Real mirror on the wall and a makeup mirror propped on the toilet tank. Jessica put it on the floor.

"Since when do bacteria have spaceships?" She pulled her sweater over her head and dropped it over the mirror.

Jessica, you're not making sense. You're confused.

She put her heel on the sweater and stepped down hard. The mirror cracked.

Go to the hospital now, if you want.

"If I take you to the hospital, what will you do? Infect other people? How many?"

Jessica, please. Haven't we helped you?

"You've helped yourself."

The room pitched and flipped. Jessica fell to her knees. She reached for the broken mirror but it swam out of reach. Her vision telescoped and she batted at the glass with clumsy hands. A scream built behind her teeth, swelled and choked her. She swallowed it whole, gulped it, forced it down her throat like she was starving.

You don't have to do this. We aren't a threat.

She caught a mirror shard in one fist and swam along the floor as the room tilted and whirled. With one hand she pinned it to the yawning floor like a spike, windmilled her free arm and slammed her wrist down. The walls folded in, collapsing on her like the whole weight of the world, crushing in.

She felt another scream building. She forced her tongue between clenched teeth and bit down. Amber fluid oozed down her chin and pooled on the floor.

Please. We only want to help.

"Night night, baby," she said, and raked the mirror up her arm.

The fluorescent light flashed overhead. The room plunged into darkness as a world of pain dove into her for one hanging moment. Then it lifted. Jessica convulsed on the floor, watching the bars of light overhead stutter and compress to two tiny glimmers inside the thin parched shell of her skull. And she died, finally, at last.

Kelly Robson's first published fiction appeared in 2015. Three short stories, one novelette, and one novella were published in *Clarkesworld*; *Tor.com*; *Asimov's*; and in anthologies *New Canadian Noir*, *In the Shadow of the Towers*, and *License Expired*. In 2016, three of her stories will be reprinted in five Year's Best anthologies. Her novella "Waters of Versailles" is nominated for a Nebula Award and a Aurora Award, and short story "The Three Resurrections of Jessica Churchill" is a finalist for the 2016 Theodore Sturgeon Memorial Award. After years in Vancouver, Robson and her wife (fellow writer A. M. Dellamonica) now live in Toronto.

The sea gnashed close to hand, to the left; it churned,
slowly, like a colossal ruminant chewing at something.

WINDOWS UNDERWATER

John Shirley

Dagon his name, sea-monster, upward man
And downward fish; yet had his temple high
Reared in Azatus, dreaded through the coast
—John Milton, *Paradise Lost*

1. Gilberto Lopez, Lymon Barnes. Summer 2014.

Lymon and Gil, both twenty-one, stood in the shade of the canopy over the festival picnic tables. Gil looked around with disgust.

Summer sunshine, green lawns, the smell of the marshes coming faintly from east of town. Tittering children eating frozen yogurt with sprinkles.

Gil was repelled by it.

"I'm sick of Rowley, man." He didn't say it too loud. That dickhead Curston was sitting at one of the picnic tables, maybe forty feet away, jawing about baseball. Deputy Curston was all full of smiles because his Red Sox had a clear road to the playoffs. He'd given Gil at least two completely unnecessary traffic tickets.

Lymon shrugged. "Rowley's okay." He was thoughtfully eating his extra large sprinkled cherry-chocolate frozen yogurt. He was the kind of guy who could eat anything and never get fat. Freckled, "pale as fishbelly, skinny as an eel," was what Lymon's dad said. Lymon's dad hinted that Lymon wasn't actually his kid. True, Lymon didn't look like his pop. Recessive genes, is all.

Gil was half Mexican, ran to chubby and always fighting it. "You got to eat that giant triple cone in front of me?"

"Surrender, surrender to the lure of the fro-gurt, Gil!"

Gil snorted. "Hell, It's not just Rowley. I'm sick of Massachusetts too."

Gil muttered. "I don't like the cops, I don't like the tourists, I don't like the ocean—especially around here. Water's too fucking murky and dark. I want to go to one of those islands where the water is crystal clear. You can see whatever's down there. And there's some kinda real culture going on. You know? Like in Hollywood."

"Kind of boring here," Lymon admitted. "Nothing to do but . . . "

"But this," Gil said. He waved a hand at the little tents and canopies and shade structures of the Rowley Arts and Crafts Festival. His other hand was holding a plastic wine glass from the "tasting booth." Eight dollars for one glass of lame wine from Virginia.

"If you left Rowley where would you go? You got free rent with your folks here."

"I'd go to California. Maybe L.A. Or San Diego. Get into film making or . . . "

Lymon looked at Gil and raised the red-blond eyebrow that was always half raised anyway. "Film making. Really."

"Okay, *listillo*. I'll start small—work for a videogame company. Do design, maybe direct cut scenes." Gil drank some of his wine. "I got an uncle in L.A. He's kind of a dick but he offered me a job. I could work there while I was getting my shit together to apply to Pixil Arts."

"You mean that uncle who has the car repair shop? You don't know anything about cars either. You've been studying to be a pharmacist, man."

"He'd teach me. I hate being in a classroom. I want to be out doing something."

"You could go back to work for your Pops."

Gil made a face. "I don't want to touch another goddamn fish. That's why I took pharmacy—there's nothing to do with fish. Dad still tries to get me to go out on Eddie's boat." His brother's name was Edwardo but he went by Eddie. "I get seasick. And it's all fished out, anyway, around here. Mostly jellyfish out there. Eddie's getting desperate—starting to fish around Innsmouth. Those reefs out there."

Lymon blinked at him, genuinely startled. "That even *legal*?"

"Sure it's legal. Nobody does it much, is all—just a tradition not to fish there. I'm not going out on the boat, no way. I'm not even working at his fish market—the smell makes me sick."

"Everything makes you sick today, man. I like fish."

"I know you do. You and your fish tanks. Come on, Lymon, we should both go to L.A. Your dad's trying to get you to move outta his place anyway. We can stay with my uncle."

"I'm doing pretty good with the bookstore. Assistant manager."

"They're gonna close that store, man. Chain's downsizing."

"Maybe." Lymon ate some more frozen yogurt. "You wanta come over, play some Skyrim? You can use my sister's computer, we can meet online."

Gil sighed. He drank a little wine. It was supposed to be cabernet but it tasted vinegary to him. "You and me used to talk about working in gaming. Gotta go to New York or L.A for that. You can code. I can draw. We can get a job at Pixil Arts."

"Yeah, right. And we could date Natalie Portman and Mila Kunis, drive em around in our new Porsches. Sure. You want some of this fro-gurt stuff? I bought too much."

"No."

"I'm playing Skyrim. You coming?"

Gil sighed. "I guess so. It's that or this. But I'm telling you . . . "

"I know. You're leaving town."

2. Gilberto Lopez, Lymon Barnes. October 2028.

"How long you back for this time, Gil?"

They were standing on the top of the dike protecting Rowley from the ever-rising sea. Lymon had taken up cigarettes, Spirit Naturals, and he was blowing smoke upward to go with the breeze sucked toward the Atlantic as the tide went out.

Gil made a faint groan. "I don't know. Maybe a long time. Lost that gig at Vapor Arts. Actually—I got mad and quit."

"You ever got past designer assistant?"

"No. Finally they offered me a job in the cafeteria."

"Christ." Lymon shook his head. "Assholes. You're a good artist."

"I don't know how to use the new e-pens, all that stuff." Gil shrugged, and admitted, "That technology's been around twenty years—I could've learned. I got all caught up in Melda and that just didn't work out. Nothing much worked out. I feel like growing up here just sapped all the life out of me. And L.A. couldn't give it back."

"Well, zip up your coat, and I'll show you something to take your mind off all that."

Gil zipped up his coat—not that easy to do. He was getting into his late thirties now and putting on significant weight, like his pops. He glanced at the sky. "Getting dark."

"Naw, won't be dark for like three hours. It's just how it *is*, now, lot of haze all the time, makes it murky out. Climate change. Florida's half underwater, north Georgia's turning into a desert. Carolinas it's storms all the time. Here, it's like this. And the ocean slopping right at our feet. But—do not despair, Gil, I got a pint of Hennessey on me too."

"You know how to get to me. Offer me liquor. I'm a cheap date. It's sad, dude."

"*Dude*, he says. The legacy of L.A. Come on."

Gil let himself be drawn along with Lymon. They tramped along the curving dike that followed the Plum Sound. The dike was high and strong, the best the Army Corps of Engineers could put up as the rising seas threatened Rowley. But if the dike cracked open, Rowley would be drowned.

Lymon handed him the pint of brandy. For something to say as he unscrewed the top—so he didn't feel like such an alky—Gil asked, "So your job's still going good?"

"Yeah. Have to learn new coding languages sometimes but—I like coding. Keeps my mind busy."

Gil glanced at Lymon and thought, *Getting fifteen years older hasn't helped him out much.* Lymon's profile seemed bloated; his lips thicker; eyes popping. Did he have some kind of thyroid issues?

Walking along the top of the dike as if it were a sidewalk, they passed the pint of brandy and looked out over the water. Up ahead, the dike curved to follow the contours of Plum Island Sound; on their right, the mirrorlike water of the marshes reflected the dull sky; a sea gull skated through the reflection.

Soon they'd left the sound behind. Now, the sea gnashed close to hand, to the left; it churned, slowly, like a colossal ruminant chewing at something. The dike curved on between sea and marsh squeezed to a thin charcoal-colored line that pointed at Innsmouth Harbor.

Gil glanced at his watch. It was low tide, but the water washed against the wall just ten feet below them. "How high's it get on the dike when the tide's full?"

"Runs over the top, sometimes, if there's a storm." Lymon sniffed, and wiped his nose with one hand. "So far, not enough to do much damage. But that dike wasn't ever high enough. Sea's rising even faster than they expected."

He passed the brandy bottle.

They fell silent for a time. The dike was flat, the brandy warming, and the miles seemed to melt away. Finally Gil said, "I kind of wonder, sometimes, why I always hated living out here. Rowley's not so bad I guess. People treated me okay. Mostly. But something was always telling me I didn't belong and—how many Mexican families in Rowley? Almost none. A few Puerto Ricans, a few Cubans. Me, I'm half—not fish nor fowl. And I don't like the fish part."

Lymon gave him a sharp look.

Gil went on, "I had this, like, fantasy, when the ocean was rising and all the dikes were being built . . . that Rowley would screw up and the whole town would be sunken. I figured my folks would get away on their boats and . . . " He shrugged and chuckled in a nervous kind of way. "Sick, I know."

"Huh. 'Kay. Kind of weird that you mentioned that but then again . . . You want to see a sunken town? You can pretend it's Rowley."

Gil started to answer, then his cell phone rang. He dug it out of his pants pocket, glanced at it, saw it was his brother's number. He thumbed *Answer*. "Eddie?" Gil listened. The phone crackled, then Eddie's voice cut through. " . . . Gil? The . . . don't . . . If they . . . that side . . . stay away . . . " Every third syllable was swallowed in a void. "They're looking from . . . "

"Eddie, what's up, I'm losing your signal, here, man. Can't make out what you're saying."

" . . . looking up at me . . . windows underwater . . . their mouths . . . windows under the . . . just don't . . . not with . . . "

A furious crackle arose on the phone, as if something in the air was angrily drowning the voice out. "Eddie?"

Eddie's voice had fallen into a void of static. Then the static ended—there was only silence. *Call ended*, it said on the screen.

"Lousy reception out here, don't even bother trying to call him back, it's hopeless, man," Lymon said. "Hey—you see that? Over there, look! There's your drowned town, man . . . "

The sun was going down behind them; the sea in front, in this light, was strangely translucent, here; as if for a moment, just before it got dark out, it had chosen to disclose what was normally hidden.

They were looking out at the sunken harbor of Innsmouth; the water had covered the old ruins. The high, razor-wired fences that had kept people out were fallen and rusting; between the remains of the fences the old brick and granite buildings were mostly tumbled into shapeless heaps; here and there in the ruins were recognizable constructions; peaked gables and gambrel roofs, a few chimney pots, something that might have been a warehouse. A narrow shape almost like an obelisk was poking out of the water, just its sharp peak showing—Gil realized, as he stared at it, that it was the top of an old church spire. No cross adorned its tip.

The warehouse, if that's what it was, had some recognizable windows, though their frames were skewed by the partial collapse of the building into rhomboids. Something moved, inside one of them—a large fish, of some kind, looking back at him. Might be the face of a big moray eel.

"Holy fuck," Gil murmured. "The water's so clear! That's . . . really not normal around here!"

"Normal for the time of day," Lymon said. His voice sounded low, croakingly low, oddly melancholy. "It's just—a trick of the light. The old town shows itself as the night comes."

"I didn't know the water had, like, totally swallowed it up. You remember when we used to come and look at the town through the fence?"

"Sure. The ruins of Innsmouth. Try to figure out which story was true. Some kind of dumping place for World War One mustard gas—that's the story my old man used to repeat. Toxic dump. People had to be evacuated and the place destroyed, so stay away."

"I always liked the devil worshipper story. That was cooler."

Lymon chuckled—again his voice had that oddly low, silky intonation Gil wasn't used to. "Devil Reef is just out there past the harbor . . . so maybe that's how the story got started. But it was never about worshipping the Devil, whoever that may be."

"I don't think it was the Devil, like Lucifer. But—some other 'devil.' Half fish and half man. From the Bible."

"Sure. He was mentioned several times in the Old Testament. Like from Judges—*Now the lords of the Philistines gathered to offer a great sacrifice to Dagon their God . . .*"

Gil glanced at him. "Impressive, dude! You memorized it!"

Lymon gazed fixedly into the sea. "My favorite is from First Samuel—*Then the Philistines took the ark of God and brought it into the house of Dagon and set it up beside Dagon . . . But when they rose early on the next morning, behold, Dagon had fallen face downward on the ground before the ark of the LORD, and the head of Dagon and both his hands were lying cut off on the threshold . . .*"

Gil stared. "That's . . . a long passage to memorize. When did you get all, uh, theological?"

"It's nothing to do with theology. It's about things that are old and powerful and different. Some creatures were simply powerful enough to be worshipped. That Bible story—a lot of propaganda. I don't imagine the Ark of the Covenant would have bothered Dagon much."

Gil licked his lips—and looked at his watch. "We got a long way to go back. I need to find out what Eddie was all worked up about . . . "

"Sure. Here—you finish the brandy. I'm going out on the fishing platform for a minute."

He handed Gil the brandy bottle, and walked off down the dike, toward a flat wooden structure Gil hadn't seen before. It was a kind of short jetty cantilevered from the dike, jutting out over the sunken remains of Innsmouth. The support beams were bolted into the dike below the water level.

As the sun went down, the sea breeze was rising, wet and cold, making Gil shiver. *Good excuse as any,* he thought, opening the brandy bottle. He drank down the last quarter of it, tossed the bottle in the water, and stuck his hands in his coat pockets to warm them as he walked over to the platform.

Lymon was standing right on the edge, looking down, as Gil joined him. "What's up with this thing, Lymon? Something for tourists?"

"It's for fishing."

"Fishing *here*? Supposedly all the fish from here is toxic."

Lymon didn't respond. He just stared down into the water.

After a long moment he said, "You ready, Gil?"

"Yeah. We should get back. Hey—when the tide goes out, does it expose the town?"

"Only some of the higher bits. The water's getting darker but you can still see . . . there! Look—you see that?" Lymon pointed.

"What?"

"Over by the spire . . . "

Something was moving toward them, making a rippling wake as it came. Gil thought it was a sea lion, probably. That was a head, sticking up out of the water, approaching them, not a fin.

"Is that a . . . " He broke off, and stepped closer to the edge to peer at the thing. "No. Not a seal—maybe a dolphin?"

"No. That's my cousin," Lymon said. "She's been down there for years."

Then Gil felt a painful punch in the middle of his back. Lymon was knocking him headfirst into the water.

Gil's mouth was open to shout and it filled with saltwater as he plunged down, toward sunken roofs, darting black shapes and rippling columns of yellow-red light.

He felt saltwater burning his throat, searing his lungs. *Drowning. Got to get to the surface.*

He flailed, but thrashing only sent him deeper.

Then a thick-bodied, naked woman rose up before him, a graceless blue-white shape, intermittently scaly—was it a woman? She was looking unblinkingly at him from enormous, bulging eyes set a little too widely. He could see the pink and blue gills respiring on her neck; he could see . . .

Nothing. Could see nothing. Darkness swirled around him, icy cold penetrated to his bones, water pressure squeezed him—and something gripped him tightly by the ankles, pulling him deeper, and he thought, *Strange way to die . . .*

Gil woke, and, after a while, decided he was alive—in some fashion.

The six-sided chamber, perhaps thirty-five feet long and twenty wide, was cut from ancient layers of coral and stone; the smell made him think of his father's fish market on a hot day. But it was cold in there, and misty.

Gil raised himself on one elbow to look around. Where was the light coming from? It pulsed softly from the corners of the room, hand-sized growths shaped something like mushrooms but filmy, transparent, laced with veins that glowed roseate-tinged blue.

On the wall to Gil's left was a bas-relief of a sort of bearded merman wearing a crown, rising up from the sea spreading his brutish claws in perverse benediction.

Dagon, Gil thought.

Now and then the walls shivered with a soft hollow booming—the sound of the sea, up above. Cracks in the ceiling dripped in rhythm with the boom.

Gil sat up, and after the throbbing in his head subsided, he found he was naked, except for a clean dry blanket. He had been laid upon a wet, plastic-wrapped mattress, probably dragged from some sunken boat; the mattress lay upon a stone slab. Where was the door to the room? He couldn't see one.

"Hey!" he called out—his voice was raspy from salt He noticed a plastic bucket on the floor holding what looked like fresh water. And a terrible thirst took hold of him.

It could be drugged . . .

But he was soon crouching beside it, drinking clean water, clearing his throat.

"I'm glad you're up," said Lymon. Gil turned to see Lymon sauntering in. There was a deep shadow behind him that emitted a grinding sound as it closed behind Lymon. Some sort of hidden door.

Gil stared at Lymon. A kind of slippery membrane oozed across Lymon's otherwise naked skin. Gill-slits had opened in Lymon's neck; his face was more elongated, now, his mouth rounder, thicker; his ears seemed to have vanished entirely; most of his hair was gone. There were only wisps of his orange hair remaining, hanging lankly to his thin shoulders. Some of the membrane had been pulled back from his head, flopped down his back like a hood made of jellyfish stuff. There were webbings of skin between his fingers.

Gil shook his head. "Jesus fuck, Lymon."

Lyon smiled. His teeth had become needlelike. "Do you like my second skin? It's alive, you know. It's a symbiotic organism, feeding off wastes from my skin and body. It protects me from cold and water pressure and salt damage. For genetic humans like you, we have another sort of second skin. It extracts oxygen right from the water, takes your carbon dioxide and—"

"Lymon—shut the fuck up! You're . . . you've . . . " Gil felt sick and the feeling overwhelmed him. He had to turn and heave out a bellyful of water.

"Yes," Lymon said, calmly, as Gil coughed and spat. "I've changed." His voice had that odd, low silkiness as he went on. "The faithful of Innsmouth were not all exterminated. Some were able to escape. They were not entirely changed, themselves. They intermarried . . . and those of us in whom the recessive gene is active—well, after a certain amount of time, as adults, we are called to the sea, and we begin to change." Lymon took Gil's elbow, helped him to sit on the mattress again. "He calls to us, Gil, and we hear him, when no one else does . . . "

The door grated again, and the female came into the room, the one who'd approached Gil underwater. She was carrying a stone jar; she wore the living ooze just as Lymon did.

"That is Darla Jane," said Lymon.

"Eat," she said, proffering the jar. Her voice had a reverberant lisp to it.

Gil looked into the jar. It looked like boiled spinach, with bits of fish; there was a rusty spoon in the jar too.

"Seaweed, a variety that will restore your strength," Lymon said. "And some fish. You'd better get used to fish. I must insist you eat—otherwise, certain persons will enter, and you will be force-fed in a particularly unpleasant way."

Gil felt heavy, weighted down by disorientation and despair. He had no strength in him to fight. He reached into the jar, scooped up some of the warm food with the spoon, and ate. It was salty, and its texture was revolting, but it restored hope and strength almost immediately.

Lymon and Darla Jane watched in silence. When he'd eaten enough, Lymon took the jar away and Darla Jane pushed him back onto the mattress.

"Breed," she said. "We breed."

"Oh . . . no, no, really, that's not going to work," Gil sputtered, looking away from her. The smell; the membrane slopping over her—unbearable. He tried to push her away. But it was like pushing away a mudslide.

"You don't understand," Lymon said. "It's not . . . about arousal, really. Not at first. But—she will show you. We need your seed, Gil. We need human seed; we only do hybrids, as children, you see. That's what works best."

"But *me*—Lymon? I'm your friend!"

"And I would miss you, Gil! So you'll be here with me. I wanted to give you a chance to live your dream. To be something that matters. To really have an impact on the world. We've been preparing the planet—encouraging those who deny climate change, through our intermediaries . . . and certain industries. The damage humanity was doing to the sea could not be tolerated. We'll end it our way. And yet, ironically, global warming is to our benefit! The sea rises! What it consumes, we too will consume. Now let Darla Jane have her way, Gil."

"No—that's completely . . . no."

"It's all right. You don't have to kiss her."

Lymon walked away, and the thing calling itself Darla Jane pressed him back, and straddled him—and the membrane parted at her groin.

Something emerged from her, there. From between her legs. *Tendrils*, thin and whipping and transparent, restless and seeking, tickling up his belly; then a red hose-like organ extruded from under the tendrils. The living hose opened itself wide, and slowly but inexorably sucked his private parts into itself—clasping testicles and all.

Gil writhed and shrieked and tried to push her away but she was far stronger than he was and he could get no grip on her slick limbs.

The tubular organ squeezed peristaltically, *milking* his blood up into it, forcing his organ to become rigid. There was a kind of sickening pseudo pleasure in the process but he was gagging at her subaquatic reek, struggling against her clamp-like hands.

The tendrils extruded spines—which stabbed into his thighs.

The pain was piercing, attenuated—but almost immediately vanished. *Some biological anesthetic*, he thought. *Like mosquitoes use so you don't feel them bite.*

Then he felt a cold pulsing from the spines—and knew he was being injected. A thick, glutinous fluid was forced into his muscles. It carried a ghastly ecstasy, a vile delight that expanded through him from his pierced thighs . . . and he found himself bucking his hips, forcing his reproductive organs deeper into the externalized genitalia of the thing that held him down until . . .

3. Gilberto Lopez, Lymon Barnes. June 2037.

Gil delighted in the feeling of being a hand in the glove of the sea. He loved being out here, free of the oppressive weight of the temple hidden under the reefs—the freedom of the open sea, the infinite possibilities. He loved kicking easily along, warm and safe within his second skin. He envied Lymon his ability to breathe directly in water—Lymon didn't have to look out through a bubble of the membrane. It blurred his vision, around the edges. But he could see well enough: the light wavering down from the surface; a school of striped fish swimming by. How had he ever felt that fish were repellent? They really were lovely—the way they all moved as one, in their school. Someday the interspecies council would move with such graceful unanimity.

The Atlantic Ocean had regained much of its ancient vitality with the awakening of Dagon and the hard work done by His people. The acidity from global warming had been much reduced, with the cultivation of the undersea forests of specially bred kelp. Mercury and other toxins were being sponged away. The council had destroyed many of the ships that had done so much damage; they had blocked the outflow from dirtwalker cities—all that had helped. The wars, too, on the surface, had helped. Struggling for resources in an overheated world, the dirtwalkers were reduced in numbers and thus in power to do harm.

It really was becoming a kind of paradise, along the northeast shore, underwater. But a number of foul dirtwalker settlements still festered on the coast.

Swimming toward the Plum Island Sound, Gil sighed, thinking that perhaps his father would have been proud of him, after all, if he could have shown him all this—his father had always loved the sea. But Pops and Mom were dead. Eddie too—Eduardo had gone a bit mad, after seeing Lymon and his brother Gil, on the trawler, that day.

I thought of him as my stronger older brother, but Eduardo was weak, and foolish, Gil thought. *A person of no vision.*

He had refused to be recruited. And Lymon's spies on the surface had reported Eddie's demise. Dead of a heroin overdose. Gil's parents had each taken their own lonely path to death. Pops had died of cancer, mom had crawled into a bottle and never gotten out. They'd wasted away in Rowley.

As he gazed out across the underseascape, Gil's only real regret was that he had no artist's supplies. How he'd love to find a way to paint this. The kelp forests; the sliding shark, the nosing dolphin. Blue-green water and diffused golden light; green going to black farther down. And the work crew, swimming briskly to the dike. What a sight they were—men and women transformed, merged with the sea.

The work was almost done, he saw, as they approached the dike. The undermining was finished. The chains were being locked into place.

Soon, the head engineer signaled to Gil—who was, now, high priest of the interspecies brotherhood—asking for permission to proceed.

Gil looked around, saw that the tide was high as it was going to be, and the others had drawn back to safety. He gestured, *Proceed*.

The engineer signaled Darla Jane—who gave that high keening call she had, that came from her vibrating gill-slits . . .

And soon the kraken came from their deep place of slumber.

Their massive oblong bodies stretched out; they turned in the water, their multiple limbs seeking, reaching for the chains; their tentacles entwined the thick steel bands. And the giant squids, bigger than any known to dirtwalker humanity, began to pull . . .

It took almost ten minutes . . . but the underpinnings at last collapsed, taking the dike with them. A great rumbling shuddered through the sea as the dike fell into it, ragged boulders of asphalt streaming bubbles as they plunged down.

But Gil was lifted up. With a cry of joy Gil felt himself carried up, bodily sluiced toward the land as the dike disintegrated into the Atlantic Ocean.

The great wave lifted him ever higher, over the sinking debris; up and up so that at last he broke the surface, and with Lymon and their companions he rode the tsunami in at dawn, the servants of Dagon astride the great wave that would be the first of many to crash down on Rowley, Massachusetts, drowning it as Innsmouth had been drowned, crushing buildings and choking the squirming dirtwalkers, so that the triumph of Dagon, and the glory of Gilberto Lopez and Lymon Barnes was complete . . .

Emmy-nominated, Stoker Award-winning author **John Shirley** has written more than two dozen novels and numerous short stories, many of which are collected in his eight fiction collections. Although best known for science fiction and horror, Shirley's most recent novel is *Wyatt in Wichita*, a work of historical fiction. A collection gathering his short Lovecraftian fiction, *Lovecraft Alive*, is forthcoming. He also writes screenplays and for television. As a musician, Shirley has fronted his own bands and written lyrics for Blue Öyster Cult and others.

"All women are balanced somewhere on the witch's scale,
but some barely make the weight requirement."

RIPPER

Angela Slatter

I

Kit hadn't seen the first one, but PC Wright told him not to worry—this one
was worse.

The throat was cut—that wasn't too bad, quite neat in fact and he had
witnessed that sort of thing before—but the woman's skirts (Kit could
see in the lamp light that she wore several against the cold, green, brown,
black, some red ruffles) had been part-pulled up, part-torn, and her fat
little middle-aged belly exposed and slashed open to leave a bloody abyss.
Intestines reached over each shoulder; a separate piece of about two feet
had been lopped off and put to one side as if whoever did it had a grander
plan. Thick wavy dark hair acted as a pillow for her head and mutilated
face; the lacerations weren't in the usual fashion of whores getting sliced
by their pimps or dissatisfied customers. There was a *design* here and that
disturbed him even more than the smell of shit and piss emanating from
the unfortunate woman, who was no longer in a position to care or to cover
herself and try to preserve a little bit of modesty. No, thought Kit, *that's*
what bothered him most, that the woman was so terribly exposed in her
death, so terribly, terribly helpless.

Hanbury Street was quiet though Kit knew that was only temporary.
PC Ned Watkins had sounded his whistle but a moment ago, and soon
the place would be crawling with bluebottles, pressmen, terrified whores,
and general gawkers. Thomas Wright, who'd been crouched down peering
closely at the body while young Watkins threw up his pint and pork pie in
a corner, made a noise—that strange noise Kit had come to associate with
police who'd found someone they knew on this kind of day. It held despair,

disappointment, disgust, rage and, peculiarly, a kind of knowing lack of surprise, as if *this* was somehow to be expected. Kit was coming to recognise it in the first pursing of the lips, the earliest expulsion of air. He wondered if he'd start doing it soon.

"It's Annie Chapman. Dark Annie," Wright said and spat. "Watkins, buck up, man."

But Watkins was having none of it and determinedly continued to dry heave after his stomach was well and truly empty. Wright shook his head, then nodded at Kit. "Off you go, lad, you're fast. Straight to Abberline and Himself at Leman Street—although, if you're passing the Ten Bells stick your head in and see if the good Doctor Bagster Phillips is in. Fair chance— he'll need to be called anyway."

Kit nodded and turned away, relieved to pour his nervous energy into a useful activity; unfortunately he bounded straight into the oncoming form of PC Airedale, the largest, most unpleasant copper in all of Whitechapel— which meant he beat out some fairly stiff competition. Kit bounced off Airedale's torso, almost ending up on his arse, and the big policeman snarled, "Watch where you're going, you half-wit."

"Leave off him," snapped Wright, "He's only doing what I told him. Get going, boy."

Kit sped off into the night as Airedale sneered, "What? You told him to run into me?"

The air was cool but Kit could feel his face burning, not only with embarrassment, but also distress at seeing the woman so abused. What had Wright called her? Chapman, Annie. The first one was Mary Anne Nichols. Although Kit hadn't seen her, he had seen the pitiable Martha Tabram, pierced all to hell by a bayonet. And still that wasn't as bad as Annie Chapman and her torn-apart belly. He rubbed a hand across his own flat stomach in sympathy.

He'd read the reports on Nichols, too, while they sat on the Inspector's desk. As a child Kit had become expert at reading upside down as much out of genuine interest as self-preservation. He'd learned early on that the only hope of conversation with his father was in discussing whatever the Reverend Caswell was reading over the breakfast table (in spite of his wife's protests).

A quick look in at the Ten Bells showed no sign of the police surgeon for Whitechapel, so he concluded the good doctor had at last gone home to his own bed. Kit hared along, barely out of breath, until he came to the steps of the nick and took them three at a time, sketched a brief wave at the sergeant on the entrance desk, and then darted up the internal staircase to the second floor.

Abberline and Himself were ensconced in the office they'd been forced to share since the former had been seconded to Leman Street in order to coordinate the Whitechapel murder investigations. This was the billet he'd occupied as head of H Division for nine years; somewhat inconveniently, its current occupant, Edwin Makepeace, had refused to move out and make way for the senior man. What had been a fair sized space for a single person, was now a rather cramped affair for two. Their desks butted up against each other like charging bulls. Neither inspector had spent much time at his individual residence since Nichols had been brought in; whether it was devotion to duty or a concern that unguarded territory might be fair game was a matter for discussion amongst the lower ranks. Kit suspected it was roughly equal measures of both.

Kit gave a hasty knock and opened the door a little before permission was given, and found himself the subject of rather steely gazes. Abberline was of middling height, in his forties, heading towards stout; a neat man with muttonchops and a meticulously tended moustache. His companion was, in contrast, tall and lean, and as neat as Abberline was, Makepeace was scruffy. Even when he was dressed for a meeting with his betters, even with all the spit-polish in the world, Kit had observed, his boss still had the air of a man who'd just been dragged backwards through a hedge.

In the no man's land where the desks met was an open bottle of whisky and a couple of tumblers, each containing differing levels of amber liquid. It seemed the masters had reached some kind of an accord. In spite of himself, Kit found his tongue tripping over words, and all he managed was an inarticulate stutter. Neither man was cruel enough to laugh, although Abberline grunted, "Spit it out, boy."

Kit took a deep breath, trying not to appear to do so, and spoke. "There's been another, sirs. Another woman's been murdered."

If it surprised the men that Kit didn't say "another whore's been ripped," that he displayed some respect, if not tenderness, for the dead woman, they didn't show it. Perhaps they just thought it a display of his youth and assumed he'd harden the longer he stayed in the job. Perhaps they were too tired to care.

"Do you have a name for this victim, Caswell?" Makepeace stood, slowly, careful not to thrust his chair back into the too-close wall. He hooked his green checkered coat from the rack and shrugged in it; the fabric seemed to shudder, unwilling to accommodate the man's shoulders. When the operation was completed and the item of clothing surrendered, Makepeace threw Abberline a tweed jacket so the inspector might make himself presentable.

"Yes, sir. Annie Chapman, sir," replied Kit, adding, rather unnecessarily, "She's another prostitute, sir."

"A wandering beauty of the night," sighed Abberline, startling Kit. He'd not given the Inspector much credit for a poetic soul. "Will you tell us where, boy, or shall we meander through the streets until we stumble upon her?"

"There's a good chance you'd find the wrong body, sir, this being Whitechapel and all," said Kit before he could help himself, then wanted to bite off his own tongue. Abberline and Himself guffawed in delight, and Kit thought the whisky had probably been his savior. "In Hanbury Street, sirs, number 29. I looked for Doctor Bagster Phillips on my way here, but he wasn't at the Ten Bells."

"Try his home. If you can't find him there then I cannot imagine which mistress he is favouring this eve, and we'll have to get some other sawbones to hack at her." Makepeace sighed. "I'd rather it be him."

"Yes, sir, I'll do my best, sir."

"Off you go, Kit, you'll have run half the city before this night's out."

II

Stopping at the Limehouse lock-up added an extra twenty minutes to the journey home, but it couldn't be helped. The seemingly ramshackle shed was hidden deep in the overgrown back garden of 14a Samuel Street, and Kit wasn't the only person with permission to use it, but he knew that his visits were carefully scheduled to ensure that no one else's tarriance clashed with his. Privacy was of the utmost importance and the Orientals understood that better than anyone Kit had ever met. Honoring debts was of equal importance, Kit had discovered, and was grateful that the debt in question was owed to him and not the other way around.

He unlocked the hut as pale rays of dawn rolled languidly across the September sky, and stepped inside, conscientiously latching the door behind him. The ever-burning lantern glowed in a corner, and Kit could make out muddy boot-prints on the pale birch of the floor, signs of other comings and goings. The interior of the lock-up would have surprised anyone who didn't have a key to it: it was (muddy prints notwithstanding) a tidy room, lined with a series of securely locked leather-bound wooden steamer trunks. Even the worst of the reprobates who used this place wouldn't dare break faith with either fellow key-holders or their Chinese hosts; it wouldn't be worth the strife. In one corner was a trapdoor, also locked. Kit didn't have a key to *that*.

His chest was located nearest the trapdoor, so he'd had plenty of time to study it in the past three months, which was also, not so coincidentally the same amount of time he'd been working for the Metropolitan Police Service. He lifted the heavy lid once the lock had been disengaged and sighed as he drew forth a dress in navy, almost as dark as his uniform, complete with bustle and ridiculously tight sleeves, and shook it to encourage the wrinkles to leave the bombazine.

The advantage of the color, she thought, *was that it didn't look as if it had been folded in the bottom of a case for almost a whole day.* She couldn't quite recall how, or indeed if, she'd ever sat comfortably in a bustled skirt. Kit—Katherine—Caswell slid the police helmet from her head and rubbed her scalp with long fingers. Her hair was cropped, a ruddy brown like her father's had been. She was thankful, in a small way, that she'd had to sell her tresses to the wigmaker so she could afford Lucius' medicine; they'd been down to her waist, as thick a mane as any young woman could have wished for and had fetched a handsome price. Since then she'd kept it neatly trimmed, surreptitiously cutting it so her mother didn't seem to notice except to comment from time to time that it was a shame the locks didn't appear to want to grow back. It—and her squarish jaw—helped Kit to pass for a boy. A girlish-looking boy to be sure, but a boy nonetheless, with a voice that was deep for a girl, light for a boy, and did not give her away for she was careful to speak in low tones.

Beneath the dress were the myriad petticoats and underclothes she'd come to loathe more and more with every passing day, particularly the corset; even the strapping across her modest breasts to keep them flat in her uniform was less uncomfortable and restricting. She shook everything out before dressing, just in case some kind of insect life had decided her drawers might make a good home. But the lock-up was very clean, and Kit knew she had no real reason for concern. And the shoes, the little black leather boots with bows and buttons up the side that made her toes hurt. In the cracked and speckled full-length mirror the owners had been kind enough to provide (Kit was under no illusions that hers was the only transformation conducted here on a daily basis), she surveyed herself and settled the silly little cream and coffee bonnet with trailing ribbons and silken butterflies onto her head, then affixed the short cape around her shoulders against the chill. She looked respectable and that was the best she could hope for.

Navigating her way through the clawing bushes and over the boggy path, she finally stepped out into the alley after taking a good look around to make sure she was unobserved. There was only the young Chinese boy, perched on a stool at the back gate, drowsy but alert enough to give her a nod as she passed by. He was one of a cadre of youngsters deployed by his community to collect information that might keep them safe, learning the business, learning to keep secrets, learning a dozen other possibly highly illegal things in regard to which Kit might one day have to glance the other way. She'd worry about that later though. For now, tolerance and willful blindness were in everyone's interests—she'd realized in the last few months that sometimes part of enforcing the law was pretending ignorance, and she was more than prepared to apply that to her current situation.

The walk to number 3 Lady's Mantle Court took ten minutes. The streets were starting to come alive, so her footsteps weren't the only sounds to be heard; bakers making deliveries, butchers lugging carcasses to restaurants and big houses, coal trucks, flower girls shouting at anyone they could see, all combined to start the beginnings of a cacophony that would grow and not subside until well after dark had fallen. Mind, things had been quieter since Mary Anne Nichols had been found. Might grow quieter still, thought Kit, now Annie Chapman had joined her compatriot. Then she wondered how long before the city's male population got up-in-arms, or at least the pimps and the bullyboys who ran the whores; those who made their living off women's backs, and who didn't mind knocking "employees' around themselves, but God help the man who hit another's whore—at least without paying extra. Finding herself at a familiar blue-painted door, Kit pushed these thoughts aside, consciously settled a blank and obedient expression on her face, and slid the neat little black key from the balding velvet drawstring purse—which also contained a dainty hanky with edges embroidered and a set of brass knuckles—into its lock.

"Did you do it? Katherine?"

Sweet Jesus, had her mother been waiting up all night until she walked in? Kit took a deep breath and paced to the tiny parlor in the rooms they rented in Mrs. Kittredge's genteelly decrepit home. Sure enough, there she was, seated by the dying fire, a frayed rug across her knee, disarrayed knitting tumbled to the floor and tangled about Louisa Caswell's worn slippers. The mourning cap she'd adopted and not relinquished, though almost three years had passed since her husband's death, sat askew on the silver-shot black hair that flowed over her thin shoulders, and her eyes, fever-bright, seemed to be trying to pierce Kit, to get inside her and determine all the secrets she might be hiding.

Kit smiled. "Yes, Mother. Good morning."

"Did you get it all done?" repeated Louisa as if her daughter had not answered. Kit nodded, crossed the room, and patted her mother's long thin hands with their spidery fingers.

"Yes, Mother. We completed the entire order. Mistress Hazleton is very pleased."

"So you are home for a while? Did she pay you? Lucius needs more medicine. Did she pay you?" Louisa had been under the impression for some time that Kit was still apprenticed to a milliner on the other side of the Thames, and that this employment sometimes required her daughter to work nights in order to fill large orders of hats—she was willing to believe that Mistress Hazleton's confections of feathers and silk, bows and beads, netting and pearls were in high demand. Louisa also had no idea that the pittance her daughter earned in that position did not stretch to the needs of three people, one of them very ill. It was four months since Kit had hit upon her plan after discovering how much improved her pay conditions might be were she a male.

"Yes, Mother. I have been paid. I will get Lucius' medicine this morning and I will pay Mrs. Kittredge the money she is owed. Then I will buy groceries and we shall have a fine luncheon before I go back to work. Put your mind at rest." She stroked Louisa's hair and face; was stunned to find how much resentment was billowing up from inside like bile, how much she hated being a parent to her mother when she'd barely finished with being a child herself. "Have you been sitting up all night?"

"Oh no, dear. I slept very well." And Kit thought she probably had after a dose of the laudanum Louisa had found was her only means to cope after the Reverend Caswell's demise. She ran tender fingers over the stump of Louisa's left ear where only a remnant of the top half remained. Louisa swatted her daughter's hand away as if the touch reminded her of things she wished to forget.

"I'll go and check on Lucius, Mother, then we shall have some breakfast. Would you like your knitting?"

The woman nodded and Kit carefully lifted the unidentifiable knotting of coarse wool and smooth wooden needles to her mother's lap and left her to get on with whatever it was she thought she was making.

Her brother's bedchamber was at the back of the ground floor flat; their entire space was small, but neat, and the paint was not peeling even if the rugs were a little threadbare. Some weeks Kit paid Mrs. Kittredge extra to help clean their rooms and the older woman was happy to help out. She was even good about sitting with Lucius when his mother and sister had to go out; and more often than not when she arrived home in the afternoons Kit would find her mother and their landlady either in the parlor drinking tea and gossiping, or in the kitchen shelling peas for a great pot of stew or soup the two households would share—and gossiping. Kit wondered if Mrs. K noticed Louisa's decaying mental state; perhaps she did and it just made her kinder. With no family of her own living close, Mrs. K had adopted the Caswells, seeming to spend more time with them than on the two floors above which were her domain. Kit didn't mind because it meant her family was watched out for while she was away.

"Get some rest," Inspector Makepeace had said when she left the station in the morning dark. *Easier said than done*, thought Kit. Lucius hadn't woken yet and Kit watched as he slept. He had their mother's coloring, black hair and palest skin, with icy blue eyes that warmed when he roused and saw his sister.

"Kit!" He struggled to sit, thin arms pushing him upwards, the weight of his wasted legs making the task harder than it should have been. She came to his aid, plumping pillows and helping him to rest against them. The room was narrow, like the whole house, with just enough space for a slender bed, a tallboy and a chair by his pillow, where a copy of Stevenson's *The Strange Case of Dr Jekyll and Mr Hyde* lay.

"You want to be careful with that. If Mother sees it we'll never hear the end of it." She lifted the book, sat down and rested the slim volume in her lap. Louisa objected to her son reading anything that wasn't "improving" and she most certainly did not consider "that Scotsman" improving. She thought his work encouraged boys to run away from home for adventure's sake. Lucius gave his most winning smile.

"She won't get angry with me, Kit, don't worry."

"No, but she will get angry with *me* and I'll be the worst person in the world for giving it to you," she pointed out, mock scolding.

"What did you do last night, Kit? What did you see?" When Kit had put her plan into action and changed jobs (to say the least), Lucius knew; he noticed everything, all the habits of the house because he had nothing better to do with himself. It was the kind of secret that was difficult to keep from him—whereas Louisa spent so much time in her own world, not caring as long as the bills were paid, Lucius had his medicine and she hers, and food made a regular appearance on the table. He read, he scribbled in the cheap notebooks Kit bought him, he read some more, he watched the garden from the tiny window of his room, he played whist with Mrs. K, although Louisa couldn't keep track of the game. But her brother, observed Kit, remained cheerful; illness and immobility hadn't soured his nature, and he looked forward to hearing about what she did when dressed as a man.

She wondered if he'd be so accepting if he'd had a father still alive, if he'd spent the better part of his thirteen years going amongst other boys and drinking in their beliefs and bigotries. Despite the hardship his sickness caused them all, a tiny part of Kit was pleased it had made him so sweet and open-minded.

She leaned forward, thinking about what to tell him—*how* to tell him, for he loved a story. So she began with her evening patrol, the three fights she'd broken up before strolling down Hanbury Street and finding Wright and Watkins in their varied positions near poor Annie Chapman. She glossed over the worst of the predations on the woman's corpse, but told him enough that a look of horrified delight sparked there even as he whispered a prayer for the soul of the dead. When finally she finished her tale and sat back in the chair, he looked as though he'd eaten a good meal; which she knew he hadn't.

"Right, I'm off to make breakfast before Mother comes looking for me."

"Five minutes more, Kit, please. Read me the chapter again that I read last night."

"But you've already read it—won't be any surprises," she teased.

"Please, Kit, I like to *hear* it too. Oh, won't you please?"

She relented and cracked the cover. "'A fortnight later, by excellent good fortune, the doctor gave one of his pleasant dinners . . .'"

III

Two in the afternoon and Kit, once again in disguise, could barely suppress her yawns. The problem with that—apart from the dagger looks Himself was giving her—was that it seemed to let the smell into her mouth, and it was bad enough that her poor nose was already getting so abused. She couldn't help imagining the odor as a taste, a contagion on the air. The Old Montague Street Mortuary stank, as one might expect, of death, a stench that had embedded itself into the very bricks of the walls, the very stones of the floor. Luckily the temperature was kind—in high summer, Kit imagined there was a good chance she'd keel over if she had to set foot in this place.

On the table in front of Dr. Bagster Phillips lay Chapman, Annie, the woman the doctor kept referring to as "an unfortunate," as if her death was some kind of inconvenience that might have been overcome in better circumstances; something from which she might *recover*. Kit kept her expression blank; Makepeace was watching her too closely to let any thoughts slip onto her face. Her camouflage was maintained by diligent discipline in all areas of her person and mentality and conduct.

She stood with her feet apart, balancing squarely and gratefully on boots with a reasonable heel, a flat sole and not a hint of buttons or bows. Dr. Bagster Phillips' voice was a buzz in her head, comments on the corpse she took in without really listening: lungs ripe with tuberculosis, the tissues of the brain diseased, abrasions on fingers where rings had been removed (and not found), the neck cleanly cut, the head almost severed, the terrible injuries to her belly and the fact that her uterus was gone. A bayonet, the doctor said quite clearly, or something very like one, wielded by someone—a man obviously, no woman would have the strength. Privately, Kit thought that untrue—if Dark Annie had been incapacitated first, there was nothing to stop a woman from hacking at her; well, apart from common decency and squeamishness.

"A Liston knife, perhaps?" asked Abberline and Bagster Phillips blew out an annoyed breath.

"Or a butcher's knife, or a circumcision knife . . . " he muttered half under his breath, then tried to rein in his temper.

"Someone with a degree of anatomical knowledge?" asked Makepeace and Kit watched the doctor squirm until he reluctantly nodded and muttered *perhaps*—he did not, Kit noted, want anyone to think a medical man might have done this. She couldn't blame him and kept her eyes on the woman as the police surgeon conducted his business. Poor Annie didn't look any better than she had the last time Kit had seen her, except she'd been cleaned up. Her face was still swollen and bruised, the slashes across her body were dried obscenely brown and black, and the cuts stood out starkly on her dead-white flesh. And the old scars, her life right up until someone had taken a blade to her, were writ large on her skin with contusions and cicatrices, scrapes and scratches. Kit had to blink to stop the heat of tears. No one else in the cold malodorous chamber was showing any sympathy for the dead woman; nor would Kit.

The doctor's commentary was occasionally interrupted by questions from Abberline and Makepeace. Both men stood near to the table on which the body rested; they leaned forward to look more closely when Bagster Phillips indicated some trauma or cut, or smudge or other trace element of the woman's murder. On either side of Kit stood Wright and Airedale, the latter looming over both his fellow PCs.

"You lot," said Makepeace, his voice echoing off the walls, "did you speak to her clients from last night?"

Wright nodded, reeled off the names of the men they'd been able to find; all had alibis, had been happily tucked up in bed with their wives after they'd availed themselves of Annie's services.

Makepeace continued, "And Chapman's husband?"

There was a silence, into which Kit, when it became apparent her betters could not fill, dropped, "John Chapman was her husband, sir, but they've been separated four years. He left London soon after their paths, err, diverged."

Airedale and Wright stared at Kit, the former with resentment, the latter with surprise.

In for a penny, in for a pound, Kit went on: "I spoke to the tarts last night, sir, those who hung around. Eliza Cooper—with whom Annie had fought over some hawker called Harry, and no I've not found him yet—told me. It seems they were friends before they became rivals. And Annie sometimes was seen in the company of one Edward Stanley, a brick layer's apprentice."

"Have you spoken to Mr. Stanley?" asked Abberline. Kit shook her head.

"I was going to try to find him today, sir, and Harry the Hawker."

"I think you'll be best spent with Mr. Stanley. Your colleagues can locate and question the mysterious Harry and see if they can learn as much as you did so quickly." Makepeace gave his other officers a look fit to melt glass; Kit knew that she was being rewarded, sent to find someone whose last name and place of work she already knew. The other two would have to start at the bottom—if they were smart they'd try Eliza Cooper first, but who knew where to find her in the daylight hours? Makepeace barked, "Well, what are you all waiting for? Get out there. And Caswell?"

She paused, side-stepping to avoid Airedale's intentional bump. "Yes, sir?"

"Mary Anne Nichols. Talk to her husband, see if he knew Chapman too."

"William Nichols. Yes, sir."

She followed Wright and Airedale into the watery afternoon sunshine. Kit took a deep breath of the air, which, although it wasn't the sweetest, was still a vast improvement on the atmosphere of the mortuary. The large copper glared at her. "Apple-polishing little bastard. Mincing, apple-polishing little bastard."

"Leave him alone. Good work's no reason to hate someone. Not his fault he's smarter than you are, Airedale." Wright crossed his arms, rolled his neck and cracked the vertebrae loudly as if limbering up for a fight. Airedale, for all his size, was unlikely to go after Wright, who was stocky and known to be a fine bare-knuckle fighter. Kit wondered what she'd do if ever the older PC's protective presence was absent and Airedale found he had free rein. Wright jerked his chin at Kit and said, "Off you go, lad, best not to keep Himself waiting when he's got such high expectations of you."

Kit shot him a grin, dodged a kick from Airedale, who muttered "mincing little bastard" yet again, and made a conscious effort to walk in a more manly way, legs apart as if large balls might be impeding his stride. She kept it up until she turned the corner into Brick Lane, finding the gait made her hip joints grind uncomfortably, and the rolled-up pair of socks in the front of her trousers had drifted uncomfortably to the left. Kit adjusted her "crotch," thinking that only as a man could she get away with such a thing in public.

A whistle, high and wolfish, caught her attention.

The previously empty street now contained a woman, small with dark brown hair, who stood at the mouth of an alley. She wore a forest-green dress, a black short jacket over the top and a clean white apron, but there was no doubt in Kit's mind what profession the woman pursued. Her skin was fair, she wore no hat, but her cheeks were rouged like a doll's, her lips painted redder than red; she stood with one hip pushed out in offering, and her gaze said "come hither" as she fluttered her lashes. She lifted a thin, graceful hand and gestured in a queenly fashion for Kit to approach.

"What are doing, you little turd? Get a move on!" Airedale growled from behind Kit and slapped a meaty hand down on her shoulder. Startled she twisted away, fish-fast, and broke into a sprint.

"Better run, you little faggot," bellowed Airedale, laughing unpleasantly.

Kit kept moving. When she drew level with the spot where the woman had been, it was empty, but somewhere back in the shadowy depths of the alley, she seemed to sense movement and the weight of a gaze still upon her.

IV

William Nichols was harder to find than Edward Stanley, but easier to talk to, Kit discovered. Stanley, at his job, was loath to take time to speak with Kit. She didn't think it was guilt—then again she couldn't be sure—but rather a wish to not be involved. He'd spent time with Annie, yes, on occasion; they'd shared lodgings now and then, yes. But he'd not seen her in a good six months and he'd met a girl, good and kind and sweet—and very religious. He was bettering himself, didn't Kit see, and he could not, would not, be associated with the likes of depraved women such as Annie Chapman. He was sorry for what happened to her, but she'd brought it upon herself by the very life she lived.

Kit found herself disliking the newly clean-living Mr. Stanley, his righteousness sticking in her throat like a chicken bone. And he had an alibi, even if she'd have preferred he didn't, just for the sheer pleasure of running him in.

"Ah, poor Polly," said William Nichols, shaking his head. Kit found him in the Bricklayers Arms, already well soused. A printer's machinist, he'd finished for the day; his employer was sitting beside him, also rather drunk. When Kit appeared that man made excuses to leave, mentioning a wife with a rolling pin and a finely tuned temper, who was expecting him home sooner rather than later. She took the seat the printer had so recently occupied, careful to sit with her legs apart and arms crossed over her chest—Airedale's comments had made her consider if she'd gotten sloppy about maintaining her masculine disguise. *Perhaps*, thought Kit wryly, *it was time to adopt all the great hallmarks of male behavior: spitting in the street, burping after a meal, and farting with enthusiasm in small airless rooms.*

"Poor Polly, poor Mary Anne," sighed Nichols. Kit pondered how whores seemed not to settle on one single name, yet created new personas for themselves—a *nom de mattress*.

"When did you last see her, Mr. Nichols?"

"Not for a few months. You know we're separated," he said, his round face sad as he sipped at his gin. Kit knew—one of the woman she'd spoken to at the time of Mary Anne/Polly's death—Nelly Holland, the tart who shared a room with her—had told how William had an affair with the nurse who'd delivered their last child, then left. He'd been forced to pay Polly maintenance, though, until it came to light she'd been on the game—her illicit earnings meant her erstwhile husband was freed from his fiscal burden.

Holland said Polly claimed they still knew each other as man and wife every so often, but Nelly'd not seen evidence of it. It was possible, Kit supposed; William Nichols appeared genuinely fond of his deceased spouse, and he didn't seem like a man with an axe to grind. To her surprise he added, "My fault entirely. I should not have laid my hat where it did not belong. Only poor Polly was so tired after that last babe and a man needs some attention. I should have been patient though."

Kit wondered if all the men of Whitechapel were coming down with the affliction of self-improvement and thought the world might not survive were it to continue unabated.

"Quite," she said. "Did she know Annie Chapman?"

He nodded sagely.

"They all know each other, don't they? Women?" he said as if the sex was some kind of tribe with an in-built knowledge of all its members, then he clarified, "The tarts. They know each other; if they're not fighting over territory and clients, they're drinking together somewhere. If they're not arguing over who stole whose best petticoat, they're sharing warnings about the bad'uns, those that won't pay what they say they will, that hurt the girls instead of simply doing their normal business."

"Were they friends?" she asked. "I mean, did they know each other well?"

He shrugged. "Knew each other well enough to have a drink at the Ten Bells, I suppose." His eyes sparkled. "Here, why are you asking? Have you found the bastard who cut my Polly?"

She shook her head and watched his interest snuff out. "No, Mr. Nichols, I'm sorry. I'm just trying to find out if Annie and Polly had any connections that might lead me somewhere useful."

"Can't help you, lad, anymore than I've said, I'm sorry." He looked so downcast she was tempted to reach over and pat his hand, but knew it would be misinterpreted and turn out badly for her no matter what. So, Kit nodded, and stood, wished him good evening and made her way through the cramped, smoky rooms of the Bricklayers Arms and out into the evening, glad for the thickness of her tunic against the coming chill.

Her footsteps sounded cold on the cobbles and carriages clattered past on their way to better places. The lights had come on, yellow beacons flickering weakly in the early hints of a night mist—of course, the alleys and courts, the side streets and lacunae between buildings did not warrant electrical illumination; darkness needed a place to thrive. After she'd moved from the door of the pub and was partway down well-lit Commercial Street, she heard a crash and a crunch as of someone dropping something and standing on something else, just inside an alleyway.

"You do make a lovely boy," said a voice from the pitchy shades, rolling effortlessly between two accents and, even though it was female, it sent a shiver through Kit. She frowned and concentrated on identifying the distinct tones as she scanned the shadows. "But I'll wager you've not got what it takes."

This last was said with a laugh and the prostitute Kit had seen on her return from the mortuary stepped out of the gloom. Irish, thought Kit, and Welsh; a smooth mix of rhythmic lilts, musical cadences and strange glottal stops. The woman moved closer and her hand snaked out, grabbing at Kit's groin, closing briefly around the rolled socks, and letting go with a laugh. The movement was so rapid, so unexpected, that she had no time to react, but stood, mouth agape, horrified. The woman turned her back, cast a look over her shoulder and said, "Will you walk with me, *lad*?"

Kit swallowed, not daring to speak, thinking only of getting this unwanted companion away from a place where they might be overheard. They fell into step and made a dignified progress towards Hawksmoor's Christ Church and its small graveyard, an island of darkness lapping against Commercial Street. They remained silent for the first minute or three, the woman nodding to other whores waiting for company. They nodded back and Kit wondered if William Nichols had been more right than he'd known when he suggested these sisters of the streets all knew each other.

"How did you know?" asked Kit quietly when they reached the metal spikes of the churchyard fence.

"Some things I just do. You're doing a fine job, though, of keeping those coppers fooled. They don't take notice, for all they're *investigators*. They take things at face value, don't you find?" She too spoke quietly, and Kit appreciated that she seemed committed to keeping Kit's secret, at least for the moment.

"What do you want? I have no money to spare," she said, thinking she simply couldn't afford to be blackmailed.

"I may be a whore, but I'm not a thief, thank you very much," said the woman, affronted dignity limning her tone.

"I'm . . . I'm sorry."

"Ah, don't be. Of course I'm a thief, we all are. I just wanted to see if you had any manners." She laughed shrilly; she was older than Kit, maybe twenty-five, and she was very pretty although, Kit observed, it wouldn't be long before the harshness of her way of life started to show itself on her face. "The other girls always say you're a polite young man, that you don't talk down to them, that you listen. Oh, don't worry, they don't know what I know and if they did, they wouldn't tell—the streets are better with you here and all. Don't want your money, Kit Caswell, but I wanted to talk to you about Polly and Annie."

"Did you know them?"

"Of course, we are of a kind," replied the woman in melodic timbre.

"Who are you?" asked Kit belatedly.

"Mary Jane Kelly," she said and nodded towards a seat inside the churchyard. "Marie Jeanette, if you prefer. Or Fair Emma or Ginger or Black Mary, if nothing else takes your fancy?"

"More names than you can shake a stick at," observed Kit and Mary Jane fixed her with a look.

"Wouldn't you? If you did what we do, wouldn't you hide your identity, try to separate yourself any way you could from what you do?" She sat on the bench, first wiping at it in a lady-like fashion with a gloved hand. "Wouldn't you take an alias and keep your real name a secret, just like the gypsies do? You—you keep your true self hidden, so you should understand."

Kit hadn't thought of it like that, but it made all the sense in the world. "I see it, yes. I'm sorry for being rude. What do you have to tell me, Miss Kelly? About the women who've been carved?"

"They've not been killed because they're whores, Kit Caswell, that's just a convenience makes them easier to find, to hunt out."

"Then why? What can they possibly have that a killer would take from them?"

"You know what he took from Annie and so do I—oh, PC Wright's a love when you get him in the mood," she sniggered smugly. "Took the very core of her, didn't he? From Polly, he took the voice-box."

No one else knew about that, Kit thought. "What could he do with body parts? You're not saying they're getting burked? What he's taking is hardly fit for commerce with the Resurrectionists and their like."

"Sweet Jesu, thought you were smarter than those with a weight between the legs, pulling their brains downwards!" Kelly shook her head. "No, he takes the things he needs, little pieces of them that the soul can cling to. He's taken two, he wants five, like the points of a pentacle."

"What?" Kit blinked.

"He can't carry away bodies, not the state they're in and he doesn't need all of them for his purposes. He just needs a little thing, a souvenir, a flesh poppet for the soul to recognize, to hang on to until he gets it to wherever he's taking them." She grasped Kit's cold hands in her own, and Kit could feel the heat of her coming through the thin-worn gloves. "He's taking them because they're witches. He's taking them for their power."

Kit didn't know which thought to follow first, so she leapt on the most obvious. "You say *he*—do you know who it is? For the love of God, don't tell me you know and haven't told!"

"Don't be a fool, Kit Caswell, if I'd knew who it was I'd have been into Leman Street so fast you'd not have seen me for the dust I kicked up." She shook her head. "I don't know who it is. I only know that when Polly and Annie died, I felt them go, and I wouldn't have felt that if their lives and power weren't taken from them so *fiercely*—with such terrible violence and with sorcery in the mix. Power travels on the air, Kit Caswell, in ways you can't understand, you can't feel—most folk can't feel. But those of us with it, we know when it shifts and shivers, we sense its passing."

"If you're so powerful, why are you all earning a living on your back?" Kit asked, eyebrows raised. "If you're witches, why not magic yourselves wealth and position or even just a tidy cottage and a comfortable living, a good husband to keep you?"

"Did I say we were powerful?" sneered Mary Jane. "Did I say we could conjure storms, fly, make great houses out of air and spit? Having magic doesn't mean you're *almighty*. There are women in Mayfair, Russell Square, in bloody Buckingham Palace, who are sisters to my kind; they can summon the wind and the lightning, but they are potent because they were born to it, they were born to *position*. But the power we have isn't of the same degree and we can't conjure a decent life out of straw and rags and shit. Sometimes we know things, sometimes we can find things that are lost, sometimes we might brew a tisane to break a fever and perhaps save a life doing it. But we can't make ourselves rich or beautiful, we can't magic ourselves *omnipotent*. Do you honestly think we'd choose this life if we had a choice?"

Kit wasn't sure, but she didn't say so. What she did say was, "I don't believe in witches. I can't take that to my inspector."

"Then how did I know what you were when I first laid eyes upon you?" Kelly challenged.

"A good guess," said Kit, making to stand. The woman grabbed her hands again and held her tight.

"Your father is dead, but he was a good man. You've a brother—he's sick, but I cannot see why. Your mother thinks you . . . make . . . hats! How precious!" She laughed nastily. Still she did not let go of Kit, though the other struggled to pull away.

"You might have asked around. You could have followed me. You could have—" Kit hissed.

"When you dream, you sometimes dream your mother dead, with a pillow over her face and all your burdens lifted," said Mary Jane Kelly flatly, and Kit deflated onto the bench beside her once again. Kelly waited until Kit had caught her breath, until she'd suppressed the sobs that shook her, until she sat straight, and raised her head to look forward into the darkness of the graveyard.

"Will you help us?" asked Mary Jane, with no pleading. "Will you? I don't know who he is, but I know he's taking us for a purpose and he's taking whores because we're easy to find, and no one cares."

"I care," said Kit, staring into the shadows, feeling as if they were opening up to receive her.

"You don't have to believe, but will you help?"

"I'll help," said Kit, and it seemed her words also meant *I believe*.

V

"Caswell, there you are." Makepeace buttonholed Kit the moment she set foot in the nick. "You're presentable and you notice things. Come along."

Kit didn't ask questions, just jogged to keep up with the Inspector's long strides as he shot out the double doors and into some unprecedentedly bright September sunshine. The tall man hailed a hansom cab, yelled an address at the driver, and jumped in, gesturing wildly for Kit to hurry up. Before she managed to sit, the cab moved off with a jerk and she lost her balance, ending up in her boss's lap. A mad scramble ensued as she slapped away helping hands and struggled to get her rear on her own side of the bench. She couldn't help the blushing, though, or the dryness in her throat at the idea the Inspector might have thought her backside too peachy, too round, the hips too broad for a boy's bony arse.

But Makepeace said nothing except, "Comfy?"

Kit nodded, then shook her head, then nodded again, then finally settled for peering out the window at the passing people and traffic and buildings. She didn't look back inside until she felt the burn of her cheeks cool. She cleared her throat. "Where are we going, sir? If I may ask?"

"We are going, young Caswell, to Mayfair."

"That's a bit posh, sir," she said before she thought that perhaps it wasn't too posh for Makepeace—didn't he have a rich wife? Hadn't the gossip called him a social climber? She added lamely, "For me at least."

"A name has come up in our investigations, a young barrister, Montague John Druitt. Doctor Bagster Phillips, upon hearing this, suggested we might talk to someone who knows him rather well, before we attempt to drag a member of the bar into our delightful premises."

"And that would be, sir?" Imagining the answer to be Druitt's parents or other family members, a wife or sweetheart of some description.

"Sir William Gull."

"The Queen's former Physician-in-Ordinary?"

Makepeace's eyebrows did their best to climb up under his hat and into his hairline. "You're awfully knowledgeable, young man."

"My brother is sick, sir," she said, honestly, having learned long ago that the best way to live a lie is to stay as close to the truth as possible. "I have spent some time researching the medical profession, looking for someone who might find out what's wrong with him."

There was a stretching silence, which the Inspector broke with, "Ah."

Kit looked out the window again and realized they'd left Whitechapel well and truly behind: the men on the footpaths were better dressed, carried canes rather than sacks; the women wore dresses that cost more than she'd earn in six months, and they'd never have to worry about being attacked on the street. She thought of Mary Kelly's words and wondered how many of those women might be the sort the killer was looking for—the sort he wouldn't touch because to do so would be to bring more attention than he wanted, more attention than he could possibly handle. Without thinking she said, "Sir, do you believe in witchcraft?"

"I believe it's illegal. Why, Kit, have you come across some gypsy offering to tell your fortune or summon a spirit?" Makepeace chuckled.

"No, sir, just . . . wondering."

Silence again, then, "Your brother, what's wrong with him?"

"If I knew that, I'd have had it fixed though it cost me a year's wages, sir." Kit rubbed her chin; Makepeace looked at her speculatively and she considered if he was noticing how lacking she was in facial hair. It didn't matter—some of the other young PCs were in the same boat, mutton chops taking their own sweet time about growing in. "He can't walk, sir, been paralyzed ever since our father died."

"Is it in the boy's head, do you think?"

Kit shrugged. "I don't know. Could be, but I think Lucius would dearly love to walk again. Doctor Gull studied paralysis especially."

"Did you bring your brother to him?"

She looked askance at her boss. "Doctor Gull hasn't practiced for some years, sir, not since his first stroke. I believe he had yet another not long ago." She didn't mention how many letters she'd written, unanswered, to the famous physician begging for a moment of his time. "Why are we going to speak to him about Druitt, sir?"

"Druitt's father was a well-known surgeon, and a friend of Gull's, who is also Druitt's godfather. Montague John teaches to make ends meet and was, for a time, tutor to one of Gull's grandsons. I'm given to understand they—that is Gull the Elder and Druitt the Younger—had a falling out some twelve months since."

"And you're hoping Doctor Gull will talk to us more frankly due to what we assume is his newly acquired dislike for Druitt?"

"Very perceptive, Caswell."

They passed the rest of the journey without further conversation. The motion of the cab almost lulled Kit to sleep, so she jumped rather more than was dignified when Makepeace boomed, "We're here."

The large house had a shiny black door, even shinier brass knocker, imposing pillars, and, like all the mansions in the square, faced a tidy private park. The glass in its white window frames sparkled and seemed to magnify the patterns on the sumptuous curtains hanging inside.

To Kit's surprise, the door was opened not by a maid, but by a tall, thin, sallow man. He did not wear the attire of a butler or the livery of a footman, but was neatly dressed in a charcoal-colored suit with matching vest and a snowy shirt. A silver chain hung from the fob pocket, signifying the presence of a watch on his person. He had a long face, grey eyes and a wary expression touched by superciliousness. He seemed reluctant to let them in, but Makepeace's best smile and the somber dignity of Kit's uniform seemed to nudge things in their favor. Still and all, Kit followed hard on the Inspector's heels just in case the door should be swiftly slammed behind him.

They stood in an impressive vestibule, punctuated by four doors (three closed, one ajar) and a long corridor that led towards an elaborately carved staircase and the back of the house. The walls were covered in a honey-golden silk paper, and any exposed wood was dark and highly polished.

"How may I help you . . . ?"

"Inspector Makepeace. And you are?" Makepeace thrust his hand at the man, who had no choice but to take it or be struck by the blade of the Inspector's fingers.

"Andrew Douglas, Sir William's personal secretary," he said, his voice vibrating a little with the force of the policeman's handshake. When he was finally released, Kit noticed that Douglas flexed his fingers as if to work out the discomfort of being grasped so securely. She noted the technique for future use, but wasn't sure she'd have the strength to deliver it as effectively as her boss. "How may I assist you, Inspector?"

"We—myself and young Caswell—are here to see Sir William. It is a matter of considerable importance." Makepeace was striding around the elegant foyer, craning his neck to see down the hallway, up the staircase, into doorways and didn't bother to hide the fact that he was doing it. Kit watched as Douglas tried to keep pace with the long-legged Inspector, but succeeded only in looking like a particularly clumsy dance partner.

"I'm afraid that Sir William is not receiving visitors this morning, nor for some time to come. He has been ill—you may not be aware," said Douglas and, seeming to finally realize he would not win this particular waltz competition, came to a halt and stared at Makepeace in a politely hostile manner. The Inspector ceased his perambulations (not because he was discomfited, Kit suspected, but because he'd seen all he could, all he needed to), and peered at the man in innocent surprise, then broke into a friendly open smile.

"I had no idea—you'll forgive me, Mr. Douglas, I do not follow gossip. I promise you faithfully young Kit and I shall not tax Sir William, but it is paramount that I speak with him—"

"And *I* said he was indisposed indefinitely," interrupted Douglas, a dark red flush creeping up from beneath his collar.

"—and I say again that I shall not leave until I have seen the good doctor." Makepeace barely paused, but raised his volume so that it was not quite a shout, yet still something that could not be ignored. In the sharp silence that followed the dying of its echoes there came a murmur, almost painfully weak, from behind the only open door. A quavering voice, however one that would not be denied.

"Let them in, Douglas, for God's sake, man. It's a police investigation, but I'm sure they're not here to drag me away."

Many times Kit had heard Mrs. K describe this person or that as having "a face like a slapped arse," but this was the first time she actually understood what that meant. Andrew Douglas' visage was pinched and red, mouth tightly puckered, his Adam's apple moved like a sphincter each time he tried to swallow his indignation. The man clicked his heels together, stretched his neck—goose-like—smoothed an errant curl back from his forehead and managed a strangled, "This way."

In his prime Sir William Gull had been a stout man, not tall, with a full head of hair and a dimpled chin; he'd strutted the halls and wards of

Guy's Hospital and traipsed his no-nonsense attitude into royal palaces, making himself a favorite with Queen Victoria, particularly after he'd saved the Prince of Wales from a bout of typhoid fever. A series of strokes had whittled him away to a bag of bones. He still had a head of thick greying locks and a thoroughly dimpled chin, though the muscles of his face seemed to struggle with gravity a little.

He sat, a small man in a large armchair beside the white marble fireplace of a room that had once obviously served as his study. He wore a red quilted robe over a white shirt; a fur rug was tucked around his legs, and his feet were firmly planted on a dark green ottoman covered in scarlet needlepoint roses. For all his diminishment his eyes were bright and blue, and showed no loss of his searching intellect.

"Sir William, I am—" began Makepeace, and found himself cut off.

"A very loud police officer. I heard, Inspector." He fixed the lanky man with a look that was part-glare, part-amusement, then addressed his employee, "Andrew, thank you, I will see to our guests. You have your duties."

"Yes, Sir William. Shall I have tea sent?" Kit could tell it almost choked him to ask.

"I think not, they shan't be with us long," said the old man pointedly, then added gently, "Off you go, Andrew."

After the door had closed, Makepeace opened his mouth, but Sir William raised a shaky hand and shook his head, waiting, listening. After a minute, they heard footsteps moving away, and the hand dropped and he smiled wearily. "Andrew is a good secretary and he has been with me a long time, but he does sometimes become over-protective and overstep the bounds of his authority, Inspector. I trust you will keep that in mind next time you're tempted to visit me?"

Makepeace, visibly chastened, but not seeming too ashamed of himself, nodded.

Sir William continued quietly, "He also sometimes listens at doors as I have learned to my chagrin. Now, how can I help you, Inspector?"

"We won't take much of your time, Sir William, but I do need to ask you some questions about your godson, Montague Druitt."

Even as Makepeace uttered the word "godson," Kit saw the old man's expression change from one of benign tolerance to disgust, which was quickly disguised again. She was impressed at how responsive his facial muscles were even though they seemed so wasted. For a moment she thought he might refuse to answer.

"All I can tell you is that he is a young man without moral compass," the doctor said, keeping his tone even with effort.

"Can you expand on that?"

The old man pursed his lips and looked away. Makepeace lowered his voice, made it quite soothing. "You may be aware, Sir William, that there have been several murders in Whitechapel, vicious and violent, of which at least two women have been the victims of the same killer. Your godson's name has been . . . mentioned."

"Then it is nothing more than an idle mention, Inspector, Druitt has no interest in women." The old man's lips thinned and compressed so they almost disappeared.

"I see," said Makepeace slowly. "He tutored your grandson—"

"I will not speak more of it, Inspector! Suffice to say that no matter what I think of Druitt's actions and his . . . personal tastes, I cannot in conscience tell you he might have done what you are suggesting. He has no interest in the female of the species, not even enough to dislike them, Inspector. Trust me when I say that Druitt is not your man." Sir William shook with the force of all the things he suppressed and Kit was concerned that he might have another stroke. A decanter of Madeira and two engraved glasses sat on the corner of a large desk, and she poured out a measure.

"Thank you, young man," managed Sir William and gulped down the proffered drink. When finished, he sighed and handed the delicate glass back to Kit with the sweetest smile she'd ever seen. "Now, Inspector, will there be anything else?"

Makepeace shook his head and moved to take the old man's hand. There was a minute hesitation, then Sir William accepted the gesture, somewhat reluctantly, but Kit thought all the more of him for it. He might have been enfeebled, but he was not broken, nor would he be bullied. And no matter how much he disliked his godson, he would not tell lies about him simply for a petty revenge.

"We'll see ourselves off the premises, Sir William. Thank you for your time."

They exited the study and let themselves out the front door before any kind of servant had a chance to make themselves known. Makepeace paused on the top step and took a deep breath, hooking his thumbs under his suspenders and surveying the empty park in front of them.

"Well, Kit, I don't know about you but I don't think well on an empty stomach. I'm sure we can find somewhere suitable around here to offer us sustenance." He strode off and Kit followed him towards where the square fed onto a busy thoroughfare. The hairs on the back of her neck crept up and she looked over her shoulder towards the fine house they'd just left. On one of the upper floors, she thought she saw a curtain twitch, but then there was nothing more, and Kit ran to catch up with the Inspector.

VI

"How long has it been now, Kit?" asked Lucius, even though he knew as well as she did.

"Twenty-two days, give or take a few hours," she answered, settling a bonnet on her hair, then tying its red ribbons beneath her chin. She'd souvenired some of her mother's old clothes from the bottom of Louisa's tallboy, things that had not seen the light of day for many years. The high-necked jacket was a deep amethyst, with pearl buttons and red lace trims; around the bottom of a skirt in the same purple hue were intricate frills, punctuated with crimson silk rosettes. The sleeves were three-quarter length and ended in a series of tiered ruffles. She'd had to pad out the chest area— her mother's assets were grander than her own. On the frame of Lucius' bed hung a damson velvet evening cape, its peacock feather design beaded in jet.

"Perhaps he's gone? Finished?" the boy ventured hopefully, but Kit shook her head.

"No. Mary Jane says not. He's just waiting for things to quieten down, for us to stop paying attention." She stood, smoothing the fabric—in an uncomfortable imitation of Annie Chapman, she wore several petticoats against the cold. "How do I look?"

Lucius shrugged. His reluctance to hurt her feelings told her she'd succeeded in her aim. She'd found her mother's face paints when she'd liberated the outfit; her cheeks were now highlighted with slashes of rouge and she'd applied a bright vermilion lipstick, then outlined her eyes with kohl. Personally, she thought she looked like a clown in the shaving mirror on Lucius' tallboy, but still she'd managed to recreate the appearance sported by most of the streetwalkers she'd seen in Whitechapel. The make-up wasn't meant to be subtle, it was there as a beacon, a red light, to say *This is what I am, get it here.*

"Will it be dangerous, Kit?" His voice quavered, and for all the occasions he'd listened with excitement as she'd recounted the tales of the crimes she'd witnessed or examined the aftermath of, this was the first instance of him being afraid. He realized that *this* time his sister was truly in harm's way.

She shook her head and lied. "No, my pet, I've got my truncheon," she tapped at it, hidden in her tight sleeve, "and the other PCs will be watching over us. All I've got to do is wander up and down the streets. Never fear, I'm not some innocent lamb."

"What if Mother sees you?"

"Mother has had her medicine, Lucius, she will sleep until morning, and Mrs. K is at her church choir meeting—or is it a séance tonight?" Kit was beginning to regret her decision to change at home, but carting more clothing and accessories to the lock-up had seemed like too much trouble at the time. And she was also beginning to regret having shared her adventures with her brother—it had been an activity designed to distract him from his four walls, not to cause him to worry. She crouched beside the bed and laid a hand on his thin shoulder. "Look at me, love: I will be as safe as houses. I'm alert and I'll be watched. Never fear. Have I ever lied to you?"

He shook his head.

"I will always come back to you, Lucius, that's the one thing you can rely on. Besides, anyone who tries to take me on will be biting off more than he can chew." She smiled and he gave a reluctant grin in return, chuckling. She wrapped her arms around him and he snaked his around her, the strength of his hug belying the frailty of his wasted form.

"Be careful, Kit."

"Always am. Now, lights out, no reading, it's late enough as it is." She opened the door. "I'll see you in the morning."

"Promise?"

"Promise."

Kit trotted swiftly along the streets, staying in the middle of the road so any attacker would have to come out into the open. Her eyes darted into the gloom of the evening, trying to detect movement and form. It was interesting, she thought, how being dressed as a woman made her feel so vulnerable. In her police uniform, with custodian helmet, truncheon swinging and silver buttons all on display, she felt invincible; she missed her bulls-eye lantern, her means of bringing light into dark places.

In the worn velvet drawstring purse were her handcuffs, whistle and the brass knuckles, her notepad and pencil. The length of painted wood in her sleeve meant she couldn't bend her arm, had to keep it straight. The heels of her shoes seemed to shout "Here I come" in much the same way as a lost lamb might bleat.

Kit shivered with more than cold and it was with some considerable relief that she entered the station to wolf whistles and mostly good-natured ribbing. Four of the other young constables, those without beards and whose skin was still soft looking (admittedly, softer-looking than that of most of Whitechapel's whores) were all in drag of various quality and degrees of taste. Kit was interested to notice that PC Watkins looked much girlier than she herself did; he also appeared pale, exhausted and troubled. Airedale, standing with the crowd of police designated as the decoy streetwalkers' protectors for the evening, sneered at each and every one of the lads, saving most of his disgust for Kit.

"That's quite enough, Constable," said Makepeace as he stepped from the stairs, Abberline behind him. "These young men are suffering for their profession and the protection of Whitechapel. There's no need to denigrate them, especially when they've gone to such trouble—lovely frock, Watkins."

A rumble of laughter rolled through the gathering. Abberline, exchanging a glance and a nod with Makepeace, stepped forward into the circle that formed around the cross-dressed PCs. He cleared his throat and clasped his hands behind his back. The glass moons of his spectacles caught the light and hid his eyes.

"You all know what you need to do, where you need to go, who you need to watch. Take no unnecessary risks, any of you. This man—this monster—has not gone away. He has not forgotten. He is waiting for us to stop attending, men. Do not give him a chance to resume his works."

Kit was heartened to hear her own thoughts echoed, but it made her shiver. Makepeace saw it, and nodded; she took *Chin up, Caswell* from the gesture and nodded back. She caught a movement—Airedale had seen the exchange and bared his teeth, apparently revolted. Kit suppressed a sigh: that was all she needed, being taken for the Inspector's "special" boy. Makepeace, however, didn't notice. He clapped his hands and shouted, "Out!" and the crowd dispersed.

Thomas Wright moved into position beside her as they pushed through the double doors. He squeezed her shoulder and muttered, "Courage, lad." She strode off ahead of him towards her allocated starting point on Commercial Road. Wright would find a spot in an alley or a darkened doorway and keep an eye on her. Kit didn't envy Watkins, who was paired with Airedale; the youngster kept his head down and she could see the large man's lips moving, pouring forth spite. She looked away, put thoughts of Airedale from her mind, and walked purposefully into the night.

She'd been on her first corner for only a few minutes before Mary Jane

Kelly appeared from the swirling mist. "You're too pretty, too fresh and you don't look anywhere near scared enough for new meat."

"I feel scared enough, believe me," muttered Kit. Kelly laughed.

"Only an idiot would come near you, you're so clean and neat!" She leaned against the brick wall casually, eyes scanning the area before them, and continued, "Men as want new young flesh don't come to the street. They go to the brothels where that can be arranged by reliable madams. People who want that sort of thing know they need to pay for it and pay a *lot*. A man knows that by the time a girl's taken to the alleys it means she can't find a place in a nice cozy bordello, that she's probably not going to be charging a premium price."

"This is all very fascinating, Miss Kelly, but you're not really helping. You're probably chasing the men away," said Kit, but she was glad for the company, however brief. With another laugh, the woman drifted off, and Kit settled into a rhythm of rambling through streets and byways, hidden squares and secret laneways known only to locals. When midnight finally passed, she had been approached by precisely no one, just as Mary Kelly had predicted. She wondered if the other PCs had had any better luck.

At the corner of Rope Walk, she bent to rub at her aching ankles through the leather of her boots. Surveying the murk she tried to divine Wright's hiding place, but failed. The air just beyond her moved suddenly and a figure ghosted through the fog. Kit straightened, fumbled with the baton in her sleeve, wishing she'd hung the whistle from her neck. Her heart clenched cold, then began to beat again as the shape resolved itself into the smallish Chinese boy who often watched the lock-up in Limehouse.

Kit pushed out a breath and leaned down so his whisper would not escape. The message made her feel ill, but she did not hesitate. With a nod to him, she set off at speed, the clatter of her heels on the pavement no longer a lamb's bleat, but a battle hymn. She surged through the streets, Wright's shouts dwindling somewhere behind her.

By the time she'd found the address—Duffield's Yard on Berner Street— it was closing on one in the morning, and a man driving a pony and trap was almost at the break in the fence that served as an ingress. The horse shied and refused to go further though the man yelled various threats. Kit stood beside the beast, put her hand on its back and felt the shudders coursing through the animal. The streetlight from outside did not reach the corners of the yard, but the pony knew something was not right.

"Hold your lantern up," Kit shouted at the driver. Grumbling the man pulled the lamp from where it hung beside him and stood, raising it as high as he could. The flame inside the glass flared and wobbled feebly with the movement, then settled and set the shadows in front of them to dancing across the old furniture, sheets of metal and general rubbish that littered the space. Kit stepped into the enclosure, searching the gloom as best she could until she spotted a supine form against the far wall.

"Hellfire," breathed the man.

Kit made her way towards the shape. Even as she crouched and pulled the whistle from her drawstring bag she knew it was too late. The woman was blond, in her forties, face hardened by the life she'd lived, and her throat was a gaping second mouth beneath a tightly pulled checkered scarf. She lay on her side, legs drawn up almost to her chest and her left hand, lying limp in a dark pool on the ground, was missing the pinky finger.

Kit blew long and hard, but before she finished the blast a figure broke from the darkest corner and rushed towards the entrance. He couldn't avoid passing Kit and struck out hard as she tried to rise. She managed to avoid falling onto the dead body, but scraped her face against the bricks of the wall before springing up and racing after the assailant.

She saw a flash of something silver—a knife—that he ran along the flanks of the horse. Kit heard the animal scream as it reared up—she wasn't able to arrest her progress quite fast enough, although she'd managed to begin the process of throwing herself backwards, so the blow the animal caught her on the shoulder was a glancing one. Nevertheless, the pain made her see stars, and she staggered away to sit before she fell beside the dead woman.

Sobbing, she found the silver whistle that she'd dropped and blew on it over and over again. She was still at it when Wright finally caught up with her, drawn by the shrilling. He pulled the thing from her mouth and gently wiped away the tears before anyone else saw Kit Caswell, one of Leman Street's up-and-comers, crying like a girl.

It wasn't long before Duffield's Yard was full of police, and the street beyond undulating with gawkers. The local doctor, Blackwell, who'd been called to the scene was soon shuffled aside when Dr. Bagster Phillips hove into view, having been rousted, on this rare occasion, from the bed of his wife.

She gave her statement to Wright, ashamed to admit that she'd not seen the murderer's face, which had been wrapped tightly in a dark-colored scarf, and a bowler hat had been firmly wedged on his head. The only thing she'd glimpsed, ever so briefly, was the pale band of flesh around his eyes, and she couldn't even remember the color of those. All she could think of were black holes, but she wasn't sure that was right.

Dr. Blackwell, not quite ready to be moved along like a common onlooker, made a point of cleaning the blood and dirt from the grazes on her cheek, and examining her shoulder. Terrified that his hands might stray lower than they should, she spent a tense few minutes lying about the amount of pain she was in, before Makepeace appeared and sent her home with orders not to return to work for an entire day.

<h2 style="text-align:center">VII</h2>

"And I tell you I'm her friend and she *will* see me!"

The yelling was loud enough to penetrate Kit's laudanum-fuelled sleep. Upon her return home she'd taken a dose of Louisa's favorite tipple and happily passed out. When her mother had come in to rouse her the next morning, she'd shrieked over the state of Kit's face and the specks of blood on the pillow. Her daughter, wanting only to keep slumbering, managed a mumbled explanation of women's problems and dizziness that had caused her to faint and fall. In the end Louisa left her alone.

There was no window in her room and, as she sat up groggily, she realized she had no idea what time it was, or indeed if she'd slept a full day and into the next. It was Louisa's voice, as strident as the first one, that propelled her out of bed and down the hallway. The front door was open, but just barely, and it was obvious that her mother and Mrs. K were trying their best to shut it. In the gap, Kit could make out a wilted bonnet that had once been very fine, and dark curls bouncing around with the force of their owner's umbrage. The familiar tones of mingled singsong accents told her who her visitor was.

"It's all right. She's a friend." Kit reached out and touched her mother's shoulder. Louisa rounded on her, eyes enormous in a bloodless face, an expression that said all her worst fears had come to fruition; as if she knew what the caller truly was.

"How can she . . . this . . . "

"Mary Jane works with me at Mistress Hazleton's."

"You've never spoken of her," hissed Louisa.

Kit fixed her mother with a long look. "And when have you ever asked me about my job, Mother, except to see if I've been paid?"

Louisa bit back a retort, all the wind taken out of her sails. Kit pushed the advantage and said, "We'll chat in the parlor. Mrs. K, won't you take Mother to the kitchen and make her some tea, please?"

Mrs. Kittredge pursed her lips in disapproval, but nodded. The two older women reluctantly receded down the hallway towards the back of the flat. Mary Jane Kelly, dressed in a peacock-blue frock and black jacket stood on the doorstep with all the dignity of a ruffled chicken. Kit half-expected to see tail feathers sprouting from her bustle in the late afternoon gloom. She wondered if the woman had made a special effort to appear "respectable" but had simply lost the knack.

"Come in, Mary Jane, please. I'm sorry for that."

In the parlor they sat, Mary Jane in her decrepit finery, and Kit in her long white nightgown, its high neck and sleeves hiding the red-purple bruising on her shoulder. The ache was beginning to eat through the comforting numbness of the laudanum. She'd slept like the dead and while it had been a relief to escape from what she'd seen last night—from what she'd failed to prevent—she was determined not to seek its balm again.

Now that they were alone, Mary Jane seemed uncertain how to start the conversation she'd so desperately sought. She cleared her throat and led with, "You're more like one of us now, the face on you. And you've got that look in your eye—a woman never looks quite the same after she's been hit, no matter that it might only happen once."

"Did you know her? Elizabeth Stride?" Kit asked, having heard the name before she'd been sent home.

"Long Liz. Swedish. Not a bad sort," replied Kelly, looking around the tiny parlor at the ambrotypes (all the Caswells in happier times) on various pieces of fine mahogany furniture jammed into the room, the loudly ticking clock on the mantelpiece, the petite point antimacassars on the wing-chairs, the lace and damask curtains over the front window with its seat that looked out on the street. Perhaps it was the nicest room Kelly had ever been in—or at least in her recent history of boarding houses and the like. "Knew Cathy Eddowes, too, her as called herself Kate Kelly."

Kit frowned. "But there was only one body in the yard—if there'd been another, I'd have noticed."

"He got Cathy at Mitre Square, about an hour after you chased him off Lizzie. That young Watkins found her—he found poor Annie, too, didn't he? He'll be a wreck." Kelly leaned back in the armchair, nestling into its folds and lumpy cushions as if it were a throne of some sort and she a displaced grandee.

Kit put her head in her hands and sobbed. She'd been too late to save Elizabeth Stride and, in failing to catch the bastard, she'd given him the opportunity to go and carve Cathy Eddowes. Mary Jane didn't comfort her—all her own tears had been wept far too long ago—just waited for Kit to pull herself together. Then she said, "He's written to the newspapers, I'm told, given himself a name. Jack. Jack the Ripper, Saucy Jack. The papers published the letter."

"*If* it's from him." Kit sniffed, wiping her eyes on her sleeve. "Why would he write, draw attention to himself? He's not doing it for that, you said."

Kelly shrugged. "Maybe it's not him, not our one. Maybe it's some Bedlamite playing games."

"Or a journalist, trying to sell more papers."

"My, what a suspicious mind you've got, little miss." Kelly picked at a speck of dirt under her nails. "Heard anything else from your Inspector?"

Kit shook her head. "We didn't really have much time to chat last night." She took a deep breath. "We spoke to Sir William Gull about his godson after Annie was murdered, but the godson's since turned up in the Thames with stones in his pockets."

"Ah, Sir William, he's an old love," sighed Kelly. Kit tilted her head.

"You know him?"

"Oh, he used to visit Whitechapel regular-like back before he got sick. Comes out sometimes, though he can't do anything but talk. Still and all, he's a darling and a great supporter of us working girls." Mary Jane snorted. Kit sat quietly for a moment.

"So, Liz and Cathy were both . . . "

"Witches? Yes." Kelly sighed. "All women are balanced somewhere on the witch's scale, Kit Caswell, but some barely make the weight requirement. Like you."

Kit nodded. "I've got nothing. No second sight or sixth sense. Mrs. K does like her séances, but I suspect she just goes for the port and biscuits afterwards. Sometimes I think my mother might see things, but that's probably just the laudanum . . . "

"She's of a type, your mother," said Mary Jane lightly, then changed the subject before Kit could ask her what she meant. "What are you going to do now, PC Caswell? You said you'd help."

Kit didn't answer. Mary Kelly watched her, face darkening.

"Well?"

"What can I do? I let two women die last night. What use am I to anyone?

What difference can I make? We don't know anything about him, we've got no clues, no direction." She shrugged.

Kelly stood, haughty as a queen. "When you've finished your wallowing, come and find me. All your self-pity isn't going to *assist* anyone—and he's got one more that he wants, needs. So don't take too much time about it."

Kit trailed her to the door and stood on the stoop as Mary Jane stepped into the night-draped street and finally disappeared, turning a corner. Kit waited, arms wrapped around herself, as if the other woman might come back, might relent. She'd not felt this hopeless or helpless, even when her mother fell apart; *then* she knew what she had to do, it was not only obvious but a matter of survival. Now she couldn't even begin to think where to start with the Whitechapel witches.

The evening cold crept through her and it was a while before she became aware of someone watching her. She scanned the area, eyes probing the scant spaces between houses, the corners, the alleys, desperately trying to pierce the darkness. She found no one and convinced herself that it was Mary Jane Kelly, peeking at her from afar. Even as she retreated inside and latched the door, though, the chain and bolt seemed nowhere near sturdy enough.

Kit stepped into the parlor to warm herself by the fire; firstly, she pulled the curtains across against prying eyes. She was still standing there, hands outstretched when she heard the mail slot rattle a little, as if someone was trying to be very quiet. Then there was the light sound of something hitting the carpet.

Padding into the corridor in her bare feet, Kit saw a creamy envelope lying there. The card of it was thick and expensively made. The flap was secured with red wax, but there was no seal stamped into it, no hint as to who it might be from. She wondered briefly if Kelly had doubled back to deliver it—then she realized she didn't even know if Mary Jane could read and write.

She fumbled with the lock and chain, and threw open the door in hopes of finding the letter's owner, but the street was empty by the time she managed to do so. Kit waited for long moments, looking up and down the thoroughfare, trying to discern if there really were eyes on her or if she was imagining it. All it did was make her certain she had not even the slightest sixth sense.

"Katherine?"

Louisa's voice traveled from the kitchen, although her mother did not show herself and Kit took the opportunity to pick up the letter and slip it into the sleeve of her nightgown. She closed and secured the door once more, moving stiffly as her injury made its position more firmly known.

"Yes, Mother?"

"Come and have some supper, if you're feeling better. You must be famished."

Kit didn't think she'd ever have an appetite again, but decided that it was in her interests to let her mother think normalcy had taken up residence in their home once more.

"Yes, Mother," she said, aware of the letter burning against her skin; she must hide it for now. "I'll just get my robe."

VIII

Watkins, thought Kit, looked worse than she felt. The deep navy of his uniform made his pallor even more striking and the circles beneath his eyes gave him the appearance of a corpse that, refusing to believe it was dead, insisted upon walking around. On her way towards Leman Street, she'd spotted her fellow PC and intercepted him as he shambled up Commercial Street in what passed for morning sunshine.

"All right, Watkins?" she asked and the young man started like a skittish horse; he peered at Kit as if unsure who she was, then seemed to relax, his shoulders dropping as he recognized her.

"Oh. It's you," he mumbled, not really looking at her but past her.

"You found the other one? Eddowes?"

He nodded. "She was cut. She was cut so bad." He began to sob. "Why didn't you catch him? You were so close, Caswell, why couldn't you just have got him so he didn't . . . so I didn't . . . "

Kit was frozen, horrified, aching with guilt and concern for Watkins, who stood before her on a crowded street, weeping like a child as people buffeted past them. She couldn't put her arms around him as she would Lucius, she couldn't walk away, and she certainly couldn't tell him to pull himself together and go to work. She hated to think what Airedale would say if he saw the youth in this state. She wondered what he'd said the night of the decoys, and where he'd been when Watkins had found Cathy Eddowes.

"I . . . I tried, Ned. I did try," she said lamely. He swallowed with effort.

"I see the other one. I seen her since I found her. Then this morning, this new one appears beside her, right next to my bed. They don't say anything, they just stand there, staring at me." He grabbed Kit's shoulders and shook her—the pain almost made her pass out. "What do they want? I've got to make them go away!"

She wrenched herself from his grip, desperate to not have his fingers clawing into the tender injured flesh. "Ned! Ned, you need to go home. You need to have a rest."

"I've not been sleeping," he said, "not since I found Dark Annie. And Airedale just keeps on at me and on at me, talking about it all the time, talking about how they come apart so easy, that it's just like butchering a cow . . . "

"Ned," she said, and gently grasped his upper arms, made him focus on her, look her in the eyes. "Ned, you need to go home. I'll talk to the Inspector, I'll let him know you're sick."

"You can't tell him! He'll think I'm mad and no one will ever let me forget it. Airedale—"

"Bloody Airedale won't bloody know!" she snapped. "Ned, I'll just tell Himself you're ill, that you've eaten something to make you sick. That's all. No more than a dodgy stomach, mate, yeah? We've all suffered from those pies at Stout Aggie's."

She nodded and soon he was mirroring her; Stout Aggie's was a byword for tasty but occasionally dangerous food that most of the local constabulary risked at least once.

"Sick," he repeated. "Sick in the guts. That's okay, then, isn't it?"

"That's okay, Ned. Off you go."

She watched him as he moved away, swaying on his feet from weariness and fear. Kit wondered if she should tell Makepeace exactly what state the young PC was in, then decided against it. She'd promised, and besides he'd never live it down if the information ever got to Airedale, which—given the way gossip, rumor and truth moved through the strangely porous walls of the station—it would. Even the other coppers weren't above tormenting the lad mercilessly, but Airedale . . . Airedale was something else, there was something wrong in him, something malicious and spiteful that liked to come out and play in the light. Kit wouldn't risk subjecting Ned Watkins to that.

Inside, Kit greeted the desk sergeant, who gave her a nod. It loosened the tightness in her chest that had taken up residence since she'd let the Ripper slip through her fingers, quite literally; she hadn't even managed to get the truncheon out of her sleeve, hadn't struck even the merest of blows on the man who'd killed four women. There would be disappointment amongst her colleagues, she knew, but how much recrimination there might be was yet to be seen. She was so caught up trying to predict the balance, she almost ran into Abberline as she made her way to the briefing room.

"Watch out, lad."

"Sorry, sir."

Abberline didn't acknowledge her apology and it made her stomach swirl. The older inspector held her accountable, she was sure of it. She couldn't say she blamed him; he was the one being torn at by the feuding eagles of Commissioner Warren, Home Secretary Matthews, and Assistant Commissioner Monro, all of whom had their particular opinions about dealing with this case, and were the kind of men who would do nothing but complain about the failure of others without ever offering concrete assistance. She wondered if Abberline's attitude towards her would trickle down; then she wondered if Makepeace shared his colleague's opinion. That thought made her feel even worse as she stepped into a room filled with stale male sweat and men in custodian helmets wearing accusing stares.

"Good of you to join us, Caswell." Makepeace said coolly, and she couldn't work out whether he was signaling his displeasure or simply trying to keep things running normally—it was his habit to greet in such a way the last PC to arrive. "Right, listen up. We had two close calls last night, and we've now two newly dead women. You can all imagine how we are being represented in the press and perceived by the public—especially with these so-called Ripper letters doing the rounds."

The mention of letters made Kit think of the one in her pocket, still unopened. She simply hadn't had either the time or the privacy since it had been pushed through the mail slot; her mother had stuck close after dinner, questioning her about her work and friends, and then insisted upon sitting beside her bed until she fell asleep—it wasn't worth it to make a fuss and arouse the woman's suspicions any further. Kit still suspected it was from Mary Jane, berating her for failing to save Liz and Cathy, for failing to catch their murderer, for failing to come up with a plan for stopping the carnage once and for all.

"No more decoys, either, after that went so well. We're being told to concentrate on the clues. The complete lack of them seems to make no nevermind to Commissioner Warren and his ilk." Makepeace proceeded to give the assembled group their assignments for the shift. Kit noted that she was the only officer not to receive a task. When Watkins was called, she didn't say anything, merely watched the annoyed look play across Makepeace's face.

She could feel Abberline looking at her and carefully kept her expression blank. She didn't see either Wright or Airedale, and their names were not called, which suggested they were elsewhere already.

Makepeace wound up, shooting a glance at Abberline whose swift shake of the head said he had nothing else to add. The older man joined the exiting flow, and Kit stayed behind, waiting for Makepeace to notice her. But he'd turned his back and was surveying the wall which was covered with maps, lists of names and places and dates, and, worst of all, the photos of the women after their deaths.

These were not gentle post-mortem depictions, but terrible facsimiles that showed in harsh black and white all of the awful things that had been done to them, all the hideous notations that had been engraved upon the victims with a sharp implement.

"Sir?"

"What is it?" Makepeace wouldn't meet her eyes.

"It's about Ned, sir. Watkins, that is—he's sick. I saw him on Commercial Street and he's gone home, sir."

"Well, why the hell didn't you say something before?" he snapped, and she remained silent until he looked at her, caught her expression and saw there that she wouldn't make her fellow constable appear weak in front of his colleagues. He nodded reluctantly. "Right. Anything else? Anything *important*?"

The night of the double event, when he'd found Kit banged up and bloody in Duffield's Yard, Makepeace had been solicitous. He'd been kind. Now he was distant, annoyed; the change, Kit assumed, was due less to the loss of Liz Stride's life than to the consequences of Kit's failure being so stunningly magnified by the death of Cathy Eddowes.

She bit her lip, uncertain what to say, what to ask. Makepeace fixed her with a look, narrowing his eyes. "Caswell, is there something you wanted?"

Slowly she shook her head, blinking hard. "No, sir, nothing. Only, I'm sorry. I did try, sir."

"Then make yourself useful." His voice suddenly sounded not so cold, somehow begrudgingly gentle. "Go and talk to Stride and Eddowes' husbands, or whatever they had that passed for husbands."

"Haven't they already been interviewed, sir?"

"Yes, but it was Airedale, so you can imagine how well that went. You might shake something loose. Off you go before I change my mind and put you to cleaning the cells."

"Yes, sir." It was busy-work, Kit suspected, but it still wasn't the worst thing he could have done to her, and it might yet yield something, some kind of connection between the women apart from their profession.

His voice stopped her. "Caswell?"

"Yes, sir?"

"It wasn't your fault." Said grudgingly, however it was as if he was happy to get it off his chest. "No matter what happens from here on in, what happened last night wasn't your fault—and quite frankly, we were lucky not to lose you too."

Kit didn't answer. She thought he was lying, but the kindness of it stoppered up her throat. She stared at the wall of evidence, taking in all the faces, the injuries, the loss. There weren't just the four, those Kelly had known and believed were being hunted for their power, Nichols, Chapman, Stride and Eddowes. The others—Emma Elizabeth Smith and Martha Tabram, Annie Millwood and Ada Wilson—to Kit's mind they didn't belong. She thought she saw the glimmer of a way to show Makepeace a path without having to mention the word "witches"; a way to make him take her seriously again. She took a deep breath, leery of breaking their fragile truce.

"They're different, sir."

Makepeace looked at her, an eyebrow raised. "Different?"

"The early ones, sir, they're not the same as the last four. Those first four were robbed and stabbed, not slashed and mutilated. Smith and Millwood survived at least for a little while, and Ada Wilson is still alive, and squarely pointing her finger at the same grenadier who was supposed to have done for Tabram. We just can't get any proof because his mates keep giving him an alibi."

Makepeace nodded for her to go on, and she took heart.

"But the last four, sir, they're different. Chapman's rings were gone, but she had coins in her pocket, which we assumed were from her last client, but maybe it was from pawning the rings. Whoever killed her didn't take that, so what if he didn't care about rings or the money because it *wasn't* about those things? We know what he *did* take from Nicholls, Chapman and Stride, sir, and that's bits of flesh. What about Eddowes, sir? Ned said she was badly cut up."

Makepeace said, "Her face was hacked at, her belly torn open and her left kidney was gone."

Kit felt her gorge rise, swallowed it down, then reinforced her point. "They're inconsistent, sir, crimes committed by discrete men—with the first four you're looking at maybe two, even three separate killers whose intent was to rob; the women died because they fought back. The second lot, our girls, that's a single killer, distinct from the others, with a stranger, darker intent."

"And what intent's that, Caswell?"

"If I knew, sir, we might be further along than we are."

Makepeace stared at Kit long and hard, then returned his gaze to the wall. Slowly he moved forward and began the process of shuffling the photos and lists into new alignments, two groups of four. Kit felt her heart lift, just a little, a kind of hope like sunlight.

"Don't you have men to interview, Caswell?"

IX

Kit strode towards the Christ Church graveyard in the late afternoon. She didn't go into the church itself, but took the gate she and Kelly had used what seemed a lifetime ago and headed towards the small cluster of figures in a back corner, huddling amongst the headstones, the shoulders of their coats lightly sprinkled with snow.

The group of seven women spotted Kit and broke apart like a disturbed swarm. Luckily not a one was inclined—or able—to run, so she lengthened her stride and managed to grab hold of the nearest. None of the others stopped to help their compatriot—the sisterhood was thin nowadays, observed Kit.

The woman, with wiry red hair, no front teeth and a scar that lifted the left side of her mouth, spat and hissed and Kit considered slapping her, then realized she'd been around men too long if she thought that was a solution.

"Eliza Cooper, pull your head in or you'll get a night in the cells whether you like it or not," said Kit, and the other seemed to calm down—although it was so cold the young PC wondered if the tart wouldn't be averse to a free bed, four walls, and a promise of warm stew. "I'm looking for Mary Kelly— still looking for her."

It was the fifth of November, and thirty-six days had passed since the double event, thirty-five since Kelly had left Number 3 Lady's Mantle Court and seemingly disappeared into thin air. The only comfort was that her body hadn't turned up anywhere. Kit almost dared hope the prostitute had packed her bags and left London for safer climes; but it seemed unlikely. Kelly, like most folk, was a creature of habit, a habitué of the city's streets and it would take more than a threat of death and dismemberment to get her to leave the place she knew best.

While Kit hadn't yet given up on finding Mary Jane, her options were thinner than workhouse broth. No one was admitting to seeing her and Kit had heard nothing from her. The letter, which still rested in her tunic pocket, made heavier by its content and all its potential consequences, had not been from Kelly.

"Ain't seen her—ain't nobody seen her in weeks," grumbled Cooper, refusing to meet Kit's eyes, but wearing a familiar expression. She'd spent so much of her time checking on Whitechapel's whores that their business was suffering—Kit's seemingly ever-present vigilance was costing them clients. Whatever gratitude there might initially have been was eaten away by her scaring off their meal tickets. There was something different, though, in Cooper's tone, an exasperation that Kit thought she might be able to swing to her own advantage.

"Eliza. Eliza, look at me."

Reluctantly, the woman did so. "What?"

"Eliza, I need to find Mary Jane. I need to know if she's all right and I need her help." The woman began to shake her head and Kit hurried on, "Please, Eliza, please. Don't think the danger's gone—Jack's still out there. He's waiting."

Kit could see the woman's resolve wavering, and she wasn't above stacking the deck; she pulled a purse from her pocket and jingled its contents. "There's enough here for a bed and a meal. You won't need to earn it the hard way. Please, Eliza, I'm not trying to hurt her."

At first it seemed her plea had failed, then Cooper made a noise of disgusted surrender and held out her hand. Kit gave her a look to say she wasn't stupid enough to give over money before she got the information and the woman laughed. "Mary Jane said you were a clever lad. Aw'right, she's at the lodging house in Flower and Dean Street—number 32, where Lizzie lived."

"Who's paying her bills?" Kit asked, as she counted coins into Eliza Cooper's grimy palms—she'd been holding something back from the housekeeping for the past weeks, set aside for this very purpose.

"She's keeping the landlord 'happy' as best she knows how," laughed the woman and gleefully pocketed the easiest money she'd ever made.

Kit frowned. "Eliza, don't spend it on drink, please. Get a room and a good night's sleep. Be safe and warm."

The woman nodded, but Kit suspected she meant the opposite, and shrugged. She'd not inherited her father's fervor for imposing salvation on those uninterested in being saved. Kit sighed and said, "Off you go, Eliza. Take care of yourself."

The woman nodded again, giving Kit a strange look. They were talking, she knew, the Whitechapel whores, about how eccentric young PC Caswell was, how he didn't want to take advantage of the favors offered him, how he didn't want to save their souls, how he just tried to help with no thought of reward. Such selflessness made them wary and suspicious.

Kit moved away quickly, wanting to ensure she got to her destination before Cooper thought better of the deal, and decided to warn Mary Jane that she'd been found.

The boarding house was like so many of its kind and there were over two hundred packed into Whitechapel alone, people crammed into tiny filthy rooms, barely able to scrape together the money for a night's sleep. Kit found the landlord's assistant—a youngish man given his lodging in exchange for looking after the degraded property in the meagrest way possible—and it didn't take long for her to coax the location of Kelly's room from him. She knocked quietly, wondering if she'd have to draw the woman out then found, to her astonishment, the door incautiously hauled open. Kelly, dressed in a simple white blouse, black shawl and blue skirt, with no trace of make-up and her hair in modest bun, seemed as surprised as Kit was.

"You. I thought it was his lordship come to collect the rent. You'd better come in then." She stood aside and let her guest past.

The room was small, but surprisingly tidy. Clothes were carefully folded on a single shelf, and the bed was neatly made. A bedside table held a lamp, a bottle of gin and two glasses. In a wicker basket at the foot of the bed was a pile of mending, and Kit could see the needle and various colored skeins Kelly had been using. Kit raised an eyebrow.

"Practicing for my new career," said Mary Jane and indicated that Kit should take the sole chair while she herself settled on the bed and took up the sock she'd been darning.

"How are you, Mary?" asked Kit as she carefully lowered herself onto the seat, somewhat concerned about how it might react to any weight greater than that of a folded blanket. The piece of furniture groaned its protest but held, and after a few moments Kit relaxed.

"Alive, which, given the circumstances, is the best I can hope for," Kelly said tartly.

Kit nodded. "I've been looking for you. I was worried."

"No need to be. I'm taking care of myself, I've a good thing going here. Only one 'client' a day and he brings me the mending to do. We've an agreement."

"You don't go out," stated Kit.

"Well, it's cold outside." Kelly tied off a thread and set the sock aside, paired it, then selected a blouse from the pile and found a matching bobbin of thread, and began the business of getting the strand through the eye of the needle. Kit found her own tongue pressing at the inside of her mouth as if to protrude in sympathetic concentration.

"Why did you disappear? Why didn't you let me know?"

"Someone started following me. Couldn't see anyone, but I just knew it. So I went to ground. Besides, you weren't looking like being any help."

Kit ignored the barb. "That last night I saw you . . . "

"Mmmmm?" Kelly sounded disinterested and kept her eyes on her task.

Kit pulled the letter from her pocket. "Someone put this through the mail slot after you left. And someone was watching my house, I'm sure of it. Was it you?"

"No. When I left, I left. And that letter's not from me either."

"I know that. It's from *him*."

Mary Jane's hands stilled, the blouse falling and slowly deflating in her lap. Kit opened the envelope, just as she had many times since she'd first cracked the wax seal. The handwriting was nothing like the red scrawl that had been reproduced in the newspapers. This was not the work of the Jack who liked to write, to communicate, to show off and revel in his notoriety. This hand was strong, graceful and in black ink; it was businesslike and focused. It was the handwriting of a proposition, an exchange. It seemed the script of a reasonable man—or at least one who considered his actions reasonable.

She held it out to the other woman, not daring to ask if she could read. Kelly took it reluctantly, and Kit watched her eyes move across the words, taking them in. Watched as the woman's thin hands began to shake. Watched as Kelly raised her stare to meet Kit's with a growing terror.

"Is that why you're here?" she asked in a strangled voice.

Kit shook her head vehemently. "No! Don't think that of me."

"Then why? Why show me this? Why find me when I'm safe?"

"Because I think I can catch him. I think I know what to do. I don't know how he knows what he knows about me, about Lucius, but I think we can lure him and catch him, Mary Jane."

"Let me get this straight: this man wants to make a deal with you. My life for a marked improvement in your brother's health? And you don't want to take him up on that?"

"Would it work?" Kit challenged.

Kelly shrugged. "It might, if this letter writer's got any power of his own. If not, then probably not."

"Well, Mary Jane Kelly, I don't believe it will. I don't believe he's got any power or he wouldn't be stealing your paltry share. I don't believe he can offer me anything and, even if he could, I wouldn't buy Lucius' health in such a way—I may not know anything about witchcraft, but I do know that a price like this is too high. If I had all the wealth in the world I'd spend it on my brother, but I won't offer one life for another. I just won't. I've got enough deaths on my conscience to last a lifetime." She rubbed her hands across her face. "And Ned Watkins is dead—did you know *that*?"

The expression on Kelly's face said she didn't. "Poor lamb. What happened?"

"He hung himself in the garden shed of his parents' house. He said he was seeing them—seeing Dark Annie and Cathy Eddowes. He said they didn't say anything, just stood beside his bed in the night and looked at him."

Kelly sighed. "Sometimes they stay around, the dead. They attach themselves to the person who found them—sometimes to their killer, but sometimes they just look for the first kind heart that happens upon them after death. You don't see Lizzie?"

Kit shook her head, wondering what that said about her heart, and leaned over to take the letter from Kelly's fingers. "I am, as you've pointed out, completely untouched by any sort of magic."

She waved the single sheet of thick cream-colored paper. "This is the only way I know how to help, Mary Jane, but I need your assistance."

"You need me to be bait," she sneered, and Kit nodded.

"Yes. Apparently no one else will do."

"Does your Inspector know about this? About this letter?"

Kit shook her head, holding the other woman's gaze.

Kelly gave a lopsided smile. "If you tell him it's about witches and magic he'll think you're mad. If you show him this letter, addressed to Miss Katherine Caswell, he'll work out that you're not what you say you are. Too many questions asked and you with not enough lies to tell."

"If he works out I'm female then my life goes back to what it was. I go back to scraping a living for three people. I *won't* be that helpless again."

"Find a rich husband, you're pretty enough."

"Where am I going to find a rich husband? If it was that easy, wouldn't you have done it by now?"

The air between them was thick and bitter. Kit took a deep breath, struggled to stop her voice from shaking. "But *this* is what I can do. If you'll help me, I can entice him out, and he will not survive, I promise you."

They both shuddered to hear the steel in her tone, to hear her say what they both knew had to be done. "He'll die for what he did to Polly and Annie and Elizabeth and Cathy. He'll die for what he'd do to you. If he's caught, he'll go to the gallows without a doubt—but he'll tell secrets and ruin lives before he does. Even if no one believes you're a witch, Mary Jane, they'll find out I'm a woman and my life will be over."

"So you'll be a murderer, too," observed Kelly.

Kit shook her head, not denying the other's words, simply not wanting to think about them. She folded the sheet of paper carefully and slid it back into the envelope as if it was the most important thing she had to do at this very moment. She stood and cleared her throat.

"I'll do it," said Kelly, voice flat. Kit froze. The other woman's consent, for all it solved one problem, created a series of others.

"Are you sure?"

"Good God, Kit Caswell, you badger me into this mad plan and now you want to know if I'm sure?" Kelly laughed harshly. "I'm sure. It's the only way I'll walk the streets safely again—well, as safe as the streets ever get for my kind."

Kit swallowed and nodded. She said, "I'll put the advertisement in the Personals section of the paper just as he asks. We'll need an address to send him to . . . "

"Not here, for God's sake."

" . . . somewhere private."

"I've got just the place."

X

Kit had only ever set foot in the store twice before. The first time was in response to a message from Mr. Wing, the week after her father's death. One of the Chinese lads had come to the rectory and Louisa, barely sentient until called to the door by Kit, had shrieked at the boy to go away. He fled, dropping a rectangle of white card in his wake, which Kit pocketed. The address on the back, inked in a fair hand, led her to Limehouse and a shop that contained all manner of herbal restoratives.

She liked the smell, incense and all the dried ingredients combined to a heady mix. Mr. Wing had seemed terribly old then as he explained his obligation to her family, and even older the second visit when Kit made the request that resulted in her being allocated space in the lock-up. This occasion, the third, she'd taken extra care with her appearance, ensuring her dress, bonnet, cape and bag were all black as a reminder of her grief— even though the mourning period was well and truly over—and the debt that was owed.

Nothing had changed, though the odor had a sickly sweet undertone— she wondered if the basement area was being used as an opium den, then shook her head. She didn't want to know and she wasn't in a position to judge anyone at this point. The light coming through windows covered in London grime was dim, the store was empty of customers, and it seemed none of the shelf contents had moved, but she knew that the Chinese apothecary did a brisk trade and Mr. Wing's reputation was such that even Harley Street specialists directed their patients here for certain types of remedies. She'd once tried Lucius on some of the old gentleman's concoctions, but the scent and taste had him refusing more than one swallow and in the end she tipped the mixture out.

Behind the counter sat the object of her search, perched on a high stool as if he was a manikin or a puppet, left as guardian. His round face showed no surprise at seeing her, although his trailing white moustaches twitched in greeting. His long robe was a curious green and she thought how well it helped him to blend in with the shadows of the interior.

"Miss Katherine," he said, his voice smooth as oil, a young man's voice. "Another social call so soon—should I be concerned?"

Kit smiled. "Hello, Mr. Wing." She wasn't entirely sure that was even his proper name, but it was the one he gave to his shop-front, to the Westerners who frequented this place, and the one his own people used at least in the presence of others. "I trust you are well."

He nodded, but didn't answer, merely waited to hear her purpose.

She hesitated, then spoke. "Mr. Wing, I must make a special request of you. I do not do this lightly, but I come to you because of our bond."

He laughed. "You mean my debt, Miss Katherine."

She half-nodded, half-shrugged.

"And what do you require of me?"

"I need a gun, sir."

He was silent for long moments, stroking his moustaches, then he did the unthinkable and got down off his throne and came toward her. His motions were not those of an aged man, and she thought he moved slowly because he wanted to, not because he had to.

"This is a very big favor, Miss Caswell," he said gravely as he came to a halt.

"You owe me a very big favour, Mr. Wing. You told me so," she said equally gravely, holding his gaze.

"What makes you think I will be interested in helping you with such an illegal thing?"

"The same reason you sent the boy to me and to tell me about the dead woman." He opened his mouth to deny it but she kept going, "Very little happens, sir, that you are not aware of—I know your runners gather information the way other boys pick berries. And I know it's to keep your people safe—forewarned is forearmed. So trust me when I say this is something I need to keep my—all people—safe. I know you will understand that and you will want to help."

He stared at her, then finally said, "Single or multiple shot?"

She blinked. "Multiple would be best."

"More than one chance, although I am told one should always make the first shot count. Do you know how to use it?"

She nodded. Her father had taught her to shoot at game birds; she'd had training in firearms when she'd joined the Met, but had not been deemed reliable enough to carry a weapon yet, being so new in the job.

"It will be with one of the boys at the lock-up."

"When? I need it . . . "

"These things are not easy to come by," he said, then laughed. "The evening of the ninth."

She thanked him and turned to go. At the door, his voice stopped her.

"Miss Katherine?"

"Yes?" She looked over her shoulder, eyebrows raised.

"Remember the steps you take cannot be taken back. Some actions are simply too serious to retreat from—this is what I always tell our young men when they must choose their paths. I think it applies to you, too. What you do next will change the direction of your life."

Kit nodded, but did not answer. Outside, she gasped and dragged the cold air into her lungs; the shop had become unaccountably stuffy and close. She closed her eyes and rubbed them until stars speckled the back of her lids. She had no choice, she told herself. Either she sat back and did nothing, pretended she was untouched by what had and might continue to happen; or she could explain everything to Makepeace and in doing so expose herself utterly and lose all that she'd fought so hard to gain; or she could do *this*, this last thing, finish it all and keep herself and her life intact.

"Where have you been?" asked Louisa as soon as Kit set foot in the door. She'd been particularly vigilant in the weeks since Mary Kelly's social call, or at least while Kit was actually home, as if whatever she might be doing would be evident when she was under her mother's watchful eye. Kit held up her purse and gave it a gentle shake so the tiny bottles clinked together, and dangled the larger bag that contained groceries.

"Medicine for Lucius and more laudanum, Mother, and food." She kept her tone even as she took off her bonnet and hung it on the hallstand, although Louisa's wariness was becoming wearying. "How is Lucius?"

"He's still running such a temperature," fussed Louisa.

Kit fished a small brown sack from the hold-all and offered it. "Boil some water and steep that in it. It's feverfew and should help."

Louisa nodded and disappeared into the kitchen. Kit made her way to her brother's room and found Mrs. K reading to him from a battered Bible. Kit couldn't tell if his expression was the result of febrile listlessness or boredom; he was staring out the pocket-sized window into the pocket-sized yard. Kit smiled. "Have a spell, Mrs. K, I'll sit with him for a while."

The older woman looked at her and nodded; she didn't seem as suspicious of Kit as Louisa did, but rather just somewhat disapproving. As if the girl had let the side down. As she passed in the doorway, Mrs. K said in a low voice, "That friend of yours from the milliner's?"

Kit tilted her head, waited for her to go on.

"I know her from somewhere, but I can't remember where."

Kit shrugged. "She lives close to Mistress Hazleton's shop. I can't think where else you might have seen her."

Mrs. K shook her head, and handed Kit the Bible. When she could hear voices from the kitchen, she sat down beside the bed and put her hand on Lucius' brow. He had a slight fever, but it was nothing like what she'd expected. "How are you feeling?"

"Fine," he said, tone light, not looking at her. "Did you find her?"

Kit had stopped sharing her adventures with Lucius—or rather, she'd been heavily censoring what she told him, and he knew it. He'd been so worried before the double event and after Kit had returned home with her face grazed and shoulder injured, he'd not looked well since. When he asked for information, it was with an undertone of distress Kit had never heard before and it added to her guilt. She'd not told him about Watkins and she'd only told him the barest minimum about her search for Mary Kelly.

"Found her, a few days ago. She's safe and well, Lucius, never fear. She's not in danger and I think he may have gone." She lied lightly.

"You said not. You said he wouldn't go away. That he wasn't going to stop until he got whatever it was he wanted."

She cursed herself for telling him everything she had. She cursed him for poking at her fear—her knowledge—that the killer was simply waiting for Mary Jane to resurface, that her plan was too risky, too ill-conceived and desperate. She leaned forward and took his hand, and spoke quietly as the sounds of tea making and her mother riffling through the groceries continued from the kitchen. "Lucius, I promise you it will all be over soon. I promise you this man will never hurt anyone ever again. And I promise you I will be so careful."

"You said that last time," he pointed out, finally meeting her eyes.

"Yes, I did. And I underestimated him. Not this time, though, not again. I just need you to trust me. Will you do that?"

Before he could answer one way or another, Louisa appeared at the door. She bore a delicate porcelain teacup, from which a scent not unlike musty camphor wafted. Lucius' nose wrinkled and he pulled a face.

"None of that, young man," said Kit. "It's for your own good and medicine isn't meant to taste like sweeties. Sometimes we all have to do things we don't want to."

He fixed her with a look and said, "I know."

XI

Waiting in the overgrown garden next to the lock-up was the lad who'd come to warn her about Liz Stride's untimely demise. She'd not seen him since then, though she'd searched. Wordlessly, he handed her a calico-wrapped package. As he made to leave, she grabbed his hand.

"How did you know? About the woman in Duffield's Yard?"

She didn't think he'd answer but she was determined not to let him go; he struggled but found her grip unbreakable. At last he went limp and said, "I saw her. Saw her body."

She let him go, knowing she'd get nothing else. He faded into the mist.

The shed was cold inside and its atmosphere seemed vaguely hostile—as if it had decided she didn't belong there anymore. Or perhaps, thought Kit, it was just her imagination. It was what she was here to do that had changed, not the space that had been her closest confidant all these months, the place that had helped her change her life and herself. The four walls that had kept her secrets hidden and safe.

She perched on the lid of her steamer trunk and stared anywhere but at the parcel in her lap. At the splinters on the walls; at the muddy footprints with an obvious void where a chunk of the thick sole of the right shoe had been taken out; at the peaked ceiling and its beams that looked too thin. Her fingers picked at the edge of the fabric wrapping and her hands shook as she took a deep breath and folded back the cloth. The revolver was a British Bull Dog—the model she'd trained with but not been issued—with six cylinders and a wooden grip. It gleamed dully at her.

Kit cracked the barrel and was greeted by the sight of bullets sleeping inside. She ran her fingers over the engraving *Philip Webley & Son of Birmingham*, that told her who had made it and where, then over the hammer. It was an older model but she didn't care about its age, just as long as it did what she needed it to.

She still could not quite believe she was going to point this thing at someone—even someone who'd done what the killer had—and fire with the intent of taking a life.

Kit closed her eyes and leaned back against the wall. The advertisement had appeared in the Personals column, stating the time and the place for the assignation, couched in terms that suggested romance was involved. She wondered if it was too late—if he'd grown bored waiting and stopped looking for a sign of contact, of agreement from her—if this was all for naught.

She had been careful each and every night since she'd first read the letter; even in the daylight hours she was wary, glancing over her shoulder, making sure she knew the number and locations of exits wherever she went, ensuring the truncheon was easily and quickly accessible, and she had developed the habit of slipping the brass knuckles on as soon as she'd taken a few steps away from the Leman Street station.

Kit had been so focused on the perceived threat that she'd ceased hearing Airedale when he sneered at her, ceased to pay attention to him at all; hadn't even really noticed when he'd quietened down these past weeks, as if there was no fun in tormenting someone who wasn't paying any mind. Wright had jokingly asked her what magic she'd worked.

Kit didn't know how long she examined the back of her eyelids, but when she felt the cold creep into her bones, she knew it had been too long. She stood and swiftly changed into her uniform, shivering. She settled her helmet on her hair, buttoned up her winter overcoat and slid the pistol gingerly into its deep pockets, praying hard that she wouldn't shoot herself in the foot.

As she passed the fence around Christ Church, she slowed, pretending to adjust her boots. She listened hard, but heard nothing until Kelly's voice swarmed out of the shadows inside the churchyard, low and clear.

"Cold night for a stroll, PC Caswell."

"Are you ready?" Kit asked, ignoring the pretend pleasantries. "Are you all right?"

"I'll take care of my part of the bargain as long as you observe yours. Just don't bloody well be late."

"I swear I won't," said Kit and Kelly's footsteps quietly crunched away on the frostbitten grass.

Kit was grateful for the warmth inside Leman Street, but didn't take her coat off as she waited impatiently through the briefing delivered by the recently promoted Sergeant Thomas Wright; neither inspector was to be seen. Wright looked harried, and when the room cleared, Kit waited behind.

"You right there, Sarge?" Kit asked.

"All the nutters are out tonight and it's not even a bloody full moon." He collected a thick ledger from the table beside him and they moved towards the door, slowing to a halt at the booking desk in the entrance hall.

"Anyone in particular?" she asked, painfully aware of the weight of the revolver in her pocket. It seemed to her that it stuck out a mile. He shook his head, and the moved into the foyer.

"Couple of old biddies arrived and demanded to speak to "Whoever is in charge, my good man" and wouldn't let up until Abberline himself heard the racket and took them up to his office."

Kit raised her brows. "They must have been raising hell—I'm amazed he didn't throw them in the cells for the night."

"I think he would have liked to, but they didn't appear to have been drinking and claimed to have important information for him. May have said he'd rue the day if he ignored them."

Kit guffawed and Wright began to speak, but was interrupted by Airedale, who stood halfway up the stairs, yelling, "Caswell!"

Kit looked at the man's face, creased into folds and red as a rolled roast, and didn't like the smile on his thick lips.

"The Inspector wants to have a word with you, immediately."

Kit exchanged a look with Wright, who shrugged that *this was news to him*, and Airedale shouted, "Quick smart!"

She set off, squeezing past the leering bobby who didn't follow her, just watched as she climbed. It made her nervous, but she tried to shrug off the feeling—she knew she was hyper-alert. She turned her thoughts to Makepeace and what he might want.

Since they'd taken the first four murders out of the investigation, two of the killers from the non-Ripper pile had been found, and watchful eyes were being kept on the grenadier who'd been seen last with both Tabram and Smith. Makepeace was very pleased with that progress, but less so with the Ripper case's lack of movement. Hundreds of men had been shuffled in and out of their doors for questioning, even more had given tips and leads, but none of them led anywhere but to dead-ends. She wished she could tell him that after tonight, the Ripper at least would no longer be a problem for the Met.

She knocked on the door of the Inspectors' office and opened it.

The cluttered billet showed no sign of Makepeace, but Abberline sat in his place, and in Abberline's usual spot were two women, respectably dressed and, as they looked at her, horribly familiar. Kit felt the blood drain from her face. Abberline regarded her coolly.

"Ah, PC Caswell. These ladies have an interesting tale to tell. Perhaps you can assist with some of the finer details?"

Louisa stared at her daughter, utterly distraught. "Oh, Katherine. How could you?"

Kit's first thought was that it seemed her mother was more upset by *this* than if she'd gone on the game, but she didn't answer. She didn't say anything except, "Where's Makepeace?"

"*Inspector* Makepeace is otherwise engaged. You are not a problem of sufficient priority."

She felt as if she was being dressed down by an outraged grandfather. The only person who didn't seemed affronted by her disguise, but rather impressed, was Mrs. K, whose countenance was that of someone who realized they've done something very, very wrong.

"I think," said Abberline in a measured tone as if he was a reasonable man taking reasonable steps, "that some time in the cells might make you more talkative."

A large hand clamped on Kit's shoulder and she didn't need to turn around to know it was Airedale, smiling as though he'd won a fortune at the races. Her mother's expression changed to one of uncertainty and she began with, "Surely, Inspector Abberline, this isn't necessary. Surely, I can simply take my daughter home and—"

"Your daughter has been committing fraud, Mrs. Caswell. She won't be going anywhere until I get to the bottom of this and establish precisely how much she has compromised investigations by her actions."

Kit wanted to defend herself, wanted to shout and scream, but the very idea of giving Airedale an excuse to either hit her or throw her over his shoulder so he could carry her to the cells like a sack of coal was enough to infuse her with an icy dignity.

He marched her to the stairs and her mother's voice, instead of fading with the distance, grew louder and more piercing. Kit almost smiled: Abberline had bitten off more than he could chew. Wright, standing behind the front desk, stared at her as she passed by and Airedale knocked the custodian's helmet from her head.

"Find Makepeace," was all she said and was roughly pushed in the square of her back for her troubles.

"Don't bother," sneered Airedale and shoved her towards the stone steps that led down.

She thought suddenly of Mary Kelly, all alone at Miller's Court while Kit sat cooling her heels. She thought of the terrible man bearing down on the woman who was trusting Kit with her life. Kit turned and opened her mouth to shout at Wright that he must find Makepeace, that he must go to Miller's Court, to tell him that the killer would be there and they could get him. It didn't matter anymore, what they knew about her, all that mattered was keeping Mary Jane safe.

Before she got a word out, Airedale's huge open palm slapped into her face, slamming her into a wall and knocking her senseless.

XII

When she came to, she was curled on the cold stone floor. He hadn't even bothered to put her on the pile of straw that passed for a bed in the tiny space. She didn't know how long she'd been out, had no idea how many of her erstwhile colleagues had wandered in to stare at her in disbelief.

She could feel the shape of the revolver pressing into her thigh—he hadn't thought to search her, to take away anything she might use. The truncheon was hanging at her belt, though her helmet was, she presumed, still sitting in lonesome fashion on Wright's desk.

What would he think, her mentor? What would he say? And Makepeace. What would the inspector say? Do? It occurred to her that she didn't care what anyone thought apart from them.

"Awake are we?" Airedale loomed in front of the bars. "Ready for some correction?"

"Where's Makepeace? Airedale, I have to speak to Himself, I have to get out of here. You don't understand—"

"I understand that you've been where you shouldn't, been meddling in things you shouldn't have. Don't you know what happens to little girls who get themselves into bad places? Little girls who don't obey the rules? Little girls who wander off the path—they get what's coming to them, that's what."

He unlocked the cell door, then pulled it closed behind him. He didn't lock it because it didn't matter—her speed was irrelevant when she couldn't get past him. He began removing his tunic and Kit backed up against the furthest wall. "Little girls who don't follow the rules learn hard lessons, *Katherine.*"

He was so certain of himself, so focused on unbuttoning his trousers, that he just laughed when she cringed away. When she spun back around and sprang at him, he was utterly unprepared. Kit swung the truncheon at the side of his left knee and heard the crack. Airedale went down with a scream, and she leapt over him as he fell. He managed to grab at her ankle and she fell too, striking her elbow on the ground so hard that it went numb. She kicked out and caught his ruddy face with the heel of her boot and heard teeth give way with a satisfying snap.

Kit scrambled to her feet and bolted, up the stairs and burst into the foyer. Wright was still at the desk, still looking perplexed. She shouted at him as she went past—no one tried to stop her—"Thirteen Miller's Court! The Ripper." Then shouldered her way out through the doors and into the night, every pump of her arms, every pound of her boots on the cobbles a prayer.

Kit didn't wait to hear if there was a rabble of coppers following her, either to give chase or assistance. She flew along the ill-lit streets, desperately trying to recall all the shortcuts she'd ever learned in her time policing Whitechapel. She got turned around twice and had to retrace her steps, sobbing and cursing, words she'd never used herself, but heard so many times from the mouths of the locale's denizens.

Miller's Court was part of the Spitalfields rookery, so dangerous it was double patrolled. It ran off the "wicked quarter mile" of Dorset Street. It was highly populated—people would *hear* an attack, she thought. The voice in her head reminded her it hadn't helped any of the other murdered women. It wasn't an area where people ran towards screams or offered help. They walked quickly the other way to avoid getting themselves into trouble.

The bulk of the Christ Church came into sight and it gave her some kind of hope—she was close. She still didn't know what the hour was. She didn't know how much time she'd lost—she should have stopped to ask before she charged off, she thought, then considered herself an idiot—as if she had any seconds to spare. And if she was too late . . . well, then time was irrelevant, wasn't it?

She threw herself to the left into Dorset Street, barely slowing down and almost slipped on the wet paving. She righted herself, kept running until she found the tiny aperture, barely a yard wide, that was the opening of the Miller's Court blind alley.

The space broadened as she got through the passage, and saw number 13 on her right. It had its own entrance, Kelly had said, and her common-law husband—no longer so—would be happy to vacate for an evening if Kelly took care of the rental areas. It stretched Kit's meager reserves, but she'd handed over the outstanding twenty-nine shillings.

Kit slowed as she approached the corner. There were two windows looking out into the court, both had rough Hessian sacks hung as curtains and the sight of the orange glow from inside calmed her for a moment—a fire meant warmth and comfort, it meant a home and a hearth. For the briefest breath of a second, Kit thought it would be okay. Then she noticed the corner of one of the windows was broken and a rag was stuffed in the gap, a piece of bleached cloth with dark stains on it.

She reached for the handle and turned it, pushing the door gently inwards.

Kit had never smelled anything like it—the other women had died outside and the scent of their deaths had been somewhat dissipated by that general condition. The air in Mary Jane Kelly's room was thick with the stink of iron and shit and piss. The dancing glow from the fireplace made it seem that what was left of the woman's chest still moved, but Kit knew that was impossible—Mary Jane had been opened up from gullet to groin. There was so much blood that Kit couldn't tell what remained on the body and what had been taken. She could tell that the breasts were gone and the legs spread, and it appeared as if most of her abdomen was scooped out. Her head was turned towards the door and the crater where her face had once been seemed to stare at Kit accusingly. Incongruously, Kelly's clothing was neatly folded on the chair beside her bed. The two rickety tables were mostly bare.

She tried not to breathe too deeply, tried not to swallow. Couldn't force herself to approach the bed, just let her eyes roam around the room, trying to take in every detail she could, everything she might be able to examine in her memory later because she knew her days with the Met were done.

There was clothing burning in the fireplace and she thought it must have come from the empty basket on one of the tables, a sign Kelly had brought her mending to occupy her; the boot prints in blood and dirt; the lack of an obvious struggle which suggested the girl had been rendered unconscious very quickly.

By the time Makepeace, Wright, and six other out-of-breath officers poured through the passage into Miller's Court, she'd seen all she ever wanted to see and taken up position on one of the old barrels that cluttered up the yard.

When her Inspector looked askance at her and asked, "How did you know?" all she could do was shrug and gesture towards the open door. What could she say, after all? That she had caused this? That she'd risked a woman's life and then lost it after she'd promised not to? He pointed a finger at her and said, "This isn't over."

"Never a truer word spoken," she muttered to his departing back.

He and Wright disappeared into the small room, and their entourage crowded around the entrance, swearing and staring. More than one of them found somewhere to throw up. When a very pale Makepeace returned, and managed to find words, they were, "Why? Why like *this*? It's not him, is it? Someone—*something*—new?"

Kit shook her head. "It's him."

"But . . ."

"He did this because she eluded him for so long. It made him angry and resentful. He could have taken someone else, but she became an obsession simply because he couldn't find her." Kit stood and rubbed at her arms, which had gone numb out in the cold. "This became *personal* and he doesn't like being defied."

She passed her gloved palms over her face, smelling the leather.

Makepeace was caught between watching his officers variously look into the slaughter room, then hurry out, and the sight of Dr. Bagster Phillips waddling along the passage from Dorset Street, almost eclipsing the entire space. The doctor's assessing gaze told her he'd heard the news. She was in no mood to be subjected to further interrogation or speculative glances, and stood.

"Where do you think you're going?" demanded Makepeace.

She looked at him. "You've got your hands full for the rest of the night, I'd imagine. I'm no longer under your control and I'm going home."

"I have questions you need to answer, Caswell."

"You know where to find me." Kit turned and walked away. The men around her stopped briefly what they were doing and watched her, but no one made any move to stop her, not even Abberline as he moved towards the scene with the gait of a condemned man.

They didn't see her the same way, she knew; somehow she'd become a criminal. She wondered if she'd find Mary Kelly's bloody shade waiting beside her bed when she got home.

XIII

Time had never passed like this, she was certain.

Each second was an hour, each hour an eternity, and the day simply stretched on as if it had transformed, somehow become an unfathomable distance. She'd lain on her bed forever it seemed, moving her gaze from the intricacies of the rug, to the painting on the wall, to the wood grain of the wardrobe, to the floral pitcher and bowl on the washbasin, to the embroidered cushion on the chair in the corner.

She did not sleep; she'd not slept in so long but still it would not come. Every so often the bubble around her was punctured by the sound of Louisa screaming, sometimes throwing the lockless door back against the wall in fury and screeching from the hallway, sometimes from elsewhere in the flat. That only stopped when Kit heard Mrs. K's soothing voice coaxing her mother away with promises of tea and something to calm her nerves. Kit hoped it was laudanum, a heavy dose, that Louisa would sleep for a very long time and perhaps forget what her daughter had done.

That was the thing, though: Louisa didn't appear to remember *precisely* what Kit had done. She was enraged, she was ashamed, she was utterly certain that her child had brought opprobrium down upon them, but it didn't seem that she recalled what her daughter had actually done. Indeed, it was apparent she'd substituted another sin altogether. As far as Kit could decipher from her mother's rants, Louisa believed Kit had become a fallen woman.

There were more accusations, each more outlandish than the next, but that was the core of it: Louisa believed Kit was a harlot and nothing anyone said could convince her otherwise. Wasn't that why she and Mrs. K had gone to the police station? To ask for an investigation? For the police to stop her daughter from doing such terrible things? Hadn't Lucius—dear sweet Lucius, concerned only for his sister's soul—sworn that was what Kit was doing?

Since arriving home in the early hours Kit had not gone to see her brother. She'd heard him through their shared wall, calling for a while, but had not been able to bring herself to answer. She could not bear to look at him and know that his actions, intended to save her, had damned Mary Kelly. She couldn't, she knew, speak to him yet without crying out all the grief building in the pit of her. If she opened her mouth, she would let something awful out, she would push a little of it—oh, just a little!—onto him just to lighten her own burden. She couldn't—wouldn't—speak to him until she could keep all her anger, her guilt, to herself. Until she could lie to him and swear he hadn't played even a tiny part in the tragedy that had reeled itself out last night.

At some point she heard Louisa's snoring begin, the nasal thunder that meant she'd had her "medicine." Soon after there was a tentative knock and it was all Kit could do to drag her attention away from the watercolor of a field of flowers—a gift from the Reverend Caswell. Mrs. Kittredge hovered tentatively on the threshold as if unsure she was welcome. Kit cleared her throat, finally found her voice.

"What is it, Mrs. K?" She'd not spoken since bidding Makepeace farewell the night before. Night? Morning? Did it matter?

"Katherine," began the woman, then stopped, moved into the room and shifted the chair beside Kit's bed so she could look directly into the girl's face, as if that was important. "Kit, I'm . . ."

Kit raised an eyebrow, unsure she was ready for any kind of interaction, but Mrs. K wasn't screaming at her, wasn't irrational, wasn't lost in the prison of her own mind. Mrs. K wanted to have a conversation, so Kit felt the least she could do was listen.

She sat up, leaning against the pillows, aware she'd not changed out of her uniform—and that it would need to be returned to the station at some point, as would the truncheon, the overcoat and whistle, and the bullseye lantern. She sighed at the thought. The boots lying in a corner, at least, were hers—or rather her father's, the Reverend having had rather small feet and Kit rather large ones.

"Yes, Mrs. K?"

"Kit, I am sorry."

Kit blinked. An apology had not been amongst her expectations.

"I'm so sorry for what we did. I thought it was right, we—your mother had her suspicions, then your brother told us what you were really doing—oh, I know she doesn't know which way's up at the moment but she'll come around—we thought we were looking after you. Only," she paused, sniffling, "only when I saw you in that room, in that uniform, so tall and proper, I knew you didn't need saving. I knew you were doing the saving and we'd ruined it. We'd ruined everything."

She broke down and began to sob. Kit wanted to join her, but tears would solve nothing. She patted Mrs. K on the shoulder and made soothing noises, managing a strangled *It's all right*, which caused the woman to rear up.

"It's *not*," she said forcefully. "It's not all right! Here's me going to all these women's meetings, listening to calls for the vote and equality, and I go and wreck your future, your steps on a path none of us are allowed to take."

"I thought you went to church and séances, Mrs. K," said Kit, somewhat bewildered. The idea of the landlady as an advocate for women's rights made Kit think she'd not known her at all. Mrs. K looked a little affronted, then abashed.

"Well, I do go to séances, yes, but where do you think we have our suffrage meetings? Where's the safest place in the world? A church. Anyway, what I need to tell you didn't come from going to church or from women's groups, but from the séances. You know I go to chat to my dear old mum?"

Kit didn't, but she nodded anyway. She felt ashamed that she knew so little about the woman who'd spent so much time looking after her mother and brother. It seemed terribly disloyal.

"Well, that poor friend of yours, Mary Jane, I *knew* I knew her from somewhere. From the séances, Kit. They bring in sensitives—mediums who can contact the spirits and the spirits speak through them. Your Mary Jane, she was one of them."

Kit felt the hairs on the back of her neck stand to attention. Séances—clairvoyants didn't perform for free. It was paid work that didn't involve being drilled up against a wall by a man you barely knew. The kind of work that Mary Kelly, who'd touched Kit's hands and accessed her worst secrets, could do standing on one leg. The kind of work at which the Whitechapel Witches would all take a punt, given the chance. Was that how he found them, this purported Jack?

"Mrs. K, did you recognize any of the other women who were killed? When the papers printed their photos, did you know any of their faces? Might they have been at the séances too, as your mediums?"

Mrs. K thought hard and finally nodded as if making a tough decision. "May well have been, Kit. May well have been at least one of them— sometimes they stank of gin when they arrived and they didn't look like good women, but they were very good mediums. Your Mary Jane gave me the best connection I've had with Mum in years."

"Do you remember anyone else there, a man showing particular interest in the women?"

Mrs. K shook her head. "Lot of different people, lot of different groups, Kit. I can't think of anyone—anyway, I'm not there to socialize with the living."

So, perhaps he hadn't been at one of the same séances as Mrs. K, but London was a veritable hotbed of people desperately looking for contact with the Other Side. Kit supposed one was bound to stumble across at least one genuine sensitive amongst all the shysters and fakes. And Jack, whoever he was, had certainly been in attendance somewhere he'd seen the power of those Whitechapel women, and he'd *chosen* them for whatever he was trying to do.

"Mrs. K," she said, swinging her feet off the bed, "I need to go out for a while. Can you keep an eye on the madhouse?"

The landlady straightened and threw back her shoulders; she seemed to regard the task as a chance to redeem herself.

It was late afternoon by the time Kit located Bagster Phillips, after traipsing far and wide. She discovered only after she'd arrived at Old Montague Street that Kelly's body had been taken instead to Shoreditch mortuary. When she'd arrived there, the autopsy was well and truly over, and there was only the attendant who told her, for an unreasonably hefty bribe, that Bagster Phillips had been joined by that unbearable snob Dr. Bond. While they'd begun proceedings with a good deal of sniping, at the end of their combined labors they seemed to have developed a kinship forged in Mary Kelly's blood and guts. Both were pale and silent when they'd finished picking through the woman's dreadful remains, said the attendant with unhealthy relish.

Kit knew Bond wouldn't have truck with her, but there was a chance Bagster Phillips would. When she at last found him at the Angel and Crown, he looked as though he'd been doing his best to wipe all memory of the morning's activities from his mind. He peered at her blearily, then gestured drunkenly to the seat beside him. He licked his lips—not in a salacious way—and chewed for a few moments as if his mouth was filled with cotton, then opened his eyes wide and tried to focus. A fat finger waggled at her.

"I always thought there was something different about you, Caswell."

"Every man is a genius with hindsight, Doctor Bagster Phillips," she said primly, her purse sitting ladylike in her lap, and he grinned.

"I used to think what a pretty boy you were, and lo, here you are, a slightly less pretty girl." He snorted with laughter. "I am willing to bet there are several coppers sighing with relief to discover that the young man they were staring at a little too long is, in fact, a damsel."

"I don't bet PC Airedale's one of them," she said, and he gave a great bellow of a laugh that almost disguised the fart that followed it.

"Oh dear, pardon me," he said and waved his hand. Kit wasn't sure if the gas was worse than the smell coming from his mouth as he belched. "Yes, you certainly took care of that great ape. I'm assuming you had good reason."

"Doctor Bagster Phillips . . . " she said. "Doctor Bagster Phillips, did you find anything in Mary Kelly's autopsy?"

He looked terribly sad. "Poor girl. Poor little girl, didn't deserve that."

"What did he take?"

"Take?" He looked confused.

"His souvenir, Doctor. He's taken something from all of them, as you well know."

He shook his head, but then answered, "The heart. Her poor heart was gone. And the baby."

Kit felt her stomach heave as it hadn't even when she viewed Kelly's remains. "She was pregnant?"

He nodded, tears in his rheumy eyes.

"Doctor, the instrument—it wasn't a bayonet, was it? I mean, there was too much—the cuts—I saw . . . "

Slowly, he nodded.

Kit continued, "Then might it not have been a Liston knife? I've seen you use one when a saw won't do . . . "

Bagster Phillips blustered—the idea that the murderer might be a medical man made him deeply unhappy, she could see—before finally agreeing. "It could have been. But he's not a doctor, Caswell, he's a butcher, make no mistake about that."

"Oh, I know, Doctor Bagster Phillips, I know." She stood, but he stopped her with a meaty hand on her arm. She raised her eyebrows.

"Be careful, Caswell. There's a man out there who really doesn't like women."

She nodded and patted his shoulder, then left him to his next swig of gin.

Out in the afternoon cold, she glanced at her father's fob watch, which she'd begun wearing since Mary Kelly's demise, in spite of Louisa's protests. She still had time, if she was swift, to go to the shop in Limehouse, to make one final request of Mr. Wing. If required, she would tell him his debt would be paid in full for this one last assistance. She wondered if that would be enough.

XIV

There was something she was missing, Kit was sure of it. Something that was in her head, certainly, something she *knew* but couldn't quite grasp the significance of—it was refusing to let itself be noticed. She picked over each tiny morsel of information, no matter how insignificant it seemed—as much to take her mind off the earlier polite but firm rebuff as to find a solution— yet her memory would still not oblige.

After leaving Dr. Bagster Phillips to his cups, she'd made her way to the apothecary's shop and found the door locked, with no sign of Mr. Wing inside. It took some determined knocking before he appeared and shook his head at her through the window. In the end, when it became obvious she was looking around for something to hurl through the glass, he gave in and opened the door but a sliver, not inviting her in.

Kit was exhausted and chilled to her bones, as if the cold had settled in them and would never go away no matter how many roaring fires she sat in front of or how many warm rugs she wrapped herself in, but she didn't press him, merely asked outright.

"Where is the boy? The youngster who came to me about the woman in Duffield's Yard? The one who brought me the gun?"

He made an exasperated sound and she knew she was very close to the borders of his patience. "Why do you ask this, Miss Katherine? What could you possibly need to know this for?"

"Because I think he saw the man who killed Elizabeth Stride. I think he came and found me of his own accord—I don't think you sent him at all. I think he found me because he was terrified—too terrified to tell me anything else—but not so scared that he didn't want someone to know." She held onto the edge of the doorframe so he couldn't close the door without hurting her. "I think when I saw him last night he made a mistake then covered it up. He said "I saw her" then he changed it to "Saw her body." I think he was saying he saw her being murdered."

"What an interesting idea, Miss Katherine. Perhaps you should take it to the police." His voice was flat as was his gaze, but she could tell that he knew what had happened, that he knew she'd lost her position, that everything was different.

She'd surrendered then, left before he could tell her she was no longer welcome to the privilege of a place at the lock-up—and frankly she'd lost enough already. She wasn't prepared to let something else slip from her grasp.

Now, sitting in the parlor as evening closed in outside, her stockinged feet were as close to the fire as she could bear, trying to melt the ice from her very core. Mrs. K had thoughtfully provided nips of port and cups of tea and they'd gone some way to helping, but she did wonder if the alcohol hadn't also dimmed her senses. Perhaps that was why she couldn't identify that essential clue.

She was so deep in thought that she didn't hear the knock at the front door, didn't rouse until Mrs. K stood poised in the doorway, the shadow of someone looming behind her.

"Katherine? Kit, you've a gentleman caller."

Mrs. K stepped back and Makepeace filled the space. Kit laughed out loud at the idea of her former boss as a gentleman caller. The Inspector held his bowler hat, twisting it around as if it was the best way to keep his hands occupied. Kit was perplexed at his demeanor. He had every right to charge in and interrogate her as if she was some stripe of criminal, in fact she'd been expecting his arrival all day—had half-expected to return from her expedition and find him furious and fuming. Perhaps it was Mrs. K's presence that kept his ire in check.

Kit carefully tucked her feet back under her skirts and nodded for Makepeace to enter. Mrs. K bustled away, muttering about tea and biscuits. Kit wondered vaguely when the landlady had last set foot in her own kitchen upstairs, or if she'd completely moved down to theirs now.

Makepeace settled in the wingback chair across from Kit and took some time crossing his legs then balancing his hat over his knee. He leaned back against the particularly lumpen cushion and tried to get comfortable. Kit watched with amusement as he wiggled as much as a man well over six feet could be said to do so, and politely tried to beat the item into submission. Finally she took pity and said, "We usually just throw it on the floor."

"Thank God for that." He whipped the thing out from behind him and dropped it beside the chair. "I will never understand the female insistence upon cushions, Caswell."

"That makes two of us, sir," she said, old habits dying hard. "But I suppose it's not 'sir' anymore. It's Mr. Makepeace."

"Edwin, if you prefer," he offered awkwardly. Kit was amazed that he wasn't angry, more aggressive and demanding. Perhaps the sight of her in a dress, knowing she was *meant* to be wearing it, calmed him down and reinstated his naturally chivalrous behavior.

"I imagine you're here, Mr. Makepeace, to ask some difficult questions." She played with the edge of the crocheted rug on her lap, tracing the knots and links carefully. "I'll answer them, of course."

"Well, that's a relief," he said dryly, then leaned forward. "How did you know? How did you know he'd be there, that it would be Kelly?"

And she told, everything, from her first meeting with Kelly, to the revelation of witchery amongst the Whitechapel whores—his face convulsed with disbelief, but she didn't care. She told him about the letter she'd received and the agreement she'd reached with Mary Jane, she told him the horrid end of that partnership and its aftermath even though he already knew. Telling and re-telling the tale of her own failure was the very least punishment she could mete out to herself, she decided.

"And you didn't tell me any of this because you thought I'd think you mad, all this rubbish about witches?"

"Don't you now? She sighed. "It doesn't matter. I've nothing to hide anymore, nothing to lose. He's got what he wants—Mary always said he only wanted five, that there's magic in the number, like the points of a star; that's what's needed for summoning and making requests. That's what she believed he was doing—that's why he kept little parts of them for the soul to cling to at least until he'd done what he needed to with that currency."

"And why this . . . Katherine?" He gestured to her clothes, to the uniform that wasn't there. "Why the disguise?"

She would not share the details of that, the *how* of her double life, about the lock-up or the help from Mr. Wing—those secrets weren't hers alone.

"Are you saying, Mr. Makepeace, that had I walked into the Leman Street nick in my bustled gown and bonnet, and asked for a job that I'd have been given a respectful hearing? That I wouldn't have been laughed out the door or threatened with a stay in an asylum until I changed my ways and ideas? I have several mouths to support, Mr. Makepeace—do you know how far the salary of a milliner's apprentice goes amongst three people, one of them ill and one increasingly . . . "

She did not finish the sentence.

"I did what I needed to. No," she corrected herself, "I did what I *wanted* to do."

"You did what you thought was right."

"Right? Or convenient? Don't think I don't know how much of this is my fault. If I hadn't been so determined to keep my secrets then this might have been over long ago. I'm very aware that I put myself and my family ahead of the lives of the streetwalkers, because I'm as bad as any man, because I didn't set sufficient store by them. I didn't think they deserved to be safe as much as I did though I didn't say it; I thought they somehow brought the violence on themselves by the very nature of their lives. I judged them less worthy than me and mine, Mr. Makepeace, and I will live with that every damned day for the rest of my life." She pointed a finger at him as he made to contradict her. "And don't tell you haven't thought the same—that they're worth less, these women. If it wasn't true then you wouldn't be sitting here so calm as you question me, acting as if I've done nothing more than steal a bag of sweeties.

"You don't think they're worth enough to get angry about—you're more infuriated that this man *dared* to defy you and make a mess on your streets, made your men look like idiots, than you're outraged by the loss of these women's lives. Deny it and I'll know you're a liar."

His lips went white and Kit thought she might have gone too far, but he didn't lose his temper, didn't deny her accusations.

"Tea and biscuits," announced Mrs. K, and entered bearing a tray. She fussed a little, making teaspoons clatter against porcelain saucers as she put the tray down on the small table beside Kit's chair.

"Thank you, Mrs. K," said Kit in a tone that said quite clearly the woman should vacate the room at speed.

As Kit poured the dark brown liquid into a rose-patterned cup, Makepeace's shoulders slumped and he said, "I heard you."

"What?"

"I heard you, when Airedale was marching you to the cells. I was in the storeroom behind the front desk and heard you tell Wright to find me. I heard it and I ignored it. I thought *Let that be a lesson to you, little miss, teach you to make a fool of me.*" He looked at the hat perched precariously on his knee.

"How long had you known?" she asked.

"The night after the double event—I came to see how you were. I was on the other side of the street and what should I espy instead of my brightest police constable but a tall woman in a nightgown freezing on her own doorstep, watching a whore wander off down Lady's Mantle Court Road."

"You knew all that time? You knew and you didn't say anything? You knew and you still listened to me when I told you about the souvenirs?" she said wonderingly.

He shrugged. "It made sense and I already knew you weren't an idiot. I didn't imagine that a change in your sex would alter that."

"Thank you," she said quietly, gratefully.

"But I was annoyed at you. Very much so. When Abberline had you locked up, I didn't intervene. I thought *that'll serve her right.*" He rubbed his face and she heard the rasping of skin against thick bristles that hadn't been shaved in a little too long. "So when you're apportioning blame, don't forget my share. I'm the one who let them lock you up. I'm the one who let Airedale cart you off—though, I swear, I didn't know he'd hit you—I'm as much at fault for Kelly's death."

She examined her hands, looking under the nails for specks of dirt, looking anywhere but at him. She was resentful, but knew she had no real right to be—it didn't matter. She'd been the one to live a lie, she'd been the one to take the risk with the other woman's life. It was all on her.

She felt suddenly very tired. She'd not slept since finding Kelly's body; only stared at the ceiling, the door, the walls, hoping Kelly might break through Kit's lack of eldritch sight and appear before her, so that she could tell the woman what had happened, that she'd not been betrayed and left to the darkness.

"I think, Mr. Makepeace, that I need to retire."

He nodded slowly and rose, hesitating until she offered her hand, which he held for too many moments as if he couldn't find the right words. Kit escorted him to the door and pulled it open just as a small Chinese boy was poised to knock. His eyes went wide at the sight of them and Kit thought he might flee, but he seemed to calm down.

It wasn't the boy she'd sought, but she thought she recognized this one from other times. He pulled an envelope, thick and pearly grey from his pocket and handed it to her, then ran away without explanation.

"What's that, Miss Caswell?" asked Makepeace.

She smiled and shook it gently. "Mr. Wing the apothecary sends herbs for Lucius, sometimes for Mother's headaches, too. He is very kind."

Edwin Makepeace nodded and restored his hat to its place and bid her farewell. She watched him lope away, not wishing to close the door too quickly lest it cause him to suspect something was not as she would have him believe.

Back in the parlor she found herself opening a mysterious missive for the second time, but at least she knew who'd sent this one. Inside was a letter and a key.

On a single sheet of thin rice paper, Mr. Wing's lovely script told her quite simply that the boy she'd wanted to speak with had been found. He'd been murdered; that the police had no interest in pursuing the crime. He wrote that yes, the boy had seen precisely what she'd thought, but he had no name to give, it was not a commodity in which he trafficked—all he had was the enclosed key, which was to the door in the floor and the door beneath. At the bottom of the page was a map, a miniature artwork in delicate pen-strokes.

Kit felt a pain in her head and spots danced in front of her eyes. Muddy boot prints on the floor of the lock-up, a void on the left side of the right sole. Bloody boot prints on the floor of 13 Miller's Court, an identical imprint. The very thing that had been staring her in the face, hidden in plain sight, one of a hundred ordinary details drifting in her memory.

Kit took a deep breath and steadied herself. She still had her kit, and the gun and the brass knuckles. She'd been surprised when Makepeace hadn't asked for the return of the Met's property. In her room, she pulled an old tweed suit that had been her father's from the back of the wardrobe and dressed carefully. The evening's work did not call for a frock. She laced up her boots, then wrapped a thick scarf around her neck. She slipped into the overcoat, feeling the weight of the revolver still lurking there, then put the knuckles and the truncheon into the opposite pocket so there would be no careless mishaps.

She told Mrs. K she was going out and not to worry, although Kit knew the woman would—but she wouldn't stop her either. The landlady stood on the stoop, a stalwart silhouette against the interior lights. Kit's bullseye lantern lit her way down the fog-obscured steps, a thin lonely band of hope piercing the moon dark night.

XV

The lock turned with no more than a whispered *click*. Kit pulled the trapdoor open and stared into the dark hole at her feet. She angled the lantern's gaze downwards and made out a metal ladder, brick walls gleaming with moisture and a paved path perhaps nine feet down. The smell wafting upwards told her that this was part of the sewer system. She wrapped the scarf tightly around her mouth and nose; it helped a little.

Tackling the rungs was a fraught exercise as she kept her grip on both the lantern—without it she was lost—and the ladder. She slipped once and almost fell, almost let go of the lamp, but recovered, breathing hard, hanging for a few moments by her injured shoulder, which had been healing well until that point.

When she reached the bottom, Kit examined Mr. Wing's map in the beam of light. She was thankful she didn't have far to go—the apothecary had considerately marked out the number of paces she needed to cover before turning left, and then right, and then left and left again until she found herself standing before a heavy door, reinforced with rusting studs. The door *beneath*.

Kit tiptoed close and put her ear to the cold surface, felt the slime of it against her cheek. She couldn't hear anything on the other side, but from behind her, back in the tunnels where she'd come from, she thought she heard a splash. A rat. She closed her eyes and shuddered.

She placed the lantern on the paving stones so she could fish around in her pocket for the trapdoor key; when she fitted it into the keyhole she was surprised that it wasn't needed—the door fell open under her touch.

Inside there was a chamber, well-lit by candles set in candelabrum of silver and gold—surely purloined—over which melted wax had spilled. A battered armchair with a fur carriage-rug folded on its seat sat in the middle of a large Persian carpet that had been ill-used. Beside it was a wide table piled with books and vials, pestles and dried ingredients, distorted things in specimen bottles and sharp surgical instruments in an open tooled-leather case, all glinting against the purple velvet lining, catching the reflections of myriad flames.

The room was surprisingly warm, and almost enough incense had been burned to subdue the sewer-stink. At the far wall was an archway hung with a thick purple curtain. Leaving her own bullseye where she'd put it, Kit entered, sliding a hand into the pocket of her overcoat and finding the grip of the revolver, pulling back its hammer so it made a distinct *snick*.

Kit froze, but there was no movement, no one charging out to stop her, and she breathed again, taking a handful of the curtain in front of her and pulling it aside.

A smaller room again, lit as the first one, but empty of all but a low circular altar in the center, a pentacle drawn on its surface. At each point was a bottle about four inches in height, inside which danced a blue-white light, and in front of each bottle was an unidentifiable rotting lump, but Kit could guess what they had been: voice-box, uterus, kidney, finger, heart.

In the center of it all was a long silver knife and a sad little gobbet of flesh, about three inches in length, like a fat worm; tiny arms, tiny legs, oversized head—it would never have a chance to grow.

Kit swallowed and turned her attention to the man who stood beside this display and smiled at her.

"Hello, PC Caswell." Andrew Douglas had lost his civilized façade in the time since she'd seen him last. Or perhaps that was just because in this location he'd reverted to what he actually was; here, he did not hide behind a veneer of sophistication. Here, he was not the valued right-hand of a rich and famous man. Here, he was a rodent at home with his kin. "How's your brother?"

Kit cleared her throat but couldn't find words. She should shoot him, she knew. She should just be done with it, but she needed—the witches needed—to know *why*. They deserved for someone to hear bear witness, for some kind of memorial even if it were an ephemeral one of words.

"Cat got your tongue? Come to think of it, if you'd had any power at all I might have taken you and your busy little tongue." He laughed at his own joke, then shook his head ruefully. "But you've got nothing, do you? Not even a tiny glimmer. You're no use to me, but you might provide some amusement."

"Why?" she managed, voice weak, throat ragged. She tried again, "Why all this? Why those poor women?"

"Poor women, poor women," he sang like some grim lullaby. "They made their choices, Katherine—is it Katherine, isn't it? Oh, I read all of your letters to Sir William, quite heart-wrenching the way you described your brother's illness, how he'd stopped walking after your father's demise, how you thought it might be psychological. What a clever girl you are," he said admiringly. "I didn't share them with him, obviously, your problems are far too small for the likes of such a great man, but they did provide me with much diversion and I was quite sad when you stopped writing.

"Imagine my surprise when a PC turned up on the doorstep by the same last name. What were the odds of a Katherine Caswell having another brother, a Kit? I was fascinated, so I found those old letters and went to your address. There you were bold as brass in your nightgown, and there she was, the lovely Marie Jeanette in all her slatternish glory. I knew she was the one. And then she went and hid from me, the bitch."

"Why?" she asked again, hating her pleading tone, hating the weakness and the fear, hating the power she was giving him by letting him know she was afraid, by letting him know she wanted an explanation before all this could end.

"Sir William, that dear man, that great man, is unwell. I've tried everything to help him, every cure, every panacea, every remedy. Everything and nothing has worked."

Kit saw, at last, a hint of sincerity, a madness tempered by a reason however wrong-headed. "But you're no doctor, and Sir William is old. He's had strokes—this is a natural progression and deterioration of the body. You cannot stop age."

He raised his finger as a conductor would a baton, a schoolmaster a cane. "I may not be a physician, but I am something else, something better, something more puissant. I am a mage. I can summon angels and demons, I have souls to offer in return for Sir William's continued good health for many years to come."

"You can barely summon the maid to bring tea. If you had any power at all you wouldn't have needed to steal from those wretched women," Kit said, unable to resist the urge to bait him. "You stole from them the way you stole from Sir William—his surgical knives, his candlesticks—that's how you repaid him. Those women had so little and you stole that from them."

"What are their worthless lives compared to his? How many has he saved? Didn't he save me from the streets, from poverty? Didn't he raise me up and make me his closest confidant?" His shout in the confined space made her ears hurt. "And didn't I know them? Didn't I know what they were when I saw them?"

"You saw them at séances, you fraud. You watched them use their abilities, you didn't divine their secrets. You saw what they openly showed."

He shook with rage, but seemed to contain himself, before continuing on. "The first one was hard, I wasn't sure of anything but my mission. It got easier, though. It got so easy I did two in one night, even though you interrupted me." He gave a proud smile. "And then the last one, your Mary Jane, she was a delight. That was when I discovered I'd got a taste for it—not just the goal, but for the activity itself! The cut and the slice of it, the color, Miss Caswell. How is your brother, by the way?"

She was puzzled by his repeated queries then realized his purpose—he wanted to hear Lucius had improved, that he was getting better. That Kit had accepted the deal Douglas had proposed, that Lucius was recovering and that Douglas' power was confirmed—he couldn't have known that Kit had been delayed that night, that she'd not intended to make a bargain with him. "He's worse. Much worse. The doctor thinks he might die."

The man flinched as if slapped.

"You are useless, powerless. All of this has been for nothing," hissed Kit. She watched as the rage welled up again and spilled across his face. He snatched the knife from the altar and threw himself at her just as she managed to bring up the gun, still in her pocket, and fired. There was the smell of gunpowder, of burnt wool, and Douglas staggered as the bullet hit him low on the waist, but he kept coming. The dagger sliced across her chest, opening coat, jacket, shirt and flesh almost to the breastbone, then he drew back and plunged the blade to the hilt into her injured shoulder. She screamed. Douglas laughed and withdrew the weapon, raising it high for another stab.

Kit reeled away, pain searing through her. She stumbled to the altar and her knees buckled, her flailing arms sweeping the glowing bottles to the floor. Douglas howled in fury as each and every one smashed on the stone flags. Kit tried to push herself up, to defend herself, to find the gun she'd dropped back into the depths of her pocket, but she fell to the side, her head landing beside the mass of broken glass and scattered spirits.

She watched as white-blue flashes swirled and rose, spiraling upwards until they coalesced into a single tongue of flame. Douglas made an inarticulate noise, and Kit guessed he hadn't really believed himself. That desperation, madness and misdirected hope had driven him. Well, she thought sleepily, now they both knew better.

She could feel blood pooling under her; her limbs becoming heavy as sin, and she was hypnotized by the blue inferno that was moving closer to her. Then it was on her chest and she felt both heat and frost on the exposed flesh, and then . . . and then it was *in* her. Roaring through her veins, burning her alive, and the voices! Oh, the voices! A chorus of joy and release, freedom and relief, all limned with a dark desire for revenge.

She only recognized one of them: Mary Jane Kelly was chattering away in Kit's skull, marshaling the others, telling them what they must do.

I didn't betray you, thought Kit, *I'm so sorry, Mary Jane, but I didn't give you up.*

And in her head, that rolling lilt of two vales, dulcet tones that sounded like a song as they said *If I didn't know that, do you think I'd be here, you idiot? Now shut up, we're concentrating.*

Kit felt herself lifted, floating up, up, until she hung, cruciform, a foot off the ground, light crackling around her, snapping like a bonfire. In front of her, Andrew Douglas stood, mouth agape, eyes empty of all reason.

He watched as she hovered, as the pulsing flare drew in on itself, concentrated on Kit's chest, then shot out like a ball from a cannon and set him alight. Where the witch-fire had not harmed Kit's skin, it incinerated Douglas, ate him from flesh to bones, until there was only a pile of smoking cinders lying where he had once stood.

Kit, momentarily still suspended, caught sight of a face in the doorway. Makepeace, disbelief and dismay scrawled across his features. Then the moment was gone and Kit dropped like a stone with a resounding thud. Her final thought before she comprehensively passed out was that she should have spoken to Lucius one last time.

XVI

"Well, Kit Caswell, you've certainly gone up in the world."

It had been almost six weeks to the day since Makepeace—suspicious enough to wait in the cold and follow her to the lock-up—had carried her out of the sewers and delivered her to the tender mercies of Guy's Hospital, where she promptly developed a fever and hung between life and death for several days.

The last time the Inspector had seen her was the morning the fever broke and she set about insisting she be sent home—and made herself thoroughly unpleasant until they discharged her. He then, by Thomas Wright's account, allowed the creative tying up of the Ripper investigation's many loose ends to keep him busy once he knew she was out of danger.

Gruff and fatherly, and seeming to have come to terms with the fact that Kit was a girl, Wright had been a frequent visitor in and out of the hospital, dragging his wife and children along to see her as if she was some kind of circus attraction. Abberline had sent flowers—she didn't know how much he really knew and didn't much care.

"Sir William is very generous," said Kit, smoothing her dark green silk poplin skirt. Her hair had grown a little and she'd had some color in the mirror this morning, but even to her own eyes she still looked too thin. She was obediently eating everything Mrs. K put in front of her.

"Very generous indeed," said the Inspector, his gaze roaming over the rich furnishings in the sitting room. The house was the smallest one in the area, not overly grand, but lovely, well-appointed, and in the most expensive square in Mayfair, right across the park from Sir William's own home.

Kit was still getting used to having a maid and a footman, but Mrs. K reveled in her new element as housekeeper—having happily rented her own home out to a family of nine—and delighted to have people to boss around in her quest to organize everything for Miss Katherine and Master Lucius. Kit had rolled her eyes and threatened to put the woman out if she ever called them that again.

"Very," she agreed.

Makepeace nodded and sipped the very fine Madeira Mrs. K had delivered earlier, then asked, "Was it by his will or otherwise?"

"More or less by his own accord, although some persuasion was required. He had no desire for his good peers to know that his very own personal secretary had been none other than Jack the Ripper, carving up unfortunates for the purposes of black magic."

"Would they have believed such outlandish drivel?"

"Doesn't matter, Mr. Makepeace. Even the smallest amount of mud makes a mark on a spotless reputation. The moment an accusation was made against Douglas, people would have been brilliant in how much they always *knew* he wasn't quite right."

"Poor Sir William," sighed Makepeace.

Kit grinned, then laughed. "Don't worry too much about the old man, he's become quite fond of Lucius and, for all his grumbling about blackmail, he quite likes me too. The deed to the house is in my name, there is a substantial sum in the bank and Sir William has engaged doctors to look into Lucius' condition."

"Will he walk again, do you think?"

She shrugged. "Perhaps, but if not, I'll be able to care for him."

Makepeace hesitated then asked, "And your mother?"

There was a long pause before she seemed to answer a question he hadn't asked. "My father died because he was kind. Almost three years ago he came across a girl in a Limehouse street, the apothecary's granddaughter. She'd been bludgeoned and stabbed—the two men who'd done it were standing over her. My father tried to defend her and the men attacked him, too. They both died watched by people too afraid to help either of them, but happy enough to recount the story afterwards."

Kit stared out the window into the pretty little garden covered in snow. "I like to think they weren't alone, then, going into the darkness." Kit thought of Mary Jane, and Cathy, Elizabeth, Polly and Annie, so isolated in their dying.

"My mother despaired afterwards. You must understand, Inspector, she is not the woman she was—I have to remind myself of that every day. *That* woman did everything to try and keep us together, to keep us fed and clothed and housed. No one wants a clergyman's family after the clergyman is gone.

"When she'd married my father, her own family disowned her—she was better than him, of course, but when a woman marries down she loses all her status, while the man's increases ever so slightly. I found a woman willing to take me as an apprentice—although truth be told, I was the least able milliner-in-training ever to grace her establishment. We struggled along on my wage for a while, but we weren't making ends meet and Lucius' condition didn't make things any easier.

"She went to her family, begged her mother to take her back if only for the sake of the grandchildren. And the woman refused. Wouldn't even offer a basket of food to help tide us over—what kind of impoverished spirit refuses such a basic kindness?" Kit looked at her hands, clasped tightly in front of her. She rose and began to pace the pretty room.

"And so, one night—this was before we moved in with Mrs. Kittredge, you understand, in another boarding house less salubrious than our last and less likely to poke into one's business. My mother would kiss us goodnight, and when she thought us asleep, she'd pinch her cheeks and carmine her lips, paint kohl about her eyes like a gypsy. She'd loosen her hair and wear the only dress she'd kept from her previous life as a rich woman's daughter, a scarlet ball gown, with black lace and jet beads sewn across it like dark stars.

"I'd hide and watch from the top of the stairs as she walked down to the front door with all the dignity of a queen and go out into the evening to earn whatever she could to keep us fed, Inspector. Judge as you will, but that was what my mother was willing to do for us."

"What happened?" asked Makepeace quietly, as if he feared the sound of his voice might break the spell of her story; that she would stop talking and he would cease to be here, in this place where she wove words to conjure another time and place, other people who were not then as they were now.

"She came home late one night, battered and bruised, one ear almost torn off, her dress ripped. They'd cut her, too, there are scars on her belly you'd never wish to see. She survived, but not really. Not up here," Kit tapped her own temple, then over her heart. "Nor here. And if that wasn't enough, one of those filthy bastards infected her."

"Syphilis?"

She nodded. "She's rotting from the inside out. She's rotting from her brain down to her very core, Inspector. Growing more unstable by the day, and I can't look after her anymore."

"So she's . . . "

"Sir William has been very generous—it makes me wonder sometimes if he knew her *before*, but he will not say. I think about what Mary Kelly said about him visiting the girls before he was incapacitated. He's arranged a place for her at a sanatorium near Windsor. Lucius, Mrs. K and I visit her once a week, although she still will not speak to me, quite rages when she catches sight of me, so mostly I sit in the foyer and read." Kit laughed mirthlessly. "I find it fascinating, don't you, Inspector, that she judges me more harshly for dressing as a man and entering your world than I ever judged her for being a whore?"

He didn't know how to reply, so he changed the subject, "And all that . . . magic I saw in you, all that fire—is it gone?"

She answered obliquely. "It wasn't me, wasn't any power of mine. It was theirs, the witches, I was just an instrument."

"What will you do now?"

"Oh, there are things to keep me busy, matters to look into," she said and offered no further explanation.

They sat in silence for a while until Kit smiled and said, "I don't wish to be rude, Inspector, but it's time for Lucius' physical therapy."

"Of course." Makepeace rose and she saw him out the door, brushing close by him and it seemed to paralyze him. He towered over her, staring down. He lifted one large hand and placed it on her shoulder, where he could feel the bandages that still bound her flesh. He opened his mouth to speak, leaning towards her.

"Do not mistake me, Makepeace. I'll be no man's whore." Kit's lips were tightly compressed into a single angry line. Makepeace blushed and muttered an apology, shrugging on his overcoat and hurrying down the steps.

Kit wondered if she would see him again or not, then decided it probably didn't matter.

She watched him stride along the street until a movement caught her eye.

Over by the fence around the private park, the spot where she would have the footman carry Lucius every day when spring came, where she hoped he would walk someday, there stood a woman.

Small with dark brown hair, wearing a forest green dress, a black short jacket over the top and a clean white apron. But she wasn't quite right—her outline shivered and shimmered, hovering between this world and the next. Behind her ephemeral skirts stood a child, holding onto her mother's legs, peeking at Kit as if shy.

Kit wondered at the ghosts, that the child who'd not ever drawn breath would look this way, then she figured Mary Jane could probably imagine her daughter any way she wanted now, could fashion her ectoplasmic flesh as she wished. The other woman smiled, a cocky sort of quirk that said *See? I'm still here. I won.*

Kit returned the grin and raised her hand in greeting, in farewell. Mary Jane picked up the little girl and set her on her hip. She gave Kit a jaunty wave and walked right through the fence into the snow-covered park, fading as she got further away. When she could be seen no more, Kit shook herself and went inside.

There were things to do.

Angela Slatter is the first Australian to win a British Fantasy Award, author of the Aurealis Award-winning *The Girl with No Hands and Other Tales*, World Fantasy Award-winning *The Bitterwood Bible and Other Recountings*, *Sourdough and Other Stories*, *Midnight and Moonshine* (with Lisa L. Hannett), *Black-Winged Angels*, and *The Female Factory* (again with Hannett). Her short stories have appeared in publications such as *Fantasy, Nightmare, Lightspeed, A Book of Horrors*, and Australian, UK, and US "best of" anthologies. Slatter's debut novel, *Vigil* will be released by Jo Fletcher Books this year, as will her first US collection, *A Feast of Shadows: Stories* (Prime Books).

All our understanding of time is made up of slipshod words that you can rearrange to cover up the fact that somewhere, somebody was wrong.

SEVEN MINUTES IN HEAVEN

Nadia Bulkin

A ghost town lived down the road from us. Its bones peeked out from over the tree line when we rattled down Highway 51 in our cherry red pickup. I could see a steeple, a water tower, a dome for a town hall. It was our shadow. It was a ghost town because there was an accident, a long time ago, which turned it into a graveyard.

I used to wonder: what kind of accident kills a whole town? Was it washed away in a storm? Did God decide, "away with you sinners," with a wave of His hand—did He shake our sleeping Mount Halberk into life? My parents said I was "morbid" when I asked these questions, and told me to play outside. So I would go outside, and play Seven Minutes in Heaven—freeze tag with a hold time of seven minutes, the length of time it takes for a soul to fly to God—with Allie Moore and Jennifer Trudeau. When the sky turned dark orange we would run back to our houses and slam our screen doors, and after my parents tucked me in I would sketch a map of the ghost town by the glow of my Little Buzz flashlight: church on the bottom of Church Street instead of the top, school on the east of the railroad tracks instead of the west. Then I would draw Mount Halberk, and take a black Sharpie, and rain down black curlicues on those little Monopoly houses until every single one was blanketed by the dark. When I got older, and madder, I would draw stick-people too—little stick-families walking little stick-dogs, little stick-farmers herding little stick-cows. And last, the darkness.

When I was in junior high school they told us the truth: the accident was industrial. The principal stood up in the auditorium and said there used to be a factory over there, in *that town*, and one day there was a leak of toxic gas, and people died over there, in *that town*. A long time ago, he said, nothing to worry about now. Some parents were angry; they said kids were getting upset. But a gas leak sounds a lot less scary than a volcano, ask any kid.

Nobody would talk about it, except when we needed to dwell on something bad. Some families said a little prayer for the ghost town during Thanksgiving, so they could be grateful for something. My uncle Ben, the asshole, told my cousins that he would leave them there if they misbehaved. Politicians in mustard suits pointed across the stage of the town hall and said, "My opponent supports the kind of policies that lead to the kind of accidents that empty out towns like Manfield." That was the ghost's name: Manfield. I lived in Hartbury.

Allie Moore was afraid of bats; she didn't like the way they crawl. Jennifer Trudeau was afraid of ice cream trucks, and nobody knew why. We only knew that when she heard the ring-a-ling song coming around the corner she'd rub her scarab amulet, to remember the power of God.

Me, I was afraid of skeletons. It was mostly the skull, the empty hugeness of the eye sockets and the missing nose and the grin of a mouth that could bite but couldn't kiss. But I also hated the rib cage and the pelvic butterfly and the knife-like fingers splayed apart in perpetual pain. It made me sick to think about what waited for me on the other side: the ugliness, the suffering. My parents took me to church and Pastor Joel promised that there would be none of that in Heaven, when I finally exhausted the cherished life that Almighty God had given me, when I finally decided my seven minutes were up and I was ready to go. "But that won't be for a long, long time from now," he said, patting my head. "So run along."

That was all well and good, but Pastor Joel didn't stop the nightmares. He didn't stop that Hell-sent skeleton from crawling out from under my box spring, clacking its teeth, tearing my sheets and then my skin. I would try to run but could never move, and those rotten bones would clamp like pliers around my neck, squeezing and squeezing until I woke up. I stopped telling my parents; their solution to everything was sleeping pills. The only thing that calmed me down was drawing and destroying Manfield, to remember that I wasn't dead like them.

It was Miss Lucy who stopped the nightmares. Miss Lucy loved Halloween, and come October she decked the classroom in pumpkins and sheet-ghosts and purple-caped vampires. She also hung a three-foot skeleton decal from the American flag above the white board. I could not stop staring at it, because it would not stop staring at me. "I know ol' Mr. Bones is kind of creepy," Miss Lucy whispered after I refused to go to the board to answer a math problem. "But you shouldn't be scared of skeletons, Amanda. You've already got one inside you." Then she reached out her finger and poked me in the chest, in what I suddenly realized was bone. I'm proud to say that I only wanted to dig myself apart for a few gory seconds before I realized that Miss Lucy was right, that a skeleton couldn't hurt me if it was already part of me.

"Memento mori," Miss Lucy said. My parents thought she was witchy, and corrected things she told us about the Pacific Wars—*we never promised that we would help Japan, we never threatened Korea.* She was gone by next September, and a woman with puppy-patterned vests had taken over her class. Mrs. Joan didn't like Halloween. Parents liked her, though.

I was seventeen the first time I went to Manfield. Allie Moore's boyfriend, Jake Felici, decided it would be a hardcore thing to do for Halloween. Jake was a moody, gangly boy who played bass guitar, and Allie's hair had turned a permanent slime-green from years on the swim team. They were the captains of hardcore. Allie invited me and Jennifer Trudeau. Jake invited Brandon Beck, who I loved so frantically that I thought it might kill me. So while other kids in Hartbury were drinking screwdrivers in somebody's basement or summoning demons with somebody's Ouija board, we piled into Jake's beat-up Honda Accord and drove down Highway 51, Brandon and his perfect chestnut hair smashed between me and Jennifer Trudeau.

We were expecting something like those old Western gold-miner towns—wood shacks, rusted roadsters, a landscape still dominated by barrels and wheelbarrows. We were expecting something that had been cut down a hundred years ago, when companies were still playing around with chemicals like babies with guns, before regulations would have kept them in line. But that was not Manfield. Manfield had ticky-tacky houses and plastic lawn gnomes and busted minivans. There was a Java Hut coffee house, a Quick Loan, a Little Thai restaurant. That is, Manfield looked just like Hartbury—only dead. Only dark.

We were standing in what had once been the town's beating heart. Jake's flashlight found a now-blinded set of traffic lights. Allie's flashlight found something called Ram's Head Tavern. Taped to the inside of the tavern's windows were newspaper clippings from twelve years back: the local high school had won a track meet; an old man had celebrated sixty years at the chemical plant that would kill them all; and they had held a harvest fair not so different from the one we celebrated in early October. Kids in flannel struggled to hoist blue-ribbon pumpkins, white-haired grandparents held out homemade pies, a blond girl with a sash that read *Queen of Mount Halberk* waved, smirking, to the camera. Hartbury was the only town on Mount Halberk now.

"Are you sure this is safe?" asked Jennifer. "What if there's still poison in the air?"

"It's not like it was radiation," said Jake, trying to muster up the certainty to be our Captain Courage. "Gas dissipates, so it's all gone now."

Allie echoed him enthusiastically, but she also pulled her plaid scarf higher up her neck. I looked at Brandon, but he wasn't looking at me. No, Brandon was hanging back with meek, slight, big-eyed Jennifer—telling her that it would be all right, kicking pebbles in her direction. None of it seemed real. I saw the five of us standing like five scarecrows, five finger puppets, five propped-up people-like things that were, nevertheless, not people. My heart was pounding like a wild animal inside my chest. I wanted to get out—out of Manfield, out of my body. I don't know what I thought was coming after me. I could only feel its rumbling, unstoppable and insurmountable, like the black volcanic clouds I had once drawn descending upon this town.

No one else seemed worried about the fact that everyone had lied about how recently the accident destroyed Manfield, and in the years to come we would never ask our parents why. I suppose we assumed that they had been so traumatized, so saddened by the loss of their sister-town, that they decided to push Manfield backward into the soft underbelly of history. "They never said when it was exactly," Jake said, in their defense, "just that it was a while ago."

A while. All our understanding of time is made up of slipshod words that you can rearrange to cover up the fact that somewhere, somebody was wrong. In a while, Brandon Beck started dating Jennifer Trudeau. In a while, I decided to leave the state for college. For a while, I dreamt of my parents driving five-year-old me to a harvest festival, buying me a pumpkin, crowning me Queen of Manfield, and then leaving me to vanish into a gently swirling fog.

I gave myself an education at Rosewood College. I learned that Seven Minutes in Heaven was not, in fact, a kind of freeze tag, because it was not, in fact, the length of time it took for a dead soul to reach God. I learned that boys would lie to you about hitchhiking across the Pampas to get you to sleep with them, and I learned they probably wouldn't call. I learned that

I had no memory of several headliner incidents that took place the year I turned six—not the three-hundred-person Chinese passenger aircraft that was mistakenly shot down over Lake Dover a hundred miles from where I grew up, not the earthquake that killed sixty in Canada, not the Great Northeastern Chemical Disaster that saw a pesticide gas cloud submerge Manfield and then float westward toward Hartbury—and that I actually had no memory of kindergarten at all.

My parents couldn't help me. I would call and they would grunt and hum and rummage through the kitchen drawers; when they got anxious, they needed to fix things. My mother remembered so many of my little childhood calamities—how I once tied our puppy Violet to my Radio Flyer and made her pull me "like a hearse"—but she didn't remember much from the year that Manfield gave up the ghost. So I tried to forget that I'd ever forgotten anything by drinking, making sure I met enough new people at each party that I'd be invited to another. I'd eventually cycle through everything and everyone, throw up in every floor's bathroom, memorize every vintage posters for every French and Italian liqueur on every dorm room wall.

I had hoped to get along with my freshman-year roommate, a poker-faced redhead named Georgina Hanssen who was also from a small town, but Georgina was not the bonding type. She lived and breathed only anthropology. She had pictures of herself holding spears in Africa and monkeys in Asia, and eventually the truth came out that her parents had been missionaries, and she had been raised Mennonite. Sometimes she ate dinner with me in the white-walled cafeteria, and we would take turns insulting the slop that passed for food, but she didn't give me any ways in, and at night she would turn down hall parties to hunch over her weird yellow books and munch her mother's homemade granola bars. One morning I woke up drunk—half in, half out of my bed—and found her staring at me like a feral animal, like she was seeing me for the first time. "What are you reading," I asked, the only question that could start a conversation with her.

"*A History of Forgotten Christianity,*" she said. Her finger scratched an itch on the open page. "For Professor Kettle's class. I'm on the chapter about cults of universal resurrection." She paused, then started reading: " '*Cults of universal resurrection have experienced cyclical fortunes throughout American history, typically reaching peak popularity during periods of economic depression.*

'*An estimated three hundred and fifty such communities have been documented across the Northeastern region. They are commonly found in small towns with high mortality rates due to exposure to natural disasters, poor medicine, and unsafe industrial conditions.'"*

Something slithered around my shoulders. "So?"

Georgina took a deep breath. *"'Cult-followers believed that God had bestowed upon them the power to return the dead to life. When an untimely death occurred in the community, church pastors and town elders would quickly perform a ritual to prevent the soul from leaving the dead person's body, holding it in a state of "limbo" until the more elaborate resurrection ritual—often involving a simulated burial and rebirth—could be performed. Although resurrection rituals varied, all cults of universal resurrection held the dung beetle—famously worshipped by ancient Egyptians for similar reasons— in high symbolic standing, as the insect's eggs emerge from a ball of its waste. Rather than Christ the divine worm, cultists worshipped Christ . . . '"*

"Christ the divine scarab," I finished. Yes, I had learned that line in Sunday school, along with God bestows the gift of life unto those who have faith, and yes, we hung scarabs on our Christmas tree, but only as a reminder that God was all-giving and we were His life-possessing children, and I had no idea what that had to do with bringing people back from the fucking dead.

"So? What happened to them?"

"'During the Great Evangelical Revival, they were mostly pressured to convert to mainstream Christianity.'" A fingernail scraped a page. Something tore inside me. "Mostly."

I left school after my freshman year. There didn't seem to be much point in staying. I went into the city, because I couldn't go home—not to that town full of the walking dead. Not to Pastor Joel and whatever he had done to us on the night of the gas leak. Not to my parents. Before I burned their pictures I would search their frozen smiles for some sign, some hollowness, some fakery, some *deadness* in their eyes. Depending on how much time I'd spent with Brother Whiskey and Sister Vodka, I sometimes found it, sometimes didn't. Regardless, I took their money—I had to, what with the economy and the price of liquor. They sent me Christmas cards with green-and-gold scarabs on them, and on the off chance that they had the right address I burned those cards along with a lock of my poisoned bleached hair, because Lily Twining said she was a witch and that was how you severed family ties. "Doesn't purify your blood, though," Lily warned me, cigarette jammed between her teeth. "Believe me, I've tried."

When I was twenty-three my Aunt Rose, wife to Uncle Ben the asshole, died of a stroke. My parents picked me up at the bus station with glassy eyes and the old red pickup, and oh how I longed to slide back into a gentler, dumber time when I could simply be their daughter, Amanda Stone, twenty-three years old. It did not work. *Memento mori.* I remembered.

Things had changed in Hartbury. My favorite Italian restaurant on Church Street had gone out of business, replaced by a plasma donation center. Everyone looked like ghouls, the skeletons that we all should have turned to grinning through their sagging skin. And a new dog—a black and white spaniel—came bounding off the porch. "Where's Violet?" I asked.

"Violet died last year," said my mother, without a hint of sadness in her voice.

"Life is cheap," I replied, rubbing New Dog behind its ears.

My parents didn't know what was happening to me. They were frightened by my tattoos: a black outline of my sternum where Miss Lucy poked me, followed by three black ribs on each side. They were worried about Brother Whiskey and Sister Vodka, not realizing that those two had seen me through a lot of darkness. They were embarrassed by how I behaved at Aunt Rose's funeral. They didn't understand why Pastor Joel's numb routine of *O death, where is thy sting?* and *O grave, where is thy victory?* made me hysterical with terror and laughter. I went to Manfield on my final night in town, and took New Dog with me—like Violet, this mutt had immediately adopted me, apparently willing to overlook the question of whether or not I was undead. I said I was going to see a friend, as in Hello darkness, my old friend, and my mother asked if I was going to see Allie Felici and her new baby. "Sure," I said, and slammed the screen door.

Manfield looked beaten-up. Windows had been broken into, storefronts had been tagged with unimaginative graffiti—a reversed pentagram here, a FOREVER LOVE there. Another car with an unfamiliar set of self-indulgent high school stickers was already parked at the mouth of the main street, and it didn't take me and New Dog long to find the occupants trudging along in the half-light, posing for pictures while making stretched-out corpse-faces. We crept behind at a safe distance, New Dog and I, just close enough to hear the sharp edges of words.

"You hear about that other town that got hit with the same stuff, except nobody died?"

"Why? They closed their windows?"

"No, joker. Look, my mom was a 911 operator. They got so many calls from Hartbury that she thought the whole town was toast, just like Manfield. But when the rescue workers got there, freaking Hartbury just closed up and told them to go home, said everything was fine."

At Aunt Ruth's funeral, my father told me that I had no respect for the life this town gave me. I said that he had no respect for death. I said that if he respected life so much then why didn't he just dig up Aunt Ruth and bring her back? His face collapsed like a withered orange. "Aunt Ruth was ready to go," he said. I flailed out of his grasp like a wildcat. I ran to the parking lot over the graves of strangers who had decided to stay dead, under the watchful eye of the great green stained-glass scarab in the window of the church. *But I am a scarab, and no man.*

It sounds romantic when you first hear it: seven minutes in heaven, seven minutes for your soul to board its tiny interstellar ship and set the coordinates for God. Seven minutes for you to change your mind. But that time is spent in nothing but the dark. The empty. Just like underneath Manfield's carefully preserved skin, behind the Ram's Head Tavern sign forever creaking in the wind, there's nothing but gas masks and body bags.

The world was changing, very fast. I had stolen food out of children's mouths, helped a man I loved pilfer from plague corpses, thanked God I wasn't pregnant because I didn't want a calcified stone baby at the bottom of my stomach. I'd seen a lot of skeletons, but only on a cross-country bus in the dead of summer did my own return to me—howling, ushered in by smoke. Its bones were just as coarse as I remembered, but its agony was so much deeper, that much richer. My skeleton had grown up. That time, I let it win. I unclenched my fists and let go. I let God.

I woke up when we stopped to let new passengers barter their way on in exchange for gas. Outside my window, one man was beating another to death for whatever the dead man had in his bag—soldiers who couldn't have been older than fifteen ran off the survivor, the killer. I might have tried to see what I could salvage from the dead one, as ghouls go after corpses, but was interrupted by an old man on the other side of the aisle with rotting teeth and a black fedora. He called me young lady, though I felt like I'd lived forever, and asked where I was from.

It was a question I hated answering. Sometimes I named the state. Sometimes I lied. Sometimes I said something crazy—"outer space" or "Hell" or "beyond." That time I told the truth. *Memento mori*—the skeleton made me. I told him about Hartbury, about the harvest festival. I told him about Seven Minutes in Heaven. I told him about playing dead—laying frozen in time in a bed of fallen leaves, waiting for someone to pluck you back to life.

"Can I tell you a secret? I died there." The shadows of nearly all my bones were tattooed across my body—I wanted to command the world to pay witness to my death. "I've died."

The old man grinned and wiggled deeper into his suit, as if he and I and every other loser on that bus were buckled into a fantastic Stairway to Heaven. "Join the club, living dead girl."

The third time I went to Manfield, I was thirty-four. I walked, because my sponsor was big on cold night walks with a backpack filled with stones, to symbolize the burdens we all carry in our Pilgrim's Progress. I was alone, save for the county dogs that smiled at me with bloody gums as they trotted up and down the cracked remains of the interstate. New Dog, whose name turned out to be Buttons, had been hit by a car on Highway 51. I invited my parents, but they frowned sadly and wondered why on Earth I'd want to go. "That's a dead town," they said.

How strange I must have always seemed to them. They must have spent my life blaming themselves for my choices, wondering why I wasn't more like sweet little Jennifer Trudeau, who had her head wrenched off in a freak accident with an ice cream truck. Seven minutes in heaven can't undo that kind of fatality. "It's peaceful there," I said.

So it was. There was a stillness in Manfield that you couldn't find in Hartbury, because when the blanket of death came for us we kicked it off. and were left naked and shivering in the world. But in Manfield there was grass carpeting what had once been the sidewalk, vines crawling up Ram's Head Tavern, rabbits nesting in the seats of long-gone drivers. Rehab always stressed peace in our time—there are some dragons you must appease, my sponsor said, because there's no fighting them. And truth's one such dragon.

A new flock of teenagers had landed in Manfield. Two girls, three boys, all on crippled bicycles whose parts had been cannibalized for the war effort. I hid behind a termite-eaten column as they wobbled past.

"You know this place is haunted. My older brother knew a guy who went up here on a dare and saw a ghost . . . a girl with a dog. One of them red-eyed demon hellhounds." In hiding, I smiled. Buttons was going to live forever. "I think that guy got deployed." As had Brandon Beck, his perfect hair shorn down to the scalp before he left for the front. The town used to hold candlelight vigils for his never-recovered body, before his parents passed and so many others followed in his footsteps. "I think he's dead."

Everyone was dead; everyone was alive. A fighter jet roared overhead, right on time for its appointment with the grim reaper. The teenagers stopped their pedaling to watch the angel pass and I took the occasion to run silent and deep, head down, fire in the belly.

Nadia Bulkin writes scary stories about the scary world we live in. It took her two tries to leave Nebraska, but she has lived in Washington, D.C. for four years now, tending her garden of student debt sowed by two political science degrees. In 2015, she had stories in the *Aickman's Heirs, Cassilda's Song*, and *She Walks in Shadows* anthologies. Nadiabulkin.wordpress.com will keep you up to date.

*"The darkness, the closeness of the place! I can scarce describe it . . .
The suffocating loneliness, the density of the forest. You couldn't
see more than five yards in any direction. It weighed on you."*

THOSE

Sofia Samatar

*" . . . how is this nonsense possible, that the enemies of Kush are copies of the
Kushite enemies of Pharaonic Egypt?"*

—L. Török, *Kush and the External World*

Sarah sets the kettle on the hob. She bends and fans the fire, her face aglow
for a moment, molten bronze. When she stands up, her color fades in the
gloom of the little house with its high windows, that house built like a ship.
Tight and trim as a yacht stands the little house, the wind beats hard against
the high windows, and Sarah's father with a blanket over his knees, her
father the old seafarer with a black-bordered card grasped tight in one hand,
draws his chair to the fire and clears his throat.

"Poor George, poor George! Well, he would keep his vow, he said; and so he
has; we shall never meet again in this life. Poor fellow! Listen, my girl, when
you go out, just stop by the Widow Cobb's, you know the place, at the end
of the lane, and see if she has any lilies. We'll send them over to George's
poor wife. It's kind of her to remember me after all these years—'remember'
in a manner of speaking—we never met. George must have spoken of me to
her, and kept my address among his papers . . . my God, Sally, but Man is a
curious beast!

"I'll tell you a strange thing. The first time I was struck by the mystery
that is Man, this same George Barnes, whose death has just been announced,
was at my side. It was in the Sudan, at Meroe, and the two of us were making
our way north to Cairo for a bit of a holiday. We were young and hardy
then, but even so, our recent misadventures in the forests had brought us

both down—George was so green about the gills, he was practically silver—and we longed for entertainment and pleasure. There was little of either in the dusty villages we passed on our way up the Nile, but the tombs of Meroe promised a diversion. At the time, I considered myself an amateur archaeologist, and it was with great excitement that I packed our Spartan picnic of bread and dried fish. There was also a jug of the native beer called *merissa*, which George wrapped in a towel as if it had been an infant. I can still see him astride his donkey, his long legs dangling comically on either side, his head swathed in a turban of blinding whiteness . . .

"He was a child, you know. Little more than a child. His father, whom George described as a 'holy terror,' had sent him to sea at the age of twelve, and George, whose nose had been permanently flattened by the fist of this same father, had set off gladly enough. The sea washed him to and fro for a number of years, with its cruelties and privations, the worst of them brought about by the men he served on ship after ship—for sea life is unkind to the small and weak, as I know from experience, though I was twenty when I left home for the waves. I was twenty, and tall, and broad, and George was a slip of a creature with gingery hair, and when we met years later in the Congo forest, natives of the same city, employees at the same plantation, I was thirty and solid as an anvil, and George, though the same age, was still a child. Was it because he'd been robbed of his childhood? Perhaps some men never grow old. What pleasure he took in our excursion to the tombs! He named his donkey Annabelle. He could whistle like a lark—it was his crooked teeth, he said. To think that George, even young George, is dead."

The kettle sings. Sarah takes it off the fire and brews the tea. Soft steam, loamy fragrance, while the wind blows. She fetches her father's pipe from the shelf and helps him to light it. He grunts his thanks, a hollow rumble deep in his wintry throat. She takes the black-bordered card from his hand and reads it beneath a window. If there are lilies, she will take them to this address. She knows the street, a poor but respectable street much like her own. It's near the Free Church—a building Sarah has passed often, but never entered. Once a young woman stopped her and gave her a pamphlet about that church, a dark and quiet woman with startling liquid eyes . . . The address on the card is just beyond there, not more than a few doors down. She'll wear her large bonnet. She'll knock at the kitchen door.

"Good afternoon, ma'am. Lilies. For the funeral."

For a moment, she will look into the woman's face. Perhaps she'll catch it before the expression twists, before it becomes like all the others, molded by the same stamp, indistinguishable. Part of the fog.

"Thank you, my dear. Would you help—just a little closer—yes, now I feel the warmth at last. I shan't scorch my beard, don't worry! Now George, as I was telling you . . . George who's laid in a box, God rest him! I suppose it ought to make us grateful we can still feel the nip of this blasted autumn . . . George was a merry lad, for all he'd been kicked about the globe like a stone in an alley. Down where we worked, at the teak plantation, the natives gave him a name I can't pronounce—your poor mother could tell you, if she weren't in Heaven—but it meant, as far as I understood it, a type of squirrel. And he was just like that, a gingery leaping squirrel with keen black eyes. I remember once at Christmas, when we were invited to dine with the plantation owner, Vermeiren, a bloodless Belgian with fangs like a mastiff, he had a bit of fun with George over that nickname. 'You do realize,' he drawled, 'that the natives eat these squirrels?'

"'Ha, ha! They are funny fellows,' laughed George.

"I laughed too, as would any man who had lived all year on millet porridge, and now found himself at the Belgian's table facing a guinea fowl poached in French wine. I laughed, I tell you; I opened my mouth and howled.

"Vermeiren showed his fangs. 'Oh yes,' he went on softly (and George and I both cut our laughter off short, so as not to drown him out), 'that little animal is quite popular with our dusky friends. Its stomach, I have been told, is full of oil. They prick the stomach—so!—collect the oil, and serve it to the chief.'

"When he said 'So!', he poked his finger in the air, toward George's midriff. His nail was long and yellow, his hand elegant and, for the tropics, marvelously clean. I noticed George turn pale, and felt a little unsteady myself.

"'They eat all sorts of disgusting things,' said George, with an effort. 'Monkeys. Grubs.'

"'So they do!' answered Vermeiren, with ghastly cheer. He addressed himself to his fowl, sawing his knife against the plate, red wine sauce mingling bloodily with the cassava that served us for potatoes. 'And men, of course!' he went on. 'You will have noticed how they file their teeth. Personally I would find it perturbing to have the name of a squirrel. I would find it most unlucky to have this name. As for me, they call me One Gun. Because of my Juliette. This satisfies me.'

"He pricked up a quivering, reddish bit of meat with his fork, and motioned with his eyes toward the rifle hanging on the wall. This was his hunting gun, called 'Juliette,' after his wife, who resided at Marseilles, where, to judge from his furnishings, she embroidered quantities of tablecloths.

"I do not know why the Belgian chose to rattle George in this manner. Perhaps he was trying, in his rough way, to put some backbone into the lad: for George was Vermeiren's overseer, charged with ensuring the productivity of the farm, and meting out punishment as required. In the early days of our employment, Vermeiren had often grumbled that George was too soft. On one occasion, I recall, the Belgian had brought forward, as evidence, a recently disciplined native called Francisco, and, exposing the native's back crisscrossed with small welts, demanded if *this* was what George called lashes? George protested that he had lashed the black soundly, as anyone could see, and Vermeiren retorted that a native's back was as insensible as teak, certainly impervious to George's paltry strokes, and that if George dared shirk again, he would be taught a lesson in lashing upon his own person. So perhaps Vermeiren's mockery that Christmas was meant to strengthen George's arm. If so, it was hardly necessary, for George had taken his earlier lesson to heart, and routinely exhausted himself in his exertions with the whip, even putting the same Francisco—apparently an habitual malingerer—into the infirmary at the Catholic Mission.

"But perhaps Vermeiren had other reasons. Perhaps he was simply possessed by that devil which leads men to tear at each other in a small space. I have often encountered this devil on board a ship; and in that house, the only white men for miles, were we not as three sailors launched on a Stygian sea? The darkness, Sally, the closeness of the place! I can scarce describe it. The windows were sheathed in white netting against the mosquitoes, and not a breath of air came through: the flames of the candles on the table stood up as straight and motionless as pikes. After dinner, George attempted to lighten the atmosphere with a carol. His voice faltered reedily into the massy night. I joined him for a few bars, but soon stopped from depression of the spirits, and he went on alone. *I gave my love a cherry.*

"The suffocating loneliness, the density of the forest. You couldn't see more than five yards in any direction. It weighed on you. It's the reason we felt so lighthearted on that trip up the Nile, the trip I was telling you about, to Meroe . . . But the forest, my God: sickness and heat and work. I kept the accounts in an office with a tin roof, so hot I'd feel my brains boiling by ten o'clock. That heat! And George stood in it all day. It took its toll on him. His fevers were terrible, enough to break your heart.

" 'Get back, get it away.' That's what he said the night your mother came to see us. She wasn't your mother then, of course, just a nurse from up the river. I'd sent word to the nuns at the Mission to rush somebody down to us, for I was sure George could not live another day. 'Easy, George,' I told him. 'This is a nurse from the Catholics come to make you well.' All the same I had to hold him down on the bed. Weak as he was, he thrashed in my arms like a seal. 'Get it away, oh God,' he moaned. And your mother bent over him in her white dress."

White, like a lily.

Sarah fingers the silver crucifix at her throat. This is her inheritance from her mother, who died when she was three years old. This, and a few dresses, and two pairs of shoes. She has let out the dresses, but she cannot wear the shoes, which are too small. She keeps them lined up under her bed. When she was very young, she used to bring them into bed with her. She gave them names: one was called *Maiyebo*. To remember this now, this naming of the shoes, causes the heat of shame to slip up her neck.

She can no longer recall her mother's face.

Her father gestures with his pipe, and she fills it. He has told her the sweet smoke does him good. She helps him light the pipe, then tucks the blanket more snugly around his wasted legs. She remembers a dream, a song.

If only it were possible to control one's dreams!

If it were, she would dream the same dream every night. One that has only come to her a few times. Fragments of glittering color and a dry, delicate scent. A memory of swinging. A dream of a structure of light.

Light. Sharp pieces of radiance. No fog. A snatch of song in a lost language. *Maiyebo.* The name of a mushroom? A comical song. Someone bounces a baby on her knee. *Mi a bi nga ro berewe te.* "I'll never see you again."

"You're not . . . you're not too lonely, are you Sal? Well, I know, but I can't help worrying. I think sometimes that we ought to have stayed in the forest. That I ought to have raised you there, among . . . But after we lost your mother, it was too hard for me, taking care of a child alone. I didn't know what to do with you, and there was your aunt, too, writing to me about my Christian duty, and the life you might have here. And, of course, there was George. Passing me like a stranger, day after day. Three years like that. Without a word. I suppose a part of me thought that after your mother was gone . . . but no. He kept his vow. 'If you do this thing,' he told me, the night before my wedding, 'if you enter into—*that*—you're dead to me." He was trembling, white, as if in the grip of one of his fevers. I thought he'd get over it.

"I thought he was still shaken up from the scare we'd had on the farm that year, and that he'd soften and come around in time. It must have affected him more deeply than I thought. I should have known, now that I think of it. I should have recognized the signs. The way he pounded on my door that night. 'Come out, come out!' That high-pitched scream. I tell you, I thought the house was on fire. I rolled out of bed and stumbled across the room, and when I opened the door he practically fell into my arms.

"'Get your gun,' he cried hoarsely. He had his own rifle, and a lantern in the other hand. As I stared, our employer Vermeiren slouched into the circle of light, casually carrying Juliette over his shoulder.

"'Stir yourself, if you please,' he said pleasantly enough. 'It seems we must make a little show of strength.'

"'For God's sake, get your gun,' repeated George, looking over his shoulder. I obeyed, donning boots, a shirt, and trousers for good measure.

"I joined them outside and locked the door behind me, and was immediately struck by the peculiar silence. There used to always be a little noise on the farm, voices of the native families, and lights, too, from their fires. Now the place was entirely deserted.

"'What's happening?' I asked softly.

"'A little fuss from our savage friends,' said the Belgian. 'Not to worry.'

"George stood so close to me, I could tell he wanted to seize my arm, though he couldn't, being encumbered by his gun and lamp. His teeth were chattering. 'Look here,' I said, alarmed by his evident panic, 'do we want to carry a light about, and make ourselves a target?'

"'By God, you're right!' cried George, and, looking at his own light in horror, he made as if to fling it to the ground.

"The Belgian snatched his wrist. 'Don't be stupid. We must not appear to be hiding. In our position, a show of fear would be catastrophic. Instead— stand up straight, little squirrel! Are you indeed a squirrel, or a caterpillar?— we must appear calm, and above all, we must shoot accurately, and to kill.'

"'Shoot at what?' I exclaimed. 'It's black as Hades.'

"Before us stretched the teak grove, like a columned ruin in the faint starlight, and beyond that, invisible to us, the damp tangle of the forest.

"'Only wait,' said the Belgian, and a spark flared as he lit his pipe.

"And so we waited. And waited. And whether it was the sound of George muttering prayers at my shoulder, the way his voice went up and down, full of little sobs, or the smell of fear that rose from him, thick and hot, I cannot say . . . Whether it was the darkness and silence around us, or the brooding, hostile forest, or the soft black of the sky in which no moon hung . . . I cannot say, Sally, why it was, but I felt something close around my heart, squeezing tight like a devil's vise. Tighter and tighter it squeezed, and my head grew light, and my body cold, and I thought of your mother, and was glad that she was away at the Catholic mission, where the nuns had given her thread, she said, to embroider a wedding veil. I clung to the thought of her face, as if it would save me . . . And perhaps, you know, it did save me. I held to that face, the face of my own Maria, as something began to happen in the dark. The darkness seemed to ripple, to stretch itself like a long snake. 'Ah,' breathed Vermeiren. 'Now it comes.'

"You were so little when we left the plantation, Sally. I wonder if you remember the soldier ants? George and I called them *siafu*, as the Belgian did, though among your mother's people they had another name. Black they were, a black and moving river, and when that river came across your path, you had best get out of the way. They'd appear after the rains, long streams of them crisscrossing the earth, and none could say whence they came or where they went. Their determination was terrible. They used to march up the walls of the house, under the roof, and straight through, across our parlor floor. I had an old Turkish *kilim* there, purchased at Istanbul in my merchant-seaman days, and where the *siafu* crossed it, they'd leave a swath clean as the noonday sky. Your mother would always laugh and say the ants proved how dusty the *kilim* was, and she'd haul it outside and beat it with the broom. But the *siafu* were nothing to laugh at. They were voracious: if they bit you, they'd draw blood. They killed chicks in the nest, and even, I heard, human babies . . .

"'Quiet!' I heard myself say. I hadn't meant to speak, but George's whimpering was breaking down my nerve. He'd given up praying now, and was simply staring at the darkness saying 'No oh no oh no oh no oh no.' The light was pitching and bobbing in his grip like a ship's lantern, and his face in the glow sweated pale as melting wax. Behind him, that ice-blooded Belgian was saying something about the seasons, and how these native disturbances came up each year as regular as the rains. It made me remember the soldier ants, which appeared after the rainstorms. Still the darkness swelled and coiled among the trees. And suddenly George let out a scream, followed an instant later by the report of the Belgian's gun: '*What the hell is that?*'

"Such a cry, Sally! My legs gave way.

"I saw the darkness bulge. It was leaking toward us, it was coming out of the trees. It was coming like a vast ocean of *siafu*, intent and ruthless and obscure like that, with a deep and cold intelligence. The terrifying thing about *siafu* is their *will*. They are utterly united, utterly faithful to their purpose. Once, I tried to snatch a tomato out of their path in our kitchen, and three of the ants went up my arm like fire.

"The Belgian was cursing. The light had gone out. I felt a kick in my ribs, the toe of Vermeiren's boot. I've never felt so grateful to be kicked. 'Get up,' he was shouting, calling us bloody cowards and other things I won't repeat in your presence.

"I realized George lay beside me on the ground. 'George, George, are you all right?'

"'I've got to get out of here,' he sobbed. 'I've got to get out.'

"Somehow, each supporting the other, we staggered to our feet. The Belgian had retrieved the fallen lantern and lit it again.

"'See!' he said triumphantly.

"There, at the edge of the teak grove, a native lay dead, shot through the heart. The darkness was natural now, empty, no longer the sentient thing it had been.

"'But—but—' stammered George, 'it is Francisco!'

"He had abandoned his gun, and clasped my arm—whether in terror or some other emotion, I cannot say.

"'Who?' inquired our employer with a frown.

"George seemed unable to speak; I explained, therefore, that Francisco was the native George had put in the infirmary.

"'Nonsense,' said the Belgian. 'As if you'd recognize him!'

"'Turn him over,' whispered George, finding his voice at last, 'and let me see his back.'

"The Belgian refused to indulge what he called my friend's 'womanish horrors'; George, to my surprise, insisted passionately; but the Belgian stood firm, finally exclaiming: 'What difference would it make? You've lashed the lot of them, as well you should.' These words seemed to throw George into a sort of frenzy. It was with difficulty that I persuaded him back to his room, and into bed. He kept repeating that Francisco commanded an army of shadow selves, which, now that their master was dead, had swarmed across the world. 'One is another,' he babbled. And though I knew he was not well—he was so broken down, indeed, that I successfully petitioned the

Belgian for a holiday—I could not shake my own sense that the darkness among the trees was *multiple*, and that George ought to have shouted, not 'What the hell is that,' but '*What the hell are those?*'"

Sarah puts on her bonnet at the glass. Neat black silk, with a generous brim that casts her features into shadow.

The wind beats the high windows. Her father sighs. Sarah touches her mother's cross.

Tonight, she will dream of tiny black eyes. A river of tiny black eyes. They're coming toward her. She lies on the grass, unable to rise. She's struggling and weeping. The eyes advance.

Waking, she will remain motionless in bed, her limbs icy. She will listen to the beating of her heart.

She will get out of bed. She'll find the matches and light the candle before the glass. Her own face will bloom toward her out of the dark. The same face that now regards her from the parlor glass, a face she has searched so often for a hint of her mother's ghost. This nose, this curving eyelid. Tonight she will take her candle and leave her room, she'll go to her father's room and shake him awake. "You called me an ant," she'll say. And he, sitting up, framed by wild white hair, "Why, Sally, what's come over you, are you mad?"

"I'm not an ant."

"But I never—"

"You said you saw her face."

"What?"

"You saw her face. In the forest. You said it saved you, the night the darkness came."

"Well, yes, I—"

"Was it the face of an ant?"

"What?"

"Did you see the face of an ant?"

And when he says nothing: "No. Of course not. An ant's face is too small."

He stares at her. White hair, white nightshirt, white wax from her candle dripping on the sheets. And his face in strange white motion. His skin quivers. She's never spoken like this to him before—has the disturbance, and the accusation, brought on some sort of attack? Gripped by remorse and terror—for how often has he told her, "Poor Sal, you have no one but me"?—she leans to touch him, and realizes just in time that his arm is also trembling, his shirt is alive, a mass of pale creatures swarms over his body.

Sarah steps back with a cry. She beats her hand against her nightdress, the hand that almost touched him. She is safe: her hand is dark and whole. She gazes at the thing in the bed, the thing in the shape of her father. It hisses softly, its tongue and teeth made of writhing maggots. "Help me." Its arms make the motions of caressing something in its lap. A few red hairs protrude from the teeming pallor. "Help my baby," it hisses, before she wakes sweating in her bed again. "Help my little child. My baby boy."

"Yes, take a little extra with you, for the lilies. For poor George. Ah, I never told you about the trip to Meroe. Wait, before you go . . . this is what I meant to say, about that trip, the last time George and I were together as friends. Yes, the last time, for when we returned to the forest, I told him about my intention to marry, and he said those final words: 'You're dead to me.' He couldn't get over it, though I explained that your mother was a good woman, a trained nurse and a Christian convert . . . Well. But at Meroe we were quite happy. George clambered about on the ancient stones, whooping like a boy. I was afraid he'd get sunstroke, to tell the truth. We sat in the shade of a cracked mausoleum wall and ate our little picnic. George was cheerful, energetic, telling me all his plans. He was going to save enough to buy a cottage back home. Enough to marry a pleasant girl. You know I almost told him about my engagement then, but for some reason I held off . . . Ah, are you leaving? Well, bring me the big book on Kush before you go. That's the one. This is a treasure, my dear, bought for a song in Cairo, probably worth more than everything else in the house put together, remember that when I'm gone! Now look here. These are some of the paintings we saw in the tombs at Meroe. Marvelous, the way the desert air protects the color. In your poor mother's country these pictures would be eaten away by the damp. Look, here's the king, and under his feet, bound captives—a conquered people. Look how they fall beneath him in a line. And their arms and legs, twisted and broken, but repeated in the same pattern, as if with a stencil. Such precision! But the odd thing, you see, is that the same images appear in the tombs of Egypt. I recognized them as soon as I saw them, for I had visited the Valley of the Kings. As I said, I thought of myself as a sort of archaeologist, and I remember I was very excited on that trip with George, thinking I might have made an important discovery. But when we got to Cairo, I found this book, and saw that the discovery had already been made. Egypt conquered Kush, you see, and the artists of Kush adopted Egypt's painting style. And generations later, these

Kushite artists used these images, images of their own people, to depict their enemies! Isn't that odd? As if the images have no character at all. As if they are vessels that can be filled again and again. Simply the enemy. And what is required of the enemy's image? Only that the figures are identical, and that they are many."

Sarah goes out. She locks the door and tucks the key in her glove. She walks with her eyes fixed on an imaginary horizon. A pale face passes her, blurred. She senses a sneer, but does not see it. She allows it to melt away like fog.

At the corner a man snarls something at her. She steps aside quickly, avoiding his lunge. He shouts at her back. Muffled by her bonnet, his voice is the honk of a goose.

There are lilies at the Widow Cobb's. Sarah buys a dozen. She will not look at the Widow Cobb's pinched, resentful face. Let it blend into fog. She takes the flowers, but she does not go to the address on the black-bordered card. She goes to the harbor.

She sits on a bench. A cold wind blows from the water.

Sarah sets the lilies beside her and takes off her bonnet.

Cold. And the sound of the gulls. She never takes off her bonnet outdoors. Her heart races. She can hear children shouting somewhere nearby. Are they coming toward her? She picks up the heavy, funereal lilies, she begins to break the flowers from their stems.

Stems fall about her feet. They shift in the wind.

Sarah takes a lily and tucks it into the black band of the bonnet in her lap.

One by one, she tucks the lilies into the band. It's delicate work, and she takes off her gloves, her skin tightening in the raw air. She continues until all twelve lilies encircle the edge of the bonnet. She puts on her gloves and places the bonnet back over her hair.

Sarah is crowned by fragrance and by snow.

Across the water, a streak of gold slips stealthily through the clouds. Sunset soon. She will sit in the cold and wait for the clouds to break, saying her usual prayer for her mother, and adding one for the man known as Francisco. She will murmur a melody under her breath, pentatonic and strange to this place. And afterward, walking home, she will pick up a low, throbbing hum in the darkened street, a hum with the same pentatonic shape as her half-forgotten song, and she will follow it through the door of the Free Church at last.

For now, she sits and waits. And the light begins to grow, to change, to take a shape rarely seen except in dreams, a shape that allows one to see, really see, and Sarah breathless and radiant in her crown perceives for a moment a world without fog, undimmed by this—that—those.

Sofia Samatar is the author of the novel *A Stranger in Olondria,* winner of the William L. Crawford Award, the British Fantasy Award, and the World Fantasy Award. She is also a Hugo and Nebula Award finalist and the recipient of the 2014 John W. Campbell Award for Best New Writer. Her most recent novel, *The Winged Histories,* was published earlier this year by Small Beer Press.

The ghost followed for a while then disappeared.
This was before he figured out what they wanted.

THE BODY FINDER

Kaaron Warren

Frank felt the back of the caravan shift to the right and knew it was time to stop for a while. He rested his hand on the device sitting on the seat beside him, looking for vibration or for warmth, as he always did. If he felt nothing in the next twenty kilometers, he'd have to stop anyway.

His destination was three day's drive away; he was in no hurry to get there. What he wanted may be there, maybe not, but it was worth a look. He'd set the address into his GPS after a police friend said to him, "You've been good to us, Frank. You've helped a lot of families. A file's just been released to the public record. Look, it's been gone over dozens of times but I dunno. There might be something."

This "help" he'd given went back decades. He remembered his first successful find. It was not long after the grave-sniffing handheld devices were released. Most considered them junk; Frank persisted until he understood how the thing worked. At first, he couldn't differentiate between adult and child.

With some fine-tuning, he could skim over the bodies of anyone over the age of sixteen. Often he didn't; he knew these lost people had loved ones somewhere regardless of their age. Someone who missed them, wanted closure. He liked to help them, as he hoped someone would help him when they found his daughter.

The first time, he was on a picnic with his ex-wife and her family. The nieces and nephews grown now, some of them parents, and he wondered how his wife could bear it. This was a year after his release from jail. He was grateful the family still spoke to him.

He wandered off, collecting wildflowers to give to her and her sisters because they were good women who deserved to be thanked. He had the device in his backpack; was never without it, especially in places where his daughter had been.

It shuddered. He dropped to his knees to twist his backpack off. He didn't want to drop it. Then he walked a slowly increasing circle until it shuddered so hard it almost vibrated out of his hands.

It wasn't her. It was another young woman and he hated himself for the relief he felt. This woman was badly damaged, cut up, and he prayed this would not be his daughter's face.

The ghost followed for a while then disappeared. This was before he figured out what they wanted.

He figured it out when he found a forty-seven year old man under the compost in a suburban backyard. The only thing the widow was surprised about was that Frank had found him. She stood, open-mouthed, glancing at the shed (she'd killed him there, Frank guessed) and back at the pile.

Frank felt a clutching at his ankle. He was only sixty-three then, still capable of rapid movement. He thought it was a cat but it was a kind of mist, or steam. As he watched, it formed into the murdered man, crawling on the ground. Frank stepped away, but the ghost followed, nudging one ankle then the next, herding him to the shed like a cat does, herding you to their food bowl.

He'd seen these ghosts before on finding bodies. Always they left him alone once he took a few steps, but this one stuck to him as he backed away. They'd shimmer when he held the gadget to them; if he didn't have it, no ghosts would appear.

As he neared the shed, the ghost reared up like an adder then thrust forward as if impatient. "Take me back," Frank thought he heard. He opened the shed door and stepped inside.

It was a concrete floor and he could see straight away where the man had died; a large, dark stain.

"Oil," she said. "Or petrol. He was always clumsy." The man sank into the stain and disappeared. It was the first time Frank realized what the ghosts wanted.

This was the first of many he took back. He kept searching, hoping and hoping to find his daughter.

He pictured his daughter doing this. Pictured her crawling. Dragging, moving through dirt like it was water.

He went time and time again to the place she'd last been seen. The ghosts wanted to go back. Had she? Had someone led her back?

It was a dance party. She was on tape there, some documentary maker, capturing the vibrancy of it all, and he watched it, they watched it, a thousand times.

He'd followed her path precisely in this abandoned factory, jumping forwards and back in moves that made him cry because she was so alive then, so full of future possibilities, so excited.

He'd watched the footage on his phone, standing as she had, on the top step, looking over the street. Then down and into the darkness. Nothing more.

Even when he wasn't looking he was looking.

He yawned and felt tiredness take him. The device was cool and silent. He carried it close by on the seat beside him in the car, or in the back of his pants when walking, where other old men carry their newspaper. He lifted his hand to wave at an old couple driving a caravan larger than his, felt his wheels veer, and that was it. Time to call it a day.

He didn't mind the grey nomads on the road, although he envied their sense of freedom. Many had suffered losses, he knew that. But none he met had caused a daughter's death. And all had buried loved ones. All had taken their loved ones back. They gave him scones, though, and the books they didn't want anymore, and made him feel as if he had a community.

His pulled his caravan into a park called River's Rest. The device buzzed hard as he neared the entrance and that was good. He hadn't found a body in months.

There were only so many bodies.

He purchased a site for three nights. The manager passed him a small plastic bag full of washing powder. "Laundry to the left, showers to the right. We do a BBQ brekkie seven to nine if you like sausages."

She managed three sites. One here, one down the road, one isolated. "We run on a trust basis, i.e. we trust you to leave the site clean and holy."

She smiled at him as if old people didn't make a mess. "If you end up staying an extra couple of days, don't worry too much. We're not booked out there. Empty at the moment so you'll have the place to yourself. Lots of peace and serenity."

It wasn't empty. A large caravan stood in the shade of a tall tree. A small boy wearing a Batman suit squatted in the dirt near the step.

Frank parked as far away as possible but distanced from the large rubbish bin as well.

He ate a ham sandwich and drank a beer, watching the river trickle by. The device hummed on his lap, eager to get moving.

He pulled on some rubber thongs, put on his sun hat, and headed down to the water's edge. He knew rivers were a popular dumping site. The men he met in jail told him that bodies were swallowed by the river bed, if you timed it right. Swallowed so far down no one would ever find them.

The kid in the Batman suit came to watch.

As Frank searched, he wished the water was higher. It was cool around his ankles, refreshing. He felt like a child again, swimming in the ocean on school holidays, or a young father, at the swimming pool with Susan learning how to swim.

"Is that a metal detector?" The little boy stood with one hand down the back of his pants, the other holding an ice block.

Frank nodded. "No luck yet."

The boy made a face of sympathy. "Sorry about that," he said. Perhaps Frank looked really sad? Too sad for one who simply hadn't found any coins? Because later the boy's mother brought Frank a plate of food, saying she'd made too much. Kind women always said things like that. His wife was still kind, although they rarely saw each other. He wouldn't let go of the grief, and she thought she had let go when she hadn't, and this clash, this wrongness of level, meant they couldn't be with each other.

And he knew she blamed him for their daughter's death. And for killing the man who killed her, without drawing out the information on where their daughter's body lay. She had stuck by Frank in jail, though, visiting every week or two, always filling his bank account with enough for treats. But he thought that was because she didn't want the guilt of abandoning him. He was the guilty one; she was happy with that arrangement.

It was his greatest regret and the one thing his wife never forgave him for, killing the man who killed his daughter. "Now we'll never know," she said. "We'll never find her."

The killer would never have told, though.

No. His greatest regret was leaving the body where it lay instead of transporting it far away. Not like his daughter, whose body was lost and whose spirit waited to be found and taken back to the place of her death.

He wished he'd known.

She was sixteen when she disappeared. Her belongings found, though, in the home of Frank's best friend. A man he'd trusted when no one else did.

This made it Frank's fault.

He was no criminal. He had no thoughts of escaping justice, no idea how to do so.

He was ten years inside and even now, thirty years later, he gloried in every day outdoors.

He used his time well in jail. He met many killers and he asked them all, *Where did you put the bodies? What sort of place?* He made a list. He wanted to understand. He wanted to know what sort of place he should look for Susan.

He learnt about true rage from these men. And that his rage was nothing compared to theirs, and that every one of them said he did the right thing in killing that man.

His cell mate, Don, was a man of his own age, a gentle soul with pink cheeks who was charged with the murders of five women. He had an impish look about him as if he held secrets, and he did; there were a dozen more.

On his release, Frank began to hunt. He spent thirty years searching for bodies. In 2010 the device was released. That took some of the guesswork out.

When Don had done his time, Frank was there to pick him up. Frank had been out twenty-five years by then; his cell mate had spent forty years inside and he was old, now, eighty-four, five years older than Frank. Fragile, pale, blinking in the light as if it was different.

"Thanks, mate," he said, his voice soft and broken. "No one else'd do it."

"I'm surprised they let you out."

"I think they forgot what I did."

Frank wasn't sure why he'd kept in touch over twenty-five years. It became habit. Through all the years of body finding, Don was interested. He'd say, "I'll never get to see another. Send me pics."

And at least they'd both been in there, and with Don around Frank was not the worst man. He and Don had traveled together, finding Don's victims.

"Not your daughter but could be." Don said it every time and Frank wasn't sure if he was trying to cause pain, or trying to make Frank feel better.

Why keep going? Because they made him believe that his little girl was waiting somewhere for him to lead her back. There were so many people to see home.

Don's memory was long since gone. He knew they were out there in the desert (I love her wide open spaces, he said) but he couldn't remember how many or where. It took a long time. Two old men, out for a ramble.

All ages, but mostly old ladies, Don said. By that he meant women over forty. Women who'd been through the worst of it, who knew themselves and were finally confident enough to be themselves. Frank loved women of that age. Loved them when they no longer stammered and kept quiet.

It was so hot out there, but there was no toilet so he didn't want to drink water. He hated pissing out in the open. He felt exposed. He didn't even like public toilets.

"Here's one," he said. They dug her up. It was a shallow grave because Don was lazy and stupid, but still, without Frank she wouldn't have been found.

They spent a week there. He found six women.

None of them were his daughter.

Don liked to hear the beeping noise telling him one of his people was there.

Don didn't mind going back to jail. He found the real world too harsh.

Frank ate the meal the mother had given him and accepted a beer from the father. They seemed a nice family. Then to bed early, and up with the sun.

Frank walked the riverbed barefoot, his toes sinking into the soft, silky mud.

The device beeped and he swept it further over to the left.

There, that was the spot.

"Found something?" It was the kid, standing there in his Batman pajamas, rubbing sleep out of his eyes. What was he, six? He was a lovely kid.

Frank would scare him, later. Make sure he never went near strangers. Had fear.

He did that with all the kids. Scared them off strangers at least, and if he got an indication, even the slightest, of anything wrong in a family, he'd dob.

The police knew him. He'd been right often enough that they listened to him.

The little boy said, "Are you a grandad?"

The question broke Frank. They only had their daughter, no more. No grandkids.

His wife married again but he never saw them.

Couldn't even remember their names.

The device shook in his hands, and he found it, the body, very fresh and new. Not his daughter.

It's not her. One day he'll find her. He'll know her bones; he saw enough X-rays when she was born, because of her shape, her "defects" people loved to say. People—more than one—had asked them, *Would you have kept her if you'd known?* The question made him and his wife both sick.

There was the feathery feeling around his ankles, like a loose hair.

The ghost herded him up the bank. He called for the boy to help, leaning on his shoulder. The boy flinched slightly and Frank saw a bruise around the area, and there was the desire to be very helpful that sometimes came with a child who was disciplined harshly.

Frank would make some calls when he got back to the city.

The boy's father met them.

"Found something?"

Suddenly fearful, Frank shook his head. "No gold here," he said, and he tried to edge past the man. But he knew the body showed clearly down there. The ghost crawled towards the family's caravan, dragging itself using dry tufts of grass, digging its fingernails into the dirt.

"Looks like you've got something down there, grandpa."

Frank shook his head. He'd been around killers enough to know this was one; he was certain of it, no matter how kind the wife was.

"Nice to meet you," Frank said and he turned putting his back to the man, wishing he'd disappear, but the man's hand fell heavy on his shoulder as it did, Frank was sure, on the little boy's. Even as he spoke the ghost writhed around his feet, mouthing *take me back, take me back.*

The man pushed him hard, into the river.

Frank landed face first.

He regretted his daughter, "take me back, Dad," she'd say, but he couldn't remember her name.

He felt bad for the little boy; no one else would save him.

But he was glad. Selfishly glad as he heard the man shouting at his family, then the caravan start and drive away, leaving him where he lay, leaving him there to die, so he would not have to crawl any distance at all to find peace.

Bram Stoker Award nominee, twice-World Fantasy Award nominee and Shirley Jackson Award winner **Kaaron Warren** has lived in Melbourne, Sydney, Canberra and Fiji. She's sold more than two hundred short stories, three novels (*Slights, Walking the Tree,* and *Mistification*) and six short story collections including the multi-award-winning *Through Splintered Walls.* Her latest novel is *The Grief Hole* (IFWG Publishing, Australia) and her latest short story collection is *Cemetery Dance Select: Kaaron Warren.*

*The Blake way is to watch the world burn from a distance
and write down what the flames looked like.*

THE DEEPWATER BRIDE

Tamsyn Muir

In the time of our crawling Night Lord's ascendancy, foretold by exodus of starlight into his sucking astral wounds, I turned sixteen and received Barbie's Dream Car. Aunt Mar had bought it for a quarter and crammed fun-sized Snickers bars in the trunk. Frankly, I was touched she'd remembered.

That was the summer Jamison Pond became wreathed in caution tape. Deep-sea hagfish were washing ashore. Home with Mar, the pond was *my* haunt; it was a nice place to read. This habit was banned when the sagging antlers of anglerfish *illicia* joined the hagfish. The Department of Fisheries blamed global warming.

Come the weekend, gulpers and vampire squid putrefied with the rest, and the Department was nonplussed. Global warming did not a vampire squid produce. I could have told them what it all meant, but then, I was a Blake.

"There's an omen at Jamison Pond," I told Mar.

My aunt was chain-smoking over the stovetop when I got home. "Eggs for dinner," she said, then, reflectively: "What kind of omen, kid?"

"Amassed dead. Salt into fresh water. The eldritch presence of the Department of Fisheries—"

Mar hastily stubbed out her cigarette on the toaster. "Christ! Stop yapping and go get the heatherback candles."

We ate scrambled eggs in the dim light of heatherback candles, which smelled strongly of salt. I spread out our journals while we ate, and for once Mar didn't complain; Blakes went by instinct and collective memory to augur, but the records were a familial *chef d'oeuvre*. They helped where instinct failed, usually.

We'd left tribute on the porch. Pebbles arranged in an Unforgivable Shape around a can of tuna. My aunt had argued against the can of tuna, but I'd felt a sign of mummification and preserved death would be auspicious. I was right.

"Presence of fish *en masse* indicates the deepest of our quintuple Great Lords," I said, squinting over notes hundreds of Blakes past had scrawled. "Continuous appearance over days . . . plague? Presence? What *is* that word? I hope it's both. We ought to be the generation who digitizes—I can reference better on my Kindle."

"A deep omen isn't *fun*, Hester," said Mar, violently rearranging her eggs. "A deep omen seven hundred feet above sea level is some horseshit. What have I always said?"

"Not to say anything to Child Protective Services," I said, "and that they faked the Moon landing."

"Hester, you—"

We recited her shibboleth in tandem: "*You don't outrun fate,*" and she looked settled, if dissatisfied.

The eggs weren't great. My aunt was a competent cook, if skewed for nicotine-blasted taste buds, but tonight everything was rubbery and overdone. I'd never known her so rattled, nor to cook eggs so terrible.

I said, "'Fun' was an unfair word."

"Don't get complacent, then," she said, "when you're a teenage seer who thinks she's slightly hotter shit than she is." I wasn't offended. It was just incorrect. "Sea-spawn's no joke. If we're getting deep omens here—well, that's *specific*, kid! Reappearance of the underdeep at noon, continuously, that's a herald. I wish you weren't here."

My stomach clenched, but I raised one eyebrow like I'd taught myself in the mirror. "Surely you don't think I should go home."

"It wouldn't be unwise—" Mar held up a finger to halt my protest "—but what's done is done is done. Something's coming. You won't escape it by taking a bus to your mom's."

"I would rather face inescapable lappets and watery torment than Mom's."

"Your mom didn't run off and become a dental hygienist to spite you."

I avoided this line of conversation, because seriously. "What about the omen?"

Mar pushed her plate away and kicked back, precariously balanced on two chair legs. "You saw it, you document it, that's the Blake way. Just . . . a deep omen at *sixteen*! Ah, well, what the Hell. See anything in your eggs?"

I re-peppered them and we peered at the rubbery curds. Mine clumped together in a brackish pool of hot sauce.

"Rain on Thursday," I said. "You?"

"Yankees lose the Series," said Aunt Mar, and went to tip her plate in the trash. "What a god-awful meal."

I found her that evening on the peeling balcony, smoking. A caul of cloud obscured the moon. The treetops were black and spiny. Our house was a fine, hideous artifact of the 1980s, decaying high on the side of the valley. Mar saw no point in fixing it up. She had been—her words—lucky enough to get her death foretokened when she was young, and lived life courting lung cancer like a boyfriend who'd never commit.

A heatherback candle spewed wax on the railing. "Mar," I said, "why are you so scared of our leviathan dreadlords, who lie lurking in the abyssal deeps? I mean, personally."

"Because seahorrors will go berserk getting what they want and they don't quit the field," she said. "Because I'm not seeing fifty, but *your* overwrought ass is making it to homecoming. Now get inside before you find another frigging omen in my smoke."

Despite my aunt's distress, I felt exhilarated. Back at boarding school I'd never witnessed so profound a portent. I'd seen everyday omens, had done since I was born, but the power of prophecy was boring and did not get you on Wikipedia. There was no anticipation. Duty removed ambition. I was apathetically lonely. I prepared only to record *The Blake Testimony of Hester in the Twenty-third Generation* for future Blakes.

Blake seers did not live long or decorated lives. Either you were mother of a seer, or a seer and never a mother and died young. I hadn't really cared, but I *had* expected more payout than social malingering and teenage ennui. It felt unfair. I was top of my class; I was pallidly pretty; thanks to my mother I had amazing teeth. I found myself wishing I'd see my death in my morning cornflakes like Mar; at least then the last, indifferent mystery would be revealed.

When *Stylephorus chordatus* started beaching themselves in public toilets, I should have taken Mar's cue. The house became unseasonably cold and at night our breath showed up as wet white puffs. I ignored the brooding swell of danger; instead, I sat at my desk doing my summer chemistry project, awash with weird pleasure. Clutching fistfuls of malformed octopodes at the creek was the first interesting thing that had ever happened to me.

The birch trees bordering our house wept salt water. I found a deer furtively licking the bark, looking like Bambi sneaking a hit. I sat on a stump to consult the Blake journals:

THE BLAKE TESTIMONY OF RUTH OF THE NINETEENTH GENERATION ON HER TWENTY-THIRD YEAR

WEEPING OF PLANTS:
Lamented should be greenstuff that seeps brack water or salt water or blood, for Nature is abhorring a lordly Visitor: if be but one plant then burn it or stop up a tree with a poultice of finely crushed talc, &c., to avoid notice. BRACK WATER is the sign of the MANY-THROATED MONSTER GOD & THOSE WHO SPEAK UNSPEAKABLE TONGUES. SALT WATER IS THE SIGN OF UNFED LEVIATHANS & THE PELAGIC WATCHERS & THE TENTACLE SO BLOOD MUST BE THE STAR OF THE MAKER OF THE HOLES FROM WHICH EVEN LIGHT SHALL NOT ESCAPE. Be comforted that the SHABBY MAN will not touch what is growing.

PLANT WEEPING, SINGLY:
The trail, movement & wondrous pilgrimage.

PLANTS WEEPING, THE MANY:
A Lord's bower has been made & it is for you to weep & rejoice. My account here as a Blake is perfect and accurate.

Underneath in ballpoint was written: *Has nobody noticed that Blake crypto-fascist worship of these deities has never helped?? Family of sheeple. Fuck the SYSTEM!* This was dated 1972.

A bird called, then stopped mid-warble. The shadows lengthened into long sharp shapes. A sense of stifling pressure grew. All around me, each tree wept salt without cease.

I said aloud: "Nice."

I hiked into town before evening. The bustling of people and the hurry of their daily chores made everything look almost normal; their heads were full of small-town everyday, work and food and family and maybe meth consumption, and this banality blurred the nagging fear. I stocked up on OJ and a sufficient supply of Cruncheroos.

Outside the sky was full of chubby black rainclouds, and the streetlights cast the road into sulfurous relief. I smelled salt again as it began to rain, and through my hoodie I could feel that the rain was warm as tea; I caught a drop on my tongue and spat it out again, as it tasted deep and foul. As it landed it left a whitish buildup I foolishly took for snow.

It was not snow. Crystals festooned themselves in long, stiff streamers from the traffic signals. Strands like webbing swung from street to pavement, wall to sidewalk. The streetlights struggled on and turned it green-white in the electric glare, dazzling to the eye. Main Street was spangled over from every parked car to the dollar store. My palms were sweaty.

From down the street a car honked dazedly. My sneakers were gummed up and it covered my hair and my shoulders and my bike tires. I scuffed it off in a hurry. People stood stock-still in doorways and sat in their cars, faces pale and transfixed. Their apprehension was mindless animal apprehension, and my hands were trembling so hard I dropped my Cruncheroos.

"What *is* it?" someone called out from the Rite Aid. And somebody else said, "It's salt."

Sudden screams. We all flinched. But it wasn't terror. At the center of a traffic island, haloed in the numinous light of the dollar store, a girl was crunching her Converse in the salt and spinning round and round. She had long shiny hair—a sort of chlorine gold—and a spray-on tan the color of Garfield. My school was populated with her clones. A bunch of huddling girls in haltertops watched her twirl with mild and terrified eyes.

"Isn't this amazing?" she whooped. "Isn't this frigging *awesome*?"

The rain stopped all at once, leaving a vast whiteness. All of Main Street looked bleached and shining; even the Pizza Hut sign was scrubbed clean and made fresh. From the Rite Aid I heard someone crying. The girl picked up a handful of powdery crystals and they fell through her fingers like jewels; then her beaming smile found me and I fled.

I collected the Blake books and lit a jittering circle of heatherback candles. I turned on every light in the house. I even stuck a Mickey Mouse nightlight into the wall socket, and he glowed there in dismal magnificence as I searched. It took me an hour to alight upon an old glued-in letter:

Reread the testimony of Elizabeth Blake in the fifteenth generation after I had word of this. I thought the account strange, so I went to see for myself. It was as Great-Aunt Annabelle had described, mold everywhere but almost beautiful, for it had bloomed in cunning patterns down the avenue all the way to the door. I couldn't look for too long as the looking gave me such a headache.

I called in a few days later and the mold was gone. Just one lady of the house and wasn't she pleased to see me as everyone else in the neighborhood felt too dreadful to call. She was to be the sacrifice as all signs said. Every spider in that house was spelling the presence and I got the feeling readily that it was one of the lesser diseased Ones, the taste in the milk, the dust. One of the Monster Lord's fever wizards had made his choice in her, no mistake. The girl was so sweet looking and so cheerful. They say the girls in these instances are always cheerful about it like lambs to the slaughter. The pestilences and their behemoth Duke may do as they will. I gave her till May.

Perhaps staying closer would have given me more detail but I felt that beyond my duty. I placed a wedding gift on the stoop and left that afternoon. I heard later he'd come for his bride Friday month and the whole place lit up dead with Spanish flu.

Aunt Annabelle always said that she'd heard some went a-cour

The page ripped here, leaving what Aunt Annabelle always said forever contentious. Mar found me in my circle of heatherbacks hours later, feverishly marking every reference to *bride* I could find.

"They closed Main Street to hose it down," she said. "There were cars backed up all the way to the Chinese takeout. There's mac 'n' cheese in the oven, and for your info I'm burning so much rosemary on the porch everyone will think I smoke pot."

"One of the pelagic kings has chosen a bride," I said.

"*What?*"

"Evidence: rain of salt at the gate, in this case 'gate' being Main Street. Evidence of rank: rain of salt in *mass* quantities from Main Street to, as you said, the Chinese takeout, in the middle of the day during a gibbous moon a *notable* distance from the ocean. The appearance of fish that don't know light. A dread bower of crystal."

My aunt didn't break down, or swear, or anything. She just said, "Sounds like an old-fashioned apocalypse event to me. What's your plan, champ?"

"Document it and testify," I said. "The Blake way. I'm going to find the bride."

"No," she said. "The Blake way is to watch the world burn from a distance and write down what the flames looked like. You need to see, not to find. This isn't a goddamned murder mystery."

I straightened and said *very* patiently: "Mar, this happens to be my birthright—"

"To Hell with *birthright*! Jesus, Hester, I told your mom you'd spend this summer getting your driver's license and kissing boys."

This was patently obnoxious. We ate our macaroni 'n' cheese surrounded by more dribbling heatherbacks, and my chest felt tight and tense the whole time. I kept on thinking of comebacks like, *I don't understand your insistence on meaningless bullshit, Mar,* or even a pointed *Margaret.* Did my heart really have to yearn for licenses and losing my French-kissing virginity at the parking lot? Did anything matter, apart from the salt and the night outside, the bulging eyes down at Jamison Pond?

"Your problem is," she said, which was always a shitty way to begin a sentence, "that you don't know what *bored* is."

"Wrong. I am often exquisitely bored."

"Unholy matrimonies are boring," said my aunt. "Plagues of salt? Boring. The realization that none of us can run—that we're all here to be used and abused by forces we can't even fight—that's so *boring*, kid!" She'd used sharp cheddar in the mac 'n' cheese and it was my favorite, but I didn't want to do anything other than push it around the plate. "If you get your license you can drive out to Denny's."

"I am not interested," I said, "in fucking *Denny's.*"

"I wanted you to make some friends and be a teenager and not to get in over your head," she said, and speared some macaroni savagely. "And I want you to do the dishes, so I figure I'll get one out of four. Don't go sneaking out tonight, you'll break the rosemary ward."

I pushed away my half-eaten food, and kept myself very tight and quiet as I scraped pans and stacked the dishwasher.

"And take some Band-Aids up to your room," said Mar.

"Why?"

"You're going to split your knee. You don't outrun fate, champ."

Standing in the doorway, I tried to think up a stinging riposte. I said, "Wait and see," and took each step upstairs as cautiously as I could. I felt a spiteful sense of triumph when I made it to the top without incident. Once I was in my room and yanking off my hoodie I tripped and split my knee open on the dresser drawer. I then lay in bed alternately bleeding and seething for hours. I did not touch the Band-Aids, which in any case were decorated with SpongeBob's image.

Outside, the mountains had forgotten summer. The stars gave a curious, chill light. I knew I shouldn't have been looking too closely, but despite the shudder in my fingertips and the pain in my knee I did anyway; the tops of the trees made grotesque shapes. I tried to read the stars, but the position of Mars gave the same message each time: *doom*, and *approach*, and *altar*.

One star trembled in the sky and fell. I felt horrified. I felt ecstatic. I eased open my squeaking window and squeezed out onto the windowsill, shimmying down the drainpipe. I spat to ameliorate the breaking of the rosemary ward, flipped Mar the bird, and went to find the bride.

The town was subdued by the night. Puddles of soapy water from the laundromat were filled with sprats. The star had fallen over by the eastern suburbs, and I pulled my hoodie up as I passed the hard glare of the gas station. It was as though even the houses were withering, dying of fright like prey. I bought a Coke from the dollar machine.

I sipped my Coke and let my feet wander up street and down street, along alley and through park. There was no fear. A Blake knows better. I took to the woods behind people's houses, meandering until I found speared on one of the young birches a dead shark.

It was huge and hideous with a malformed head, pinned with its belly facing whitely upwards and its maw hanging open. The tree groaned beneath its weight. It was dotted all over with an array of fins and didn't look like any shark I'd ever seen at an aquarium. It was bracketed by a sagging inflatable pool and an abandoned Tonka truck in someone's backyard. The security lights came on and haloed the shark in all its dead majesty: oozing mouth, long slimy body, bony snout.

One of the windows rattled up from the house. "Hey!" someone called. "It's you."

It was the girl with shiny hair, the one who'd danced like an excited puppy in the rain of salt. She was still wearing a surfeit of glittery eye shadow. I gestured to the shark. "Yeah, I know," she said. "It's been there all afternoon. Gross, right?"

"Doesn't this strike you as suspicious?" I said. "Are you not even slightly weirded out?"

"Have you ever seen *Punk'd*?" She did not give me time to reply. "I got told it could be *Punk'd*, and then I couldn't find *Punk'd* on television so I had to watch it on the YouTubes. I like *Punk'd*. People are so funny when they get punk'd. Did you know you dropped your cereal? I have it right here, but I ate some."

"I wasn't aware of a finder's tax on breakfast cereal," I said.

The girl laughed, the way some people did when they had no idea of the joke. "I've seen you over at Jamison Pond," she said, which surprised me. "By yourself. What's your name?"

"Why name myself for free?"

She laughed again, but this time more appreciatively and less like a studio audience. "What if I gave you my name first?"

"You'd be stupid."

The girl leaned out the window, hair shimmering over her One Direction T-shirt. The sky cast weird shadows on her house and the shark smelled fetid in the background. "People call me Rainbow. Rainbow Kipley."

Dear *God,* I thought. "On purpose?"

"C'mon, we had a deal for your name—"

"We never made a deal," I said, but relented. "People call me Hester. Hester Blake."

"Hester," she said, rolling it around in her mouth like candy. Then she repeated, "Hester," and laughed raucously. I must have looked pissed-off, because she laughed again and said, "Sorry! It's just a really dumb name," which I found rich coming from someone designated *Rainbow.*

I felt I'd got what I came for. She must have sensed that the conversation had reached a premature end because she announced, "We should hang out."

"In your backyard? Next to a dead shark? At midnight?"

"There are jellyfish in my bathtub," said Rainbow, which both surprised me and didn't, and also struck me as a unique tactic. But then she added, quite normally, "You're interested in this. Nobody else is. They're pissing themselves, and I'm not—and here you are—so . . . "

Limned by the security lamp, Rainbow disappeared and reappeared before waving an open packet of Cruncheroos. "You could have your cereal back."

Huh. I had never been asked to *hang out* before. Certainly not by girls who looked as though they used leave-in conditioner. I had been using Johnson & Johnson's No More Tears since childhood as it kept its promises. I was distrustful; I had never been popular. At school my greatest leap had been from *weirdo* to *perceived goth.* Girls abhorred oddity, but quantifiable gothness they could accept. Some had even warmly talked to me of

Nightwish albums. I dyed my hair black to complete the effect and was nevermore bullied.

I feared no contempt of Rainbow Kipley's. I feared wasting my time. But the lure was too great. "I'll come back tomorrow," I said, "to see if the shark's gone. You can keep the cereal as collateral."

"Cool," she said, like she understood *collateral*, and smiled with very white teeth. "Cool, cool."

Driver's licenses and kissing boys could wait indefinitely, for preference. My heart sang all the way home, for you see: I'd discovered the bride.

The next day I found myself back at Rainbow's shabby suburban house. We both took the time to admire her abandoned shark by the light of day, and I compared it to pictures on my iPhone and confirmed it as *Mitsukurina owstoni*: goblin shark. I noted dead grass in a broad brown ring around the tree, the star-spoked webs left empty by their spiders, each a proclamation *a monster dwells*. Somehow we ended up going to the park and Rainbow jiggled her jelly bracelets the whole way.

I bought a newspaper and pored over local news: the headline read GLOBAL WARMING OR GLOBAL WARNING? It queried alkaline content in the rain, or something, then advertised that no fewer than one scientist was fascinated with what had happened on Main Street. "Scientists," said my companion, like a slur, and she laughed gutturally.

"Science has its place," I said and rolled up the newspaper. "Just not at present. Science does not cause salt blizzards or impalement of bathydemersal fish."

"You think this is cool, don't you?" she said slyly. "You're on it like a bonnet."

There was an unseemly curiosity to her, as though the town huddling in on itself waiting to die was like a celebrity scandal. Was this the way I'd been acting? "No," I lied, "and nobody under sixty says *on it like a bonnet.*"

"Shut up! You know what I mean—"

"Think of me as a reporter. Someone who's going to watch what happens. I already know what's going on, I just want a closer look."

Her eyes were wide and very dark. When she leaned in she smelled like Speed Stick. "How do you know?"

There was no particular family jurisprudence about telling. *Don't* appeared to be the rule of thumb as Blakes knew that, Cassandra-like, they defied belief. For me it was simply that nobody had ever asked. "I can read the future, and what I read always comes true," I said.

"Oh my *God*. Show me."

I decided to exhibit myself in what paltry way a Blake can. I looked at the sun. I looked at the scudding clouds. I looked at an oily stain on our park bench, and the way the thin young stalks of plants were huddled in the ground. I looked at the shadows people made as they hurried, and at how many sparrows rose startled from the water fountain.

"The old man in the hat is going to burn down his house on Saturday," I said. "That jogger will drop her Gatorade in the next five minutes. The police will catch up with that red-jacket man in the first week of October." I gathered some saliva and, with no great ceremony, hocked it out on the grass. I examined the result. "They'll unearth a gigantic ruin in . . . southwestern Australia. In the sand plains. Seven archaeologists. In the winter sometime. Forgive my inexactitude, my mouth wasn't very wet."

Rainbow's mouth was a round *O*. In front of us the jogger dropped her Gatorade, and it splattered on the ground in a shower of blue. I said, "You won't find out if the rest is true for months yet. And you could put it down to coincidences. But you'd be wrong."

"You're a *gypsy*," she accused.

I had expected "liar," and "nutjob," but not "gypsy." "No, and by the way, that's racist. If you'd like to know *our* future, then very soon—I don't know when—a great evil will make itself known in this town, claim a mortal, and lay waste to us all in celebration. I will record all that happens for my descendants and their descendants, and as is the agreement between my bloodline and the unknown, I'll be spared."

I expected her to get up and leave, or laugh again. She said: "Is there anything I can do?"

For the first time I pitied this pretty girl with her bright hair and her Chucks, her long-limbed soda-colored legs, her ingenuous smile. She would be taken to a place in the deep, dark below where lay unnamed monstrosity, where the devouring hunger lurked far beyond light and there was no Katy Perry. "It's not for you to do anything but cower in his abyssal wake," I said, "though you don't look into cowering."

"No, I mean—can I help *you* out?" she repeated, like I was a stupid child. "I've run out of *Punk'd* episodes on my machine, I don't have anyone here, and I go home July anyway."

"What about those other girls?"

"What, them?" Rainbow flapped a dismissive hand. "Who cares? You're the one I want to like me."

Thankfully, whatever spluttering gaucherie I might have made in reply was interrupted by a scream. Jets of sticky arterial blood were spurting out of the water fountain, and tentacles waved delicately from the drain. Tiny octopus creatures emerged in the gouts of blood flooding down the sides and the air stalled around us like it was having a heart attack.

It took me forever to approach the fountain, wreathed with frondy little tentacle things. It buckled as though beneath a tremendous weight. I thrust my hands into the blood and screamed: it was ice-cold, and my teeth chattered. With a splatter of red I tore my hands away and they steamed in the air.

In the blood on my palms I saw the future. I read the position of the dead moon that no longer orbited Earth. I saw the blessing of the tyrant who hid in a far-off swirl of stars. I thought I could forecast to midsummer, and when I closed my eyes I saw people drown. Everyone else in the park had fled.

I whipped out my notebook, though my fingers smeared the pages and were so cold I could hardly hold the pen, but this was Blake duty. It took me three abortive starts to write in English.

"You done?" said Rainbow, squatting next to me. I hadn't realized I was muttering aloud, and she flicked a clot of blood off my collar. "Let's go get McNuggets."

"Miss Kipley," I said, and my tongue did not speak the music of mortal tongues, "you are a fucking lunatic."

We left the fountain gurgling like a wound and did not look back. Then we got McNuggets.

I had never met anyone like Rainbow before. I didn't think anybody else had, either. She was interested in all the things I wasn't—Sephora hauls, *New Girl*, Nicki Minaj—but had a strangely magnetic way of not giving a damn, and not in the normal fashion of beautiful girls. She just appeared to have no idea that the general populace did anything but clog up her scenery. There was something in her that set her apart—an absence of being like other people—and in a weak moment I compared her to myself.

We spent the rest of the day eating McNuggets and wandering around town and looking at things. I recorded the appearance of naked fish bones dangling from the telephone wires. She wanted to prod everything with the toe of her sneaker. And she talked.

"Favorite color," she demanded.

I was peering at anemone-pocked boulders behind the gas station. "Black."

"Favorite subject," she said later, licking dubious McNugget oils off her fingers as we examined flayed fish in a clearing.

"Physics and literature."

"Ideal celebrity boyfriend?"

"Did you get this out of *Cosmo*? Pass."

She asked incessantly what my teachers were like; were the girls at my school lame; what my thoughts were on Ebola, *CSI*, and Lonely Island. When we had exhausted the town's supply of dried-up sponges arranged in unknowable names, we ended up hanging out in the movie theater lobby. We watched previews. Neither of us had seen any of the movies advertised, and neither of us wanted to see them, either.

I found myself telling her about Mar, and even alluded to my mother. When I asked her the same, she just said offhandedly, "Four plus me." Considering my own filial reticence, I didn't press.

When evening fell, she said, *See you tomorrow*, as a foregone conclusion. *Like ten-ish, breakfast takes forever.*

I went home not knowing what to think. She had a bunny manicure. She laughed at everything. She'd stolen orange soda from the movie theater drinks machine, even if everyone stole orange soda from the movie theater drinks machine. She had an unseemly interest in mummy movies. But what irritated me most was that I found her liking *me* compelling, that she appeared to have never met anyone like Hester Blake.

Her interest in me was most likely boredom, which was fine, because my interest in her was that she was the bride. That night I thought about what I'd end up writing: *the despot of the Breathless Depths took a local girl to wife, one with a bedazzled Samsung.* I sniggered alone, and slept uneasy.

In the days to come, doom throttled the brittle, increasingly desiccated town, and I catalogued it as my companion caught me up on the plot of every soap opera she'd ever watched. She appeared to have abandoned most of them midway, furnishing unfinished tales of many a shock pregnancy. Mar had been sarcastic ever since I'd broken her rosemary ward so I spent as much time out of the house as possible; that was the main reason I hung around Rainbow.

I didn't want to like her because her doom was upon us all, and I didn't want to like her because she was like other girls, and I wasn't. And I didn't want to like her because she always knew when I'd made a joke. I was so *angry,* and I didn't know why.

We went to the woods and consolidated my notes. I laid my research flat on the grass or propped it on a bough, and Rainbow played music noisily on her Samsung. We rolled up our jeans—or I did, as she had no shorts that went past mid-thigh—and half-assedly sunbathed. It felt like the hours were days and the days endless.

She wanted to know what I thought would happen when we all got "laid waste to." For a moment I was terribly afraid I'd feel guilty.

"I don't know." The forest floor smelled cold, somehow. "I've never seen waste laid *en masse*. The Drownlord will make his presence known. People will go mad. People will die."

Rainbow rolled over toward me, bits of twig caught in her hair. Today she had done her eyeliner in two thick, overdramatic rings, like a sleep-deprived panda. "Do you ever wonder what dying's like, dude?"

I thought about Mar and never seeing fifty. "No," I said. "My family dies young. I figure anticipating it is unnecessary."

"Maybe you're going to die when the end of this hits," she said thoughtfully. "We could die tragically together. How's that shake you?"

I said, "My family has a pact with the All-Devouring so we don't get killed carelessly in their affairs. You're dying alone, Kipley."

She didn't get upset. She tangled her arms in the undergrowth and stretched her legs out, skinny hips arched, and wriggled pleasurably in the thin and unaffectionate sunlight. "I hope you'll be super sad," she said. "I hope you'll cry for a year."

"Aren't you scared to die?"

"Never been scared."

I said, "Due to your brain damage," and Rainbow laughed uproariously. Then she found a dried-up jellyfish amid the leaves and dropped it down my shirt.

That night I thought again about what I'd have to write: *the many-limbed horror who lies beneath the waves stole a local girl to wife, and she wore the world's skankiest short-shorts and laughed at my jokes.* I slept, but there were nightmares.

Sometimes the coming rain was nothing but a fine mist that hurt to breathe, but sometimes it was like shrapnel. The sun shone hot and choked the air with a stench of damp concrete. I carried an umbrella and Rainbow wore black rain boots that squeaked.

Mar ladled out tortilla soup one night as a peace offering. We ate companionably, with the radio on. There were no stories about salt rain or plagues of fish even on the local news. I'd been taught better than to expect it. Fear rendered us rigidly silent, and anyone who went against instinct ended up in a straitjacket.

"Why is our personal philosophy that fate always wins?" I said.

My aunt didn't miss a beat. "Self-preservation," she said. "You don't last long in our line of work fighting facts. Christ, you don't last long in our line of work, period. Hey—Ted at the gas station said he'd seen you going around with some girl."

"Ted at the gas station is a grudge informer," I said. "Back on subject. Has nobody tried to use the Blake sight to effect change?"

"They would've been a moron branch of the family, because like I've said a million times: it doesn't work that way." Mar swirled a spoon around her bowl. "Not trying to make it a federal issue, kid, just saying I'm happy you're making friends instead of swishing around listening to The Cure."

"Mar, I have never listened to The Cure."

"You find that bride?"

Taken aback, I nodded. Mar cocked her dark head in thought. There were sprigs of grey at each temple, and not for the first time I was melancholy, clogged up with an inscrutable grief. But all she said was, "Okay. There were octopuses in the goddamned laundry again. When this is over, you'll learn what *picking up the pieces looks like*. Lemon pie in the icebox."

It was *octopodes*, but never mind. I cleared the dishes. Afterward we ate two large wedges of lemon pie apiece. The house was comfortably quiet and the sideboard candles bravely chewed on the dark.

"Mar," I said, "what *would* happen if someone were to cross the deepwater demons who have slavery of wave and underwave? Hypothetically."

"No Blake has ever been stupid or saintly enough to try and find out," said Mar. "Not qualities you're suited to, Hester."

I wondered if this was meant to sting, because it didn't. I felt no pain. "Your next question's going to be, *How do we let other people die?*" she said and pulled her evening cigarette from the packet. "Because I'm me, I'll understand you want a coping mechanism, not a Sunday School lecture. My advice to you is: It becomes easier the less you get involved. And Hester—"

I looked at her with perfect nonchalance.

"I'm not outrunning *my* fate," said Aunt Mar. She lit the cigarette at the table. "Don't try to outrun other people's. You don't have the right. You're a Blake, not God."

"I didn't *choose* to be a Blake," I snapped, and dropped the pie plate on the sideboard before storming from the room. I took each stair as noisily as possible, but not noisily enough to drown out her holler: "If you *ever* get a choice in this life, kiddo, treasure it!"

Rainbow noticed my foul mood. She did not tell me to cheer up or ask me what the matter was, thankfully. She wasn't that type of girl. Fog boiled low in the valley and the townspeople stumbled through the streets and talked about atmospheric pressure. Stores closed. Buses came late. Someone from the northeast suburbs had given in and shot himself.

I felt numb and untouched, and worse—when chill winds wrapped around my neck and let me breathe clear air, smelling like the beach and things that grow on the beach—I was happy. I nipped this in its emotional bud. Rainbow, of course, was as cheerful and unaffected as a stump.

Midsummer boiled closer and I thought about telling her. I would say outright, *Miss Kipley.* ("Rainbow" had never left my lips, the correct method with anyone who was *je m'appelle* Rainbow.) *When the ocean lurker comes to take his victim, his victim will be you. Do whatever you wish with this information.* Perhaps she'd finally scream. Or plead. Anything.

But when I got my courage up, she leaned in close and combed her fingers through my hair, right down to the undyed roots. Her hands were very delicate, and I clammed up. My sullen silence was no barrier to Rainbow. She just cranked up Taylor Swift.

We were sitting in a greasy bus shelter opposite Walmart when the man committed suicide. There was no showboating hesitation in the way he appeared on the roof, then stepped off at thirty feet. He landed on the spines of a wrought-iron fence. The sound was like a cocktail weenie going through a hole punch.

There was nobody around but us. I froze and did not look away. Next to me, Rainbow was equally transfixed. I felt terrible shame when she was the one to drag us over to him. She already had her phone out. I had seen corpses before, but this was very fresh. There was a terrible amount of blood. He was irreparably dead. I turned my head to inform Rainbow, in case she tried to help him or something equally demented, and then I saw she was taking his picture.

"Got your notebook?" she said.

There was no fear in her. No concern. Rainbow reached out to prod at one mangled, outflung leg. Two spots of color bloomed high on her cheeks; she was luminously pleased.

"What the fuck is *wrong with you*?" My voice sounded embarrassingly shrill. "This man just killed himself!"

"The fence helped," said Rainbow helplessly.

"You think this is a *joke*—what *reason* could you have for thinking this is okay—"

"Excuse you, we look at dead shit all the time. I thought we'd hit jackpot, we've never found a dead guy. . . . "

Her distress was sulky and real. I took her by the shoulders of her stupid cropped jacket and gripped tight, fear a tinder to my misery. The rain whipped around us and stung my face. "Christ, you think this is some kind of game, or . . . or a YouTube stunt! You really can't imagine—you have no *comprehension*—you mindless *jackass*—"

She was trying to calm me, feebly patting my hands. "Stop being mad at me, it sucks! What gives, Hester—"

"*You're* the bride, Kipley. It's coming for *you*."

Rainbow stepped out of my shaking, febrile grip. For a moment her lips pressed very tightly together and I wondered if she would cry. Then her mouth quirked into an uncomprehending, furtive little smile.

"*Me*," she repeated.

"Yes."

"You really think it's *me*?"

"You *know* I know. You don't outrun fate, Rainbow."

"Why are you telling me now?" Something in her bewilderment cooled, and I was sensible of the fact we were having an argument next to a suicide. "Hey—have you been hanging with me all this time because of *that*?"

"How does that matter? Look: This is the beginning of the end of you. Why don't you want to be saved, or to run away, or something? It doesn't *matter.*"

"It matters," said Rainbow, with infinite dignity, "to me. You know what I think?"

She did not wait to hear what I imagined she thought, which was wise. She hopped away from the dead man and held her palms up to the rain. The air was thick with an electrifying chill: a breathless enormity. We were so close now. Color leached from the Walmart, from the concrete, from the green in the trees and the red of the stop sign. Raindrops sat in her pale hair like pearls.

"I think this is the coolest thing that ever happened to this stupid backwater place," she said. "This is awesome. And I think you agree but won't admit it."

"This place is literally Hell."

"Suits you," said Rainbow.

I was beside myself with pain. My fingernails tilled up the flesh of my palms. "I understand now why you got picked as the bride," I said. "You're a sociopath. I am not like you, Miss Kipley, and if I forgot that over the last few weeks I was wrong. Excuse me, I'm going to get a police officer."

When I turned on my heel and left her—standing next to a victim of powers we could not understand or fight, and whose coming I was forced to watch like a reality TV program where my vote would never count—the blood was pooling in watery pink puddles around her rain boots. Rainbow didn't follow.

Mar had grilled steaks for dinner that neither of us ate. By the time I'd finished bagging and stuffing them mechanically in the fridge, she'd finished her preparations. The dining room floor was a sea of reeking heatherbacks. There was even a host of them jarred and flickering out on the porch. The front doors were locked and the windows haloed with duct tape. At the center sat my aunt in an overstuffed armchair, cigarette lit, hair undone, a bucket of dirt by her feet. The storm clamored outside.

I crouched next to the kitchen door and laced up my boots. I had my back to her, but she said, "You've been crying."

My jacket wouldn't button. I was all thumbs. "More tears will come yet."

"Jesus, Hester. You sound like a fortune cookie."

I realized with a start that she'd been drinking. The dirt in the bucket would be Blake family grave dirt; we kept it in a Hefty sack in the attic.

"Did you know," she said conversationally, "that I was there when you were born?" (Yes, as I'd heard this story approximately nine million times.) "Nana put you in my arms first. You screamed like I was killing you."

My grief was too acute for me to not be a dick.

"Is this where you tell me about the omen you saw the night of my birth? A grisly fate? The destruction of Troy?"

"First of all, you know damn well you were born in the morning—your mom made me go get her a McGriddle," said Mar. "Second, I never saw a thing." The rain came down on the roof like buckshot. "Not one mortal thing," she repeated. "And that's killed me my whole life, loving you . . . not knowing."

I fled into the downpour. The town was alien. Each doorway was a cold black portal and curtains twitched in abandoned rooms. Sometimes the sidewalk felt squishy underfoot. It was bad when the streets were empty as bones in an ossuary, but worse when I heard a crowd around the corner from the 7-Eleven. I crouched behind a garbage can as misshapen strangers passed and threw up a little, retching water. When there was only awful silence, I bolted for my life through the woods.

The goblin shark in Rainbow's backyard had peeled open, the muscle and fascia now on display. It looked oddly and shamefully naked; but it did not invoke the puke-inducing fear of the people on the street. There was nothing in that shark but dead shark.

I'd arranged to be picked last for every softball team in my life, but adrenaline let me heave a rock through Rainbow's window. Glass tinkled musically. Her lights came on and she threw the window open; the rest of the pane fell into glitter on the lawn. "Holy shit, Hester!" she said in alarm.

"Miss Kipley, I'd like to save you," I said. "This is on the understanding that I still think you're absolutely fucking crazy, but I should've tried to save you from the start. If you get dressed, I know where Ted at the gas station keeps the keys to his truck, and I don't have my learner's permit, but we'll make it to Denny's by midnight."

Rainbow put her head in her hands. Her hair fell over her face like a veil, and when she smiled there was a regretful dimple. "Dude," she said softly, "I thought when you saw the future, you couldn't outrun it."

"If we cannot outrun it, then I'll drive."

"You badass," she said, and before I could retort she leaned out past the windowsill. She made a soft white blotch in the darkness.

"I think you're the coolest person I've ever met," said Rainbow. "I think you're really funny, and you're interesting, and your fingernails are all different lengths. You're not like other girls. And you only think things are worthwhile if they've been proved ten times by a book, and I like how you hate not coming first."

"Listen," I said. My throat felt tight and fussy and rain was leaking into my hood. "The drowned lord who dwells in dark water will claim you. The moon won't rise tonight, and you'll never update your Tumblr again."

"And how you care about everything! You care *super* hard. And you talk like a dork. I think you're disgusting. I think you're super cute. Is that weird? No homo? If I put *no homo* there, that means I can say things and pretend I don't mean them?"

"Rainbow," I said, "don't make fun of me."

"Why is it so bad for me to be the bride, anyway?" she said, petulant now.

"What's *wrong* with it? If it's meant to happen, it's meant to happen, right? Cool. Why aren't you okay with it?"

There was no lightning or thunder in that storm. There were monstrous shadows, shiny on the matt black of night, and I thought I heard things flop around in the woods. "Because I don't want you to die."

Her smile was lovely and there was no fear in it. Rainbow didn't know how to be afraid. In her was a curious exultation and I could see it, it was in her mouth and eyes and hair. The heedless ecstasy of the bride. "Die? Is that what happens?"

My stomach churned. "If you change your mind, come to West North Street," I said. "The house standing alone at the top of the road. Go to the graveyard at the corner of Main and Spinney and take a handful of dirt off any child's grave, then come to me. Otherwise, this is good-bye."

I turned. Something sang through the air and landed next to me, soggy and forlorn. My packet of Cruncheroos. When I turned back, Rainbow was wide-eyed and her face was uncharacteristically puckered, and we must have mirrored each other in our upset. I felt like we were on the brink of something as great as it was awful, something I'd snuck around all summer like a thief.

"You're a prize dumbass trying to save me from myself, Hester Blake."

I said, "You're the only one I wanted to like me."

My hands shook as I hiked home. There were blasphemous, slippery things in each clearing that endless night. I knew what would happen if they were to approach. The rain grew oily and warm as blood was oily and warm, and I alternately wept and laughed, and none of them even touched me.

My aunt had fallen asleep amid the candles like some untidy Renaissance saint. She lay there with her shoes still on and her cigarette half-smoked, and I left my clothes in a sopping heap on the laundry floor to take her flannel pj's out of the dryer. Their sleeves came over my fingertips. I wouldn't write down Rainbow in the Blake book, I thought. I would not trap her in the pages. Nobody would ever know her but me. I'd outrun fate, and blaspheme Blake duty.

I fell asleep tucked up next to Mar.

In the morning I woke to the smell of toaster waffles. Mar's coat was draped over my legs. First of July: The Deepwater God was here. I rolled up my pajama pants and tiptoed through molten drips of candlewax to claim my waffle. My aunt wordlessly squirted them with syrup faces and we stood on the porch to eat.

The morning was crisp and grey and pretty. Salt drifted from the clouds and clumped in the grass. The wind discomfited the trees. Not a bird sang. Beneath us, the town was laid out like a spill: flooded right up to the gas station, and the western suburbs drowned entirely. Where the dark, unreflective waters had not risen, you could see movement in the streets, but it was not human movement. And there roared a great revel near the Walmart.

There was thrashing in the water and a roiling mass in the streets. A tentacle rose from the depths by the high school, big enough to see each sucker, and it brushed open a building with no effort. Another tentacle joined it, then another, until the town center was alive with coiling lappets and feelers. I was surprised by their jungle sheen of oranges and purples and tropical blues. I had expected somber greens and funeral greys. Teeth broke from the water. Tall, harlequin-striped fronds lifted, questing and transparent in the sun. My chest felt very full, and I stayed to look when Mar turned and went inside. I watched like I could never watch enough.

The water lapped gently at the bottom of our driveway. I wanted my waffle to be ash on my tongue, but I was frantically hungry and it was delicious. I was chomping avidly, flannels rolled to my knees, when a figure emerged at the end of the drive. It had wet short-shorts and perfectly hairsprayed hair.

"Hi," said Rainbow bashfully.

My heart sang, unbidden.

"*God*, Kipley! Come here, get *inside*—"

"I kind've don't want to, dude," she said. "No offense."

I didn't understand when she made an exaggerated *oops!* shrug. I followed her gesture to the porch candles with idiot fixation. Behind Rainbow, brightly colored appendages writhed in the water of her wedding day.

"Hester," she said, "you don't have to run. You'll never die or be alone, neither of us will; not even the light will have permission to touch you. I'll bring you down into the water and the water under that, where the spires of my palace fill the lost mortal country, and you will be made even more beautiful and funny and splendiferous than you are now."

The candles cringed from her damp Chucks. When she approached, half of them exploded in a chrysanthemum blast of wax. Leviathans crunched up people busily by the RiteAid. Algal bloom strangled the telephone lines. My aunt returned to the porch and promptly dropped her coffee mug, which shattered into a perfect Unforgivable Shape.

"I've come for my bride," said Rainbow, the abyssal king. "Yo, Hester. Marry me."

• • •

This is the Blake testimony of Hester, twenty-third generation in her sixteenth year.

In the time of our crawling Night Lord's ascendancy, foretold by exodus of starlight into his sucking astral wounds, the God of the drowned country came ashore. The many-limbed horror of the depths chose to take a local girl to wife. Main Street was made over into salt bower. Water-creatures adorned it as jewels do. Mortals gave themselves for wedding feast and the Walmart utterly destroyed. The Deepwater Lord returned triumphant to the tentacle throne and will dwell there, in splendor, forever.

My account here as a Blake is perfect and accurate, because when the leviathan prince went, I went with her.

Tamsyn Muir is from New Zealand, but also spends time in Oxford, England. A graduate of the Clarion Writers' Workshop, her fiction has appeared in *Fantasy, Weird Tales, Nightmare,* The *Magazine of Fantasy & Science Fiction, Clarkesworld,* and a couple of other "year's best" volumes. Her work has been nominated for the Shirley Jackson and Nebula Awards.

Then I saw it, a long tank along the back wall. The snake was magnificent, from the pale skin on her belly to the brown scales on her back.

FABULOUS BEASTS

Priya Sharma

"Eliza, tell me your secret."

Sometimes I'm cornered at parties by someone who's been watching me from across the room as they drain their glass. They think I don't know what's been said about me.

Eliza's odd looking but she has something, don't you think? Une jolie laide. A French term meaning ugly-beautiful. Only the intelligentsia can insult you with panache.

I always know when they're about to come over. It's in the pause before they walk, as though they're ordering their thoughts. Then they stride over, purposeful, through the throng of actors, journalists, and politicians, ignoring anyone who tries to engage them for fear of losing their nerve.

"Eliza, tell me your secret."

"I'm a princess."

Such a ridiculous thing to say and I surprise myself by using Kenny's term for us, even though I am now forty-something and Kenny was twenty-four years ago. I edge past, scanning the crowd for Georgia, so I can tell her that I've had enough and am going home. Maybe she'll come with me.

My interrogator doesn't look convinced. Nor should they be. I'm not even called Eliza. My real name is Lola and I'm no princess. I'm a monster.

We, Kenny's princesses, lived in a tower.

Kath, my mum, had a flat on the thirteenth floor of Laird Tower, in a northern town long past its prime. Two hundred and seventeen miles from London and twenty-four years ago. A whole world away, or it might as well be.

Ami, Kath's younger sister, lived two floors down. Kath and I went round to see her the day that she came home from the hospital. She answered the door wearing a black velour tracksuit, the bottoms slung low on her hips. The top rose up to reveal the wrinkled skin that had been taut over her baby bump the day before.

"Hiya," she opened the door wide to let us in.

Ami only spoke to Kath, never to me. She had a way of ignoring people that fascinated men and infuriated women.

Kath and I leaned over the Moses basket.

"What a diamond," Kath cooed.

She was right. Some new babies are wizened, but not Tallulah. She looked like something from the front of one of Kath's knitting patterns. Perfect. I knew, even at that age, that I didn't look like everyone else; flat nose with too much nostril exposed, small eyelids and small ears that were squashed against my skull. I felt a pang of jealousy.

"What's her name, Ami?"

"Tallulah Rose." Ami laid her head on Kath's shoulder. "I wish you'd been there."

"I wanted to be there too. I'm sorry, darling. There was nobody to mind Lola. And Mikey was with you." Kath must have been genuinely sorry because normally she said Mikey's name like she was sniffing sour milk. "Where is he now?"

"Out, wetting the baby's head."

Kath's expression suggested that she thought he was doing more than toasting his newborn. He was always hanging around Ami. *Just looking after you, like Kenny wants*, he'd say, as if he was only doing his duty. Except now that there were shitty nappies to change and formula milk to prepare he was off, getting his end away.

Ami wasn't quite ready to let Kath's absence go.

"You could've left Lola with one of my friends."

Ami knew better. Kath never let anyone look after me, not even her.

"Let's not fight now, pet. You're tired."

Ami's gaze was like being doused in ice water. It contained everything she couldn't say to me. *Fucking ugly, little runt. You're always in the way.*

"You must be starvin'. Let me get you a cuppa and a sandwich and then you can get some sleep."

We stood and looked at the baby when Ami had gone to bed.

"Don't get any ideas. You don't want to be like your aunt, with a baby at sixteen. You don't want to be like either of us."

Kathy always spoke to me like I was twenty-four, not four.

Tallulah stirred and stretched, arms jerking outwards as if she was in freefall. She opened her eyes. There was no squinting or screaming.

"The little scrap's going to need our help."

Kath lifted her out and laid her on her knee for inspection. I put my nose against the soft spot on her skull. I fell in love with her right then.

"What do you wish for her?" Kath asked, smiling.

Chocolate. Barbies. A bike. A pet snake. Everything my childish heart could bestow.

Saturdays were for shopping. Kathy and I walked down Cathcart Street towards town. We'd pass a row of grimy Victorian mansions on our way that served as a reminder of once great wealth, now carved up into flats for social housing or filled with squatters who lay in their damp dens with needles in their arms.

After these were the terraces, joined by a network of alleyways that made for easy assaults and getaways. This model of housing was for the civic minded when everyone here had a trade, due to our proximity to the city of Liverpool. The ship-building yards lay empty, and the 1980s brought container ships that did away with the demand for dockers. The life inside spilled out into the sun; women sat on their steps in pajama bottoms and vest tops, even though it was lunchtime. Fags in hand, they'd whisper to one another as Kathy passed, afraid to meet her gaze. A man wore just shorts, his pale beer belly pinking up in the sun. He saluted when he saw Kathy. She ignored him.

I followed Kathy, her trolley wheels squeaking. The sound got worse as it was filled with vegetables, cheap meat shrink wrapped on Styrofoam trays, and bags of broken biscuits.

Kathy stopped to talk to a woman with rotten, tea-stained teeth. I was bored. We were at the outskirts of town, where the shops were most shabby. House clearance stores and a refurbished washing machine outlet. I wandered along the pavement a way until something stopped me. The peeling sign over the shop window read RICKY'S REPTILES. The display was full of tanks. Most were empty, but the one at the front contained a pile of terrapins struggling to climb over one another in a dish of water.

The shop door was open, revealing the lino floor that curled up at the corners. It was a shade of blue that verged on grey, or maybe it was just dirty. I could see the lights from the tanks. The fish were darting flashes of wild color or else they drifted on gossamer fins. I was drawn in. The man behind the counter looked up and smiled, but to his credit he didn't try and talk to me, otherwise I would've run.

Then I saw it, a long tank along the back wall. I went closer. The snake was magnificent, from the pale skin on her belly to the brown scales on her back.

She slithered closer, eyeing me and then raised her head and the front third of her body lifted up as if suspended on invisible thread. I put my forehead against the glass.

"She likes you," the man murmured.

She moved up the side of the tank. I realized that I was swaying in time with her, feeling unity in the motion. I was aware of her body, each muscle moving beneath her skin, her very skeleton. I looked into the snake's black eyes and could see out of them into my own. The world was on the tip of her forked tongue; my curiosity, the shopkeeper's sweat and kindness, the soft flavor of the mice in the tank behind the counter.

A hand gripped my shoulder, hard, jerking me back to myself. It was Kathy.

"Get away from that thing." Her fingers were digging into me. "Don't you ever come in here again, understand?"

She looked at the snake, shuddering. "God, it's disgusting. What's wrong with you?"

She shouted at me all the way home, for putting the wind up her, letting her think some pervert had taken me. I didn't realize just how afraid she was. That she was looking at me like she didn't know what she'd birthed.

The novelty of motherhood soon wore off. Ami sat in the armchair of our flat, her toenails painted in the same tangerine shade as her maxi dress. She was sunbed fresh and her lips were demarcated in an unflatteringly pale shade of pink. Her hair was in fat rollers ready for her evening out.

"Guess where I went today?" she asked, her voice bright and brittle.

"Where, doll?" Kath puffed on her cigarette, blowing a stream of smoke away from us.

If Ami was slim, Kath was scrawny. The skin on her neck and chest was wrinkled from the lack of padding and twenty-five cigarettes a day. She wore a series of gold chains and her hands were rough and red from perpetual cleaning. Her face was unbalanced: nose too small and large ears that stuck out. Round eyes that never saw make-up. I forget sometimes, that she was only twenty-four then.

"To see Kenny."

Tallulah got up and I thought she was leaving me for Ami but she was just fetching her teddy. When she sat back down next to me, she wriggled against me to get comfortable. Ami bought Tallulah's clothes. Ridiculous, expensive things to dress a toddler in, old fashioned and frilly.

"Kenny always asks after you." Ami filled the silence.

"Does he?" Kath tipped the ash from her cigarette into the empty packet. God love her, she didn't have many vices.

"He never says but he's hurt. It's all over his face when I walk in and you're not with me. You're not showing him much respect or loyalty. All he wants to do is look after you and Lola, like he looks after me and Tallulah."

"I don't want Kenny's money. He's not Robin Hood. He beat a man to death."

"He's our *brother*."

Which was funny, because I didn't know that I had an uncle.

Kath's face was a shutter slamming shut.

"He loves to see pictures of Lola."

"Photos? You showed him photos?" Kath was blowing herself for a fight.

"I only showed him some pictures. He wanted to see her. What's up with you?"

"Lola's *my* business. No one else's."

"Well, I'm taking Tallulah for him to see next time."

"No, you're not. Not to a prison."

"She's mine. I'll take her where the fuck I want."

"You've done well to remember you've got a daughter."

"What's that mean?"

"You're always out with your bloody mates. You treat me like an unpaid baby sitter. She spends more time here than with you and then you've got the cheek to tell me to mind my own."

"So it's about money?"

"No," Kath threw up her hands, "it's about you being a selfish, spoilt brat. I'm your *sister*, not your mum. And it's about how you treat Tallulah."

"At least I know who her dad is."

Kath slapped her face. A sudden bolt that silenced them both. It left a red flush on Ami's cheek. Whenever I asked about my dad, Kath told me that she'd found me in a skip.

"I'm sorry, Ami..." Kath put out her hands. "I didn't mean to. I mean..."

"Tallulah," Ami snapped, holding out her hand.

Tallulah looked from me to Kath, her eyes wide. Ami pulled her up by the arm. She screamed.

"Be careful with her."

"Or what, Kath?" Ami lifted Tallulah up, putting her under one arm like she was a parcel. "Are you going to call Social Services? Fuck off."

Calling Social Services was a crime akin to calling the police.

Tallulah was in a full on tantrum by then, back arched and legs kicking. Fierce for her size, she proved too much for Ami who threw her down on the sofa. She lay there, tear stained and rigid. Ami had started to cry too. "Stay here then, see if I sodding care."

There are times when I feel lost, even to myself, and that what looks out from behind my eyes isn't human.

I'm reminded of it each day as I go to work at the School of Tropical Medicine.

Peter, one of the biochemists from the lab downstairs has come up for a batch of venom. He watches me milk the snakes when he can overcome his revulsion.

Michael, my assistant, tips the green mamba out of her box. I pin her down with a forked metal stick, while Michael does the same, further along her body. I clamp a hand just beneath her neck, thanking her silently for enduring the indignity of this charade. If it were just the two of us, she'd come to me without all this manhandling. I'll make it up to her later with mice and kisses. She's gorgeous in an intense shade of green, her head pointed.

"You have to stop that work when you get too old," says Peter, "you know, reflexes getting slow and all that."

The deaths of herpetologist are as fabled as snakes are touchy. There's no room for lax habits or slowness. Handled safely for years, a snake can turn on you, resulting in a blackened, withered limb, blood pouring from every orifice, paralysis and blindness, if not death.

Peter's a predator. He's been a swine to me since I knocked him back. I turn to him with the snake still in my hand. She hisses at him and he shrinks away.

I hook the mamba's mouth over the edge of the glass and apply gentle pressure. The venom runs down the side and collects in a pool.

What Peter doesn't know is that when my darlings and I are alone I hold them in my arms and let them wind around my neck. Our adoration is mutual. They're the easy part of my job.

"They like Eliza," Michael is offended on my behalf. There's not been a bite since I've been here.

"Concentrate." I snap at him as he brings the mamba's box to me. I regret my churlishness straight away. Michael is always pleasant with me. He never takes offence at my lack of social graces but someday he will.

Snakes are easy. It's people that I don't know how to charm.

Tallulah trailed along beside me. She looked like a doll in her school uniform; pleated skirt and leather buckled shoes. I didn't begrudge her the lovely clothes that Ami bought her. She jumped, a kittenish leap, and then she took my hand. We swung arms as we walked.

We turned onto Cathcart Street. Laird Tower was ahead of us, dwarfing the bungalows opposite. Those used by the elderly or infirm were marked out by white grab handles and key safes.

A pair of girls sat on a wall. They jumped down when they saw us. School celebrities, these playground queens, who knew how to bruise you with a word. They'd hurt you for not being like them, or not wanting to be like them.

"Is she your sister?" Jade, the shorter one asked Tallulah.

"No," Tallulah began, "she's . . . "

"Of course not," Jade cut across her, keen to get out the rehearsed speech. Jade didn't like my prowess in lessons. I tried to hide it, but it occasionally burst out of me. I liked the teacher. I liked homework. I even liked the school, built in red brick that managed to still look like a Victorian poorhouse.

Jade was sly enough not to goad me for that, going for my weakness, not my strength. "You're too pretty to be Lola's sister. Look at her ugly mug."

It was true. I remained resolutely strange; my features had failed to rearrange themselves into something that would pass for normal. Also, my sight had rapidly deteriorated in the last few months and my thick lenses magnified my eyes.

"Be careful." Jade leaned down into Tallulah's face. "You'll catch her ugliness."

Tallulah pushed her, hard, both of her small hands on her chest. Jade fell backwards a few steps, surprised by the attack. She raised a fist to hit Tallulah.

My blood was set alight, venom rising. Water brash filled my mouth as if I were about to be sick. I snatched at Jade's hand and sunk my teeth into her meaty forearm, drawing blood. I could taste her shock and fear. If she was screaming, I couldn't hear her. I only let go when her friend punched me on the ear.

• • •

After I'd apologized I sat in the corner of the room while Kath and Pauline, Jade's mum, talked.

"I thought it would be good if we sorted it out between us, like grown ups," Pauline said.

Social Services had already been round to confirm that I was the culprit. *Has she ever done anything like this before?*

No, Kathy was calm and firm, *Lola wasn't brought up that way.*

"I'm so sorry about what happened." Pauline lifted her mug of tea, her hand trembling a fraction. She took a sip and set it down, not picking it up again.

"Why?" Kath sat up straighter. "Lola bit Jade. *I'm* sorry and I'll make sure that she is too by the time I'm done with her."

"Yes, but Jade was picking on her."

"That's no excuse for what Lola did. She should've just walked away."

"It's time that someone cut Jade down to size."

"My daughter *bit* yours." Exasperation raised Kathy's voice a full octave.

"She was asking for it."

Kathy shook her head. Then, "How is she?"

Jade had lain on the pavement, twitching. Red marks streaked up her arm, marking the veins.

"She's doing okay," Pauline swallowed. "She's on antibiotics. She's a bit off color, that's all."

"The police and Social Services came round earlier."

"I've not complained. I'm not a nark. I'd never do that."

"I didn't say you had."

"You'll tell Kenny, won't you? We're not grasses. We won't cause you any bother. I'll skin Jade if she comes near your girls again." We were known as Kathy's girls.

"Kenny?" Kathy repeated dully.

"Please. Will you talk to him?"

Kath was about to say something but then deflated in the chair.

"Ami's says she's visiting him soon, so I'll make sure he gets the message."

Kathy closed the door after Pauline had gone.

"What did you do to her?" It was the first time she'd looked at me properly since it had happened.

"It wasn't her fault." Tallulah stood between us. "She was going to hit me."

"What did you do to her?" Kathy pushed her aside. "Her arm swelled up and she's got blood poisoning."

"I don't know," I stammered. "It just happened."

She slapped me. I put my hands out to stop her but she carried on, backing me into the bedroom. She pushed me down on the floor. I curled my hands over my head.

"I didn't bring you up to be like that." Her strength now was focused in a fist. Kathy had hit me before, but never like that. "I swear I'll kill you if you ever do anything like that again. You fucking little monster."

She was sobbing and shrieking. Tallulah was crying and trying to pull her off. Kathy continued to punch me until her arm grew tired. "You're a monster, just like your father."

We stayed in our bedroom that night, Tallulah and I. We could hear Kathy banging about the flat. First, the vacuum hitting the skirting boards as she pulled it around. A neighbor thumped on the wall and she shouted back, but turned it off and took to the bathroom. She'd be at it all night, until her hands were raw. The smell of bleach was a signal of her distress. There were times when I thought I'd choke on the stench.

The skin on my face felt tight and sore, as if shrunken by tears. Tallulah rolled up my T-shirt to inspect the bruises on my back. There was a change coming, fast, as the shock of Kathy's onslaught wore off.

It hurt when Tallulah touched me. It wasn't just the skin on my face that felt wrong. It was all over. I rubbed my head against the carpet, an instinctual movement as I felt I'd got a cowl covering my face. The skin ripped.

"I'll get Kathy."

"No, wait." I grabbed her wrist. "Stay with me." My skin had become a fibrous sheath, my very bones remolding. My ribs shrank and my slim pelvis and limbs became vestigial. My paired organs rearranged themselves, one pushed below the other except my lungs. I gasped as one of those collapsed. I could feel my diaphragm tearing; the wrenching of it doubled me over.

I writhed on the floor. There was no blood. What came away in the harsh lamplight was translucent. Tallulah held me as I sloughed off my skin, which fell away to reveal scales. She gathered the coils of me into her lap. We lay down and I curled around her.

I couldn't move. I could barely breathe. When I put out my forked tongue I could taste Tallulah's every molecule in the air.

• • •

The morning light came through the thin curtain. Tallulah was beside me. I had legs again. I put a hand to my mouth. My tongue was whole. My flesh felt new. More than that, I could see. When I put my glasses on the world became blurred. I didn't need them anymore. The very surface of my eyes had been reborn.

My shed skin felt fibrous and hard. I bundled it up into a plastic bag and stuffed it in my wardrobe. Tallulah stretched as she watched me, her hands and feet splayed.

"Tallulah, what am I? Am I a monster?"

She sat up and leaned against me, her chin on my shoulder.

"Yes, you're *my* monster."

I ache for the splendid shabbiness of my former life, when it was just Kath, Tallulah, and me in the flat, the curtains drawn against the world and the telly droning on in the background. Tallulah and I would dance around Kath, while she swatted us away. The smell of bleach and furniture polish is forever home. Kath complaining when I kept turning the heating up. Being cold made me sluggish.

Endless, innocuous days and nights that I should've savored more.

"How was your test?"

"Crap." Tallulah threw down her bag. "Hi, Kath."

"Hi, love," Kathy shouted back from the kitchen.

Tallulah, school uniformed, big diva hair so blond that it was almost white, a flick of kohl expertly applied at the corner of her eyes.

"I'm thick, not like you." She kicked off her shoes.

"You're not thick. Just lazy."

She laughed and lay on her belly beside me, in front of the TV. She smelt of candy floss scent she'd stolen from her mum. Tallulah was the sweetest thing.

There was the sound of the key in the door. I looked at Tallulah. Only her mum had a key. We could hear Ami's voice, followed by a man's laugh. A foreign sound in the flat. Kathy came out of the kitchen, tea towel in hand.

Ami stood in the doorway, flushed and excited, as if she was about to present a visiting dignitary.

"Kath, there's someone here to see you."

She stood aside. I didn't recognize the man. He was bald and scarred. Kathy sat down on the sofa arm, looking the color of a dirty dishrag.

"Oh, God," he said, "aren't you a bunch of princesses?"

"Kenny, when did you get out?" Kath asked.

"A little while ago." He took off his jacket and threw it down. A snake tattoo coiled up his arm and disappeared under the sleeve of his T-shirt. It wasn't the kind of body art I was used to. This hadn't been driven into the skin in a fit of self-loathing or by a ham fisted amateur. It was faded but beautiful. It rippled as Kenny moved, invigorated by his muscles.

"Come and hug me, Kath."

She got up, robotic, and went to him, tolerating his embrace, her arms stiff by her sides.

"I've brought us something to celebrate."

He handed her a plastic bag and she pulled out a bottle of vodka and a packet of Jammy Dodgers.

"Just like when we were kids, eh?" he grinned.

"See, Kenny's got no hard feelings about you staying away." Ami was keen to be involved. "He's just glad to be home."

They both ignored her.

"Now, girls, come and kiss your uncle. You first, Tallulah."

"Well, go on." Ami gave her a shove.

She pecked his cheek and then shot away, which seemed to amuse him. Then it was my turn. Kath stood close to us while Kenny held me at arm's length.

"How old are you now, girl?"

"Eighteen."

"You were born after I went inside." He sighed. "You've got the family's ugly gene like me and your mum but you'll do."

For what? I thought.

Kenny put his fleshy hand around Kath's neck and pressed his forehead against hers. Kathy, who didn't like kisses or cuddles from anyone, flinched. I'd never seen her touched so much.

"I'm home now. We'll not talk about these past, dark years. It'll be how it was before. Better. You'll see. Us taking care of each other."

Georgia's unusual for a photographer in that she's more beautiful than her models. They're gap toothed, gawky things that only find luminosity through the lens. Georgia's arresting in the flesh.

I hover beside our host who's introducing me to everyone as though I'm a curio. We approach a group who talk too loudly, as if they're the epicenter of the party.

"I find Georgia distant. And ambitious."

"She lives on Martin's Heath. In one of the old houses."

"Bloody hell, is that family money?"

"Rosie, you've modeled for Georgia. Have you been there?"

"No."

Rosie sounds so quiet and reflective that the pain of her unrequited love is palpable. At least I hope it's unrequited.

"Have you seen her girlfriend?"

"Everyone, meet Eliza," our host steps in before they have a chance to pronounce judgment on me within my earshot, "Georgia's partner."

I shake hands with each of them.

"Georgia's last shoot made waves. And I didn't realize that she was such a stunner."

We all look over at Georgia. Among all the overdressed butterflies, she wears black trousers, a white shirt, and oxblood brogues.

"Don't tell her that," I smile. "She doesn't like it."

"Why? Doesn't every woman want that?" The man falters, as if he's just remembered that I'm a woman too.

These people with their interminable words. I came from a place where a slap sufficed.

"Don't be dull," I put him down. "She's much more than her face."

"What do you do, Eliza?" another one of them asks, unperturbed by my rudeness.

"I'm a herpetologist."

They shudder with delicious revulsion.

I glance back to Georgia. A man with long blond hair reaches out to touch her forearm and he shows her something on his tablet.

I'm a pretender in my own life, in this relationship. I know how my jealousy will play out when we get home. I'll struggle to circumnavigate all the gentility and civility that makes me want to scream.

Eventually Georgia will say, *What's the matter? Just tell me instead of trying to pick a fight.*

She'll never be provoked, this gracious woman, to display any savagery of feeling. I should know better than to try and measure the breadth and depth of love by its noise and dramas but there are times that I crave it, as if it's proof that love is alive.

Ami took Tallulah away with her the first night that Kenny came to the flat.

"But it's a school night. And all my stuff's here."

"You're not going to school tomorrow." Ami picked up her handbag. "We're going out with Kenny."

Tallulah didn't move.

"Mind your mum, there's a good girl." Kenny didn't even look up.

After the front door closed, Kathy locked and chained it.

"Get your rucksack. Put some clothes in a bag. Don't pack anything you don't need."

"Why?" I followed her into her bedroom.

"We're leaving."

"Why?"

"Just get your stuff."

"What about college?"

Kathy tipped out drawers, rifling through the untidy piles that she'd made on the floor.

"What about Tallulah?"

She sank down on the bed.

"There's always someone that I have to stay for. Mum. Ami. Tallulah." She slammed her fist down on the duvet. "If it had been just us, we'd have been gone long ago."

"Stay?"

She wasn't listening to me anymore.

"I waited too long. I should've run when I had the chance. Fuck everyone."

She lay down, her face to the wall. I tried to put my arms around her but she shrunk from me, which she always did when I touched her and which never failed to hurt me.

If we were his princesses then Kenny considered himself king.

"Kath, stop fussing and come and sit down. It's good to be back among women. Without women, men are uncivilized creatures." He winked at me. "Tell me about Ma's funeral again, Kath."

Ami sat beside him, looking up at him.

"There were black horses with plumes and brasses. Her casket was in a glass carriage." Kath's delivery was wooden.

"And all the boys were there?"

"Yes, Kenny. All the men, in their suits, gold sovereign rings, and tattoos."

"Good," he said, "I would've been offended otherwise. Those boys owe me and they know it. I did time for them. Do you know the story?"

"Bits," Tallulah said.

"I told her, Kenny." Ami was keen to show her allegiance.

"You were what, twelve?" He snorted. "You remember nothing. We did a job in Liverpool. A jeweler who lived in one of those massive houses around Sefton Park. We heard he was dealing in stolen diamonds. I went in first," he thumped his chest. "At twenty-three I was much thinner back then, could get into all sorts of tight spots. I let the others in afterwards. We found his money but he kept insisting the diamonds were hidden in the fireplace, but his hidey-hole was empty. He kept acting all surprised. He wouldn't tell, no matter what." Kenny shrugged. "Someone grassed. A copper picked me up near home. Under my coat, my shirt was covered in his blood. I kept my trap shut and did the time. The others were safe. Eighteen years inside. My only regret is what happened to Ma. And missing her funeral."

"There were white flowers, everywhere, spelling out her name." Ami said. He patted her arm in an absent way, like she was a cat mithering for strokes.

"I wish they'd let me out for it. Ma was a proper princess, girls. She was touched, God bless her, but she was a princess."

Kath sat with her hands folded on her knees.

"Do you remember what Dad said when he was dying?"

Kath stayed quiet.

"He said, *You're the man of the house, Kenny. And you're the mother, Kathy. Kenny, you have to look after these girls.* Poor Ma, so fragile. When I heard about her stroke, I was beside myself. It was the shock of me being sent down that did it. Whoever grassed me up has to pay for that, too. I should've been here, taking care of you all."

"I managed," Kathy squeezed the words out.

"I know. I hate to think of you, nursing Ma when you also had a baby to look after. You were meant for better things. We didn't always live in this shithole, girls. We grew up in a big rambling house. You won't remember much of it, Ami. Dad bred snakes. He was a specialist. And Ma, she was a real lady. They were educated people, not like 'round here."

The words stuck in my gut. 'Round here was all I knew.

"Happy days, weren't they, Mouse?" Kenny looked directly at Kathy, waiting.

"Mouse," Ami laughed like she'd only just noticed Kathy's big eyes and protruding ears, "I'd forgotten that."

Mouse. A nickname that diminished her.

"What's *my* pet name?" Ami pouted.

"You're just Ami." He said it like she was something flat and dead, not shifting his gaze from Kathy.

There it was. Even then, I could see that Kathy was at the center of everything and Ami was just the means to reach her.

There's a photograph in our bedroom that Georgia took of me while we were traveling around South America. It embarrasses me because of its dimensions and scares me, because Georgia has managed to make me look like some kind of modern Eve, desirable in a way that I'll never be again. My hair is loose and uncombed and the python around my shoulders is handsome in dappled, autumnal shades. My expression is of unguarded pleasure.

"Let's stay here, forever," I said to her when she put the lens cap back on. "It's paradise."

What I was really thinking was *What would it be like to change, forever, and have the whole jungle as my domain?*

"Do you love it that much?" Georgia replied in a way that suggested she didn't. "And put him down. Poor thing. If he's caught he'll end up as a handbag."

So it is that serpents are reviled when it's man that is repulsive.

I got off the bus at the end of Argyll Street and walked towards home. Kenny sat on a plastic chair outside The Saddle pub, drinking a pint. He was waiting for me.

"What have you been doing today?" He abandoned his drink and followed me.

"Biology." I was at college, in town.

"Clever girl. That's from your grandparents. I used to be smart like that. You wouldn't think it to look at me."

There was an odd, puppyish eagerness to Kenny as he bounced along beside me. I darted across the road when there was a gap in the traffic. The railway line was on the other side of the fence, down a steep bank. Part way down the embankment was a rolled up carpet, wet and rotted, and the shopping trolley that it had been transported in.

"Let me carry your bag. It looks heavy."

"I can manage."

"I wasn't always like this. I had to change for us to survive. Fighting and stealing," he shook his head, embarrassed. "I only became brutal to stop us being brutalized. Do you understand?"

The sky had darkened. Rain was on its way.

"We lost everything when Dad died. The house. The money. Your grandma lost her mind. It was the shock of having to live here. We were posh and we paid for that. On our first day at school a lad was picking on Kathy. Do you know what I did? I bit him, Lola. Right on the face. He swelled up like a red balloon. He nearly choked. Nobody picks on my princesses."

Nobody except him.

"Are you special, Lola?"

"I don't know what you mean."

I dodged him as he tried to block my path. Tallulah wouldn't have told him anything. Ami though, she had told him to prevent Pauline and Jade getting a battering.

"I can wait," he didn't pursue me, just stood there in the drizzle. "We have lots of time now."

"We're going for a ride today." Kenny followed Kath into the kitchen. He'd started turning up at the flat every day.

"I can't, Kenny, I've got loads to do."

"It can all wait."

Kenny had the last word.

"Where are we going?" Tallulah asked.

"You're not going anywhere except to Ami's. She needs to get her house in order. A girl needs her mum. She's sorting your bedroom, so you're going to live with her. Properly."

"I don't want to."

"Want's not in it."

Kathy stood between them. He pushed her aside.

"I live *here*." Tallulah wouldn't be moved.

"You live where I tell you." He had this way of standing close to you, to make himself seem more imposing, and lowering his voice. "You act like you're something with that pretty little face of yours. Well, I'm here to tell you that you're not special. You're fucking Mikey Flynn's daughter. And he's a piece of dead scum."

Poor Mikey Flynn, rumored to have done a runner. I wondered where Kenny had him buried.

"Go home, Tallulah." Kathy raised her chin. "Kenny's right. You're not my girl. You should be with your own mother."

Tallulah's eyes widened. I could see the tears starting to pool there.

"Go on, then," Kathy carried on, "you don't belong here."

"Mum," I opened my mouth.

"Shut it." Kathy turned on me. "I've been soft on you pair for too long. Now help Tallulah take her stuff to Ami's."

"No," Kenny put a hand on my arm, "Lola stays with us."

As Kenny drove, the terraces changed to semis and then detached houses. Finally there were open fields. It felt like he'd taken us hours away but it wasn't more than thirty minutes. We turned up an overgrown drive. Branches whipped the windscreen as Kenny drove.

"Kenny." Kath's voice was ripped from her throat. He patted her hand.

The drive ended at a large house, dark bricked with tall windows. It might as well have been a castle for all its unfamiliar grandeur. Overgrown rhododendrons crowded around it, shedding pink and red blossoms that were long past their best.

"Come on."

Kenny got out, not looking back to see if we were following.

Kath stood at the bottom of the steps, looking up at the open front door. There were plenty of window bars and metal shutters where I grew up, but the windows here were protected by wrought iron foliage in which metal snakes were entwined. The interior was dim. I could hear Kenny's footsteps as he walked inside.

"This is where we used to live." Kathy's face was blank. She went in, a sleepwalker in her own life. I followed her.

"Welcome home." Kenny was behind the door. He locked it and put the key on a chain around his neck.

Kenny showed us from room to room as if we were prospective buyers, not prisoners. Every door had a lock and every window was decorated in the same metal latticework.

I stopped at a set of double doors but Kenny steered me away from it. "Later. Look through here, Kathy. Do you remember the old Aga? Shame they ripped it out. I thought we could get a new one."

He led us on to the lounge, waving his arm with a flourish.

"I couldn't bring you here without buying *some* new furniture." He kept glancing at Kathy. "What do you think?"

The room smelt of new carpet. It was a dusky pink, to match the sofa, and the curtains were heavy cream with rose buds on them. Things an old woman might have picked.

"Lovely, Kenny."

"I bought it for us." He slung his arm around her neck. It looked like a noose. "You and me, here again, no interference." His face was soft. "I've plenty of money. I can get more."

"Go and play," Kath said to me.

It'll shame me forever that I was angry at her for talking to me like I was a child when all she was trying to do was get me out of his way.

I went, then crawled back on my belly to watch them through the gap in the door.

Kath broke away from him and sat down. Kenny followed her, sinking down to lay his head on her knee. Her hand hovered over him, the muscles in her throat moving as she swallowed hard. Then she stroked his head. He buried his face in her lap, moaning.

"What happened to us, Mouse?"

Mouse. He'd swallow her whole. He'd crush her.

"You said you can get more money. Do you mean the money from the job in Liverpool?"

He moved quickly, sitting beside Kathy with his thigh wedged against the length of hers.

"Yes." He interlaced their fingers, making their hands a single fist. "I want you to know that I didn't kill anyone."

"You didn't? You were covered in blood."

"It was Barry's son, Carl. He always had a screw loose. The man wouldn't tell us where the diamonds were and Carl just freaked. He kept on beating him."

"But you admitted it."

"Who would believe me if I denied it? I did the time. Barry was very grateful. I knew it would set us up for life. I hated waiting for you. I imagined slipping out between the bars to come to you. I was tempted so many times. I hated the parole board. There *were* diamonds, Kath. I took them before I let the others in. I stopped here and buried them under the wall at the bottom of the garden. I nearly got caught doing it. Then the police picked me up, on my way back to you. That's why I had to do the stretch, so nobody would suspect. They're safe, now. Shankly's looking after what's left of them." He laughed at his own cryptic comment. Every Merseysider knew the deceased Bill Shankly, iconic once-manager of Liverpool Football Club. "Did I do right, Kath?"

Then she did something surprising. She kissed him. He writhed under her touch.

"Mouse, was there anyone else while I was inside?"

"No, Kenny. There's never been anybody else."

He basked in that.

"It'll be just like I said."

I sensed her hesitation. So did he.

"What's wrong?"

"It won't be like we said though, will it?"

"Why?"

"It should be just us two." She leaned closer to him. "Lola's grown up now. She can look after herself."

"Lola's just a kid."

"I was a mother at her age." She put her hand on his arm.

"No, she stays."

Her hand dropped.

"Lola," Kenny called out. "Never let me catch you eavesdropping again. Understand?"

"I'll just say goodnight to Lola." Kath stood in the doorway to my new bedroom, as if this game of fucked-up families was natural.

"Don't be long."

I sat on the bed. The new quilt cover and pillowcase smelt funny. Kenny had put them on straight out of the packaging without washing them first. They still bore the sharp creases of their confinement.

"Lola," Kathy pulled me up and whispered to me. "He said to me, when we were kids, 'I'm going to put a baby in you and it's going to be special, like me and Dad,' as if I had nothing to do with it. I can't stand him touching me. When I felt you moving inside me, I was terrified you'd be a squirming snake, but you were *mine*. I'd do anything to get him away from us and Ami. I was the one who told the police."

Uncle. Father. Any wonder that I'm monstrous?

"Kenny's always been wrong. He thought it was from Dad, although he never saw him do it. It's from Mum. It drove her mad, holding it in. She nearly turned when she had her stroke. I have to know, can you do it too?"

"What?"

"We can't waste time. Can you turn into," she hesitated, "a snake?"

"Yes." I couldn't meet her gaze.

"Good. Do it as soon as I leave." She opened the window. "Go out through the bars. Will you fit?"

"I don't know if I can. I'm not sure that I can do it at will."

"Try. Get out of here."

Panic rose in my chest. "What about you?"

"I'm going to do what I should've done a long time ago." She showed me the paring knife in her back pocket and then pulled her baggy sweater back over it. It must've been all she had time to grab. "I won't be far behind you."

"What if you're not?"

"Don't ask stupid questions," she paused, "I'm sorry for not being stronger. I'm sorry for not getting you away from here."

"Kathy," Kenny's voice boomed from the corridor, "time for bed."

After she left I heard the key turn in the lock.

I went through the drawers and wardrobe. Kenny had filled them with clothes. I didn't want to touch anything that had come from him. There was nothing that I could use as a weapon or to help me escape.

I'd not changed since the time I'd bitten Jade. I lay down, trying to slow my breathing and concentrate. Nothing happened. The silence filled my mind along with all the things he would be doing to Kathy.

I dozed, somewhere towards early morning, wakening frequently in the unfamiliar room. I missed Tallulah beside me in the bed we'd shared since childhood. I missed her warmth and tangle of hair.

When Kenny let me out it was late afternoon.

"Where's my mum?"

"Down here."

There was a chest freezer in the basement. Kenny lifted the lid. Kathy was inside, frozen in a slumped position, arms crossed over her middle. Frozen blood glittered on the gash in her head and frosted one side of her face.

Kenny put his hand on my shoulder like we were mourners at a wake. I should've been kicking and screaming, but I was as frozen as she was.

One of Kathy's wrists was contorted at an unnatural angle.

"She betrayed me. I always knew it, in my heart." He shut the lid. "Now it's just you and me, kid."

He took me up through the house, to the room at the back with the double doors. There were dozens of tanks that cast a glow. Some contained a single serpent, others several that were coiled together like heaps of intestines.

"My beauties. I'll start breeding them."

There were corn snakes, ball pythons, ribbon snakes—though I had no names for them back then—all of which make good pets. I stopped at one tank. He had a broad head with a blunted snout.

"Ah, meet Shankly." Kenny put his hand against the glass. "He was hard to come by. They're called cottonmouths because they open their mouths so wide to show their fangs that you see all the white lining inside."

The cottonmouth must have been young. I remember his olive green color and the clear banded pattern on his back, which he would lose as he got older.

"Are you special, Kathy?"

"I'm Lola."

"Yes, of course you are. Are you like me?"

"I'm nothing like you. Leave me alone."

"I'll look after you. Like you're a princess. You'll want for nothing. And you'll look after me because that's how it works."

"Don't fucking touch me."

Kenny pressed my face against the tank. Shankly showed me his pale underbelly as he slid towards me.

"Be afraid of him," Kenny nodded at the snake, "he still has his fangs. I'll make a mint from his venom."

Shankly climbed up a branch in his tank and settled there.

Kenny pushed me down with one hand and undid his belt buckle with the other.

"I'm your daughter." It was my last defense.

"I know."

Then he put his forked tongue in my mouth.

I couldn't move. The place between my legs was numb. I'd already tried sex with a boy from college. I knew what it was about. We'd fumbled and fallen in a heap in the bushes by the old boating lake one afternoon. It wasn't an experience to set the world alight but it was satisfactory enough.

This wasn't just a sex crime, it was a power crime. Kenny wanted my fear. I shrunk into the distant corners of myself trying to retreat where he couldn't follow. His orgasm was grudging, delivered with a short, gratified moan.

Afterwards he sat with his trousers open, watching me like he was waiting for me to do something. I was frozen. I'm not sure I even blinked. That was how Kathy must have felt, forever stuck in that single moment of inertia and shock that kept her in the same spot for a lifetime. She was right.

She should have run while she had the chance. Fuck her mother. And Ami, for all the good she'd done her.

Kenny stood up. I thought, *It's going to happen again and then he's going to dump me in the freezer.* Instead, he went upstairs, his tread heavy with disappointment.

"Don't stay up too late, pet."

I think I was waiting for something too, when I should've been searching for something sharp to stick between his ribs. I couldn't summon anything; I was still too deep inside myself.

I was colder than I'd ever been before, even though the summer night was stifling. The room felt airless despite the window being wide open and butting up against the grille. Sometimes, when Georgia's away, I feel that cold.

Get up, get up before he remembers you and comes back down for more.

"Lola." A voice carried through the window.

It was Tallulah, a pale ghost beyond the glass. Her mouth was moving as she clutched at the bars.

I turned my face away, in the childish way of *if I can't see her, then she can't see me.* I didn't want her to see me like this. It occurred to me that she might have been a witness to the whole thing. I turned back but she'd gone, so I closed my eyes.

I should've known that Tallulah would never leave me. The snakes swayed in their tanks, enraptured. Tallulah was long and white, with pale yellow markings. Slender and magnificent. She glided over me and lay on my chest, rearing up. I couldn't breathe because she took my breath away. I could feel her muscles contracting and her smooth belly scales against my bare chest.

Get up, get up, or he'll come down and find her like this.

Are you special?

Her tongue flicked out and touched my lips. I had no choice. I had to do it, for her. There was the rush of lubricant that loosened the top layer of my skin. The change was fast, my boyish body, with its flat chest and narrow hips perfectly suited to the transformation.

I crawled out of my human mantle. Molting was good. I shed every cell of myself that Kenny had touched.

Both Tallulah and I are unidentifiable among my extensive research of snakes, bearing properties of several species at once. We made a perfect pair for hunting. The pits on my face were heat sensitive, able to detect a variation of a thousandth of a degree, feeding information into my optic nerves. I saw the world in thermal. Kenny's heart was luminous in the dark. I slid up the side of his bed and hovered over his pillow. Tallulah lay beside him on the mattress, waiting.

Look at your princesses, Kenny. See how special we are.

Kenny snored, a gentle, almost purring noise.

It's a myth that snakes dislocate their jaws.

I opened my mouth as wide as I could, stretching the flexible ligament that joined my lower jaw to my skull. I covered his crown in slow increments. He snorted and twitched. I slipped down over his eyes, his lashes tickling the inside of my throat. He reached up to touch his head.

Tallulah struck him, sinking her fangs into his neck. He started and tried to sit up, limbs flailing, which was a mistake as his accelerating heartbeat sent the venom further around his circulation.

Trying to cover his nose was the hardest part, despite my reconfigured mouth. I thought my head would split open. I wasn't sure how much more I could stomach. Not that it mattered. I wasn't trying to swallow him whole. A fraction more and I was over his nostrils completely.

There was only one way to save himself. I recognized the undulations he was making. I could feel the change on my tongue, his skin becoming fibrous. I had to stop him. I couldn't imagine what he'd become.

He was weakening with Tallulah's neurotoxins, slumping back on the bed, shaking in an exquisite fit. He'd wet himself. I stretched my flesh further and covered his mouth and waited until long after he was still.

I woke up on the floor beside Tallulah. We were naked. My throat and neck were sore. The corners of my mouth were crusted with dried blood. We lay on our sides, looking at one another without speaking. We were the same, after all.

"How did you find me?" I was hoarse.

"I had to wait until Ami went out. I found the house details in her bedroom drawer. I didn't have any money so I had to get a bus and walk the rest of the way. I'm sorry that I didn't get here sooner."

"It doesn't matter now."

Tallulah picked up our clothes and then our skins, which lay like shrouds. It was disconcerting to see how they were molds of us, even down to the contours of our faces.

"I'll take these with us. We can burn them later."

I went upstairs. I edged into the darkened room as if Kenny might sit up at any moment. He was a purple, bloated corpse with fang marks in his neck. I fumbled with the chain around his neck, not wanting to touch him.

"Where's Kathy?" Tallulah asked.

I told her.

"Show me."

"No, I don't want you to remember her like that." I seized Tallulah's face in my hands. "You do know that she didn't mean what she said, about you not belonging with us? She was trying to protect you."

Tallulah nodded, her mouth a line. She didn't cry.

"We have to bury her."

"We can't. Tallulah, we have to get out of here. Do you understand? Ami will come for you when she realizes you've gone. There's something else."

I put my hand in the cottonmouth's tank. It curled up my arm and I lifted it out, holding it up to my cheek. He nudged my face.

"Lift out the bottom."

Tallulah pulled out bits of twisted branch and foliage, then pulled up the false base. She gasped. Out came bundles of notes and cloth bags. She tipped the contents out on her palm. More diamonds than I could hold in my cupped hands.

We loaded the money into Kenny's rucksack and tucked the diamonds in our pockets.

"What about the snakes?"

We opened the tanks and carried them outside. I watched them disappear into the undergrowth. Except for Shankly. I put him in a carrier bag and took him with us.

There are days when I wake and I can't remember who I am, like a disorientated traveler who can't recall which hotel room of which country they're in.

I'm hurt that Georgia didn't want me to collect her from the airport.

There's been a delay. I won't get in until late. Go to bed, I'll get a cab.

I wished now that I'd ignored her and gone anyway instead of lying here in the dark. The harsh fluorescent lights and the near-empty corridors of the airport are preferable to the vast darkness of our empty bed.

Not going is a stupid test with which I've only hurt myself. I've resolutely taken her consideration for indifference. I want her to be upset that I wasn't there, as if she secretly wanted me there all along.

See, I confuse even myself.

The front door opens and closes. I should get up and go to her. She comes in, marked by the unzipping of her boots and the soft sound of her shedding clothes.

Love isn't just what you feel for someone when you look at them. It's how they make you feel about yourself when they look back at you.

Georgia is the coolest, most poised woman that I know. We're older now and our hearts and flesh aren't so easily moved but I still wonder what she sees when she looks at me.

"Do you love me?" It's easier to ask it with the lights off and my head turned away from her.

Everything about us is wrong. We're lovers, sisters, freaks.

She answers in a way that I have to respond to. I glide across the floor towards her and we become a writhing knot. We hunt mice in our grandiose pile and in the morning we are back here in our bed, entwined together in our nest.

When we wake again as human beings she says, "Of course I love you, monster."

When we shed the disguises that are Georgia and Eliza, and then the skins that are Lola and Tallulah, we *are* monsters. Fabulous beasts.

Priya Sharma lives in the UK. Her stories have been published by *Tor.com*, *Black Static*, *Interzone*, *Albedo One*, and *Alt Hist*, among others. She has been anthologized in various "best of" anthologies edited by Ellen Datlow, Paula Guran, Jonathan Strahan, Steve Haynes, and Johnny Mains. "Fabulous Beasts" has been nominated for a Shirley Jackson Award in the novelette category. Her short story, "Lebkuchen," was reprinted earlier this year in *Into the Woods: Fairy Tales Retold*. More information about her writing can be found at priyasharmafiction.wordpress.com

Below the falls the waters teem with light,
the glint of gold like the flash of drowned skin.

BELOW THE FALLS

Daniel Mills

Gentlemen, I am tired of ghost stories. In my lifetime, I have heard a hundred such tales, a hundred variations on the same tired formula. We have the respectable narrator, the decrepit country house. A series of unsettling incidents: disembodied footsteps, say, or voices in the night. Finally there is the ghost itself, which bursts upon the narrator's mind like the swift and violent intrusion of the repressed id. His faith is shattered, his sanity. He is never again the same.

But there is life in the old form yet. If we take the defining quality of a ghost to be its attendant sense of mystery, its otherness, then I propose to you that we are surrounded by such spirits at all times whether we choose to admit it or not. In pain the mind hides even from itself, becoming a darkened star around which light bends but does not pass through.

I hope you might allow me to read from an old diary. The tale it relates is, I aver, a kind of ghost story, though the dead do not walk in its pages, except in the usual way by which the words of the deceased survive on paper long after their graves have been filled.

The diary came into my possession some years ago when I was practicing medicine in Lynn, MA. A nurse at the hospital in Danvers, knowing of my interest in psychoanalysis, mailed it to me upon the death of its author, a young woman by the name of Isabella Carr.

Mrs. Carr was born in Walpole, NH, and lived there with her mother and stepfather until the age of eighteen, when she was married to Horace Carr, Esq, of Beacon Hill, Boston. The diary begins shortly after her wedding and depicts the weeks immediately prior to her committal.

Aside from these few facts, the nurse's letter was tantalizingly vague, and in the same spirit, I present the diary to you now without further prelude.

• • •

APR 2

Alfie was here again last night.

I heard him at the door, his faint scratching. He was just outside the room, waiting for that late hour when the whole of the house lay sleeping and there was only me to hear him.

I opened the door. He scuttled inside, dragging his belly on the floor. He was terribly thin, his hair all in patches. It came away in tufts beneath my fingertips, baring the pitted skin beneath, the sallow flesh speckled with rot: they had buried him alive.

I dropped to my knees and wrapped my arms around him. He did not resist but merely lay with his head against my chest as I whispered into his ear.

I'm sorry, I said. I thought you were dead.

His breathing was strained and rapid but still he did not stir. He listened as the words poured out of me, an undammed torrent. I spoke for hours, or what seemed like hours, and later, I awoke to find him gone with the bars of sunlight on my face.

Bridget woke me. She entered the room while I slept and now applies herself to the tasks of stripping the bed, taking down the curtains. She whistles as she works—an Irish song, I suppose, for I do not recognize the tune.

Downstairs, the clocks all sound the half-hour, and I know that I have overslept. Mr. Carr awaits me in the breakfast room. He will be dressed for his clients, his club, checking his watch as the minutes tick past and still I do not come—

APR 7

A letter from Uncle Edmund—

This morning I woke early, before dawn, and padded downstairs in my nightgown. In the hall I found the mail where it had been dropped through the slot. In amongst my husband's correspondence was a letter addressed to me in my uncle's hand.

I recognized it at once. Edmund is my father's brother, his senior by ten years or more. He is a big man, like Father was, and likewise well-spoken, if occasionally given to maundering, and his avowed agnosticism had once made him a figure of some controversy in our household.

When Father died, Edmund took to writing me long letters, and these I cherished like jewels, for I heard my father's voice in his words and seemed to catch his scent upon the page. The letters ceased with Mother's marriage to Mr. Orne, who is a Methodist of the meanest sort, though it was months before I realized they had hidden them from me.

Uncle Edmund had obtained my husband's address from a gentleman friend in Walpole "of some slight acquaintance" with Mr. Carr. He rarely speaks of it, but Mr. Carr was born there as well and is, in fact, my mother's cousin—though he relocated to Boston as a young man and was subsequently estranged from his family for years.

Now Edmund writes to say that Father's house has been sold and is soon to be demolished. My mother has moved with Mr. Orne to Vermont, so as to be nearer his church, while our neighbors the Bosworths have bought the property. They have plans to erect a gristmill, damming the creek where it plunges to the falls.

Soon it will all be gone: the gardens, the paths down which we walked on summer evenings, Father and I, when the damp lay thickly on the air and the rosebushes rustled all round. I remember. We crossed the creek at the footbridge, where the petals lay like a blood-trail, and sat together in a place above the falls while the current frothed and broke among the rocks below.

APR 8-9

Midnight—

I hear the church bells tolling, the passing of the mail coach. An old man sings his way home, and a young girl weeps in the alley. In the silence of this hour, each sound recalls to me my shame and the solitude that followed. Days and nights in that bedroom with the curtains drawn while Mr. Orne kept watch outside and Mother walked the halls, screaming.

From the bed I watched the curtains change in color from grey to yellow to crimson. On cloudless nights the moon shone through the fabric, flesh-white and glistening with grease, making stains on the bedclothes and running like an oil in the blood—

For months I listened for the swollen creek, fat with autumn rain, white water roaring as it fell. Sometimes I thought I was dying. Other nights I was certain of it. In the evenings, I heard the winds blowing outside, and Mother weeping, and Mr. Orne ascending the stairs—

Then one night he unlocked the door and entered the room with his Bible under his arm and the usual prayers upon his lips. He knelt beside me and took hold of my wrist. He said some words. There was a sharp pain, then, and a light washed over me, cool as spring rain or the touch of God's breath on my forehead, and finally, I slept.

• • •

APR 11

Sunday, no church—

I will not go. Mr. Carr is away on business, and for all of her coaxing, Bridget could not rouse me from the bed. She is a Catholic girl, of course, and quite devout. From the window I watched her hurry off to mass, wearing her Sunday hat with the brim pulled down to her ears.

Then I dressed myself in the blue silk he had loved and sat by the window with my diary in my lap. As I write, I watch the birds circle the rooftops opposite. I admire their ease, their lightness. They drift like bracken on the churning current, carried this way and that with the wind through the chimney-pots, dropping like stones when they sight the river.

The ice is out of the Charles. Every morning reveals a surface more degraded, riven with forks of liquid water. Last week Mr. Carr walked home with me after church. He was meeting a client after lunch, a young man of my own age, and was in rare good spirits. The day was fair and warm and we took the bridge over the Charles.

Halfway across, I paused and gazed down at the river with its plains of blue-grey ice and glimpsed the creek behind them like the words in a palimpsest. I could hear the falls, too, over the clatter of wheels and footsteps, and recalled the garden at night. The rush of water spilling over rocks, foaming far below. The answering hum of the blood running through me.

Mr. Carr joined me at the railing. I asked him of what the ice reminded him. He thought for a moment and said that it resembled a map.

Yes, he said, more confident of himself. It is much like a map of the city. Do you see? he asked, pointing. There is my street, my house.

April 11th and the ice is gone and Mr. Carr's map with it. Beacon Hill has dwindled away into the black water, and soon my father's house will follow. There will be only the river, only the creek, two channels feeding the same sea. I must go back—

APR 15

This morning at breakfast I raised the matter of the house in Walpole and asked Mr. Carr for his leave to travel there. At first I thought he had not heard me, for he did not answer, and did not wrest his gaze from the newspaper.

I must see it, I said. While it is still standing.

He turned the paper over. He continued to read.

Hmm? he murmured.

Father's house, I said. Our neighbors, the Bosworths—

Mr. Carr slapped down the paper.

His cheeks were flushed. They had darkened to purple and the pores stood out below his eyes. We have been married three months, but I have never before seen him angry.

And how is it you have heard of this? he demanded.

Uncle Edmund, I said. He wrote to me.

Is that so? How interesting.

He reached for his coffee cup. He sipped from it, seemingly lost in thought as a carriage passed in the street outside, rattling the buds on the trees.

He shook his head slowly. When he spoke, his voice was low and level.

He said: It is entirely out of the question.

I will be discreet, I said. Say nothing—

He slammed down his cup. The saucer cracked beneath it, upturning the cup and sending the hot liquid spilling across the table. He leapt up and called for Bridget. The girl appeared in the doorway with her eyes downcast, looking terrified.

Clean this up, he said. He indicated the mess before him.

Yes, sir.

He glared at me. Leave us, he said.

And I left—but I listened outside the door.

Mr. Carr was furious with Bridget. He hissed and spat at her and threatened her dismissal. It would seem he believes that she sneaked a letter to my uncle on my behalf. The good Catholic girl, Bridget did deny the accusation, but bowed her head and accepted this punishment as her due, speaking up only to voice her agreement, and later, her apology.

See that it does not happen again, he said. Good day.

Bridget swept out in her apron and skirts. She scurried past me with her face in her hands, reaching the staircase at a near-run.

For his part Mr. Carr pushed back his chair and vanished through the opposite doorway. I heard the front door shut behind him, his footsteps on the stoop.

He will visit his club when the working day is done. He will not return for hours.

Bridget

[The next page appears to have been removed.]

I still think of it, that first sight of the Atlantic. When I was sixteen, we visited the coast south of Portland and stayed with Uncle Edmund in a cottage on the sea.

Evening fell, and we followed the reach of the shore beyond the lighthouse. By then the tide had gone out, leaving the dead fish piled all round and the great ropes of seaweed like sheaves in a summer field, waiting to be taken up and carried in.

The stench was overwhelming, sour and sweet and sharp with the tang of the sea. Father fell ill. He broke from me without warning and stumbled to the water's edge where he emptied his guts into the ocean. Afterward, he lay feverish on the cobble and muttered to himself of the battlefields of his youth: Fredericksburg, Chancellorsville.

I held his hand. I listened. The waves went out from us as the rains moved in, sweeping the shore and eclipsing the light on the rocky headland. There was thunder, then lightning, and Father stirred, moaning with the dark that lived inside him.

I shook him, gently. Father, I said.

He opened his eyes.

APR 19, 5 O'CLOCK—

I have seen to everything. It can do no harm now to write of it.

The carpetbag is packed and secreted beneath the bed, and I am alone, waiting for Bridget to return. She left the house at noon to pawn my wedding ring. With the money she will purchase two tickets for a northbound train that will bring us to Walpole in the morning.

Tomorrow! I am frayed and shaking, a cord drawn taut. I can smell the old garden, the roses. The scent is more vivid in memory than it was in life, mingled with the perfume of soil and damp and that of the blooming linden. I close my eyes and hear the creek, sending up spray where it drops beneath the bridge, and remember the great clouds of dragonflies and the way they drew near us at dusk, wings flashing—

LATER—

I am locked in. The door is shut, the key turned fast.

Bridget has betrayed me. She now keeps watch outside, walking up and down the hallway and singing to herself in Irish. Moonlight spills in a fan across the floorboards, shining on broken glass and specks of hanging dust. I had time only to hide this diary before Mr. Carr stormed inside with Bridget following him meekly.

He was livid, incandescent with rage. He swept the bottles of my medicine from the dressing table and stomped down on the remnants, grinding the glass beneath his shoes.

Bridget retrieved the carpetbag from under the bed. At first I thought she meant to spare it his fury, but instead, she merely placed it wordlessly into his hands. He snarled and tossed the bag on the fire. The fabric caught light, then the clothes inside, the blue silk Father loved—

I threw myself at the fireplace, but Mr. Carr caught me by the wrists and pushed me to the floor at his feet. Throughout this time he said nothing, but his eyes were black and shrunken to points, like those of Mr. Orne, when he ministered to me in the dark of that winter, or those of my mother when first she found us out in sin—

Mr. Carr produced his ring from his coat pocket and jammed it down the middle finger of my left hand, forcing it past the joint so I knew I should not be free of it.

You made a promise, he said. To me, as I did to your mother. We mustn't forget that.

Come, he said to Bridget, and they were gone.

APR 21?

Mr. Orne is here. He paces beyond the door. In his tread I hear the echo of steps from long ago and imagine the house in Walpole where I watch the faceless mourners come and go.

Some hold dresses or kitchen implements, bed-sheets caked with red and yellow filth. One man carries the charred remnants of my carpetbag while another walks with fistfuls of broken glass, blood dripping from his hands. They proceed with unearthly slowness, with all the gravity of pallbearers: rolling up the rugs, wheeling out the cradle, carrying off the materials of home like the seashell spoils of some god-conquering army.

Now the house stands empty. It is a ghost of itself, an absence made visible, like the clothes Father wore that morning, when he left the house, and which the Bosworth boy found above the falls. They were neatly laid out, the boy said, the pants folded in quarters, the wedding ring left in his shoe.

That ring: its smoothness on my skin. Whatever became of it? After the funeral, when the mourners had gone, Mother plucked the band from her own finger and flung it into the creek, as though to sink Father's memory with it, and now I am her cousin's wife.

The lamp is dim. Mr. Carr's ring glitters. It casts a white smear on the wall, *an inverted shadow which moves in time with the rhythm of my hand on the paper so that I think of the moon in Maine as it rose over the headland, dragging the waves behind it, water and light trapped in the song they sang between them until at last you woke and looked at me—*

Dusk when I reach Walpole. From the station I walk to the house, lifting my skirts and sprinting when I hear the singing creek.

I am too late. Little remains save rubble. The floors have been torn out, the walls collapsed into the cellar, and the garden, too, has been plowed under.

The flowers are gone, the rosebushes. Uprooted and piled on the brush heap. Burned. The smell of wood-smoke lodges like cotton in my throat, stopping the air in my lungs. I can't breathe—can't walk—a fever is on me—

It pulls like the spring current. It drags me through the ruined garden on hands and knees and down the path that leads to the footbridge. Here the water ripples, waves within waves. The creek is running high. Below the falls the waters teem with light, the glint of gold like the flash of drowned skin. Mother's ring—or yours—and my blue dress charred and floating—

This was where it happened, where they found you.

Alfie is in the hall. I hear him scratching. I must

The diary ends there. The remaining pages are blank.

In those days, my interest in the abnormalities of the human brain took me to Danvers at least once a month. On my next visit, I sought out the nurse who had sent the diary.

She was a young woman of pretty coloring and sensitive disposition. She was, in fact, nothing at all like the matronly figure I had imagined. I gathered that she had been quite close to Isabella Carr and considered herself to be something much nearer a friend than a caretaker. She thanked me for coming, and for my kindness in reading the diary, and showed me into the room, as yet vacant, in which Mrs. Carr had lived out the final years of her life.

From the nurse, I learned that Mrs. Carr had been committed by her husband following an incident in their Beacon Hill home in which the family's Irish maidservant had been attacked and nearly killed. Edmund Ashe had contested the committal order on his niece's behalf but his efforts failed when evidence of opiate dependency came to light.

Throughout her time in the hospital, Isabella was never seen to write letters or keep a diary but instead spent her days beside the window, absorbed in silent contemplation of the grounds below. When she was twenty-eight, she sickened with pneumonia and died. Afterward the nurse found the diary tucked up inside the lining of the feather bed, where it had languished, apparently forgotten, since Mrs. Carr's arrival at Danvers some years previously.

"I'm not ashamed to say that it gave me the chills," the nurse said. "For a moment I even imagined that she had wanted me to find it. Nonsense, of course. She was ill. Probably she had hidden it inside the bed and forgotten about it. Of course it should have been sent to her family—her mother, if not her stepfather—but after reading it . . . well, it didn't seem right, somehow. And Edmund Ashe is dead these two years."

"Had she no other family?"

"No," she said. "She hadn't."

Her eyes moved over the empty walls and she was suddenly far away.

"It's sad, really. As I said, her uncle tried to fight the committal order. In the courts it emerged that Isabella had mothered a child some years previously, a little boy. She was unmarried at the time, and it had all been hushed up. Her mother and stepfather conspired to hide the pregnancy from their neighbors and married her off to Horace Carr soon afterward. He was Mrs. Orne's cousin, as you know, a man of certain habits, and it was rumored that the marriage had not been consummated."

"And the little boy? What became of the child?"

"He went to an orphanage. A woman came by and carried him away. I don't believe Isabella ever recovered from that—though I was often uncertain of how much she remembered. In any case, the poor babe didn't see his first birthday. Cholera, I believe it was."

"What was his name?" I asked. "The baby's."

She did not answer me immediately. Instead, she went to the window and closed the curtains halfway, drawing a shadow across the bed. She filed from the room but paused in the doorway to address me a final time.

"The child's name," she said, "was Alfred."

She disappeared into the hallway. Her footsteps retreated down the corridor. The sun broke through the parted curtains, and I was alone with my thoughts.

Daniel Mills is the author of the novel *Revenants: A Dream of New England* (Chomu Press, 2011) and of the short fiction collection *The Lord Came at Twilight* (Dark Renaissance Books, 2014). His stories have appeared in numerous magazines and anthologies, including *Black Static*, *Shadows & Tall Trees*, and *The Mammoth Book of Best New Horror*. His second novel will be released in 2017 by ChiZine Publications. He lives in Vermont.

Vampires are haunted, obsessed things, every one among them.
But some much more so than others.

THE CRIPPLE AND STARFISH

Caitlín R. Kiernan

Almost three thousand feet above sea level, the ruins of the Overlook Mountain House squat silent and barren on the crest of its namesake. It is a bleak, disowned place, left for timber rattlers and roosting birds, black bears and chipmunks, visited now only by the occasional sightseers curious and intrepid enough to make the two-hour hike from Woodstock. The hotel burned on a February night in 1923, and all that now remains is a towering grey, right-angle maze of cement poured in 1878, under the direction of architect and builder Lewis B. Wagonen of nearby Kingston, New York. These walls were raised one hundred and thirty-seven years ago, and ninety-two years ago the hotel was razed. There is about this lonely place a mute and inescapable arithmetic—dates, altitude, time, geometry. It is the sum of its history, and little else remains. And, too, there are ghosts, of the fifteen women and men who perished in the fire and of four laborers who died during the hotel's construction. Though, by ghosts nothing more is meant than fading memory, lingering, voiceless echoes trapped forever in empty window casements and in reinforcing iron bars exposed by crumbling concrete and rusting down all the long decades since the fire. Lost souls with names that are nowhere now remembered, faces forgotten, whispers. In the summer, the ruins are wreathed in a riot of green—bracken and saplings and poison ivy, red oaks, mountain paper birch, balsam fir and red spruce, blackberry, blueberry, huckleberry.

But this is not summer. This is a freezing night late in January, and a storm front from Ontario has swept across the Great Lakes to dump its burden of snow on the peaks and ridges and deep glacier- and river-carved valleys of the Catskill Escarpment. The moon, waxing gibbous, is hidden behind the low violet-blue-oyster clouds racing by overhead, occasionally so low that they scrape their underbellies on the mountains, fog-shrouding secrets, concealing those who wish concealment. Those who have come; those who have gathered. Another age might have pulled punches and called this a fairie court, though it is surely nothing of the sort.

All the same, there is a court here.

Below the open sky, where once were the second and third stories and the wide peaked roof of Mr. Wagonen's stately pleasure dome, sits the Queen of Blades, Madam of Keen Steel and Obsidian Massacres, most often known as the Lady of Silver Whispers (she has so, so many sobriquets, but not a proper name among them). She reclines upon her throne. She *names* it her throne, as does her retinue, the attendants and sycophants and hangers-on, but in truth it's nothing more than a broken-backed, mildewed récamier, the upholstery so threadbare and rotted than it hangs in faded strips the black and golden yellow of a yellowjacket wasp. She is naked, save the charcoal smears painted on her white skin, skin as pale and cold as the falling, drifting snow. Her eyes are rubies. Her lips are the deep, poisonous black of drooping clusters of belladonna berries, and her kiss is loaded with the same hyoscine, atropine, and hyoscyiamine compounds found in those very same deadly nightshades. Her nails are carved of cobalt glass, as good as.

The court teems around her, frenetic, freed on nights like this from their necessary seclusion, from the shadow sorceries that conceal them from the eyes of men—save on those rare instances when they choose to reveal themselves. They mutter delightful obscenities among one another, they argue philosophy and history and fashion, they prostrate themselves at her feet. Some among them caper and dance, fuck and engage in acts so perverse that no one would ever deign to call those acts mere fucking. Most nights here there is only hunger, their mutual craving shared and unsated, but not tonight. Tonight there has been a feast, a carload of unwary travelers whose Prius broke down on Route 212, three warm bodies stolen like children from their cribs—father, mother, daughter—and presented to the Lady of Silver Whispers. All here have drunk; not their fill, for there is not ever any genuine satiation. But the bill of fare was enough that the nagging emptiness has been dulled for a time.

They are not all her progeny. Some have come here from as far away as Chicago, Manhattan, Ottawa, Boston, Philadelphia, traveling long night-bound miles to witness her glory and to be counted among this number. One of these is a coal-haired woman named Marjorie Marie Winthrop, who was only nineteen years old the night the Overlook Mountain House burned. She's one of the youngest among the court, and she comes and goes, erratic as the weather. The Lady would never count her as loyal; Marjorie Marie has always been too distant and consumed by her own hauntings and obsessions. Vampires are haunted, obsessed things, every one among them. But some, like Marjorie Marie, much more so than others. She sits on stairs that once led up to the hotel's wide south piazza, smoking, wrapped in the raw-bone wind and trying to recall how it felt to shiver.

She isn't alone on the stairs. The man with her was a colonel in the War Between the States, a Union soldier in Lincoln's army, and for decades he has loved Marjorie Marie, in the careless, detached way that vampires love. He sits with her, listening to the laughter and screams and catcalls of the court. His mother named him Hiram Levi, but somewhere down more than a century and a half of life and this existence stranded between life and the grave, somewhere and somewhen he sloughed that name off, like an old skin. Marjorie Marie knows him only as Willie Love, the name he adopted because of his fondness for the harmonicas, guitars, and the voices of the Delta Blues.

"You talk an awful lot," she says to Willie Love. She's soft spoken, and her voice still carries a hint of a Southern Appalachian accent. "Sometimes, I think you're the wordiest dead man whom I've ever met."

Willie Love is always going on about writing books, though, to Marjorie Marie's knowledge, he's never set a single word down on paper. Instead, he seems to carry it all filed behind his red eyes.

He smiles and spares a quick glance at the swirling sky, then continues as if he hasn't been interrupted.

"I was saying, if we conceive of any given human being as the embodiment of the Taoist concept of yin and yang, and of the *taijitu*—which symbolizes yin and yang—each body being black and each soul being white—two distinct things that form a complete whole, distinguishable, divisible, but also intrinsically linked—then what occurs in our passage is that our souls have been, as it were, *inverted*—in part, the white turning to black—and then melded with our flesh. Refashioned, made *in*divisible, *in*extricable, *in*distinguishable.

"Inextricable," she says, and Marjorie Marie takes a long drag on her cigarette. The smoke reminds her of being alive and her breath fogging in the cold. Even though she can't inhale, she *has* long since learned the trick of drawing the smoke into her mouth, then letting it leak slowly from her nostrils and lips. She doesn't feel the nicotine, her metabolism—as much a ruin as the hotel at her back—being entirely incapable of taking it up. Those intoxicating molecules are not passed along through her sluggish bloodstream to cross the blood-brain barrier and act upon waiting acetylcholine receptor proteins in the adrenal medulla, the autonomic ganglia, and the central nervous system. But it helps, regardless, just having something in her mouth, something to take the edge off the endless oral cravings and keep her hands busy.

"Imagine," he continues, "the yin and yang as a paint bucket full of black and white paint, and a stick is inserted into the paint, and it's stirred until it's not black and white, but only a uniform black."

"Wouldn't it come out grey, instead?" she asks him. "Not black, but grey?"

"You're being pedantic," he says.

"Yeah, but black and white make grey."

"Pedantic and too literal. It's a metaphor."

"Still, black and white make grey."

Then Marjorie Marie and Willie Love are both silent for a time, letting the cold night hang heavy between them, filled with the noise from the court. And the ceaseless wind. It's a wild night on the mountain, a wendigo's breath rattling through the trees and roaring across the snow gathered between their trunks, burying root and stone and last autumn's rotting leaves beneath crystalline dunes.

"Is there more?" she asks, finally.

"There's always more," he replies. "Isn't that the way it works?"

"I don't know. You're older than me."

"Older don't make me no way wise, girl."

Marjorie Marie has smoked her cigarette down almost to the filter; she drops the butt and grinds it out against the concrete step with the ball of her bare left foot. Then she lights another. The smoke, seemingly immune to the wind, hangs about her face like a question mark. She has the amber eyes of a lynx. She took her dinner from the mother, and the woman looked into those eyes, and the vampire looked into the woman's soul, her divisible soul that would soon be freed by her death.

Willie Love continues:

"There's that dot of white in the black and, likewise, that point of black in the white half. I think of them as the eyes of the *taijitu*. When we died, you and me, those eyes were plucked from out their rightful places and swapped, so all the white was then in the white and all the black was then in the black. The inherent *balance* of yin and yang was pried apart. Violated. So, our bodies have no soul remaining to keep them alive and animate, and our souls have no body to tether them to the earth. But, see, instead of death, dissolution, whatever, our souls are tied down to—well, I'm not precisely sure what—a piece of magickal material and secreted away. What remains of our souls, now fused, returns as ghosts to haunt our corpses. Our bodies should be decaying away to nothing but bones or less, right, right? Dust. But, no, *instead* they are puppeteered around by our fused black souls, and so long as we feed on the life of others—"

"It sounds to me, Willie, like you're rambling, just pulling this stuff outta your ass. We should go back to the party."

"You hate those fucks, and you know it," he sneers. "I know you know it. You don't want to be in there, not any more than I do."

"Whatever," she says, shrugs, and takes another drag on her cigarette. The tobacco is good. She can't inhale; her lungs have nor drawn breath, haven't inflated, in all those one hundred and eleven years since her death at the hands of a pretty Romanian *moroi*.

"As I was saying," he continues, " Let's take it just one step further, and let us say that the process our transubstantiation and rebirth, that it seared out the *eyes* of the yin and yang—"

"The black and white dots?"

"Right. The black and white dots. So the pieces of our bodies that were in our souls—existing there to maintain balance—are gone. And see, Marjorie Marie, this is why we cast no reflection, why holy water and crucifixes burn us, why our unhallowed flesh cannot bear the touch of sunlight. Because the pieces of our soul that existed within our bodies are gone. Hence no breath, no pulse, no heartbeat or blood pressure. No shitting, no pissing, no fucking ejaculations."

"You miss those, do you?" she smirks.

"Fuck you," he says, then laughs and tosses a dumpling-sized lump of shale towards a paper birch. It hits the trunk with an audible thump, audible at least to their ears, even over the cacophony of the wind and the Lady's bacchanal.

"I used to miss orgasms," she says, "but I got over that a long time ago."

"You were just a kid," he says. "A kid in nineteen aught four, at that. And unmarried. How many orgasms did you ever have?"

"A few," says Marjorie Marie, and she says it a little defensively. "I had a few. Enough to miss them for a time." And wanting desperately to change the subject, to divert his attention from whatever had passed for her sex life before her death at the hands of the Romanian vampire, she says, "There's more, isn't there."

"There's always more," he replies. "Isn't that the way it works?"

"You say so, yeah, that's the way it works."

She smokes, and Willie Love talks.

"Yeah, so maybe it goes like this. The magick of our passage, I mean. Rather than looking soulless, we look like haunted, possessed corpses."

"Speak for yourself, dead man."

"But there's something *different* about her," he says, lowering his voice to a conspiratorial whisper. And he turns his head and points back towards the Lady of Silver Whispers.

"Of course there's something *different* about her," says Marjorie. "Otherwise, she wouldn't be her, now would she? She'd be just be another one of us leeches. I figure it's cause she's older, because she's been around since God was in diapers"

"No," he says, frowning a slight sort of frown. "No, it not so simple as that, I think. You look at her, or I do, and what I see is a *weak* vampire— because I'm only seeing the original black half of her, not the white and black made into one blackness. Whatever happened to her, she lost her soul. It wasn't fused like yours and mine. We assume she's like us, but she isn't. And what we see, that ain't the all of it. She's like an iceberg, and what we see is only *half* of what's really there to *be* seen. If you look hard, if you look really long and hard, you start to glimpse what's hidden below the surface."

"Honestly, I'd prefer not to."

"I know," says Willie Love. "I see how you are around her."

"She's a bag of spiders," says Marjorie Marie.

He laughs again, then adds, "You best be careful what you say aloud, girl. Don't ever think no one's listening in. There's always ears. There's always eyes. *De mortuis aut bene aut nihil*, as they say."

"I've made it this long, haven't I? And without you to play the good shepherd?"

There's a sudden, violent gust of wind, howling past at thirty miles per hour, thirty or forty or fifty, and trees bend and trees snap. Branches tumble to the ground, and snow devils whirl like dervishes in the Ulster County night. But that wind doesn't touch Marjorie Marie or Willie Love. Their life-in-death curse sets them well beyond the reach of the elements, and the gust parts for them like the Red Sea for Moshe *Rabbenu*. Not so much as a hair on Marjorie Marie's head is stirred by the blow's fury.

She shuts her eyes, bored with thinking on Willie Love's metaphysical prattling. He's not the first vampire she's known who cobbles together absurdities and nonsense in a topsy-turvy attempt to understand a thing that cannot be understood, not by minds that once were human. Minds that are still—for all their newfound alienness—not much *more* than the minds of humans. Marjorie Marie pushes his voice aside and lets her thoughts wander, instead, back through decades, through a century and then some, and she can hear the gentle conversations of the women and men, the privileged, monied families, who've come from bustling Eastern and Midwestern cities to spend lazy summer days and easy warm nights in the hotel, to gaze out at the majestic view. She sees them plainly, seated and standing, arranged along the south piazza at her back, attended by black servant boys with cool drinks. The women in their fine gingham and calico day dresses, hems lined with Irish lace, their wide hats adorned with feathers and silk flowers. The men in their tall beaver-skin top hats, playing checkers and cribbage and cards, string ties, bow ties, spats and frock coats. Billy Murray is singing "I'm Afraid To Come Home in the Dark" from the silver horn of a Victrola. It is a perfect summer day, and the fire that will bring down the Overlook Mountain House is more than two decades away. The new century holds in store horrors these people do not even begin to suspect, not from the gentle, sun-washed perspective of the south piazza. They are protected, momentarily, and the future is a slow train coming, with neither the wail of a steam whistle nor the rumble of steel wheels on steel rails to warn them of its murderous intent. They're babes left alone on the tracks.

"Did you hear that?" Willie Love asks, and she opens her eyes.

"I hear lots of shit, old man." And she does. She hears the fractal whisper of the spiraling snowflakes as they brush one against the other. She hears the heartbeat of a fisher cat sleeping in its den not far from the ruins. She hears the footsteps of a red fox, padding along a fallen log, as it stalks a rabbit, and she hears the lazy blink of an owl watching the fox. She hears the court, like a lesser storm raging beneath the clouds. She hears the flow of xylum sap in a maple's trunk.

"You'll have to be more specific," she adds.

"It was nothing."

Marjorie Marie glances back over her shoulder towards the ragged throne of the Lady of Silver Whispers and all the noisy debauchery, and then she stares up into the falling snow and the low clouds, scanning the sky for any hint of dawn.

"They'll be at it all night," says Willie Love.

"Why the fuck do we even fucking come up here every year?"

"Where else, love, would we go?"

Baby dear, listen here—

I'm afraid to come home in the dark.

The fox pounces. The rabbit screams. The owl flies away.

"We're like the demons down under the sea, the tenants of Ol' Sheol," Willie Love says, and he lights the ragged stub of a cigar. "The flesh and life forces as one, rather than two discrete things. Which is, of course, *naturellement*, soulless in the way that humans understand souls. There is nothing remaining to transcend. Nothing has survived that is able, upon the final destruction of the flesh, to flee the body. There are nails, carpet tacks, hammered in all about the tatty edges of our vanquished *élan vital*.

"Willie, do ever actually bother to think about this shit before it comes tumbling out of your mouth?"

Singing just like a lark ,

There's no place like home .

But I couldn't come home in the dark.

"But," he goes on, undaunted, "this means there is still a consciousness, a spark, the *qi* if you wish—the Hebraic *ruah,* the *lüng* of Tibetan Buddhism, *ad infinitum, ad nauseaum*—a *force* there animating the dead flesh, and the dead flesh can be both summoned and guided by magick the way a human soul can—if one is so disposed and has at his disposal the tools, the acumen, and the etheric, nether connections. Ergo, our souls didn't pass on to heaven or hell or whatever, whatever and whichever somewhere. We are, by the curse of our makers, no more than pretty, hungry birds with broken wings."

He rubs at his forehead, then just stares at her awhile.

"What?" she asks. finally, his eyes beginning to make her uncomfortable.

"You're still out there rooting about for your own answers, however much you might mock my suspect conjectures."

And at first she doesn't reply. It's her own goddamn business and certainly none of his, and she has the decency to keep it to herself, not hold forth on the steps of the Overlook Mountain House, lecturing to her indifference and the freezing night and all passing nocturnal beasts.

"Marseilles?" he asks, pushing, apparently done torturing her with his treatise on the trapped souls of the undead.

"No," she says. "Not fucking Marseilles."

"Well, sure as shit not that delusional cobblestone alleyway in le quartier du Montparnasse, within spitting distance or a stone's throw from Cimetière du Montparnasse. Not *that*, sweets, no matter how romantic would have been your undoing so near to the final resting places and narrow houses of Maupassant, Man Ray, Baudelaire, Samuel Beckett, Simone de—"

"It wasn't Marseilles," she says again, interrupting his catalog of those interred in Montparnasse Cemetery.

"I heard you went back to Bucharest," he says. "So, I just assumed—"

"Who told you I went back to Bucharest?"

Willie Love takes the damp, smoldering cigar stub from his mouth and frowns at her. "Well, did you? I thought you were past this, Marjorie?"

And for a week he never got home till the break of day.

At last poor Mabel asked the reason why.

Said Jones, "I'm goin' to tell the truth or die."

She rubs at her lynx-gold eyes, trying to drive away the unwelcome ghost of a song committed to an Edison hard black wax cylinder in 1907. That and all those mumbling, well-heeled Edwardian phantoms who haven't a clue their time on earth has come and gone and will not come again.

"I spoke with Constantin Vasile," says Willie Love.

"You were checking up on me?" Marjorie Marie asks, not bothering to hide her incredulity or to mask the anger creeping into her voice. *Fuck this,* she thinks. *I was better off back there with the Lady's three-ring circus of freaks and fuckwits.*

"No, I wasn't checking up on you. There was another matter. And Constantin mentioned that you were in Bucharest, that you spent a few nights in his attic. He's worried about you."

In a workshop on Strada Pericle Gheorghiu, Constantin Vasile carves crucifixes and rosary beads and miniature wooden saints.

Marjorie Marie shuts her eyes again.

Baby dear, listen here—

I'm afraid to come home in the dark.

On the south piazza, a chubby red-headed man from Boston is complaining about Roosevelt's increasingly radical economic policies. No one seems to be listening to him. Children are laughing.

Was it Marseilles?

Wasn't it?

Here she has a jigsaw puzzle with a thousand pieces, does Marjorie Marie Winthrop, and she's never been especially good with puzzles. And, what's more, what's worse, this is a puzzle missing at least half its pieces.

Missing because they were stolen—those memories of her death—by the one who murdered her. Marjorie Marie doesn't know why. She's never had a chance to ask the bitch, the creature who's chosen never to be anything more substantial than a shadow at the corners of Marjorie Marie's vision.

She said she loved me. She said she loved me, and that she would not see me age and die and be lost to the world.

So, she killed me, emptied my head, dragged me back from the void, and then abandoned me.

The Romanian vampire, whose name Marjorie Marie was forced to forget and has never has learned again—though not for lack of trying—used to send her letters, postcards, vials of perfume, jewelry, packages wrapped in brown butcher's paper that always found her, no matter where she was. But they stopped coming decades ago. For all Marjorie Marie knows, the woman is dead, having at last met her well-deserved undoing at the sharp end of a white-oak stake, purity punching its way through her rotten black heart. Maybe a hunter took her head. Maybe she was burned to ash and the ashes stirred with salt and holy water and scattered across the sea.

"Yeah," says Marjorie Marie, "I was in Bucharest."

"Well, did you find what you were looking for this time?" he asks, even though he knows she knows he already knows the answer.

Her existence has become convoluted sentences.

"It comforts me, that city does," she says, instead of answering his question.

"You're picking at scabs."

Above them, a thunderclap rumbles, like the wrath of an angry god, and Marjorie Marie thinks of Washington Irving's "odd-looking personages playing at nine-pins," attired in their "quaint outlandish fashion." *I could lie down beneath a tree*, she thinks. *I could turn my own Rip Van Winkle trick and sleep away a hundred years. I could dig deep, down past the burrows of groundhogs and the trails of earthworms, into the shale and limestone bones of the mountains, and there I could sleep until this world and all my regret and even the Lady of Silver Whispers has passed from the world.*

"Then why don't you?" asks Willie Love.

"Shit," she says, lighting another cigarette, the last from the pack of Camel Lights she took off the man from the car on 212. "You'd miss me too much."

But I could, thinks Marjorie Marie Winthrop. *I could do just that. Before too long, even Willie Love would forget me.*

"I might," he tells her. "But I might not."

The wind carries the ecstasy and smells and tastes of the court's orgy, and it carries the voices of the tourists on the south piazza. She can hear the roar of the flames that devoured the Overlook Mountain Hotel, the screams of those burning alive, the crash of the roof coming down in a shower of sparks that sailed away into the night, an ember cloud to rain charcoal and soot on the streets of Woodstock and Bearsville. Behind Marjorie Marie and Willie Love, the Lady calls for blood—not the blood of unfortunate mortals, but the blood of her own kind, so much richer, aged in dead veins that are as good as wine or whiskey kegs. It always comes to this, on these long winter evenings, that her appetite turns to cannibalism, and the illusion of immortality, the lie of life everlasting, comes crashing down for the one who loses the lottery.

She reaches into a velvet sack the deadly, sinful crimson of holly berries and draws out the astragulus bone of wild boar. The bag holds an assortment of foot bones from a dozen or more species and each has engraved upon it a Roman numeral. Likewise, a Roman numeral has been drawn with blue chalk upon the forehead of every one of the vampires who has answered the Lady's beck and call to gather with her in the ruins at the top of the mountain. They all came knowing the risk, the price of her company and of the pleasures of her court. But that doesn't make this moment any less terrible, and it doesn't diminish the dread in each unbeating heart as she hands the bone down to her hierophant to be read out. On the stairs leading up to the south piazza, Marjorie Marie and Willie Love fall silent. He chews at the stub of his cigar, and her left hand goes to the mark above her eyebrows: XVII.

"It's a razor-sharp, crap-shoot affair," whispers Willie Love, parroting the lyrics of a song he heard way back in 1995. He smiles. "There is no Hell," he says. And then, "There is no Hell like an old Hell."

They wait for the number to be read, and Marjorie Marie knows that there's some defeated sliver of her that is praying it will be her number, her time, her judgment justly handed down for every misdeed and for daring to play roulette by coming to this high, haunted place on this stormy night.

"You're so full of shit," she says to Willie Love.

"That I am, love. That I surely am."

The Lady of Silver Whisper's jester plays on his tin penny whistle, and even above the storm, the notes are clear as lead crystal, C and F major, the rise and fall, manic cross-fingering, dry lips and breathless breaths blown through the wooden fipple. It's a ritual as old as her reign. It's a ceremony as immutable as the Stations of the Cross, the Lady's own Via Dolorosa.

"Twelve!" cries the hierophant, when the jester's song is finished.

"Twelve," echoes the Lady of Silver Whispers.

Marjorie Marie feels a shiver down her spine, ice in her atrophied guts, though she could not say if these sensations are born of relief or disappointment.

"'Prepare the table,'" says Willie love, "watch in the watchtower, eat, drink: arise ye princes,'" And then he laughs a dry and humorless laugh.

Marjorie Marie turns and peers at him with those shimmering, unreadable lynx eyes of hers.

"Isaiah, Chapter Twenty-One, verses five through nine. 'Babylon is fallen, is fallen, and all the graven images of her gods he hath broken unto the ground.'"

Within the three-story cement walls of the Overlook Mountain House, beneath that roiling blizzard roof, the sacrifice is led through the muttering throng and up to the Lady's yellowjacket récamier. The sacrifice's name is Daciana Petrescu, who died in 1976 in Braşov. Marjorie Marie marvels briefly at the coincidence, that tonight the Lady would be treated to the blood of a Romanian, this tinker's daughter born in a Căldărari village on the banks of the wide Danube Delta. It will only seem a coincidence to Marjorie Marie, of course, striking only the wearisome nerves of her own obsessions. Daciana Petrescu doesn't struggle, and she doesn't cry out or protest in any way; she goes to her doom with dignity, head held high and whatever fear she may feel she doesn't let show. It will be a bad death, an ugly and violent death, but she'll not give the Lady of Silver Whispers the satisfaction of seeing her terror.

"She stole so much of you," says Willie Love. "Whoever she was, whether it was Marseilles or Paris. She mined your memories, scooped you out clean. She left you lost to fill in the gaps, to weave false recollections that may, perhaps, approach the truth, but which will never touch it"

"You're a bastard," she replies.

"Like Constantin, I worry for you."

The Lady's fangs sink into Daciana Petrescu's throat, tearing open the carotid, and what passes for her life is sprayed across the frozen crust at the her killer's bare feet. It wasn't her blood, anyway; easy come, easy go.

"I should leave," says Marjorie Marie. "I never should have come here, and I should go."

"Will you be back next year?" asks Willie Love, doing a shoddy job of disguising his anxiety that she might not, that he might never see her again.

"I should go," she says again, as if that's meant to count as an answer.

"We have expended our souls," he says. "Our creators, our executioners, they expended our souls, which are now one and the same as our flesh, in that implosion of yin and yang. And so, sweet, the only thing awaiting us is oblivion. Not Hell nor Heaven nor Purgatory. Not some pagan, pantheistic underworld. Only nothingness. Me, I take that as a scrap of comfort."

"I'm going now. Take care of yourself, Willie Love. Watch your shadow."

And then she breaks apart, the body of Marjorie Marie exploding into five hundred, six hundred, a thousand shrieking sparrows, a miraculous flurry of tiny bodies and frenetic wings. For a moment, all the Lady's court—and even the gore-lipped Lady herself—turns towards that mad twittering, and the dead man who was born Hiram Levi watches as the flock disappears into the sanctuary of the forest.

Caitlín R. Kiernan's award-winning short fiction has been collected, to date, in fourteen volumes, one of which, *The Ape's Wife and Other Stories* received the World Fantasy Award. Novels include *The Red Tree* and *The Drowning Girl: A Memoir* (winner of the James Tiptree, Jr. Award and the Bram Stoker Award, nominated for the Nebula, Locus, Shirley Jackson, World Fantasy, British Fantasy, and Mythopoeic awards). Mid-World Productions has optioned both to develop into feature films. Kiernan is currently writing the screenplay for *The Red Tree*.

That door led to terrible things . . .

THE DOOR

Kelley Armstrong

Her earliest memory was of the door.

She'd woken in the night, hearing a noise, and padded into her parents' room to see her mother sound asleep. Then the noise came again, a bang from the front of the house. From beyond the door.

She crept down the hall, through the living room and into the kitchen. The door was there. She inched closer, barely daring to breathe.

What if it opened?

What if something was on the other side trying to get in. Some monster from her fairy tale books. An ogre or a troll or a wicked witch.

The house was so silent she could still hear her mother breathing. Then the noise came again.

She swallowed and wrapped her arms around herself.

Something *was* there. Beyond the door.

She was not supposed to open the door. That was the rule. The only real rule she'd ever known. Do not open the door. Never open the door.

But if a monster was out there . . .

She had to peek. Just a peek to be sure before she ran and woke her mother.

She slid toward the door, one stockinged foot and then the other, making as little noise as possible. Then she gripped the knob and turned.

The door opened easily. On the other side . . . Well, she knew what was *right* on the other side, because she'd caught glimpses before. It was a tiny room with boots and shoes and other stored items. And a second door. When Momma or Daddy went out, they'd go through the first one, and then they'd close it before she'd hear them open the other. That was the real door. The one that led to terrible things, and she had no idea what those things were, nor had her parents even said they were terrible, but she knew. She just knew.

The noise came again and she struggled for breath and then continued her sliding walk toward that second door—

It opened and a figure filled it. A huge figure carrying a huge bag, and she had one brief flash of all the monsters it could be—all the trolls and the ogres—and then she heard, "Oh! What are you—?" and it was her father's voice, and he hurried in and quickly shut the door and put down the bag before scooping her up. "What are you doing here, sweetheart? You know you aren't supposed to open the door."

"I heard a noise."

"Ah, well, that would be me, very happy to be home. I didn't mean to get in so late. But I brought you treats. Lots of treats."

With the bag dragging from his other hand, he carried her through the inner door and kicked it shut behind them. Then he set her on the table and opened the sack. Inside she saw food. He dug down and pulled out a long box covered in bright pictures.

"Do you know what this is?" he asked.

She shook her head.

"Candy Land. It was my first game when I was your age. Now it's yours. And to go with it . . . " He dug deeper and pulled out something that made her squeal, and he chuckled and handed her the red lollipop. "Candy Land and candy. The perfect match. And books, too. I brought lots of books. Now, let's find one, and we'll read it while you eat that lollipop, and then you'll be ready to go back to bed. We have a big day tomorrow, putting away all the food. I have more on a wagon outside. I'll bring it all in while you find a book you like."

That was her first memory. Her first game, too. The first of many. Many games and many days spent playing them, the three of them. Even more than the games, her father brought books. He'd read them to her or her mother would, and soon, she could read them to herself, at least the easy ones.

There were toys, too. Action figures and stuffed animals and building blocks, and she'd act out the scenes from the books, sometimes by herself, sometimes for her parents.

Her mother would tease that Daddy brought back more books than food. Once, when she was supposed to be asleep, she heard Momma doing more than teasing about it, talking to her father in a low, anxious voice.

"She doesn't need so much. The toys, the books, the games. Not if it means you have to stay out there longer."

"I'm fine," he said. "And if it makes her happy, it makes me happy."

They were happy. Just the three of them, in their house. There was a yard, too. In books, every house had a yard, and theirs was no different. A backyard with a swing and a slide and grass and a fence, and she was not supposed to climb the fence, but she could lean against it and gaze out at the endless blue sky, the sun shining down from above.

Then, when she was old enough to read all the books, she got a surprise. They all got a surprise, or so it seemed from her parents' whispered conversations. A baby. A girl. A little sister. Then it was the four of them, and it was as if everything started over again. Out came the baby books, with her reading them to her sister, and then Candy Land, pulled up from under the house where they'd stored it.

Some of the old toys and games and books—the ones she'd outgrown— would go away with Daddy, but the ones she couldn't bear to part with were still there, in the storage space under the house and, later, piled up outside along the fence. She remembered once, after reading about a storm, her sister had panicked on seeing the piles of books and games along the fence.

"We have to bring them in!" she said. "They'll get wet when it rains."

She'd laughed at that, laughed and scooped her sister up. "Have you ever actually seen it rain, silly?"

"Well, no, but it must, right? When we sleep?"

She shook her head. "Rain is only in books. Like snow and storms and polar bears. Now, speaking of polar bears, there's a book over here that I think you'll like . . . "

It was not long after that that Daddy got sick. The arguments, still quiet ones, held behind their parents' closed bedroom door happened more often.

"I'll go out instead now," their mother said. "It's my turn. You're sick and—"

"—and I will not get any less sick by staying indoors. I'll do it for as long as I'm able, gather as much as I can, while I can. You'll need to go out soon enough."

Momma cried at that. Cried so softly that she had to put her head against the door to hear the quiet sobs and their father's equally quiet voice, soothing her, calming her, until the bed creaked and there were more whispers and sighs and then all went quiet.

Their father did not go out for as long after that. Short trips, but more of them, until the space under the house was teeming with more food than she'd ever seen. And then he could not go out, could barely leave the couch, and they'd take turns sitting with him and reading to him, or just playing and reading in the same room until, one morning, he did not wake up.

"But we'll see him again, won't we?" she said to their mother, after the days of crying, of grief. "That's what the books say. That we'll see him when we go wherever he is."

"That sounds about right," their mother said and hugged her hard.

Time passed. Their mother went out now, often for days on end, and despite what she'd said about their father bringing back too many books and games and toys, she did the same.

Her sister was old enough to read all the books when their mother took ill. It was as it had been with their father, a slow progression of wasting, with more frequent but shorter trips out as she filled the stockpile below the house.

When their mother became too sick to leave her bed, she stayed with her, bringing food and books and games. Then came the night when their mother woke her and motioned not to wake her sister, sound asleep on the other side of the bed.

"I have one more book for you to read," Momma said, her voice a papery whisper, so soft that she had to bend to hear her.

Momma pressed a thin leather journal into her hands. "I wrote this for you. It explains everything—what happened here, what you'll need to do, how to get food and water." Momma took her hands and wrapped them around the book. "You will need to make a decision when you read it. What to do about the door. For your sister."

She nodded.

"Your father did all this for you," Momma said. "He loved you so much. We both did." A moment's pause and then, "Were you happy?"

She frowned, not understanding the question.

"Were you happy? Here? Like this?"

"Of course."

Momma took her face in her hands and kissed her forehead, her lips so light she barely felt them. "I hope you still can be. I hope you both always can be. We were. In spite of everything."

Momma lay down and rested and then, as dawn's light slipped into the room, she gave a long rattling sigh, and her chest stopped rising and stopped falling.

She leaned over their mother and kissed her cheek. Then she carried her sister into the living room and put her on the couch. Once her sister was tucked in, she retrieved the book from her mother's bedside and headed for the kitchen.

• • •

The door.

She'd not seen it in so long. The inner one would open and close, and she would not even bother trying to peek through anymore. She didn't care what was out there.

Yet now . . .

She looked down at the book. She could read it first. Get answers that way. But she set it on the kitchen table and walked to the door instead. She opened the inner one. Then she moved through the tiny room that still held their father's shoes and jacket.

There was a lock on the outer door, up high where the children could not reach it. But she wasn't a child anymore, and when she stood on her tiptoes, she could turn it easily. She did, and she pulled open the door and stepped out.

Light. That was the first thing she saw, and it was all she saw, the light so bright it hurt and she doubled over, shielding her eyes. At first it seemed to come from everywhere. As her eyes slowly adjusted, she realized that the light came from an opening nearly as tall as her. She could see nothing except that opening. She walked toward it and ducked and went through it and—

Her stockinged toes touched down on nothing, and she pulled back quickly. She put her hands over her eyes to block the light, and then peered through her fingers. She saw . . . sky. That was all. Sky. Except it didn't look like the sky behind the house. This blue was pale, almost white, and the clouds moved. She blinked hard and stepped back, and when she did, her gaze dropped and she saw a city.

She knew it was a city from pictures in her books. A city below, sprawled out beyond the forest.

A dead city.

That was the phrase that sprang to her mind. She didn't know from where until a memory flashed, of her father speaking to her mother long ago.

"It's a dead city now," he'd said. "Everyone who could leave is gone. Everyone who stayed . . . The radiation . . . "

"Is it safe to even be going there?"

"Do we have a choice?"

She could only vaguely recall reading about radiation in a book and knew nothing more about it. Her mother's journal would explain. For now, she understood this—that the food and water they needed to survive was out there, where it wasn't safe, but there was nothing they could do about that except not eat, not drink.

Her eyes had adjusted enough that she could look around and when she did, she saw that she was standing in the mouth of a cave high above the city. A cave in a mountainside.

She looked behind her, and there was their house. Built inside a cave. She walked back through the hole, exhaling in relief as the light dimmed and she could see better.

She looked at the walls, painted bright blue. Her sky. She glanced down to see the green underfoot, not like the green beyond the cave's mouth at all, but short and prickly and never growing any longer. Her grass. Her gaze turned up to see a hole in the roof of the cave, with light streaming through. Her sun.

She heard a click and then the padding of feet in the small room and a voice calling her name. With a gasp, she raced to the door and through it, and scooped up her sister as she pulled the door shut behind her.

"And what are you doing, missy? You know you aren't supposed to open the door."

"I heard a noise. And Momma won't wake up."

Grief surged as she buried her face in her little sister's hair. "I know. We'll talk about that. First, though, don't ever open the door. There's no reason to. Everything you need is in here."

And with that, she made her decision. Without even considering an alternate choice, she made it.

She put her sister down and prodded her into the kitchen. "Let's go play a game. Maybe Candy Land. I know it's a baby game, but I feel like playing it today. Later, we'll have breakfast and talk about Momma. In a few days, I'll need to go out, like Momma and Daddy did. But not yet. Not just yet."

She stepped into the tiny room and locked the outer door. Then she walked into the kitchen, shut the inner door firmly behind her and went to play Candy Land with her sister.

Kelley Armstrong is the author of the Cainsville modern gothic series and the Age of Legends YA fantasy trilogy. Past works include Otherworld urban fantasy series, the Darkest Powers & Darkness Rising teen paranormal trilogies, and the Nadia Stafford crime trilogy.

Mom's theory was that some people are born for a reason;
born to do a specific thing.

DANIEL'S THEORY ABOUT DOLLS

Stephen Graham Jones

I'm twelve when this all starts, and Daniel's about to be five. And I thought he was like the rest of us, then. I thought he was like I had been, at his age. But he wasn't. It could be he had been born different, of course. Or maybe one day, walking down the hall on his short legs there had been a click in his head, a deep, wet shift in his chest that made him roll his right shoulder, look at all of us in a colder way. Not just me and Mom and Dad. After that click, he looked at *people* in a colder way. I should have been watching him the whole time. I should have never slept. Then I could have seen him in his twin bed across from mine one night, when he coughed up a shiny black accretion, studied it in the moonlight sifting through our bedroom window, then wrapped it in a tissue, leaving it on the nightstand for Mom to throw away.

It was his soul.

None of us would know for years.

For our whole childhood he was just Daniel, always the full name. My little brother seven years younger, the accident that almost killed my mom, being born, like he'd been picking at the walls of her womb, latching his mouth onto places not made for feeding. He didn't talk until he was four. The doctors said not to worry, that some kids just took their time.

This isn't about him getting all the attention, either. This isn't about me growing up off to the side, taping and gluing my action figures and trucks back together and starting them on another adventure I was going to have to make up alone.

I'm good with the alone part. Really.

Those first four years when Daniel wasn't talking, the house was always buzzing anyway. New wallpaper, the trim painted over and over, slightly different shades each time, like a bird's egg fading in the sun, its inside baked rotten.

Our mom and dad were preparing for our little sister. Trying to make her room at the end of the hall so perfect that she couldn't help being born. Perfect enough that she wouldn't listen to the doctors, who told Mom there was no way, that Daniel had messed her up too bad, too forever.

Dad wanted a little princess, see. And our mom would kill herself to give him that princess, if she had to.

So, when the baseboards finally matched the color of the new knobs on the cabinets, when the corners had been sanded off all the coffee table and footboards, when Dad had parked all the tractors in a line by the barn, then re-parked them again, it finally happened: Janine.

Our mom and dad named her early so they could coo to her through the tight wall of skin my mom's stomach became. They named her so they could lure her out, so they could talk her through.

To explain it to us, what was happening, my dad got a black marker with a sharp point and drew the outline of a sideways baby onto Mom, like a curled over bean with fingers and toes and an open eye watching us. If we'd been a family that already had a daughter, we might have had a leftover doll to use, to explain this process with, but what we had instead was Dad's strong bold lines on our mom's belly.

Years later, at a movie theater, I would see the outline of a person taped off on the street, where they'd died their dramatic movie death, and I would lean forward, away from my date. I would lean forward and turn my head sideways, to see if I could hear that person under the asphalt, whispering.

Daniel told us it's how he learned to talk: hours on the couch with Mom in her seventh month, his head pressed flat to her bared stomach, Janine whispering to him.

When she died just like the doctors had said she would, Dad had to break down the bathroom door to keep Mom from eating all the soap from the towel cabinet. I remember him carrying her down the hall, bellowing at us to get out of the way. How her mouth was foaming, how her eyes were so blank.

I don't know if she was trying to choke herself to death or if she thought she was dirty on the inside.

After she was sedated on the couch, and Dad was pouring me cereal at the formal dining room table we never used, I heard Daniel speaking words for the first time.

I stood from my chair, peered over the back of the couch.

Daniel had rolled Mom's shirt up, had the side of his head pressed to her stomach.

He was talking to Janine.

It was the only time I ever hit him.

Mom's theory. when she checked back into the world, was that some people are born for a reason. That they're born to do a specific thing. And, in teaching Daniel to talk, Janine had done that specific thing. It released her from having to be born at all.

We held a private service for her in the woods behind our house. I got dressed up and combed my hair flat and everything.

We walked single-file out to where we'd used to have picnics, under the big tree. It was maybe five minutes past the edge of the pasture. Our dad was trying not to cry. Our mom was squeezing his hand. Daniel was standing on the other side of the hole from me. I guess our dad had dug the hole the night before, or early that morning.

"Will the ants get her?" Daniel asked.

Because they always found our watermelon as soon as we cut it.

Mom shook her head no, not to worry.

The box they had for her was cardboard and waxy and as long as Dad's arm. It smelled like flowers, and, because Mom's stomach was still big, that box made less sense than anything else in the history of the world, ever.

They didn't explain it to us.

We raised our voices, sang one of the children's songs Mom had been humming down to Janine since the first month.

It was nice, it was pretty, it was good.

Except for that box.

It fit into the hole perfectly, and all four of us used our hands to clump the dirt back in over it. Then my dad pulled a little sharpshooter shovel from behind some tree and scooped a little more on, and tamped it all down into a proper mound.

"No marker," our mom said, her hand over her own heart, like cupping it. "*We'll* be the marker, okay?"

This is how families survive.

"Okay," Daniel said, trying the sounds out.

Dad rustled Daniel's mop of hair. It was like a hug, I guess.

"I think he's had the words in there the whole time," Dad said.

"My big boys," Mom said, and lowered herself to her knees, pulled Daniel and me to her and held on, her belly between us, a hard, dead lump.

"Okay," Daniel said again, quieter.

He wasn't talking to us.

Three nights later I woke softly, my eyes open for moments before I could see through them, I think.

They were fixed on Daniel's bed.

It was empty.

I trailed my fingers on the walls, felt my way through the darkened house. Living room, kitchen, utility. Dad's study, Mom's sewing room. Their bedroom, the two of them breathing evenly in their musty covers.

Then Janine's room at the dead end of the hall.

I would get in trouble if the sound woke my parents—Janine's room was already in the process of becoming a shrine—but I clicked the light on.

It was like stepping into a cupcake. Everything was lace and pink and white-edged, like a thousand doilies had exploded, fell into an arrangement that before had only existed in our dad's head.

Daniel wasn't there either.

I turned the light off, trying to muffle the sound in the warmth of my palm, and in that new darkness I saw a firefly bobbing outside the window.

Except it was a yellowy flashlight, moving through the trees.

Daniel.

I pulled my shoes on without tying the laces and crept out the front door, left it open a crack behind me.

Five minutes later, I caught up with him.

He'd seen where Dad put that little sharpshooter shovel. It was just his size.

By the time I got to Janine's grave, he'd already dug down to the waxy cardboard-box center.

I reached out to stop him—he didn't know I was there—but it was too late.

He'd already stepped down into the open grave, the box not supporting his weight, the sound of a jumbo staple popping loud in the night.

And then I didn't say anything.

What he pulled up from that box, holding it under the armpits like a real baby, was the doll Dad had bought for Janine, the doll he hadn't had to demonstrate the baby in Mom's stomach.

She'd been stripped naked, of course.

If her eyes rolled open, it was too far for me to see, and too dark.

• • •

Because I'd left the door open, when I got back to the house there was something turning in slow deliberate circles on the couch.

A possum. It was following its rat tail around and around, like it had lost something, or was patting down a bed for itself.

It hissed at me, showed it rows of teeth, sharp all the way back to the hinge of its jaw.

I fell back, clutching for the coat rack, to pull it down in front of me, maybe, to hide what was going to be my screaming escape, but what my fingers dug into, it was the shirt of Daniel's pajamas.

He didn't even look over at me as he crossed the living room, the shovel held over his shoulder like a barbarian axe.

The possum screamed when he swung the blade into it, and by the time our mom and dad had clambered into the living room, my dad with his pistol held high like a torch, my mom's silk sleep mask pushed up on her forehead like a visor, the possum was biting at its own opened side, and rasping.

Daniel looked up to Dad, then to Mom.

The shovel was twice as tall as he was.

"*Daniel*," our dad said, his voice trying to be stern, I think.

It didn't work.

"Oh," Mom said then, and stepped back from the bloody couch. From the dying possum.

The possum's babies were calving off. They'd been hidden under the dark back fur on her back. They looked like malformed mice.

I clapped my hand to my mouth, threw up between my fingers.

Daniel brought the flat of the shovel down on the fastest of the babies, was, as our dad said later, too young to know better, too young to understand.

Dad wasn't standing where I was, though. He wasn't close enough to hear Daniel.

Daniel was whispering to someone.

I'm thirty-eight now, and that night under the tree, The Night of the Possum, as we came to call it, it's still as clear in my mind as if it just happened.

Daniel would be thirty, I guess.

And, I wish I could trace a line from the year Janine died to now, and put hashmarks on it. This is Daniels' first date. This is the neighbor's new colt. This is when he figured out the bus lines—when he figured out he could go into the city by himself. This is him in the guidance counselor's office, the counselor not finding an explanation for him in any of the college textbooks she'd saved.

This is Mom and Dad, watching him return again and again back into the trees.

This is me, growing up to the side.

My first date was with Chrissy Walmacher. The neighbor's new colt is hers. I sat with her while it was dying, for horse reasons I never really understood. This is me and Chrissy, riding the bus to a concert in the city. This is the guidance counselor, veering her to this school, for that life, and veering me to a different school, for a different life.

This is me at thirty-four, standing at my dad's funeral, my mom there, Daniel pulling up at the last moment, his suit perfect, his face set to "mourning," his eyes drinking the scene in for cues.

We had had the same grades, played the same sports.

Without me providing the model of what to do, I think Daniel would have had to reveal himself. As it was, he could just step into my shoes, follow my lead, fit in, attract zero attention.

What Dad died of, it wasn't anything. Just cigarettes. Just too many years.

Standing there, I was only on my second job of the year. I'd tried normal jobs, offices, even manual labor, but indexing books in the privacy of my apartment on the second floor was finally the only thing that fit. It was work that made sense.

Contracts were getting fewer and farther between, though. There's software that can do what I do, more or less. With a little fine-tuning afterward, even I have a hard time telling any substantial difference.

Dad dying, it wasn't a windfall for me, or for Mom or Daniel either, but it was going to help. My grief was a little bit of a mask as well.

After the funeral, to escape the house, I drove Daniel down to the bar my dad had been loyal to, the years after Janine—before he cut drinking off altogether, at my mom's request.

This was the real funeral. Walking through a space he had walked through, at our age. Moving as he moved, our reflections in the smoky mirror perhaps vague enough to fall into step with his. We were trying his life on, and, before we'd even sat down, we were finding his life not that interesting.

Saying goodbye, it's complicated.

Daniel ordered the same beer I did. He'd never cared about beer, probably wasn't even going to drink this one to the bottom.

"So what's what these days?" I asked.

I'd seen actors on TV open conversations exactly like that, in places like this.

"You know," he said.

He'd bloomed into an electrical engineer. In his senior year, when I was first getting on the job market, I remember him building model intersections on Dad's shop table, and wiring stoplights, giving them this or that trigger, this or that safety. The traffic was imaginary, but the lights always clicked through their cycles perfectly.

Mom and Dad would stand in the doorway, Mom's hands balled at her throat with pride.

Everything they'd been saving for Janine, they heaped it onto Daniel.

My one-time girlfriend Chrissy Walmacher's second wedding had been two weeks ago. She'd invited me, and it had put a picture in my head of me standing at a white fence, looking over. Just another sad postcard I sent to myself in a weak moment. One of many.

"Any girls to speak of?" I asked.

Daniel leaned back, shrugged his right shoulder in that way he had, like he was about to shove his right hand deep into his pocket for the perfect amount of change. He wasn't looking at me anymore, but at a college girl with hair so metallic red it had to have just been dyed, or colored, however that happens. She was sliding darts from the dartboard, one booted foot pulled up behind her like she was kissing someone in a movie.

"Stay single," I told him, raising my glass. "These are your good years."

He came back to me, his fingers circling his own mug.

What he didn't say, what he didn't ask, was How would I know this gospel I was preaching?

Big brothers are required to say certain things, though. To give advice, whether it's from experience or from a book of celebrity interviews that now has a comprehensive index.

"You going to miss him?" Daniel said then, watching my eyes for the lie.

"He's Dad," I said, taking another long drink.

"But still."

Behind me a dart struck home, and the redhead tittered.

"I miss him for Mom," I said.

"Yeah," Daniel said, nodding like this was true. Like this was something he hadn't thought of.

"I saw you that night," I said then, trying to spring it on him. "Did you ever know?"

I'd been saving it for more than half my life.

Daniel looked to me, his head turned sideways, like for clarification.

"Night of the Possum," I said, in our family way.

"Oh, yeah," Daniel said. "The possum. Man. I'd nearly forgotten her."

Until just that exact moment, I'd never once thought of that possum as having a sex. But of course it had been a mom. It had had babies. Of course. *Her.*

The way he said it was so personal, though. So intimate.

"*What* did you see?" he said, setting his mug down after touching the beer to his lips again. He wasn't drinking it, I didn't think. He was just doing what I did. He was fitting in. He was looking like one of us.

He wasn't, though.

Not even close.

According to Daniel, he'd been out to Janine's grave in private in the weeks since her funeral—a behavior learned from Mom and Dad, he claimed, from following them on the sly, making their little pilgrimage of grief before dinner two or three times a week, if it was just a casserole cooking. He'd been there, sure, but never with a shovel. Never to dig that little cardboard coffin up. What did I think he was, a ghoul? Can a kindergartner even *be* a ghoul?

"That's what I'm saying," I told him, a beer deeper into this night of nights. "You were just, like, curious, I think. As to what we'd actually buried."

"Janine," he said.

I stared at him about this, waiting for him to see it.

I'm an indexer, Daniel an electrical engineer, but still, we'd both figured out long ago that what happens with Mom's kind of miscarriage is that the body either reabsorbs the fetus or the body chunks it up, delivers it bit by bit, to be assembled never.

Not pleasant to think about, but the human body's crawly and gross when you look too close.

Each of us figuring that out about Janine, it was probably why we'd gone into comparatively sterile work settings: desks, drafting tables.

Nothing with blood.

"It would have messed me up, though, right?" Daniel said, touching that warm beer to his lips again. "Given me a unique perspective on—on *life*."

I took a real drink, waited for him to say the rest.

I didn't want to disturb this moment.

He was watching the redhead behind me again, talking to the two girls she was with. It was like he was taking a series of still shots with his mind. With his heart.

The reason he was dismissing my question about girls was because girls were all there was for him. I could tell by the way he watched her. But it would cruel for him to flaunt it in front of his big brother. In front of his practically celibate big brother.

"If I'd dug her up like you say, I mean," Daniel said, coming back to me for a moment. Holding my eyes with his, probably so he could gauge how I was taking this: as hypothetical, or as confession.

"You did dig her up," I said. "That's why you had that shovel. For the possum."

"It was right there on the porch," Daniel said, his voice falling into that little-brother whine I hated. "I was on my way back from the bathroom and I heard you, came to see. The door was open behind you, man. The shovel was right there where Dad left it. It's where he always left it, for snakes. Remember?"

I studied the grain of the table top, trying to track this version.

Mom *had* had an encounter with a king snake. That little sharpshooter shovel *did* have a handle at top, perfect for holding the shovel blade steady over a snake's head.

But I'd seen.

"So, *if* you'd dug her up," I finally said. Because there had to be *some* ground he would cede.

Daniel pushed air out his nose in a sort of one-blow laugh, a version of the way Dad used to dismiss our pleas for money or keys or permission, and said, "Then . . . she would have been dug up?"

"We should go out there," I told him.

He wiped his mouth with the back of his hand. "There wouldn't be anything," he said. "Not after all these years. Maybe an eyeball. Those are hard plastic, right?"

"You're talking about Janine," I said.

"We're talking about a doll," Daniel said. Obviously. "And, say we go out there, and that doll's still there," Daniel said, leaning over his beer. "Would that somehow prove that I dug up the . . . the surrogate of Janine, and then put her *back* exactly as she'd been?"

He was right.

"Or it would prove that nobody'd ever dug her up at all," he said, lifting his beer and setting it down, for emphasis.

"I thought—" I said then, looking behind to the group of college girls as well, "I guess I just thought that . . . you were a kid, man. I thought that, that you might really think that stupid doll *was* Janine. Whether you dug her up or not."

"It. Whether I dug *it* up or not."

"I thought you'd think that that was what Mom had had inside her all along. That, I don't know, she would have grown up into a mannequin or something. That everybody was always walking around with these dolls lodged in them, waiting to get out."

"The women at least," Daniel added, in his playing-along voice.

"It's your theory," I said. "Or, I mean, it would have been."

Daniel wasn't watching the college girls anymore. Just me.

"I was five," he said, finally. "Not stupid. But thanks, big brother."

I nodded like I deserved that, and kept nodding, drank another beer, talked about nothing, and left him there with the college girls, didn't talk to him for two years, I think it was. And that was just for Mom's funeral.

Her granite headstone came in two months later.

Carved into it was that she'd been mother to three beautiful children.

I ran my fingers over the jagged valleys of those letters, and watched cars pass on Route 2.

"Guess you can die of being alone," Daniel had said to me earlier that day, about Mom.

Or, not about Mom, but *because* of Mom.

He was talking about me, though.

I was becoming the male version of a spinster.

It can happen when you grow up without enough light.

Ask anybody.

For the next year and a half or two years, Daniel was a ghost. He lived in the city, I even knew where, but the life he led—it wasn't even a mystery to me, really. I assumed it would be a follow-through of who he'd been before. And I was happy for him. One of us deserved that.

I was out at the farm, sleeping in the same bedroom I'd slept in as a boy.

Someday I'd move into Mom and Dad's room, I told myself. Someday.

The lacy drapes in Janine's room were so fragile now that touching them made them crumble. Nearly three decades of sunsets can do that.

At night, crossing to my desk for another round of pages, I would find myself watching the window over the kitchen sink. For fireflies. For Janine.

She never came, though. She'd never even been born. Finally, as I'd known all along was going to happen, I walked out into the trees with a new shovel, to settle this argument.

Our big tree was the same as it had always been. In tree-years, the intervening decades hadn't even been a blink.

The grave mound was long gone, of course. Now there were beer bottles and old magazines scattered around, meaning teenagers had discovered our idyllic spot. The models in the magazines were wearing clothes from years ago, staring up at me from the past.

I pushed the blade of the shovel into the ground, leaned over it, gave it my meager weight and dug deeper than my dad had, just to be sure.

Nothing.

That night I dug two holes.

The next night, three.

On the fourth night, angry, I raised the shovel before me formally, like a cross I was about to plant once and for all, and sliced down through a long slender root. I closed my eyes, sure this had been the tap root. That this tree had lived two hundred years just to have me kill it by accident. Kill it to settle a debate that was only happening in my head.

If it had been the taproot, and if my dim recollection that this was a good way to kill a tree was accurate, it would be a week or more before the leaves wilted at the edges, anyway.

I didn't know if I could force myself to watch. Meaning this tree was either going to be alive or dead to me for the next few decades. When I'd think about it, the picture of it in my mind would shudder between possibilities, and that clutch in my gut would either be guilt or relief. Either absolution or condemnation.

And Daniel was right: the waxy cardboard box, it had long since been reclaimed. I kept hoping for at least a rusted staple to prove the burial, the coffin, the funeral we'd all been complicit in staging, but even staples would have turned back to earth, this long after.

It was about this time that something started going wrong with my stomach. With my digestion. The doctor my plan allowed told me it was nerves, it was stress, that I would push through, get better. Not to worry. Then he clapped my shoulder, guided me back out into the daylight of the city.

I stood in the parking lot by my car for longer than the attendant understood. He watched me the whole way past his little guard booth, perhaps trying to gauge for himself the news I'd just received. It would be a game you would come up with just to stay sane, sitting in that guard booth day after day.

I was dying, I didn't tell him.

It was that house. Living there, it was killing me the same way it had Dad, the same way it had Mom. Because I had no real connections to the world, no fibers or tendrils reaching out from me, connecting me to people, the world was letting me go. Letting me slip through. Maybe it was even mercy.

And the house was the mechanism. My stomach had been fine before, my digestion nothing I'd ever had to think about.

Radon, lead paint, asbestos, contaminated water, treated lumber sighing its treatment back out: it could be anything poisoning me.

I had to warn Daniel. Sell the house after my funeral, I would tell him. After I'm gone, get rid of it. Don't keep it because of Janine. She was never even real, man. And she's not there anymore, either. I looked. I looked and I looked. She's gone. And it's for the best.

Driving to the address I had lodged in my head like a tumor, the townhouse listed under Daniel's name for years in our shared legal documents and invoices, I indexed in my head the talk I was going to give him. It made it more real, having an index. Being able to turn to this page for that part, another page for a different part.

It calmed me, kept me between the lines the whole way over.

I parked behind his garage, blocking him in if he was there—the visitor slots were all taken—knocked on his door. No answer. I didn't knock again, just sat on his patio and studied the sides of my hands, my stomach groaning in its new way. After twenty or thirty minutes, the super or maintenance man came by, greeted me by Daniel's name.

"Brother," I corrected, stopping him, waving off the apology already coming together on his face.

"Oh, yeah," the super or maintenance man said, close enough now to see. "Mr. Robbins not home yet?"

"Guess not," I said. "I can wait. He didn't know I was coming by. Kind of a surprise reunion."

"Here," the maintenance man said, and stepped past, and, just on the authority of family resemblance, opened the door with the master key, pushed it open before me as if to prove this was really happening.

It was an indication of how little of a threat I looked to be. An indication of how frail I must appear, that sitting on patio furniture in the sunlight could be considered cruel, could be something he would want to save me from.

"You can die of being alone," I said to myself, once I had Daniel's door pulled shut behind me.

Daniel's place was much as I guess I'd imagined it: black-and-white prints bought as a set—some national park, and the sky above it—a sectional leather couch, a large television set rimed with dust. An immaculate kitchen. Ice-cold refrigerated air.

I called Daniel's name just to be sure.

Nothing.

I settled into the couch, couldn't figure out his remote control.

I felt like an intruder. Like one of those people who break into vacation homes and move through them like ghosts, running their palms over the statuettes, over the worn arms of the dining room chairs.

I almost left, to do this right, to call him, arrange a proper visit.

For all I knew, when he came home, there would a girl under his arm, fresh from happy hour, him having to guide her shoulders so she could find the couch. So she could find the couch occupied by her date's pale reflection.

I stood, breathing harder than made sense for somebody alone in a room, and told myself just the bathroom, and that I was to leave it exactly as it was, no splashes, no drops, no towels hung obviously crooked, no smudges on the mirror. And then I would leave.

Except, on the back of the toilet was a mason jar, one of those kinds with the lids that have wire cages on them, to trap all the air. Behind the thick glass was what I assumed to be potpourri, or some sort of collection of dried moss strands. I picked it up gingerly, turned it to the side.

It was hair. Long winds of dry hair.

I rolled the jar in my hand, studying it. The hair was in sedimentary layers. Like a curio from a gift shop.

I shook the jar timidly. All the hair stayed the same. And it really was hair. I set it down, zipped up, and was going to leave it there, had told myself it was the only sensible thing to do. It wasn't sensible to interrogate stranger's decorations. And that's what my brother was, by now, a stranger.

Still. I came back to the jar, tried to twist the top off to smell—this *had* to be something decorative, something all other single men knew about as a matter of course—but the lever had rusted shut, from the steam of a thousand showers.

"Good," I said out loud. This wasn't my business anyway. This wasn't my life.

When I saw the metallic red hair a few layers up from the bottom, though, my fingers opened of their own accord.

The jar shattered on the side of the toilet, the hair unwinding on the tile floor, taking up the space of a human head, and still writhing, looking for its eventual shape.

I could still hear that red head's dart sucking into the dartboard. Could still see her standing at the line painted onto the floor of that bar. But I couldn't see the rest of her life.

She hadn't been the first, and she hadn't been the last.

The way I made it make sense was that Daniel had become a hair stylist instead of an electrical engineer. That, when he'd hit thirty, he'd changed professions, gone with his heart instead of a paycheck. He got more interested in the people in the crosswalk than in the traffic cueing up at the lights.

Daniel who was just as indifferent with his wardrobe and appearance as I'd always been. He'd be no better a hair stylist than I would.

Still, this couldn't be what it seemed.

I felt my way out of the bathroom, made myself walk not into his bedroom—smelling where he slept would be too intimate—and not back down the stairs like I'd promised myself, but to the only other door on this floor I hadn't been through. The only door that was closed.

I told myself I was just going to reach in, turn the light on in there long enough to catalog it as storage or living space—I might need to stay here one night someday, brother—but then, the door open just enough for my forearm, my hand patting the wall for a light switch, something scurried behind me.

I turned, didn't catch it.

The sense the sound left in my head, though, it was an armadillo, somehow.

No: a possum.

I clutched the door frame, my heart slapping the inside walls of my chest, a sweet, grainy smell assaulted the inside of my head, and looked into what was neither living space nor storage, exactly.

This was an operating room.

On the table, tied down at all four corners, was the latest woman.

All Daniel's attention had been focused on her stomach.

He'd been looking for something, I could tell.

Above the table, on the ceiling, was a large mirror. Meaning the girl had been alive when this started.

I shivered, hugged my arms to my side, and felt my chin about to tremble.

On one of the flaps of skin that had been folded back from her middle, there was still a black line.

Daniel was drawing that baby shape on the body before he cut in. And he was cutting in to free the doll, the doll he knew had to be there, the doll Mom and Dad had practically promised was going to be there.

Janine was still whispering to him.

I shook my head no, no, please, and when I turned to leave, there they were on the wall. All the dolls he'd—not *found*, that was impossible, that was wrong.

The dolls he'd bought and salvaged and sneaked home. The dolls that completed the ritual he'd learned at five years old.

They were all wired to a pegboard, their smooth plastic bodies covering nearly every hole, and the pegboard was the whole wall, by now. This was the work of years. This was a lifetime.

To honor them, the blood and meat the dolls had been wrapped in to simulate the birth for Daniel, it had been left to dry on them.

I threw up, had to fall onto my hands to do it, it was so violent.

And then the scurrying again. In the hall.

I looked up just after *some*thing had crossed from one side of the doorway to the other. And where my ears told my eyes to look, it wasn't up at head-level, at person-level, but at knee-level.

Instead of a possum now, what I saw in my head was the doll my dad had bought for Janine. The one we'd buried. Only, it was crawling around on all fours, its elbows cocked higher than its back, its face turned up, to keep its eyes opened.

And when she talked, it was going to be that same language she'd taught Daniel. That same dead tongue.

I stood, fell back, dizzy, not used to this kind of exertion, and my hand splashed into the insides of the girl on the table, and I felt two things in the same instant. The first was the warmth of this girl's viscera, when I'd assumed she'd been dead for hours, long enough to have cooled down. The second thing I felt was what Daniel was always looking for: a hard plastic doll foot. From the doll inside each of us, if you know where to look. If you cut at the exact right instant, and reach in with confidence, with faith.

My hand closed on the smooth foot and the moment dilated, threatened to swallow me whole.

I brought my hand back gently, so as not to disturb. So as to pretend this hadn't just happened.

Whatever was in the hall had seen, though. Or heard the girl's insides, trying to suction my hand in place.

Save her, a hoarse voice whispered, from just past the doorway. *Don't let her drown.*

I stared at the wall of dolls, none of their lips able to move. I stared into the black abyss of the doorway. I studied the front- and backside of my gore-smeared hand.

"Daniel?" I said. Because I'd recognized the voice. Because who else could it be.

"Save her," the voice whispered again, from lower in the hallway than a person's head would be.

Unless that person was *crawling*. Unless, in the privacy of his own home, that person flashed around from room to room like that. Because that was who he was. That was *what* he was.

"Please," I said.

No answer.

I backed to the wall shaking my head no, shaking my head please, and, from this new angle, could see into the supply closet, the one Daniel had taken the door off of. Probably because his hands, in this room, didn't want to be touching doorknobs.

The doll our father had buried in our childhood, she was standing between two stacks of foggy plastic containers.

She'd been dressed, was just staring, her eyelashes black and perfect, her expression so innocent, so waiting.

Janine.

I wanted to fall to my knees—to give up or in thanks, I wasn't really sure. I put my hand to my face and didn't just smear my cheek and open eyes with the black insides of this dead girl, but my lips as well. My tongue darted out like for a crumb, just instinct, and the breathing in the hall got raspier. Less patient. Like this was building to something for him.

It made me cough that kind of cough that comes right before throwing up.

Out in the hall, Daniel sighed from deep in his mania, and then there was sound like he'd fallen over. From my wall, I could see one of his bare feet through the doorway, toes-up.

It was trembling. Like something was feeding on his face. Like the possum had come for him after all these years.

I crashed to the doorway to protect him, my little brother, to kick away whatever had him by the face.

It was just Daniel, though. He was spasming, his whole body, his eyes closed. It was a seizure. It was ecstasy.

"Daniel, Daniel," I said, on my knees now, taking his head in my lap.

He trembled and drew his arms in tight, his mouth frothing.

After a whole life of being alone with his task, with his compulsion, with his crusade, I'd finally joined him, I knew.

This wasn't a seizure, it was an orgasm. A culmination of all his dreams. I was the only one who could possibly understand what he'd become. What he was doing. And I was here.

His breath, it smelled like soap, and I had to picture him flaking a bar into a pile then lining his gums with it.

I sat down farther, to better cradle his head, and, when I had to angle him up to an almost sitting position, his eyes rolled open and he looked over to me, then down to my stomach as well, for the gift he'd been denied. The miracle he'd trained himself to sense.

My stomach. My digestion.

It wasn't nerves. What I was experiencing, what I was feeling, it was smoother than nerves. More plastic.

I unsnapped my shirt, looked down where Daniel was, and the vague outline of a tiny hand pressed against the backside of my skin when I breathed in, like it was stable, it was steady. It was me doing the moving.

I pushed away, into the hall wall, let Daniel's head fall to the carpet and bounce, his eyes closing mechanically, his right foot still trembling.

I was breathing too fast and I was breathing not at all.

And I could hear it now too, the whispering.

From the shop.

A whispering, but a gurgling, too.

The doll in the dead girl's still-warm entrails. The doll Daniel had wanted me to save.

The whole wall watched me cross the room on ghost feet. I looked to Janine for confirmation, and when she didn't say this was wrong, I plunged my hand back into the remains on the table, found the foot I'd felt earlier, and birthed this smooth plastic body up into the light, the body's corruption stringing off it.

When I turned the doll rightside up, its eyes rolled open to greet me, its lashes caked with blood.

I carried the doll by the leg to Daniel, and brought it up between us like a real fresh-born baby, but it only made him shake his head no, like I wasn't getting it. Like I didn't see.

"Over, over, over again," he said, turning sideways to reach down the hall. He tried to stand to go down there but wasn't recovered from his fit yet. He fell into the wall, slid down.

I looked where he'd meant to go, though.

The only light that way was the bathroom.

I drifted there, the doll upside-down by my leg again, its hard plastic fingers brushing my calf through my slacks.

The hair. The sedimentary tufts of hair.

That had to be what he meant. Over, over: *start* over. The traffic light goes red, then it cycles back to green again, and hovers on yellow, spilling back to red.

I carried the tufts of hair back, jewels of glass glittering on those dried strands.

When I knelt down by Daniel again, he opened his mouth like a baby bird and I knew I was right: this was part of his process. You save one doll from inside a woman, and you start over with hair from one of the other women. Like paying. Like trading. Like closing a thing you'd opened.

"Here, here," I said, fingering the hair from the jar, packing his mouth with it. His eyes watered, spilled over with what I took to be joy. "It'll be all right," I whispered. "We're saving her, Daniel. We're saving her."

He coughed once, hearing his name, then again from deeper, and, using two fingers, I shoved the wad of hair in deeper, so it could bathe in his stomach juice like a pearl. So it could become a soul for him again.

I kissed him once on the forehead when his body started jerking again, this time for air, and, when he bit the two fingers I was using to make him human again, I inserted the new doll's hand instead.

It held the hair in place until Daniel calmed. Until he went to sleep. Until there was no more breath.

I moved his right foot, to get his tremble going again, but there was nothing left.

My little brother was dead. His mission was over.

I kissed Daniel's closed eyes, my lips pressing into each thin eyelid for too long, like I could keep him here, at least until I removed my lips.

Behind those eyelids, though, the balls of his eyes were already turning hard like the yolks of boiled eggs.

This is how you say goodbye.

I stood, wiped that new doll's ankle clean—plastic holds prints—and stepped back into the shop, used a scalpel to remove the patch of carpet I'd thrown up into. I rolled that carpet up like a burrito.

Without looking up to them, I nodded to the open-eyed dolls then turned the light off with my wrist, stepped over what was left of Daniel, and made my way through the living room, out the front door.

"He ever show up?" the super or maintenance man asked, suddenly pruning something in the flowerbed that didn't need pruning. Meaning he'd had second thoughts about letting me in. He was standing guard, now. He was on alert.

In one hand I was clutching a small patch of rolled carpet I'd never be able to explain.

On my other hip, her cool face in my neck, was Janine.

I looked back to the door I'd just locked.

"No, never did," I said, "but there's water on the floor in his kitchen."

The super or maintenance man stood, his brow furrowed.

"Sink?" he said.

"Refrigerator," I said back, and followed him back in, pulled the door shut behind us, twisting the deadbolt.

Ten minutes later I stepped out again, my breathing back to normal, almost.

"Well that was different," I said to Janine, and hitched her higher.

Walking along the side of the house back to the garage, to my car, I had to turn my head away from her to cough, and then place my hand on the wall to steady myself.

What is it? she asked

Her voice was perfect.

I spit a shiny conglomerate of segmented blackness up into my palm, and studied it.

"Nothing," I told her, and somewhere between there and the car, I left my soul behind me on the ground.

Stephen Graham Jones is the author of fifteen novels and six story collections. His most recent book is the novel *Mongrels,* from William Morrow. Jones lives in Boulder, CO.

When we introduce the heroic factor into the population, and give rise
to a superhuman élite, let us not have forgotten the heart . . .

KAIJU MAXIMUS®: "SO VARIOUS, SO BEAUTIFUL, SO NEW"

Kai Ashante Wilson

It hadn't come down since great-grandparent days, but as its last descent had left no stone on stone—nor man, woman, child alive—anywhere people had once dwelled aboveground on the continent, the hero would go up before it came down again, and kill the kaiju *maximus*. They would go too: the hero's weakness, and her strength.

For long cool days, she led them up the old byways toward the specter of the mountains. Finally they reached the foothills. Here and there leaves of the deep green forest had just begun turning red or gold in the last days of summer. He and the children were all fit, all well, and so most days the hero could get about twenty kiloms out of them. She carried the food, that pack twice the weight of his, which was plenty heavy enough. She brought down game for them if he asked, a turkey, or ducks. They did just as that old sciencer in the last cavestead had counseled: every morning a drop of her blood under the children's tongues and his, and indeed the heroic factor served to ward them all from sickness. No more fevers, not a cough. The scaled dry patches on the boy's neck and hands cleared up, and he suffered no more frightening episodes of breathlessness. In little more than a month the baby, looking all the time more and more like poor Sofiya, shot up several centimets, five or six, and put on as many kilos. And him? That ankle he'd twisted back in the spring stopped aching during the first and last hours of a long day's hike, stopped aching at all. You don't really know, until it's gone, how much the pain was wearing on you all along.

Come downhill one bright chill afternoon, he and the baby and boy were resting in the swale, eating apples, when the hero came down from the sky.

She gave him the choice of the last hill they'd climb that day. "Which one?" she said. Just north of them two hills overlapped in east-west adjacency. "Where's the good water?"

He thought about it and said, "That one," holding out his apple toward where, unseen and unheard, a freshwater spring bubbled up from cloven rock, and ran down down the chosen hill's farside. Though much higher, the other hill looked easy-hiking. The hill awaiting them was squat, not half so high: but they'd end up climbing its height four or five times, after all the switchbacks, its sides being steep and densely forested, interrupted by brief sheer bluffs. There never really was a chance, was there, the easy hill might have had the water?

"Saw some duck while I was up flying," the hero said. (They only ever argued over the children—food for them, water for them, rest.) "But just those spoonies with orange fat."

"That's okay."

"Kids won't eat that kind, you said." The hero's latest eyes caught the light funny, as if prismatic oil were wetting them, not saltwater tears. "They taste too nasty."

"It's okay," he said. "Really."

"You gotta speak up if you want me to hunt."

It was nice, he told himself, that she thought to offer. "Tonight I meant to finish up what we brung fresh from the last cavestead. So please don't worry yourself." He didn't need some special solicitude that came out of the blue every once in a while. What he needed was not to be argued against, and never, ever overruled, when the hero wanted to wring a few more kiloms from the day—and so skip some meal, rest stop, or water break—and he said to her, "They can't; the kids are tired. We need rest."

I don't think Sofiya should do that. I don't think she's ready.

"You hurting for water? I can take the canteens and fill em."

"We're okay. Early tomorrow morning we should hit the trickle, otherside of that west hill there. We got plenty till then." He smiled up at her (irises glinting jewel-like in the oblique fall of light). "And you know I know my water."

"Yeah." She touched his head and ran fingers through his hair which, not easily, he kept washed and combed for her. "You do, don't you?"

Now, his father: *there* had been a dowser, the old man able not just to find the water but call it from the ground, however dry. He himself could feel the water pumping or at rest in the earth well enough to say where the nearest creek or pond lay, and to judge at a glance whether this standing pool or that mineral-stained leak was poisonous or potable. And the boy could as well: grandson's talent biding fair to rival his grandfather's, for already son could often pinpoint what father could only be vague about.

The hero looked at her weary children half-eating, half-sleeping on their weary father's lap. "We'll rest here a bit longer, then head up when the sun touches the top of those trees there."

Mouth full of apple, he nodded. On rare occasions the hero drank thirstily from a spring, or returned to camp with the haunch of some deer she'd devoured out of his and the children's sight; and he'd roast it up for their supper and next-day's eating. But she took neither food nor water more than once a month. All the good that a daily two leets of water, full night's sleep, and three squares did for you, the hero got from a quiet half hour's sit-down in the sun. She found a bright spot now and partook.

He unraveled a cocklebur from the boy's head propped on his thigh. "What say you, buddy? How was your papa's waterwitching that time?"

Eyes closed, the boy held an apple to his mouth, nibbling at it; he spoke with quiet dreaminess. "We're gonna get to that water today, Papa—right as the sun's going down. And the spring's a good gushy one, not no little trickle like you said."

Still with a couple nice bites on it, the baby chucked her apple-core to the mangy pup that had crept after them since midmorning. "I wanna'nother one, Papa," she said. "I'm still hungry."

"We ain't got apples to waste, pumpkin." He handed her the half left of his. "Now, just you get to eat this, okay? It's yours, all by yourself."

> *Dr. Anwar abu Hassan, psychogenomicist:* To us who still flounder in the storms of the untamed heart, the awakened mystics have explained just what good, in the cosmic sense, is this folly called erotic love. Lust and passion are early doors, first steps away from pure self-concern; and later doors, further steps, lead even as far as the mystic arrives: to that love surpassing understanding, which may encompass a whole planet, and every living creature on it. And so, when we introduce the heroic factor into the population, and give rise to a superhuman élite, let us not have forgotten the heart. Predilection for the pretty face is a precursor of universal caritas. And in defense of one beloved earthling some hero may well save us all.

> *At the* RITUAL BENISON *before each boss-fight, a hero will temporarily advance +1000 XP for every point of comeliness their spouse possesses. But the hero must ensure that his or her spouse always has food, water and rest enough to maintain this attribute. And* SUPERHEROES *must consider the welfare of their children as well, for the sword and the wings can only . . .*

Twilight was setting fire to the clouds as they reached the flat top of the hill. Up there was rocky, windswept and bush-covered; or, no—these were all trees, dwarfish kin to the lower forest, with not one gnarled cousin reaching even shoulder-height. All sense of accomplishment from so many steps taken thus far, from so much ground covered, can be voided by a single majestic vista. The prospect overlooked a broad and forested valley, compassed by distant hills, and marching thence to the very limits of sight: ever-higher mountains, some peaks snowtopped, a few piercing the clouds. Let it not be said that he knew even a moment's despair—for he was loyal to the hero, and steadfast to her cause: humanity's salvation—but neither could such a view hearten anyone so footsore. *How far must they go?* At his feet the children sat down together, stretched out side-by-side, and went to sleep: not a full minute passing between these progressions. The hero didn't want your chatter, your second guesses, nor to be pestered with ten thousand questions. But he dared ask this one aloud, although quietly, and well softened up:

"I guess we got quite a ways further to go, huh?"

"We're here. This is it," the hero said. "I'll kill it tonight."

According to the maps a city of millions had nestled in this valley before the age of monsters cut short the Anthropocene. Now, only a howling green wilderness filled the lowlands, and on the sixth day God might have called it quits in the morning, finishing with the beasts: never having put people in the garden at all. For miles and miles—forever—there was nothing to see, save rock, tree and mountain: certainly no kaiju *maximus.* "Where is it?" he said. "I don't see anything."

The hero took his shoulders in hand, turned him bodily about, and let go; she pointed.

Knowing that her finger pointed west, even so he was confounded for a moment, and thought *east,* where sooty night had fallen already. Never before had he seen such insombration as covered over a deep groin between western mountains. This wasn't the smoky gloom that *minores* carried about with them, those mighty shambling towers. Nor yet was it the terrifying local midnight in which the hero had fought and killed a kaiju *plenus*, fully mature, while that great beast hove up over the world nearly lost in darkness, although it had been sunny midafternoon. No, the insombration that blackened the valley's western reaches didn't so much dampen ambient radiance as seem a positive dark in its own right: the opposite, not merely absence, of light. The bright fires of sunset had no power to penetrate those malignant shadows, which gave up not even the faintest conjectural hint of the *maximus* within.

A chill wind blew on this hilltop. He shuddered. "I can't get the least little glimpse of it through that. Can you?"

The hero nodded. She shrugged off the pack of food, and unbuckled and dropped her heavy sword as well. "Y'all get yourselves settled up here." Carapace flipping open, her wings extended. "I'll be back shortly to get ready for the fight."

"Is it woke already?" he said. "Or still sleep?"

But with a swiftness just faster than his eyes could track the hero plunged upwards into the lowering dusk and sped away west.

If you'd crouched next to him while he checked on the children, you'd have judged them much too wiry for their age. Where was the baby fat? you'd wonder. The chubby thighs and soft bellies? And though one was six, and the other three-and-a-half, brother and sister were very close in size; for the boy's dead heroic twin had hogged the womb, and been born with not a fair half but nearly fourth-fifths the share of health, size and strength. Sofiya had been a little frightening, so fiercely had she rejected any helping—any intercessory—hand, although in the end she'd needed her papa no less than this baby and boy, hadn't she? And please don't say these sleepers looked uncared for, like no one worried over them always conniving for their well-being. But he feared you probably would. Who *loves* these children? you'd cry out, looking all around you, hot-eyed and accusatory. Who *feeds* them? The heart wrung in his chest taking in their gaunt exhaustion. He took off his coat and draped it over them. With just his grandfather's woolen sweater against hawk on the hilltop, he set about gathering wood for the fire.

Onions and potatoes sizzling in bacon fat was a smell to wake any hungry youngster, however deeply asleep. The children pressed close to him at either side, staring lustfully into the pan. The baby made to stick tender fingers right into hot popping grease; he caught that hand. "Whoa there, pumpkin."

"I'm hungry though."

"We'll be eating in two shakes." He chopped up most of the remaining ham for the hash and stirred the pan. Still, supper could use some more stretching. He tapped the baby's nose and pointed. "You see that bent-over tree, the little'n? Just looky at all that good dandelion growing under it. How about you go pull us two big ole handfuls for the pan? And make sure to shake off all the bugs and dirt. *You* know how."

"But I'm *hungry*, Papa."

"Soon as I get me some greens, you get your supper."

After the baby jumped up, he said, "And, buddy, will you gather up everybody's canteen for me? Just a few steps thataway, over behind the big boulder you see right there, I judge it's a nice spring of water just bubbling up—"

Sassy, and with voice raised: "I know already, Papa." The boy shouldered up the baby's canteen beside his own.

"Well, all right." The outburst surprised him. It wasn't a tone the boy would ever dare take with his mother, and so neither should he with his father. But a bit of backtalk was, in this case, good news. Trekking twenty kiloms everyday kept the boy so doped with fatigue, the sun could rise and set without him showing any glimmer of personality or preference, much less temper. So, yes: shout at Papa if you would! "Go on, then. Pour out the old water, and rinse them canteens out good, you hear? Top em all back up full too."

"I know." The boy stamped a foot, holding out his arm to receive the last canteen strung up over his shoulder.

"Best not be super long about it either, buddy. Or me and the baby might get so hungry we gobble up your supper too. *Whew*, don't this pan just smell wonderful?"

"You better not, Papa!" In their leather sleeves, the winebottles under his elbows and pinched to his sides, the boy hurried round the boulder toward the stream's source.

While they ate he told the children that this was the night Mama would fight the kaiju. Strategic, this timing; for very little news was so upsetting it could ruin a good hot supper, served up right now. "The big one?" said the baby. "Yes, pumpkin." "The *maximus*?" said the boy. "Yes, buddy." And that seemed to be that, for at least so long as they scraped their forks into the pan.

After supper he found himself taking in anew their grimy little faces, all smeared and content, and he heard his mother's voice. *When you fixing to wash these babies, man? Been three weeks now.* It's cold and windy out here, Mama. I can't wash them in this weather. *Boy, it's getting into the fall. Ask yourself: is it gon' get warmer and warmer, or will you be breaking ice to get at the creek soon? They'll cry, Mama; that's how cold it is.* I don't want my children hating me. *Well, all right—keep doing what you doing, then. I'm just sorry I musta not taught you anything about where sickness come from, or the kind of infections won't nothing cure. Myself, I'd just build up this fire good, and see the babies get nice and warm afterwards . . . but you grown! Do it your way.*

"Y'all," he said, "it's been a long time now, right? I think we all might need a bath."

There was an uproar, and tears to break your heart. Possessing nothing like the necessary fortitude, he pretended to be his own implacable mother, and dug out the little cake of soap, everyone's change of underthings, and after doubling the fire marched himself and the children round the boulder to the near-freezing gush of mountain spring.

"I can do something," the boy screamed. "The fire underground, Papa."

Children spoke wildly at bathtime, and you learned to harden your heart and pay no attention. He put hands on the boy to undress him for soap and water.

"Wait," said the boy. "I can make the water hot. I can, Papa."

He let the boy go and sat there on a rock beside the stream. Sucking her thumb, the baby leaned heavily against his side, as she did when upset. "What do you mean, buddy?"

"There's . . . fire in the ground, Papa. Real deep down," said the boy. "And there's steamwater sitting on top of it." His hands swooped and gestured to map these geologic interrelations. "I can ask that hot water to mix with this cold, so the spring comes up here feeling nice."

"Can you, buddy? I never heard of such a thing. My own papa couldn't . . . Well, go on; let's see." He watched the boy's face go demented with effort, with concentration, and his heart sank realizing the son he thought he knew was in fact unknown to him; but it lifted up too, for the boy had genius. The candlelight of his dowsing gift blazed high into roaring flames. And, oh, *how* had he ever forgotten this?—how the twenty-times-brighter gift of his father at work on some feat used to cast illumination by which he himself could plumb depths, discerning subtleties ordinarily far beyond him? From some superheated pool a full subterranean mile down, the boy caused geothermic steam to vent upwards through intervening strata, and that terrifically hot water to temper the icy flow of the mountain stream warmer, and warmer still, until even bloodwarm—

"*There*, buddy," he said. "That's hot enough."

White plumes of vapor were emerging from the cracked boulder's underside with the cascade of water. He quickly got off his own coat and sweater and all the baby's things and ducked her into the balmy waters. While his son stood there with face set, eyes squinched closed, body all a-tremble, he bathed his daughter.

Soaping her feet a second time, he tore open a fingertip on some errant shard of glass—but, no; for apparently this glass was somehow *in* his daughter's foot, or *on* it. He asked the baby to sit down there in the water and let papa see that foot. It gave him a nasty scare, seeing what he saw. By the campfire's dim filterings from the boulder's farside, and by the guttering embers of sunset: the baby's toenails had all gone black and strange-shaped. Then, gingerly pricking his thumb against the sharp downcurved points of them, he understood that his daughter wasn't taken ill at all—indeed she was soon to transcend the question of illness altogether. The lusciously heated water delighted the baby and she wanted to linger and splash. But the fires of the boy's gift were by now dwindling fast, and the spring beginning to cool. "Can't play in the water, pumpkin." He soaped her hair and rinsed it squeaky. "Bud's working real hard to keep it warm for you. We gotta hurry."

The boy said, "Papa . . . "

"It's all right, buddy." He lifted the baby out, towel-swathed. "Let go."

The spring resumed its arctic flow, the steam dispersing at once. The boy took weary seat upon a rock nearby.

He had the baby dry and in her change of longjohns and fresh socks, all snugly bundled up and booted again, in about a minute flat.

"Well, buddy," he said. "My dowsing's nowhere near as good as yours. So we'll just wait till morning"—what *optimism*, the apocalypse being scheduled for tonight!—"and you can have a bath when you feel strong enough to call up more hot water. Okay?"

"Okay, Papa."

"Hey, pumpkin—*hey* there—you come back here! What you running off for all by yourself, like you don't know better than that? Mmhmm, you just sit down right here beside your brother. Buddy, you hold my baby's hand, you hear?"

"Okay, Papa."

Never in your life did you see somebody wash up quicker. Dunking himself, he yodeled once from sheer cruel iciness, and then kind of hopped from foot to foot while scrubbing himself with soap, hooting sadly both times he crouched to splash himself over with frigid rinsewater. It was a pathetic and undignified show—nevertheless hilarious to the children, who shrieked with laughter.

He led them back to the fire. The gusts were cutting northerly across the hilltop, and so he'd built the fire in the windshadow of a depression, and stacked up stones for a further break, but still the flames leaned and shuddered. The children tried to talk to him of such little events of the day past as the three of them would hash over nightly before bed—for instance, that poor little puppydog. "What you thinks gon' happen to him, Papa?" But hunkered down before the fire, he only shook his head, teeth chattering while he pulled the comb through his hair. So the boy began telling the baby that same old made-up story, about the nice family with three little kids, who lived together in a tent set up beside a stream on a green field, where the kids could play all day in that good, sunny place. As usual, the baby wanted to know *Was it warm? How warm was it?* And the boy laid out for her again how wonderfully warm it was there, the sun shining everyday.

Sounds nice, he thought, but as always wished to object that people couldn't just live out in the open like that. If ever people dared to gather in numbers on the planet's surface, and especially when they began to cultivate, and build, and knock down trees, a perturbation intensified in the leylines. Kaiju felt such human activity as a worsening itch in need of a good hard scratch. The children knew perfectly well that people had to live underground in cavesteads; they'd visited plenty. But they spent most of their lives in the wind and rain and sunlight, campfollowing after the hero with their papa; and so naturally the great outdoors, and tents beside sweetwater streams, seemed to them pleasures anyone might know.

Warmed through and dry, he dressed. There was cutlery and the pan to put up. With no threat of rain, he decided against the tent, but got out the ground pads and bedrolls. After a word to the children—*stay put, behave*—he went to launder his and the baby's soiled underthings.

Dr. Anwar abu Hassan, psychogenomicist: While we are contending, still, with the problem of human survivability vis-a-vis the existential alien threat, please, my dear colleagues, heed this warning: The Hero Project will have thought too small, and perforce must fail, if we discard all but the mechanistic solutions. I submit these questions for your consideration.

How does the martyr remain true, although put to the ultimate test? Whence comes the endurance of the last man standing, his unbroken will to survive? And what *is* that moral fiber investing the woman who runs always to the succor of other lives, never balking at risk to her own? *Can a coward fight the kaiju—will a selfish woman, or a waffling, indecisive man?* So, yes, then, to near-sonic flight, to static apnea *in vacuo*, to electrogenerative plaxes; and, yes, as well, to all the various exoskeletal enhancements: But as we engineer the superhuman *corpus*, again I say, let us not neglect the heart!

And should the spouse freely offer up the greatest sacrifice, then the hero's biomagicite shall become charged with +100 mana: finally sufficient to induce a VOLCANIC HOTSPOT, *whereby a perforation in the earth's crust causes superheated magma to discharge explosively from the aesthenosphere, instantly destroying kaiju* minores, *and causing* pleni *and the* maximus . . .

Spraying the sky the count of stars must go to billions, and the singular moon shone down as well, just a sliver waxing from new. From unlit lunar lands far from the bright crescent—still burning more than a century on—the wrecked mothership winked and flared with eerie phosphorescence. Yet apart from their fire on the hilltop, not another light could be seen over the whole dark and untenanted earth. Barring this one little camp, there was nothing to proclaim that apes had ever come down from the trees, or women once decked themselves in silk and diamonds, or men in times past waged war upon each other.

Lest the wind blow it away, he tangled up their laundry to dry in the boughs of a tree-canopy all knotty and interlaced as arthritic fingers. By the time he'd rejoined the children fireside and stretched out his hands to ease their cold-ache, the boy and baby's talk had turned to chocolate.

He protested. "But if we make it tonight, there's none for later. That's it, all gone."

The boy extended a litigious forefinger. "*You* said we'd have our chocolate when Mama fights the kaiju. You *promised*, Papa."

No, he'd said "maybe," for he never made promises. What on earth could he guarantee? "It's the last little bit, y'all." He could feel himself doing the ugly, tiresome thing, whereby you put off some pleasure best enjoyed now, for fear nothing good will come again. "Are you both sure?"

Yes!

So he put on water to boil and shaved the chocolate into their tin cup and, finishing the honey as well, sweetened it all up. Sitting between them with the cup, he parceled sips back and forth, but could as well have left the arbitrage to them. For sister and brother were best of friends tonight—angels of fairness—and this camp saw such smiles as none had in some time. What else do you hope to see? Only that your children be warm and well and glad. While they ran fingers round the inside of the cup, chasing dregs, the hero came down from the air and it was time.

Her wings folded invisibly into her carapace. And two mettes tall and more, she, kneeling, brought herself down to child's-reach. "Bless me for the fight," the hero said, and all the lightness left their camp, as if hawk, suddenly switching quarter, had blown the fire out. She picked up her scabbard from where it lay, pulled forth the sword, and beckoned the boy forward to kiss the flat of the blade.

"Papa," said the boy.

"I'm here." He set the baby back safely from the fire and took his son's hand. "I'll catch you, buddy. You won't be hurt." Last time, a bolt of lightning had struck down abruptly from the cloudless sky: charging the sword, but also felling the boy in passing. For a week he lay shivering and mumbling in some half-awake state, and thereafter for months was ill and weak.

They walked over to the hero at his son's slow pace. Small folk know that unreckonable caprice flickers through the heart of the great, and they know as you may not that so-called love—that the benevolent smile—may turn on the instant to wrath and ruination. Therefore the children never approached the hero with steps less wary than those of the old Israelites coming before Yahweh.

The boy looked up into his mother's face: her stillness and regard, insectile or statuesque. Going to his knees beside his son, he whispered urgingly of the planetary importance of this single fight above all the rest that had ever gone before.

The boy said at last, "I hope you win, Mama," and touched his puckered mouth to the sword even taller than himself. At once the pommel in the hero's grip took light, brilliance spilling out between her fingers. The cold grey steel began turning to white-hot fire.

He snatched the boy back into his arms, tumbling over, and kicked desperately against the ground to get distance between them and that incinerative heat. Their coats smoked, hair crisped. "Take it away from us," he shouted at the hero. "It's too hot." She got up holding the incandescent beam, and with each step farther seemed to bear away a furnace going full blast, its doors ajar, and then some vagrant midsummer's day, and thereafter lesser and lesser warmth, until the cold of the boreal night closed rightfully about them again. At the summit's edge the hero plunged the sword down into solid rock that sputtered and smoked like grease scorching in a pan much too hot. Leaving the bright blade bobbing in liquid stone, the hero came back and knelt as before. Then she bowed until her forehead rested on the ground, for the baby's kiss upon her back.

Already the hero had wonderful wings, but to fight the *maximus* she'd need much better. As a rocky shelf, one thousand tons, falls off some mountainside and onto the unlucky walker below, just so did the kaiju hit, with as much force. And their alien effluents, whether spat, shat, or bloodlet, reduced the flesh of earthly creatures to runny sludge, a fertile dung for the world's resurgent wilderness, feed for the forests that arose where every city fell. They couldn't guess what shape, this time, the hero's metamorphosis would take; she had no idea herself. Their only forewarning was that, whatever changes, they would be always perilous, always a shock.

"Pumpkin," he said and squatted on his haunches. He reached out his arms and sucking her thumb the baby came to him. But when he urged her from his embrace and toward the hero, saying, "Give Mama a kiss, just like you did before," the baby seized a fistful of his coat, nor wished to let it go. "Are you scared?" He stroked his daughter's hair and smiled at her in complicity, allowing a little of his own fear to show. "I know; me too. But I need you to do this one little thing for me. Just for your papa: won't you give Mama a kiss on her back?" (A kiss compelled held no power—nor did a loveless one.) His appeal shifted something in the child's heart prior words had not, and her fear-blank eyes began to clarify. He said, "Please?" and the baby nodded. Toward the hero and away from him, he set her walking with gently propulsive hands.

The baby cast back one uncertain glance. At his nod, she bent to kiss the hero's dorsal carapace. Fretfully his two hands hovered to grab his daughter back. No sooner did the baby's lips alight than her mother's torso—indeed limbs and whole self—returned to a more human shape, but not made of flesh and bone, rather become some kind of living marble.

At dead center of the hero's smooth adamantine back, a thin-lipped mouth pursed open. From this hole erupted a long and rotary tentacle of spiked stone. With full decapitatory powers, this flailing rotor tore the air just centimets overhead where he cringed, pressing the baby and himself down, noses flat to earth. Hysterical from terror the baby fought to get free and run, while he shouted at the hero to go up into the air before she killed them both. When the hero had gone aloft, he let the baby go. Sister fled back to brother fireside where the children clung together like half-drowned co-survivors who had won to shore by grace of God alone, and through shark, shipwreck, and storm, had not gone down with all the rest.

The hero could not lift much more than her own weight off the ground ordinarily, but now without effort she stooped from the sky and plucked him up into her arms. They hovered midair.

Her mouth by his ear to be heard above the roaring downdraught of that strange, singular wing: "Do you love me?"

"Yes."

"Really?" Her lips were stone, and if not soft at all, entirely smooth. "I wonder. Love me enough to do anything? No matter what?"

"Whatever," he said. Could she even feel his fingertips caress her face? "I'll do anything." She was hard to embrace, hard to come close to, being made of stone and so much bigger. "I love you."

"To fight the *maximus* I need more than you ever gave me those other times. A whole lot more."

He said, "How much?" and she said,

"How much can I get?"

Even then the hero waited on him to press his lips to hers.

If you've ever sucked and chewed on sugarcane, then you have the right image. Vigor, youth, beauty—something on that order—was wrung out of his body like water from a sodden rag, or sweetness chewed from sugarcane. But the agony made no difference to how readily he opened his mouth to the requited passion of her stony kiss. Suppose that some small sacrifice were asked of you as helpmeet and shieldbearer for the greatest hero who has ever lived, and suppose that in fulfilling your role *she* might deliver the homeworld. Would you do it? *He* would. She hardened to some much denser substance than living marble, and the arms about him caused his bones to creak and ache. Becoming a chevaux-de-frise of sharp diamond, her lips began to abrade his, drawing blood as the kiss went on.

As he grew feeble she held him closer, until desire and will notwithstanding, his body just could no longer. The hero held her lips one short millimet from his, begging, "Kiss me, kiss me," and he tried, oh he did, always whispering back when she asked, "Do you love me?" "Yes, yes."

Let him go. There was a gravelly clatter, rock-on-rock, as pebbles bounced off much harder stuff. Dimly he became aware that his children were screaming and throwing stones at their mother again. *Let him go. I hate you.* Had the kiss gone so far already? Not too far yet, he hoped. Someone must see the baby and boy tucked into their blankets tonight. And who but him would see them fed a hearty warming bowl in the morning? Such terror these thoughts inspired, he turned his face from hers. Released, he felt himself fall through the air, and hitting the ground saw rainbow-bright glitter and then darkness.

He woke to the baby and boy saying *please don't be dead.* Prostrate on the ground he scrabbled there unable to turn faceup, without the strength even to lift his bloody mouth from the dirt. *Get up, Papa, get up.* Trying to say anything that might comfort the children, he made only the mewling of a kitten which alone of its litter tossed overboard had washed ashore undrowned. These efforts to speak and rise, strenuous to no effect, wearied him so that finally he lay for a long time with quietude hardly to be distinguished from that of a corpse on its bier. The children as well exhausted themselves, and their howls waned to grizzling; their yanking at his coat, to a small hand each stroking at his hair.

From faraway in the night there came at random either one vast crash or repeated booms, as if contending gods took and threw godlike blows. Once, a tremendous though faint echo of the hero's anger resounded out of the distance, her voice pitched such that blood would have spurted from their ears, had he and the children heard that blast near at hand.

Time did what it does and by and by he felt himself drift from merest proximity to death, into slightly more distant purlieus. He splayed one withered claw under each shoulder and pushing against the ground—pushing as hard as he could—came somehow up to sit. Just the sweet Lord can say how he got up on his two stick legs and made it over to the fire where he sat again, or fell. They paced him there, a child at either side; patient, silent, good as gold.

"Buddy."

"Papa?"

"Look in the pack there. Get me out the cut-ointment and a clean rag."

The boy did so.

It wasn't too bad dabbing the mud from his lips with the dampened rag, but smearing his lacerated mouth with the astringent ointment, he made noises that couldn't be helped.

"All right," he said once he'd caught his breath. "Put it up now, bud. Rag goes with the dirty ones."

"Okay, Papa."

Exactly once before had the baby seen the toll of this dire miracle, though she might not remember. Standing beside him, she groped with bemittened hands at his slack-seamed cheeks, his thin white hair, as if only by touch could she grasp this onset of morbid age. He smiled at her and said, "Mama will turn me back like I was after she beats the kaiju." *If* she does . . . "Don't you worry, pumpkin." But not even the voice was his own: higher, breathy, querulous. Her face crumpled, tears welling in her eyes, and none of his friendly words were reassuring to the baby.

The boy came back to sit, and lean, gingerly against him. Had you trotted the globe around and come home again, having despaired that day would ever arrive, so too might you breathe out as the boy did then, as long and slow, a shudder passing also through you. Many times he'd seen his papa go suddenly grey, though never before this stooped and frail, a spotted scalp visible like dirt and stone under a dusting of snow.

To distract the baby's unhappiness, he said, "Want to hear something wonderful?" Brightness pulsed in the western dark, like the traffic of thunderbolts between stormclouds. "Let me tell you what happens sometimes, pumpkin."

Between hiccups: "What, Papa?"

"Sometimes, when a hero's got no son or daughter with the factor—that's still alive, I mean—then it starts expressing in the *other* same-sex child. That happens a lot with heroes, actually. Your papa should've been on the lookout." His tone was light, as at storytime, or telling jokes.

"What you mean, Papa?"

"I think, pumpkin—" he kissed her teary cheek "—*you're* gonna wake up just like Mama one day real soon. A hero. How about that?"

The baby reached a hand to his mouth as she'd done when almost newborn, still an infant, and pressed his lips together in a buttoning gesture. She let the hand fall and said, "No," as decisively as when refusing despised foods. "I don't want that."

"Well," he replied (as always when the sequel would come soon enough, nor be anything the children desired): "We'll just have to see then, won't we?"

"No, Papa!" The baby grabbed his coat and gave him a good shake—he so weak, she could do so. "*Not* see. I want to stay *people*."

He tapped the little fist clinched in his coat and raised his brow at her. The baby turned him loose.

"Aww, don't say that." He shook his head sadly at her. "I really wish you wouldn't, pumpkin. Mama is people too."

"I mean, I mean." The baby was still at that age when words tend to fail, and anger or tears have to fill the gap; her voice broke. "Like you and buddy."

"Shh," he said, "Okay, then," as if she might not rise to *Homo sapiens heroïcus* on his mere say so. "All right, all right." He rubbed circles on her back, she quieted, and the whole world tipped nauseously then. He heard himself shout.

"What's that?" Terrified, the baby embraced him round the neck. "What *is* it, Papa?"

The ground beneath them was yawing as if the sea, the planet itself groaning deeply bass and agonized as some old sinner repentant on his deathbed. Abruptly, some twenty kiloms down the valley, a bright volcanic arm—a hand of fire—thrust up from the earth and made a credible grab for the moon, incandescent fingers raking across the sky. Brilliance snatched aside the black of night as though it were a flimsy curtain, the truth behind it high noon. They cried out, throwing up a hand or both as the dark cold valley was relit to midday green. The gushing white blaze spewed comets as a geyser does waterdroplets, these fiery blue offshoots waning yellow-orange-red as they fell to earth, as the sourcefire itself discolored: now dimming to ochre and yet still painful to see, even squinting through their fingers; now dimmer still, ruddy-black as the glowing crumbs of their own little campfire; now going out.

In that awful first glare, though, they glimpsed the kaiju *maximus*, its shape like some conjuration out of all the earth's collective nightmare, reminiscent of a creature he'd seen once in a picturebook, some beast of the forgotten world—and called what? He couldn't remember. Bright-lit, that apparition stuttered in stark chiaroscuro, wallowing in magma: horrific, bigger than could be put into words. The eruption, dwindling, and burnout endured only for a slow five-count, but it seemed as if hours passed. Nor did they look away even once, not one time blink, until the veils of starless insombriate night fell over that vision again. After this sign and wonder, the baby turned to him expectantly, to see whether Papa might interpret, but he could only shake his head.

The end of days—what is even this, to a child's need for sleep? He looked to the boy and saw that his son's eyes were closed, mouth softly open. To the baby he said, "Let me go tuck in buddy-man." She released her hold round his neck and stood by watching while the boy was chivvied to his feet and, eyes closed, mumbling irritably, not really awake, was led over to his bedroll where, coaxed, he laid himself down, at once dead to the world again, while the boots were pulled off him, the covers tucked up around him. Heart rattling so in his chest you had to hope it could last the night through, he clambered to his feet after these exertions and saw that far hills were burning like victims in flight from some holocaust, their hair alight, their heads bewreathed in flames, all ablaze with forest fires. The wind began to taste of ash. He sought his spot by the fire again and the baby climbed into his lap. "Ain't you sleepy at all yet, pumpkin?"

"No," the baby said, and then: "Did you love Sofiya?"

"*Yes.*"

Again the earth moved as it should not, making unwonted sounds, but by then they were inured.

"And did Sofiya love you, Papa?"

"Well," he began, and was by fortuity saved from a lie and the truth alike. "Oh, looky there!" He pointed into the darkness just over the marge of their campfirelight. "See who came up to join us." From those respectful shadows doomed spaniel eyes watched them. For even after hope, it seemed, hopeful forms and strategies survived.

The baby said, "Puppy!" and jumped up. "Can we keep it, Papa? Like the family in the tent by the river? *They* got a dog."

That ole mangy mutt, there? *Of course not*, child: it's no telling what diseases that thing's got! "All right," he said, and sent the baby over to the hero's pack.

"Well, you ain't pulling, pumpkin," he said. "How you fixing to get that knot loose if you don't pull good? *Pull*, girl. There you go, there you go. See? Now loosen it up, reach in, and should be right there on top: the hambone left from supper, wrapped in one of them ole-timey plastic bags."

Kai Ashante Wilson's stories, "Super Bass" and "The Devil in America," can be read for free at Tor.com. His novella *The Sorcerer of the Wildeeps* is available for purchase from all fine ebook purveyors. His novelette, «Légendaire.», can be read in the anthology Stories for Chip, which celebrates the legacy of science fiction grandmaster Samuel R. Delany. Kai Ashante Wilson lives in New York City.

Workings have a price, you see, and the single best
currency for such transactions is blood, always.

HAIRWORK

Gemma Files

No plant can thrive without putting down roots, as nothing comes from nothing; what you feed your garden with matters, always, be it the mulched remains of other plants, or bone, or blood. The seed falls wherever it's dropped and grows, impossible to track, let alone control. There's no help for it.

These are all simple truths, one would think, and yet, they appear to bear infinite repetition. But then, history is re-written in the recording of it, always.

"*Ici, c'est elle,*" you tell Tully Ferris, the guide you've engaged, putting down a pale sepia photograph printed on pasteboard, its corners foxed with age. "Marceline Bedard, 1909—from before she and Denis de Russy met, when she was still dancing as Tanit-Isis. It's a photographic reference, similar to what Alphonse Mucha developed his commercial art pieces from. I found it in a studio where Frank Marsh used to paint, hidden in the floor. Marsh was Cubist, so his paintings tend to look very deconstructed, barely human, but this is what he began with."

Ferris looks at the *carte*, gives a low whistle. "Redbone," he says. "She a fine gal, that's for sure. Thick, sweet. And look at that hair."

" 'Redbone?' I don't know this term."

"Pale, ma'am, like cream, lightish-complected—you know, high yaller? Same as me."

"Oh yes, *une métisse, bien sur.* She was cagey about her background, *la belle Marceline*, liked to preserve mystery. But the rumor was her mother came from New Orleans to Marseilles, then Paris, settling in the same area where Sarah Bernhardt's parents once lived, a Jewish ghetto. When she switched to conducting séances, she took out advertisements claiming her powers came from Zimbabwe and Babylon, darkest Africa and the tribes of Israel, equally. Thus the name: Tanit, after the Berber moon-goddess, and Isis, from ancient Egypt, the mother of all magic."

"She got something, all right. A mystery to me how she even hold her head up, that much weight of braids on top of it."

"Mmm, there was an interesting story told about Marceline's hair—that it wasn't hers at all but a wig. A wig made *from* hair, maybe even some scalp, going back a *long* time, centuries . . . I mean, *c'est folle* to think so, but that was what they said. Perhaps even as far as Egypt. Her mother's mother brought it with her, supposedly."

"Mummies got hair like that, though, don't they? Never rots. Good enough you can take DNA off it."

You nod. "And then there's the tradition of Orthodox Jewish women, Observants, Lubavitchers in particular—they cover their hair with a wig, too, a *sheitel*, so no one but their husband gets to see it. Now, Marceline was in no way Observant, but I can see perhaps an added benefit to her *courtesanerie* from allowing no one who was not *un amant*, her intimate, to see her uncovered. The wig's hair might look much the same as her own, only longer; it would save her having to . . . relax it? *Ça ira?*"

"Yeah, back then, they'd've used lye, I guess. Nasty. Burn you, you leave it on too long."

"*Exactement.*"

Tully rocks back a bit on his heels, gives a sigh. "Better start off soon, you lookin' to make Riverside 'fore nightfall—we twenty miles up the road here from where the turn-off'd be, there was one, so we gotta drive cross Barker's Crick, park by the pass, then hike the rest. Not much left still standin', but I guess you probably know that, right?"

"Mmm. I read testimony from 1930, a man trying for Cape Girardeau who claimed he stayed overnight, spoke to Antoine de Russy. Not possible, of course, given the time—yet he knew many details of the events of 1922, without ever reading or hearing about them, previously. Or so he said."

"The murders, the fire?" You nod. "Yeah, well—takes all sorts, don't it? Ready to go, ma'am?"

"If you are, yes."

"Best get to it, then—be dark sooner'n you think and we sure don't wanna be walkin' 'round in *that*."

• • •

A mourning sampler embroidered with fifteen different De Russy family members' hair once hung upstairs, just outside my husband's childhood bedroom door: such a pretty garden scene, at first glance, soft and gracious, depicting the linden-tree border separating river and dock from well-manicured green lawn and edging flowerbeds—that useless clutter of exotic blooms, completely unsuited to local climate or soil, which routinely drank up half the fresh water diverted from the slave quarter's meager vegetable patch. The lindens also performed a second function, of course, making sure De Russy eyes were never knowingly forced to contemplate what their *negres* called the bone-field, a wet clay sump where slaves' corpses were buried at night and without ceremony, once their squeamish masters were safely asleep. Landscaping as *maquillage*, a false face over rot, the skull skin-hid. But then, we all look the same underneath, no matter our outward shade, *ne c'est pas*?

In 1912, I took Denis's hand at a Paris *soiree* and knew him immediately for my own blood, from the way the very touch of him made my skin crawl—that oh-so-desirable *peau si-blanche*, olive-inflected like old ivory, light enough to shine under candle flame. I had my Tanit-wig on that night, coils of it hung down in tiers far as my hips, my thighs, far enough to brush the very backs of my bare knees; I'd been rehearsing most of the day, preparing to chant the old rites in Shona while doing what my posters called a "Roodmas dance" for fools with deep pockets. Frank Marsh was there, too, of course, his fishy eyes hung out on strings—he introduced Denis to me, then pulled me aside and begged me once again to allow him to paint me "as the gods intended," with only my ancestors' hair for modesty. But I laughed in his face and turned back to Denis instead, for here was the touch of true fate at last, culmination of my mother's many prayers and sacrifices. Mine to bend myself to him and bind him fast, make him bring me back to Riverside to do what must be done, just as it'd been Frank's unwitting destiny to make that introduction all along and suffer the consequences.

Antoine De Russy liked to boast he kept Denis unworldly and I must suppose it to be so, for he never saw me with my wig off, my Tanit-locks set by and the not-so-soft fuzz of black which anchored it on display. As he was raised to think himself a gentleman, it would never have occurred to Denis to demand such intimacies. By the time his father pressed him to do so, I had him well trained: *Something odd about that woman, boy*, I heard him whisper more than once, before they fell out. *Makes my blood run cold to see it. For all she's foreign-born, I'd almost swear I know her face. . . .*

Ha! As though the man had no memory, or no mirrors. Yet, I was far too fair for the one, I suspect, and far too . . . different, though in "deceitfully slight proportion"—to quote that Northerner who wrote your vaunted *testimony*—for the other. It being difficult to acknowledge your own features in so alien a mirror, not even when they come echoing back to you over generations of mixed blood, let alone on your only son's arm.

You got in touch with Tully last Tuesday, little seeker, securing his services via Bell's machine—its latest version, any rate—and by yesterday, meanwhile, you'd flown here from Paris already, through the air. Things move so fast these days and I don't understand the half of it; it's magic to me, more so than magic itself, that dark, mechanical force I hold so close to my dead heart. But then, this is a problem with where I am now, *how* I am; things come to me unasked-for, under the earth, out of the river. Knowledge just reveals itself to me, simple and secret, the same way soil is disturbed by footfalls or silt rises to meet the ripple: no questions and no answers, likewise. Nothing explained outright, ever.

That's why I don't know your name, or anything else about you, aside from the fact you think in a language I've long discarded and hold an image of me in your mind, forever searching after its twin: that portrait poor Frank did eventually conjure out of me during our last long, hot, wet summer at Riverside, when I led my husband's father to believe I was unfaithful expressly in order to tempt Denis back early from his New York trip . . . so he might discover me in Frank's rooms, naked but for my wig, and kill us both.

Workings have a price, you see, and the single best currency for such transactions is blood, always—my blood, the De Russys' blood, and poor Frank's added in on top as mere afterthought. All of our blood together and a hundred years' more besides, let from ten thousand poor *negres'* veins one at a time by whip or knife, closed fist or open-handed blow, crying out forever from this slavery-tainted ground.

After Denis's grandfather bred my mother's mother 'til she died—before his eyes fell on her in turn—*Maman* ran all the way from Riverside to New Orleans and farther, as you've told Tully: crossed the ocean to France's main port, then its capital, an uphill road traveled one set of sheets to the next, equal-paved with vaudeville stages, dance floors, séance rooms, and men's beds. Which is why those were the trades she taught me, along with my other, deeper callings. Too white to be black, a lost half-girl, she birthed me into the *demimonde* several shades lighter still, which allowed me to climb my way back out; perception has its uses, after all, especially to *une sorciére*. From earliest years, however, I knew that nothing I did was for myself—that the only reason I existed at all was to bring about her curse, and her mother's, and her mother's mother's mother's.

There's a woman at Riverside, Marceline, ma mie, my mother told me before I left her that last time, stepping aboard the steamship bound for America. *An old one, from Home—who can say how old? She knew my mother, and hers; she'll know you on sight, know your works, and help you in them.* And so there was: Kaayakire, whom those fools who bought her named Sophonisba—Aunt Sophy—before setting her to live alone in her bone-yard shack, tending the linden path. It was she who taught me the next part of my duty, how to use my ancestors' power to knit our dead fellow captives' pain together like a braid, a long black snake of justice, fit to choke all De Russys to death at once. To stop this flow of evil blood at last, at its very source.

That I was part De Russy myself, of course, meant I could not be allowed to escape, either, in the end. Yet only blood pays for blood, so the bargain seemed well worth it, at the time.

But I have been down here so long, now—years and years, decades: almost fifty, by your reckoning, with the De Russy line *proper* long-extirpated, myself very much included. Which is more than long enough to begin to change my mind on that particular subject.

So, here you come at last, down the track where the road once wound at sunset, led by a man bearing just the barest taint of De Russy blood in his face, his skin, his veins: come down from some child sold away to cover its masters' debts, perhaps, or traded between land-holders like a piece of livestock. One way or the other, it's as easy for me to recognize in Tully Ferris by smell as it'd no doubt be by sight, were I not so long deep-buried and eyeless with mud stopping my mouth and gloving my hands, roots knot-coiled 'round my ankles' bones like chains. I'd know it at first breath, well as I would my own long-gone flesh's reek, my own long-rotten tongue's taste.

Just fate at work again, I suppose, slow as old growth—fate, the spider's phantom skein, thrown out wide, then tightened. But the curse I laid remains almost as strong, shored up with Kaayakire's help: Through its prism, I watch you approach, earth-toned and many-pointed, filtered through a hundred thousand leaves at once like the scales on some dragonfly's eye. I send out my feelers, hear your shared tread echo through the ground below, rebounding off bones and bone-fragments, and an image blooms out of resonance that is brief yet crisp, made and remade with every fresh step: you and Tully stomping through the long grass and the clinging weeds, your rubber boots dirt-spattered, wet coats muddy at the hem and snagged all over with stickers.

Tully raises one arm, makes a sweep, as though inviting the house's stove-in ruin to dance. "Riverside, ma'am—what's left of it, anyhow. See what I meant?"

"Yes, I see. Oh, *pute la merde!*"

Tree-girt and decrepit, Riverside's pile once boasted two stories, a great Ionic portico, the full length and breadth necessary for any plantation centerpiece; they ran upwards of two hundred slaves here before the War cut the De Russys' strength in half. My husband's father loved to hold forth on its architectural value to anyone who'd listen, along with most who didn't. Little of the original is left upright now, however—a mere half-erased sketch of its former glory, all burnt and rotted and sagging amongst the scrub and cockle burrs. Like the deaths of its former occupants, its ruin is an achievement in which I take great pride.

"Said this portrait you come after was upstairs, right?" Tully rummages in his pack for a waterproof torch. "Well, you in luck, gal, sorta . . . upstairs fell in last year, resettled the whole mess of it down into what used to be old Antoine's ballroom. Can't get at it from the front, 'cause those steps is so moldy they break if you look at 'em the wrong way, but there's a tear in the side take us right through. Hope you took my advice 'bout that hard-hat, though."

You nod, popping your own pack, and slip the article in question on: It even has a headlamp, bright-white. "*Voila.*"

At this point, with a thunderclap, rain begins to fall like curtains, drenching you both—inconvenient, I'm sure, as you slip and slide 'cross the muddy rubble. But I can take no credit for that, believe it or not; just nature taking its toll, moisture invading everything as slow-mounting damp or coming down in sheets, bursting its banks in cycles along with the tea-brown Mississippi itself.

Ownership works both ways, you see. Which is why, even in its heyday, Riverside was never anything more than just another ship, carrying our ancestors to an unwanted afterlife chained cheek-by-jowl with their oppressors, with no way to escape, even in death. No way for *any* of us to escape our own actions, or from each other.

But when I returned, Kaayakire showed me just how deep those dead slaves had sunk their roots in Riverside's heart: deep enough to strangle, to infiltrate, to poison, all this while lying dormant under a fallow crust. To sow death-seeds in every part of what the De Russys called home, however surface-comfortable, waiting patient for a second chance to flower.

Inside, under a sagging double weight of floor-turned-roof, fifty years' worth of mold spikes up the nose straight into the brain while shadows scatter from your twinned lights, same as silt in dark water. You hear the rain like someone else's pulse, drumming hard, sodden. Tully glances 'round, frowning. "Don't like it," he says. "Been more damage since my last time here: there, and there. Structural collapse."

"The columns will keep it up, though, no? They seem—"

"Saggy like an elephant's butt, that's what they *seem* . . . but hell, your money. Got some idea where best to look?" You shake your head, drawing a sigh. "Well, perfect. Guess we better start with what's eye-level; go from there."

As the two of you search, he asks about *that old business*, the gory details. For certainly, people gossip, here as everywhere else, yet the matter of the De Russys is something most locals flinch from, as though they know it to be somehow—not sacred, perhaps, but *significant*, in its own grotesque way. Tainted and tainting, by turns.

"Denis de Russy brought Marceline home and six months later, Frank Marsh came to visit," you explain. "He had known them both as friends, introduced them, watched them form *un ménage*. Denis considered him an artistic genius but eccentric. To his father, he wrote that Marsh had 'a knowledge of anatomy which borders on the uncanny.' Antoine de Russy heard odd stories about Marsh, his family in Massachusetts, *la ville d'Innsmouth* . . . but he trusted his son, trusted that Denis trusted. So, he opened his doors."

"But Denis goes traveling and Marsh starts in to painting Missus de Russy with no clothes on, maybe more. That part right, or not?"

"That was the rumor, yes. It's not unlikely Marceline and Marsh were intimates, from before; he'd painted her twice already, taken those photos. A simple transaction. But this was . . . different, or so Antoine de Russy claimed."

"How so?"

You shrug. "Marsh said there was something inside her he wanted to make other people see."

"Like what, her soul?"

"*Peut-etre.* Or something real, maybe—hidden. *Comme un*, eh, hmmm . . . " You pause, thinking. "When you swallow eggs or something swims up inside, in Africa, South America: It eats your food, makes you thin, lives inside you. And when doctors suspect, they have to tempt it out— say 'aah,' you know, tease it to show itself, like a . . . snake from a hole. . . . "

Tully stops, mouth twitching. "A *tapeworm*? Boy must've been trippin', ma'am. Too much absinthe, for sure."

Another shrug. "Antoine de Russy wrote to Denis, told him to come home before things progressed further, but heard nothing. Days later, he found Marsh and Marceline in Marsh's rooms, hacked with knives, Marceline without her wig, or her, eh—hair—"

"Been scalped? Whoo." Tully shakes his head. "Then Denis kills himself and the old man goes crazy; that's how they tell it 'round here. When they talk about it at all, which ain't much."

"In the testimony I read, de Russy said he hid Marsh and Marceline, buried them in lime. He told Denis to run, but Denis hanged himself instead, in one of the old huts—or something strangled him, a big black snake. And then the house burnt down."

"Aunt Sophy's snake, they call it."

"A snake or a braid, *oui, c'est ca. Le cheveaux de Marceline.*" But here you stop, examining something at your feet. "But wait, what is—? Over here, please. I need your light."

Tully steps over, slips, curses; down on one knee in the mud, cap cracking worryingly, his torch rapping on the item in question. "Shit! Look like a . . . box, or something. Here." As he hands it up to you, however, it's now his own turn to squint, scrubbing mud from his eyes—something's caught his notice, there, half-wedged behind a caryatid, extruding from what used to be the wall. He gives it a tug and watches it come slithering out.

"*Qu'est-ce que c'est, la?*"

"Um . . . think this might be what you lookin' for, ma'am. Some of, anyhow."

The wet rag in his hand has seen better days, definitely. Yet, for one who's studied poor Frank Marsh's work—how ridiculous such a thing sounds, even to me!—it must be unmistakable, nevertheless: a warped canvas, neglect-scabrous, all morbid content and perverted geometry done in impossible, liminal colors. The body I barely recognize, splayed out on its altar-throne, one bloated hand offering a cup of strange liquor; looks more the way it might now were there anything still unscattered, not sifted through dirt and water or filtered by a thousand roots, drawn off to feed Riverside's trees and weeds with hateful power. The face is long-gone, bullet-perforated, just as that skittish Northerner claimed. But the rest, that coiling darkness, it lies (*I lie*) on—

You make a strange noise at the sight, gut-struck: "Oh, *quel dommage!* What a waste, a sinful waste. . . . "

"Damn, yeah. Not much to go on, huh?"

"Enough to begin with, *certainment*. I know experts, people who'd pay for the opportunity to restore something so unique, so precious. But why, why—ah, I will never understand. Stupid superstition!"

Which is when the box in your hands jumps, ever so slightly, as though something inside it has woken up. Makes a little hollow rap, like knocking.

As I've said, little seeker, I don't know you—barely know Tully, for all I might recognize his precedents. Though I suppose what I *do* know might be just enough to feel bad for what must happen to you and him, both, were I any way inclined to.

Frank's painting is ruined, like everything else, but what's inside the box is pristine, inviolable. When my father-in-law disinterred us days after the murders, too drunk to remember whether or not Denis had actually done what he feared, he found it wound 'round Frank's corpse, crushing him in its embrace, and threw burning lamp-oil on it, setting his own house afire. Then fled straight to Kaayakire's shack, calling her slave-name like the madman he'd doubtless become: *Damn you, Sophy, an' that Marse Clooloo o' yours . . . damn you, you hellish ol' nigger-woman! Damn you for knowin' what she was, that Frog whore, an' not warnin' me . . . 'm I your Massa, or ain't I? Ain't I always treated you well . . . ?*

Only to find the same thing waiting for him, longer still and far more many-armed, still smoldering and black as ever—less a snake now than an octopus, a hundred-handed net. The weight of every dead African whose blood went to grow the De Russys' fortunes, falling on him at once.

My cousin's father, my half-uncle, my mother's brother: all of these and none of them, as she and I were nothing to them—to him. Him I killed by letting his son kill me and set me free.

I have let myself be dead far too long since then, however, it occurs to me. Indulged myself, who should've thought only to indulge them, the ancestors whose scalps anchor my skull, grow my crowning glory. Their blood, my blood—Tully Ferris' blood, blood of the De Russys, of owners and owned alike—cries out from the ground. Your blood, too, now.

Inside the box, which you cannot keep yourself from opening, is my Tanit-Isis wig, that awful relic: heavy and sweet smelling, soft with oils, though kinked at root and tip. You lift it to your head, eyes dazed, and breathe its odor in, deeply; hear Tully cry out, but only faintly, as the hair of every other dead slave buried at Riverside begins to poke its way through floors-made-walls, displace rubble and clutter, twine 'round cracked and half-mashed columnry like ivy, crawl up from the muck like sodden spiders. My wig feels their energies gather and plumps itself accordingly, bristling in every direction at once, even as these subsidiary creatures snare Tully like a rabbit and force their knotted follicles inside his veins, sucking De Russy blood the way the *lamia* once did, the *astriyah*, demons called up not by Solomon, but Sheba. While it runs its own roots down into your scalp and cracks your skull along its fused fontanelles to reach the grey-pink brain within, injecting everything which ever made *me* like some strange drug, and wiping *you* away like dust.

I *would* feel bad for your sad demise, little seeker, I'm almost sure; Tully's, even, his ancestry aside. But only if I were anyone but who I am.

Outside, the rain recedes, letting in daylight: bright morning, blazing gold-green through drooping leaves to call steam up from the sodden ground, raise cicatrix-blisters of moisture from Riverside's walls. The fields glitter like spider webs. Emerging into it, I smile for the first time in so very long: lips, teeth, muscles flexing. *Myself* again, for all I wear another's flesh.

Undefeated, *Maman*. Victory. I am your revenge and theirs. No one owns me, not anymore, never again. I am . . . my own.

And so, my contract fulfilled, I walk away: into this fast, new, magical world, the future, trailing a thousand dark locks of history behind.

Previously best-known as a film critic, teacher, and screenwriter, **Gemma Files** has published around seventy-five short stories since 1993. Some of them have been compiled in two collections. She is also the author of the Hexslinger trilogy of novels and *We Will All Go Down Together*, a story cycle. Files most recent book is novel *Experimental Film* (2015). She lives with her husband and son in Toronto, Ontario.

*And now she was here, the place to which she had been traveling
for decades, since the first landing team shot images back to Earth ...*

THE GLAD HOSTS

Rebecca Campbell

Mai knew them from photographs back on Earth, but she was still mesmerized by the creatures overhead. They were neither mammalian nor insectoid, not birds nor lizards, but the first denizens of a new kingdom, their temporary, webbed wings filling the sky with a murmuration that collected, diverged, dissolved as they ran their courses to the northern roosting grounds. Her first week on Shanti, she spent a very, very long time staring at the sky, at both the unnamed constellations and the creatures, and thought about how they would soon shed their filamentary wings and come to ground in a shallow bay off Shanti's enormous, singular ocean. She watched the strange stars wheel, and said to herself, This is home, this is home, this is home.

She had awoken six weeks early, a month before landing. Time, which had stopped for the ten subjective years of her voyage, had begun again with a snap like a slingshot. She knew this not because of menopause, or grey hairs, or radical changes in earthly politics, but because of her inbox, which was filled with thousands of messages she could not yet bring herself to read. During all those years asleep, Mom had written weekly about what she put in the garden, who was married, what books she read. Her messages amounted to more than a million words by the time Mai woke. A million words she could not yet bring herself to read, because they unsettled the persistent sense she had that everyone was as they had been before stasis-time, all of them awaiting ignition as she had done at the beginning of her multi-generational tenure, losing consciousness before synthetic umbilicals snaked into her body. Ten years gone in a single moment so brief that when she woke she wondered if something had gone wrong and they were still circling Earth. But it was Shanti below them, and she had become a woman past forty, floating in placental goo that had not been there a moment before.

She had swallowed against the tubes down her throat. The panic started. She began to feel the calluses and sores of a decade suspended. She threw up and a hose carried off her yellowish effluent. She felt the slither of internal machinery, and as it withdrew she felt how deeply infested she was by plastic and metal. A voice in her ear—no, not her ear, in the middle of her head, a friendly voice: Do not panic do not panic. When she could raise her wet, entangled hand to her face she found she had no eyebrows or lashes.

And now she was here, the place to which she had been traveling for decades, since the first landing team shot images back to Earth and she, only twelve, fell in love with Shanti the greenskinned. Shanti, who surpasseth understanding, even when Mai spent a whole afternoon with her eyes turned upward, wondering at the flutter of translucent wings.

It happened on an afternoon she didn't notice, walking barefoot near the river, maybe, or staring up into Shanti's aurora. Some dormant wisp breached her body on an in-breath among billions of other in-breaths. Her hand rose to scratch the inside of her elbow and through the abraded skin slid the spore. Something kindled, something single-celled, a bubble suited only to drift, rudderless, with each heartbeat until it rose through the permutations of its life cycle from spore to something larval, or like a nematode, and then some terminal, adult shape she could not imagine.

There are analogues on Earth, and she's afraid her mother will find them and learn about parasitic horrors: the fungus that permeates the exoskeleton of an ant and drives it upward along a stem to the underside of a leaf, where the punctuating explosion of its possession rains infection down on its sisters.

There's the flick of a small fish in the water, the light catching its silver belly, and the flash catching the eye of a heron, who catches the fish and—in eating—catches the parasite. The spreading brain-lesions that tell the fish: Flash, flick your tail up through the water to the air, to the beak of the waiting bird. Go. Go. Go. They say it over and over. Go.

Or the rat who rushes the cat. Or the man who rushes the telephone pole in a sports car because recklessness is a lesion on his brain and *Toxoplasma gondii* exploits his nervous system. The tongueless fish. The caterpillar who is nurse and nursery to a family of wasp larvae.

• • •

Her first impulse was always to lie. *No, everything's great*, she always said. She wrote a letter to her mother, about how beautiful Shanti was. Lovelier than the pictures. Everyone was kind. The fruit trees were always in flower. The ocean was a deep aquamarine, shading into an orange like a traffic cone when the sun descended. There were no traffic cones on Shanti, so she deleted that bit, and added something about a mandarin orange from the shop Mom liked on Fisgard Street. She wondered if Mom had bought oranges there this last Christmas, or any of the intervening Christmases. She hoped nothing had happened to stop the yearly ritual of oranges in green tissue paper.

She wrote a(nother) letter to her mother. *I've been infected by a parasite. I won't tell you what because I don't want you to search for it. By the time this reaches you it won't matter much, anyway. In fact, I'm forbidding you right now from looking for anything or asking anyone. Apparently I have about twelve hours as myself. They won't say what happens next, because it's kind of unpredictable. There are lots of animals who've had it, but only two people. They won't tell me.*

I can't stop thinking about the time we climbed up Mount Tolmie, the Christmas after Dad died, and you asked me something about agriculture in a seasonless ecology. And it was such a stupid question, I wouldn't answer it properly.

I keep thinking I feel them—every itch, every little nerve-wriggle—though they're too small to feel, so it's all in my head. I know it's all in my head. But they're not in my head. Or, not yet. The blood-brain barrier is the last redoubt, and then—I don't know.

I keep thinking about Mount Tolmie, and looking down at the lights when the city's fogged over. I keep thinking about the oak trees on the way up, on either side of the path, and the Easter lilies in February and March. Then maybe walking down to the beach and getting gelato, maybe a sugar-cone, and sitting on the beach, and trying to pick up as much Styrofoam out of the high-tide line as we could find. If you want to know, Shanti's seasonlessness is not much problem for permaculture, at least. Parasites, on the other hand, are a

She wrote the letter again, but differently, with no mention of the parasite or Mount Tolmie. She screamed at the doctors outside her isolation bubble: extract it, cell by bloody cell. Flood me with all the old cures—malaria or mercury baths, chemotherapy, kill it with radiation. Kill me on the way, if necessary. Kill it, kill it, just kill it I can feel it. Let me go home so they can get it out.

Overhead the convoy still floated, awaiting its return voyage, and she begged them to put her back in her pod and send her to Earth, hoping stasis killed it dead, or at least delayed its colonization. But the possibility of cross-contamination, the invasion of Earth's ecosystem by what amounted to a biological weapon already embedded in what might become a compliant host. Besides, she had years ahead of her, probably, maybe. Shanti is always a one-way journey.

Do something with the last minute you have. Scream. Again. Scream. Hack yourself open and let the invading legions spill out through the wound you make in your own gut. No.

Write another letter home warning them that though they may, later, receive letters from a Mai-shaped creature, it will not be her. No, go for a walk. No, eat a meal as a human being. Use the most dire and terrifying pickup line of all time: I'm about to become a composite entity, governed by an occupying host of single-celled aliens, and I'd like to get laid one last time as a person. No. Whatever you do, don't go to sleep, because then you won't know when it happens. Just wait, all night if necessary, in the little hut on the edge of the settlement to which you have been exiled for the village's safety because they really don't know what happens next. Wait for each little spore to flower in your brain and affix itself to your very substance. No.

She wrote a letter to her mother: *Does the fish flash in the shallows where the bird can see it because it is the parasite's creature, or because of the pleasure it takes in sunlight? Does the caterpillar love the little wasps, and the rat feel a transfiguring passion for the cat?*

She deleted it.

Mai seemed to remember that she had felt lonely in quarantine at first, maybe because it had frightened her, spending her nights outside the walls in the little hut. The loneliness, however, was temporary, because the first symptom of the Shanti Parasite's successful colonization was that she stopped hating the Shanti Parasite. On the afternoon of the second day of her infection she looked down and was surprised to find she had broken two fingers in some struggle against the interior of her own body. There were gouges and deep bruises on her face and belly. That was when it had her, a species better adapted, wilder, subtler, more lovable than any creature any human had ever encountered.

She healed quickly. She re-read the first letter home, the one about the little dear ones, written in panic, but she could still remember the day on Mount Tolmie. How her mother had wanted to climb it at Christmas in some weak simulacrum of holiday tradition. They'd take the dogs along the winding path to the top, she said, and sit in a patch of sunlight for a few minutes as they had done before Dad died. Mom brought shortbread, Christmas baking that was also a remnant of that other world. To Mai, they all seemed like marionettes, following the forms of a family that no longer existed, and that wouldn't exist—in the same way—ever again. She wished she'd declined to climb, as her sisters had done, but together she and Mom looked down at the city and Mom tried to make conversation, asking that stupid question about Shanti's axial tilt. Mai could not control her irritation, nor the anger that flared at this question, since she had explained in great and pedantic detail about axial tilts and seasons and permaculture.

She remembered thinking: You should have known better than to come home for Christmas, because it was not home, but a husk, remarkable only because it possessed the shape of the thing it once held, which had been your family.

She'd left her mother to clean up the waxed paper and the Thermos, and gone back to the husk, taking the short, fast route down the mountain, her mother trailing behind her with the dogs. On Shanti, parasitized, Mai remembered the day with the disinterested gaze of a woman staring through a telescope at a tiny, perfectly focused star. The winter jasmine had been in bloom. She wanted gelato from the place down on the beach, and without looking back to see if her mother was still following she had turned away from the house and toward the water.

On Shanti, she stopped being afraid. She stopped sneezing. That was good. She didn't mind that no one talked to her anymore because after the dissolution of fear and anger, and after her instantly cured hay fever, came love, which her doctors called a side-effect of *the excessive production of oxytocin and phenethylamine, as well as other as yet unidentified endogenous opiates* in the reports they sent back to Earth. It would have been easier to call it love, she told them, and they ignored her. The *excessive production* was exactly what she told them it was: love passionate. Tender. Erotic. Love familiar, and love affectionate. All possible shades rushed her at once: love unspeakable, love irresistible, love both angelic and animal, love that burst her heart like a shell, her pupils permanently dilated as her blood boiled with the little dear ones, and those *as yet unidentified endogenous opiates*.

The earlier, earthly passions were only harbingers of Shanti, and she remembered each as a prefigure of the first real love she ever knew: her little sister's babyhood when she was just four; her cat; her first love, at fifteen. Her second love, at eighteen. Her first adult love, which was also her terminal passion, when she was twenty-one. Then the years of stasis as she awaited Shanti in the library or on the starship, the blank years, during which time passed, but seemed not to.

And now: the little dear ones who kindled in her blood regulated—blindly, she thought, with the instinctively perfect manipulations of infancy—the operative chemicals in her brain, filling her with all shades of affection. All possible degrees and experiences telescoped into a passion for the single-celled creatures who floated through the viscera of her eye, droplets that cast translucent shadows in the day, and hazed her sight with the bioluminescence of Shanti's night. She felt the rush of them through all the corridors of her body, the multitudes, the civilizations under her skin, whose shapes she could not imagine, whose futures were inaccessible to her, and whose language she did not speak, though she heard its murmur everywhere.

She scares the colonists, like she's a time bomb about to cover them all with *Ophiocordyceps unilateralis*, which is silly, because she couldn't if she tried, and it doesn't exist on Shanti, anyway. That's okay, she says to the one doctor who's stuck doing physicals and tracking the Shanti Parasite's progress. When she goes in for her monthly examinations he is masked and latexed. She points out that the whole planet is teeming, and he goes pale and queasy and she feels sad that she's upset him, but isn't quite sure why.

The secret they won't mention in their reports—though she tells them over and over again—is that the Shanti Parasite makes her a better person. Definitely a better daughter. She reads all her letters from Earth one after another without being afraid of what she'll find. She wonders why Mai's first thought was to lie to her mother, and is troubled by this, and by the memories that she possesses but no longer understands. With her astronomer's gaze she remembers that other life: Mai's mother on the last morning, in the garden, barefoot in her nighty. Mai in pajamas, sitting on the step with her very last cup ever of morning coffee, watching Mom pull a dandelion—its root as large as a carrot—from the bed beneath the pink rhododendron. Mai watched her snap the root, then scatter the leaves. Dandelions, an old-world invader species, arriving with the first North American settlers, and equally voracious. There were—so far—no dandelions on Shanti. Which was too bad, Mai thought, because dandelion root made a coffeeish sort of drink. Not a substitute, but something you could drink and remember coffee by.

The sun in the garden now, on the still-unopened buds of the lavender in the border that lined the path, in among the rosemary and low thyme bushes. Mom picked lavender stems, and the young branches of the rosemary and thyme.

She carried them to Mai, wrapping them with a blade of grass, and handed Mai the tiny nosegay. Mai held it, and the faint stickiness of the herbs' oily stems spread on her fingers.

Mai thought of Shanti's permanent spring, the long, temperate year at the mid-latitudes of the settlement, the heat of the equator, the glacial mountains above the treeline. She held the bunch tight to her lips and breathed through their leaves. She did not look to see, but she thought her mother's mouth twisted, her eyes fixed steadily on the ground under her bare feet.

"Take it with you?"

"I don't know if they'll let me."

"Mai, you're crawling with organisms. You're a generation ship. A little bunch of flowers from your mother isn't going to destroy Shanti's ecosystem. We've probably already done that, anyway."

Mai looked away from the garden, into which she, and her mother, and her sisters had been born, and said to herself, Never anything so familiar, ever again.

The little bunch of flowers and leaves are still with her, in a baggy, in a locker, with other things she does not use: notebooks, some jewelry still vacuum-packed that fit into her ten-kilo personal allowance. Like most colonists she had loaded up on information, the nearly weightless petabytes of data: favorite books, photographs, patterns and programs, recordings of her sister's children telling stories.

The flowers, now scentless, their petals nearly grey, are the only things that demonstrate in their substance the passage of time. Other than her face, of course, which despite the no-doubt moisturizing unguents of the pod, shows years of existence, though not years lived. She and the flowers know it.

The developing Shanti Parasite: from the single-celled to something like a nematode in the fourth year of her infection. She was sick for three weeks, shedding most of the original millions so only a few thousand survived to settle into lesions on her brain and along her spine. The doctors won't even touch her anymore. No one touches her, which is less troubling than the die-off that meant she no longer thrums inside like a salmon-river in spring. She misses them.

The new lesions brought the first of the neurological symptoms: the fingers of her left hand curled around the palm. She often wakes up with a thin film of some flexible amber spread over her face, tinting Shanti's blue-green palette a warm, nostalgic gold.

Carriers—two others in the settlement, a few animals outside—recognize one another by the faint scent of what would on Earth be called orange blossoms, though it is unpleasant and fetid to the uninfected settlers, the doctor told her. He doesn't use a mask anymore, but he breathes through his mouth when she visits. Even when she is out of quarantine, she avoids the canteens because faces change when she comes too close. She's pretty sure some of them also think she should be executed. She is glad they are outnumbered, but she still stays away, in case of accidents. That is okay. The one night a few drunk kids from the village found her in her hut and called her out she hid in the closet until security cleared them away. She stayed there for a day and a night, her arms wrapped around her body, and the darkness lit by her own luminous excretions.

After that she stays away. She walks farther than any of the survey teams, farther than the scouts, or the trackers. She sleeps rough, alone, though never alone. Sometimes, together and without speaking—because to be a carrier is to be always in the wordless company of one's beloved—she and the other two from the settlement climb mountains to the thin, high reaches of Shanti's atmosphere, and bathe in a flood of cosmic radiation visible only to their naked, decaying eyes. Mai swims—the dormant creatures oxygenating her blood—an hour underwater. Her skin, once brown, now mottled a faint blue-green, pearlescent as it grows luminous in the blue glow of Shanti's night sky. Everywhere she sees a new color adjacent to violet, something outside the human spectrum for which there is no name. She calls it *Shanti*.

She hears them teeming above her and underground, the littlest dear ones, the single-celled, the unattached, their bioluminous glow lighting the sky, and running through the water when, at night, she creeps from her hut and climbs the escarpment above the village, the last ridge before the ocean.

• • •

Even now Mai-who-is-no-longer-quite-Mai remembers to write letters to Mai's mother, because to do so is kind. She does this monthly, and it is very difficult. She reads earlier letters in order to understand what letters to one's mother are supposed to sound like. The problem is that, while she remembers, quite clearly, Mai's life from before she became no-longer-Mai, she suspects she's still missing something in the letters: some pain, some history that is no longer relevant or explicable in her new, composite existence.

She remembers a handful of lavender, which she held in her palm, and sniffed that first week on Shanti. The leaves were so old she wondered if the scent was a phantom of her desire to smell this last gift of her mother's, which had traveled so far with her, and which had faded to grey-purple, the scent of something once green, of Earth. How she had kept it in the little pouch—the white one onto which her niece had embroidered three spears of lavender blossoms on their grey-green stems, her large, uneven stitches marked—so Mai's sister had pointed out—with a drop of blood where the needle had dug deep by accident. Despite this mishap the girl had finished the little project, and Mai loved the stitches, down to the knots on the back, where her cotton had got tangled. The niece was in her twenties now. Out of school. Married. A mother. A religious zealot. An officer. A lesbian. A diplomat. A retail clerk. A slacker. An activist.

Mai-who-is-no-longer-exclusively-Mai feels the swelling along her spine, where in their dormant stage the creatures fixed themselves and now dream through the last sleep of their infancy. She thinks of all the shapes through which they traveled, of spore-consciousness and single-celled-consciousness, of jellyfish blooms, the lesions of recent years, and then quiescence, the latent promises of the pupal stage, which is also the nearly last stage of Mai.

She wishes she could smell it again. Lavender. They started a lavender hedge in one of the gardens, but the scent is different here, though equally beautiful. Or perhaps her memory is unreliable, and the thing she smells is lavender as it has always been.

She wishes the gardeners weren't so uncomfortable around her. She could go visit the lavender more often then.

Mai-who-is-not-Mai knows these things, and knows that—somewhere inside, somewhere deep—there is a hurt, a structural break that will never come un-broken, even if she goes back home, even if they let her, even if she wanted to.

Mai is sorry, she writes on behalf of her addressee's daughter, *for that Christmas you climbed Mount Tolmie together. She remembers that after the mountain you both walked all the way to the gelato place that's practically on the beach, and she told you that she'd been accepted in the third wave of settlers. You began to cry. It was chilly, but she bought a raspberry sugar cone, and you kept sniffling, and she could only think about how awful your sniffles sounded, and how she wished you'd brought a hanky, which you hadn't, so in this imperious way she handed you a handful of napkins, and you sniffled into them, but you wouldn't talk because your voice tore, so it was better to be quiet. Mai remembers looking across the water toward the Olympic peninsula, and the day was flat and she thought about how worn-out the world was, how crowded, how grotty, how back-of-beyond, how provincial. And how, winking invisibly at you, though you were both blinded by daylight, lay Shanti. And that was the future, not the tired old world where mothers could sniffle their tears into napkins from a gelato stand. Mai crunched through her sugar cone, and asked—angrily, and without compassion—why the most important decision of her life was more about her mother than it was about her. Mai is sorry for this. Mai would like you to know that she understands now why you were crying. I write on Mai's behalf, but I am not, exactly, Mai. I am aware that this statement will hurt you further, but I think you would also prefer to hear this than to hear untruth, or nothing.*

I wish I could tell you that Mai is doing well, that she's not in pain, that she loves Shanti and is happy here, but I am not sure what these words mean, exactly. I wish I could give her the fingers with which to type this letter, but that is no longer possible. I know she wants me to say goodbye, though.

More than that, she wants to say she's sorry.

She is relieved to wake up one day and know—without knowing how she knows—that it is the last day. The knowledge is not painful, because it comes with the love that always floods what's left of her body. She knows what the other ones—the humans—expect her to do with this knowledge, which is to quarantine herself and alert the hospital, so they can destroy the creatures before they flower. They've talked about how they'll handle it, which comes down to a fatal dose of morphine derivatives, and then something she does not wish to know regarding the destruction of her body.

She is no longer human enough to feel that silly sort of loyalty to the settlement. In the manner of hosts before her—none of them settlers, because she is the first one to bring the dear ones to term—she limps up the escarpment above the village before the sun rises. The instinct is as inexorable as the spawning runs of Pacific salmon, so she walks listening to the impulse, driving her upward. She hears their teeth, and—the part of her mind that was still Mai—imagines that somewhere, she is in pain. They are kind, though, they do not wish her to hurt, only want her to hear the grinding of tooth on bone, and the softer sound of something wearing away at the cartilage of her ribcage. When she holds one hand to her throat she feels through her fingertips a new vibration.

Her spine snaps as she reaches the top of the escarpment and she topples, her head turned enough so that one cheek presses into Shanti's light soil, and one eye—the eye uppermost that survives the fall—staring now into the darkness that is no longer darkness to her, that glows with the faint phosphorescence of all the winged ones, all the dear creatures of the air, the glad host of Shanti's heaven. Not long now, the first breaches her skin in a rush of blood, and then another, the once-limitless universe of her body too small to contain them all.

Her skull cracks, and she still loves them. Her brain, sentient a moment longer, hung about with the tiny creatures—their carapaces pale brown like her skin, and possessing her dark eyes—wriggling out into the sunrise, their long bodies, their damp limbs already knitting spider-web wings to catch the breeze. They flicker through her peripheral vision, gleaming in the ultraviolet spectrum. She thinks, How lovely, how lovely, as they leave afterimages and light trails in her eye.

Out in the sky, above the settlement, among the glad hosts of the infected. Go on. She expects no response, but she hopes they sense her as she senses them, and thinks, Go on go on go on.

Rebecca Campbell is a Canadian writer and academic. She attended Clarion West in 2015 and her work has appeared in *Beneath Ceaseless Skies*, *Interfictions Online*, and *Interzone*. NeWest Press published her first novel, *The Paradise Engine*, in 2013. You can find her online at whereishere.ca.

I imagine her cocooned in a soft grey gel that presses on the skin of anyone approaching her—cold, firm, resistant. No such gel is visible in real life,

THE ABSENCE OF WORDS

Swapna Kishore

Music blasts my ears when Mom opens the door. A glance to check that Mom's okay—no bandages anywhere, nothing wrong with her walk, face not particularly tenser than normal—then I put down my overnight bag, kick off my high heels, and stride across to switch off the over-energetic, ear-splitting disco music. Things must be worse with Gran if Mom needs such cacophony.

"So, what happened?" I say.

Mom had summoned me by using the "emergency" word and then emailed the Delhi-Bangalore-Delhi e-ticket. *Three days, Nisha, that's all I need*, she had said over the phone. *It's a three-day weekend, no, Good Friday morning through to Sunday night? I'll tell you when you come. Please?*

Our project didn't "do weekends" as my boss put it—we worked all seven days and late hours at that—but I had been sufficiently alarmed by Mom's desperate-sounding parental pleading. And here I am, tired because I woke up at 2:00 a.m. to catch the flight. I'm still clueless about the problem.

Mom waves me to the sofa.

"I've bagged a two-year assignment in New York," she says. "Researching and writing on a series of health topics. Prestigious stuff."

"Congrats," I say tentatively. My gaze snaps to Gran's bedroom door.

Mom sighs and plunks on a chair opposite me. There are traces of white at the roots of her hair. Her housecoat is crumpled, smudged with turmeric splotches, and her slipper strap is frayed. She used to be so particular about remaining meticulously groomed even at home. Things change over the years, I guess.

"You've accepted?" I say. I already suspect the summons is related to Gran. Gran's eighty years old, frail but with no known problems other than the one we never talk about. Still I can't imagine Gran living alone, doing stuff like buying groceries, getting gadgets repaired, ordering gas, taking auto-rickshaws to the nearest ATM, and I guess Mom can't imagine it, either.

"I shortlisted some old age homes where I can pull strings and get bumped up the queue," Mom says. "I contacted a couple." She pushes her bifocals up her nose and tucks back a wayward strand. "One said they don't accept elective mutes. The other wanted a medical certificate and full psychiatrist evaluation."

Fifteen years ago, I'd been away at boarding school when Mom called to inform me of the diagnosis. That someone would choose not to speak creeped me out; for a while I blamed myself for my spat with Gran, even wrote a bunch of letters promising to be a good girl if she started speaking, but Gran never replied. Then I came home and saw the rest of the problem. It still creeps me out, Gran's muteness and the weird stuff around it.

"You could refer them to the psychiatrist you used earlier," I suggest. I can't imagine what any doctor would say now about Gran. How would they even ask her any questions?

"Actually, Nisha," Mom smoothens her gown over her knee, "I didn't take her to any doctor at that time."

I gape at her. "But you had told me . . . " So she had lied fifteen years ago. I feel rage rise in me, sizzling, in my core, branching through me, dividing, narrowing, till I am a network of fire. I force my anger to invert into ice. It turns shard-sharp under my skin, solid as icicles. But my incomplete sentence lies heavy between us.

Red splotches stain her cheek.

"Amma and I had argued," she says. "I'm not sure you remember what had happened the night before you left for school that year. You'd returned late because of some silly friend's party and I'd scolded you."

Of course I remember. "Scolded" was a mild word for the fury Mom had unleashed on me for a minor teenage mistake, but I'd managed to stay absolutely quiet by freezing in my rage. That time, after Mom stormed out, was probably the only time Gran scolded me. I hadn't known that Gran argued with Mom afterwards.

Mom continues, "So later that night Amma barged into my bedroom all preachy and saintly. Apparently my—" she annotates the air with curly quotation marks "—*legacy of anger* would spoil your life." Her chest heaves, her voice is ragged. "I just lost it. I told Amma she had screamed often enough herself. At least I hadn't abandoned my daughter."

"Abandoned?" I repeat.

"I—" Mom's mobile rings. She blinks at the display, clears her throat, and begins speaking in a smooth voice with a cultured BBC accent. Her shoulders straighten, completing her morphing into her competent journalist persona. I wonder whether to head for Gran's door and finish off the obligatory visit, but Mom's call is over and she's glaring at me.

"About Gran's silence," I prompt. "If you think she's not speaking because she's angry with you, have you tried apologizing to her?"

Mom's glare could frizzle anyone normal, but me, I have my ways to meet her crest of rage with my troughs.

"Fine," she says. "*Fine*. One more time won't hurt." She snaps her fingers, like she's saying, *Nisha, heel*. I keep myself cool, distant, visualize my return ticket right down to its Times New Roman font and the airline's logo, and tell myself it is just a few days.

Mom strides towards Gran's room, her housecoat swishing at her ankles. I follow her. An abrupt halt at the door, with me just a step behind. I am aware of the thud in my chest, the clamminess of anticipation on my skin.

Gran's room is still like a world in a time warp. Dust motes thicken the slants of light. Gran is sitting near the window, her wrinkled skin translucent in the morning sun. There are no other sounds, of course, none of the tiny sounds that define us: a throat being cleared, dry hair crackling, the gentle swoosh of breath, the rustle of Gran's starched cotton sari.

Gran looks up at us, sensing us in spite of the absent footsteps.

"I said something fifteen years ago," Mom shouts from the door. "I'm sorry, *okay*? How many times must I say that! You can start talking again, can't you?"

Horns on Mom's head would have matched that tone.

"Your voice doesn't reach her," I remind Mom.

Mom frowns and steps into the room, her footfalls cushioned into nothingness. Whenever I dream of Gran, I imagine her cocooned in a soft grey gel that presses on the skin of anyone approaching her—cold, firm, resistant. No such gel is visible in real life, but even so, Mom takes tiny steps, as if she, too, is forcing her way past some invisible gel.

When Mom is a couple of feet from Gran, she opens her mouth. Her face twists like she is screaming, her mouth keeps opening wide, closing, opening, closing. I hear nothing. I know Mom can't hear herself, either. How the hell does Mom tell Gran anything? Food's ready. Geyser water is hot enough for a bath. Do you want this sari starched? Stuff needed to coordinate the minutiae of life.

Mom's expression stiffens. She presses her lips together as if to catch words before they are swallowed. She grabs a notepad, probably kept handy for this purpose. She scribbles something and holds it in front of Gran, who glances at me, then adjusts her spectacles and squints at the pad. No nod, no shaking her head, no twitch of her face. Her hands remain folded restfully on her lap. I retreat to the living room.

Mom follows me a few moments later, crumpling the note. "Breakfast?"

Spoons clang against plates, cupboards and drawers are opened and closed with violent bangs. But apparently the noise is an inadequate antidote for Mom, because her eyes are over-bright—this, the woman who has never cried in my presence.

I wish I was far away, safe from whatever is about to tumble out. It is as if we are both standing at the edge of something dark and viscous that we have been avoiding all these years. I wonder if we will finally admit that "elective mute" cannot explain that gobble-all-sound sphere that's been growing around Gran all these years.

Mom gulps hard. She cracks an egg with unnecessary force. Whisk, whisk. Chops onions. Whisk, splatter, mop, curse. A pat of butter sizzles in the pan. In goes the omelet mixture, and then Mom finally looks at me. "She walked out on me again that time."

The toaster belches out toast charred at the edges. I place it on a plate. I absorb the words. *Walked out. Again.*

"After I dropped you off at the railway station the next morning, Amma wasn't there and her clothes were missing. She had left a two-line note saying I shouldn't worry. I didn't tell you because you'd get tense. You were so fond of her." Jealousy tinges Mom's voice in spite of the stretch of years.

I run my finger across the rough, burned edge of the toast, stare at the charcoal on my fingers. "Then?"

"I called up friends and relatives acting casual and probed them without explaining why. No one mentioned Amma. I wondered whether to report her as missing, but she'd said, *Don't worry.* A week later, she rang the doorbell and marched to her room with her bags. That's when it started, her refusal to talk and the . . . rest of it."

I wonder how it must have been, that week of uncertainty, then Gran returning, and Mom not getting any explanation or even the satisfaction of a good slinging match. I wonder how it must have been, sensing that zone of silence and fearing showing it to a doctor. That summer, when I'd come home for vacations and noticed how sound got deadened when I approached Gran, I'd felt so frightened I'd pretended there was no problem. Back then the sound-soaking shroud extended a foot around her; now it fills her room.

"Bloody-minded, that's what she is," Mom murmurs.

I am about to ask whether bloody-mindedness explained the gobbled words when I remember something else. "You said she'd walked out before."

Mom hesitates.

"Tell me," I say. "I'm old enough to know family secrets."

"Fair enough." Mom nods. "When I was a child, your Grandpa and Gran had a major fight." She sips her coffee. "She stalked off to an ashram at Rishikesh. Everyone was upset with her. Women aren't supposed to abandon a husband and daughter for spiritual practice. Besides, no one believed she was religious."

I am careful not to look up as I quarter the omelet and place it over toast, edges aligned. I've seen a couple of photographs of Gran as a young woman, faded sepia photos of a slender woman in a cotton sari with a broad border, a face that was overwhelmed by fiery eyes and a frown. I try to imagine Gran as an impetuous woman leaving a family and boarding a crowded train to the Himalayas, a small cloth *jhola* on her shoulder as her sole worldly possession. No internet to get an advance hotel booking, probably no safe hotels for women. No mobile phones, only trunk calls that needed to be booked from post offices, and telegrams that could be sent. Gran arriving in an ashram in the foothills of the snow-covered mountains, shivering in a cotton sari, or perhaps snug and warm in a pashmina shawl.

"Five months later," Mom continues, "your Grandpa got into a legal hassle, and they somehow managed to inform Amma, and she returned. She'd changed. Earlier she would just get angry all the time, but now her moods swung between rage and a fake sort of calm during which she spouted condescending platitudes." Mom pours herself some more coffee. "Once, reprimanding me for something, she blamed our entire family because she had left a critical *siddhi* work midway and her guru would not accept her back."

"You think she's been struck silent because some spiritual *siddhi* accounting system kicked in?" I can't help the sarcastic edge in my voice. "Or are you saying some other guru started her on another siddhi in that week she went missing later?"

"Let's stay focused," Mom says, as if I've been the one reminiscing. "The problem I'm facing is finding a place for her when I'm away."

"How does she interact with others? Milkman, car wash man, whoever. What do they think of that, er, stillness around her?"

"She just folds her hands when anyone approaches her and gives that saintly smile. She takes her morning walk on the terrace when people are barely awake. I've not heard her talk to anyone when I'm there." Mom pauses a beat. "As for that penumbra around her, well, people don't come close, and I avoid talking when I'm close to her, so I don't look like a cartoon character opening and closing my mouth soundlessly."

"No risk-taking, eh?" I blurt out. My words sound more caustic than I intended.

I sense the heat of her rage even before her face contorts, and instantly I am ice, I am far away. I don't live here, I don't have to do anything. I only have to survive for two days and then return. She runs the course—the tightening body, the clenched fists, the eyes bulging out just a teeny bit more. I wait for the outpouring. Minutes pass like hours. But she presses her lips tight. I guess she realizes I am older and can walk out.

Finally, I decide to take a risk myself and lower my rigid, distant stance. "I guess we have a—what they call—situation. Now?"

Mom face deflates like a punctured balloon; this is how her rage always dies—like a tornado hitting a black hole.

"I just don't get it, Nisha," she says. "If I leave an alarm clock near her and go away, it rings. I hear it ring. But if I am holding it, even if it is rocking like mad in my hands, there is not even a *chooo* of a sound."

"How does she handle something like, say, a dentist trip?"

Mom squiggles and squirms. "The last trip was almost five years ago. She didn't talk in my presence. The dentist took her in, and she gestured to me to stay out. I have no clue what happened inside, and I couldn't ask the dentist, could I?"

So Mom's been avoiding Gran's checkups. I bite back my comment about health journalists not doing what they preach. Who am I to criticize Mom when I have been avoiding visits?

"But now . . . " Mom mumbles.

We sip our coffees, and then Mom's lips part, her eyes soft-focus on me, like she's got a brain wave.

My stomach cramps. Surely Mom isn't thinking, no, she *can't* think, that Gran should stay with *me*? I'm holed up in an itsy-bitsy one-room *barsati* in Delhi. Heck, I don't even take Mom there when she visits Delhi for short trips; we do the mother-daughter ritualistic cozying up in a coffee shop, or her hotel, or just talk on the phone.

I want to cut Mom's suggestion off before she makes it. "I think," I say, stalling for time, when the answer flashes upon me, brilliant in its simplicity, "I have an idea."

"What?" Mom's eyebrows arch.

"Ashrams accept inmates, no? And silence is respected as a *sadhana* amongst spiritual seekers. Spin a yarn about her having taken a vow of silence or elective isolation or something."

It takes but a moment for a smile to fill Mom's face and crinkle her eyes, and the wrinkles suddenly transform into a poster for dignified ageing. Then she's calling people, gathering information, invoking favors with her contacts.

I steel myself and step into Gran's room. I break into a run when I cross her threshold, only too aware that I will not be able to enter the sound-deadening zone if I stop to think. Then I am there, standing an arm's width from her. "Hello, Gran, how are you," I say, and my voice is lost in the silence she enforces on me. Gran smiles at me. Nothing in her shows the energy and animation she had when I was much younger. Her fragility intimidates me.

She extends her hand tremulously.

The last time we'd touched was when she hugged me years ago, the night after my minor teenage mistake and Mom's explosion. First Gran had begun scolding me, saying I shouldn't have got so "angry" at Mom, though I'd not said anything to Mom, just stayed silent and kept my eyes lowered, masking my curled-up rage with a docile expression. I'd expected sympathy from Gran for my self-control, even praise, so when she began admonishing me my rage uncurled and erupted at her. I yelled at her how nasty she was, flinging, for good measure, words I'd seen scratched on school desks and in the toilets, hoping to slice through right to her core, slash her. Gran, after a few moments of stunned silence, said, *You want to hurt me, Nishi, have I hurt you so much?* And she smiled as if she'd received some life-saving insight. Then she hugged me tightly, forgiving, consoling me. That evening, the evening of the last hug I'd accepted from her, was also the last time I'd heard her voice.

Now her frail hand remains extended, but I cannot get myself to even touch her. I stand awkwardly for a couple of minutes and then tiptoe out.

A duly deferential *darshan* of the ashram's Swamiji is obligatory before we can leave Gran for her week's experimental stay at the ashram. Gran, Mom, and I wait in the hall, surrounded by scores of devotees including parents and kids. Kids laugh and play and hit one another, embarrassed parents scold them, women chatter, men argue. Noise engulfs us, but Mom and I cannot speak because we are throttled by Gran's proximity. Her sphere has shrunk but not vanished. I find myself missing work—lovely, stressful work, predictable random crises, buzzing with the challenge of office politics.

A baby bawls loud enough to hush the room into silence. The hapless mother cajoles the baby, offers her breast, rattles a colorful *jhunjhuna*, all to no avail. Kids, really!

Gran stretches her arms out. The mother's eyes blaze with fierce protest; I shrink, embarrassed. But strangely, the woman passes the baby to Gran, who cradles it. It stops wailing, and contemplates Gran with wide-open eyes, beautiful, kohl-lined. Its face squeezes a bit, and I fear a renewed audio output, then fear that the output will be seen but not heard, and how weird that would seem, exposing us as freaks. But what erupts is a gentle burp as its mouth softens into what doting adults consider a smile. A burp that can be heard.

Gran returns the baby to the mother.

Mom walks off and returns within a minute with the ashram manager. "Please come in, madam," he says. I assume Mom's handed in an over-generous donation.

Swamiji is in his eighties, more wrinkled than Gran, with matted locks and sandalwood paste on his forehead, very stereotypical. We fold our hands in greeting. For an awkward moment, his disciples seem to expect us to prostrate, something neither Mom nor I are comfortable doing. Gran beams, Swamiji smiles back, the tension breaks, and a disciple grabs the offerings I have assembled—coconuts, flowers, sweets.

"God bless you, children," Swamiji says. "Anger is bad, love is good. Regret paves the way for good actions, but correct action needs love and wisdom."

Yeah, sure. We've driven a hundred kilometers for this unique advice. I move away from Gran so that my voice can be heard.

"My grandmother has not spoken for many years." I gesture at Gran. "Silence surrounds her. We worry about it."

"People choose paths based on their karma." He chuckles. "*Shanti, shanti.*"

I hurry to add, "She was once trying for *siddhis*. We wonder whether—"

"Tranquil minds hear eternity. *Shanti, shanti.*" He nods at his disciples, who herd us aside. The next devotee in the queue proffers flowers and hard cash. We weren't expecting answers, I console myself. We are here to settle Gran in, not play Sherlock Holmes. Besides, our stay in the hall has confirmed that Gran's sound-deadening weirdness affects only Mom and me, so Gran's stay should pose no problems. Gran can pass for a pious lady who has taken the vow of silence, the revered *maun vrat.*

The room allotted to Gran is small but well lit. Gran sits on the bed while Mom unpacks her suitcase into a cupboard. Outside the window is a sprawl of low buildings and geometric gardens. Residents with serene but vacuous expressions weed vegetable patches and teach kids under canopied neem trees. So very idyllic. I shudder.

Mom pulls out a pad and scribbles: *I am going to New York for two years. If you like this place, you can stay here.*

Gran's head snaps up. Mom had only mentioned a week's retreat to her earlier. I feel ashamed of this way to break the news, but I can't fault Mom; I hadn't helped her, either. Gran extends her hand towards Mom, who quickly steps back. She scribbles again: *We will find another place if you don't like this ashram.*

Gran starts neatening the pleats of her sari.

My mobile vibrates. I step outside to take the call: a crisis at work. I calm down my boss, then blow up at a subordinate before instructing him on how to resolve the problem.

By the time I finish, Mom is outside, talking to the ashram manager.

"Your Mataji will be happy here." His reassuring way smacks of practice. "She looks peaceful."

A prominent lump bobs up and down Mom's throat.

"I'm sure she will," I tell the manager, and lead Mom away.

Mom's knuckles are white knobs on the steering wheel and her shoulders are hunched. I'm scared a single wrong word can shatter her. Sounds abound near us—the grunt of gear change, the swish as she swerves the car to avoid potholes, my own heart, thudding loudly. Car horns penetrate our closed windows. But loudest of all is the silence between Mom and me, thick-textured, dark with foreboding.

Later, while clearing up after dinner, Mom scrubs a plate clean with unnecessary vigor. "You must be having a sleep backlog."

I nod and escape to my room upstairs.

I lie awake for a long time. Past midnight, I dash off an email to my boss, pleading an emergency. Then I resume staring at the fan overhead and the ominous shadows it casts on the ceiling thanks to the neon street lights outside.

• • •

On Sunday, I mall-walk, shopping for gifts. I am clueless about what Gran likes. And Mom's a successful career woman, articulate, energetic, but what sort of books does she like? Does she enjoy clothes, jewelry? Does she party? Which movies does she see? I have stayed safely distant for too many years—after college, I found internships, summer courses, residencies, jobs, anything that kept me away. Not that Mom tried to get closer.

I select a small sandalwood owl for Gran because she often called me *ullu* as a kid, her affectionate way of saying I was as silly as an owl. For Mom, I buy a Parker pen, a congratulatory gift for the prestigious assignment we haven't talked about.

When I return home, I tell Mom I have rescheduled my ticket for Monday night and will visit Gran before that.

"Tomorrow? I won't be able to come with you. I'm interviewing a doctor for a lead article," Mom says.

"No problem," I say, relieved.

A small girl holding a doll is sitting near Gran. "Dadima, will you play with me?" When the child sees me, her smile wavers and dissolves. It reminds me of my office, of the wariness springing onto the faces of my juniors when I approach. I try to remove the snarl underneath my smile, the tension beneath my skin, but the girl scurries away.

I approach Gran, allowing myself to hope that things will be normal now, but when my footfall is smothered by her, I feel rejected, slapped shut, and the twinge in my chest leaves me breathless for a moment.

Paper does not rustle as I unwrap the owl. My fingers trace the carved wings; hesitant, I hold out my present. Gran cups her palms, and I lower the owl into them. My fingers brush hers. I stiffen, but force myself to relax. It could be the last time I'll be seeing Gran. I can handle it.

Gran grasps my hand; her skin is baby soft, even softer than it used to be long ago, when she hugged me at every pretext, back in those days when I would let her hug me. Why have I hesitated to touch her all these years? My eyes smart. I think of blinking away my tears, but what's wrong if a tear or so meanders down?

"Gran," I say.

Waves of silence absorb my voice, cool like an evening breeze. Not like the brittle ice I use to form my protective guard when yelled at—no, this is a soothing, caressing cool shell. I feel all soft and liquid inside.

"I've been an *ullu* all these years." My words are lost as sound, but they make my skin tingle.

Tears stream down Gran's cheek in rivulets, dividing, combining, dividing. Tears drip onto her lap, and some of those tears are mine.

Gran's lips move soundlessly, but the air suddenly has a hint of jasmine, like an offering to gods unknown. A blessing? Perhaps she has been speaking thus for years, words lost to me because of my frigid distance. Perhaps this gift of calming me is what she traded her voice for. Not stubbornness, not hypocrisy or anger, but quiescence—only I had held myself rigid against it.

Maybe Gran didn't know that Mom and I were too busy being bristly and angry, one by yelling, another by freezing.

I snuggle into Gran's lap as if I were a child again.

Mom chatters continually as she drives me to the airport, churning out tidbits about this person and that, people I don't know or care about, about her new project, about some press coverage she got. I let the words float around me, an alphabet soup devoid of anything meaningful. It is only after she parks at the airport, after we are safe and crowded in the rush of humanity, that she asks, "How is she? Does she speak there?"

"She was very peaceful. Happy."

"Obviously she'd be happy, now that she's away from me." Mom's eyes blaze with a familiar, corrosive rage.

"Mom, please."

"Okay, so I was not the best of daughters. I tried but Amma never . . . "

The gravel in Mom's voice, that tautness, tenses me against her assault. But even as my defense snaps in place, her voice loses meaning. Her lips move, but all I hear is a gurgle and burble of something rushing at me, searing-hot waves of lava, wave after wave, lapping, foaming. And then the sounds vanish. It's just silence all around me. I wince and jerk back, shocked.

Shock has paled Mom's face, too—she has noticed the absence of her words.

I inhale deeply, unfreezing the tightness inside me, trying not to resist. *Please*, I plead to gods I have never worshipped, *this sort of silence is not my way.*

Mom's face turns rigid, turns soft, her lips quiver.

I wonder whether to risk speaking.

"Mom?" I cannot hear my own voice. I try again, and again, and finally I hear my whisper. Thank the gods, if they exist.

Mom looks sadder than I have ever seen her. "I will book my flight via Delhi so that we can meet."

I nod. "Good."

We continue walking, the brief aberration unacknowledged, my throat clogged with doubts I dare not utter. I soak in every little sound—the swish of my clothes against hers, the drag and creak of my wheeled bag rolling behind me. Mom clears her throat every few seconds—just checking, perhaps.

Standing at the entrance of the passengers-only area, Mom's smile is forced, woebegone. Perhaps she dreads returning home, a lonely home even more silent without Gran. I surprise myself by pulling Mom into a hug. She tightens, but then lets her body yield to my contours. Last we hugged was probably when I was five years old.

"Take care," I say.

Swapna Kishore lives in India and writes fiction and nonfiction. Her speculative fiction has appeared in *Nature (Futures), Fantasy Magazine, Strange Horizons, Ideomancer, Sybil's Garage, Warrior Wisewoman 3, Breaking the Bow, Apex Book of World SF (Volume 3), Mythic Delirium 1.3,* and various other publications and anthologies. She has published books on software engineering and process management, including a business novel. She is currently focusing on supporting dementia care in India and she blogs about it and creates online resources for caregivers in English and Hindi. Her website is at swapnawrites.com.

You are not a fate-spun heroine from one of those
Gothic Romances you so despise . . .

MARY, MARY

Kirstyn McDermott

The woman in the bed makes a soft, parched sound that might be a groan, that might be a name long carried, never forgotten, or else a name more recently brought in careful, eager hands to the heart-shaped cage in her breast. *Fanny*, she might be saying, or *William*. Or perhaps she merely moans as thin rivers of fire course beneath her skin and her throat closes dry around each breath. A minute passes, or several, sickroom time stretched far beyond compassion, before her eyelids rasp open once more.

"Patience," she mutters. "A little patience."

In a chair near the door, a man sleeps slumped against the curl of his fist. Carlisle, the woman remembers, her husband's surgeon-friend with his large, kindly hands and eyes that fail altogether to mask his dismay, no matter the words of comfort he proffers. Carlisle, the good doctor, not the one who came before: those brusque and brutal fingers scraping at her womb, tearing the reluctant placenta loose piece by grisly piece; eighteen hours of labor and she would have suffered that pain tenfold in trade for its bloody aftermath.

Bear up, Mrs. Godwin. We must have the whole of it out.

The woman has crafted her life in words; she can find none with which to approach such an agony.

A movement by the window on the other side of the room snares her attention and she rolls her head on the pillow. At first she surmises that a witching-hour breeze has billowed the drapes—though they have been drawn close now for days, the glass behind them a shield against the noxious vapors of London's air—but now a tall, dark shape frees itself from the shadows and moves towards the bed. Tallow-light flickers across a familiar countenance; narrow hands clasp and unclasp.

"I cannot help you this time," the Grey Lady says. "This is not a mouthful of laudanum. It is not the foul waters of the Thames with boatmen ready at hand. This is . . . beyond me."

The woman in the bed swallows. "I have never asked it of you."

"And yet."

"And yet."

The Grey Lady leans forward, nostrils flaring. Perhaps she smiles.

"I apologize." The woman in the bed averts her gaze. "The . . . odors are unpleasant." Sweat and blood, the stench of putrid flesh; she is rotting from the inside out and knows it, catches the smell of herself whenever she moves: arms lifted to steady a glass against her lips; the anguish of negotiating the chamber pot. Her body tells more truths than a priest— ah, how William's jaw would clench at such superstitious fancies. *I feel in heaven*, she recalls confessing, words floating on the tincture Carlisle had administered. A turn of her husband's mouth, his hand swaddling her own: *I suppose, my dear, that is a form for saying you are in less pain.* Her own dear Horatio.

"Mrs. Godwin?" The good doctor himself, as though stirred by these recollections, rises from his chair. "How do you feel, may I enquire?"

"No worse," she says. "I fear, no better."

"There's naught to be gained from such conjecture, Mrs. Godwin." He crosses to the bed and presses a hand first to her brow, then to her left cheek. The coolness of his skin is welcome; the accompanying concern that pinches at his face, less so. "I shall rouse your husband. He wished to be fetched when next you woke." Carlisle leaves the room in hurried strides, sparing not a glance for the tall figure standing opposite.

"He did not see you," the woman in the bed remarks. Her tone is one of confirmation rather than surprise. "Good men would see angels, would they not?"

"I am not an angel," the Grey Lady says. "We have traversed this ground many times."

"A devil then. A demon."

"I know of no such creatures."

"Nor of Heaven, nor Hell."

"I cannot say such places do not exist, only that I know nothing of them."

"Yet, if shades such as yourself exist, might not angels? Might not Heaven?" After so many years, the conversation is rote; it has worn grooves in her tongue.

The Grey Lady smiles. "I cannot say otherwise."

"I—" The woman in the bed grimaces against a sudden spike of pain. "I am dying."

"Yes."

"You are the first to speak it."

"There have never been untruths between us. There should be none now." Again, she leans close. Again, her nose twitches. "Mary Wollstonecraft, you smell of burnt sugar, and hyacinth, and . . . " Those colorless eyes widen. "And *hope*? Even at this juncture?"

"I am frightened," the woman in the bed whispers. Within her, a renewed heat builds and she can feel sweat beading fresh on her skin. The pain worsens. "I am very frightened."

The Grey Lady smooths a place in the rumpled bedclothes and sits. "I will not leave." A small yellow wasp emerges from the collar of her blouse to crawl over her clavicle and along her throat. She moves as though to swat it, then pauses, hand hovering by her face. The insect takes flight and describes a slow, buzzing circle before alighting on the Grey Lady's knee. Its segmented body twitches. "She, too, will stay."

The woman in the bed closes her eyes. Blood simmers in her veins. This is not her end.

"This is not my end."

"There is always an end," the Grey Lady reminds her. "What fascinates is the beginning."

Rehearsing the words of aggrieved indignation she would consign to paper the very moment she returned home, Mary Wollstonecraft stalked across Westwood Common. How bitterly disappointing to have believed Miss Arden worthy of the highest friendship, only to find herself scorned once again in favor of other girls. Those whose better circumstances, no doubt, saw them placed unforgivably higher in Miss Arden's affections.

Mary could scarcely be blamed for her family's diminishing standing, or her father's foul temper and weakness for gambling. She suspected the whole of Beverley made barbed sport of Edward Wollstonecraft, yet it wasn't a single one of them who slept sentry on the landing outside her mother's door those nights he staggered home with pockets barren and fists full of drunken rage. On brash, abrasive Mary, he would not dare to lay a finger, and often she found herself regarding a new bruise on her mother's face with seething, unexpected contempt.

If only Elizabeth Wollstonecraft would refuse to yield to her husband. If only she would not succumb.

If that soulless bond was marriage, Mary wanted no part of it.

Nor friendship either, certainly not friendship with Jane Arden, who deigned to offer tea and lemoncake to Mary merely as an afterthought, it seemed, having first seen to the care and comfort of the evidently superior Miss Jacobs. Even Jane's mama had behaved with more politeness towards the girl, complimenting her pretty muslin petticoats and the stylish manner in which her blond hair had been curled and cleverly pinned.

Mary fumed. She would demand the letters she had written Jane Arden be returned forthwith, lest her words pass between vulgar hands and be made the subject of gossip and scorn. The very notion of enduring such slights from a person she loved—and which affection she had supposed returned!—was too much to bear.

Her foot splashed the edge of a puddle and she recoiled, breath hissing sharp through her teeth at her own carelessness before a bright scrap of yellow attracted her eye: a bee struggled on the surface of the murky water, damp wings aquiver in their valiant effort to attain the sky. Sympathies aroused, Mary bent closer. Not a bee, she realized, but a wood wasp. Autumn winds had shed the surrounding oak trees of most of their foliage and it took Mary scarcely a moment to find a suitable leaf, brown and curled at the edges like a small boat. Gathering her skirts about her, she crouched by the puddle and extended the makeshift vessel.

"Do you suppose that a wise course of action?"

The voice was unexpected and Mary started, dropping the leaf in the puddle and almost toppling backwards. Regaining her balance, she looked up to see a tall, elegant lady in a grey silk redingote and matching gloves standing but a few yards from where she herself crouched, undignified as a washerwoman.

"That is a wasp, child," the lady said. "Rescue it and you'll likely be stung for your trouble."

"I am not a child," Mary retorted. "Nor do I see why the poor creature would have any reason to do me harm."

"It is a wasp. What greater reason would it seek?"

Ignoring her unwelcome interlocutor, Mary retrieved the leaf and positioned it beneath the creature in question, which was now clearly tiring. Carefully, she raised the leaf up, allowing the water to drain over an edge while the wasp remained safe, albeit sodden, within.

"There," Mary said, gaining her feet as she brandished her trophy for closer inspection. "She merely needs to dry her wings."

The lady stepped closer, right to the edge of the puddle. She bent forward as if to study the proffered leaf but her gaze never shifted from Mary's. Her irises were a pale, watery grey and strangely flat, without hint of sparkle or sheen, as though they drew light into themselves yet, covetous, hoarded all outward reflection. After too long a moment, her eyelids shuttered and she sniffed; a subtle, delicate motion that reminded Mary of nothing so much as the family's tabby cat taking scent of the kitchen while supper was being prepared.

At last, the lady opened her eyes. "Ah," she said. "You see?"

The wasp had crawled from the leaf and was making cautious progress along Mary's palm. Mary held her breath as spindly yellow legs tickled her skin. "If I remain still, she shall not sting me."

"But is that within your nature, Mary Wollstonecraft? To remain still?"

Startled, Mary glanced up. "I did not give you my name."

Without warning, a gloved hand snaked out and plucked the wasp from Mary's wrist. Wings pinned together, the insect twitched furiously between gentle fingers, its black-barbed abdomen seeking a target. "You smell of rising dough and jonquils and, ah, such willful ambition," the lady in grey said. Then she thrust the wasp into her mouth as though it were nothing more than a boiled sweet and began to chew.

Mary looked on in horror. And with no small amount of curiosity. "But does it not sting?" she asked.

The lady's thin lips spread into something resembling a smile. Scraps of semi-chewed wasp blackened the gaps between her teeth. "I intend to keep a watch on you, Mary Wollstonecraft. I believe there will be much of interest to observe."

William Godwin, eyes red-rimmed and puffy, encloses her hand within his own. "Mary, my dear, it is necessary to talk of the children. Respecting their care while you are ill, as you may be for . . . for some time to come. Are there especial instructions you would leave me? For the children?"

The woman in the bed blinks. "The children?" He has a kind face, her husband. She has always thought so.

"The children," he echoes. "Little Fanny, and the baby. Remember, they have been sent to stay with Mrs. Reveley until . . . until you are well once more."

She remembers, of course she remembers. Her daughter, Fanny, named in dearest memory of one by whose side she herself had kept helpless vigil so many years ago. Watching day and night while her sallow friend sickened and rallied and sickened once more. Watching, too, as the weak little creature her friend had birthed succumbed with barely a whimper, his gummy mouth limp against the wet nurse's breast.

"The baby is dead," the woman in the bed whispers.

"No, Mary," William says. "Our daughter is strong and in good health. Do not weep for her sake, I beg you; she is in no danger."

"The baby is dead," she insists.

On the other side of the room, the Grey Lady speaks up. "It was Fanny's baby who died, Mary, not yours."

"And Fanny, too. Fanny is dead."

"Yes, Fanny is dead," the Grey Lady agrees. "But your *daughters* are both alive."

Her husband pushes more words across the coverlet but the woman in the bed pays them no mind. "So many dead babies, and their poor mothers with them." Tears scald her eyes. "Oh, for naught, for naught."

On this matter, the Grey Lady remains silent.

In Lisbon, the late November weather was more clement than what London might have offered, but Mary Wollstonecraft nevertheless harbored a deep chill in the marrow of her bones. She stood with her arms crossed, her back turned away from the bed where Fanny Blood—nay, Fanny *Skeys*, as her tombstone would newly have it—lay motionless and cold beneath the coverlet. If she had permitted herself a glance, Mary knew that she would see a yellow wasp perched on the dead woman's brow, its forelegs bent as though in prayer. But she would not look. Around her finger, she curled and uncurled a lock of brown hair, recently snipped.

"If Skeys had but married her sooner," Mary said bitterly. "If he had brought her across to Portugal a year or two ago rather than leave her behind to languish in London, her health might have been perfectly restored."

Beside her, the Grey Lady tilted her chin. It was a gesture approaching acknowledgment more than agreement, and one Mary had come to find exceedingly irritating. "Fanny was consumptive for a long time," the Grey Lady said. "An earlier marriage—an earlier pregnancy—might have equally exacerbated her condition."

Mary exhaled sharply. "You cannot know this."

"No, but I may decline to play such fateful games."

Pressing her lips tightly together, Mary shook her head. Her heart felt empty, scoured out by this most recent blow. Surely, if she closed her eyes and allowed her imagination free rein, she might follow once more the footfalls of her sixteen-year-old self. Might step into that neat little house and meet afresh the slender and elegant girl who had instantly and irrevocably captured the entirety of her passion, of her desirous soul, with the turn of a gentle cheek and diffident flash of a smile.

And might Mary not then hold this girl in safer keeping than the world hence had done? Might they not set up a home together, alone, Fanny with her painting and clever seamstress fingers, and Mary able to find like employment perhaps, or perhaps even secure a teaching position? Might she not be permitted to then love Fanny as she truly wished, wholly and without censure or rejection, to feel that small, flushed hand clasped tight within her own, until their breaths jointly expired?

Instead of this. A fractured and disparate decade, so small a span, passed in such grievous haste.

"What will you do now?" the Grey Lady asked.

Mary wiped tears from her face. "Once matters here are settled, I expect I shall return to Newington Green—though I fear my sisters will have sorely neglected our little school in my absence. Everina does well enough if someone is nearby to drive her along, but Eliza . . . Eliza is a helpless thing."

"Your own contribution to her state is not insignificant."

Mary stiffened. "My *contribution* was to remove a near-deranged young mother from her *oblivious* husband lest she commit some dreadful harm to her own person. She did not wish to remain with him; you heard her speak it on several occasions."

"She might not have wished to leave her infant daughter behind."

"Do not scold me for that in which I was given no choice. If children were not deemed to be the property of husbands, how many more wives might seek to escape their arduous marriages?"

The Grey Lady tilted her chin. "I apologize. This is not the time to remonstrate on such subjects."

"I could not know the baby would die. It was always my hope to reunite them once my sister was well."

"That is true, but it provides no comfort to Eliza."

Mary pulled the lock of Fanny's hair even tighter around her finger until the tip darkened and swelled. To attend so frequently upon illness and death might be thought to numb a person utterly, but Mary had been left in a state of raw sensitivity. It was she who had nursed her abject, querulous mother throughout the months of her final lingering disease, changing dressings that did little more than hide the seeping necrotic flesh beneath, all the while managing her father's ill-tempered impatience. It was upon her shoulders that care for poor, distraught Eliza had fallen—care and responsibility and blame for executing the only plan she thought viable, the sole desperate avenue of escape at their disposal.

And now Fanny, dearest Fanny, and her tiny newborn son.

Mary was exhausted, in her body and in her heart. "I cannot continue. Not without her."

"And yet you will," the Grey Lady said. "As you always have."

"Has it grown dark?" the woman in the bed asks. "I cannot see you."

"I am here, Mary," the Grey Lady says. Her tone is smooth as velvet curtains.

Deeper, more strained voices entreat from the wings, but the woman in the bed pushes them aside. She will no longer be corralled by the demands of men.

"I am here," the Grey Lady repeats.

When she'd set off for St. Paul's to see her publisher that evening, Mary Wollstonecraft's mood had been one of anxious despondency. As much as the decision grieved her, she would need to abandon her rebuttal of Edmund Burke's recent attack on the French Revolution, on the principles and passionate character of a people determined to dismantle a pernicious monarchy. Who was she to tackle so protracted and presumptuous a project, one so removed from her usual territory of pedagogy, fiction and the criticism, however barbed and insightful, that she regularly contributed to the *Analytical Review*?

Joseph Johnson had been encouraging of the proposed pamphlet, certainly, and she was painfully aware that he'd already had her first pages printed in anticipation of their completion, but her mind now floundered within its own argument. Clamorous ideas buzzed and batted within the confines of her skull, refusing to be pinned to the page: feckless parents, irresponsible aristocrats and spoiled eldest sons—her own brother, Ned, came readily to mind—who inherited familial wealth yet neglected to care for poverty-struck sisters; the inherent privilege entrenched in class and gender that bred selfishness and injustice within men, and forced desperate women into marriages little better than legal forms of prostitution; the dire need for social and economic reform, rather than dependence upon charity, which did merely gratify wealthy sensitives seeking to congratulate themselves on their benevolence while continuing to indulge in the vices of inequity.

So vast a problem, so much of which to speak, and—most insistent among her thoughts—who was Mary Wollstonecraft, former governess, sometime author and literary critic, to write *A Vindication of the Rights of Men*?

Now, as she mounted the steps to her George Street home, Mary did so with clenched teeth and renewed vigor. Her hands shook as she peeled away her gloves and hung her beaver-fur hat on its stand. She was not at all surprised to find a familiar figure waiting in her study.

"You are returned early," the Grey Lady remarked as Mary seated herself at her desk. "I thought you might have stayed for dinner."

"I find myself quite without appetite for food."

"Did Mr. Johnson take your decision well?"

"Mr. Johnson said that I should not struggle against my feelings. That I should indeed lay aside the work if that would better my happiness. That he would destroy all that had already been written and printed, and do so cheerfully." Mary snorted. "*Cheerfully* was the precise word he used. For such a *mutilation*."

The Grey Lady smiled. "All is well then, and you may continue with your other work. A review of that play you attended with *Henry Fuseli*, perhaps?"

At the mention of the name, Mary felt her stomach flutter. She released a deep breath and steeled herself. No matter how great their genius, no matter how seductive their whispers, certain Swiss artists could be given no place in her heart this night, nor for many nights to come.

"I will put nothing aside," Mary said. "Effusions of the moment these pages might be, but the moment is of no small import." Unhappy with its banishment, Fuseli's visage flitted across her mind. Undaunted, she flicked it away. "Tell me, why should genuine passion be so well regarded when it flows from the paintbrush of a man, but not from the pen of a woman?"

"It is the way of things," the Grey Lady said. "As those with means and power govern those without, that which is male governs all that is female."

"It need not be so," Mary countered. "France shines hope upon us, no matter the worn and tired nostalgia that Burke and his ilk parade as vaunted tradition. We should yet see a progressive society built upon talent and ambition, rather than unearned privilege. Why should it be our continued duty to repair an ancient castle, built in barbarous ages, of Gothic materials?"

"Do you say, we should allow such edifices to crumble?"

"I say . . . " Mary paused. Her eyes narrowed dangerously. "We should bring them to rubble ourselves."

The Grey Lady clasped gloved hands together at her waist. "I would very much like to see such a world as you describe."

Mary picked up her pen and found the place among her papers where her thoughts had stumbled and trailed off earlier in the day. Frowning, she crossed out a line or two. Then she cleared her throat, dipped nib into ink and began anew, words flying from her as furious wasps provoked from their nest.

She was called *a hyena in petticoats, a philosophizing serpent.* She was accused of lacking reason, of seeking to poison and inflame the minds of the lower classes, of being too shallow a thinker.

Those at the *Gentleman's Magazine* confessed themselves astonished that a fair lady might seek to assert the *rights of men*, remarking that they were always taught to suppose that the *rights of women were the proper theme of the female sex.*

By *rights*, they did not refer to those of education or self-determination.

While Romans governed the world, they pointed out, *the women governed the Romans.* The age of chivalry having thankfully not yet passed, women should content themselves with ruling from the boudoir—though it remained questionable that such a viper as Mary Wollstonecraft might gain for herself so coveted a position.

The rights of women, indeed! Oh ho, what fertile ground for sarcasm and jest!

Lips moving silently as she walked, Mary Wollstonecraft rehearsed the words she would soon say to Sophia Fuseli, sounding them for depth and clarity. Hers was an inarguably practical solution, a proposal that would surely suit all parties, and a *rational* one at that. Despite her many impassioned letters to the man, Mary suspected a recent cooling of Henry's sensibilities and she required the situation between them to be resolved. Her mind would otherwise remain fragmented, her thoughts unmarshalled.

The printing of a second edition of *A Vindication of the Rights of Woman* had allowed Mary not only to correct some glaring errors of grammar and spelling, but to bolster arguments she feared too weak in the version Johnson had rushed to press this January—yet again! the Devil coming for the conclusion of a sheet before it was written!—but still she was unhappy. Although gratified by the book's reception—more welcoming than her previous *Rights of Man* had enjoyed—a second volume remained to be written, her ideas expanded beyond the core theme of female education. If women were ever to be the equal of men, they would need to be treated thus, with responsibilities greater than coquetry, manners and marriage placed upon their dainty shoulders.

Why should they not aspire to autonomy? To their proper place within governance, commerce and the intellectual life of their society? A woman who had not power over her own self would remain forever a slave, and surely no true progressive argument could seek to deny universal rights to one half of the population . . .

Residual anger warming her cheeks, Mary paused to compose herself; she could not arrive in such a visible state of consternation.

Sophia Fuseli was already seated by the window when Mary was admitted into the modest but charmingly appointed parlor.

"Miss Wollstonecraft." The younger woman scarcely smiled as she gestured towards a chair opposite. Her pretty face, those model features her husband so adored, remained stiff and unyielding. "May I offer you tea?"

Mary accepted both seat and beverage, though she perched nervously upon the edge of one and took little more than a sip of the other. Less than a quarter of an hour later, it was Sophia Fuseli whose complexion reddened and flushed. Her cup trembled on its saucer as she reached to place them on the table.

"You insult both my husband and his wife, Miss Wollstonecraft." The woman's tone was chilled, crisp as frosted glass. "And you make yourself a fool."

"You misunderstand me," Mary said. "I do not wish to share Henry with you in the manner of wife—"

"Kindly take your leave, *Miss* Wollstonecraft."

But how could she, when Sophia was clearly confused as to her intentions—for why else would the woman take such prompt and livid offense? "Please, I do not mean to insult your marriage. My proposal arises solely from the sincere affection which I have for Henry, I can assure you. We have an *intellectual* affinity, he and I, and I plainly find that I cannot live without the satisfaction of seeing and conversing with him daily."

"You shall have to find a means of living so."

"But if we all inhabited the same household—"

"Will you not quiet your tongue?"

"Consider the practicalities, Mrs. Fuseli, if nothing else. We are none of us people of great means; to combine resources and share expenses within one household—"

"*Miss Wollstonecraft!*" Sophia Fuseli rose up in one violent motion. She thrust a finger at Mary, who struggled to gain her feet as readily. "You shall leave my house this moment and never again *stain* its rooms—or my husband's studio—with your presence. You are no woman of principle, to speak so boldly of your rights and yet seek to trample roughshod over mine. You are no woman at all, but a monster."

Escorted to the street by the Fuselis' housekeeper, Mary stumbled but a dozen steps before stopping to brace herself against a wall. Around her, London bustled through its afternoon. Pedestrians passed oblivious to her humiliation as the clatter of hooves on cobblestones, the wooden groan of coaches, assaulted her ears. Her heart was an empty, gnawing thing within her. She had lost Henry.

She had lost Henry.

Her scalp prickled with sudden regard. Blinking away tears, Mary looked about her. On the opposite side of the street, still and perfectly unjostled by the milling foot traffic, stood a tall woman wearing a hat dressed with ostrich feathers. The woman's face was stern, reproving, and even at this distance, Mary could glimpse the disappointment in those steely eyes.

Well? Though she but mouthed them, the Grey Lady's words pealed loud as funeral bells in Mary's mind. *Did I not warn you, Mary Wollstonecraft? Did I not say?*

If her heart was a cage, she was unduly careless of its latch.

Fleeing the whispers and sneers of London, she sought refuge in Paris scant weeks before the execution of the king, and so became witness not to her beloved revolution but to the bloody terror that would claim it. Helpless to do aught but write, she took up her pen with fervor, heedless of the danger in her very English observations. In her politics, in her words, Mary Wollstonecraft was fearless.

But her heart was a cage, and its door remained open long after Fuseli had slipped featherless from its hold. Open, inviting another who alighted upon the flimsy bars and sang of love and desire and the untasted delight of sweat-salted skin. Another who skipped inside to settle for a while, or at least to give appearance of settling, his brash American plumage so bright and strange that Mary found *herself* wholly captivated—in her mind and soul and finally, wondrously, in her body.

"She is exquisite, is she not?" Mary Imlay, as she now styled herself, held her newborn daughter against her breast. "Ten perfect fingers in miniature, and look! Eyes the very shade of my darling Gilbert's. Surely now that our Fanny is here, he will stay in Le Havre with us. Whoever could resist such eyes as these?"

"She is indeed a most agreeable child," the Grey Lady said.

Frowning, the new mother glanced up. "You mock me?"

"I have never mocked you, Mary Wollstonecraft. But I do worry."

Such concern was not misplaced.

Barely three months of shared parenthood were hers to enjoy that summer before Gilbert Imlay, her once-soulful lover, now less-than-official husband chafing under harness, left for London on matters of business similar to those that had dragged him away during her pregnancy. As before, he promised to send for her when matters were settled. As before, months slid past with no firmer word on when that might occur.

Her treatise on the French Revolution completed prior to Fanny's birth, Mary was without a literary project with which to occupy herself. Instead, her word-churned mind bloated and burst itself over a near constant production of correspondence to Imlay—longing, scornful, desirous, admonishing letters that scarce received a satisfactory reply. Bodily, she devoted herself to Fanny, nursing the baby through smallpox, encouraging her efforts first to crawl and then to stand, rubbing her gums with chamomile as the first tooth began to cut.

"She will need to be weaned," Mary said, wincing as the child mauled a nipple between her newly armed gums.

"She is not the only one," the Grey Lady remarked.

Abandoned and friendless in the port city of Le Havre, Mary bundled up her daughter and returned to Paris. With Robespierre fallen, the streets were at last clean of the bloody work of the guillotine, but that winter proved the harshest of her thirty-six years. It was a winter of poor harvests and famine-priced food, a winter of unobtainable coal and wood cut laboriously by her own chapped hands, a winter of despair and burgeoning suspicion.

Imlay, came the whispers from foe and well-meaning friend alike, never intended to send for her or Fanny. Instead, he frittered his money away on the company of pretty London actresses.

On one pretty London actress in particular.

She tried to not heed them, but the words sank into her marrow.

Mary's latchless heart was ill. Her soul was weary. The impish, smiling face of her daughter undid her daily; she loved the child more than she would have once thought possible, and yet those soft and vivacious features bore so solid a stamp of Imlay upon them, it was sometimes nearer cruelty than kindness to behold them.

At night, alone with the darkness and a silence that no sound save Fanny's fluttering breath could penetrate, Mary's thoughts thickened and set. She pitied the poor mite for being born a girl into a world run by men for their own ends, and wondered what earthly good she was showing herself to be as a mother. Certainly no better a mother than wife, or sister, or any kind of *woman* at all, and now that the child was no longer in need of her milk—

"I am nothing," Mary whispered to the empty air.

She required, and received, no reply.

Finally, there came a summons to London, though she set off with little more than resignation in her breast. This was for Fanny, who deserved more from a father than the pauper-gift of his name, and it was for Fanny too that Marguerite accompanied them. The efficient new maid seemed as excited to see England as Mary had once been to visit France.

Mary's gelid, smoke-grey thoughts trailed them all.

They were settled at Charlotte Street, the lodgings comfortably furnished with all but Imlay himself who vacillated between affection and apology, but remained acutely stubborn in his refusal to adopt the role of *paterfamilias*. A refusal of which, it seemed, all of London was jovially aware.

The laudanum, she later insisted, was an error of judgment.

She had not intended—

Certainly not—

She had once been Mary Wollstonecraft.

Movement was the key, as it always had been. If she remained still, in her body or in her mind, thick-thumbed gloom would smother her alive.

And so, to the astonishment of many, she agreed to Imlay's proposal of a Scandinavian journey—some long-outstanding business she might follow up on his behalf, a traitorous ship captain to track down in Sweden, a purloined cargo of silver and gold to pursue in foreign courts—with the insinuation that their personal situation might be further resolved over the months of her—and Fanny's—absence. Having sighted once more the woman who had so inflamed his passions in Paris, having held again the child those passions had born, might it not be that Imlay merely required time and space in which to unfetter himself from present entanglements?

At this barest hint of oil, Mary's heart flung open with a shriek.

It was dim inside the carriage, and her clothing was wet and stinking of the Thames. She stared at her trembling hands, at fingernails still tinged corpse-blue, as though they alone had managed to resist the pull of the wakeful world.

"You are a foolish, obstinate woman, Mary Wollstonecraft." The Grey Lady sat opposite, arms crossed over her breast, mouth drawn pencil thin.

"Mary Imlay," she corrected, as she had done countless times this past year. Her throat rasped with the sting of a thousand wasps; she would never forget the unexpected agony of drowning, the furious burn of all that water rushing to fill her. If she had been foolish, it was only in her expectation that such an end might be painless.

The Grey Lady snorted. "You have never been Mrs. *Imlay*, in truth, and pray never shall be."

"He is resolved that another might take that name."

"You knew this."

"Until yesterday, I only suspected."

"You *knew*, Mary, let us not pretend otherwise."

Mary shook her head. All those letters sent speeding back through Denmark, Norway, Sweden, all those notes received in turn from his deceitful hand, all those hints and promises that she and Fanny might still have a place by his side—only to return to find him setting up house with his *actress*. With the whole of London witness to her humiliation, to Imlay's callous desertion, she had seen no other way to extricate herself or her daughter from the wretchedness into which they had been plunged.

"It was you who saved me," Mary said.

"I breathed upon a fisherman's nape," the Grey Lady replied. "Encouraged him to turn towards Putney Bridge at the moment of your leaping; that was the furthest of my ability. It was he, and those in the tavern, who effected your resuscitation."

"You would play my guardian angel, then?"

"I am no angel, Mary. Must we tread this patch anew?"

"A monster then, to see me dragged back to life and misery."

"To life, yes, and to your child."

Tears coursed down her cheeks but Mary made no move to wipe at them. "I had—I had made provisions for Fanny. She was to return to France, to be raised safe from the taint of her mother's errors, beyond the scorn of those who would damn her for her parents' degradation."

"This performance is wasted," the Grey Lady snapped. "You are no martyr to wail in sackcloth and ashes."

"You cannot know what I endure! What I have endured these past months—"

"But I do. Each passion, each *degradation,* that has e'er passed through you, I have felt most keenly. I know you, Mary Wollstonecraft. I know that you suffer, I know that your suffering is genuine—but, oh, how you delight in *feeding* it."

"Do not *presume* to tell me—"

"I shall do more than presume and, for once, you shall do naught but listen." The Grey Lady leaned forward; her eyes were flat metal discs in their shadowed sockets. "You make of people what you would have them be— such superior beings! so worthy of your heart!—and then you mourn their failings, when you are not blinding yourself to them. Imlay, Fuseli, even Fanny Blood—yes, Fanny; do not appear so shocked—they are more vital to you in their absence, for their presence can never approach the chimeras you have fashioned in their stead."

"You take Gilbert's side in this?" Beneath her despair, a renewed anger simmered.

"Never." The Grey Lady's voice was softer now, its barbs for the moment withdrawn. "I will always stand with you, but I will not tip soothing lies into your ear, nor will I aid this melancholy. You are stronger than you imagine, Mary, and I would have you see *yourself* through clear, unclouded eyes."

Shivering, Mary rubbed her cheeks. Rain pattered on the carriage roof and she found herself wishing the journey would never reach its end. For all her intellectual accomplishments, her much-prized rationality, she was terrified. Alone and abandoned she had been on several occasions, and penniless too, but never in so dire a situation as this. Never with a child—a girl child—for whom to care and somehow shield from the world's most outrageous fortunes.

"Oh!" she cried as her daughter's round and rosy face flashed into her mind. "My little Fanny, I would have left you to them. How could I have thought . . . "

"Your thoughts were elsewhere," the Grey Lady said. "They have been elsewhere for too long now, and it is past time you collected them." She sniffed the air, her nose wrinkling in displeasure. "Spoiled yeast and calla lilies and desperation, still."

"I can smell only mud and sewage."

The Grey Lady chuckled. "That too, of course."

"My heart beats, yet this feels a living death."

"While it seems so, I will not leave you."

Mary pressed her face to the window. "It is dark outside."

"It is October; the days grow short."

"It is so very dark." For the barest of breaths, Mary imagined she could feel the squeeze of gloved hands about her wrists. She closed her eyes. "I am frightened."

"Know that I am here," the Grey Lady said. "And cling to this, if nothing else: you are not a fate-spun heroine from one of those Gothic Romances you so despise."

This time she was certain that she felt it, the touch of flocked velvet soft as infant skin against her bare, chilled flesh. The impossible pressure of those thin and gentle fingers.

"You are Mary Wollstonecraft, and you will die for no *man*."

Even in darkness, words glimmered and beckoned, drawing her outwards. First, the mixed blessing of her journals, notes for the travelogue that Joseph Johnson had commissioned upon learning of her Scandinavian endeavor. She wrought from them an epistolary elevated by personal circumstance: a woman journeying alone with an infant; a woman caught in the process of betrayal and abandonment; a woman traversing the masculine spheres of commerce, politics, creativity and philosophy—and crafting such clever, such *candid* dispatches.

Behold: Mary Wollstonecraft, Traveler-Philosopher!

Her mind flexed, and lightened.

Invigorated, finding solid footing once more among the literary circles of London, she conceived a fresh project by which she rapidly became consumed. *Maria*, the novel would be titled, or *The Wrongs of Woman*, and from the first she was resolved on a slow and calculated execution. The crafting of a truly *excellent* book was an arduous task, and this time Mary would not allow herself to be rushed. This time, she would reflect and revise and reconsider. This time, her words would ring with utter clarity.

Behold: Mary Wollstonecraft, Polemic Novelist!

Her heart, too, discovered a new fascination. Or perhaps rediscovered it.

Upon the occasion of their first meeting years before at one of Johnson's weekly dinners, Mary had found William Godwin irksome in his undiscerning admiration of supposedly eminent men. He had, in turn, thought her too outspoken in conversation, especially when he would have preferred to imbibe the opinions of others around the table. Other eminent *men*, an unspoken qualification she had perceived only too well.

Newly reacquainted within overlapping social circles, they found themselves drawn to one another with the inexorable, near imperceptible weight of planetary bodies whose orbits, previously misaligned, now moved in startling synchronicity. Mary's passions, never cooled, rekindled. William's, to his own astonishment, burned all the bolder for their hitherto untested state.

But non-planetary bodies, bodies of flesh and flagrant blood, follow their own particular, if not wholly predictable, paths and thus conceive *projects* of their own.

See William Godwin, famous for his very public repudiations of marriage as a moral institution.

See Mary "Imlay," already sensitive to gossip and the subject of much speculation.

Then imagine—oh imagine!—the fraught negotiation of these two proud and independent souls around the sudden expectation of a third. The small, private ceremony at St. Pancras. The quiet series of announcements to friends. The united front against those who shunned them, those who mocked and scorned and professed outrage, or merely snide amusement, at a marriage for which the catalyst would soon become roundly apparent.

Behold: Mary Wollstonecraft, Mother-To-Be, Redux.

The woman in the bed opens her eyes and tries to focus on the figures surrounding her. There is William, dear William, his tired face so pale, his eyes sunken. The doctor, the good doctor, whose name she cannot for the moment recall. And, of course, the other.

"I did not finish," the woman in the bed croaks. "I thought there was time, at last, to be still."

William clutches her hand. "There is time, my love."

"There is no time," the Grey Lady says quietly.

No attention is paid to her by any soul present save the woman in the bed, who struggles now to sit up, who is restrained by the gentlest of palms placed against her panting sternum, who is entreated to rest, to save her words for when she is well. William's eyes are glossy with tears.

The woman in the bed stares past him. "My baby, who will teach her, who will protect her?"

"Hush." William brushes damp hair from her face. "There will be time to talk of such matters."

"There is no time," the Grey Lady repeats. "I will not lie to you, Mary."

"You must look to her," the woman in the bed pleads. "Look to her as you have me."

Hush, my love, do not worry yourself so needlessly.

"That is not my purpose," the Grey Lady says.

"Then *make* it your purpose. My daughter will not know her mother."

Carlisle? Carlisle, she is raving; see how her face contorts?

Mr. Godwin, I can do nothing further to help her.

The Grey Lady moves closer to the bed. A yellow wasp crawls down her sleeve and into the palm of her hand. "I am sorry, Mary. If it were in my power, I would ease all the suffering in the world, beginning with your own."

"It is dark," the woman in the bed whispers. "It is dark as the Thames."

Carlisle, fetch that lamp here. Mary, see? There is yet light.

I fear it will not be long, Mr. Godwin.

"I felt as one standing on a precipice," the woman in the bed says. "All the world bustled and buzzed below me and for once I need not race away. There would be time, the baby would come, and there would yet be time for all I wished to do." Her chapped lips crack around a smile. "I should be at my desk."

Mary, be still now. Hush.

"Do not leave me, I beg you."

Never, my love. I am here always.

"I will not leave you." The Grey Lady extends a hand. "But here, open your mouth."

Insect legs scratch and tickle as they crawl over her tongue. The woman in the bed presses the wasp against her palate, feels its barbed abdomen burst even as it sinks its sting into her flesh. Where she expected pain, there is instead a spreading languid heat and the taste of molasses on fresh-baked bread.

"It is all I can do," the Grey Lady says.

It is enough.

• • •

Do not suppose this to be her ending.

It is a play truncated in its second act, a journey derailed before its terminus, a cloth cut short by miser's blades; you cannot decipher the whole pattern from but a fragment in your hand.

She would not have remained still. She *could* not have remained still.

There would have been more words. There would always have been more words.

Her story cannot be shaped to a convenient arc, to a neat and satisfactory conclusion.

This is not her ending; it is merely where she left off.

It is not her purpose and yet the Grey Lady comes regardless, propelled by curiosity perhaps, or perhaps by some deeper compulsion. The baby is sleeping in a simple wooden crib which once rocked the Reveleys' own children to slumber, now retrieved from storage and pressed into tragic and unexpected service. Nearby, little Fanny plays mother to a favorite doll, fussing with its hair and dress and planting noisy kisses upon its porcelain cheeks. The child does not notice the Grey Lady's arrival in the room, just as she has never noticed her myriad comings and goings. That is as it should be.

The Grey Lady approaches the crib, drops to one knee beside it. "Let me look at you, then." Her eyes scan the infant's chubby features, hoping to discern some familiarity in the shade of the nose, in the turn of the mouth, but her efforts are ill-rewarded. Babies are, after all, babies. In time, there might be something of the mother in this one, or the father, but that time will not be the Grey Lady's to witness.

She sighs. "Good life to you, child, and to your sister."

The baby opens her eyes. Dark brown as her mother's were, and curious, they fix themselves upon the Grey Lady's face. Those eyes see her.

"Oh my," she whispers. Leaning forward, her nose inches from the newly fascinating creature in the crib, she takes a delicate sniff. Oh my, indeed. "Mary Godwin . . . " The Grey Lady frowns; the name feels unfinished on her tongue. "Mary *Wollstonecraft* Godwin, or however you shall be someday known, you smell of thunderstorms and secret truths and . . . and monsters?"

The baby makes a soft, gurgling sound. Tiny fingers flex.

"Oh, my dear girl," the Grey Lady tells her. "I shall be keeping a very close watch on you."

Kirstyn McDermott has been working in the darker alleyways of speculative fiction for much of her career and her two novels, *Madigan Mine* and *Perfections*, have each won the Aurealis Award for Best Horror Novel. Her most recent book is *Caution: Contains Small Parts*, a collection of short fiction published by Twelfth Planet Press. When not wearing her writing hat, she produces and co-hosts a literary discussion podcast, *The Writer and the Critic*, which generally keeps her out of trouble. She can be found online (usually far too often) at kirstynmcdermott.com.

The future is not knowable until it has become the past . . . right?

CASSANDRA

Ken Liu

πόλλ ξ, ἀλλ' ἐχῖνος ἕν μέγα
The fox knows many things, but the hedgehog knows one big thing.
—Archilochus

"Just doing my job." He mugs for the cameras, that magnificent smile, that ridiculous cape and costume, that stupid quirk of the brow. Behind him is the unharmed research center building. Overhead the brilliant fireworks of the bomb he had heaved into the sky light up the scene, the sparks drifting down over his shoulders like confetti.

He could have tossed the bomb into the river, of course, but this makes for better TV. This is why I've taken to calling him *Showboat*, which happens to also work well with the soaring "S" on his chest.

"What do you have to say to her?" some reporter shouts.

"Villainy doesn't pay," he says, like some baseball player with a repertoire of a dozen clichés that will play well for any purpose. *Don't be evil. Surrender and face a fair trial. The American people will not tolerate terrorism. Open your heart to the goodness around you.*

I flick off the TV. He had probably figured out my plans with the city's help. With thousands of surveillance cameras everywhere these days, it's almost inevitable that my image was captured by some of them. Computers and his super-vision would have done the rest. He does believe in at least one form of anticipatory knowledge then, the kind that concerns me.

I'll keep on trying, though I'll need a better disguise.

The apartment is well appointed, comfortable. The man who owns this place won't be back until tomorrow morning; I'll be safe here. I fall asleep almost immediately after a long day of crawling through ventilation ducts and utility crawlspaces carrying explosives.

I dream about the building I failed to blow up, about the humming servers and cluttered labs I saw, about the knowledge that is stored within, about automated drones sweeping across the sky, over a busy market, over a remote hamlet, raining death upon the people below implacably. I feel the terror of the man through whose eyes I see these things, and the knowledge that it is wrong, all wrong, and yet also necessary, because war has its own logic, the perennial excuse of cowards trying to evade responsibility.

But *I* am the villain. Right?

You want to hear some dark, twisted origin story, some formative experience that explains how I've come to be me. That's what Showboat wants, too. "I feel sorry for her," he tells the cameras. "No one is born evil." I want to throw the remote at the TV every time he says that.

The real story is pretty mundane. It started with a search for cool air.

It's summer and there's no air conditioning in my apartment. Buying a window unit and installing it and figuring out how to pay for the extra electricity—the very thoughts exhaust me. Planning has never been my strong suit. I like to take things one step at a time. It's why I'm still in the city with no job after college, trying to put off making that phone call to my parents about possibly moving back home. *You're right, Dad; it looks like that degree in literature and history really isn't so useful.*

So I go out for ice cream, for cold smoothies, for the cool air in discount stores where they sell everything you desire and nothing you need.

There's a family near the TVs with their color saturation turned up so high that the skin on the white actors look orange. The woman stands next to one of the 72-inch beasts, looking skeptical.

"I think it might be a bit too big," she says.

The man looks at her, and I see his face go through this weird transformation. It was a handsome face, but now it's not. It's like she has just insulted him in some unforgivable manner.

"I said I like this one," he says. I don't think I'm imagining that thing in his tone, the thing that makes the skin on the back of my neck cold, makes me want to cringe.

She must be hearing it, too. She tenses, straightens up. One of her hands goes to the TV, leaning on it for support; the other hand reaches down and grabs the hand of her little boy, who's maybe four and tries to shake her off but she refuses to let him go.

"Sorry," she says.

"You think our place is too small, is that it?" he asks.

"No," she says.

"You make ten dollars an hour and complain about not getting enough hours, but you think we should be in a bigger place."

"No," she says. Her voice gets smaller. The boy has stopped struggling and lets her hold his hand.

"I guess it must be my fault. I should be working more. That must be what you mean."

"No. Look, I'm sorry—"

"I tell you I like this TV and you start this again."

"I like the TV."

The man glares at her, and I can see his face grow redder and redder as if he's still figuring out all the ways she's insulted him. I realize what a big man he is, how this rage magnifies him, gives him that aura of power. Abruptly, he turns around and heads for the exit.

The woman lets out a held breath, as do I.

She takes her hand off the TV and starts to follow the man, the boy obediently trailing her. Our eyes meet for a moment and her face flushes, embarrassed.

I want to say something but don't. What am I supposed to say? *He's got a temper, doesn't he? You going to be okay? Is he hitting you?* What do I know about the lives of strangers? What do I know about the right thing to do?

So I watch as they leave the store, the fog from the air conditioning over the automatic doors enveloping her for a moment as she steps through.

I go up to the TV they had been looking at, and for some reason that I can't even explain, put my hand on the TV, put my hand where she put hers earlier. It's like I'm seeking the lingering trace of the warmth of her hand, some assuring sign that she'll be all right.

And it feels electric, feels like the moon opens up and the stars are singing to me.

An apartment a few tiny rooms the bed the table the kitchen the carpet a mess Damn you're lazy I'm sorry I was late Teddy was sick had to take him Damn you're lazy

A toy piano is like a window a handle on a polished shoe grinding mezzo soprano Daddy is angry He is he is my darling Let's be quiet

The link is with us woman with woman. Your eyes your face It's nothing Why do you not leave Because So Because

Why did you look at him?

I wasn't I wasn't I wasn't

Lets dance So tender sometimes I'm sorry I was angry forgive me but sometimes you push me

He can be so sweet

A girl is a woman because a woman is an omen Oh man a whole man a hole in a woman a wholesome woman.

An awl is a drill some sharply polished nail

Broken dish a wailing a crying a tantrum Get him to stop! I'm trying I'm trying Damn you're lazy I'm tired Talking back I told you not to push me Don't don't you're scaring him get away from me

A burst of crimson of red ink iron sweet

Screaming and screaming and screaming he's not stopping Call the police call

My first vision leaves me breathless and ill.

I ask myself questions in an attempt at persuasion: What have I seen? What am I supposed to do with these images? What is their epistemological status? What is the rational reaction?

So I plead ignorance and do nothing.

Then there she is in the news: on TV, on the web, in the stacks of papers they still put in the convenience stores.

She was getting ready to leave him. Already found an apartment.

He came at her with that awl while their son watched. I couldn't stop him, and I tried. I tried.

I show up to the funeral, where lots of strangers have gathered outside the chapel to lay flowers around a fountain. I watch the bubbling water and imagine the blood gushing out of her. Guilt gnaws at my insides like an iron file, but the rest of me feels numb. I catch sight of the boy once, and his stoic eyes stab at me like a pair of awls.

And then he swoops in like some butterfly, dressed in his flowing cape and skintight costume. With his hair slicked back, his square jaw steeled, and his arms akimbo—arms that could bend beams of titanium and hold up a falling airplane—he poses. The cameras flash. Despite my cynical nature, I feel my heart lift up. We all need a hero, especially a superhero.

He gives a speech in that familiar baritone. He declares war on domestic violence; he promises to keep his super eye out for signs of trouble; he asks neighbors and friends to see something and say something. "Women shouldn't have to fear the men in their lives."

He doesn't explain how he's going to accomplish this. Is he going to examine every family in the city? Ferret out the poison from the root of our fucked up culture? Maybe he thinks it's enough for him to pay attention to the problem, to muscle his way to victory the way he grabbed that burning plane out of the sky, set it down by the shore, and peeled it open like a banana so everyone inside tumbled out and said *oh thank you thank you.*

But really, what right do I have to mock him and his platitudes? I should have done something. I saw what was going to happen.

His eyes sweep over the crowd, and our gazes meet for a moment. His eyes linger on my face just a second too long, and I wonder what he sees.

The next time it happens I'm about to enter the convenience store.

The man comes barging out the door with his head down and eyes on the ground. He doesn't hold the door open for me and I have to duck out of the way before he runs me over. He gives me a quick glance as he passes by and I see something in his face that makes my heart stop—intense anger at the world, anger at everybody and everything, anger at me.

I pull the door open, unsettled; an old lady is trying to come out with a bag of bananas and crackers; I put my palm on the inside of the door to hold it open, put it on the spot where the man had slammed his hand a moment earlier.

A winter a splinter I'm a nice guy ice guy my life is not nice Why don't you why
You owe me you owe me you all owe me
The girl who said no the boy who laughed why does he He doesn't deserve it nobody does and they say I'm the weird one
A gun
Look at me look at me look at me you can't hear me screaming you don't know how much the silence and an island and a new land and it's the same the same nothing ever changes
Two guns
I can see you I see all of you cowering terrified shivering shaking trembling leaves that you are should I let you live Why
I'm a nice guy ice thrice bang bang bang yes oh yes now you wish you were nice
Three guns

• • •

You're supposed to get in touch with him by calling 911. He monitors that. If it's the kind of emergency that can use his help, he'll come.

This *is* an emergency, but the police will mock me if I call and maybe charge me for wasting their time. *Sure, officer, happy to repeat my story. I followed a man home and got his address because I saw a vision that he was going to go on a mass shooting.*

So I write to him at his fan club email. I try to keep it vague but promise him IMPORTANT URGENT INFORMATION. I try not to use any capital letters in the rest of the email. To get to the superhero I have to defeat the spam filter first.

It's afternoon and there's a thundershower. He hovers outside the window and taps the glass lightly. I rush over to open it.

"Thanks for coming," I say, as though it's perfectly normal to have a superhero step through my window. "You must be really busy."

He shrugs and gives me a smile that shows off his perfect teeth. "When it rains really hard, the crime rate goes down."

It has never occurred to me that villains, super or otherwise, might have plans derailed by the weather. I suppose it makes sense. Even henchmen don't like to get wet.

"I have a crime to report."

He listens to my story, nodding encouragingly from time to time. I tell him about my newfound power and dead Annie, whose funeral he attended, and angry Bobby, who's going to kill.

He looks at me with those eyes that exude practiced kindness. "I'll take care of it."

And he opens the window and leaps out, as smooth as a fish leaping back into the ocean. I run to the window, my heart so full of happiness that I'm half expecting to see a rainbow. I watch his figure shrink over the rooftops, a blue-and-red angel of justice, truth, and all that is good and worthy.

I pace around my apartment, unable to remain still for even a minute.

He comes back an hour later, tapping on my window. The rain hasn't let up, and he shakes himself off like a wet dog before alighting gently in my living room.

"Did you see him?" I ask.

He nods but says nothing. I scrutinize his face, and something in me wilts, dies.

"He's a perfectly nice young man," he says. "Away from home, living on his own for the first time. He's a bit shy, is all."

"But the guns!"

"He doesn't have any guns."

"Maybe they're just really well hidden."

"I have X-ray vision."

"Maybe he's going to get them." I realize that I don't know anything about the timing of my vision. Maybe Bobby will buy the gun tomorrow, maybe not until twenty years from now.

I think of Annie's picture and how she looked embarrassed the only time we looked at each other. *I knew something. And I did nothing.*

"You have to believe me. I saw Annie die."

He sighs and shakes his head. "Nobody knows the future."

"They used to think nobody could fly. Or dodge bullets. Or see through walls. Or pluck a burning airplane out of the sky before it crashed."

He looks at me, his face hardening. "Then tell me how I'm going to die."

I look at him, my mouth opening and closing wordlessly. Finally, I say, "I don't know. It doesn't work like that."

He nods. "Nobody knows the future."

I become obsessed with Bobby. I stalk him from a distance, watch his comings and goings, try to piece together his life. I buy directional microphones and long-range zoom lenses. I download manuals written by private detectives and read them late at night.

I find out just how good my tradecraft is one day on the subway. I follow him onto the platform and get into the same car, at the other end. The train starts to move. He turns, looks me straight in the eyes, and walks over.

"You've been following me around."

I try to deny it, but I don't even have a story ready.

"Why?"

His eyes are confused, but his tone is polite.

I mumble something about living in the same neighborhood and having the same schedule. He asks for my name. He seems ill at ease but not in a way that appears dangerous—though to be honest, how is he supposed to act when he thinks he's confronting a stalker? We shake hands and tell each other it's nice to meet you.

His hand is warm, damp. I don't get any visions.

I ask him to dinner.

• • •

Bobby doesn't know anything about guns. He's never gotten into a fight. He's lonely but likes to read and play video games. He's thinking about becoming vegan. This is the extent of what I find out about him by the end of dinner.

He's awkward but polite. Our conversation doesn't flow smoothly because he seems to try out everything he says in his head ten times before he says it. Not my type. But dangerous? I can't see it.

We walk back together from the restaurant and stop in front of my building.

I look at him. He's nervous and expectant. I comb through our conversation. *Nobody knows the future.*

Before he can ask for a hug or a kiss, I shake his hand and step back, "I'll see you around the neighborhood."

He looks dejected but not surprised. "Why did you follow me around if you aren't interested?"

I think about how to answer this in a way that is truthful but not too truthful. "Because I wanted to know if I'm special."

"Special how?"

Just then Showboat zooms over us in the evening sky, a patriotic-color-schemed comet. We stare up at him together.

"A bit like that," I say.

"I bet he gets all the girls," Bobby says. "I bet it's nice to have that kind of power."

"Maybe," I tell him. "I don't know. Goodnight."

I try to go on with my life. The visions come more frequently now, are more vivid. I don't see visions of happy strangers; my gift is for brutal, bloody futures.

I take to wearing gloves marketed for germaphobes, made of some space age material that's supposed to be able to breathe while killing germs—pure lies. In fact, they make my hands sweat and the germs probably think of them as Club Med.

But they do keep me safe, safe from myself.

Once in a while, when I must touch something that hold traces of other hands—a touch screen tablet repurposed for taking credit cards or a restroom faucet—the visions leave me with a headache and palpitating heart.

• • •

There is a silence in singing, a violence in wringing, a justice and a tenderness and a rustiness in anything sweet and needs no explaining

The path all knowing everywhere sharp objects regret dark and thick and tangy as undersea molasses

Here is your attempt at explication but listen to the sound of sweet sweet sweet wee wee wee like some foundation in a room full of inattention which is death miles and miles of death

There is a mention of a tension that is quite an extension of my intention. For a rose is a rose is a rose is a briar a poke at a nose a bloody nose a gory a glory the same as flag waving.

Then comes the shooting, the bodies, the note left behind by Bobby in which he recounts his years of rejection and rage. My name shows up near the end, the stuck-up girl who thinks she's special and is obsessed with guns and who comes on to him only to reject him like everyone else. He talks about the desire to experience power, like the man with the red cape and blue tights. He writes about guns and their ability to remake the meek into the mighty, into superheroes. He speaks in the language of vengeance and unstanched wounds bleeding for years.

"You're responsible for this," he says, his cape looking cheap in the fluorescent light of my apartment.

I hear in his voice the voice of easy accusation, the pinning of blame upon imagined proximate causes. It's disappointing to see your heroes fall.

"That's absurd. He has been building up this delusion of rejection and hatred for years. He was just good at hiding it. You should have listened to me. You're just as responsible."

"Sophistry," he says. "You made the future you claim you saw. That's your power."

"No," I tell him. "We make the future together."

I suppose I could have just kept the gloves on all the time or moved back to my parents' house and never emerged, never touched anything that might still hold the heat and sweat from someone else.

It's one thing to be ignorant, but another to refuse to know.

If I can see the future but decline to, how am I different from a man passing by a pond and averting his eyes from the drowning child?

So I learn to live with the visions, to interpret them, to do what I can to thwart fate. I learn how to filter out the noise and blur and shifting lights, to focus and make sense of what I see and turn it into a scene, a sequence, a narrative. I learn to pay attention to details in the fleeting images: to clocks, to newspapers, to the lengths of shadows and the density of crowds.

At the ATM I see money being hidden in a locker in a changing room, a bribe to a woman in charge of something or other. I go to the gym and wait until five minutes after she's gone. I go in, take the money, and leave.

I don't know if that did any good. Maybe she'll just go back and ask for more, or demand payment from someone else. Maybe whatever she's being bribed for, she ends up doing anyway. But at least I have money to live on and to devote to my new career.

The man emerging from the elevator holds the door open for me.

"Thanks."

He nods and leaves. I put my hand on the door where his hand had been. I'm compelled to know.

I see a street corner. A tourist couple with a little daughter.

"Carla!" the father calls out. "Don't run so far ahead."

She turns down a narrow alley, in which I'm hiding. The parents follow their daughter in, admonishing her.

I go up to them and demand their money. I speak in the voice of the man who had held the elevator door open. The father refuses, and I take out my gun. Instead of complying, he lunges at me, trying to disarm me. I squeeze the trigger and he crumples to the ground, his face fixed in disbelief. The woman tries to flee, pulling the little girl behind her, and I shoot her also. Then I stare at the little girl standing next to her dead mother. She doesn't understand what has happened. She looks back at me, confused.

Why not? I think. One more isn't going to make any difference now.

I glance down at my watch and make a note of the time.

I shake off the cold desolation of the killer's mind. I get into my car and drive, frantically looking for that street corner on the GPS. I have only a few minutes.

There he is, loping along on the sidewalk, heading for his destiny. What am I going to do? Tell him I've seen him kill? If he backs off today, what about tomorrow, and the day after that? Can fate be so easily averted?

I ram my car into him as he starts to climb up a hill. A jolt of adrenaline, the pure thrill of thwarting the future.

Then I spin the wheel and back up, and speed away with screeching tires and the smell of burnt rubber in my nose. As I crest the hill I think I see Carla and her parents, obliviously happy.

I drive. And drive.

• • •

That one is simple. Most futures are far more complicated. There's Alexander, for example, hard working and well meaning.

From a distance, I see him standing at the street corner and mashing the button for the crosswalk impatiently. By the time I arrive at the corner he's already dashed across and the light has changed.

I tap the button and am overwhelmed by what I see: he's working on machines that will massacre a village of old people and children. He doesn't know it yet and he doesn't intend to. But it will happen. Intent is not magic.

How do I stop him? Could I intervene along the way, use some gentler roadblock to divert him from this future? But there are a thousand visions screaming for my attention, a thousand future victims to save. If I devote all my time to diverting Alexander, I will have also made the choice to let Hal go through with his kidnapping or Liam succeed in strangling his ex-wife.

We know what we know. What we do with that knowledge makes the future.

In the end, I opt for killing Alexander also. He's at the corner again, oblivious, a creature of habit with a set routine. I have a new car, a guided missile of future vengeance, or anticipatory justice. I step on the gas.

I stay where I am.

I turn around, and he's there, the red cape whipping in the wind.

"I've been watching you," he says. "You aren't very good at this, repeating the same modus operandi. But then again, most villains don't know any better. I'm taking you in."

He rips the top of the car off for dramatic effect. People exclaim in the distance. I hear the sirens of police cars.

I don't try to resist. "If you don't stop him"—I lift my chin in the direction of Alexander—"you'll have the blood of dozens, maybe hundreds, on your hands." I sketch my vision for him in a few sentences. "You could claim ignorance before, but not any more. You know I'm right."

Alexander, some distance away, is still trying to recover from the shock of his near encounter with death. He looks like a mild-mannered bureaucrat, his lips moving like a fish's.

"I don't know any such thing," Showboat says.

"Wouldn't it be better," I plead, "to kill the man long before he got on the plane rather than having to rescue the plane as it plunges toward the ground?"

He shakes his head adamantly, confident in his faith, his liberty, his justice, his truth. "We're not going to live in a society of pre-crimes."

"We're not as free as we think. There are tendencies, inclinations, forces that compel us—what we call fate."

"But you think you're free," he says. "You think you're qualified to judge."

He has me in a bind. If I succeed in thwarting the future, then my vision was wrong. If I don't succeed, then I may be said to be a proximate cause. If I do nothing, I can't live with myself.

"Is it so hard to believe someone can look through time as easily as you can through solid walls? Do you really believe it a mere coincidence that what I spoke of came to pass, that I might have been its sole cause?"

For a moment, the face of our caped hero shows doubt, but it's fleeting, and the resolute expression quickly returns like a mask. "Even if you're right, what makes you think you have seen the *whole* future? Maybe he'll also save the lives of dozens of soldiers; maybe his machines will kill a kid who grows up to be a dictator. The future is not knowable until it has become the past. But I just stopped you from murder. I know that. It is enough."

I think about my fragmentary visions. What do I *really* know?

"And you can't stop what you think will happen by killing him," he tells me. "He's just one man out of many others working on the same thing. Fate, if it exists, is resilient."

He's not entirely wrong, I suppose. I am a time traveler in a sense, and stories about time travelers changing history are often frustratingly stupid. The larger trends of history are rarely dependent on a single individual. Who would you have had to kill to prevent the destruction of the native peoples of the Americas, of Australia, of Hawaii? To stop the Atlantic slave trade? To avoid the mass atrocities of the wars in Indochina and East Asia? You could have killed every named explorer and general and emperor and king in the history books and the currents of colonial conquest probably wouldn't have shifted by much.

But that way lies madness. We'll never have complete knowledge. I know what I know, but he refuses to learn what he can. That makes all the difference.

The police car screeches to a stop nearby. He reaches for my hand to pull me out of the wreck of my car. His hand is warm and dry; it doesn't feel like the hand of someone who kills by refusing to believe, who takes refuge in the assumed condition of our ignorance, secure in his knowledge.

A blur that resolves into flashing images. Clarity.

Through his eyes, I see him regretting not following me in the squad car to be sure I'm put away; I see him examining the drive-through window of the fast-food restaurant and the bank across the street, where the robbers had emerged, his super-vision picking out the bullet holes in the sidewalk and walls and calculating their trajectories; I see him taking in the site of the shoot-out and clench his jaws; I hear the officers apologizing for rushing to confront the robbers without having secured me properly.

His visions are as orderly and predictable as his clichés.

Our hands separate. "Goodbye," he says, that familiar smug smile on his face again. "The city is safer today with you out of the way."

I look out the back window. He can't resist the cameras. He's going to give another impromptu press conference. The city's criminals, say, bank robbers, like to wait until he's on TV before making their moves.

Perfect.

The car starts to move. "You hungry?" one of the officers asks the other.

"I can eat."

"What are you in the mood for?"

I pipe up, "There's a Pollo Pollo on Third Avenue, across from the Metropolitan Bank."

The one in the passenger seat turns to look at me.

I put on a hungry and pleading look. "I have a coupon if you also get me something. My treat."

The officers look at each other and shrug. "All right. You aren't going to get a chance to use that coupon for a while."

"My loss. Say, do you work out or is that a bullet-proof vest under the jacket?"

I train. I learn to shoot, to fight, to become the super villain he aready thinks I am.

If killing one man is not enough stop all the abusers, to reverse the momentum of culture, to uninvent the machinery of death, to change the currents of history, then I have to kill more.

I move from the empty apartments of vacationing couples to houses that had just been moved out of and not yet moved in—a touch on the doorknob is enough to tell me the story. I get good and then better at my craft.

I kill violent boyfriends in their sleep, poison future gunmen over meals, plot the erasure and destruction of clean, dust-free laboratories where they design weapons that kill while minimizing guilt. Sometimes I succeed; sometimes he stops me. He becomes obsessed, the anticipation of my next move haunting him as my visions haunt me.

I know a little about many things: snippets from people's futures, paths that will cross and uncross. I can't see that far into the fog: every action has a consequence, and consequences have other consequences. It's true that only when the future has become the past can it be seen as a whole and understood, but to do nothing because you don't know everything is not a path I can follow. I know that a little girl named Carla is alive because of me. It is enough.

He and I are not so different, perhaps, just a matter of degrees.

So we dance across the city, he and I, antagonists locked in the eternal struggle between the scattered knowledge of fate and the ignorant certainty of free will.

Ken Liu is an author and translator of speculative fiction, as well as a lawyer and programmer. A winner of the Nebula, Hugo, and World Fantasy Awards, he has been published in *The Magazine of Fantasy & Science Fiction, Asimov's, Analog, Clarkesworld, Lightspeed,* and *Strange Horizons,* among other venues He also translated the Hugo-winning novel, *The Three-Body Problem,* by Liu Cixin, which is the first translated novel to win that award. Liu's debut novel, *The Grace of Kings,* the first in a silkpunk epic fantasy series, was published by Saga Press in April 2015. A collection of short fiction, *The Paper Menagerie and Other Stories,* was published earlier this year. He lives with his family near Boston, Massachusetts.

Thigh-deep in the ocean, Billy-Rid crooned a lullaby.

A SHOT OF SALT WATER

—◆—

Lisa L. Hannett

Accordions unpleated welcoming songs the day the mermaids returned.

The first notes droned joyful at dawn, played by young men with wool collars unrolled against the wind. Mattress-clouds bulged above land and water, miles of damp cotton dulling the fishermen's music. As the sky blanched, fiddlers sawed harmonies, horsehairs screeching on weather-warped bows. Bodhráns were rescued from blanket boxes and cupboards, clatter-spoons from the backs of junk drawers. Soon drummers thumb-pounded down autumn-gold slopes from the village. Beats jigged and reeled past the wharves, along the coast, then splashed through froth seething to shore.

Sparking a cig, Billy Rideout watched the procession from the dunes. Nodded at the lack of flute-wailing. That hollow music wasn't fit for a homecoming, he thought. Too much like drowning-storms. Like last breaths blown through old bones.

There'd be singing later, in Ma Clary's kitchen. And in the tavern. In the shipyards. Up and down the waterfront, men were already warming throats with liquor and oil, preparing for tonight. Mermaids liked a bit of haze in his tenor, or so Billy-Rid told himself, sucking smoke.

Half a day's sail away, the first tall masts striped the gunmetal surf.

"Get your arse down here, Rid," called Eli Stagg from the strand, carrying an armload of tinned gooseberries. "Grab a basket on the way."

Billy-Rid pocketed the half-burnt stub, did as told.

On the beach, musicians and local b'ys milled. Horsing around between tunes, they swigged from jars while uncles and grandys set up trestles. Ankle-deep in the shallows, ancient sea-salted women supervised, criticizing with squints and scowls but few words. Pointing out which tablecloths needed pinning down. *Tsking* at the smell of charred griddle-cakes. Snapping knot-knuckled fingers as Billy-Rid made a mess of the buffet, jumbling savouries and sweets on the boards. Between snorts, the matrons snacked on baked haddock. Sucked on bottles of spiced rum, dipper, screech.

"Full sail," said the eldest, her white hair still plaited in maid's ropes. Keen eyes trained on the horizon, she talked around a half-chewed wad. "Fleet's racing the rain."

Innards clenched, Billy-Rid pretended not to see the sharp-nosed schooners spearing closer. Distant fuzz-dots slowly hardening into crows-nests, smudged lines into hemp ropes. Coffin-dark jibs fading to shades of burgundy and mud on approach.

Beneath the proud sails, tall figures flitted to and fro on deck. They climbed the rigging, easy as flies. They swung the boom. They white-waked it for home.

Rid turned away, fumbling a plate of currant loaves. Gulls swooped, crammed their gullets with sweet white bread, as rowboats were lowered over gunwales a mile off shore. Ducking to avoid claws and beaks and wings, the b'ys each took up a shot of salt water.

"Fill yer guts," they said, tossing it back for luck.

"Good lads," said the nans, shooing the squawkers. Smirking when Rid suggested a second shot.

"Only takes one," they said.

"Better safe," Billy Rideout replied, upending another glass. Failing to drown the squirm in his guts.

The mermaids far outnumbered their rowboats, neither so many as when they'd first set out.

Clinker planks and women both were hard-worn from their travels. Hulls were mottled, keels paint-flaked. Otter-skin slickers were ripped and sleeveless, showing off oar-muscled arms. Canvas pants were ragged, storm-chewed at the hems; some hung like skirts, revealing tattooed thighs. Short-straw girls remained out on the ships—so close but still so far from home. Guarding the profits of their time abroad, the yield of raiding and trading. Scoping the waters for ill-omened shadows.

The shore party leapt overboard, hauled tired skiffs from hard-packed to soft sand. Their hair was dreadlocked, rimed with spray. Ten months at sea had staved in their cheeks, chiseled the roundness from hips and breasts. Blubber-treated packs were slung cross-body, leaving their arms free for fighting. Several hefted short-swords, others had daggers—though weapons weren't needed for *this* landing. There were no screams at the seafarers' approach, no terror at the sight of harpoons. Instead a baritone chorus whooped its greetings, singing tunes that beckoned them, one and all, inland.

Blood-cracks split the maids' smiles as they ran to their dads, their b'ys, their lovers. Only one made the trip from water to welcome slowly. Concentrating, stepping carefully, she waddled across the flats with buckler-strap loose around a misshapen belly.

"Reckon your lass is carrying," Ma Clary said to Billy-Rid, lifting her pipe at the girl he loved. Then the old sailor bent, knees cracking, and palmed a handful of shells off the strand. Whispering a blessing, she threw the lot like confetti. "First time lucky."

"Lucky," said Rid's mouth, while the rest of him gaped. Sweat pricked his brow, despite the chill air. The sky puckered and began to spit.

Lord look at her, he thought, fumbling for a stiff whiskey to keep him upright. For nigh on ten months—a whole season's sailing—he'd packed every minute with distraction. Full days on the wharf, full nights at Kelloway's pub. Cod-fishing, carousing, pickling his brain. Trying not to think of this moment. Of her.

Alberta Stagg.

His Beetie.

Lord *look* at you, he thought, lungs floundering. His gaze skimmed the cords of Beetie's flaxen hair, the many hoops in her ears, the welts around her knees, the mermaid-cut of her calves.

Just look at you, he thought, and look he did; returning, again and again, to the bulge slung at his girl's waist. The bundle cloak-shielded from the elements, the spatter now a steady drizzle. *She's carrying*, Ma Clary had said—and so she was. Hefting a child Billy-Rid might have given her. A baby she might have gone and got for them both.

They ate everything the gulls hadn't scabbed, drank till the rain seemed a joke. Gingham blew off tables, cartwheeled into the waves. Crocks were dropped, broken, buried under the skip and twirl of dancing feet. *A waste*, potters would say the next morning, but for now these losses were celebrated. They were expected. Annual tributes to the gods of wind and water.

Rum doubled Billy-Rid's vision, ale blurred its edges. Swept into the sodden crowd, he swigged from any jar that passed. One minute he was on the sand, numb legs failing to reach Beetie three tables over; a blink later, he was reeling up the path into town, beach at his back. He was battered and tossed onto the road leading to Kelloway's, a flurry of strong palms beating across his shoulders as the other b'ys tried to slap up some of his fortune.

"Filled her guts," they said, all ruddy-cheeked, butcher-built men like himself. Thumping and clapping, the lads passed him shot after shot of salt water, whooping til he threw them down, howling when he threw them back up. Leaving Rid to contemplate the mess on his boots, they stomped up the planks to the pub. The din inside roared when the double doors opened: slurred voices, shrill pipes, the barman shouting out orders. Before they swung to, Billy-Rid heard the b'ys cheering his mermaid. And quieter, but distinct, Beetie's giggled delight as the babe in her arms started baying.

Might be they're right, Rid thought, straightening. The kid *could've* been my doing. It happens. It has happened.

Stumbling, he took a step toward the pub for each of the land-births they'd had on this rock they called home. Beetie was one, no doubt about it; not a snip or surgeon-scar on her. But that was eighteen-odd years ago, he thought, shaking the rum-fog from his head. Ma Clary's niece? Yeah, she and the bottleman from Bonnebay had themselves a small brood of landlubbers. No gills, no fins in the bunch. Half a dozen of Rid's dockside mates were earth-stock, like him; no merchild he'd ever seen could grow *their* class of beard or bulk.

Not every babe was fished, Rid thought. He paused on the stoop, listened. This one *could* be mine.

Inside, the baby cried, a liquid mewl with a note of whale-song about it.

Alberta had once been Billy's alone, his own shy girl who'd beet-blushed at his swagger, his attention, his gut-twisting love. She'd been his long before her summer-ship weighed anchor. And everyone knew he'd been hers.

As was custom, he'd ringed a reef-knot of silk round Beetie's finger, making their intentions plain.

As was custom, he'd knotted his body around hers, morning and night, making the most of spring.

As was custom, when her bloods kept coming despite Rid's best efforts, when the tides changed and currents warmed, when the cannery reeked to the high heavens and barley began greening the fields, his Beetie had bodied the very schooner that had carried her back again today, carrying.

It wasn't *that* long ago, Rid thought, pushing into a blue fug, heavy as the clouds outside. The guppy *could* be ours.

On the pub's threshold, he stopped, fought for breath. The air was humid with merriment and music. Standing on chairs near the hearth, Dana and her water-born son added banjos to the fiddlers' medley. Over at the bar, Vin Clary out-plucked them all on his mandolin. Harmonicas jangoed between verses, competing with the lonesome burtle of uillieann pipes. Between cups and jars, hands pounded stained barrels. Heel-rhythms had the floor quaking, pleasure thrumming across puddles trekked in with the rain.

At the room's heart, Beetie was surrounded by cheek-pinchers, back-thumpers, drunken coo-cluckers. Her fair hair browning with sweat. Broad face living up to her nickname. Rawhide jerkin unlaced, revealing a strong collarbone and the kelp necklace she'd made for their tying day. Billy-Rid fancied the links still had some wet to them, though the roe-beads had well and truly dried. The little gems were grey, now, as the pebbles in her gaze.

Meeting it unsteadily, he flubbed a grin. A tiny hand had reached up from within Beetie's vest, its blunt fingers groping for the seaweed chain. Hard to tell from this distance if the bluish cast of its skin was more than a trick of grog-tinted light. If its little digits had been tipped with nails, or anemones. If it looked anything at all like him.

Don't go, he'd wanted to beg, all those months ago. Beetie had woken hours before dawn. Her gear waited by the front door; it hadn't taken long for her to dress, to shoulder a hooded harpoon. The weapon had been a gift from her da, the blades vicious, star-shaped. The same one her late mam had wielded. It suited her, Rid had thought, but couldn't bring himself to mention it. Beside him, the pillow still cupped the space where Beetie's head had rested. The linens were still soft with her warmth. Billy-Rid had inhaled the beeswax scent of her, refusing to get out of bed, to say goodbye.

I can be enough, he'd wanted to lie. *We have more than enough, with us two.*

Instead, he'd whistled for fair winds and Beetie had turned a pretty crimson, self-conscious in her new skins and leathers. It was her first voyage, her first chance to hunt and shoal and multiply. She would have gone with the mermaids no matter what he'd said.

He only wished he'd said more.

"Good on you, lad," Eli Stagg said now, full-proud with drink. Rid's teeth rattled as Beetie's old man threw an arm round him. Nodding thanks, he wriggled free only to be swept away in a current of dancers. The music capered, tempo unpredictable. Suddenly Billy-Rid was gripped under the pits, lifted like a child, then twirled and twirled and twirled. Lanterns pitched overhead, shadows tipsy. Awash in the stench of wet wool, beer and eel, Rid swooned. Clipped his chin on someone's sharp elbow. Bit his tongue. Saw stars.

" 'Bout time," Beetie said, yanking him straight. Herself nearly tall as he, even barefoot. The hand she'd extended streaked red with rope-burns. Her laugh sun-bleached, voice barnacled. "Thought you were avoiding me." She glanced down at the gup. "Us."

" 'Course not," Rid said, barely hesitating.

Uncertainty flickered across Beetie's face—half a second's flinch—but she squashed it with a pickled-egg kiss. Almost a year at sea had livened her tongue but sapped its honey. Billy-Rid recoiled.

"Aren't you going to introduce us," he said, too stiffly. Trying again, he wiped his mouth and dimpled at the mermaid, his once-darling girl.

"Go on then," Rid prompted, as the musicians mopped their brows, drained the dregs of Kelloway's black ale. A few began packing their instruments, aiming to reach Ma Clary's before the crowds. "Let me see it."

"*Her*," Beetie said, pulling back the sealskin swaddling.

No quick-mustered charm could keep the pleasant in Rid's expression. His smile-muscles went slack as paste.

"Gorgeous, isn't she?"

Fronds of skin dripped from the bub's angled jaw, waxen flaps the hue of new leaves. Her chest jutted as she grizzled, the strakes of her ribs visible through a thin smock. The arms were slender but stunted; fern shoots partly unfurled. Rid took in the equine nose and winced at the strange list of her gaze. One deep brown eye turned up at Beetie; the other swivelled its iris 'round at him. Translucent lids blinked independently, or not at all.

Billy-Rid searched for signs of gills, for coronet bumps on the fry's skull, found none. Yet.

Beetie beamed. "Isn't she the prettiest little thing you ever saw?"

Around them, mermaids raised jars, bellowing shanties. Kelloway tapped the last keg, uncorked the final two barrels of mash. Tin pipes whistled for all the luck in the world, their empty wind blowing beautifully nowhere.

"Never seen one quite like her," he said at last, earning another strong-armed embrace. The stolen bub pipped and squirmed between them.

Quivering, Rid buried his face in his wife's brackish locks and wept.

For a month they called her Guppy, same as every other sea-child. A month for her to earn a name, to thrive on land. A month for Billy-Rid to adjust.

Drinking mostly brine, the bub grew plump and fast.

While Rid nursed the thirsty thing, Beetie and the mermaids disappeared over the rim of the world. Twice daily, fish drew them oceanwards and fish brought them back. The routine kept the town's pantries full, the lasses' figures hard. Before long they'd be pointing bowsprits east again, raising sails, whetting harpoons; until then, the women would work. Keep the iron in their muscles. It wouldn't do for the island's best hunters to run to suet in the off-season. It took steel to replenish stocks.

Billy-Rid knew this as well as anyone.

Folk wouldn't survive without them.

With the b'ys at Kelloway's, Billy-Rid laughed it off. His failure. He was no different from his mates, really. None of them had managed to cast their lines through a mermaid's salt—except Tuck, just that once, when he'd barely learned how to handle his rod. That kid hardly counted, though. Within a day, the poor thing suffocated with a bellyful of air.

Even so.

By now Beetie must've been raw as Rid was, after a fortnight of his contributions. His trying and trying and trying for a bub of their own.

A *real* one.

One *he'd* made, not one she'd snatched.

Maybe the sea had grown too strong in Beetie's blood. Maybe, or too weak in his. Maybe it was the way she rode him now, as she never had before. Maybe it was the bile in Rid's thoughts, the burn of wondering where *exactly* she'd got the gup, from whom *exactly*, and *how*. Maybe it was the ache of not-asking.

Maybe it was that Beetie didn't—wouldn't—need him.

Maybe that's what left him so empty.

The gup's not right, Rid thought.

All afternoon on the quay, she'd huffed and chortled in Ma Clary's lap, gumming a piece of dried cod. The gran doted on Beetie's girl, watched after her while Rid sorted and cleaned and filleted a half-ton of trout. When name-day planning had called Ma up to the bingo hall, she'd passed the bub on to the coast guard. Taking turns, the young men harnessed Gup to their backs, buoyed by her weird fluting as they patrolled the harbour. At last, when no one else had been free, Billy-Rid was forced to bring the baby and her noise home.

The cottage had been dank as a bait-house when they'd got in—Beetie'd had the windows open again, despite the autumn squalls. Rid hadn't bothered to sop the puddles beneath the casements, knowing they'd soon be propped and dripping again. Beetie claimed to like it that way, cool and blustery. Said it reminded her of being on deck.

Rid lowered the baby into clean bathwater, then dragged the tin tub near the hearth. Hunkering beside it, he sat back on his heels. Paddled his fingers down by Guppy's feet, avoiding the spiked-curl of her toes. She sputtered strange notes, maw agape.

As if it hasn't mastered its nostrils, Rid thought. As if the damp air up here is too dry for its mouth.

With one hand he soaked a square of flannel, wrung it out, soaked and wrung, soaked and wrung, splashing himself more than her. The other cupped his chin, held his head up. Orange pennants rippled in the flue-draft, tips jigging, hooking Billy-Rid's lashes, dragging his lids to half-mast. Logs sighed and settled. Heat lulled like nostalgia, like sun-baked memory.

In the yawning flames, Rid saw golden days; time he'd spent with Beetie *before*. When there'd been no ships or guppies for them. No bucklers or harpoons. No tying ceremonies or name-days. No bub that wasn't theirs, not really. When they'd been kids, and sweet on each other. When they'd taken shifts at the guttery together, quick-slicing salmon bellies, carp heads. When they'd snuck to the rock pools at lunch, smoked stolen cigs. When they'd decorated each other's faces with iridescence, scales stuck to their overalls, and they'd pretended—Lord how they'd pretended—they were magical.

She was, Billy Rideout thought, now as then. Salt glistening in her hair. Freckles on her nose, blue and yellow in the sunlight. *The chunk torn from her gums an inheritance*, Ma Clary once said, *of the first mermaid, the first hook that failed to snag her. It was the second cast that had done the trick, taken the girl home.*

The second cast, Rid thought, up to the elbow in suds and warmth. The second had been strong and true . . .

"What the blight are you doing?"

At the cottage door, Beetie dropped her cloak and bag. Cold night gusted in as she dashed across the small room. Five strides and she'd shoved Rid away from Guppy, the bub burbling, submerged to the nose.

"A splash in the basin is more than enough," Beetie said, scooping the child, voice lowered, aiming to soothe. "*More* than enough. You don't want her to drown."

Of course not, Rid thought, sinking to the floor. Beetie slapped his hands

A SHOT OF SALT WATER 425

when he reached for a towel. Cooing and fussing, she turned her back. Swaddled the girl tight, held her close. Bounced the near-miss from her nerves.

Left eye trained on Rid, right on the overfull tub, Guppy keened. A rippling, uncertain song.

Oh, how the b'ys would snort to see Billy-Rid acting so mawkish.

Steaming Gup's bottles, scrubbing her unders, airing quilts between downpours. Plumping Beetie's pillow with fresh-plucked down. Roasting stones in the fire, slipping them under the blankets, keeping the ice from her toes while she napped. Bartering crayfish for spuds, onions, carrots; sweet-talking Ma Clary out of a vat of new cream. Cooking huge batches of the Staggs' favorite chowder. Bypassing Kelloway's in the evenings, heading straight home to see Beetie off to the docks. Waking early to greet her at dawn. Brewing new leaves for her after-sail tea.

The week leading up to Gup's naming-day party, Billy-Rid did what he could. To help. To make things right. He threaded garland after garland of urchins, ribbons, coral, and kelp. He hung them from the bingo hall's rafters so Beetie wouldn't have to do it. He lugged tables and benches galore, set them all up, leaving plenty of room for dancing. When Kelloway came to stock the bar, he stayed the hell out of the way.

But still.

Even so.

Beetie had stopped tangling her legs 'round his at night. She'd started bringing Guppy with her down to the docks. Saying: the nans loved the girl so. Saying: they cared deeply and dearly. Saying: they wanted nothing but to spend time with the child.

"It would be cruel to deny them," Beetie said, freeing Guppy from Rid's grasp. "They're only trying to make her feel welcome. They're doing their best."

As if Rid wasn't.

That night, Kelloway's overflowed with rum and revelers. The whole town was expected to show the next morning, bow-tied and be-gartered, before mermaids lifted anchor for the first catch. But a naming-day just wouldn't be a naming-day if folk weren't fur-tongued and skull-sore, retching into the buckets Billy-Rid had scattered around the hall. The whole island was expected at dawn: sea-striders and sand-runners, tykes and cane-toters. Those born to men, and those taken.

Every last soul would *have* to be out of their blimmin senses come morning, to pretend that Guppy belonged.

"Limber up," Rid said to Eli Stagg, flexing and throwing back another belter of screech. His words burred, slow in coming. "Got a big ask tomorrow."

One minute Beetie's da was tilting the rim, the next his glass was drained on the bar in front of an empty seat. Rid's neck swerved. A pint foamed in his grip. A second later it was shards glinting beneath his stool, replaced by a plastic kiddie-cup. Black mash and sour-cherry swilled down his craw, scorching a path to his stomach. Behind the taps, Kelloway scowled as Billy-Rid ordered another, but served it up anyway.

"Good man," Rid said, or something like. Maybe, "Lucky man." The barkeep leaned over the counter, lit the cig Rid had stuffed arse-end into his gob. The publican never had gups of his own, lucky man, never had planted nor sea-sowed. Good man.

"How about a splash of the bland stuff," Kelloway said, sliding a pitcher of melted ice down the plank. "Might be you've had enough of the harsh."

"Might be," Rid agreed, but it felt good in him, the blaze in his heart, the lava in his belly. It got him up off the stool, onto the dance floor, where Beetie spun and spun, locks flying loose, baby on her hip. Squeezeboxes hawed and fiddles wheezed as Rid barged through the crowd. Flutes, real flutes, no mere ha'pennies these, tootled like Gup as he wrenched her away from the mermaid. His wife.

"Thing's squawking for a feed," he said, cradling the bub. "Look how thirsty—"

"Give her back."

Around them, sailors thumbed knife hilts, toyed with sword belts. Pipers trilled, undaunted, while wooden spoons clacked, missing beats. String-pluckers and sawyers climbed off stage, tension bloating into the gaps of their music.

"She's thirsty," he said quietly, enunciating precisely. "I'll take care of her."

Beetie rested her palm on Billy-Rid's forearm, firm but gentle. She smiled, a spark of fun in her expression. Humor he hadn't seen in weeks. "Do what you gotta do, Billy-b'y," she said, patting him like a child. "But mind you keep her wee snorter above water this time."

Through the hot rush of blood in his ears, Rid couldn't hear every mermaid's laughter. Only the one closest to him. The loudest and least shy.

• • •

Outside, threadbare clouds blanketed the navy sky. Stars peeped through holes here and there, silvering billows above and swells below. Thigh-deep in the ocean, Billy-Rid crooned a lullaby. In his shaking arms, Guppy added garbled notes, high as the moon-chunk overhead. Its reflection hazed around them, wavering on the expanse of wet black. In the distance, dorsal fins broke the surface. Two. Four. Seven. Too rigid to blend with the whitecaps. Rid stood and watched like the sentries weren't; the men slunk off for a stint of elbow-raising down at the pub. *It's been a month*, they'd no doubt reasoned. *Surely a month gone is time enough for the damned fish to forget.*

Rid studied Gup's elongated features, saw their likeness cresting the waves.

Still singing, he trudged further into the wash. Winter lurked in the deeps, shrivelling him. Shame boiled anew, thoughts of Beetie scorching his cheeks. How she'd left him. How she'd returned.

The baby gurgled as Rid plunged her. In and out, in and out, in and out of the water. She giggled as if it was a game, her skin-fronds flapping and floating, dripping. Sodden, her mess-cloth sagged, slid off, sank. Switching tunes, Billy-Rid disentangled Gup from her smock, let her ridges free, the hard clay of her skin. All spine and cartilage and bone. Better, he decided. The bub honked, wide-gummed with agreement. More natural, he thought. The way she would've been for her naming-day dip come daybreak.

The sea foamed as Rid churned. Submerged or not, Guppy was alert, eyes ever open, ever swerving. Salt water rushed in and out; her protruding lips sucked, spurted. Hoarse, Rid hissed "Come on, come on," avoiding the bub's mouth-fountain. Her odd gaze. Its unblinking ease, its alien color.

He played deaf to the squelch of liquid burps.

"Come on," he repeated, louder now, holding the girl under.

Forearms straining, Rid whispered, "Come on, come on," as ten seconds passed, twenty, the baby's slow-wriggle turning full-squirm.

"Come *on*," he said again and again, voice cracking, *"Come on,"* until, finally, she was wrenched from his grasp.

The creature was more man than seahorse, more stallion than pony. A trumpet nose dominated his long face; traces of sorrow in the round black eyes were undermined by the angry trumpeting of his snout. Spikes lined his muscular arms. Fronds the same shape and hue as the bub's dangled from a strong jaw. A carapace of ribs toughened his chest, accentuating the round softness of his stretch-marked belly. His were a warrior's shoulders: broad, ink-marked, boasting scars. Squiggles puckered the flesh on biceps and delts. A vicious, spark-shaped scab livid between clavicle and neck. Beetie's wound.

Treading water for a moment, the hippocampus cradled his squeaking child. Mesmerized by her existence. Tail curled around weeds, the creature stretched to his full height—shorter than Billy-Rid.

Our Guppy would've been quite the runt, he realized. From the looks of it.

The seahorse nipped gills into his baby's neck, then immersed her slowly, gently. As though afraid she'd vanish if let out of sight. As she was lowered, Guppy exhaled without music. Quietly grateful. The dissonant strain of her land-breathers hushed.

Not ours, Rid corrected as the bub drank the sea into her lungs. As she and her da sank into the star-speckled blackness, without a word. She was never ours.

Ripples arrowed east, flippers and arms slicing away toward plundered isles. Waiting for his pulse to slow, Rid tapped out the jig-splash of seahorses departing. When he could no longer tell the difference between liquid-peaks and fins, he turned and faced shore. Saw the yellow glow of Kelloway's atop the hill, spilling like weak ale across the boardwalk. Snippets of song drifted on the quickening breeze. Caws of joy. Back-slaps of mirth.

Shivering, Rid gauged the distance between *here* and *there*.

A far walk, he decided. Farthest he might ever take.

Wilting to his knees, Rid felt his limbs vaguely, steeped in chill. Just a minute's rest, he told himself, looking down at his freezing hands, flipping them a couple of times to make sure they were still there. On his palms, a swathe of scales shimmered in the moonlight. Had he touched the stallion? Had he soaked up some of his magic?

I must have, Rid thought. I must have.

Inspired, he sloshed to his feet. Shy Beetie always hated dancing and parties; he'd rescue her from the crowd, take her to the rock pools, freckle her pink prettiness with scales. Oh, how she'd glisten, then. How she'd love.

You're a fool, Billy Rideout, he thought a second later, flopping into the shallows. Part-squatting, he rubbed his hands together, watched the iridescence flake slowly away. His body aching with cold. Useless cock shriveled. Balls in his belly. Overalls heavy with naught but seawater.

Only one way to fetch a bub, he knew. Only one that he could accept.

From the shallows, Billy-Rid swore he heard his wife's heels skip-stepping on Kelloway's floorboards. Emptied glasses thunking on the bar. Spoon-beats and hide-rappings and harmonica wails. Tilting his head, he listened to another, closer, deep-wooden rhythm. Tethered ships colliding with rails. Hulls bumping against pilings. Ropes creaking between gunwales and jetty. Masts swaying. Figureheads stretching, pointing to the fecund east.

Mind awhirl, Rid calculated.

He measured the span between *here* and way up the hill *there*.

Here and just over to the docks *there*.

Deciding, he bent and scooped a shot of salt water. Swallowed for luck. Steeled himself to go.

Lisa L. Hannett has had over sixty short stories appear in venues including *Clarkesworld, Fantasy, Weird Tales, Apex, The Year's Best Australian Fantasy and Horror,* and *Imaginarium: Best Canadian Speculative Writing.* She has won four Aurealis Awards, including Best Collection for her first book, *Bluegrass Symphony,* which was also nominated for a World Fantasy Award. Her first novel, *Lament for the Afterlife,* was published in 2015. You can find her online at lisahannett.com and on Twitter @LisaLHannett.

"Let's say a soul is what makes men different from animals . . . "

STREET OF THE DEAD HOUSE

Robert Lopresti

What am I? That is the question.

I sit in this cage, waiting for them to come stare at me, mimic me as I once mimicked them, perhaps poke me with sticks, and as they wonder what I am, so do I.

I don't think Mama had any doubts about what she was. I don't think she could even think the question. That is the gift and the punishment Professor gave me.

I remember Mama, a little. We were happy and life was simple, so simple. Food was all around us, dangers were few, and there was nothing we needed. When I was scared or hungry Mama would pick me up and cradle me to her furry breast.

I was never cold. It was always warm where we lived, not this place, called *Paris* or *France.* Goujon cannot talk about anything without giving it two names. Sometimes he calls me an *Ourang-Outang,* and sometimes an *ape.*

Mama called us nothing, for she could not speak like people, or sign as I have learned to do. That did not bother her. She was always happy, until she died.

The hunters came in the morning, firing guns and shouting. Mama picked me up and ran. She made it into the trees but there was another hunter waiting in front of her. He made a noise as if he were playing a game, but this was no game. He fired his gun and Mama fell from the tree. I landed on top of her but she was already dead.

My life has made no sense since then.

I remember the first time I saw Professor. He tilted his head when he looked at me and spoke. We were in his house. The smell of the hunters was finally gone.

He gave me food and tried to be kind but I was afraid. The food tasted wrong and soon I got sleepy, but not the kind of sleepy I knew with Mama.

I know now something in the food made me sleep. Things were confused after that and I would wake up with pain in my head.

He did things to my head. Each time I woke the room looked different, *clearer,* somehow. And one day when Professor spoke I understood some of his noises.

"Ah, Jupiter. You are with me again. And you are grasping my words, aren't you? The chemicals are working just as I predicted."

He held out a piece of fruit. "Are you hungry, Jupiter?"

I was. I reached for it.

He pulled it away and moved his other hand. "Do this, Jupiter. It means *orange.* Tell me you want an orange."

After a few more tries I understood. I copied his hand and he gave me the orange.

That was my first lesson. That was my first surrender.

Many more sleeps, many more words, many more pains in the head.

Soon I knew enough gestures to ask Professor questions.

Where is Mama?

"Dead. Hunters killed her. When I heard they brought back a baby I bought you from them."

Do you have a mama?

"I did, Jupiter. Everyone does. I will show you a picture of mine. I grew up in a place called Lyon. It is far from here, and full of men like me."

Where is your mama?

"She died when I was young."

Killed by hunters?

"No, Jupiter. She got sick. Not sick like you did last month. Much worse."

Where did you live?

"With my papa. Oh dear. A papa is something like a mama. You had one too but *Ourang-Outang* papas don't live with their children. I don't know why. My papa was a baker. That means he made bread, like I eat with my meals."

I tried bread once. It had no taste.

Did your papa die?

"Yes, but that was much later. There was an accident, he was hit by a wagon. You've seen pictures of wagons." His face changed again. "I had to go to the morgue to fetch him. I knew then I would leave Lyon, because it made me so sad."

What is that?

"What is . . . oh, morgue? It is a house where they put the dead."

Did they put my mama there?

"No, Jupiter. Only men."

Why?

"Well." He scratched his head. "I think it is because men think that only they have souls."

What is that?

Professor waved his arms. "I was afraid you would ask! I know nothing about souls. We would need a priest to explain that—and don't bother asking me what a priest is, because I can't explain that either. Let's say a soul is what makes men different from animals."

A soul lets you speak?

More head scratching. "I'll have to think about that one, Jupiter."

I lived in the middle of the house, where there were trees to make nests in. It was surrounded by white walls, and Professor lived on the other side of the walls. There were some windows, spaces in the walls with bars, through which I could see into his rooms. There were also bars on the top of my part of the house.

One day Professor came to me, excited. "We are to have a visitor, Jupiter! A man who speaks French."

What is that?

"The words I speak, that I have been teaching you. Men from different places use different sounds, and French is how they speak where I was born. Most men here speak English, or Dutch, or Malay."

He made the playing noise. "So many ways to talk, Jupiter. But until now none here have spoken as I do."

Is that why they are afraid of me? Because they cannot speak to me?

His face changed. "Why do you say they are afraid?"

I can smell it on your helpers. The men who clean and cook.

"Have any of them bothered you, Jupiter?"

No. But they peek in my room when you are not there. Some of them speak but I do not know what they say. And when I tried to sign back they did not understand.

Professor got quiet. "I am sorry they are afraid of you, Jupiter. Men fear what they don't understand. Perhaps I should have let my helpers visit you, but I didn't want to confuse you with many kinds of words."

He stood up. "We will see how things go with the sailor, yes? Maybe we can find more friends for you."

What is that?

"What, friend?"

No.

"Hmm. Then . . . *sailor*? A sailor is a man who travels on boats. I have shown you pictures of boats, yes? We need a sign for sailor, I see."

Boat man.

His face changed. "Very good, Jupiter. You are getting better and better at thinking of signs."

I want to see the sailor.

I smelled him as soon as he came into the house. The sailor smelled like the fish Professor sometimes eats, and like the smoke some of the helpers smell of.

I heard them while they ate.

"So, where are you from, Monsieur Goujon? Is that a Norman accent?"

"It is, Professor. I was born near Caen, but I have lived most of my life with my uncle near Paris. That is actually why I am here in Borneo. He asked me to supervise a load of precious cargo so I left my ship and will take another back."

"Excellent. I trust you will visit me often while you are here. It is a rare treat to chat with someone who speaks the mother tongue."

"How can I resist such a charming host? Not to mention this wonderful food."

It didn't smell wonderful to me. Mostly bread and burnt meat.

"I am amazed that you can survive here in this primitive land. Pirates, natives, opposing armies . . . and yet here you sit in this beautiful villa! How do you do it?"

"Ah well, it is a little miracle, I suppose. The English assume I am a French spy, and would root me out if they could, but this end of the island is run by the Dutch and the Dyaks, and they have no desire to lose the only physician in their territory.

"When I first reached Borneo some of the Malay pirates tried to take me as their personal physician, but I told them I couldn't work that way. If they wanted my services they would have to set me free—and they did! I suspect they feared I could make them sick as well as heal them. But they come by cover of darkness, when they need me."

"Professor, if I am not being rude, may I ask what a scholar like yourself is doing out in the wilderness? It amazed me to hear about you."

ROBERT LOPRESTI

"Hmm." Professor's voice got quieter. "What *did* you hear, exactly?"

The sailor made the playing noise. "Oh, you know what the locals are like. The natives are pagans and the Dutch aren't much better. They say that you have turned animals into servants!"

"I suppose that is better than if they thought I turned my servants into animals." They made the playing sound. "In fact, my friend, they are closer to the truth than you might imagine. But they are far away, too."

"Really? I am fascinated! Please explain."

"Very well. I should tell you I was trained as a doctor in France. I found myself working in a rural area and, alas, there were many feeble-minded people there."

"Very sad, but I have heard that that condition runs in families."

"It does. And often a healthy member of such a clan will produce feeble-minded offspring, even though both parents seemed completely normal."

"Perhaps the family is cursed by God."

"I know nothing of curses, my friend. As a natural philosopher I can only deal with *this* world. But my breakthrough came when a fever struck our village and, alas, killed a number of small children, both the normal and the feeble-minded."

"Death makes no distinctions, I know."

"Very true. But it occurred to me that I had a great opportunity here that for the sake of all mankind I could not let slip away. As you know, what we call the mind is contained here, in the skull."

"The brain, yes. I saw one once, when a man was killed by an explosion."

"Ah. Then you understand that there is nothing magical about the brain. It is just a pile of meat, one might say. And yet all art and literature and wisdom spring from it, yes? So I decided to see if there was a difference between the healthy and feeble-minded brains."

I heard nothing for a moment. When the sailor spoke he sounded different. "You cut open dead children? Is that *legal*?"

"No. Autopsies, for that is the word, are not legal in France. But they should be or how can medicine advance? My so-called crime was discovered and I had to flee the country. How I wound up in Borneo is a long story. But the important thing is what I learned. The feeble-minded brain looked different; there were variations in shape. It did not smell like a normal brain, and I became convinced that there were chemical differences. I thought, perhaps, it might be possible to improve the little ones."

"Surely you have not been experimenting on living children, Professor!"

"No, my friend. Not even on feeble-minded ones, although I hope I will get the chance to do so. Out here I was able to try my ideas out on apes. Have you seen them?"

"I have, here and in Africa."

"And what do you think of them?"

"I hardly know. They seem like a joke the devil played on mankind. A satire."

"Hmm. I think they are more likely a rough draft, if I may call it that. The Bible tells us God made animals before man, after all. I have worked on almost a dozen of them over the years, trying to improve their brains."

"With what goal, professor? To turn them into men?"

"No, my friend. That would be neither possible nor moral. But if I can improve their ability to think, imagine what I can do for the feeble-minded children!"

I heard a chair scrape back. "That is the most fantastic scheme I have ever heard! Has there been any success?"

"Ah! There has indeed. The latest subject has been a marvel. Come with me, my friend, and you can meet my greatest triumph. He lives in my courtyard."

I heard them coming so I backed away from the door.

The sailor was big, higher and wider than Professor or his servants. He had fur all around his face, and where there wasn't fur his skin was red.

He stared at me, eyes and mouth wide.

"Jupiter, this is my guest, Goujon. Goujon, let me introduce you to Jupiter."

I am happy to meet you.

"What is it doing?" said Goujon, quietly. I smelled his fear.

"The gestures? That is how Jupiter speaks. You will notice I sign while I speak to him. What is it, Jupiter?"

Is he the sailor?

"Yes, the boat man. Boat man. You see, Goujon, he invented this combination of signs to mean *sailor* when he heard you were coming."

"This is amazing, Professor! I wouldn't have believed it possible. How long have you had him?"

"I purchased him almost three years ago. He was a baby and hunters had killed his mother. He is by far the brightest and most trainable subject I have been lucky enough to encounter."

Goujon said more and I got angry. He backed up, toward the door.

"What is it?" Professor asked me. "What is the problem?"

Cannot understand.

"Oh. The sailor has an accent. He learned to speak far from my home. I am sorry, Goujon. Jupiter gets frustrated when he can't understand what is said to him."

The sailor looked at me. His face changed. "You know what? So do I."

Professor made the playing sound. "Ah, very good!"

"Could you teach me to sign, Professor? I would like to speak with your amazing friend."

It was exciting to be teaching instead of learning.

The sailor came every day. He would say a word and I would show him the sign, then he would copy it.

Professor sat and watched. He helped when I could not understand, or when there was a word there was no sign for.

"Gold," said Goujon.

What is that?

"Ah!" Professor said. "It's a metal, Jupiter, like iron, but yellow and heavier. It shines. How about this for a sign? Yellow metal."

"You leave out the most important thing about gold, Professor," said Goujon. "It is valuable."

What is that?

"Valuable? You can get things with it. Here." Professor pulled flat metal things from his pocket and handed them to me. "These are coins. Here's a sign for coin, yes? I give these to the fruit man and he gives me fruit. Then he can give them to, say, the fish man, and get a fish."

Are they gold?

"No, Jupiter. Gold coins are very valuable. That means you would have to trade a lot to get them."

"Or trade something very valuable," said Goujon.

One day the sailor told us he would be leaving soon. A boat had come that would take him and the things his uncle wanted away. After that he kept coming over, but not for lessons. I heard him and Professor talking. They sounded angry.

"You can find another one. My God! With the money he would fetch in France you could hire armies to hunt the deep woods for them."

"What do you think he is, a circus act? This is a great experiment. My greatest! I may never find another I can train so well. And when he starts to decline I will examine his brain and see how my chemicals altered it. Then I can apply what I learned to the children—"

"That's another thing. Do you think anyone, *any* civilized country would let you cut up people the way you have done with that thing in there? That is madness."

"Get out of my house! You are not welcome here! Go back to France, or to the devil!"

After a few minutes Professor came into my room. "How are you, my friend?"

Well. Where is the sailor?

"Ah. He is gone. He is going home. I am sorry he couldn't come to say goodbye to you. Did you like him, Jupiter?"

I liked teaching him.

Two sleeps later and I woke, hearing screams and smelling blood.

I screamed too.

I left my nest and climbed to the top of the tallest tree. I heard more screams. Professor's helpers were running away from the house.

The door opened and the sailor ran in. "Jupiter! Where are you? Come down!"

I stayed in the branches.

"Jupiter! The hunters are here! The professor says I must take you away or they will kill you. Hurry!"

I came down and followed him out of the house, the first time I was outside since I was a baby.

There was a cart at the door with many men. I screamed and tried to back away but Goujon was behind me. "It's all right, Jupiter. They are my friends. They will help us get away from the hunters. Climb into the cart."

I did, but Goujon did not. The door closed and I saw that the walls were bars, like the top of my room. I screamed.

"Shut the brute up!" said one of Goujon's friends.

"Let him prattle. Go!"

I could smell animals I had only had hints of before. Those must be horses, I thought. Professor had shown me pictures of horses pulling carts.

And then there were so many smells and sights that nothing made sense.

There were many sleeps on the boat. I was never out of the box of bars and I was too sick to eat. No one came except Goujon.

"How are you, Jupiter?"

Sick. Where is this?

"We are going to France. That is where the professor was born."

Where is Professor?

"He died. The hunters killed him."

Is he in the dead house?

"The dead house? I suppose he is. But don't worry. You will be safe from the hunters in France. There are many people there who will want to see you. No one has ever seen an *Ourang-Outang* who could talk before! They will pay a fortune."

What is that?

Goujon called the place where we lived a *barn* and a *house*. It did not look like the Professor's house. It was dark and cold and there were no trees to sleep in.

Trees wouldn't have mattered because he did not let me out of the box.

Two sleeps after we arrived Goujon came in, excited. "Good news, Jupiter! Some professors from the university want to meet you."

Professor is dead.

"Yes, yes, but these are other men like him. You will sign for them and they will want you to come live with them in a beautiful house full of trees and fruit and people. You will be famous, Jupiter!"

What is that?

As usual, he didn't answer.

I heard the professors arrive. I was excited to meet them. Perhaps they would be my friends like Professor was.

But I heard Goujon talking on the way up the stairs. "The man who trained him was mad, gentlemen, quite mad. He wanted to experiment on children! I don't pretend to understand what he did to this poor beast. The scars on his head have healed. But we had to stop the professor before he engaged in more such crimes. I'm afraid he fought to the death."

Then I knew how Professor died.

Goujon entered the room with two other men. They had white hair like Professor and one wore circles that made his eyes look big. They stared at me.

"He can't speak, gentlemen," said Goujon. "You will have to learn the signs he uses, but it is not hard. Even I can do it. Jupiter!" He started signing. "Here are two new friends for you. Say hello."

I looked at them.

"Come, Jupiter," said Goujon. "Show them the sign for your name. Or for sailor! You created that yourself. Boat man! Remember?"

I hooted.

"He's a fine specimen," said the man with the circles. "The Jardin des Plantes would be pleased to have him, but not at the price you are asking."

"He's not a zoo animal," said Goujon. "He can talk! Or sign, anyway. Ask him about life in Borneo."

The younger man came closer to my box. "Oh, why not? We've come this far. Jupiter, my name is Pierre. Are you hungry?"

I said nothing. I did nothing. Soon they left.

Goujon was angry. "What was that for, you brute? They would have taken good care of you!"

You killed Professor.

He backed away. "How—? Oh. You heard what I told them. I didn't mean that, Jupiter. It was just . . . just . . . Well, they wouldn't have understood about the hunters."

You killed Professor.

He made the playing sound. "I'm afraid your evidence would not hold up in a court, even if you knew what a court was. You don't want to set a quarrel with me, Jupiter. The sooner you cooperate, the sooner you can live with someone you prefer."

I will not help you.

"No? We will see about that."

He took the lamp and left.

Two sleeps passed. I had no food. No one cleaned my box.

On the third morning Goujon came in with a basket of fruit. "Are you ready to be sensible, Jupiter?"

You killed Professor. I will not help you.

He waved his arms. "If you starve to death it won't help anyone! The professor is dead, Jupiter. What do you want?"

Home.

"Where do you think that is, exactly? You think you can go back to the professor's house and live there again? Will the Dyaks bring you food and clean up your mess? You could never survive in the forests. In the name of the good god, let me help you."

What is that?

He didn't answer. He took the food away.

The next morning Goujon came back with more fruit. "Don't eat so fast. You'll get sick."

When I was done he said. "All right. You want to go back to Borneo, do you? Very well. It will take money."

What is that?

"Money? The professor told you about that the first time I met you. Remember? Gold coins?"

Why do I need them?

"Because the captain—the big boat man—won't take you to Borneo without them. Now, my uncle keeps an eye on all the important things that happen here in Paris, and he knows of a caper that is perfect for us."

What is that?

Goujon said his uncle knew of an old woman, a fortune-teller, who was going to buy a shop. I didn't know what most of those words meant but Goujon just waved a hand.

"Never mind. All that matters is this: On Friday she will have a big bag full of gold coins in her house. If we get them there will be enough to send you back to your Malayan hellhole and for me to live here for many years."

He told me that the woman was a mama and her child lived with her, but the child was grown. They lived on the fourth floor of a house.

"My uncle says there is no way to get into the building but through a window on the fourth floor that can be entered from the yard; I have seen it and you could do it easily." He made the playing sound. "Easy as climbing a tree."

That night he let me out of the cage. We went outside where he had a closed wagon waiting. Two horses pulled it. The man in front was so frightened I could barely smell the horses.

"Come inside, Jupiter," said Goujon.

I didn't want to. It was dark and small and the air was cold.

"If you run away, you will never get home. Do you understand that? You can't get home except by boat and only I know which boats go there."

I will go.

Goujon turned to the driver. "Rue Morgue. Jupiter, what's wrong? Calm down."

Why are we going to the dead house?

"The dead . . . the morgue? No, *morgue* is just the name of the street. We won't be going to the morgue at all. Just calm down and get in the carriage. Please."

We traveled through the place Goujon called Paris, although sometimes he called it France. The windows were shuttered but I could hear and smell. It was like the boat ride; too much to remember.

The house where the woman lived was not the dead house. Goujon told me the dead house was far away and I shouldn't think about it.

This house was bigger than the professor's had been.

"The door is always locked."

What is that?

"Locked? Closed so no one can get in. Like your cage or your room back in the Professor's house in Borneo." He led me to a yard at the rear of the building. "Look at the windows on the top floor. The woman lives there with her daughter. Could you get in?"

I looked up at it and felt happy. I had never been able to climb so high.

I can.

"Are you sure, Jupiter?"

I can. Now.

Goujon put a hand on my arm. "Not now. She will not have the coins until the end of the week. Let's go back home."

I pulled my arm away. *Practice.*

"Practice? That makes sense. But not here." He leaned out of the box and spoke to the man who helped the horses.

"We will go to an empty building I know. You can climb there without being seen."

We went. The building was not as tall as the one where the woman lived, but it was still wonderfully high. I stretched out my arms and began to pull myself up the outer walls.

I felt my heart beating. I had done nothing like this in my life. I had only climbed the trees and walls in Professor's house. I never wanted to stop. I swung from one piece of wall to another. Swung again and caught a window with my leg. I could have gone on forever.

Goujon yelled. "Jupiter! We have to get going! It will be morning soon."

I wanted to ignore him. He said we were going home, but where was home? The cage?

"Jupiter! There's no food here. If you don't come with me you will never get back to Borneo!"

He was right. I climbed to the top once more and then rushed all the way to the street beside him.

Goujon's face changed. "You liked that, didn't you?"

Yes.

"It was very cruel of that professor to keep you locked up like that. Jupiter, what's wrong?"

I never thought Professor was cruel to lock me up. Why didn't he let me climb the trees outside his house?

I got in the wagon. When we went into the house Goujon said: "I won't ask you to get in that cage again, Jupiter. We have to trust each other, yes?"

Yes.

Each night Goujon took me out to practice at a different empty building.

"That metal tree is a lightning rod, Jupiter. There is one on the roof of the fortune-teller's house, near the chimney. It is much higher. Can you climb it? Yes? Very good!"

I enjoyed the practice so much I did not want it to end, but on the third night Goujon said, "I think you are ready, Jupiter. Tomorrow the old woman will buy another house. So tonight we must move, eh?"

Yes.

I didn't know why the old woman wanted another house. But I was sure she didn't need it as much as I needed to go home.

When the carriage arrived, the street was empty and silent. I could hear that no one moved inside. I could smell how nervous Goujon was.

"Ready, Jupiter?" he whispered. "Excellent, excellent. I will be down here waiting. I'm sure the women are asleep by now."

I climbed the tall lightning rod. It was easy. The shutter was open against the wall. I grabbed it with both hands and swung across to the open window. That was easy too.

Inside the room was one bed, the kind Goujon sleeps on, the head against the window. I squeezed through the window and landed on the bed.

The old woman sat in a chair beside the bed, a metal box full of papers on the table beside her, and she slept. Her eyes were closed, and she growled.

I crept to her. The bags of gold coins Goujon described were lying on the table beside her. I tried to pull one but there were strings on it, and they were wrapped around her wrist.

She growled again. What could I do?

I went back to the bed and stuck my head out the window. I tried to sign my problem, but Goujon didn't understand. Finally he climbed up the pole, badly, and reached the top.

I crawled out the window, hanging onto the sill, and when our heads were as close together as they could get he looked up and me and whispered, "What's wrong?"

Woman asleep. Bags tied to hand.

Goujon took one hand off the pole and almost fell. He pulled something from his pocket and held it up to me. "Razor. You know how to open it?"

Yes. I had seen him shave.

I reached down to take it. I opened the razor and made sure I knew how to hold it. Then I crept back to the woman. I took hold of the first string and started cutting. The woman kept growling.

I caught the bag so it didn't make a sound. I put it on the floor. Then I started to cut the other string.

I heard a door close. A young woman had come in. Her back was to me and she was doing something to the door.

What could I do?

She turned and saw me. She screamed.

The old woman woke. She saw me and screamed.

Now I was scared. I wanted to scream too.

Before I could back away the old woman hit me in the face. Then she grabbed me by my fur. I tried to push her away but the razor caught her in the throat. Her eyes went wide and blood squirted out poured down.

I smelled blood. I was scared. I dropped the razor and jumped back. The old woman fell to the floor.

The daughter screamed louder than ever.

Outside from below the window, I heard Goujon shouting, "My God! You devil! What have you done?"

The daughter would not be quiet. I put a hand over her mouth.

She bit me.

I put my hands on her throat. I made her quiet. She fell down.

"Get out of there, Jupiter! Take the coins and come!"

I was scared. I had never done anything so bad before.

I tried to pick up the old woman by her fur but pieces of it came out. I grabbed her by the middle and rushed up the bed to the window. I held the woman outside so Goujon could see her. Maybe Goujon could help her?

His eyes went wide. "What have you done?" he yelled, frightening me. I lost my grip and the old woman fell out the window to the yard below.

"My God! What have you done?" Goujon slid down the lightning rod. He ran from the yard. I heard the carriage with the horses pull away.

I lifted the daughter and looked for a place to hide her. The door was locked. I didn't want to throw her out the window.

There was no fire in the fireplace. I hid her in there.

I heard people running up the stairs, banging on the door.

I left the coins on the floor and climbed out the window, and it slammed shut behind me. I climbed up to the roof.

I kept going from roof to roof until I could not hear the screams, or smell the blood.

Before the sun rose I found a forest. There were many trees and a grassy place with a path where people walked. I climbed into a tree and hid.

I had not meant to hurt anyone, but I think those two women were dead. I had killed them like the hunters killed Mama. Like Goujon killed Professor.

Professor whipped me once for hurting one of his helpers. This was worse. What would happen now?

I stayed in the tree all day. People walked by on the path but they never saw me. I don't think they were looking for me.

After dark I went down and searched for food. I found a place where there had been many kinds of food and carts. I found bins where old food was piled and found fruit I could eat. Then I went back to the trees and made a nest.

That's how I lived for many sleeps.

The food was bad. It was making me sick. Professor could make me better but he was dead. Goujon killed him but maybe he did it to help me.

One night I knew I couldn't stay there anymore. I climbed down and followed the smells back to the place where Goujon lived.

The door would not open but I knew what to do. I climbed in a window on the top floor. Goujon was in a bed growling like the old woman had done.

That made me sad.

I touched him on the arm. He woke with a jerk and sat up. He was afraid.

"Jupiter! Is that you?"

I touched his hand.

Goujon leapt out of the other side of the bed. "Wait, just wait." He lit a lamp.

"It is you! I thought you were lost forever. Where have you been?"

Food and water.

"Of course! Where are my manners? Come with me."

I ate. He drank something that smelled spoiled.

I told him what happened.

"What an amazing adventure, Jupiter. I never would have thought you could survive for so long in this city. I am glad to have you back."

Are the women in the dead house?

"Yes. You know you killed them, don't you?"

I didn't mean to.

"Yes. But I doubt anyone else would believe it." He put down his glass. "Listen, Jupiter. There was one man clever enough to realize that only an animal like you could have broken into that house. A strange fellow named Auguste Dupin who lives in a ruined house with his boyfriend, I suppose. You should see the place! Nothing but moldy furniture and books, hundreds of books.

"This Dupin is both a genius and a fool, I think. He tricked me, convinced me that he found you, but he wasn't clever enough to realize that you are an animal who *thinks.* And that's the point, Jupiter. Do you know what they do to murderers in France?"

What is that?

"A murderer? Someone who kills people, like you did. They kill murderers; chop off their heads. Do you want them to chop off your head, Jupiter?"

My hands trembled as I signed *no.*

"And I don't want them to cut off mine, either. Understand me, Jupiter. If you are a mere animal then you are not a murderer. But if you are smart enough to help me *steal* then you are smart enough to kill, and they will *kill* you for it. Do you understand, Jupiter?"

No.

He sighed. "If they see you signing they will know how smart you are. Then I will be killed as a thief and you as a murderer. But if you don't sign, if you can keep from ever letting anyone see you do it, then they will think you are just a brute, and neither of us will be punished. What do you say, Jupiter? Can you keep the secret?"

Could I? Could I pretend to be as empty and silent as the horses and the dogs?

"Jupiter?"

I didn't answer. I have never answered.

Goujon had no money to send me home. I understood. This is my punishment.

He couldn't sell me as a talking beast but he sold me to the Jardin des Plantes. There are many animals here.

I live in a box of bars in a big house that is always cold. That is my punishment, too.

There are other apes, but they don't like me. The Professor made me different and they can tell. So I live in another building, alone.

Goujon came once and talked to me. I didn't answer.

He thinks I am afraid. He thinks I pretend to be an empty beast because they will kill me if they find out I can think.

I am not afraid. But after I killed those women I knew I had to decide.

What am I?

Professor tried to turn me into a man. I am not a man. I will not be part of a man.

So I must be a beast. I have decided.

Beasts do not speak. Beasts do not sign.

Yesterday there were a lot of excited men in front of my cage. They were all facing one man, who was pointing at me and talking. I couldn't understand what they were saying until one of them called him by name: *Dupin*.

That was the man Goujon told me about, the one smart enough to realize an *Ourang-Outang* killed the women, but not smart enough to know that I was also smart.

Now he was telling everyone how he figured out that it was me and the men were telling him how clever he was.

He looked at me and I thought: if I sign now and he is so clever he will know that I am signing, even if he cannot understand the words. Would he tell everyone or would he be ashamed that he was mistaken?

My fingers itched to sign: *You are the fool.*

But I am a beast. Beasts are silent. I let him pass me, still thinking that I cannot think.

There are more people outside my box now. They yell at me and make the playing sound. I do nothing.

They look at me and I look back. I look back.

Robert Lopresti is the author of more than sixty mystery stories, so it is no surprise he wrote this retelling of the very first detective story. His latest book, *Greenfellas*, is a comic crime novel about a mobster who learns about climate change on the day he becomes a grandfather and decides to save the environment. Lopresti's short stories have won the Derringer and Black Orchid Novella Awards, as well as gaining an Anthony nomination. He is a librarian in the Pacific Northwest. "Street" is his third published fantasy story.

Even the newspapers had started to notice the high incidence of death in that area of the city. It was odd, these clusters of death . . .

THE GREYNESS

Kathryn Ptacek

Angela gazed down at her husband's body in the hospital bed and wondered what it was like to be dead.

This isn't what I should be thinking, she told herself, and yet it was. She reached out and placed her fingertips on his arm. Warm. Her fingers trembled as she watched his chest, waiting for him to draw in that next breath, waiting to hear the exhalation, waiting, waiting, waiting.

They were all waiting out in the hall for her, too . . . Waiting ever so politely before they bustled in, before they intruded upon her last time with her husband.

They told me to take as long as I wanted. She put her other hand up to her mouth to stifle a giggle. As long as I wanted—an hour, a day, a week? How long was too long? Too short? What if she swept out of the room right now? Would they think less of her? Think she wasn't a very good wife?

She rubbed her fingers across his skin. It still felt like him. She bent down and kissed him and closed her eyes and remembered all the times they had embraced and explored each other with their lips and tongues.

Her husband hadn't been old, hadn't been young, hadn't been sick. Apparently something was going on inside Ben, something that she hadn't noticed, something no one realized. *Had he known?* she wondered. If so, he hadn't said anything, but then he wouldn't have. He would not have wanted to worry her, to make her wonder what was going to happen.

She inhaled deeply. All she smelled was the antiseptic tang of the hospital room, but beneath it lay a faint odor. Death? She opened her eyes, but didn't see the grim reaper or anything remotely like it lurking in the corner. Again, she almost laughed. Why would she see that now when her husband died an hour before? His spirit or soul or anima or whatever was gone—it had slipped away into the night, and left his shell, had left her behind.

She traced the curling hair on his forearm, smoothed a rough patch of skin—hadn't she suggested he have his doctor check it out?—intertwined her fingers with his . . .

Beneath her palm resting on the top of his hand she felt a brief warmness, and for a wild moment she thought he was alive, that he was moving. But she opened her eyes and all the joy that had surged through her in that instant drained, and there lay his body. Dead. Dead is dead.

Only then did she laugh, loud and long, not even stopping when the two nurses and administrator with all the pesky paperwork stepped into the room and gaped at her. She laughed even harder—papers to fill out when her love was dead. She laughed until the tears washed down her cheeks.

Days blurred by . . . all the little things, all the big things she had to do. All the things she and Ben hadn't thought about, because, surely, death was a long way away.

That's what he always said, but every so often she saw something in those yellow-brown eyes—those wolf eyes—that said otherwise. But she had thought he was just fearful, as she was, and so they never talked about what had to be done. More papers to fill out; the meetings with the lawyer; arrangements, arrangements, arrangements. She was self-employed, so there was no boss to call to say she wouldn't be returning to work for a while.

In the old days, she thought as she stared into the closet to pick out clothes for him to wear in the casket, *he would have died at home, and his sister and I and maybe another woman would have washed the body carefully, with respect, and we would have dressed him in his finest suit, and he would have laid in the coffin in our parlor.*

Except we don't have a parlor, she thought, her lips twisting into a bit of a smile as she thought of the two-bedroom apartment. No, far from it. A chuckle threatened to escape, and she wondered why she thought it was funny. Nothing was funny now; yet everything was funny.

She found the charcoal grey suit he wore on business trips, the pale grey shirt he liked, the tie adorned with red koalas that she had given him one birthday, the black socks and shoes. Belt? Of course. What about underwear? Once more she found herself laughing aloud. She did that a lot lately. People stared at her, too. She laughed sometimes in the middle of the grocery store. Just stopped pushing the cart and stood there, veggies on one side of the aisle, pasta on the other, and laughed and laughed, like seeing a can of corn was the most amusing thing. Sometimes, the laugh started out as a chuckle; sometimes it bloomed into a full-blown guffaw, and she would find her shoulders shaking, and she'd realize she had tears in her eyes.

Carefully, she folded his clothing and placed it into the large shopping bag. Then she grabbed the handle of the bag, locked the apartment, and headed to the funeral home. She walked because it was only a few blocks away—Ben used to joke that it was certainly convenient to have a mortuary nearby!—and because it was a warm autumn day, the kind of day they both enjoyed so much, the kind of day they would have gone walking with the dog. Her hand holding the bag trembled, and then she was there and up the steps to ring the doorbell. Again, she felt that bit of warmth on her palm, and she rubbed her hand against her jeans. *Oh, good*, she thought, *I'm getting hot flashes now.*

"Come in, Mrs. Martinson," the undertaker said as he opened the door. Joseph Whyte reached out to take her hand, and once more she felt the warmth. She looked past his shoulder because she couldn't bear to meet his too-kind eyes and saw a number in his office just off the parlor: 57. She blinked, and the number shimmered, then disappeared gradually, leaving an after-image in her mind.

"Are you all right?" Whyte asked, then said quickly, "I'm sorry . . . of course, you're not. Come this way." He led her into his office, and she sat, the bag at her feet.

As he talked, he showed her catalogs, and she marveled that there was such an industry built up around death. In the end she handed over the shopping bag when he said he would see to it himself. For that, she was glad. Whyte had a cousin who worked with him, and she didn't like the man; the first day she had gone to the funeral parlor the cousin had swept her up into a hug. She had pulled away and had seen unshed tears in his eyes, and for some reason that bothered her.

Now that she was in the office, she studied the furnishings. She didn't see that number at all, and that worried her. She was seeing things, feeling things . . . did grief cause hallucinations? She didn't know.

Could she have been thinking of something else and then thought she saw the number? But what? Heinz 57 ketchup? *Too absurd, even for me,* she told herself. She rose and thanked the man, but she did not shake his hand again.

• • •

Angela got through the funeral at the church, with its solemn music and the too-sweet scent of dead lilies, and she nodded when people she knew and didn't know approached and told her how sorry they were. She kept her hands clasped lightly around her clutch purse, as if holding onto that would keep her anchored somehow. She found she didn't want to touch anyone, didn't want anyone to touch her. She'd built up this little cocoon of . . . whatever . . . around herself like an invisible force field, and she didn't want it breached. She knew that if anyone put a hand on hers or slipped an arm around her shoulder she would break down and laugh and cry and howl until they took her away and sedated her. She couldn't take it . . . not now, not yet.

So she nodded and nodded and nodded, and all she could think about was going home and laying down for a nap, retreating from the greyness that shrouded her.

She rode in the car behind the hearse, and she endured the rest of the ceremony beside the open grave. It started to rain, but the funeral director had anticipated the bad weather, so canopies protected her and the others seated there. Then it was over. She wanted to get home, get into bed, not think, not do anything, not—

Someone called her name, and she turned and saw it was Tommy. Without thinking, she reached out because, after all, this was Ben's dear friend from college, and the warmth blossomed beneath her palm, and past him, on a gravestone in the next row over, she saw a black numeral: 1. She blinked—and he gave her the look, the one that always made her cry, and now she began weeping uncontrollably.

"I'll take you home," Tommy said, and she nodded against his shoulder.

There were more pats on her back from other friends and neighbors now as they crowded around her, tapping and touching, and she felt like the world was shrinking in on her, like she couldn't breathe. Tommy saw the desperation in her eyes, pulled her away, and escorted her to his car.

He didn't talk on the drive back to the apartment, nor did she. She thanked him as she got out, then he followed her inside and made coffee and sat down in the kitchen and said nothing. She changed into comfortable clothes and once more in the kitchen, she sat and sipped her coffee, and still they didn't talk.

Tommy just gazed out the window, while she continued staring down into her coffee mug. How could her husband have died so quickly? Didn't he know they had so many things left to do? They hadn't finished all the trips they planned, and she hadn't given him the present for his birthday next month, and . . . and . . . and . . .

She tried to stop thinking.

Tommy made dinner for them both that night, and she pushed the food from one side of the plate to the other. She suspected that he had talked to the other friends, and they had decided to stay with her for the next few days. Tonight would be his tour of duty, as it were. She wondered briefly who would show up tomorrow . . .

She went to bed an hour or so later, while he bunked out on the couch, and in the morning he fixed them breakfast. She nibbled on the toast, then he kissed her cheek and said he had to leave. She nodded and thanked him. She listened to him leave the apartment, and she went to the window. She saw him get into the car and pull out of the parking lot, and she watched as the dump truck barreled along the street and smacked into the convertible.

She screamed and flung herself out the door and ran down the stairs . . . but it was too late. Her husband's best friend was dead.

Another funeral. Angela stayed in the back, spoke to no one, and left before everyone drove to the cemetery. At home, she made herself some coffee, then stood at the window while the coffee cooled.

If he hadn't come back here . . . if he had stayed for another hour . . . if, if, if.

If.

Hours became days, and days became weeks. The grey still enveloped her, still made her numb at times. She did things out of rote. She got up, went to the store, walked the dog, made a meal now and then, watched TV without seeing it, walked the dog again, went to bed. The next day was just a repeat of the day before . . . and the day before that.

Friends dropped in, bringing casseroles that she dutifully stored in the freezer, and they told her about all the things she was missing, and she nodded.

"And isn't it just weird?" Leslie said on the first day of winter as they sat in the kitchen. "Mr. Whyte and all."

The greyness shifted a bit. Angela frowned. "What are you talking about?"

Her friend glanced over. "Oh, I guess you're not keeping up with the papers."

She shook her head. "No. I get them, then don't read them. Maybe one of these days I will."

"Then I guess you didn't hear about Mr. Whyte."

"The funeral director?"

"Yeah, he died. Some rare fast-growing tumor. And isn't it just so weird . . . Ben hasn't been gone for even two months, and then Tommy, and now this guy."

"Yeah." Two months . . . "He didn't seem sick when I saw him."

"Well, he was kind of old."

"Not that old, I thought."

Two months. "This was in the paper, right?" Leslie nodded. Angela went to the stack of papers and flipped through them until she found the right issue . . . and yes, there was his obituary. She checked the date of his death, and it had been almost two months since she had taken her husband's clothes to him. Almost two months, but not quite. Just a few days under.

Fifty-seven days, to be precise.

Abruptly, she sat down.

Her friend left shortly after that, and Angela was glad. She needed to think, not talk . . .

She had shaken Mr. Whyte's hand at the funeral home. She saw the number *57*. He had died that many days later.

She had shaken Tommy's hand at the graveside ceremony. One . . . the number she had seen on a gravestone. *1*. And he had died the next day.

What the hell? What is this? And she remembered that both times she had felt a warmth on the palm of her hand. And she remembered that day when she'd sat by Ben as he lay in the hospital bed, with her hand atop his . . . and the warmth had been there, even though it wasn't possible. His skin was already cooling off; there should have been no warmth, and yet, she knew that's what she felt.

She put her face in her hands and closed her eyes, and told herself it couldn't be. *But it was. Wasn't it?*

Somehow this . . . thing . . . this ability had transferred from her dead husband to her. She stared at her hands. They appeared no different than before, and slowly she traced the life line across her palm and thought about all the times as a kid when friends had "read" her palm and said she would live a long life and have a loving husband and four kids or more. They had all giggled because at that point they weren't even that interested in boys.

She felt a wet nose against her leg and glanced down to see the mutt there. He wanted his walk. She stared at him and remembered that Ben had taught the dog to shake hands. No, she thought; I won't do it. She retrieved the leash, snapped it to his collar, and headed out to the park.

How do I prove this? she wondered. *Not everyone I shake hands with will die in the next week or month or year or two. Will I meet someone and then see a number that's so huge that it indicates years or even decades?*

There was only one way to find out.

Angela saw someone at the park whom she'd seen before, and she stopped to chat, and before she walked away, she extended her hand and shook with the other woman. 14. She saw the shimmering number on the wall of the building across the street.

Now to keep track, and she wondered that she could think about this so coldly, so objectively. She rushed home and found a pocket-sized notebook and made a note of the day and the shimmering number. She knew the woman's name, so that could be verified.

Every day for two weeks Angela chatted with the woman while their dogs sniffed each other, and when she went home that night, she thought that perhaps she had been wrong. But when she saw the headlines in the newspaper the next morning, she knew she wasn't. Her park acquaintance had gone home the night before, drowned her little child, then killed herself.

Angela put the paper down and squeezed her eyes shut. How could this woman have done something like that? She didn't seem like she was unraveling. Each time Angela had seen the woman in the park, she had been friendly and had talked about her daughter and the plans she had for the four-year-old in the spring. In the spring. She had been looking forward to the new year, and now she was dead.

For several days Angela didn't budge from the apartment. She took the dog out for a quick walk twice a day, then she raced home. She didn't want to see anyone, she didn't want to talk to anyone. She ignored phone calls; she refused to come to the door when someone pounded there. She just called out that she was fine.

Except she wasn't fine, and she realized she couldn't hide any longer. What must her friends think? They were already worried, but now they left messages for her. Don't give into the grief! they said. You have to move on! they counseled. Don't become a hermit! Think of yourself; you're still young! Go out and try not to think!

In the morning, when it wasn't quite as grey as it had been, Angela showered, dressed, and left the apartment.

She greeted everyone she met warmly, and she shook hands with the shopkeepers and their customers and the delivery man and mail carrier, and after each instance, she saw a number. She had her notebook with her, so each time she jotted down the number and the occasion of the meeting. She did that all day long, walking along the streets, greeting people she knew—after all, she and Ben had lived there a long time and had come to know a lot of people, if just even by sight—and then she headed home.

She kept tabs on the obits in the newspapers, and each time someone she'd shaken hands with died, she put a little check mark by the notebook item.

There were, she thought some three months later, *a lot of obits, a lot of dead people.* And even the newspaper reporters had started to notice the high incidence of death in that area of the city. It was odd, these clusters of death, authorities said, because the deaths weren't all murders or suicides. *Bummer about the stats not working out,* she thought, and almost laughed aloud.

She watched from her window and wondered how long the people out there had to live. What about the people in the apartment building? Wasn't there supposed to be an association meeting that night? She imagined she would have to shake a lot of hands; it was the courteous thing to do, after all.

She laughed, this time long and hard, and the dog raised his head and whined softly.

She couldn't stay in. She had to find out about more numbers. Wasn't there someone who didn't have a number?

She went back out again, and headed in a different direction. *Time to skew the stats some more.*

She shook hand after hand all along her walk. She was the epitome of a friendly person. She smiled. She laughed when she chatted with acquaintances. *3. 17. 41. 65.* The numbers shimmered and flew by her, and once she reached out to touch the numeral, but there was nothing there, of course.

She paused when she saw a patrol car cruise by, and thought the two cops inside must be searching for something, anything!

But they won't find anything, she told herself, *because who would believe it?* She paused in front of a shop window and wondered who the haggard woman staring at her was. She grimaced and realized it was her own reflection. *I look like hell,* she thought. *I have to work on myself. I have to eat better; I have to get some sleep. I have to remember to comb my hair before leaving the apartment.* But as she stared at the circles under her eyes and at the hollows in her cheeks, she wondered if it was worth it.

Should I shake my own hand? she thought, trying not to giggle. Will I see a number? Did Ben do this? How long had he had this ability? And why hadn't he said anything to her? Did he think she wouldn't believe him? Well, maybe she wouldn't have. But maybe she would have. He should have warned her!

And as she stared at her gaunt face—like death warmed over, her dad always said—she wondered something else.

What if . . . she took a deep breath . . . what if she wasn't just seeing the number of days left in someone's life? What if this whole thing was something more, something like—No. It couldn't be, but yet . . . What if she was the one who caused these people to die? After all, there had been a lot of deaths in the area since Ben's death. Surely, not all those people had been about to die. What if, somehow, she helped them along? Maybe it was like a roulette wheel, and when she held someone's hand, the spinning wheel stopped, and the little death ball jumped and bounced and the number that came up was the number of days left in that person's life.

So, if she didn't shake someone's hand, she wouldn't know, and they wouldn't know, and maybe they would live forever and ever. Or at least for another decade or two.

Interesting. She chuckled, and she watched as a man walking behind her glanced over at her, then looked sharply away. *Don't like what you see, eh? Me, either.*

She spun away from the shop window and thrust her hands into her pockets. What now? Home to the greyness and the dog and staring out the window, or . . . or something else.

Only one way to find out, she told herself, and she walked down the street, heading to the hospital. She had to see the doctors and nurses who had worked on her husband, who had failed to save his life. She wanted to shake their hands and tell them she knew they had done all they could. Except they hadn't. She knew that somehow they had messed up . . . or Ben would still be alive today!

And maybe when she got to the hospital, she'd find the ambulance crew there, too . . . She'd shake their hands as well, and thank them, all the while thinking they could have worked on Ben faster, could have made better time to the hospital.

And when she was done there, perhaps she would stroll to some other wards to pay a few visits. Maybe the maternity ward. She glanced down at the lifeline on her hand . . . *No loving husband and no four kids, and if I can't have them,* she thought, her dried lips quirking into a smile, *maybe others shouldn't, either.*

She started whistling as she walked into the greyness.

Kathryn Ptacek's novels (in various genres) are being re issued as ebooks from Crossroad Press and Necon Ebooks. Check out her Facebook page for updates. She lives in the beautiful northwest corner of New Jersey where she keeps a lively garden. She collects teapots and beads.

"Thing about music is in the end, all we can do is face our own. I hope yours has some bop to it."

THE DEVIL UNDER THE MAISON BLUE

Michael Wehunt

Gillian notices that no one ever closed Mr. Elling's attic window. A week has passed since the brief swirl of ambulance lights near dawn. Already his house seems decades older.

She's staring across at it when she hears his voice say, "Lord, child, you about run as far as you can get." He has a rich and rumbly cadence. There's a crackle in it, too, faint as a needle at the end of one of his records. Somehow she is not startled, though he might as well be perched right here beside her, on the high sharp peak of her house. That's how close his words are; she feels them in the shingles under her hands, and in the cups of her ears.

She sees him (for a second she's sure of it) in his old chair, rocking slowly toward and away from her, in and out of the pool of a hanging bulb. Even from a distance he looks ancient, his skin like dried dates. The silver of his hair glints and fades. She can't see his eyes, but she pictures them, heavy-lidded, stained the yellow of a smoker's teeth.

He was the only person she could talk to in her six months here, though most days she'd just listen. Stories about his life in the big jazz towns; who played what with whom before when. He could talk the sun down, tapping the valves of his battle-tarnished trumpet idly in his lap. Betty, he called the old horn, with something in his voice that said she was his one true love. His lungs couldn't handle her anymore, but sometimes, just to get a smile, he'd lift her up and blow his cheeks out into great globes. Then cough a while after.

For the first time she wonders if maybe he knew that listening would do her more good. Her father had pulled her out of school after the day in the maple trees, and the weeks had grown into one long, opaque strand. Now Mr. Elling's words carry clear through the space between their houses like the few stray starlings (they're late flying south) calling to one another above. Faraway cars on the highway sound like the ocean. She can pretend the starlings are gulls and she is somewhere else, a place that, if only for a little while, doesn't have her father in it.

She calls across asking Mr. Elling if he is a ghost. He breathes a deep sigh. "You just hush," he says. "No need for you to be yelling. It don't much matter what I am. I ain't haunting nobody, that's for sure. Just lingering. I got a story I kept letting myself not tell you. Before, it was a story about my daddy and me. Now it's maybe got room for you and yours, and that's a terrible thing to come to."

A minute unravels. She listens to the birds. "Look at that sky, Gillian," he says. She has to grip the shingles, so wide and heavy is the shock of hearing that. To Mr. Elling they're just words. He says them kindly, like another sigh, but she remembers (she's always thinking of) the backseat of her father's convertible after a sudden detour into a clump of maples, her mouth still sticky from ice cream. Her father whispered those words and then sneaked a kiss along her neck, as she peered up between the full trees, into blind blue and clouds like stuffing pulled out of dolls.

Today's sky is much the same, a little whiter. The clouds hang closer. Someone is burning leaves, but not nearby. She presses her hand to her belly, cold against the tight warmth there.

"I will surely miss this northern sky," Mr. Elling says, and makes a close-mouthed little *mmhm* sound before he goes on. "But one last story before I move on to wherever it is I'm headed. Betty and me had us some good years, and I'm satisfied.

"See, the best times were bebop, hard bop, all the bops. The birth of the cool. I'm lucky those times were the ones I happened to be in. The greats slipped on more new styles than a woman in a shoe store. They always were looking for the next big groove, the next big rule-breaker. And you might ask how a brokedown young fella from South Carolina with a drunk waste of a daddy could bus hisself down to Louisiana, with just a dream in his head of playing with actual *gods*. Well, there's a reason us old folks get to say we were young once."

The handful of starlings has fallen quiet. Nothing moves through his attic window now, if anything ever did. She can almost pick out the last few patches of red paint on the rocking chair's pale arms. She can come close to riding the swells of his voice, the pop and hiss of a well-worn tune.

"But piss on all that history lesson talk," Mr. Elling goes on. "You don't know the insides of jazz aside from my jawing, but just know that folks like

Coltrane and Monk—never Miles, wasn't nobody blowing trumpet beside that man and not coming off like a bugler in a doomed infantry—they were reason enough to sell your soul."

And for a moment, just one, she seems to hear her mother singing Billie Holiday under her breath, seems to see her far below (in a yard she never knelt in) stabbing at the soil with her spade. As though both of Gillian's important ghosts are here. She seems to smell her, too, not the powdered lavender of her hugs but something that traces her mother's freckled skin further down in her mind: honeysuckle, like the vines that spread wild in the woods behind the old neighborhood, before the hospital, before the house went dusty and full of echoes and she and her father moved away. To here.

And she almost says that, yes, she does know the insides of jazz.

Mr. Elling's old voice drifts on. "Like I told you a time or three, I came to the Big Easy late in the game. It was a frying-pan August, 1958, about as humid as humid gets. Beautiful city, crumbling slow and majestic. Green growing on everything. The day I got there my precious mama was in her grave just shy of three weeks and my daddy wasn't worth the dirt in it.

"I could play a mean trumpet, had been since I was fifteen until my daddy put a stop to it. And I had big plans to travel around, looking up at my name in tall letters on marquees. But I was a beanpole with the lungs to match. I didn't have the soul of the greats. Betty and me got to perform with some guys exactly twice between then and October of '59. That night was set to be my third, as I'd just started making some regular friends by then, something like a crew. Strictly small-time, but it was better than *no*-time, if you catch my drift.

"Except thirty feet outside the back door of the Maison Blue, on Frenchman Street, I met myself four and a half white fellas all liquored up and looking for somebody like me—the biggest one I'm counting as a fella and a half. I didn't know them from Adam, and they didn't know me from whoever was the first black boy in the Bible. Well, suffice it to say I never stepped foot in the Blue that night. Later I found out a kid called Rett Wilson sat in for me. Not half bad for a tin ear. He did some session work on a few records.

"Excuse an old-timer, Gillian. I never told this story before, but that's no excuse for all my other recollections to come seeping in the cracks. Even passed on I may be longwinded, but I mean to get through this quick, so that we can see what we see."

He laughs and there's not a drop of wheeze in it. And no humor, either. She watches for the faded bronze of her father's old Cabriolet. Her hand rubs nervous circles on her belly.

"I don't know what I had more of on me," Mr. Elling says, "blood or dirt. I made quite a dust cloud in that back lot, what from hitting the ground over and over. Them fellas left, brushing off their white, white shirts. I could see two of my teeth right in front of my eyes, and judging from the inside of my mouth I figured there were probably a few more scattered around. My Betty, I could just see her down by my feet. She was streaked with some red, too.

"One of my eyes was already swelled shut, but the other one saw something gleaming at me from the crawlspace under the Blue. Flashlight eyes, like a cat. There was a little door dragged open along the dirt, and they were staring out from the black square behind it. I could feel my busted ribs and I was spitting out blood so I didn't drown in it. That is, I was fine where I was; at some point somebody would step out back for some air and fetch me to the hospital.

"But damned if those eyes didn't get bigger and yellower. Damned if they weren't looking at me with something deeper than a cat's cool regard. Then they pulled back into that dark, lamps trailing off down a mine. Might be the cat's supposed to be the curious one, but that long evening it was me.

"Most folks wouldn't have gone hauling themselves through the dirt toward that hole, grinding broken parts inside with every inch. Most folks would've passed out from the pain of it, and in that way, I was most folks. But I came to and I crawled some more, and when I made it to that black opening, I peered in, smelling sour dirt and cool dark."

She almost tells him she's on the edge of her seat—this would get a laugh out of him, ghost or no—but she keeps quiet. The street is empty and breathless, the sun sliding on its track, closer to the line of coloring trees.

"But I supposed that was no cat. Just like I supposed if I squeezed into that hole, it would be like no dark I ever saw. So I went on ahead and did it. There was a lot inside me that wasn't doing so hot; them white boys had wanted to beat me within an inch of life, and they measured good. Stands to reason they knocked something loose in the clear thinking part of my head.

"About the second my feet were inside, the door scraped shut behind me. The ceiling wasn't two feet above my head. I couldn't hear even a floorboard creak from inside the Blue. It was like climbing into my own grave.

"And I felt something come right up to my face in that pitch dark. It felt bigger than the Maison Blue itself. I went cold all over. I was already in shock, if not from the beating then for sure from dragging my cracked self across the Blue's lot and through that hole.

" 'What do you want?' I asked the blackness, and it came right back with a silence that stretched out like a line of mountains way off in the distance. I held my breath and heard my heart."

His own voice trails off much the same way—Gillian knows the Adirondacks are out there, past her eyes around the curve of the earth—and now she sees the convertible, black canvas top up for the cold season, slide down the street to her left. It pulls into their driveway, earlier than most days. Her father steps out and gazes up at the roof, his head tipped back. The house is tall and skinny, so unlike her; at more than thirty feet up, it's easy to pretend she doesn't hear him call her name.

"Well, speak of the devil," Mr. Elling says, and this time there is some shine to his laugh. Again she almost sees his hands gripping the chair, ticking back and forth in time with her heartbeat. Those hands he would always describe as coffee up top, cream on the bottom.

"I thought I was messing with something bad under there, something *biblical*, but I was a long way off from being too old to make a boy's mistakes, if ever a man is. To go looking for trouble. So I told the dark, 'I want to be one of the greats.' I was flat on my stomach from having to worm inside that thin space, so can you blame me? I had already assumed a worshipping position. 'I want Betty and me to travel the world and sit in with the giants and to see their eyes like dinner plates when they hear me play.'

"Back then most folks, myself included, hadn't ever heard the story of Robert Johnson, him cradling his old guitar at the crossroads, the devil holding out a heap of genius in exchange for his soul. He'd been dead going on twenty years, but his brand of fire and blues hadn't caught on yet. I hadn't ever heard of Faust and his bargain, neither, so mercy knows what got that idea in my head that night, that old Satan was crouched up in the dirt looking to add one more soul to Hell. I suppose I just wanted to play the trumpet that bad. I laid there in that crawlspace, waiting for fire to light it up, and I knew I'd see a hole gaping in the world, and an oily goat-skinned man. Big perfect square teeth and eyes blacker in the flaming light than I'd ever be. He'd drip all colors on the ground and I'd choke on musk thick in my nose.

"But that quiet just went on and that dark kept pressing against me. I had no business still being conscious so I slept a while."

Mr. Elling falls silent, waiting and watching. Gillian's father climbs out the attic window and sits beside her, still in his suit, checkered tie loosened at his throat. One hand is full of wildflowers tied with string. She stares at his other hand, the one that wastes no time dropping onto her thigh, then peeks over at the sculpted beard on his cheeks, the wiry eyebrows, the hair turning winter at his temples.

A fresh sheet of wind carries again the scent of honeysuckles. A summer smell in the fade of November, a smell from before she came here and she was still allowed to be just a girl with scabbed knees and tangled hair, ranging the woods behind the house she was born in. A girl who had friends at school and a living mother whose arms she could tuck herself beneath.

"I wish you wouldn't come out here, sweetheart," he says. His fingers squeeze, relax.

Her father does not smell of the grave, or the dark under Mr. Elling's jazz club. He is cinnamon gum and aftershave curling through the sweetness of the honeysuckle. The man beside her is calm and king of his world. The one in her memory, just five months younger, panted as he pushed her dress up around her waist.

Since that day in the backseat, she can't run through the woods, trying to keep ahead of her beating, squishing heart. There are no woods anymore. Behind the new house are only more houses, boxing her in at each turn. She can't bury her face in a wild flush of honeysuckle vines like she used to, before, when her mother's chemo was at its worst and her father began coming into her bedroom in the evenings. When it was still just his callused hands, his thin lips emerging from the nest of beard, wanting to be fed.

"You're in a delicate condition," her father says, and gives her the flowers. They smell of nothing.

She looks at him again. Fear and love like the two halves of the gold heart hanging around her neck.

"Some places in the light," Mr. Elling says, "are worse, Gillian." Her father doesn't hear. His face remains soft and his hand kneads and slides. "You're up in the sky but you'd be better off in the dirt under the Blue with the devil you don't know. Fortunately for you, child, I got a tune that was never pressed on no wax."

And now she does see the old man. She sees him lift the trumpet up, the sun flashing off the brass as he brings it to his lips. The chair rocks once, twice, then comes to a stop, the lined face in shadow. And she hears him play, really play, for the first time.

Her father's head turns toward the sound, eyes squinting. The horn comes wafting across, clean and bright, and it's hardly music, she's never heard anything that serves as a point of reference. There are many-petaled syllables, there are quick snaps like sheets on a clothesline in the wind.

"Pretty, isn't it?" she says, and pats the slim space between her and her father. "Here, scooch closer to me." He grins and shifts over, the tacky grit pulling at his slacks. His hip touches hers; his hand drops back down, higher this time, at the crook where her legs join in reluctant heat. And the horn slips into an impossible key, slow notes clouding the air. The two of them gasp as one, only this time he does not gasp in release; nor is her own in tearing pain.

Maybe the atoms of the fall day tremble. They seem to. Briefly, everything is more, the roof slanting up to her like vast, brooding hands, the distant ocean cars full of unwritten stories.

Except her father. He looks so small up here.

For the first time in shameful weeks she aches to have her mother back. She aches even for the glances she'd catch toward the end, as though his fingerprints stood out on her skin like brands. She aches for another chance to sit by her hospital bed, to drape the sheaves of her hair across her mother's (their neighboring shades of rusty orange) and translate the emotion that turned her head away on the pillow.

Her father leans close and breathes into her ear, "It's beautiful. Just like our new family."

Mr. Elling's cheeks go on blowing a mournful joy between his house and hers. The sun rubs the trees and Betty sours, her tone darkening. Her father leans his head against her face; his eyelashes are wet. The halves of her heart gain dreadful weight.

The trumpet dips and rises and cuts out. Mr. Elling says to her, not even having to catch his breath, "That next morning I came out from under the Blue streaked with dirt, Betty tucked beneath my arm. And you know what came traipsing out of that hole with me? A mangy old tabby cat, ordinary as daylight. She glanced at me, licked herself a minute, and went off to find breakfast.

"Later on I'd wonder if the devil had been anywhere near New Orleans that night. And I ain't saying God Himself came down from on high and slithered into that grave beneath the Blue, getting dirt under His fingernails just for me. I haven't ever been able to say that. But it sure feels closer to the truth, somehow. I was all mended up, you see. My back popped as I bent and touched my toes. I ran my tongue across every single one of my teeth.

"And right then I felt I'd given up my soul. I could feel that empty space in me, all hollowed out. Even so, I didn't go seeking fortune and fame, no, not then. I didn't even touch lips to Betty quite yet. I never would go white fella hunting, neither. I put myself on a bus back to South Carolina, and I went to see my own daddy."

She wishes her father would jump. She waits for it, her fingers clenched tight upon the peak of the roof.

"You need to realize," Mr. Elling says, "that your daddy ain't going nowhere on his own. Folks like him never do, and I can't help you there. Betty had something special in her, but she never had no magic, bless her heart. For a minute, though, riding on that bus, I just knew she did."

Her father kisses the hinge of her jaw. She feels his mouth smile.

"Now my mama was a proud, good woman," Mr. Elling says, and there are rough edges in his voice. "The kindest mother a boy could want. She was in the ground hardly a year by then, and my daddy's fists was mostly the reason she was there. And he still walked his little patch of earth, or he did those rare days he wasn't curled up in drink.

"It was surprising cool in Greer when I stepped off that Greyhound. I found him snoring in his bed. I stood over him and me and Betty played him something awful. And we played him something sweet. By the time the sun set on us, he was hanging from the big oak behind the house. I sat on a patch of dirt and watched him twitch and swing. That patch had been scrubbed clean from years of my feet scuffing it, the times I'd sit listless on my old tire swing, hearing my mama cry through the kitchen window. The light painted my daddy in blood and I wasn't happy, but I wasn't sad, neither, no ma'am."

She waits (look at that sky) but her father does nothing. The horn cries out again, only for a beat, and then bleeds into silence. In the distance she expects a wet coughing to start up in its place, but of course Mr. Elling's lungs aren't clogged with age anymore. They are reborn.

And under her palm, Gillian feels the baby kick. The strangeness of it pulls the air from her.

"Now here's where the deal gets sweet," Mr. Elling says. "There is no deal. All a child's got to do is pick up the telephone, and your daddy will face the music, same as mine. I didn't do nothing except pass on and play you a tune. You were a good friend to an old man these last months. But you don't have to be in that story I told. What you want to do is yours to want, and you ain't got to give me or God a thing. Being happy sure would be nice, though."

She turns to her father for a long moment. "Do I look pretty from down there?" she asks, and points down to the lawn, as perfectly trimmed as his beard. Her face is full of heat. The baby kicks again, demanding to be known.

"Of course you do, honey." He smiles inside the beard. "You look just like your mother."

Gillian places her hand against his side. He leans over and kisses her ear, breathes cinnamon fog into her hair. She gently digs her fingers into the meat of him. He giggles for a bare second, twisting away, and then he's gone. By the time she hears the mundane thump on the ground, she's already watching the sky stain at the edges. The air is still flushed with that misplaced summer sweetness. The tree line, the sinking sun, the starlings blur in her eyes.

There's a wink of light across the way, the silver of close-cropped hair and the battered gold of Betty. Mr. Elling lifts her in a wave, says, "Thing about music is in the end, all we can do is face our own. I hope yours has some bop to it." He steps away into his dark. The chair slows and stills.

She raises her own hand for a second. Below her is silence. She knows she should get inside. There's a bundle of shingles she saw once in the garage. They'll need to be dragged up to the attic and opened up. There's a pouched belt heavy with hammer and nails that will buckle around her father's waist. A tearful phone call to make, a swirl of ambulance lights, before she can at last return to her own narrow bed in her own narrow room.

She knows she should get inside. But she goes back to rubbing the curve of her belly in quiet, calming circles.

Michael Wehunt grew up in North Georgia, close enough to the Appalachians to feel them but not quite easily see them. His short fiction has appeared in *Cemetery Dance*, *Shadows & Tall Trees*, *The Journal of Unlikely Entomology*, *Aickman's Heirs*, *The Dark*, and *The Mammoth Book of Cthulhu: New Lovecraftian Fiction*, among others. His debut fiction collection, *Greener Pastures*, is out now from Shock Totem Publications. Find him online at michaelwehunt.com.

*I have chosen the menu of our war as carefully as the stones
in my hair. All my art has bent upon it.*

THE LILY AND THE HORN

Catherynne M. Valente

War is a dinner party.

My ladies and I have spent the dregs of summer making ready. We have hung garlands of pennyroyal and snowberries in the snug, familiar halls of Laburnum Castle, strained cheese as pure as ice for weeks in the caves and the kitchens, covered any gloomy stone with tapestries or stags' heads with mistletoe braided through their antlers. We sent away south to the great markets of Mother-of-Millions for new silks and velvets and furs. We have brewed beer as red as October and as black as December, boiled every growing thing down to jams and pickles and jellies, and set aside the best of the young wines and the old brandies. Nor are we proud: I myself scoured the stables and the troughs for all the strange horses to come. When no one could see me, I buried my face in fresh straw just for the heavy gold scent of it. I've fought for my husband many times, but each time it is new all over again. The smell of the hay like candied earth, with its bitter ribbons of ergot laced through—that is the smell of my youth, almost gone now, but still knotted to the ends of my hair, the line of my shoulders. When I polish the silver candelabras, I still feel half a child, sitting splay-legged on the floor, playing with my mother's scorpions, until the happy evening drew down.

I am the picture of honor. I am the Lily of my House. When last the king came to Laburnum, he told his surly queen: *You see, my plum? That is a woman. Lady Cassava looks as though she has grown out of the very stones of this hall.* She looked at me with interested eyes, and we had much to discuss later when quieter hours came. This is how I serve my husband's ambitions and mine: with the points of my vermilion sleeves, stitched with thread of white and violet and tiny milkstones with hearts of green ice.

With the net of gold and chalcathinite crystals catching up my hair, jewels from our own stingy mountains, so blue they seem to burn. With the great black pots of the kitchens below my feet, sizzling and hissing like a heart about to burst.

It took nine great, burly men to roll the ancient feasting table out of the cellars, its legs as thick as wine barrels and carved with the symbols of their house: the unicorn passant and the wild poppy. They were kings once, Lord Calabar's people. Kings long ago when the world was full of swords, kings in castles of bone, with wives of gold—so they all say. When he sent his man to the Floregilium to ask for me, the Abbess told me to be grateful—not for his fortune (of which there is a castle, half a river, a village and farms, and several chests of pearls fished out of an ocean I shall never see) but for his blood. My children stand near enough from the throne to see its gleam, but they will never have to polish it.

My children. I was never a prodigy in the marriage bed, but what a workhorse my belly turned out to be! Nine souls I gave to the coffers of House Calabar. Five sons and four daughters, and not a one of them dull or stupid. But the dark is a hungry thing. I lost two boys to plague and a girl to the scrape of a rusted hinge. Six left. My lucky sixpence. While I press lemon oil into the wood of the great table with rags that once were gowns, four of my sweethearts giggle and dart through the forest of legs—men, tables, chairs. The youngest of my black-eyed darlings, Mayapple, hurls herself across the silver-and-beryl checked floor and into my arms, saying:

"Mummy, Mummy, what shall I wear to the war tonight?"

She has been at my garden, though she knows better than to explore alone. I brush wisteria pollen from my daughter's dark hair while she tells me all her troubles. "I want to wear my blue silk frock with the emeralds round the collar, but Dittany says it's too plain for battle and I shall look like a frog and shame us."

"You will wear vermillion and white, just as we all will, my little lionfish, for when the king comes we must all wear the colors of our houses so he can remember all our names. But lucky for you, your white will be ermine and your vermillion will be rubies and you will look nothing at all like a frog."

Passiflora, almost a woman herself, as righteous and hard as an antler, straightens her skirts as though she has not been playing at tumble and chase all morning. She looks nothing like me—her hair as red as venom, her eyes the pale blue of moonlit mushrooms. But she will be our fortune, for I have seen no better student of the wifely arts in all my hours. "We oughtn't to wear ermine," she sniffs. "Only the king and the queen can, and the deans of the Floregilium, but only at midwinter. Though why a weasel's skin should signify a king is beyond my mind."

My oldest boy, Narcissus, nobly touches one hand to his breast while with the other hand he pinches his sister savagely and quotes from the articles of peerage. "'The House of Calabar may wear a collar of ermine not wider than one and one half inches, in acknowledgement of their honorable descent from Muscanine, the Gardener Queen, who set the world to growing.'"

But Passiflora knows this. This is how she tests her siblings and teaches them, by putting herself in the wrong over and over. No child can help correcting his sister. They fall over themselves to tell her how stupid she is, and she smiles to herself because they do not think there's a lesson in it.

Dittany, my sullen, sour beauty, frowns, which means she wants something. She was born frowning and will die frowning and through all the years between (may they be long) she will scowl at every person until they bend to her will. A girl who never smiles has such power—what men will do to turn up but one corner of her mouth! She already wears her red war-gown and her circlet of cinnabar poppies. They brings out the color in her grimace.

"Mother," she glowers, "may I milk the unicorns for the feast?"

My daughter and I fetch knives and buckets and descend the stairs into the underworld beneath our home. Laburnum Castle is a mushroom lying only half above ground. Her lacy, lovely parts reach up toward the sun, but the better part of her dark body stretches out through the seastone caverns below, vast rooms and chambers and vaults with ceilings more lovely than any painted chapel in Mother-of-Millions, shot through with frescoes and motifs of copper and quartz and sapphire and opal. Down here, the real work of war clangs and thuds and corkscrews toward tonight. Smells as rich as brocade hang in the kitchens like banners, knives flash out of the mist and the shadows.

I have chosen the menu of our war as carefully as the stones in my hair. All my art has bent upon it. I chose the wines for their color—nearly black, thick and bitter and sharp. I baked the bread to be as sweet as the pudding. The vital thing, as any wife can tell you, is spice. Each dish must taste vibrant, strong, vicious with flavor. Under my eaves they will dine on curried doves, black pepper and peacock marrow soup, blancmange drunk with clove and fiery sumac, sealmeat and fennel pies swimming in garlic and apricots, roast suckling lion in a sauce of brandy, ginger, and pink chilis, and pomegranate cakes soaked in claret.

I am the perfect hostess. I have poisoned it all.

This is how I serve my husband, my children, my king, my house: with soup and wine and doves drowned in orange spices. With wine so dark and strong any breath of oleander would vanish in it. With the quills of sunless fish and liqueurs of wasps and serpents hung up from my rafters like bunches of lavender in the fall.

It's many years now since a man of position would consider taking a wife who was not a skilled poisoner. They come to the Floregilium as to an orphanage and ask not after the most beautiful, nor the sweetest voice, nor the most virtuous, nor the mildest, but the most deadly. All promising young ladies journey to Brugmansia, where the sea is warm, to receive their education. I remember it more clearly than words spoken but an hour ago—the hundred towers and hundred bridges and hundred gates of the Floregilium, a school and a city and a test, mother to all maidens.

I passed beneath the Lily Gate when I was but seven—an archway so twisted with flowers no stone peeked through. Daffodils and hyacinths and columbines, foxglove and moonflower, poppy and peony, each one gorgeous and full, each one brilliant and graceful, each one capable of killing a man with root or bulb of leaf or petal. Another child ran on ahead of me. Her hair was longer than mine, and a better shade of black. Hers had blue inside it, flashing like crystals dissolving in a glass of wine. Her laugh was merrier than mine, her eyes a prettier space apart, her height far more promising. Between the two of us, the only advantage I ever had was a richer father. She had a nice enough name, nice enough to hide a pit of debt.

Once my mother left me to explore her own girlish memories, I followed that other child for an hour, guiltily, longingly, sometimes angrily. Finally, I resolved to give it up, to let her be better than I was if she insisted on it. I raised my arm to lean against a brilliant blue wall and rest—and she appeared as though she had been following me, seizing my hand with the strength of my own father, her grey eyes forbidding.

"Don't," she said.

Don't rest? Don't stop?

"It's chalcathite. Rub up against it long enough and it will stop your blood."

Her name was Yew. She would be the Horn of her House, as I am the Lily of mine. The Floregilium separates girls into Lilies—those who will boil up death in a sealmeat pie, and Horns—those who will send it fleeing with an emerald knife. The Lily can kill in a hundred thousand fascinating ways, root, leaf, flower, pollen, seed. I can brew a tea of lily that will leave a man breathing and laughing, not knowing in the least that he is poisoned, until he dies choking on disappointment at sixty-seven. The horn of a unicorn can turn a cup of wine so corrupted it boils and slithers into honey. We spend our childhoods in a dance of sourness and sweetness.

Everything in the Floregilium is a beautiful murder waiting to unfold. The towers and bridges sparkle ultramarine, fuchsia, silvery, seething green, and should a careless girl trail her fingers along the stones, her skin will blister black. The river teems with venomous, striped fish that take two hours to prepare so that they taste of salt and fresh butter and do not burn out the throat, and three hours to prepare so that they will not strangle the eater until she has gone merrily back to her room and put out her candles. Every meal is an examination, every country walk a trial. No more joyful place exists in all the world. I can still feel the summer rain falling through the hot green flowers of the manchineel tree in the north orchard, that twisted, gnomish thing, soaking up the drops, corrupting the water of heaven, and flinging it onto my arms, hissing, hopping, blistering like love.

It was there, under the sun and moon of the Floregilium, that I read tales of knights and archers, of the days when we fought with swords, with axes and shields, with armor beaten out of steel and grief. Poison was thought cowardice, a woman's weapon, without honor. I wept. I was seven. It seemed absurd to me, absurd and wasteful and unhappy, for all those thousands to die so that two men could sort out who had the right to shit on what scrap of grass. I shook in the moonlight. I looked out into the Agarica where girls with silvery hair tended fields of mushrooms that wanted harvesting by the half-moon for greatest potency. I imagined peasant boys dying in the frost with nothing in their bellies and no embrace from the lord who sent them to hit some other boy on the head until the lord turned into a king. I felt such loneliness—and such relief, that I lived in a more sensible time, when blood on the frost had been seen for obscenity it was.

I said a prayer every night, as every girl in the Floregilium did, to Muscanine, the Gardener Queen, who took her throne on the back of a larkspur blossom and never looked back. Muscanine had no royal blood at all. She was an apothecary's daughter. After the Whistling Plague, such things mattered less. Half of every house, stone or mud or marble, died gasping, their throats closing up so only whines and whistles escaped, and when those awful pipes finally ceased, the low and the middling felt no inclination to start dying all over again so that the lordly could put their names on the ruins of the world. Muscanine could read and write. She drew up new articles of war and when the great and the high would not sign it, they began to choke at their suppers, wheeze at their breakfasts, fall like sudden sighs halfway to their beds. The mind sharpens wonderfully when you cannot trust your tea. And after all, why not? What did arms and strength and the best of all blades matter when the wretched maid could clean a house of heirs in a fortnight?

War must civilize itself, wrote Muscanine long ago. *So say all sensible souls. There can be no end to conflict between earthly powers, but the use of humble arms to settle disputes of rich men makes rich men frivolous in their exercise of war. Without danger to their own persons, no Lord fears to declare battle over the least slight—and why should he? He risks only a little coin and face while we risk all but benefit nothing in victory. There exists in this sphere no single person who does not admit to this injustice. Therefore, we, the humble arms, will no longer consent to a world built upon, around, and out of an immoral seed.*

The rules of war are simple: should Lord Ambition and the Earl of Avarice find themselves in dispute, they shall agree upon a castle or stronghold belonging to neither of them and present themselves there on a mutually agreeable date. They shall break bread together and whoever lives longest wins. The host bends all their wisdom upon vast and varied poisons while the households of Lord Ambition and the Earl bend all their intellect upon healing and the purifying of any wicked substance. And because poisons were once a woman's work—in the early days no knight could tell a nightshade from a dandelion—it became quickly necessary to wed a murderess of high skill.

Of course, Muscanine's civilized rules have bent and rusted with age. No Lord of any means would sit at the martial table himself nowadays—he hires a proxy to choke or swallow in his stead. But there is still some justice in the arrangement—no one sells themselves to battle cheaply. A family may lift itself up considerably on such a fortune as Lord Ambition will pay. No longer do two or three men sit down simply to their meal of honor. Many come to watch the feast of war, whole households, the king himself. There is much sport in it. Great numbers of noblemen seat their proxies in order to declare loyalties and tilt the odds in favor of victory, for surely someone, of all those brawny men, can stomach a silly flower or two.

"But think how marvelous it must have looked." Yew said to me once, lying on my bed surrounded by books like a ribbonmark. "All the banners flying, and the sun on their swords, and the horses with armor so fine even a beast would be proud. Think of the drums and the trumpets and the cries in the dawn."

"I do think of all that, and it sounds ghastly. At least now, everyone gets a good meal out of the business. It's no braver or wiser or stranger to gather a thousand friends and meet another thousand in a field and whack on each other with knives all day. And there are still banners. My father's banners are beautiful. They have a manticore on them, in a ring of oleander. I'll show you someday."

But Yew already knew what my father's banners looked like. She stamped our manticore onto a bezoar for me the day we parted. The clay of the Floregilium mixed with a hundred spices and passed through the gullet of a lion. At least, she said it was a lion.

Soon it will be time to send Dittany and Mayapple. Passiflora will return there when the war is done—she would not miss a chance for practical experience.

Lord Calabar came to the Floregilium when I was a maid of seventeen. Yew's husband came not long after, from far-off Mithridatium, so that the world could be certain we would never see each other again. They came through the Horn Gate, a passage of unicorn horns braided as elegantly as if they were the strands of a girl's hair. He was entitled by his blood to any wife he could convince—lesser nobles may only meet the diffident students, the competent but uninspired, the gentle and the kind who might have enough knowledge to fight, but a weak stomach. They always look so startled when they come a-briding. They come from their castles and holdfasts imagining fierce-jawed maidens with eyes that flash like mercury and hair like rivers of blood, girls like the flowers they boiled into noble deaths, tall and bright and fatal. And they find us wearing leather gloves with stiff cuffs at the elbows, boots to the thigh, and masks of hide and copper and glass that turn our faces into those of wyrms and deepwater fish. But how else to survive in a place where the walls are built of venom, the river longs to kill, and any idle perfume might end a schoolgirl's joke before the punchline? To me those masks are still more lovely than anything a queen might make of rouge and charcoal. I will admit that when I feel afraid, I take mine from beneath my bed and wear it until my heart is whole.

I suppose I always knew someone would come into the vicious garden of my happiness and drag me away from it. What did I learn the uses of mandrake for if not to marry, to fight, to win? I did not want him. He was handsome enough, I suppose. His waist tapered nicely; his shoulders did not slump. His grandfathers had never lost their hair even on their deathbeds. But I was sufficient. I and the Floregilium and the manchineel tree and my Yew swimming in the river as though nothing could hurt her, because nothing could. He said I could call him Henry. I showed him my face.

"Mummy, the unicorns are miserable today," Dittany frowns, and my memory bursts into a rain of green flowers.

I have never liked unicorns. I have met wolves with better dispositions. I have seen paintings of them from nations where they do not thrive—tall, pale, sorrowfully noble creatures holding the wisdom of eternity as a bit in their muzzles. I understand the desire to make them so. I, too, like things to match. If something is useful, it ought to be beautiful. And yet, the world persists.

Unicorns mill around my daughter's legs, snorting and snuffling at her hands, certain she has brought them the half-rotted meat and flat beer they love best. Unicorns are the size of boars, round of belly and stubby of leg, covered in long, curly grey fur that mats viciously in the damp and smells of wet books. Their long, canny faces are something like horses, yes, but also something like dogs, and their teeth have something of the shark about them. And in the center, that short, gnarled nub of bone, as pure and white as the soul of a saint. Dittany opens her sack and tosses out greying lamb rinds, half-hardened cow's ears. She pours out leftover porter into their trough. The beasts gurgle and trill with delight, gobbling their treasure, snapping at each other to establish and reinforce their shaggy social order, the unicorn king and his several queens and their kingdom of offal.

"Why do they do it?" Dittany frowns. "Why do they shovel in all that food when they know they could die?"

A unicorn looks up at me with red, rheumy eyes and wheezes. "Why did men go running into battle once upon a time, when they knew they might die? They believe their shield is stronger than the other fellow's sword. They believe their Horn is stronger than the other fellow's Lily. They believe that when they put their charmed knives into the pies, they will shiver and turn red and take all the poison into the blade. They believe their toadstones have the might of gods."

"But nobody is stronger than you, are they, Mum?"

"Nobody, my darling."

He said I could call him Henry. He courted me with a shaker of powdered sapphires from a city where elephants are as common as cats. A dash of blue like so much salt would make any seething feast wholesome again. *Well, unless some clever Lily has used moonseeds, or orellanine, or unicorn milk, or the venom of a certain frog who lives in the library and is called Phillip. Besides, emerald is better than sapphire.* But I let him think his jewels could buy life from death's hand. It is a nice thing to think. Like those beautiful unicorns glowing softly in silver thread.

I watch my daughter pull at the udders of our unicorns, squeezing their sweaty milk into a steel pail, for it would sizzle through wood or even bronze as easily as rain through leaves. She is deft and clever with her hands, my frowning girl, the mares barely complain. When I milk them, they bite and howl. The dun sky opens up into bands like pale ribs, showing a golden heart beating away at dusk. Henry Calabar kisses me when I am seventeen and swears my lips are poison from which he will never recover, and his daughter feeds a unicorn a marrow bone, and his son calls down from the ramparts that the king is coming, he is coming, hurry, hurry, and under all this I see only Yew, stealing into my room on that last night in the country of being young, drawing me a bath in the great copper tub, a bath swirling with emerald dust, with green and shimmer. We climbed in, dunking our heads, covering each other with the strangely milky smell of emeralds, clotting our black hair with glittering sand. Yew took my hand and we ran out together into the night, through the quiet streets of the Floregilium, under the bridges and over the water until we came to the manchineel tree in the north orchards, and she held me tight to her beneath its vicious flowers until the storm came, and when the storm came we kissed for the last time as the rain fell through those green flowers and hissed on our skin, vanishing into emerald steam, we kissed and did not burn.

They call him the Hyacinth King and he loves the name. He got it when he was young and ambitious and his wife won the Third Sons' War for him before she had their first child. Hyacinth roots can look so much like potatoes. They come into the hall without grandeur, for we are friends, or friendly enough. I have always had a care to be pregnant when the king came calling, for he has let it be known he enjoys my company, and it takes quite a belly to put him off. But not this time, nor any other to come. He kisses the children one by one, and then me. It is too long a kiss but Henry and I tolerate a great deal from people who have not gotten sick of us after a decade or two. The queen, tall and grand, takes my hand and asks after the curried doves, the wine, the mustard pots. Her eyes shine. Two fresh hyacinths pin her cloak to her dress.

"I miss it," she confesses. "No one wants to fight me anymore. Sometimes I poison the hounds out of boredom. But then I serve them their breakfast in unicorn skulls and they slobber and yap on through another year or nine. Come, tell me what's in the soup course. I have heard you've a new way of boiling crab's eyes to mimic the Whistling Plague. That's how you killed Lord Vervain's lad, isn't it?"

"You flatter me. That was so long ago, I hardly remember," I tell her.

She and her husband take their seats above the field of war—our dining hall, sparkling with fire and finery like wet morning grass. They call for bread and wine—the usual kind, safe as yeast. The proxies arrive with trumpets and drums. *No different, Yew, I think.* My blood prickles at the sound. She is coming. She will come. My castle fills with peasant faces— faces scrubbed and perfumed as they have never been before. Each man standing in for his Lord wears his Lord's own finery. They come in velvet and silk, in lace and furs, with circlets on their heads and rings on their fingers, with sigils embroidered on their chests and curls set in their hair. And each of them looks as elegant and lordly as anyone born to it. All that has ever stood between a duke and a drudge is a bath. She is coming. She will come. The nobles in the stalls sit high above their mirrors at the table, echoes and twins and stutters. It is a feasting hall that looks more like an operating theater with each passing war.

Henry sits beside his king. We are only the castle agreed upon—we take no part. The Hyacinth King has put up a merchant's son in his place—the boy looks strong, his chest like the prow of a ship. But it's only vanity. I can take the thickness from his flesh as fast as that of a thin man. More and more come singing through the gates. The Hyacinth King wishes to take back his ancestral lands in the east, and the lands do not consider themselves to be ancestral. It is not a small war, this time. I have waited for this war. I have wanted it. I have hoped. Perhaps I have whispered to the Hyacinth King when he looked tenderly at me that those foreign lords have no right to his wheat or his wine. Perhaps I have sighed to my husband that if only the country were not so divided we would not have to milk our own unicorns in our one castle. I would not admit to such quiet talk. I have slept only to fight this battle on dreaming grounds, with dreaming knives.

Mithridatium is in the east. She is coming. She will come.

And then she steps through the archway and into my home—my Yew, my emerald dust, my manchineel tree, my burning rain. Her eyes find mine in a moment. We have done this many times. She wears white and pale blue stitched with silver—healing colors, pure colors, colors that could never harm. She is a candle with a blue flame. As she always did, she looks like me drawn by a better hand, a kinder hand. She hardly looks older than my first daughter would have been, had she lived. Perhaps living waist-deep in gentling herbs is better than my bed of wicked roots. Her children beg mutely for her attention with their bright eyes—three boys, and how strange her face looks on boys! She puts her hands on their shoulders. I reach out for Dittany and Mayapple, Passiflora, and Narcissus. *Yes, these are mine. I have done this with my years, among the rest.* Her husband takes her hand with the same gestures as Henry might. He begs for nothing mutely with his bright eyes. They are not bad men. But they are not us.

I may not speak to her. The war has already begun the moment she and I rest our bones in our tall chairs. The moment the dinner bell sounds. Neither of us may rise or touch any further thing—all I can do and have done is complete and I am not allowed more. Afterward, we will not be permitted to talk—what if some soft-hearted Horn gave away her best secrets to a Lily? The game would be spoilt, the next war decided between two women's unguarded lips. It would not do. So we sit, our posture perfect, with death between us.

The ladies will bring the peacock soup, laced with belladonna and serpent's milk, and the men (and lady, some poor impoverished lord has sent his own unhappy daughter to be his proxy, and I can hardly look at her for pity) of Mithridatium, of the country of Yew, will stir it with spoons carved from the bones of a white stag, and turn it sweet—perhaps. They will tuck toadstones and bezoars into the meat of the curried doves and cover the blancmange with emerald dust like so much green salt. They will smother the suckling lion in pennyroyal blossoms and betony leaves. They will drink my wine from her cups of unicorn horn. They will sauce the pudding with vervain. And each time a course is served, I will touch her. My spices and her talismans. My stews and her drops of saints' blood like rain. My wine and her horn. My milk and her emeralds. Half the world will die between us, but we will swim in each other and no one will see.

The first soldier turns violet and shakes himself apart into his plate of doves and twenty years ago Yew kisses emeralds from my mouth under the manchineel tree while the brutal rain hisses away into air.

Catherynne M. Valente is the *New York Times* bestselling author of over two dozen works of fiction and poetry, including *Palimpsest*, the Orphan's Tales series, *Deathless*, *Radiance*, and the crowdfunded phenomenon *The Girl Who Circumnavigated Fairyland in a Ship of Own Making*. She is the winner of the Andre Norton, Tiptree, Mythopoeic, Rhysling, Lambda, Locus, and Hugo Awards. She has been a finalist for the Nebula and World Fantasy Awards. She lives on an island off the coast of Maine with a small but growing menagerie of beasts, some of which are human.

Not with a bang, but a whimper.

SNOW

Dale Bailey

They took shelter outside of Boulder, in a cookie-cutter subdivision that had seen better days. Five or six floor plans, Dave Kerans figured, brick façades and tan siding, crumbling streets and blank cul-de-sacs, no place you'd want to live. By then, Felicia had passed out from the pain, and the snow beyond the windshield of Lanyan's black Yukon had thickened into an impenetrable white blur.

It had been a spectacular run of bad luck, starting with the first news of the virus via the satellite radio in the Yukon: three days of disease vectors and infection rates, symptoms and speculation. Calm voices gave way to anxious ones; anxious ones succumbed to panic. The last they heard was the sound of a commentator retching. Then flat silence, nothing at all the length of the band, NPR, CNN, the Outlaw Country Station, and suddenly no one was anxious to go home, none of them, not Kerans and Felicia, not Lanyan or his new girlfriend, Natalie, lithe and blonde and empty-headed as the last player in his rotating cast of female companions.

On the third day of the catastrophe—when it became clear that humanity just might be toast—they'd powwowed around a fire between the tents, passing hand-to-hand the last of the primo dope Lanyan had procured for the trip. Lanyan always insisted on the best: tents and sleeping bags that could weather a winter on the Ross Ice Shelf, a high-end water-filtration system, a portable gas stove with more bells and whistles than the full-size one Kerans and Felicia used at home, even a Benelli R1 semi-automatic hunting rifle (*just in case*, Lanyan had said). The most remote location, as well: somewhere two thousand feet above Boulder, where the early November deciduous trees began to give way to Pinyon pine and Rocky Mountain juniper. Zero cell-phone reception, but by that time there was nobody left to call, or anyway none of them cared to make the descent and see. The broadcasts had started calling it the red death by then. Kerans appreciated the allusion: airborne, an incubation period of less than twenty-four hours, blood leaking from your eyes, your nostrils, your pores and, toward the end—twelve hours if you were lucky, another twenty-four if you weren't—gushing from your mouth with every cough. No-thank-yous all around. Safe enough at seventy-five-hundred feet, at least for the time being—the time being, Lanyan insisted, lasting at least through the winter and maybe longer.

"We have maybe two weeks' worth of food," Kerans protested.

"We'll scout out a cabin and hunker down for the duration," Lanyan said. "If we have to, we'll hunt."

There was that at least. Lanyan was a master with the Benelli. They wouldn't starve—and Kerans didn't have any more desire to contract the red death than the rest of them.

All had been going according to plan. Inside a week they'd located a summer cabin, complete with a larder of canned goods, and had started gathering wood for the stove. Then Felicia had fallen. A single bad step on a bed of loose scree, and that had been it for the plan. When Kerans cut her jeans away, he saw that the leg had broken at the shin. Yellow bone jutted through the flesh. Blood was everywhere. Felicia screamed when Lanyan set the bone, yanking it back into true, or something close to true, splinting it with a couple of backpack poles, and binding the entire bloody mess with a bandage they found in a first-aid kit under the sink. The bandage had soaked through almost immediately. Kerans, holding her hand, thought for the first time in half a dozen years of their wedding, the way she'd looked in her dress and the way he'd felt inside, like the luckiest man on the planet.

Luck.

It had all turned sour on them.

"I'm taking her down, first thing in the morning," he told Lanyan.

"What for? You heard the radio."

"You want to die, too?" Natalie asked.

"I don't want *her* to die," Kerans said. That was the point. Without help, she was doomed, anybody could see that. There wasn't a hell of a lot any of them could do on their own. A venture capitalist and a college English professor and something else, a Broncos cheerleader maybe, who knew what Natalie did? "Even if it's as bad as we think it is down there," he added, "we can still find a pharmacy, antibiotics, whatever. You think there's any chance her leg isn't going to get infected?"

Grim-faced, Lanyan had turned away. "I think it's a bad idea."

"You have a better one?"

"How are you going to get down, Dave? You planning to use the Yukon?"

Kerans laughed in disbelief. "I can't believe you'd even say that."

"What?" Lanyan said, as if he didn't know.

"You were the best man at my wedding. Hell, you introduced me to Felicia."

"We have to think of ourselves now," Natalie said.

"Fuck you, Natalie," Kerans said, and that had been the end of the conversation.

He was wakeful most of the night that followed. Felicia was feverish. "Am I going to die, Dave?" she'd asked in one of her lucid moments. "Of course not," he'd responded, the lie cleaving his heart.

Lanyan woke him at dawn. They stood shivering on the porch of the cabin and watched clouds mass among the peaks. The temperature had plunged overnight. The air smelled like snow.

"You win," Lanyan said. "We'll go down to Boulder."

The snow caught them when they were winding down the rutted track from the cabin, big lazy flakes sifting through the barren trees to deliquesce on the Yukon's acres of windshield. Nothing to worry about, Kerans thought in the backseat, cradling Felicia's head in his lap. But the temperature—visible in digital blue on the dash—continued to plummet, twenty-five, fifteen, ten; by the time they hit paved road, a good hour and a half from the cabin, and itself a narrow, serpentine stretch of crumbling asphalt, the weather had gotten serious. The wipers carved slanting parabolas in the snow. Beyond the windows, the world had receded into a white haze.

Lanyan hunched closer to the wheel.

They crept along, pausing now and again to inch around an abandoned vehicle.

"We should have stayed where we were," Natalie said, and the silence that followed seemed like assent.

But it was too late to turn back now.

Finally the road widened into a four-lane highway, clogged with vehicles. They plowed onward anyway, weaving drunkenly among the cars. By the time they reached the outskirts of Boulder, the headlights stabbed maybe fifteen feet into the swirling snow.

"I can't see a thing," Lanyan said. They turned aside into surface streets, finding their way at last into the decaying subdivision. They picked a house at random, a rancher with a brick façade in an empty cul-de-sac. The conventions of civilization held. Lanyan and Kerans scouted it out, while the women waited in the Yukon. They knocked, shouting, but no one came. Finally, they tested the door. It had been left unlocked; the owners had departed in a hurry, Kerans figured, fleeing the contagion. He wondered if they'd passed them dead somewhere on the highway, or if they'd made it into the higher altitudes in time. The house itself was empty. Maybe they'd gotten lucky. Maybe the frigid air would kill the virus before it could kill them. Maybe, Kerans thought. Maybe.

They settled Felicia on the sectional sofa in the great room, before the unblinking eye of the oversized flatscreen. Afterward, they searched the place more thoroughly, dosing Felicia with the amoxicillin and oxycodone they found in the medicine cabinet. Then the food in the pantry, tools neatly racked in the empty garage, a loaded pistol in a bedside table. Natalie tucked it in the belt of her jeans. Kerans flipped light switches, adjusted the thermostat, flicked on the television. Nothing. How quickly it all fell apart. They hunched around a portable radio instead: white noise all across the dial.

Welcome to the end of the world, it said.

Not with a bang, but a whimper.

The snow kept coming, gusts of it, obscuring everything a dozen feet beyond the windows, then unveiling it in quick flashes: the blurred limb of a naked tree, the shadow of the Yukon at the curb. Kerans stood at the window as night fell, wondering what he'd expected to find. A hospital? A doctor? The hospitals must have been overwhelmed from the start, the doctors first to go.

The streetlights snapped alight—solar-charged batteries, the death throes of the world he'd grown up in. They illuminated clouds of billowing white that in other circumstances Kerans would have found beautiful. Cold groped at the window. He turned away.

Lanyan and Natalie had scrounged a handful of tealight candles. By their flickering luminescence, the great room took on a cathedral air. Darkness encroached from the corners and gathered in shrouds at the ceiling. They ate pork and beans warmed over the camp stove, spread their sleeping bags on the carpet, and talked. The same goddamn conversation they'd had for days now: *surely we're not the only ones* and *how many?* and *where?* and *what if?*

"We're probably already dying," Natalie said, turning a baleful eye on Kerans. "Well, we're down here now," she said. "What's your plan, Einstein?"

"I don't have a plan. I didn't figure on the snow."

"You didn't figure on a lot of things."

"Cut it out," Lanyan said.

"We didn't have to do this, Cliff," Natalie said.

"What did you expect me to do? I've known Felicia for years. I've known Dave longer. It's not like we had access to weather reports."

No, Kerans thought, that was another thing gone with the old world. Just like that. Everything evaporated.

By then the cold had become black, physical.

Kerans got to his feet. He tucked Felicia's sleeping bag into the crevices of the sofa. She moaned. Her eyes fluttered. She reached for his hand.

Kerans shook two oxycodone out of the bottle.

"These'll help you sleep."

"Will you stay with me, Dave?"

All the way to the end, he thought, and he knew then that at some level, if only half-consciously, he had accepted what he had known in his heart back at the cabin. She was gone. She'd been gone the moment she'd slipped on that bed of scree. And he'd laughed, he remembered that, too. Whoops, he'd said, and she'd said, *I'm hurt, Dave,* her voice plaintive, frightened, tight with agony. He'd never heard her use that voice in seventeen years of marriage, and he knew then that she was beyond help. There was no help to be had. Yet Lanyan had surrendered the Yukon all the same, and they had knocked on the door before barging into this house, just as they had knocked on the door of the summer cabin in the mountains before that. How long, he wondered, before they reverted to savagery?

"Will you stay with me, Dave?" she said.

"Of course."

He slid into his sleeping bag. They held hands by candlelight until the oxycodone hit her and her fingers went limp. He tucked her arm under her sleeping bag—he could smell the wound, already suppurating with infection—and lay back.

The last of the tealights burned out.

Kerans glanced at the luminescent dial of his watch. Nine-thirty.

The streetlight's spectral blue glow suffused the air.

He closed his eyes, but sleep eluded him. An endless loop unspooled against the dark screens of his eyelids: Felicia's expression as the earth slipped out from under her feet. His helpless whoop of laughter. *I'm hurt, Dave.*

He opened his eyes.

"You awake, Cliff?" he said.

"Yeah."

"You think Natalie's right? We're all going to wind up coughing up blood in twenty-four hours or so?"

"I don't know."

"Maybe the snow," Kerans said. "Maybe the cold has killed the virus."

"Maybe."

They were silent.

"One way or the other, we'll find out, I guess," Lanyan said.

Snow ticked at the windows like fingernails. Let me in. Let me in.

"About the Yukon—" Kerans said.

"It doesn't matter, Dave. You'd have done the same for me."

Would he? Kerans wondered. He liked to think so.

"I'm sorry I was an asshole," Lanyan said.

"It doesn't matter."

"Felicia's going to be okay."

"Sure she is. I know."

Kerans gazed across the room at the shadowy mound of the other man in his sleeping bag.

"What do you figure happened?"

"Hell, I don't know. You heard the radio as well as I did. Something got loose from a military lab. Terrorists. Maybe just a mutation. Ebola, something like that."

Another conversation they'd had a dozen times. It was like picking a scab.

A long time passed. Kerans didn't know how long it was.

"It doesn't matter, I guess," he said, adrift between sleep and waking.

"Not anymore," Lanyan said, and the words chased Kerans down a dark hole into sleep.

Lanyan woke him into that same unearthly blue light, and for a moment Kerans didn't know where he was. Only that strange undersea radiance, his sense of time and place out of joint, a chill undertow of anxiety. Then it all came flooding back, the plague, Felicia's fall, the blizzard.

Lanyan's expression echoed his unease.

"Get up," he said.

"What's going on?"

"Just get up."

Kerans followed him to the window. Natalie crouched there, gazing out into the sheets of blowing snow. She held the pistol in one hand.

"What is it?" he whispered.

"There's something in the snow," she said.

"What?"

"I heard it. It woke me up."

"You hear anything, Cliff?"

Lanyan shrugged.

Wind tore at the house, rattling gutters. Kerans peered into the snow, but if there was anything out there, he couldn't see it. He couldn't see anything but a world gone white. The streetlamp loomed above them, a bulb of fuzzy blue light untethered from the earth.

"Heard what?" he asked.

"I don't know. It woke me. Something in the snow."

"The wind," Kerans said.

"It sounded like it was alive."

"Listen to it blow out there. You could hear anything in that. The brain, it"—he hesitated—

"What?" Natalie said.

"All I'm saying is, it's easy enough to imagine something like that. Voices in the wind. Shapes in the snow."

Natalie's breath fogged the window. "I didn't imagine anything."

"Look," he said. "It's late. We're all tired. You could have imagined something, that's all I'm saying."

"I said I didn't imagine it."

And then, as though the very words had summoned it into being, a thin shriek carved the wind—alien, predatory, unearthly as the cry of a hunting raptor. The snow muffled it, made it hard to track how far away it was, but it was closer than Kerans wanted it be. It held for a moment, wavering, and dropped away. A heartbeat passed, then two, and then came an answering cry, farther away. Kerans swallowed hard, put his back to the wall, and slid to the floor. He pulled his knees up, dropped his head between them. He could feel the cold radiating from the window, shivering erect the tiny hairs on his neck. He looked up. His breath unfurled in the gloom. They were both watching him, Lanyan and Natalie.

"It's the wind," he said. Hating himself as he said it, hating this new weakness he'd discovered in himself, this inability to face what in his heart he knew to be true.

Came a third cry then, still farther away.

"Jesus," Lanyan said.

"They're surrounding us," Natalie said.

"They're?" Kerans said. "They're? Who the hell do you think could be out there in that?"

Natalie turned and met his gaze. "I don't know," she said.

They checked the house, throwing deadbolts, locking interior doors and windows. Kerans didn't get the windows. You wanted to get inside bad enough, you just broke the glass. Yet there was something comforting in sliding the little tongue into its groove all the same. Symbolic barriers. Like cavemen, drawing circles of fire against the night.

As for sleep, forget it.

He leaned against the sofa, draped in his sleeping bag, envying Felicia the oblivion of the oxycodone. Her skin was hot to the touch, greasy with perspiration. He could smell, or imagined he could smell, the putrescent wound, the inadequate dressing soaked with gore.

Across the room sat Lanyan, the Benelli flat across his legs. At the window, her back propped against the wall, Natalie, cradling the pistol in her lap. Kerans felt naked with just the hunting knife at his belt.

The snow kept coming, slanting down past the streetlamp, painting the room with that strange, swimming light. Lanyan's face looked blue and cold, like the face of a dead man. Natalie's, too. And he didn't even want to think about Felicia, burning up under the covers, sweating out the fever of the infection.

"We should look at her leg," he said.

"And do what?" Natalie responded, and what could he say to that because there was nothing to do, Kerans knew that as well as anyone, yet he felt compelled in his impotence to do something, anything, even if it was just stripping back the sleeping bag and staring at the wound, stinking and inflamed, imperfectly splinted, oozing blood and yellow pus.

"Just keep doling out those drugs," Lanyan said, and Kerans knew he meant the oxycodone, not the amoxicillin, which couldn't touch an infection of this magnitude, however much he prayed—and he was not a praying man. He couldn't help recalling his mother, dying in agony from bone cancer: the narrow hospital room, stinking of antiseptic, with its single forlorn window; the doctor, a hulking Greek, quick to anger, who spoke in heavily accented English. *We're into pain management now,* he'd said.

"How much is left?" Natalie said, and Kerans realized that he'd been turning the prescription bottle in his hands.

"Ten, maybe fifteen pills."

"Not enough," she said. "I don't think it's enough," and a bright fuse of hatred for her burned through him for giving voice to thoughts he could barely acknowledge as his own.

After that, silence.

Kerans's eyes were grainy with exhaustion, yet he could not sleep.

None of them could sleep.

Unspeaking, they listened for voices in the storm.

At two, they came: one, two, three metallic screeches in the wind.

Lanyan took one window, Natalie the other, lifting her pistol.

Kerans stayed with Felicia. She was stirring now, coming out of her oxycodone haze. "What is it?" she said.

"Nothing. It's nothing."

But it was something.

"There," Natalie said, but she needn't have said it at all.

Even from his place by the sofa, Kerans saw it: a blue shadow darting past the window, little more than a blur, seven feet long or longer, horizontal to the earth, tail lashing, faster than anything that size had any right to be, faster than anything human. There and gone again, obscured by a veil of blowing snow.

Kerans's own words mocked him. Imagination. Shapes in the snow.

He thought of that icy tapping, like fingernails at the window.

Let me in.

Felicia said, "Dave? What is it, Dave?"

"It's nothing," he said.

Silence prevailed. Shifting veils of snow.

"What the hell was that thing?" Lanyan said.

And Natalie from her window. "Let's play a game."

Nobody said a word.

"The game is called 'What if?'" she said.

"What are you talking about?" Kerans said.

"What if you were an alien species?"

"Oh, come on," Kerans said, but Lanyan was grim and silent.

"Way ahead of us technologically, capable of travel between stars."

"This is crazy, Dave," Felicia said. "What is she talking about?"

"Nothing. It's nothing."

"And what if you wanted to clear a planet for colonization?"

"You read too much science fiction."

"Shut the hell up, Dave," Lanyan said.

"We're intelligent. They would try to—"

"We're vermin," Natalie said. "And what I would do, I would engineer some kind of virus and wipe out ninety-nine-percent of the vermin. Like fumigating a fucking house."

"And then?" Lanyan said.

"Then I'd send in the ground troops to mop up."

Kerans snorted.

"Dave—"

"It's craziness, that's all," he said. He said, "Here, these'll help you sleep."

Nothing then. Nothing but wind and snow and the sound of silence in the room.

After a time, they resumed their posts on the floor.

Felicia, weeping, lapsed back into drugged sleep.

"We're going to have to get to the Yukon," Natalie said.

"We can't see a fucking thing out there," Kerans said.

"At first light. Maybe the snow will stop by then."

"And if it doesn't?" Lanyan said.

"We make a run for it."

"What about Felicia?" Kerans said.

"What about her?"

Kerans looked at his watch. It was almost three o'clock.

He must have dozed, for he came awake abruptly, jarred from sleep by a distant thud. A dream, he thought, his pulse hammering. It must have been a dream—a nightmare inside this nightmare of dark and endless snow, of a plague-ravished world and Felicia dying in agony. But it was no dream. Lanyan and Natalie had heard it, too. They were already up, their weapons raised, and even as he stumbled to his feet, shedding like water the sleeping bag across his shoulders, it came again: a thump against the back of the house, muffled by snow and the intervening rooms.

"What is it?" Felicia said, her voice drowsy with oxycodone.

"Nothing," he said. "It was nothing. A branch must have fallen."

"That was no branch," Natalie said. "Not unless it fell twice."

And twice more after that, two quick blows, and a third, and then silence, a submarine hush so deep and pervasive that Kerans could hear the boom of his heart.

"Maybe a tree came down."

"You know better," Lanyan said.

"Dave, I'm scared," Felicia whispered.

"We're all scared," Natalie said.

Felicia began softly to weep.

"Shut her the fuck up," Natalie said.

"Natalie—"

"I said shut her up."

"It hurts," Felicia said. "I'm afraid." Kerans knelt by the sectional and kissed her chill lips. Her breath bloomed in the cold air, sweet with the stink of infection, and he didn't think he'd ever loved her more in his life than he did at that moment. "There's nothing to be afraid of," he whispered, wiping away her tears with the ball of his thumb. "It's just the wind." But even she was past believing him, for the wind had died. The snow fell soft and straight through the air. The streetlamp was a blue halo against the infinite blackness of space. Natalie's game came back to Kerans—what if—and a dark surf broke and receded across the shingles of his heart. Felicia took his hand and squeezed his fingers weakly. "Just don't leave me here," she said. "Don't leave me here to die."

"Never."

The glitter of shattering glass splintered the air. Felicia screamed, a short, sharp bark of terror—

"Shut her up," Natalie snapped.

—and in the silence that followed, in the shifting purple shadow of the great room with its sectional sofa and the grey rectangle of the flatscreen and their sleeping bags like the shucked skins of enormous snakes upon the floor, Kerans heard someone—something—

—*let's play a game the game is called what if*—

—test the privacy lock of a back bedroom: a slow turn to either side. *Click. Click.*

Silence.

Felicia whimpered. Kerans blew a cloud of vapor into the still air. He clutched Felicia's fingers. He remembered a time when they had made hasty love in the bathroom at a friend's cocktail party, half-drunk, mad with passion for each other. The memory came to him with pristine clarity. He felt tears upon his cheeks.

And still the silence held.

Lanyan snapped off the safety of the Benelli.

Natalie put her back to the foyer wall, reached out, and flipped the deadbolt of the front door. She pushed it a few inches ajar. Snow dusted the threshold.

"The Yukon locked?" she whispered.

"No."

Once again, the thing tested the lock.

"Dave, don't leave me—"

"Natalie—"

She froze him with a glance. God help him, he didn't want to die. He choked back a sob. They had wanted children. They had tried for them. In vitro, the whole nine yards.

"I won't leave you," he whispered.

Then the privacy lock snapped, popping like a firecracker. The door banged back. Something came, hurtling down the hallway: something big, hunched over the floor, and God, God, shedding pieces of itself, one, two, three as it burst into the room. Guns spat bright tongues of fire, a barrage of deafening explosions. The impact flung the thing backward, but the pieces, two- or three-foot lengths of leg-pumping fury, kept coming. Snapping the Benelli from target to target, Lanyan took two of them down. Natalie stopped the third one not three feet from Keran's throat. It rolled on the floor, curving needle-teeth snapping, leathery hide gleaming in the snow-blown light, and was still.

Those alien cries echoed in the darkness.

"Time to go," Natalie said.

Lanyan moved to the door.

Felicia clutched at Kerans' hand, seizing him with a tensile strength he did not know she still possessed. The cocktail party flashed through his mind. They had wanted children—

"Felicia—" Kerans said. "Help me—"

"No time," Natalie said.

And Lanyan: "I'm sorry, Dave—"

The moment hung in equipoise. Kerans wrenched his hand away.

"Time to go," Natalie said again. "We can't wait. You have to decide."

She ducked into the night. A moment later, Lanyan followed.

Glass shattered at the back of the house, one window, two windows, three.

"Don't leave me, Dave," Felicia sobbed. "Don't leave me."

Outside the Yukon roared to life.

"Dave," Felicia said, "I'm scared."

"Shhh," he said, brushing closed her eyelids with his fingers. "Never. I'll never leave you. I love you."

He bent to press his lips to hers. His fingers fumbled at his belt. They closed around the blade.

A moment later, he was running for the Yukon.

A winner of both the Shirley Jackson Award and the International Horror Guild Award, **Dale Bailey** is the author of *The End of the End of Everything: Stories* and *The Subterranean Season*, both published in 2015, as well as *The Fallen, House of Bones, Sleeping Policemen* (with Jack Slay, Jr.), and *The Resurrection Man's Legacy and Other Stories*. His work has twice been a finalist for the Nebula Award and once for the Bram Stoker Award, and has been adapted for Showtime Television's *Masters of Horror*. He lives in North Carolina with his family.

There was something I wasn't seeing, a presence weighting the scene in front of me. It was waiting at the corners of my vision, huge and old and empty. Or, not empty so much as hungry.

CORPSEMOUTH

John Langan

I

In July of 1994, the year after my father died, my mother, youngest sister, and I went to Greenock, Scotland, from which my parents had emigrated to the United States almost thirty years before. Mom and Mackenzie flew over for a month; I joined them two weeks into their trip. The three of us stayed with my father's mother, who owned a semi-detached house set near the top of a modest hill. From the window of its front bedroom, on the second storey, you could look out on the River Clyde, here a tidal estuary, which had allowed the region to become a center for British shipbuilding for over two centuries. Two miles across, the river's far shore was layered with green hills, the Trossachs, long and sloping, the markers of geological traumas ancient and extreme.

I actually arrived a day late, because of a mechanical difficulty with my plane that was not detected until we were ready to pull away from the gate. The pilot's intimation of it in his message to the passengers caused a woman seated ahead of me to start shouting, "Oh my God, I had a dream about this last night. We're going to crash. The plane is going to crash. We can't take off." Fortunately for her—and possibly, for the rest of us—we were removed from the plane and bused to one of the airport's hotels, where we were put up overnight.

I spent part of that time trying to phone someone on this side of the Atlantic who could call my relatives overseas to let them know not to go to the airport for me. I had no luck, and passed the remainder of the night restless from the knowledge that I would have to be up early if I didn't want to miss the return bus to the terminal. I wasn't certain why I had taken the time off from the optometrists' office I was managing for this trip. Obviously, it had to do with the loss of my father, with an effort to address the gap his death had left in my life by returning to the place of his birth and early life, by spending time with the members of his family who still lived there, as if geography and blood might help to heal the edges of what remained a ragged wound. Already, though, my plan seemed off to a dubious start.

II

The sleep I managed was troubled. I fell into a dream in which I watched my father as he sat with a handful of other men in the back of a van speeding along a narrow street that ran between high brick walls blackened by age. Overhead, what might have been the gnarled branches of trees peeked down from the tops of the walls. My father looked as he had during my later childhood, slender, his hair already fled from the top of his head. He was dressed in a denim worksheet and jeans, as were the rest of the men. Although he did not look at me, I was certain he knew that I was watching him, and I waited for him to turn to me and say something. He did not.

III

Despite my concerns, I woke in plenty of time, and had an uneventful flight across the ocean, and was met at the airport in Glasgow by one of my older cousins and my mother and sister. They had checked the flight information before leaving for my original arrival, learned of the alteration to my trip, and saved themselves the earlier run to the airport. Although the ride to my grandmother's wasn't especially long, I was still feeling the effects of my night in the airport hotel (I was too much of a nervous flyer to have napped during my time in the air), and I struggled to hold open my eyelids, which felt weighted with lead. I had a confused impression of stone and steel buildings, of cars and trucks flowing around us, of a strip of blue river speeding by on my right. When we arrived at my grandmother's house, I succeeded in greeting her and one of my aunts and a couple of my cousins, but it wasn't long before I climbed the stairs to the front bedroom, assuring everyone that I just needed a little nap, and slept straight through to the next morning.

IV

Somewhere deep in that sleep, I dreamed I was standing at the picture window overlooking the Clyde. It was night, but the sky shone silver-white with the gloaming, casting sufficient light for me to see that the river was dry. Its bed was a wide, muddy trench bordered by rocky margins draped with seaweed. At points further out in the mud, boulders sat alone and in clumps.

Thousands, tens of thousands of fish lay on the mud and rocks, their long, silver bodies catching the light. Most of them were dead; a few still thrashed. All along the riverbed, a great line of people walked downstream, towards the ocean. Male, female, old, young, tall, short, fat, thin: they were as varied a group as you could assemble. As was their dress: some were in their work clothes, some their pajamas; some in formal wear, some in hospital gowns; some wearing the uniforms of their professions, some stark naked. The only detail they shared was their bare feet. They trudged through mud that sucked at their ankles, that slurped at their shins, that surged around their thighs. If they were closer to shore, they stumbled on seaweed, slid on rocks. They trod on fish, kicked them out of the way. It seemed to me that there was something I wasn't seeing, a presence weighting the scene in front of me. It was waiting at the corners of my vision, huge and old and empty. Or, not empty so much as hungry. There was no sound from the crowd, but overhead, I heard a high-pitched ringing, like what occurs when you run your damp finger around the rim of a wineglass.

V

The following morning, I came downstairs to the smells of the breakfast my grandmother was cooking for me, fried eggs and bacon, fried tomatoes, buttered toast, orange juice, and instant coffee. She had insisted to my mother and sister that she was going to make breakfast for me, and that she wanted us to have some time alone. Mom and Mackenzie had removed themselves to my Aunt Betty and Uncle Stewart's house, a short distance along the road.

I wasn't certain what my grandmother wanted. While we had seen my father's parents during our previous visits to Scotland, it had seemed to me that we spent more time with my mother's mother, who had come to stay with us in America (though I didn't remember her visits). The most I had spoken to my father's mother was immediately after his death, when I had done my best to console her over the phone, assuring her that he had been suffering and was at least out of pain, and she had said, "It's like it's himself talking to me."

Now, she sat down with me at her small kitchen table and said, "Tell me about your dad, son."

I didn't know what to say. Her question should not have caught me off guard. My father had been his parents' acknowledged favorite—as one of his younger brothers had told me, their mother's golden boy. Although Mom, my siblings, and I had visited Scotland only every few years, for a good part of my childhood, Dad's job with IBM had necessitated regular international travel, to Paris and Frankfurt, and he was usually able to arrange an extra couple of days' stay with his parents. Despite his geographical distance from them, he had been able to maintain a close relationship with his mother and father; whereas myself, my brother, and my sisters knew our paternal grandparents mostly as names Dad and Mom discussed now and again. Occasionally, my father would mention his father as the source of an old song he was singing, or relate an anecdote about my grandfather's days in the shipyards, when he'd argued with his fellow workers against unionizing. He didn't say much about his mother; though his affection for her was palpable. For her to want me to tell her about him now was no surprise. Quite reasonably, she assumed that he was what we had in common, and she assumed that I felt about him the way she did.

This was not exactly the case. I loved him, fiercely, the way I had as a small child. For almost as long, though, that love had been complicated by other emotions, ones that, at twenty-five, I was nowhere near reckoning with. There was fear, of him and the temper that could ignite without warning, and for him and the heart whose consecutive infarctions during my eighth grade school year had left me in constant dread of his mortality. There was anger, at his stubborn insistence on his point of view, at his tendency to cut short so many of our more recent arguments by threatening to put my head through the wall if I didn't shut up. There was embarrassment, at the prejudices that had trailed him from his upbringing, against everyone who was not white, Catholic, and Scottish, at his tendency to point out the flaws even of people he was praising. And there was guilt (as some comedian or another said, the gift that keeps on giving), at my inability to love him as simply, as straightforwardly, as did my siblings. In the year or so leading up to his death, he and I had seemed to be moving, slowly, tentatively, toward some new stage in our relationship, one in which the two of us might be less on guard around one another, more relaxed, but his two months in Westchester Medical Center, his death, had forever kept us from reaching that place.

None of this could I say to my grandmother. Eyes wide behind her glasses, lips pressed together, she inclined ever-so-slightly toward me, her attitude one of anticipation, for anecdotes and details that would allow her son to live again in her mind's eye. So that was what I gave her, a morning's worth of stories about Dad. I couldn't not talk about his final stay in the hospital, the open heart surgery from which he had never fully recovered, becoming steadily weaker, until testing revealed that he had late stage cirrhosis, his liver was failing, and the situation roared downhill like a roller coaster whose brakes had sheared off. But I could balance that story with others, most of them focusing on his pride in my brother and sisters. I told her about the cross country and spring track practices and meets he picked them up from and drove them to. I narrated his help with and participation in their assorted science projects (including letting Mackenzie wake him throughout the night in order to assess the effects of an interrupted sleep schedule on his ability to perform a set number of tasks). I shared with her his delight in my brother's acceptance to medical school, and his pride in Christopher's commission in the Navy. I expressed his admiration for my middle sister, Rita, who managed a schedule that included teaching dance classes at the school at which she was a student, playing guitar with the church folk group, and working a part-time job at an optometrist's office, all the while completing high school. I considered it an achievement that, not once during our extended breakfast, did my grandmother ask about my father and me.

VI

The remainder of the day consisted of a visit to my aunt and uncle's house, a few hundred yards up the road, for a loud and cheery dinner of meat pies, sausage rolls, bridies, chips, and beans, with Irn Bru to drink. We were joined by Stewart and Betty's children and children-in-law, and their grandchildren, who were fascinated by my American accent and kept asking me to pronounce words in it. Uncle Stewart promised to drive me around to see the local sights; one of my cousins and his wife invited Mackenzie and me to watch a movie at their place; another of my cousins said that my sister and I had to come fishing with her and her dad another night. Oh, and there was a fair down by the water next weekend . . . In a matter of two hours, my schedule for most of my remaining time in Greenock was arranged. I didn't mind. I had grown up without much in the way of extended family nearby; really, it was just Mom, Dad, my brother, sisters, and me. During the months after my father's death, when the flood of calls and visitors that had swept over us in the immediate aftermath of his passing diminished to a stream, then a trickle, then dried completely, I had felt this lack acutely. To be here, taken into the bosom of Dad's family, was like being gathered into an incredibly soft, comfortable blanket. I loved it.

VII

Later that night, though, as I was sitting up in bed, trying to read by the astonishing late light, I found myself unable to concentrate on my book.

Had Mackenzie been awake, I would have talked to her, but I could hear my sister snoring in the back bedroom, which she was sharing with Mom. I could have checked on my mother, but even if she was awake, I was reluctant to disturb her with what was on my mind. It concerned my father, and his final stay in the hospital.

The morning after he emerged from surgery, the nurses propped him up in bed and gave him a pen and pad of paper with which to communicate. (He was, and would remain, intubated, his breathing assisted by a ventilator.) Due to the ICU regulations, only three of us could visit him at a time, so my sister, Rita, and I waited and sent Mom, our brother, and Mackenzie in first. Rita and I made small talk for five or ten minutes, then Chris and Mackenzie came out to trade places with us. I had seen my father in the hospital before, many times, and the sight of him in his hospital gown, the top of the white ridge of bandages visible at its collar, below the trach tube, was not shocking. What was strange, off, was the expression on his face, his brows lowered, his jaw set, a look of concern tinted with anger. Rita and I crossed the ICU cubicle to him and embraced him, both of us delivering deliberately casual greetings, trying to act as if everything was fine, or was going to be fine. He returned our hugs, then turned his attention to the pad of paper propped on his lap. He took his pen and carefully wrote a sentence. When he was finished, he held the pad up for my inspection.

The line he'd written was composed of characters I didn't recognize. There was what might have been a square, except that the upper right corner didn't connect. There was a triangle whose points were rounded. There were parallel lines drawn at an angle, descending from right to left. There was a circle with a horizontal line bisecting it, an upside-down crescent, and a square whose bottom line turned up inside the shape before connecting with the line on the left, and which continued to turn at ninety-degree angles within the square, making a kind of stylized maze. I stared at the symbols, and looked at my father. My lack of comprehension was glaringly obvious. I said, "Um, I'm sorry—I don't understand what you're trying to tell me."

In response, he underlined the strange sentence several times and showed it to me again.

"Dad," I said, "I don't understand. I'm sorry. I can't read this."

His eyebrows raised in frustration. Although he was on the respirator, I could practically hear him blowing out his breath in exasperation. Employing the pen as a pointer, he moved it from symbol to symbol, as if taking me slowly through a simple statement.

I could feel my face growing hot. I shook my head, held up my hands. He glared at me.

"Let me see," my mother said, leaning over from the other side of his bed. She didn't have any more luck with what Dad had written than had I. He was irritated with both of us—Rita refrained from looking at the pad—but his annoyance with me felt as if it had a particular edge, as if I, of all people, should understand what he was showing me.

After that, it was time to go. When we returned for the next visiting session, two and a half hours later, Dad was surrounded by several nurses, all of whom were focused on preventing him from leaving his bed, which he was trying to do with more vigor than I would have anticipated from a man who had just had his chest cracked open. Mom talked to him, as did the rest of us as we came and went from the room, but though the sound of her voice, and ours, calmed him slightly, it wasn't enough to make him abandon his efforts. This led to him being given a mild sedative, then put in restraints. For the next two weeks, he struggled with those restraints daily, pulling at the padded cuffs buckled to his wrists. His features were set in a look of utter determination; if any of us spoke to him, he regarded us as if we were strangers.

My mother was afraid he had suffered a stroke, one of the possible complications of the surgery about which she and Dad had been warned. In the notes to his chart, the nurses described his new condition as a coma. Neither diagnosis seemed right to me, but where was my medical degree? All I knew was, he wasn't there, in that writhing body—or maybe, we weren't there for him, he was seeing himself in surroundings foreign and frightening. Finally, at the end of fourteen days of watching him wrestle with his restraints, one of the doctors realized that Dad might be having an allergic reaction to a drug they had been giving him (we never learned which one) and ordered it stopped. With the cessation of that drug, he returned to normal within a day. The restraints were removed, and although he only left his room for follow-up X-rays and further surgery, at least he was himself.

Those symbols, though, I had not forgotten. The most likely explanation was that they were an early product of my father's drug allergy. Had any of my siblings, my mother, asked me about them, I would have offered this rationale, myself. Yet on some deeper level, I didn't buy this. He had exhibited too much focus in writing them. Had he ever been well enough to be removed from the ventilator, I would have asked him about them. Since that hadn't happened, they remained a mystery. I might be transforming the scribbling of a mind frightened and confused into a coded message of great import, but I could not forget the expression on my father's face as he showed me what he had set down.

After all, during the surgery, his heart had been stopped, and although a heart-lung machine had continued to circulate and oxygenate his blood, who could say what state he—his self, his soul—had been in for that span of time, how far he might have wandered from his body? Sometimes, I imagined him, waking from his surgery to find himself in an unadorned room with a single chair and a single door, and being told by a man in a drab suit that this was where he had to wait until the operation was completed and the doctors found out whether or not they could restart his heart. I imagined the man offering him a newspaper, its headlines the row of symbols he would copy for me.

To what end, though? I recognized the scenario I had invented, the speculation that prompted it, as magical thinking of the most basic kind, driven by longing for my father to have been involved in something more than the slow and painful process of his death. In his writing, I hoped for clues to another state of being, evidence of the place he had entered when he died.

I sat my book down on the nightstand. I eased out of my bed and crossed to the large window that gave a view of the Clyde and its far shore. In the late light, the river was the color of burnished tin, the Trossachs purple darkening to black. My father had not lived in this house—one of his mother's cousins had bought it for her after my grandfather died. But the river it surveyed had shaped his life as definitively as it had the land through which it flowed. The shipyards on its banks had brought my great-grandfather here from Ireland. A younger son of a farming family, disqualified from inheriting the farm by his order of birth, he had booked passage across the Irish Sea to find work as part of the industry building the vessels with which the British Empire maintained its quarter of the globe. Beyond that, I didn't know much about the man. I presumed he had obtained my grandfather's job in the shipyards for him, which I knew had consisted at one point of painting the hulls of ships. I wasn't sure why my father hadn't followed him in turn, unless it was because my grandfather (and probably, grandmother) had wanted something else for him, an office job, which he eventually found with IBM. All the same, Dad had courted Mom on the Esplanade that ran along the Clyde on the eastern side of town, and he kept newspaper clippings about the river that his relatives mailed to him folded and tucked within the pages of his Bible. I wasn't any closer to knowing what I expected from this trip. But gazing out at the river, the hills, felt strangely reassuring.

VIII

That night, my dreams took me down to the Clyde. A chain link fence kept me from a flat, paved surface above which cranes rose like giant metal sculptures. I turned to look behind me, and almost toppled into a chasm that dropped a good twenty feet. The gap ran parallel to the fence, to the river beyond. Maybe ten feet across, its walls were brick, old, blackened; although its bottom was level—a road, I realized when I saw a white, boxy van drive up it. At once, I knew two things with dream certainty: my father was in that van, and there was something at my back, on the other side of the paved lot. The hairs on the back of my neck prickled at it. Old—I could feel its age, a span of years so great it set me shivering uncontrollably. I did not want to see this. I shook with such intensity, it jolted me from sleep. Awake, I could not stop trembling, and wrapped the bedclothes around me. I took a few minutes to return to sleep, and once I did, it was to a different dream.

IX

Once he was home from work the next day, Uncle Stewart made good on his promised tour of the area. Mackenzie came, too. The three of us squeezed into his car, a white Nissan Micra whose cramped interior lived up to its name, and off we went. A soft-spoken man, Stewart kept a cigarette lit and burning between his lips for most of the drive. He worked for a high-tech manufacturer who had moved into one of the old shipping buildings. He was what my parents called crafty, which meant he had a knack for artistic projects. Fifteen years before, when he'd been laid off his job at the shipyards and unable to find another, he had turned his efforts to building doll-sized replicas of old, horse-drawn travelers trailers. He'd gifted one to my parents, who placed it in their bedroom, where my siblings and I went to admire it. The detail on the trailer was amazing, from the flowered curtains hung inside the small windows to the ornaments on the porcelain horse's bridle. (He bought the horses in bulk from a department store.) Stewart had sold his trailers, first to family, then to friends, then to friends of friends, then to their friends, the money he earned helping to keep his family afloat until he found a new job.

He was also a repository of local knowledge, some of which he shared with Mackenzie and me as he steered the Micra up and down Greenock's steep streets. He showed us the house our father had grown up in, the apartment where our mother had been raised by her mother, the church where our parents had married. He drove us down to the river, to the Esplanade, and along to where a few cranes stood at the water's edge like enormous steel insects. He drove us east, out of town, towards Glasgow, so that he could show us Dumbarton Rock across the Clyde, a great rocky molar whose ragged crown stood two hundred feet above the river. A scattering of stone blocks was visible at the summit. Nodding at the rock, Stewart said, "There's been a castle of some sort there forever," the words emerging from his mouth in puffs of cigarette smoke that his open window caught and sucked out of the car. "Back when the Vikings held the mouth of the Clyde, and the islands, that was the westernmost stronghold of the British. Before that, the local kings ruled from atop it. Like the castle in Edinburgh—Sterling, too. There's a story that Merlin paid the place a visit, in the sixth century."

"King Arthur's Merlin?" I said.

"Aye. The king at the time was called Riderch. They called him 'the generous.' King Arthur's nephew, Hoel, was passing through, and he was injured. Fell off his horse or the like. King Riderch put him up while he was healing. When Riderch's foes learned he had King Arthur's nephew under his roof, they laid siege to the place. Riderch had a magic sword—*Dyrnwyn*—that burst into flame whenever he drew it, but he and his men were pretty badly outnumbered. There was no way he could get word to King Arthur down in Camelot in time for it to do him any good. It looked as if Arthur's nephew was going to be killed while under Riderch's care. So was Riderch, himself, but you see what I'm saying. It would be a big dishonor for Riderch, alive or dead."

Stewart steered toward an exit on the left that took us to a roundabout. He followed it halfway around, until we were heading back toward Greenock. As he did, he said, "This was when Merlin showed up. He'd been keeping an eye on Hoel, and he'd seen the trouble Riderch was in for his hospitality to Arthur's kin. He presented himself to the King, and offered his assistance. 'No offense,' says Riderch, 'but you're one man. There's a thousand men at my front door. What can you do about a force of that size?'

"'Well,' says Merlin. The King has a point. He is only one man, and although his father was a devil, there is a limit to his power. 'However,' says he, 'I have allies I can call upon for help. And against them, no force of men can stand.'

"'Then I wish you'd ask those friends for their aid,' says Riderch.

"Merlin says okay. He tells the King he needs a corpse, the fresher, the better. It just so happens that, earlier that very day, Riderch's men caught a couple of their enemies attempting to sneak over the castle wall. He has his men bring them before him, and right on the spot, executes the pair. 'There you go,' he says to Merlin. 'There's two corpses for you.'

" 'Good,' says Merlin. He has the King's soldiers carry the bodies right outside the front gate. It's going on night time, and Riderch's foes have withdrawn to their tents. Merlin instructs the soldiers to dig a shallow grave, one big enough for the two dead men. Once it's been dug, he has them lay the corpses in it and cover them over. Then he sets to, using his staff to draw all manner of strange characters in the soil. He was a great one for writing, was Merlin. If you read some of the older stories about him, he's always writing on things, prophecies of coming events, usually. King Riderch watches him, but he doesn't recognize the characters Merlin's scratching into the dirt.

"When he's done, Merlin steps back from the grave. Pretty soon, the earth begins to tremble. It moves from somewhere deep below them, as if something's digging its way up to them. Over in the siege camp, a few of Riderch's enemies have been watching Merlin's show. As the ground shakes, more of them run to see what's causing the disturbance. The soil over the grave jumps, and a great head pushes its way through the dirt. It's a man's head, but it's the size of a hut. The hair is clotted with earth. The skin is all leathery, shrunk to the skull. The eyes are empty pits. The lips are blackened, pulled back from teeth the size of a man's arm. The arms and legs of the bodies the King's men buried hang out over the teeth, the remainder of the corpses inside the huge mouth. It's a giant Merlin's summoned, but no such giant as anyone there has ever heard tell of. It's as much an enormous corpse as those it crunches between its teeth. It keeps coming, head and neck, shoulders and arms, chest and hips, until it towers above them. You can imagine the reaction of Riderch's foes: sheer panic. The King and his men aren't too far away from it, themselves. Merlin touches his arm and says, 'Steady.' He points to the siege camp and says to the monster, 'Right. Those are for you.'

"The giant doesn't need to be told twice. It takes a couple of steps, and it's in the midst of the enemy fighters, most of whom are trampling each other in their haste to get away from it. It leans down, sweeps up a handful of men, and stuffs them into its mouth. It stomps others like they're ants. It kicks campfires apart, catches men and tears them to pieces. A few try to fight it. They grab their spears and swords and stab it. But that leathery skin is too tough; their blades can't pierce it. Soon, the giant's feet are covered in gore. Its lips and chin are smeared with the blood of the men it's eaten. There's no satisfying the thing; it continues to jam screaming men into its mouth. In a matter of a few minutes, Merlin's monster has broken the siege. In a few more, it's routed Riderch's foes. Some of them flee to the ships they sailed here. The giant pursues them, smashes the prows of the ships, breaks off a mast and uses it as a club on ships and men alike.

"King Riderch turns to Merlin and says, 'What is this thing you've brought forth?'

"'That,' says Merlin, 'is Corpsemouth.'

"'Corpsemouth,' says Riderch. 'Him, I have not heard of.'

"Merlin says, 'He and his brethren were worshipped here many a long year ago. He was not known as Corpsemouth, then, but what his original name was has been lost. He and his kindred were replaced by other gods, who were replaced by newer gods than those, and so on until the Romans brought their gods, and now the Christians theirs. All of Corpsemouth's fellows went to the place old gods go when men are done with them, the Graveyard of the Gods. Corpsemouth, though, refused to suffer the same fate as his kin. Instead, he lived on their remains. If any men stumbled across him, they were his. As later generations of gods came to the Graveyard, so Corpsemouth had them, too. Down through the ages he has continued, losing hold of everything he used to be, until all that remains is his hunger.'

"Riderch watches the giant crushing the last remnants of his enemies. He says, 'This is blasphemy.'

"'Maybe,' Merlin says, 'but it saved King Arthur's nephew, and it saved you, too.' Which Riderch can't argue with.

"Once the last of the enemy fighters is dead, the giant, Corpsemouth, turns in the direction of Merlin and the King. Riderch puts his hand on his sword, but Merlin tells him to keep it in its sheath. He points his staff at the hills behind Dumbarton Rock. Corpsemouth nods that great, gruesome head, and walks off in that direction. That's the last Riderch sees of him, and of Merlin, for the matter. I don't suppose he was too upset about either."

Stewart's story had taken us all the way back to his front door. He pulled the parking brake and turned off the engine. "And that," he said with a grin, "is a wee bit of your local history."

Mackenzie and I thanked him, for the story and for the tour. While we were walking up to the house, my sister said, "Where did Merlin send the monster—Corpsemouth?"

Our uncle paused at the front door. "The story doesn't say. Maybe north, to the mountains. That's where many terrible and awful beasts were said to dwell. I'll tell you what I think. A few miles east of Dumbarton Rock, there was an old burial place unearthed in the 1930s. It was the talk of this part of the country. I remember my father speaking about it. The fellows who dug it up said they found evidence of an ancient temple there. 'Scotland's Stonehenge,' the papers called it."

"What happened to it?" I said. "Can you visit it?"

"They put a pair of apartment buildings over the spot," Stewart said. "The war interrupted the excavation, then, when the war was over, another group of scientists said the chaps who'd discovered the place had overstated its significance. There were a few rock carvings that were of interest, they said, but as long as they were removed and sent to the museum in Glasgow, they saw no reason not to build the high rises there. So the men from the museum came and cut out the pieces of rock to be preserved and the rest became part of the foundation for the new construction. My father was upset about it, about all of it, but especially about the carvings being taken away. 'There's folk put they things there for a reason,' he says, 'and yon men from the museum would do well enough to leave them be. There's no telling what trouble they'll stir.' I suppose he had a point. Although," Stewart added, "I've yet to see any giants prowling the hills. But if you ask me, that's where Merlin told Corpsemouth to go."

X

That night, I lay in bed thinking about Stewart's story, wondering what my father would have made of it. Mackenzie was sleeping over at Stewart and Aunt Betty's house, or I might have asked her. My mother was long since unconscious. I was sure Dad would have enjoyed Stewart's tale as entertainment. He was a great fan of adventure stories of all stripes, with a soft spot for horror narratives, too. Mostly, he watched them as movies and TV shows; although he might read a book like *Firefox* or *Last of the Breed*. Whenever he saw a new movie, especially if it had been on TV too late for me and my brother, he would describe it to us the next day, in a scene-by-scene retelling no less detailed than the story Stewart had told. In this way, I knew the plots to most of the Connery and Moore James Bonds, a number of Clint Eastwood thrillers, and an assortment of films focused on mythological figures such as Hercules. He would have appreciated the way Stewart's tale blended the historical with the horrific; though he might have preferred a different, more dramatic end to the monster, blasted by Merlin's magic, say, or set alight by King Riderch's fiery sword.

I was less sure how he would have dealt with the story's pagan elements, especially, the idea that gods came and went over time. I knew he'd been interested in mythology. Exploring the basement as a child, I had found stacked in the shelves near the furnace a half-dozen issues of a magazine called *Man, Myth & Magic*, whose title had appealed to me instantly but whose pages, full of reproductions of old woodcuts and classical paintings, not to mention, articles written in a dry, academic language, left me confused. I'd wanted to ask him about the magazines, but had the sense that I shouldn't. There was a reason they were in the basement, after all. Plus, puzzle me though they did, I didn't want to lose access to them, which I might if he realized I was paging through them. So I kept quiet about the magazines, but I noticed that, whenever I brought up stories from the Greek or Norse myths I was reading, he usually knew them, though he tended to downplay his knowledge.

I wasn't sure to what extent this was because he was a devout Catholic, his faith fire-hardened from having grown up in a Protestant culture of institutionalized religious prejudice. He was leery of anything that might contradict the Church, his faith threaded through with a profound anxiety about Hell. Occasionally, he spoke about the Passionist fathers who visited his local church when he was a boy to deliver terrifying sermons on the fate of the damned. (I wondered if this was part of the attraction horror films had for him, their glimpses of the infernal.) The standard by which a soul would be judged after death was a source of concern, even worry, for him. We had discussed the apparition of the Virgin Mary to the children at Fatima, during which, she had told one of the boys to whom she revealed herself that he was destined to spend a great deal of time in Purgatory. While Purgatory was not Hell, neither was it a place to which you would have expected a young child to be sent. What could he have done, Dad said, to merit such a punishment? With the perspective of the last year, it had become clear to me that his questions about my church attendance during the two years I lived in Albany, his concern about my dating a girl who wasn't Catholic, were rooted in an honest desire to keep me out of Hell, whose smoky fires burned low and red in the corners of his mind.

I didn't believe my father had anything to fear from eternal damnation. I wasn't sure there was anything for him to be concerned about, one way or the other. During my youth, I had been as devout as my father. To be honest, I had loved my religion, which was full of all manner of marvelous stories, those in the Old and New Testaments, yes, and those in the lives of the saints, too. I shared some of dad's nervousness at the threat of Hell, but I grew up in the post-Vatican II Church, when the rewards of salvation were emphasized over the torments of damnation. Once I entered adolescence, however, the joys of the opposite sex became vastly more compelling than the strictures of faith. If I was hardly original in this—indeed, compared to the rest of my high school classmates, I was the latest of late bloomers—I roamed off the beaten path in my growing intellectual disagreement with the Church. I found its positions on most social matters riven by contradiction; nor did it help that so many of the men who pronounced them did so with an air of self-righteousness that set my adolescent teeth on edge. The ritual of the Mass, and its central conceit, the intersection of the numinous with the mundane, continued to speak to me, albeit, in a more figurative sense than I was sure my father would have approved. Religion in general seemed to me increasingly figurative, less a description of some ultimate reality than, at best, another human invention to help us through the struggle of living. At worst, it was another way for a small group of men to hold sway over a significantly larger of people, politics with more elaborate costumes. Either way, it had nothing to do with any life after this one.

To be sure, I had taken comfort from the Church and its rituals during the days and weeks after Dad had died. By the following winter, though, my attendance at Mass had lapsed almost entirely. Even when my work schedule permitted me to take my mother and Mackenzie to church, I sat through the service listening with one ear, especially when the priest stood to deliver the sermon. Sometimes, I thought that I could have been a better Catholic if I lived in a country whose language I did not speak, so that I wouldn't realize the priest was summarizing a *Peanuts* comic to explain God's love for us. I missed the faith I'd had in my childhood, and I regretted its loss because it had been so important to my father, and had remained so for the rest of my family. Its loss filled me with a kind of terror, because it had taken with it my father, consigning him to a void in which I and everyone else I knew would, in the end, join him.

XI

No surprise: that night, I dreamed of Corpsemouth. I was standing on the shore of the Clyde. It was the same, twilit time I'd encountered in all my recent dreams. In front of me, the river was at low tide, exposing an expanse of waterlogged sand studded with rocks of varying size. Behind me, the

Battery Park, Greenock's riverfront park, stretched flat and green. Beyond where the water lapped the sand, a wall of yellowish fog sat on the river, veiling the opposite shore. From within the fog, I heard the slosh of water being parted by something large. Goosebumps raised on my arms as the air chilled. An enormous silhouette loomed through the fog. Fear filled me like water bubbling into a glass. The fog churned at its edge; waves splashed the beach. A leg taller, far taller, than I pushed into view. The color of brackish water, its flesh was dried and wrapped around enormous bones. There were figures tattooed on the skin, but the creases and folds from its withering rendered them indecipherable. A second leg appeared, carrying the rest of the monster with it, but I didn't wait to see any more of it. I turned and ran for the edge of the park, which had receded almost to the horizon. Sand grabbed at my feet. I slipped on a rock and fell into another. When the giant hand closed on me, I wasn't surprised. I woke as it lifted me into the air, my heart pounding, relieved that I didn't have to see the old god's face, its terrible mouth open for me.

XII

The following day, my cousin, Gabriel, and his wife, Leslie, drove me, Mackenzie, and our mom to Glasgow. Gabriel was Uncle Stewart and Aunt Betty's second oldest, which made him five years older than I was. The times my parents had taken my brother and sisters and me to Scotland when we were growing up, Gabriel had always been the kindest of my cousins, willing to talk to my brother and me as equals about all manner of serious subjects: nuclear war, the fate of the human race, life on other planets. He worked for the railroad, in what capacity I wasn't clear. Leslie was an elementary school teacher; she and Gabriel had been married for eight years.

After we found a parking spot, Leslie, Mom, and Mackenzie set off for Sauchiehall Street and its assorted shops, Gabriel and I for the West End Museum, a sprawling, Victorian extravagance in red stone whose center was crowned by a selection of turrets that suggested a fairy tale castle full of treasure. The museum, I had learned from a follow-up conversation with Uncle Stewart, was where the engraved rocks removed from the burial site east of Dumbarton Rock had been sent and were currently on display. I wasn't sure why I wanted to see them; it might have been for no more complicated a reason than that my uncle had told me about them. I hadn't shared my objective with my cousin, but he was happy to accompany me across the museum's wide, green lawn.

Inside, we traversed a large, echoing gallery to the stairs to the third floor, where the exhibit on Scotland's Ancient Cultures was located. The display was at the far end of the level. It had been organized around a half-dozen modest display cases, each of which contained a handful of relics of the country's oldest-known inhabitants. Large photographs of the Scottish countryside, each seven feet high by five wide, had been hung in the midst of the cases. Gabriel strolled over to a display case showing the rusted blade of an old sword. In front of a picture of a shallow brook running at the base of a snow-topped mountain, I found what I had come to see.

The only thing in its case, the piece of grey stone was rectangular, larger than I had anticipated, the size of a small table. The white lettering on the glass cover identified it as having been unearthed in 1933 on Gibbon's Farm in Dunbartonshire. The description pointed out the pairs of concentric circles visible on the stone's upper right quadrant, as well as the U-shape directly below them, which I thought resembled a horseshoe. The approximate date given for the stone was 500 ACE. I crouched to get a closer look at the stone, which brought me level with its base. From that position, I noticed a series of marks in the rock. At first, I took them for the scrapes and scars left by whatever tools had been used to extricate the slab. Then they came into focus, and I was looking at a row of characters. A rough square whose upper right corner didn't connect was followed by a triangle with rounded ends, which was succeeded by a pair of parallel lines slanting from right to left. Fourth was an approximate circle with a line through its center, a crescent like a frown fifth. Last was another square, only, this one's edges failed to connect in the lower left corner, instead turning inside in a series of right angles to form a stylized maze.

It was as if I were looking at the figures through a tunnel. Everything except that patch of rock was dark. I could hear the steady click and sigh of my father's respirator, the faster, high-pitched beep of the heart monitor, the intermittent beep of a machine keeping track of some other function. I could smell the antibacterial foam we applied to our hands every time we entered his room. I could feel the thin blanket we helped him pull up because the room was too cold. My heart fluttered in my chest. I went to stand, and fell onto my butt. I looked up, and still saw the symbols on the stone. I remembered the expression on my father's face when he showed them to me, the frustration.

Gabriel's hand on my shoulder brought me back to myself. "What happened?" he said. "Are you okay?"

"Lost my balance," I said, pushing to my feet. "I squatted down to get a better look at the exhibit, and I fell right over. I'm fine."

"So you wanted to see this, eh?" Gabriel gestured at the stone. "Let me guess: Dad told you his Corpsemouth story, didn't he? Including the part about the mysterious graveyard whose sacred stones were removed. Am I right?"

"Yes."

"You know he made up all of that."

"Not this." I nodded at the display case.

"No, but it's only a piece of rock with a couple of circles on it. There's nothing magical about it."

I was surprised by his bluntness. "I don't know," I said, "it's kind of cool. We don't have anything like this in New York."

He shrugged.

"What about the figures on the end, there?" I said.

"What do you mean?"

"These ones," I said, pointing to the half-dozen characters on the stone's base.

He bent to inspect them. "Looks like someone was playing with their penknife. What's the display say about them?"

"Nothing."

"That's your answer, then."

I was tempted to tell Gabriel about the last time I'd seen these same figures, but saying that my late father had written them on a piece of paper for me after emerging from surgery during which his heart had been stopped sounded too lurid, too melodramatic. Instead, I said, "I suppose you're right. Why don't we go see what the ladies have been up to?"

XIII

On the way to our meeting spot on Sauchiehall Street, though, past shop windows full of high end clothes, shoes, and liquor, I asked my cousin if he truly believed his father had invented the story of Corpsemouth. "Not completely," he said. "Dad reads all kinds of books; I'm sure he's run across something like his monster in one of them. The king that's in the story, Riderch, he was real, and had his castle at Dumbarton Rock."

"But no Merlin," I said.

"Actually, there is a story about Merlin showing up there," Gabriel said. "What is it they say? If you're going to tell a lie, make sure to fit as much of the truth into it as you can manage."

"It's not exactly a lie," I said, "it's a story."

Gabriel didn't answer.

XIV

For the rest of our excursion, which ended with dinner at Glasgow's Hard Rock Café, and for the return drive to Greenock, which took us past Dumbarton Rock, those symbols floated near the surface of my thoughts. As far as I could remember, my father hadn't taken us to visit the West End Museum during any of our family trips to Scotland. Nor, as far as I knew, had he gone to the place on his own, although this was difficult to the point of impossible to be certain of. He'd never mentioned it, and he'd had no trouble telling us about his visit to the Louvre, while he'd been in Paris on one of his business trips. I asked my mother about it during our dinner at the Hard Rock, delivering my question at the end of a short appreciation of the museum. "There was a lot of fascinating stuff in it," I said. "Did you and Dad ever go there?"

A year past his death, Mom's eyes could still shine with tears, her cheeks blanche, at the mention of my father, of their life together. She reached for her napkin, dabbed the corners of her eyes. "No," she said, returning the napkin to the table. "I think I went on a school trip there—I don't remember how old I was. Just a girl."

"What about Dad?" I said. "Did his school visit the museum, too?"

"I don't know," Mom said. "They probably did, but he never mentioned it to me."

"Oh," I said. "I was wondering. Because, you know, you guys took us to a lot of museums when we were young." Which was true.

"That's what happens when you're traveling with children," she said. "No, in our younger days—BC, we used to say, Before Children—Dad and I went on picnics, or out dancing."

So perhaps my father had been to the museum as a boy, and perhaps on that occasion he had seen the weird symbols carved on the base of the rock. And perhaps his brain had tossed up that memory as his anesthesia wore off. The last perhaps, however, seemed one too many. Yes, the mind was a complex, subtle organ, and especially after a dramatic experience, who could predict its every last response? Yet this felt more like special pleading to me than admitting that something strange had happened to my father, and whatever its parameters, it had left him with a message for me written in characters I couldn't read.

• • •

XV

Back in Greenock, we dropped Mom, Mackenzie, and Leslie off at Stewart and Betty's. Gabriel and I drove back to his house, in order, he said, for him to initiate his American cousin into the mysteries of the single malt. He and Leslie lived on a steep street that gave a view of the Clyde. The houses along it sat on a succession of terraces, like enormous stairs descending the hillside. He parked in a short gravel driveway, and led me first into his and Leslie's house, to deposit her day's purchases on the living room couch, then out a pair of French doors, into the back garden. A brick path took us through rows of flowering bushes to a wooden hut whose door was flanked on the right by a large window. A hand-painted sign over the door read GABE'S HORN; under the name, the artist had drawn a simplified trumpet from whose mouth alcohol poured. My cousin opened the door, flicked a light switch within, and ushered me into the building.

To the right, a short bar stood in front of a shelf lined with bottles of Scotch, with some better varieties of vodka and bourbon to either side of them. Behind the bottles, a mirror the length of the bar doubled the size of the room. To the left, a quartet of chairs surrounded a round table. Beyond the table, a chrome jukebox stood against the wall. Posters and pennants of the local soccer team, the Greenock Morton, decorated the walls, with framed photographs of Gabriel and Leslie in assorted vacation settings among them. Gabriel made for the bar, which he slipped behind to survey his selection of whisky.

There were a couple of tall stools in front of the bar. I settled onto one of them and said, "This is great."

Gabriel glanced over his shoulder at me. "Do you think so? It's just something Leslie and me put together in our spare time."

"It's fantastic," I said.

"We like to come out here after a day at work, or if we're having friends over."

"It reminds me of a place my dad took me to," I said. "There was a guy who was a friend of his—through work, but he was from Scotland, too. One night, Dad had to go over to his house—to pick up something for work, I think—and he brought me along with him. I was thirteen or fourteen. This man led us down to his basement, which he had set up as a bar—though not as nice as this one. He passed my dad a glass of something—I don't know what it was, but Dad told me afterwards that our host had not been stingy with his booze. I had a ginger ale, which he gave to me out of one of those specialized dispensers you see in real bars, with the hose and all the different buttons on top of it. I was thoroughly impressed. The guy had been in the RAF during the war—he had a couple of big pictures of planes on the wall. The three of us sat around talking about that for an hour. I felt so grown up, you know?"

"Aye." Gabriel nodded. He had picked three bottles and set them on the bar. "I have some ginger ale in the refrigerator, but I think it's time for something a wee bit more mature." From under the bar, he produced a pair of whisky glasses, along with a small pitcher of water. He opened one of the bottles and tipped respectable amounts of its amber contents into both glasses. To each he added a literal drop of water. I picked up the one closest to me, and raised it to my nose. The odor of its contents, sharp, threaded with honey, was the smell of I couldn't count how many family parties. It was me playing waiter to my father's bartender, gathering drink orders from whichever guests were there for the latest First Communion, or Confirmation, or Graduation, and conveying them to Dad, who had opened the liquor cabinet in the kitchen and stood ready to dispense its contents. It was me returning to those guests with one or two or three glasses in my hands, delivering them to their recipients, and hurrying back to the kitchen for the next ones. It was me carrying to a particular friend a liquor my father had secured specifically for them, making sure to let them know Dad had said this was something special for them.

"Cheers," Gabriel said, lifting his glass to me.

"Cheers," I said, repeating the gesture to him.

The whisky flared on my tongue, and flamed all the way down my throat to my stomach, where it detonated in a burst of heat. Eyes watering, I coughed, and set the half-empty glass on the bar.

"You said you're not much of a Scotch drinker," Gabriel said.

"Not much as in, never," I said. "Which is strange, considering it was the drink of choice at family get-togethers."

"Try sipping it," Gabriel said. "You want to be able to savor a good single malt."

"Okay." I took a more measured drink, and tasted honey mixed with something woody, almost bitter. I described it to Gabriel. "That's the peat," he said. I nodded, trying more. The flavor was not what I was used to: it filled the mouth, asserting itself as did none of the mixed drinks I'd previously had. I'd never been much of any kind of drinker, and I felt the liquor's potency before I was finished with the glass. My cousin's bar and its contents softened, their edges slightly less defined. Something inside me loosened. I said, "All right. What's wrong with your dad's monster story?"

Gabriel raised an eyebrow. "You mean Corpsemouth?"

"Yes," I said, "that. In the museum, I had the impression you were less than enchanted with it."

"Ach, it's fine," he said. "Dad's always been a great one for the stories."

"Mine, too," I said.

"That story—the Corpsemouth one—you know what it's really about, don't you?"

"A giant monster?"

"It's death," Gabriel said. "It's a way of picturing death, of representing the way death feels to us."

"Sure," I said. "It's like—there's a line in one of Stephen King's books—I think it's '*Salem's Lot*—this kid is asked if he knows what death is, and he says yeah, it's when the monsters get you."

"Aye," Gabriel said, "that's what I'm trying to say."

The second Scotch my cousin served tasted less of honey and more of smoke, and something peppery. The knot within me that had started to loosen slid away from itself. Gabriel leaned across the bar and said, "So. How're you finding it, being here?"

The row of strange symbols flickered behind my eyes. "It's different than I was expecting," I said.

"It's bound to be."

"Yeah. It's funny. I thought that coming here would let me feel more in touch with my dad. Granted, it's only been a few days, but so far . . . "

"You don't."

"I don't."

"How could you? You didn't know him here. You knew him in America. It's okay."

"Maybe you're right. If that's the case, then what am I doing here?"

"You're with family."

"Yeah," I said. "I didn't have much of that when I was growing up, you know? It was just the six of us. It's kind of nice."

The third and final Scotch Gabriel poured was thinner, the peat combining with a briny flavor to give the liquor an astringent taste so blunt it was oddly appealing. "Thank you," I said to my cousin, speaking with the deliberation of someone whose tongue was heavy with alcohol. "I appreciate you sharing your expertise with me."

"I'm hardly an expert," Gabriel said.

"Regardless. You know what's funny?"

"What?"

"I can picture my dad enjoying the whole Corpsemouth story. It reminds me of movies we watched when I was a kid, *The Golden Voyage of Sinbad*, *Clash of the Titans*, *Dragonslayer*—these stories about heroes fighting enormous monsters."

"I suppose," he said.

"Well, you two appear to be having a merry time," Leslie said. She was standing in the open doorway to the bar.

"We were talking about monsters," I said.

"I'm sure you were," she said. "Stewart gave me a lift home. I'm not rushing you out, but he says if you want, he can run you back to your Gran's."

"That is probably a good idea," I said. "I'm fairly confident I've reached my limit for alcohol. Honestly, I think I passed it a while ago."

I thanked Gabriel for his generosity with his spirits, and him and Leslie for having squired my mother, sister, and me around Glasgow, today. "We've got to have you back for another tasting before you leave," Gabriel said.

"From your mouth to God's ear," I said.

XVI

Outside, night had fallen, the last of the gloaming retreated to the horizon. Stewart was waiting in his Micra at the end of the driveway. I lowered myself into the front passenger seat. He'd been listening to a news program on the radio; as I buckled my seatbelt, he turned it off. "And how was your education?" he said.

"Great," I said. "Gabriel introduced me to some quality stuff."

"Aye, he's a great one for the single malt, our Gabriel." He released the parking brake and reversed into the street. "Are you up for a wee jaunt?"

"Sure."

"Good man." He shifted into first and started downhill.

"Where are we headed?" I said.

"The river."

"Oh."

The whisky I'd consumed made the steep road seem almost vertical, the Clyde below rather than ahead of us. Retaining walls raced toward us and swerved right and left. The river grew larger in fits and starts, as if it were a series of slides being snapped into view. The car's engine whined and growled as Stewart worked back and forth among the gears. If not calmer, I was at least less terrified than I would have been without the Scotch insulating me.

At the foot of the hill, the street leveled and ran straight to the river. One hand on the steering wheel, Stewart depressed the car's lighter and fished a cigarette from the packet in his shirt pocket. Rows of squat apartment houses passed on either side. Stewart lit his cigarette and drew on it till the tip flared. Exhaling a cloud of smoke, he said, "Did you see that stone in the museum?"

"I did," I said.

"Not much to look at, is it?"

"I don't know. When you think about what it represents—how old it is and everything . . . I'm glad they have it at the museum, but it's kind of a shame they couldn't leave it where it was."

"Aye."

"The exhibit said no one's sure exactly what the symbols on it mean. Maybe images of the sun."

"They're for binding," Stewart said.

"Binding?"

"Aye, for keeping a spirit or a creature in one place. You bind them by the sun and the moon. That's why there's two sets of circles on the stone. It's a very old rite."

"What was bound there?"

Stewart shot me a sidelong glance. "I told you and your sister yesterday."

"Corpsemouth? For real?"

He nodded.

"I thought that was . . . "

"A story?"

"Yeah. No offense."

"There was something called up at Dumbarton Rock when Riderch was king. It was older than ancient, and it was terrible. Maybe it was summoned to help the king against his enemies. Maybe it was summoned to fight Riderch. Maybe someone was playing around and opened a door that should've been left shut. It took a powerful man to send the thing back where it belonged, and lock the gate after it. That stone was part of the locking mechanism."

"Wait. You're serious."

"I am."

"But . . . "

"That's impossible? Ridiculous? Insane?"

"I'm sorry, but yeah."

"It's all right. I wouldn't expect you to believe it, even with a few drams in you."

We had crossed the major east-west highway through town and come to a short road, which passed between an inlet of the river on the left, and a couple of apartment buildings on the right. Stewart drove to the end of the road, where a chain link fence sectioned off a stretch of pavement that went another twenty yards to the river. He parked the car and exited it. I followed. This close to the water, the air was cool bordering on cold. While Stewart popped the trunk, I surveyed the fence, which continued to the right, guarding the edge of a much larger paved area, which was filled with large metal shipping containers, some of them sitting on their own, others stacked two and three high. In the near distance, a trio of cranes faced the Clyde, weird sentinels looking out over the dark water. Tall sodium lights gave the scene an orange hue that made it appear slightly unreal.

Behind me, Stewart shut the trunk. He was carrying a pair of metal poles, each about a yard long, one end wrapped in duct tape. "Here," he said, handing one to me.

I took it. The pole was hollow, but heavy. "What's this?"

"Protection."

"From what?"

"Come this way." He set out to the right. I hurried after. Together, we walked the fence for a good hundred yards, until we came to a wire door set in it. The entrance was locked, but Stewart withdrew a ring of keys from his trousers, which he thumbed through until he arrived at one that slid into the lock and levered it open. The door's hinges shrieked as he pushed it in. I cringed, expecting the angry shout of a security officer. None came. Stewart stepped through. I pushed the door closed behind us, to minimize suspicion.

Keeping to the shelter of the containers, Stewart and I made our way across the paved expanse, he moving quietly, gracefully, I with the exaggerated care of someone contending with too much alcohol. We headed steadily in the direction of the river. A light mist floated around us, waist-high. This close, the cranes were gigantic, monumental. Stewart stopped, raised his hand. "Do you hear that?" he said quietly.

"What?"

"Listen."

Ahead and to our left, on the other side of a pair of stacked containers, something scraped over the pavement. Holding the metal pole in both hands, the tip low, as if it were a sword, Stewart crossed to the metal boxes. I kept a few steps behind, in a half-crouch. He moved right, to one end of the containers. The sound continued in alternating rhythm, a short scrape followed by a longer one. Before continuing to the other side of the boxes, Stewart stopped and ducked his head around for a look at whoever was there. He jerked back. Closing his eyes, he inhaled, then blew out. He murmured something I couldn't hear, raising and lowering the end of the pole while he did. As the light played up and down the metal, I saw writing on it: the symbols I had seen in the Glasgow museum, on a piece of paper in my father's hospital room. Heart lurching, I straightened. I tilted the pole I was holding back and forth, and sure enough, there were the same half-dozen characters cut into it. In an instant, I was sober, the effects of Gabriel's drinks swept away by the sensation of standing within the current of something immense and strange.

"Right," Stewart said. "There's something coming up to the end of this box. When it reaches us, I'll step out and see to it. You shouldn't need to do anything. This one isn't big. If it gets past me, though, you'll have to slow it down. Go for its legs, but mind its hands. Here we go."

The scraping was right next to us. Stewart moved out into the alley formed by our containers and one beyond it. As he did, he pivoted, slashing the pole from right to left at whatever was still hidden from me by the edge of the container. There was a heavy crunch, a sharp clang, and the pole flew out of Stewart's hands, ringing on the pavement to his right. A wooden club swung at him from his left. He ducked, but it caught him high on the shoulder with sufficient force to knock him from his feet. He landed hard.

I took a deep breath and stepped out from the container, in front of Stewart's opponent. I couldn't bring myself to strike someone I hadn't seen, but I held the pole up in what I hoped was a menacing fashion. I intended to shout, "That's far enough!" What I saw, however, stilled the voice in my throat.

It was as big as a large man. At first, I thought it was a man, dressed in a bizarre costume. Much of it was mud, thick, dripping with water. Its surface was clotted with junk, crushed beer cans, shards of broken glass, saturated cardboard and newspaper, pieces of plastic, metal, wood. Here and there, rocks studded with barnacles tumored its skin. In other spots, clumps of mussels clustered black and shining. Seaweed draped its shoulders, to either side of a head fashioned from the broken skull of either a cow or horse. The lower jaw was missing, the mouth a hole gaping in the muddy throat. The thing advanced, the scraping I'd heard the debris in its flesh rasping the pavement. I retreated. The club with which it had struck Stewart was in fact its right arm, a single piece of driftwood. Its left arm was a mannequin's, wound in rusted wire and strands of seaweed.

This was not a man in a suit—which was impossible, and hurt to think. It swept the wooden arm at me. I leapt back, just out of reach. Stewart was on his hands and knees, grabbing for his weapon. I jabbed at the thing, trying to keep its attention. The wooden arm held straight, like a spear, it lunged at me. I sidestepped, swinging my improvised sword against the arm. With a flat clank, arm and pole rebounded from one another. The creature turned, whipping the wooden arm back at me. I went to duck, slipped, and fell. The arm struck the container behind me with a gong. This close, the smell of the thing, a stink of sodden flesh and vegetation, made my eyes water. Swiveling on my butt, I chopped its right leg with the pole, hammering the approximate location of its knee. The leg buckled inward, tipping the creature toward me. I scrambled away from it. Attempting to maintain its balance, it propped itself on its wooden arm, but Stewart hit its other leg from behind with a blow that sent the creature crashing on its back. Before it could recover, he brought the pole down on its head like an executioner swinging his axe. The animal skull rattled across the pavement. The rest of the thing, however, continued to move, doing its best to raise itself on its broken legs, dropping mud and bits of glass, pebbles, on the ground. My stomach churned at the sight. Ignoring the body, Stewart strode to the skull. He struck it twice with the pole, cracking it into several large fragments, which he stomped underfoot until they were unrecognizable. As if it were an engine running down, the body gradually ceased its motion.

Stewart dropped the pole and crossed to the creature's remains. Careful of its rusted wire sleeve, he caught the mannequin arm at the elbow. "You take the other side," he said.

Leaving my weapon, I did as he instructed. The wood was slimy, as if it had sat underwater for a while.

"Into the river," he said, nodding toward the end of the alleyway.

Together, we hauled the heavy form to where the pavement ended at a concrete ledge. Ten feet below, the Clyde lapped at the wall. "On three," Stewart said. "One, two, three!" I threw so hard I almost overbalanced myself into the water along with the creature's body. Stewart caught my arm. "Steady, lad." What was left of the thing struck the water with a considerable splash. It sunk quickly, leaving clouds of mud in its wake.

"What about the rest—the skull?" I said.

Stewart shook his head. "Leave it there. It's better to keep it separate from the rest."

Adrenaline lit my nerves, rendering everything around me painfully sharp. "I cannot believe I am standing here having this conversation with you," I said. It was the truth. Had Stewart said to me, "You're not. This is a dream," I would have had little trouble accepting his words.

Instead, he shrugged, turned, and started in the direction of the gate we'd entered.

I joined him. "What was that?" I said.

"Corpsemouth," he said, stooping to retrieve his weapon.

"I thought he was supposed to be taller," I said, picking up mine.

"In his proper form, he is," Stewart said. "Fortunately for you and me, enough of the old binding remains to keep him from appearing that way. What he's able to do is put together versions of himself, avatars, out of whatever's lying around. We call them his fingers."

"Who's 'we'?"

"A group of concerned citizens. We came together after the war. That was when Corpsemouth first made himself known, again, once the binding stone was removed. No one knew what they were doing. It had been too long since anything like this had happened. A couple of the founders were able to lay their hands on a few old books that gave hints of how to confront the monster, but a lot of it was learn as you go."

"I'm sure," I said. "Does Gabriel know about any of this? What about the rest of the family?"

"No, that isn't how it's done," Stewart said.

"How is it done?"

"Why? Are you interested in being part of it?"

"No," I said. "No, this was more than enough."

Stewart smiled thinly.

"Was my father part of this?" I thought of those old issues of *Man, Myth & Magic*.

"No," Stewart said. "Though I wondered a few times if he wasn't aware of more than he let on."

"Does this—tonight—does this kind of thing happen often?"

"More than I'd like."

As we walked, the mist thickened around us, rendering the shipping containers, the cranes, faint, ghostly. It didn't affect Stewart's sense of direction. He continued forward.

"What about this?" I said, holding up the pole. "Not the pipe, I mean, the writing on it."

"That depends on who you ask," Stewart said. "There's some who say that those are connected to old gods. Not as old as Corpsemouth, but not too far off. When they were young and strong, he wasn't of much concern to them. As they grew older, though, and saw themselves being supplanted by newer powers, their strength ebbed and his hungry mouth became a worry. They thought that if they gave up their divinity, the monster wouldn't want them. So they put their godhood into these symbols, and ever since, anyone who uses them has been able to draw on their power."

"Did it work? Did they escape?"

"No one knows," Stewart said. "I doubt it. Corpsemouth eats gods, but he's happy to consume whatever he can get his claws on."

Overhead, a lamp lit the mist orange. Somewhere in the distance, I heard voices, faint, indistinct.

"That's one explanation," I said. "What's the other?"

"You're sure you don't want to be part of this?"

"Is that why you brought me with you?"

"You haven't answered my question."

"Nor you mine," I said.

"Some folk say the symbols come from a fabulous city, one on the shore of a black ocean, where they were the inhabitants' most closely guarded treasure."

"That's interesting," I said, "but it's not the question I meant."

"I know," Stewart said.

Through the mist, the gate swam into view. Stewart pushed it open and walked out. I went to follow, but before I could, a shout drew my attention to the left. No more than twenty yards away, through a clearing in the mist, a white van was parked. At the sight of it, my heart knocked. I knew this vehicle, had watched it drive through my dreams. For this to be the same van was impossible, of course, but on a night such as this one had proved to be, it could be none other. I was suddenly sick with dread and grief. To walk to the van was terrifying, but to remain in place, let alone, to leave, was worse. Legs shaking madly, I stepped toward it. Stewart said something, but whatever it was didn't register.

The mist was full of yells and calls whose locations I couldn't pinpoint. Was one of those voices my father's? I wasn't sure. The mist muffled the sounds, as if I was hearing them from the other side of a thick wall. I was almost at the van. Its interior was dark. Was it empty? Half-expecting my hand to pass through it, I reached for the handle to the driver's door. It was solid to the touch, and when I pulled, it clicked and the door opened. There was no one behind the wheel. Kneeling on the seat, I leaned into the van.

It was empty. There was no evidence of its passengers left behind; although, for a second, two, I caught the faintest odor of dried sweat and laundry detergent, the scent I'd breathed whenever I'd rested my head against my father's chest at the end of the day, when I wished him goodnight. Then it was gone.

I exited the van, closing the door. Stewart was standing behind me. "Is . . . " I started, and paused, unable to utter the remainder of the question.

"Aye," Stewart said.

"Where is he?"

He tipped his head toward where the mist was thick. "Out there."

"So if I go there, I'll find him?"

"You might," he said, "or you might not. You could spend an hour searching this lot, or you could wander off someplace else, and be lost."

Without warning, I was crying, tears streaming down my cheeks. I felt every bit as bad as I had the night my father had died, when it seemed a spear had been driven straight through my chest, as if his death were a pin that had fixed me forever in place. To see him one more time, to speak to him, to tell him I loved him and was sorry I hadn't been a better son, was a prospect almost too much to bear. To fail, though, to walk away and not return, was not something I could do to my mother and sister. I turned from the van and headed for the gate.

The shouts and calls persisted. "What's happening?" I said to Stewart. "What are they doing?"

"The same thing we were."

"Corpsemouth?"

"It's not just our world he wants to break into. There are folk on the other side who do their best to keep him out of there, too."

"Can he hurt them?"

"Oh aye, he eats the dead same as anything else." Seeing the expression on my face, he added, "But your dad was always a capable fellow. I'm sure he'll be fine."

XVII

After the night's events, I did not anticipate sleeping. Almost the instant I settled onto my bed, though, my arms and legs grew heavy, my eyelids struggled to stay open, and I slid into unconsciousness. For an indeterminate time, I drifted in a blank, not unpleasant place. Slowly, a long, black cord came into view. It corkscrewed around and around, the way the cord on our old telephone had. It faded, and was replaced by the interior of the white van.

This time, it was full of the handful of men I'd seen in it a few days ago. My father was among them. All of the passengers looked worse for wear, their shirts and pants torn and dirty, their arms and cheeks cut and bruised. Dad was leaning forward, a black telephone receiver held to his ear. I couldn't hear every word he was saying, but I understood enough to know that he was saying he was okay.

With a start, I realized he was speaking to me. For the dream's brief duration, he continued to reassure me, while I said words he could not hear. The connection, it seemed, was one way. Then the call was finished, and I was awake—though not before a last glimpse of the white van, speeding along through high, brick walls black with age, carrying my father to the next stop on his long, strange death.

John Langan's most recent book is a collection, *Sefira and Other Betrayals* (Hippocampus, 2016). He is the author of two previous collections, *The Wide, Carnivorous Sky and Other Monstrous Geographies* (Hippocampus, 2013) and *Mr. Gaunt and Other Uneasy Encounters* (Prime, 2008), and a novel, *House of Windows* (Night Shade 2009). With Paul Tremblay, he co-edited *Creatures: Thirty Years of Monsters* (Prime, 2011). He is one of the founders of the Shirley Jackson Awards, for which he served as a juror during its first three years. He lives in New York's Hudson Valley with his wife, younger son, and so, so many animals.

ACKNOWLEDGEMENTS

"The Door" © 2015 Kelley Armstrong. (*Led Astray: The Best of Kelley Armstrong*, Tachyon Pubications).

"Snow" © 2015 Dale Bailey (*Nightmare*, June 2015).

"1Up" © 2015 Holly Black (*Press Start to Play*, ed. John Joseph Adams, Vintage).

"Seven Minutes in Heaven" © 2015 Nadia Bulkin (*Aickman's Heirs*, ed. Simon Strantzas, Undertow Publications).

"The Glad Hosts" © 2015 Rebecca Campbell (*Lackington's #7*).

"Hairwork" © 2015 Gemma Files (*She Walks in Shadows*, eds. Moreno-Garcia & Stiles, Innsmouth Free Press).

"Black Dog" © 2015 Neil Gaiman (*Trigger Warning: Short Fictions and Disturbances*, William Morrow).

"A Shot of Salt Water" © 2015 Lisa L. Hannett (*The Dark #8*).

"The Scavenger's Nursery" © 2015 Maria Dahvana Headley (*Shimmer #24*).

"Daniel's Theory About Dolls" © 2015 Stephen Graham Jones (*The Doll Collection*, ed. Ellen Datlow, Tor).

"The Cripple and Starfish" © 2015 Caítlin R. Kiernan (*Sirenia Digest #108*).

"The Absence of Words" © 2015 Swapna Kishore (*Mythic Delirium #1.3*).

"Corpsemouth" © 2015 John Langan (*The Monstrous*, ed. Ellen Datlow, Tachyon Publications).

"Cassandra" © 2015 Ken Liu (*Clarkesworld # 102*).

"Street of the Dead House" © 2015 Robert Lopresti (*nEvermore*, eds. Nancy Kilpatrick & Caro Soles, EDGE Science Fiction and Fantasy Publishing).

"Mary, Mary" © 2015 Kirstyn McDermott (*Cranky Ladies of History*, eds. Tansy Raynor Roberts & Tehani Wessely, Fablecroft).

"There is No Place for Sorrow in the Kingdom of the Cold" © 2015 Seanan McGuire, (*The Doll Collection*, ed. Ellen Datlow, Tor).

"Below the Falls" © 2015 Daniel Mills (*Nightscript 1*, ed. C.M. Muller, Chthonic Matter).

"The Deepwater Bride" © 2015 Tamsyn Muir (*The Magazine of Fantasy & Science Fiction*, Jul-Aug 2015).

"The Greyness" © 2015 Kathryn Ptacek (*Expiration Date*, ed. Nancy Kilpatrick, EDGE Science Fiction and Fantasy Publishing).

"The Three Resurrections of Jessica Churchill" © 2015 Kelly Robson (*Clarkesworld #101*).

"Those" © 2015 Sofia Samatar (*Uncanny #3*).

"Fabulous Beasts" © 2015 Priya Sharma (*Tor.com*, 27 July 2015)

"Windows Underwater" © 2015 John Shirley (*Innsmouth Nightmares*, ed. Lois Gresh, PS Publishing).

"Ripper" © 2015 Angela Slatter (*Horrorology*, ed. Stephen Jones, Quercus)

"The Lily and the Horn"© 2015 Cathrynne M. Valente (*Fantasy #59*).

"Sing Me Your Scars" © 2015 Damien Angelica Walters (*Sing Me Your Scars*, Apex Book Company).

"The Body Finder" © 2015 Kaaron Warren (*Blurring the Line*, ed. Marty Young, Cohesion Press).

"The Devil Under the Maison Blue" © 2015 Michael Wehunt (*The Dark #10*).

"Kaiju *maximus*®: "So Various, So Beautiful, So New" © 2015 Kai Ashante Wilson (*Fantasy #59*).

OTHER NOTABLE STORIES: 2015

Allan, Nina: "A Change of Scene" (*Aickman's Heirs*, ed. Simon Strantzas)

Allen, Mike: "The Spider Tapestries" (*Lackinton's #8*)

Anders, Charlie Jane: "Ghost Champagne" (*Uncanny #5*)

Anderton, Joanne: "2B" (*Insert Title Here*, ed. Tehani Wessely)

Armstrong, Kelley: "We Are All Monsters Here" (*Led Astray: The Best of Kelley Armstrong*)

August, Julia: "Unravelling" (*Lackington's #5*)

Ballingrud, Nathan: *The Visible Filth* (novella)

Barron, Laird: "Fear Sun" (*Innsmouth Nightmares*, ed. Lois Gresh)

Barron, Laird: "In a Cavern, in a Canyon" (*Seize the Night*, ed. Christopher Golden)

Barron, Laird: "The Blood in My Mouth" (*Madness of Cthulhu II*, ed. S.T. Joshi)

Barron, Laird: "We Smoke the Northern Lights" (*The Gods of H.P. Lovecraft*, ed. Aaron J. French)

Barron, Laird: *X's For Eyes* (novella)

Biancotti, Deborah: "Look How Cold My Hands Are" (*Cranky Ladies of History*, eds. Tansy Rayner Roberts & Tehani Wessely)

Bolander, Brooke: "And You Shall Know Her By Trail of Dead" (*Lightspeed #57*)

Bradley, Rebecca: "An Inspector Calls" (*Expiration Date*, ed. Nancy Kilpatrick)

Bulkin, Nadia: "Violet is the Color of Your Energy" (*She Walks in Shadows*, eds. Silvia Moreno-Garcia & Paula R. Stiles)

Burke, Chesya: "For Sale: Fantasy Coffins" (*Stories for Chip: A Tribute to Samuel R. Delany*, eds. Nisi Shawl & Bill Campbell)

Cameron, Dana: "Whiskey and Light" (*Seize the Night*, ed. Christopher Golden)

Campbell, Rebecca: "Unearthly Landscape by a Lady" (*Beneath Ceaseless Skies #161*)

Claus, Jennifer: "The Room is Fire" (*New Genre #7*)

DeMeester, Kristi: "To Sleep in the Dust of the Earth" (*Shimmer #28*)

McDonald, Sandra: "Rules for Ordinary Heroes" (*Nightmare #32*)

Duffy, Steve: "Even Clean Hands Can Do Damage" (*Supernatural Tales 30*)

Etchison, Dennis: "Don't Move" (*F&SF*, Sep/Oct 2015)

Files, Gemma: "The Salt Wedding" (*Kaleidotrope*, Winter 2015)

Ford, Jeffrey: "The Thyme Fiend" (*Tor.com*, 11 Mar 2016)

Ford, Jeffrey: "Winter Wraith" (*F&SF*, Nov/Dec 2015)

Gregory, Eric: "March Wind" by Eric Gregory (*Lady Churchill's Rosebud Wristlet #33*)

Hao, Jingfang (trans. Ken Liu): "Folding Beijing" (*Uncanny #2*)

Helms, Alyc: "The Blood Carousel" (*Lady Churchill's Rosebud Wristlet #32*)

Hodge, Brian: "This Stagnant Breath of Change" (*Shadows Over Main Street*, eds. Doug Murano & D. Alexander Ward)

Hodge, Brian: "One Possible Shape of Things to Come" (*Eulogies III*, eds. Jones, Kalanta & Tremblay)

Hopkinson, Nalo & Nisi Shawl: "Jamaica Ginger" (*Stories for Chip: A Tribute to Samuel R. Delany*, eds. Nisi Shawl & Bill Campbell)

Jager, Michelle: "Home Delivery" (*SQ Mag #21*)

Jones, Stephen Graham: "The Man Who Killed Texas" (*Nightmares Unhinged*, ed. Joshua Viola)

Kalin, Deborah: "The Cherry Crow Children of Haverny Wood" (*Cherry Crow Children*) (novella)

Kalin, Deborah: "The Briskwater Mare" (*Cherry Crow Children*)

Langan, John: "Underground Economy" (*Aickman's Heirs*, ed. Simon Strantzas)

Lee, Karalynn, "Court Bindings" (*Beneath Ceaseless Skies #176*)

Lee, Yoon Ha: "Variations on an Apple" (*Tor.com*, 15 Oct 2015)

Lee, Yoon Ha: "Two to Leave" (*Beneath Ceaseless Skies #173-174*)

Leslie, V. H.: "Precious" (*The Outsiders*, ed. Joe Mynhardt)

Littlewood, Alison: "Wolves and Witches and Bears" (*Nightmare #34*)

Machado, Carmen Maria: "I Bury Myself" (*Lady Churchill's Rosebud Wristlet #33*)

Malik, Usman T.: "The Last Manuscript" (*Exigencies*, ed. Richard Thomas)

Mannetti, Lisa: *The Box Jumper* (novella)

Markov, Haralambi: "The Language of Knives" (*Tor.com*, 4 Feb 2015)

Marshall, Helen: "The Vault of Heaven" (*Aickman's Heirs*, ed. Simon Strantzas)

Maruyama, Kate: "Akiko" (*Phantasma*, eds. J.D. Horn & Roberta Trahan)

McDermott, Kirstyn: "A Song For First Hours" (*SQ Mag #20*)

McGuire, Seanan: "Something Lost, Something Gained" (*Seize the Night*, ed. Christopher Golden)

McGuire, Seanan: "The Myth of Rain" (*Lightspeed #60*)

McHugh, Maura: "Family" (*Cassilda's Song*, ed. Joe S. Pulver)

Moraine, Sunny: "It is Healing, It is Never Whole" (*Apex #75*)

Muir, Tamsyn: "The Woman in the Hill" (*Dreams from the Witch House: Female Voices of Lovecraftian Horror*, ed. Lynne Jamneck)

O'Keefe, Megan E.: "Of Blood and Brine" (*Shimmer #23*)

Parks, Richard: "The Bride Doll" (*Beneath Ceaseless Skies #183*)

Randall, Jessy: "Maybe a Witch Lives There" (*Mythic Delirium #1.3*)

Russell, Karen: "The Prospectors" (*The New Yorker*, 8 & 15 June 2015)

Schanoes, Veronica: "Ballroom Blitz" (*Tor.com*, 1 April 2016)

Sharma, Priya: "The Absent Shade" (*Black Static #44*)

Shearman, Robert: "Blood" (*Seize the Night*, ed. Christopher Golden)

Slatter, Angela: "Bluebeard's Daughter" (*SQ Mag #20*)

Slatter, Angela: "Lavinia's Wood (*She Walks in Shadows*, eds. Silvia Moreno-Garcia & Paula R. Stiles)

Slatter, Angela: *Of Sorrow and Such* (novella)

Snyder, Lucy A.: "The Yellow Death" (*Seize the Night*, ed. Christopher Golden)

Taylor, Keith: "Herald of Chaos" (*That Is Not Dead*, ed. Darrell Schweitzer)

Taylor, Lucy: "In the Cave of the Delicate Singers" (*Tor.com*, 15 July 2015)

Tem, Steve Rasnic: "Between the Pilings" (*Innsmouth Nightmares*, ed. Lois Gresh)

Tem, Steve Rasnic: "Deep Fracture" (*Madness of Cthulhu II*, ed. S.T. Joshi)

Tem, Steve Rasnic: "The Grave House" (*Strange Tales V*, ed. Rosalie Parker)

Tem, Steve Rasnic: *In the Lovecraft Museum* (novella)

Trent, Letitia: "Wilderness" (*Exigencies*, ed. Richard Thomas) (novella)

Valente, Catherynne M.: "The Long Goodnight of Violet Wild" (*Clarkesworld #102*)

Valentine, Genevieve: "Given the Advantage of the Blade" (*Lightspeed #63*)

Valentine, Genevieve: "Visit Lovely Cornwall on the Western Railway Line" (*The Doll Collection*, ed. Ellen Datlow)

Vaughn, Carrie: "Bannerless" (*The End Has Come*, John Joseph Adams)

Vaughn, Carrie: *El Hidalgo de la Noche* (*El Hidalgo de la Noche*)

Vernon, Ursula: "Pocosin" (*Apex #68*)

Vernon, Ursula: "Wooden Feathers" (*Uncanny #7*)

Walters, Angelica Damien: "Tooth, Tongue, and Claw" (*Nightscript 1*, ed. C.M. Muller)

Warren, Kaaron: "Mine Intercom" (*Review of Australian Fiction Vol. 13, Issue 6*)

Warrington, Freda: "Ruins and Bright Towers" (*Night's Nieces: The Legacy of Tanith Lee*, ed. Storm Constantine)

Wong, Alyssa: "Hungry Daughters of Starving Mothers" (*Nightmare #37*)

Yang, J. Y.: "A House of Anxious Spiders" (*The Dark #9*)

Yap, Isabel: "The Oiran's Song" (*Uncanny #6*)

Yoachim, Caroline M. "Seasons Set in Skin" (*Beneath Ceaseless Skies #177*)

ABOUT THE EDITOR

Paula Guran is senior editor for Prime Books. In addition to the Year's Best Dark Fantasy and Horror series, she has edited and continues to edit a growing number of other anthologies as well as more than fifty novels and single-author collections. She is the recipient of two Bram Stoker Awards and an IHG Award, and has been nominated for the World Fantasy Award twice. Mother of four, mother-in-law of two, grandmother to three, she lives in Akron, Ohio.